FROM THREE TO FIVE

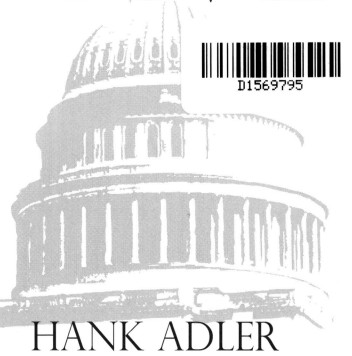

HANK ADLER

JULY, 2012

Domestically, by the summer of 2012, the President could only point to a small handful of extremely unpopular legislative successes accompanied by general policy failures. The economy had fallen to the floor and then crashed. Reported (real) unemployment exploded to almost thirteen percent by the end of 2010 and had leveled off at eleven percent by the summer of 2012. The President had signed legislation that ultimately spent more than $2 trillion to get the economy back on track and all it had appeared to do was increase the deficit.

After sinking a South Korean ship early in 2010 and the shelling of a South Korean island in late 2010 without any meaningful consequence, North Korea demonstrated its nuclear capabilities in the fall of 2011. Their action was the real-time delivery of an armed nuclear missile to a small nearly uninhabited island off the coast of South Korea. While the population of the island had been only a few individuals, the use of nuclear weapons by North Korea in this third and far more frightening hostile action against South Korea had again caught the world off guard. China and Japan had immediately provided a clear and unambiguous message to North Korea that any follow-up North Korean missiles would be closely followed by the total decimation of their country. The North Koreans took these threats at face value and quickly backed down with a commitment to no future actions. These pronouncements were accompanied by the reality that Japan had become a competent nuclear military power without anyone in the administration so much as considering they were moving in that direction. The President's response of a call for yet more negotiations with North Korea had been a cause for many nations to look more towards China and Japan than the United States as the world's new superpowers.

Mexico and the accompanying drug trade had Americans in border states terrified of illegal immigration and the drug trade. The Mexican drug cartels seemed to be moving deeper and deeper into the United States.

Relations for the United States in the Middle East were at their worst historical levels. With Iran now openly a nuclear threat, no Middle Eastern nation was comfortable relying on the United States for protection and each was following the international lead of Iran. The rest of the Middle East was in political turmoil. Afghanistan had been fought to a military standstill and the troops of the United States were slowly returning home. The reality on the ground for Afghan citizens was very dangerous. It was safe to be a Taliban leader outside the cities; it was safe to be a Taliban member in the cities. If one was not a Taliban, leaving the cities was often a death sentence.

~

FRIDAY, AUGUST 3, 2012

There are many large, plush hotels in Los Angeles. The city also has a selection of fine restaurants and exceptional conference centers. Max's Place is not a plush hotel, a fine restaurant or an exceptional conference center. While Max's Place is well known in Los Angeles and has been in business for well over thirty years, the restaurant is best known as a banquet facility for companies that would prefer to spend a bit less on their annual corporate party.

One of the chief advantages of Max's Place is that it is located very close to the San Diego freeway and is within a reasonable drive time for most Los Angeles citizens for their annual corporate extravaganzas. There is a huge parking lot next to the facility, which combined with proximity, makes it a wonderful location for corporate events. Max's Place is also very close to both the Los Angeles and Santa Monica Airports.

On this particular Friday morning at 7:00 a.m. in early August, Max's Place was well appointed with spotless white tablecloths and white covered chairs. While capable of serving several hundred meals at near the correct temperature and with reasonable—though certainly not exceptional—quality, this particular morning the single buffet table included only coffee brought in from *Starbucks* and untoasted bagels with cream cheese from a local delicatessen. There were no wait staff in the building and for this day only, the Friday morning guard was given the morning off and the security was provided by about two dozen very large and intimidating security men. Each gentleman with the security team had prior military experience and worked for one of the major Los Angeles security firms. All were armed and

had meaningful additional armaments in their cars. These men were profes-
sionals. One needed to look very closely be able to see that each member of
the security team was packing. Each was attired in dark suit coat and tie. The
wardrobes did nothing to cloak the intimidation factor of each individual.

Both the parking lot and the restaurant were protected by these pro-
fessionals, the type of security men reserved for the rich and famous. In
the parking lot, drivers sat in their cars waiting for their clients. Not one
ventured from his or her car after receiving very specific verbal and written
instructions as they entered the parking lot. As one might expect, many of
the drivers were also security men or women and more than a few had additional security team members in their front passenger seats. A significant
number of these individuals were also licensed for the weapons under their
coats and several maintained small arsenals in the trunks of their vehicles.

The local neighborhood also had the attention of the security forces. The
surrounding neighborhoods near the Los Angeles airport never saw a gathering
similar to that which was taking place on this day. As a result, even at this early
hour, there were a few security vehicles roaming the neighborhood to ensure
that the visitors to Max's Place could arrive and leave with total anonymity,
safely and without any involvement with the community. While there was only
a tiny concern about the neighbors at 7:00 a.m., the security team recognized
that if the event was twelve hours later there might have been a great security
concern. If the neighborhood knew the names and bank accounts of those attending this meeting, at the very least, there would be significant gawking.

To be conservative, a decision had been made to assume it was actually
7:00 p.m. so that the security teams would be exceptionally alert. When
one purchases highly paid and highly competent security personnel, one
is paying for *exceptionally* alert. Payment had been made and security was
exceptionally tight.

When some of the drivers and the additional security individuals initially attempted to accompany their clients from the parking lot to the front
door of Max's Place, they had been waved back to their cars. Most returned
to their cars and drove their clients the less than one hundred yards to the
front door where the drivers were again informed that they were expected
to remain in the comfortable seats of their Lincoln Town Cars and other
luxury drivables. They were instructed to either pick up their charges at the
door when the meeting was complete or to wait *in*, not by, their cars for
their clients to reappear.

6

It was more than a bit unusual for most of the clients, drivers or security men to be at a B-list restaurant like Max's Place. The parking lot was not a priority of ownership and urgently needed a few hundred thousand dollars in asphalt repairs. It would not have been a shock if one or two of the passengers slipped and fell in this pothole-filled parking lot when returning to their vehicles. Therefore, the parking lot itself was a serious concern to those trapped in their cars and facing the possibility of dealing with a passenger who had just slipped on the way back to their car. That being said, the repeated warnings to stay in their cars were adhered to by every driver and every security person.

Given the experience of the men and women in the vehicles in the parking lot and the arsenals in their trunks, an attack by a light armored division probably could have been held off for several hours. While the security patrolling the neighborhood had given that fact no thought, at least a few drivers recognized that while there might still be security issues around this parking lot, there were surely no issues about protecting the lives of their clients. That was unless one recognized that with the number of air conditioners and car engines running while the meeting at Max's Place continued, the air pollution counts were frightening.

Max's Place had probably not—or actually, never—had clientele with the combined amount of net worth that was in the building. Major corporate executives, heirs to fortunes created over decades, a few current and retired athletes (including one who was pitching Monday evening at Dodger Stadium), a number of people from the film industry, and a significant number of self-made men and women sat with paper cups filled with *Starbucks* coffee and an untouched cold bagel.

If someone had taken the time—and probably at least two-dozen people in the room were thinking about it—the net worth in the room could have been calculated at well over $400 billion. With that amount of net worth and the accompanying egos to support it, there was no seating chart and no sign-in list. In the front of the room, one small table was set up with four chairs and a single microphone. In the back of the room, there was a second table with a few note pads placed without any particular order. Great care had been taken to ensure the speakers' table did not appear to be more significant than any other table. While covered by a white tablecloth, it was the only table in the room without covered seats. Each of the folding chairs at the head table could easily have been fifteen or twenty years old.

~

7

Beth Midlands, Reesa Jonathon and Father Miles Woods began to sit down at the head table after Ross Anderson, standing at the head table, had asked the attendees to find a seat. Surprisingly, the almost three hundred attendees instantly went to various tables and took their seats.

Anderson was dressed in "California casual," befitting his business interests in surfwear and hotels. Once a three star athlete at the University of Southern California, he had converted his senior thesis for his class in entrepreneurial management into a multi-billion dollar business empire. Anderson's flowered shirt, khaki pants, yellow socks and brown loafers were his daily business attire and for this group, carefully selected to show his personal confidence by not dialing up the three-piece suit or exaggerating his power by appearing in jeans and a t-shirt. Anderson's audience had arrived in all three choices of wardrobe.

Like many Southern California executives, Ross Anderson had found great happiness on a surfboard since before his teens and he continued to surf a few mornings a week before work. If surfing was leisure as opposed to exercise, surfing was the only leisure he had during most weeks. If surfing was exercise as opposed to leisure, surfing was the only exercise he had during most weeks. He worked at his companies like the most devout followed their religion. He had used his little spare time to become a philanthropic powerhouse during the past two decades. It was this very public philanthropic success that allowed him to convene this meeting and not be looking at merely a half dozen people rather than the three hundred people in the room at this early hour on a very hot day in early August in a B-list Los Angeles restaurant.

Anderson ignored the microphone and asked if everyone could hear him. As he did this, he moved his wiry frame to the left side of the table and positioned himself, stage right, to the audience. His favorite economics professor at USC taught from that spot and whenever Anderson spoke to a large group, he always tried to emulate that specific favorite professor. For reasons Anderson did not understand, but knew to be true, being to everyone's front right and not in the middle of the stage or behind a podium made any speaker more approachable and believable.

No one indicated they could not hear him and Anderson began with what he hoped would be an easy presentation.

"So, I am Ross Anderson and with Beth Midlands, Reesa Jonathon and Father Woods, we have invited you today for the purpose in participating in something that I would call a reverse revolution. As may surprise you, this is not a morning where we are going to ask you for tens of billions of dollars for some worthy charitable purpose. The four of us are here on a political mission." This line produced a groan from the audience. Ross Anderson smiled a toothy grin that showed his family could not afford braces when he was a kid and, in his best unaccented Southern California manner, continued a presentation that he hoped and believed might change the world as most knew it.

"OK, this is your official welcome and thank you for attending. Everyone in this room is a very busy person. I suppose that the size of the audience is a tribute to Beth, Reesa and Father Woods. Of course, Father Woods, in my experience, does not exactly ask people to do anything.

"Normally, I would ask Father Woods to offer a prayer before a meeting like this, but he and I agreed that this was a purely secular event and our goal today is to embrace everyone that is here and, well, we thought a quick silent offering might be the best way to start and not offend anyone. So, let us just have a silent moment and I ask you to think great thoughts and if you believe in any particular deity, try to get him or her to help us along this morning."

After no more than fifteen seconds of silence, Anderson began again: "Thank you. And again, thank you for attending today and thank you for leaving the personal and corporate airplanes either at home or someplace other than LAX. Apparently, by keeping the airplanes scattered, *TMZ* is not in Max's parking lot this morning. And thank you for not bothering each other for autographs, although I have to admit, I wouldn't mind a new picture with you, Carolyn." A ripple of laughter followed this comment as Carolyn, a middle-level country and western singer, was Anderson's wife of more than twenty years.

"We have done our best with security today and apologize to those of you uncomfortable leaving Vito in your car.

"We are realists and while we can only hope that this meeting is kept confidential, at least through the end of this weekend, if we ultimately do read about it in the press, at least we didn't have the photographers here to verify anyone and everyone's presence.

"And again, I do ask—actually I beg you—to keep this meeting confidential, at least for a few days. And if you cannot keep the meeting confidential, try to keep who was here confidential. There will be people here who want no part of what we are selling and it would be very unfair to connect them to this event.

"As you obviously know, we asked that everyone leave their cell phones, Blackberries, iPods, iPads, and for all I know, their centrifuges in their cars and then we made you all walk through a metal detector and tried to get any remaining cell phones. If somehow you have a recording device of any kind, please don't record this meeting. We are all adults here and it would be inappropriate for anyone to violate anyone else's confidentiality.

"I think you all know at least one of us, but if not, I am going to admit for the four of us, none of us has ever made a significant political contribution other than when one of you calls to tell us we are, quote, wanted to attend some political event." This brought another gentle chuckle from the assemblage.

"So, without any further foreplay, let's talk. We will open this up for discussion after each of the four of us speaks and each of us will speak for less than fifteen minutes. I promise you that we will have you out of here at a very reasonable time this morning."

Anderson took a full step toward his audience. "The four of us are terrified about this election. The four of us are terrified about the direction of the country. Two of us are lifetime Republicans and two of us are lifetime Democrats. As I previously mentioned, none of us have been what anyone would refer to as politically active.

"We each describe, remember, as two Republicans and two Democrats, the relationship of our personal philosophies to the philosophies of our two parties with the same language, not an original quote, but the same language: *There has been no change in my political philosophy, it is my political party that has moved.*"

There began some applause and Anderson quickly responded, very loudly, "Thank you, but no applause this morning please, this is not a political stump speech and I want to respect everyone's time. But I will say, the common thread among disaffected voters, I believe, is that they feel—as do we—that their political parties have been stolen from them by the politically active wings of their party, left or right.

"Agree with that premise or not, let's assume that many of us will agree on some, but not *all*, key points here this morning and we can listen to each other without cheering…"—Ross smiled—"…or booing. This will save a bit of time.

"Father Woods suggested that the four of us get together a month ago and talk about the political landscape. We met several times, mostly by telephone, and today's meeting is the sole outcome of our efforts.

"What may surprise you is that none of us believe that we are some crazy Diogenes out there looking for an honest man. In ethereal terms, however, we do not believe that the quest for a successful third-party presidential candidate is an impossibility and in specific terms, we believe Senator Vincent is undisputedly an honest man of the middle. Undoubtedly, there are things each of us finds in Senator Vincent that are disappointing or perhaps very disappointing. But, we believe, Senator Vincent is America's best hope, maybe our only best hope.

"Maybe it is what each of us disagrees with Senator Vincent about that makes him the best candidate for president. He is not willing to make all of his decisions based upon what the far left side of his party believes. We believe it is okay not to tow the political party line on every issue. It is okay to generally believe in what the party believes and disagree on some issues. We think of his political philosophy as a bit like ordering a BLT, hold the mayo. Generally, he wants to go in the direction of his party, but he is not going to conform to every position enunciated by the politicians controlling his party; he can actually think for himself.

"As you know, in just four days, this American Exceptionalism Party is having their one day political convention in Cleveland. And yes, Cleveland is not where I would launch a political campaign, or pretty much anything else. But it is a one-day convention. One day, the kind of political convention that suits me—no nonsense, a couple of nominations, a couple of speeches and home. But, I digress." As with the first speaker at most conferences, Anderson was maintaining the interest of his audience.

"The four of us agreed, again, as two Republicans and two Democrats, that at the end of the day, we have politically more in common with each other than we do with our historical political parties. We also agreed that while we have less and less to agree with in our own parties, we have more and more to disagree with in the opposite party. This appears to be the nature of today's political landscape as the fringes control both parties. We agreed that this was unhealthy and egos aside, we believe that our feelings are common to tens of millions of Americans, actually we believe they are common to far more than tens of millions of Americans. We also agreed that interestingly enough, on some serious issues such as abortion, we had more

11

in common with our competing views than with the extreme views of the politically active controlling the Democratic and Republican Parties"

At this point, the six-foot-four-Inch, one hundred and ninety-five pound Anderson smiled and looked at his audience. As he did when he was nervous, he instinctively scratched the hair behind his right ear and laughed to himself because whenever he effectuated this mannerism, it reminded him that he was a bit out on a limb, intellectually or stylistically. He continued: "Can you believe that? The four of us, two pro-abortion and two anti-abortion have more in common with each other than our respective political parties." There were a couple of hundred nods in the audience.

"None of us want a poor woman who has been raped to be forced to carry that child to full term and none of us want a baby aborted in the eighth month because she has changed her mind. And yet, these combined views are out of step with each of our political parties." He paused. "Uh, I haven't exactly posed this specific question to Father Woods, but you get my point. Heads nodded and there was some exchange of words at every table as the reality of the commonality of this point hit home.

"Another example would be on tax policy where none of the four of us want confiscatory rates or a stupid national sales tax instead of an income tax. Further, each of us believes that if there were some reasonable expectations that spending and debt repayment would be linked to tax collections, we would be willing to pay higher tax rates for a very short period of time to get the country's finances back in order.

"Of interest here, I think, none of us are comfortable with the status quo on many, many issues, but we are convinced that both parties are already unbelievably far from our political sweet spots and moving further away every day. Each of our political parties seems to want to move in the wrong direction from the status quo on far too many issues. Whatever the issue, each of the political parties is moving to the extremes. Perhaps it is a symptom of the age of extreme sports and extreme solutions. We do not believe, regarding virtually any major issue, that either the extreme solutions being offered by the left or the extreme solutions being offered by the right, or the Democratic or Republican Parties alike, are frankly worth a damn!"

Among those in the audience who were pretending they were at the final table at the World Series of Poker and trying desperately not to have anyone know what they were thinking, there were both perceptible and almost perceptible nods of agreement. A few attendees lightly applauded these remarks by Ross Anderson.

"None of us know if the American Exceptionalism Party is a place we will want to reside for the long term. I think each of us hopes that following the election"—at this point, Anderson was intentionally not using the names of the AEP candidates as he wanted to keep the conversation at a big picture level with as little discussion of candidates or specific issues as possible— "that our political parties will move back towards the center. I will admit that none of the four of us truly believes that this will happen as the activists seem to control far too much of each parties' political apparatus, but one can always hope. A discussion for another day.

"I will add, and I know many of you will disagree, but I would like to discuss at some future time a way to somehow achieve the re-democratization of the Senate and the House of Representatives. I don't know exactly what that means, but I do know I don't want a congressman from another state or district telling my guy or gal how to vote."

Anderson had by now walked to the middle of the room. "So, why did we invite you here? We could have just sent you a letter. We invited you this morning for this exceptional breakfast of coffee and cold bagels because we want you to conduct independent campaigns for both specific issues and the presidency. And we want and hope the individual campaigns will elect George Vincent to the presidency. And we mean independent campaigns and we mean you, not us, not groups of us, but individuals. Let me repeat that, we want you to conduct independent, yes independent, campaigns to support George Vincent. And asking three hundred people to fund independent campaigns is a reason to try to get us all under one roof, once." Anderson's speaking style was non-descript as was his accent. He easily could have been an anchor newsman, the one who apparently had never lived in any section of the country when he was being raised and had no defining accent. "Once." he repeated.

"We know that everyone, literally everyone, in this room has the financial capability to mount a significant campaign, on their own, if they believe the cause is right. You may each define what that financial capability means to you individually, but if you are thinking $10,000 or even $100,000, you are not in the same zip code as Beth, Reesa, Father Woods and me. We are talking about each of you allocating millions of dollars towards saving our nation!" As the reality of the *ask* set in on the audience, there was near silence accompanied by a large number of looks between individuals. One movie producer in the back quietly said, "Are they fucking kidding?" to no one in particular, but it echoed across the room and a few heads turned.

"No, we are not f–ing kidding. And," Anderson continued, "we want to make it crystal clear that we have no intention of violating a single law, regulation or anything that would result in anything worse than a lawsuit from someone trying to get some attention." He emphasized, "We, I repeat, *we* do not expect or want any of you to violate a single law, regulation, or anything that could get you into trouble. In fact, we expect and demand the opposite. We expect and demand that everyone be pristine in his or her political efforts. This means that if you go forward, you will be conducting an independent campaign on your own, without anyone else in this room. Let me repeat this a third time…" and he did.

"The good news is that this every-person-for-themselves approach requires that this meeting be the last meeting of our group. This means that for those of you who determine to go forward and run your own independent campaigns, we do not expect to have so much as a telephone call from you over the next four months unless you already happen to be someone we talk to on a regular basis. We absolutely do not want so much as a call or e-mail indicating that you are moving forward. And I am absolutely serious about this; independent means independent and that means not so much as a discussion of election strategy on the fairway at Brentwood Country Club up the street or at some posh restaurant in Santa Monica. We want each of you to be as clean and pure as Caesar's wife.

"And there is a reward for this decision to be an independent ship during the campaign. Yes, a reward. What is that reward? To ensure that you are independent, it is highly recommended that you not attend so much as a single political event through November. You can tell all of your political buddies that your lawyers have told you not to attend so much as a bake sale in support of one of the candidates!"

"Hallelujah!" hollered a self-made billionaire on Anderson's immediate right. "To me, that is a get out of jail free card." The laughter erupted, in part because he had expressed the thoughts of eighty percent of the people in the room, but more fully because the extent of the proposal and the potential personal cost of this meeting were becoming fully apparent and the audience needed a breather.

Anderson continued: "There is a quasi-independent part of the game. Groups are allowed to run campaigns as groups on specific issues. But even though these campaigns are run by independent groups interested in special issues, they cannot be coordinated with any other campaign, in particular the presidential campaign. The fact that issues are relevant and meaningful to the election is legal, so long as the campaign does not expressly help a single candidate.

"With respect to the specific issues campaigns, all we want to do today is identify five specific issue campaign funds to which you can contribute. But, we mainly want to beg you to consider running your own independent presidential campaigns. And we beg you not to take this idea to the dark side and use it to support one of the main party candidates. And by the way, they really do not need your money. They have already hit all of the special interests.

"All of you knew that the price of admission today was going to be substantial if you decided to join our little non-existent gaggle. There are only five different signup sheets for this morning's meeting where others will organize independent issue specific campaigns. You can see the five issues. We are not going to discuss these this morning. You may agree or disagree, but they are not our focus. The sign-up sheets are at the back of the room.

"On each individual table, there is a long list of individuals throughout the country who can help you run independent political campaigns and a long list of legal beagles who know how to keep you out of trouble. There is no sign-up sheet for independent campaigns and again, frankly, we literally do not want to know who is doing what.

"And, oh yes, Hale Funk is sitting on the left side of the room here. He is with Kilony, Bass and Bren, a fine Los Angeles law firm with great credentials in political campaigns. Should I decide to run an independent campaign, which I promised to them would not be a firm decision until after this meeting, I will be using Hale. He is also here this morning to jump up in the air and yell *FIRE* if anyone says a single word that would be illegal or restrict anyone in the room from taking future independent actions that before this meeting would have been perfectly legal." Hale Funk, resplendent in Beverly Hills' classic overkill lawyer attire, uninvited, stood up, turned to face the crowd, and waived. Hopefully, he thought that his wave and his decision to accept the invitation to be there this morning would be worth millions to him in legal fees. While he had agreed with virtually every word

15

that had been expressed so far and would be expressed before the end of the meeting, his compelling interest and goal in attending the meeting was a personal financial opportunity and now, it had been accomplished through merely being acknowledged and standing up. He hoped to later be asked for the dozens and dozens of business cards he had brought to the meeting.

"You are all adults and I am certain that your good ethics and brain-power will cause you to seek excellent legal counsel and not violate any laws of the land. In our four minds, we are a nation of laws and we do not want anyone to decide that the ends justify the means and do something illegal or, frankly, something stupid.

"I have spoken too long. Let me give the floor to Reesa. One more thing before I hand off the microphone, the little calculator machines in front of you are to determine if we have all wasted our time here today. There was no assigned seating, so no one will know who entered what on these calculators, but when we are done we are going to ask a question, which roughly says if you expect to conduct an independent campaign or plan to participate in a special issue campaign, how much do you expect to spend? On our end and on the screen, all that will be seen is a total number and therefore you will know exactly what we know. You guys know me, at least by reputation, there will be no follow-up nonsense like, 'You can do better.'" Pause. "It will be what it will be. While we will not know who said they would do what, many of us will only spend our money if we have your absolutely non-recourse promise to spend your money. Reesa?"

About a dozen of the attendees took the microphone handoff as an opportunity to head for the door. Included in this group were mainly entertainment related individuals who were firmly committed to the current president. But there were also two extremely wealthy Republicans headed to their cars, and they, especially, were likely to use their cell phones to let the leadership of the Republican Party know what was happening. (There are no secrets in politics.)

Ross Anderson watched these individuals head for the door and called out: "Dear God, at least give us the courtesy of a few hours before your outgoing calls cause the press to descend on Max's Place! We would all like to go home without battling past satellite trucks."

Heather Goldman, Democrat, president of a small independent movie studio in Culver City stopped and turned towards Ross Anderson. Goldman was dressed in a gold pants suit, a cotton blouse and high heels. With her

16

long blond and far out-of-style ponytail, she looked a bit like a palomino horse, a beautiful palomino horse, but a palomino horse nonetheless. Goldman looked at the others who were departing, stopped, and loudly offered: "Ross, I admire what you are doing. I truly do and I appreciate this morning's invitation. This is just not what I have in mind for myself. That being said, would you folks"—looking at the others headed for the door—"stop, join me and put up your hand to promise no cell phone calls before noon." Everyone stopped as if a staff sergeant had ordered *Halt!*, looked at the others, and affirmatively raised their hands.

Anderson breathed an audible sigh of relief. "Thank you, Heather. Good luck on your next movie and thank you all for coming."

Anderson walked back to the Spartan head table, picked up the microphone and handed it to Reesa Jonathon. It was likely that virtually everyone in the room knew who Reesa was and yet very few, if any, had ever met her or seen her in person. Reesa was the only heir to an oil fortune resulting from some serious wildcatting by her grandfather in the 1920s. She did not stand up because she could not stand up. Once a hopeful Olympic swimmer, she had been in a serious traffic accident almost thirty years before and was now a paraplegic.

Reesa Jonathon had struggled with alcohol for almost a decade after her accident. This was well chronicled and now one of the other reasons she was well known to this group. Unknown to this group or virtually anyone else, was that one morning she got up, went to the telephone book, got the number for Alcoholics Anonymous and had not had so much as a sip of wine at dinner after her first AA meeting in Indianapolis. That day and that meeting changed her life in more ways than most people's lives generally changed between birth and death. Her only remaining vice became coffee and she made not the slightest attempt to limit her input, which could be mammoth. She often kidded herself that coffee was the fourth food group. With her last glass of scotch and that first cup of coffee, she seemingly disappeared from the face of the earth. There had not been a picture of her in the papers in nearly twenty-five years.

A married woman who had been less than faithful to a faithful husband before and after her accident, after she found AA, Reesa Jonathon became a model of fidelity. She even returned to the church she had left when she was swimming seven hours a day in high school.

17

"Thank you, Ross. I think most of you know my story. Short form: great athlete, lousy person, horrible accident, alcoholic, then found AA and lost Jameson Scotch on the same day almost twenty-five years ago. Found God and peace thereafter."

While Ross Anderson had held the attention of this money-laden group, Reesa Jonathon, in just a few sentences had them spellbound. Had anyone ever filleted themselves in front of a group of strangers like that in less than forty-five seconds?

"So here is the deal. I know about two things. I know about health care and I know about philanthropy. The President doesn't understand either one. Paul Roland, the Republican, wants to ignore that either exists." Each sentence or small cluster of sentences sounded as if it was all she had to say. Her voice was unusually deep, possibly the result of her accident as she was a timid, quiet, almost silent youth. In the days of swimming hour after hour in the pool every day, she tended to speak no more than a few hundred words a day. Her speech pattern, not the sound or the volume, was the same when she was eight years old, a blast of words and that was the end of it.

"The President, if given the chance, will ultimately eliminate our ability to get good health care if you are over a certain age or have certain health characteristics, etc. Think of an aging woman in a wheelchair, or think of a seriously disabled four-year-old, your choice. I guess at the moment, it would not be difficult to imagine an old hag in a wheelchair." Nervous laughter was heard in the audience. "And, the other thing I know something about, where the President continually proves he has no clue is charity. Every time he talks about eliminating or reducing allowable deductions for charitable purposes, he proves he knows nothing about charitable giving. The President is setting out to kill many charities and all churches. And again, I don't believe that Paul Roland wants to help anyone, the ill, churches or the charities. He has that very strict every-man-for-himself philosophy. He would have made a great Puritan in New England in 1650.

"This president will put in place heath care regulations under his 2010 health bill, probably the day after the election if he is elected, that will cause some of us to die and Paul Roland would eliminate current regulations that permit us to live. Now there is a Hobson's choice if I ever heard one.

"So, in my opinion, neither the Democrats nor the Republicans represent the America that has existed for two hundred plus years, or the America I think we should be. Period.

18

"Let me talk about charity for a minute first, and in a global sense. I'll tell you about my world of charity in a minute. The President wants to reduce the tax deduction for charitable contributions for wealthy taxpayers. Now there is an incentive to give! All this does is increase the cost of giving and this will undoubtedly result in a reduction in large charitable gifts across the country. Strangest thing I have ever heard. Doesn't he understand that most of what we give to non-church charities will become a government expense if the donations are not made? Of course, when the President makes $5 million a year and gives only a few thousand dollars a year to charity, you know where he stands on charity. He and his wife gave away almost nothing, maybe a few thousand dollars a year, when they were making over $300,000 a year before he was a presidential candidate. And there is the Vice President giving away about eight dollars a year to charity!" She paused for just a moment. "That is crazy. Of course, Congressman Roland and his group want to eliminate any incentive for giving, so to the charitable world, each is an unacceptable candidate. To Roland's credit, although I disagree, his elimination of charitable incentives is based in his deep conservative philosophy. The President has no underpinnings to his beliefs on contributions; he has only politics.

"We need to get back to the middle folks or one of these two sides is going to kill us. They may have different political weapons and goals, but the message is the same and it is not good. If you go far enough right in the Republican Party, there is chaos from a lack of adult supervision; if you go far enough left in the Democratic Party, you become communist, a communist, not a socialist! And darn it, Socialist is unacceptable as well. Oh yes, in my opinion, this is also chaotic in both parties, resulting from complete lack of adult supervision. I don't think either candidate knows what he is talking about in this specific area. Knowledge may be power, but words seem to be the fuel of politicians. Two very bad choices by our two parties.

"This will surprise you folks, but I gave away $175 million to charity last year and because of my great grandfather, if I choose to, I can continue to do that every year, forever." This sentence brought about some serious murmurs in the crowd, as no one really understood how much money and annual income Reesa had and no one knew she was philanthropic at any level. "Yes, for you tax accountants, that means my annual taxable income is about $350 million if I give away the maximum fifty percent and since it is all from oil and gas, I'm probably worth about $4 billion.

19

"Now, I hope that number does not leave this room, although it would take a great deal of faith to believe that will not happen. Please don't tell Steve Forbes. As my gay friends in AA say, I guess I have *outed* myself, but that does not mean I want to read articles about Reesa Jonathon and her fight from deprivation in *Parade Magazine*." This produced some uncomfortable laughter as the gay community was well represented in the room and she, along with most of this audience, was aware of it. Reesa Jonathon paused.

"We have managed to give away literally billions over the past couple of decades and I bet, until today, Sam and I have received very few serious requests for donations. Of course, this is because we always say no, often rudely, and then if we think it is a worthy cause, we make the contribution through a myriad of institutions and names organized specifically to protect our privacy."

The silence in the room was deafening. While there were one or two philanthropists in the room who were well known as philanthropic deities, literally no one was in the same league claimed by Reesa Jonathon and not a single person in the room had an inkling that she had ever donated dollar one to anything. Most, if not all, philanthropy of the scope being exposed by Reesa Jonathon was done through estate planning or large charitable foundations, not through gifts by individuals. Given that based on their personal statements, the charitable funds from Bill Gates' and Warren Buffet's estates are going to go towards global issues, Reesa was essentially claiming the title of the largest charitable giver to American charities.

She rolled her wheelchair to the right side of the table, stage left. Reesa was wearing an Armani top and blue pants. Reesa Jonathon was fairly unremarkable in appearance, not too heavy, not too light. Under her Armani top was a powerful set of shoulders from years both swimming and from dealing with a wheelchair. Above the Armani top was a simple, short hairdo for her brown hair.

"We have damn near funded one particular academic institution in this country by ourselves and I believe I could roll myself onto that campus, find the University president's office and have his secretary tell me that he is catching up on his e-mails at the moment and he does not have time to meet with me. Of course, if I mentioned the name of the foundation that appears on his checks, he would throw his mistress off the couch and be out in the waiting room while buttoning up his trousers in fifteen seconds." Reesa gave the room a good chance to laugh.

"Oh, golly, I don't mean that we hide our money from the IRS; I buy a fleet of new military jets for the Air Force every year through the income taxes we pay whether I want to or not because they still get a fortune from us. You do have to laugh, last year we went to a football game and three F-22 Raptors flew overhead before the national anthem. As we were walking out of the stadium, Sam walked, I rolled past the pilots who had arrived at half time and I thanked them for their service. One bright, young face looked at me and thanked me for the airplane. Little did he know…" Laughter covered the room. In just a few minutes, Reesa Jonathon had gone from an intriguing known, yet unknown, asterisk of sports history to one of this group's new heroes.

"Well, that is how I have wanted it and how I want it in the future, but I suspect that I lost my anonymity a minute or two ago. Frankly, my anonymity is not as important as the United States of America. That being said, wearing a wig of choice to change my brown hair color doesn't provide the same disguise to one who travels horizontally instead of vertically.

"Everyone gives to charity for different reasons and I admire those of you who give serious money and enjoy seeing your names on buildings or receiving honorary degrees. I would just rather be left alone and observe whether the charities do what they have promised to do. It is probably a character flaw for me. Sam thinks so. Anyway, the President does not seem to understand that after I give away that $175 million, I don't have it anymore. And from that money that I don't have anymore, he wants me to pay additional Federal tax of about $20 million on my contributions. Is he crazy or does he just not understand?

"The one thing I can tell you about that crazy idea of limited tax deductions for charitable contributions is that big contributions everywhere will collapse or be greatly reduced if he has his way. I intend to do everything I can to stop it. It is the mega-contributions that build great institutions. No one can build a serious building without a few whales as contributors."

The thoughts, political and charitable, stirring in Reesa Jonathon's mind were special and could not help but to continue to alter her remaining years. She was very much enjoying her little presentation and had focused her eyes on some of the big name givers as she dropped her numbers on the assemblage. Maybe this was a new calling for her. She began to think about how much money she might be able to raise for her favorite charities with matching gifts. She began to think about convincing some of these captains of industry and princes and princesses of Hollywood that they should currently support charities for all of the right reasons and leave the most significant portion of their estates to well-run public charities. *Oh well,* she thought, *that is all in the near distant future. Today, this morning, is about changing the political landscape. This morning is solely about political action.*

"I have always laughed when I think about that term, charitable whale, and little old me. In many instances, if in the future the President's plan is enacted and I decide the tax benefits are too little and my contributions are not made, the President's plan means that the government will have to pay one hundred percent of the cost of those facilities or charitable activities that I would have financed. Let's say I decide not to give $1 million to the Red Cross, does he not understand that the Federal government will end up paying $1 million for the necessary services to victims of disasters? Thus, instead of having taxpayers make the same payments with deductible charitable dollars. I lose my tax deduction and the government now pays one hundred percent directly to the Red Cross instead of roughly thirty percent by giving me my tax deduction. Now there is a wonderful result that the President's administration must clearly not understand.

"And since the government will not subsidize churches, there may be no church building starting at day one. That is nuts. And the Tea Party, they want to have a FairTax, some FairTax; it would reduce my annual Federal taxes by more than $150 million by my calculations and that means some group of poor laborers is going to have to pay those taxes. How could I, or we, ever live with that?" There were a few FairTax supporters in the room and each of them supported the FairTax for the identical reasons Reesa found repugnant. Their reactions, beneath their smiling faces, were mixed, at best.

"Health care...the President wants to make it available only to those who quote, unquote, deserve it. What do you think my chances will be if I live into my eighties?" She raised her voice and allowed her New York accent to escape, not a very pleasant sound, and said: *"Hey, we have an eighty-year-old cripple out here who needs an appointment to see if that twitch means she has a brain tumor."* Pause. *"Well, tell her we have three children with tonsillitis and a young woman with a broken arm; tell her to give us a call in a few weeks and we will see if we can work her in. She is way down in the point system and very expensive to treat...* Terrific, I'll miss you guys.

"And Paul Roland, I think he wants to ask a traffic accident victim to produce a birth certificate in the emergency room. These two candidates do

22

not represent Reesa Jonathon. I hope they don't represent your view of the world on these issues.

"As I told Ross yesterday, my grandpa would be proud to know that I will be kicking off an independent campaign for Senator Vincent with a starting budget of $100 million. And if that is not enough, I will up the ante. And don't worry; we will not reduce our charitable contributions by one cent. Father, do you have some thoughts?"

While Reesa Jonathon did not want so much as a single clap, every member of the audience was instantly standing and more than a few had at least a single tear in each eye. One guest looked at her neighbor and said: "This feels like a scene from *Butch Cassidy and the Sundance Kid*, 'Who is that woman?'"

Father Woods could have been sent to Max's Place by central casting. Perhaps, central casting for an old black and white movie including Bing Crosby as the star, but central casting for sure. White as a freshly washed and starched T-shirt and red cheeks, that was Father Woods. He would have given Bing Crosby a run for his money portraying a priest. He was not a tall man and, although born in Boston, he had been blessed with many years in Ireland, where his family lived until he was fourteen years old and where he ultimately returned and took his undergraduate studies at Trinity, in the heart of Dublin. He had a great deal more than a hint of an Irish accent. He was the second son of a family with two sons and three daughters; his fate to become a priest was effectively written prior to birth. Most described the Father as a lovely and gentle man.

The priest would use the microphone. While a brilliant orator, he rarely raised his voice above an Irish whisper. As Ross Anderson handed him the microphone, the Priest thought about how important his next few words were to his church and his life mission.

"Oh Reesa, have you thought about accepting Catholicism?" His Irish whisper put the emphasis on *thought*. Great laughter followed. "There are several, actually many churches in Boston that are in great need of rebuild-ing. Reesa, let's do lunch and talk philanthropy!" The audience laughed.

"Friends, we need to talk for a moment about both Almighty God and the church. While that seems extreme, it is in fact, exactly what I mean." Father Woods' voice sounded exactly as if it was sent to the meeting by Bing Crosby, that simple, gentle Irish tilt. Father Woods' Irish speaking style placed his word emphasis on his verbs. It was delightful.

23

"This morning, while Ross Anderson served what he seems to think is a healthy breakfast, Ross carefully instructed each of us to talk about issues and asked us not to bash either candidate. Sorry Ross, but I need to talk about an issue where I feel betrayed, betrayed with respect to that which my entire life and being have been consumed.

"I supported the President in the last election. I suspect some of the actions I took and some of the things I said from the pulpit were inappropriate from a church/state prospective. But I believed. I believed this president would be good for America. Yes, I believed that he was everything that President George Boone was from a religious perspective and everything that President Bill Cloud was from a policy standpoint. For me, this was a perfect match. I believed that this president was a religious man. I believed that because he talked about it and because he seemed to relish the opportunity to go to church and share his thoughts. While having a religious president is not a necessity from a legislative sense to me, and the United States has had some fine presidents who were not particularly religious, but if you are a Catholic priest as myself, it is more than a helpful addition to a candidate's resume. Maybe, it is the promise not fulfilled that drives me crazy.

"I remember the scandal with Reverend...whatever his name was in Chicago and the President's response. I first thought his response was eloquent and appropriate and then I thought to myself, this is"—the priest emphasized the verb *is* a bit more than the emphasis in his other offerings—"really odd. This is a smart man, a smart politician, and yet he was silly enough to sit in a pew and listen to a man who had a view of the United States that, at best, would be inconsistent with the view of more than ninety percent of most Americans. Why would he sit there? Why wouldn't he find a new church? And I can remember thinking to myself as if it were yesterday, maybe, just maybe, he was not in church quite as often as the rest of his rhetoric would imply. But I put that aside because I wanted to believe. Boy, did I want to believe.

"And then that young minister, the one down in Orange County here, asked the President about conception and the President replied that the date life begins was *beyond his pay grade*. Beyond his pay grade? Nothing more than a prepared dodge! I bristled and found myself yelling at the television set for the good minister to ask a follow-up question or simply repeat the question. Nothing. And again, silly me, I wanted to believe." The verb *wanted* again was dominant in this sentence. "I *wanted* to believe!" he repeated. "I convinced myself that this was just politics at work."

"And we win. We elect a black President of the United States who believes in healing the sick, talking to foreign leaders who we do not talk to because we disagree on matters of state, and believes deeply in Christ. Winner, winner, winner!" The priest raised his arms as if a touchdown had been scored. "How good does it get for me? And then he spends what seemed like years selecting a church and at the end of the day he never chooses a church. The family does not attend any church in Washington D.C., any church at all. Some crap about impacting Sunday services. He claims his church is the chapel at Camp David and that he gets daily devotionals on his Blackberry. His Blackberry? Give me a break. Great way to raise your kids. Apparently, the only time he attends church is when he wants to give a political speech. And I feel betrayed. Yes, betrayed.

"Those of you who know me know I read everything. I read all of the political books, left, far left, right, far right...ok, ok, I skip far right." A kind of snort of a laugh came from the priest and a bit of laughter from his audience. "I pick up *Game Change* and there it is on page 235; his wife admits that the President stopped going to church a decade, yes, a *decade* before the presidential election. He stopped going to church when his first child was born. And I feel used and betrayed. My instincts had told me there was something wrong with the picture and I wanted so much to believe that I ignored all of the signs.

"Now, I am not remotely indicating that the President is not a Christian. Many good people and many good Christians only attend church on occasion. But a good Christian does not go out of his way to give an incorrect impression of his religiosity. From a religious standpoint, as a Priest, I forgive him completely, but as just a citizen who thinks hard about his vote, I feel betrayed."

Father Woods took a moment to gather his thoughts. For him, this was a catharsis and he felt much better having admitted that he was wrong about the President; at least wrong in his own mind. The audience listened attentively without applause or any other definitive reaction. Probably a little better than one-half of this audience had voted for the President and certainly many of them were not inclined to agree with this priest or manage to find anything wrong with this president as a person.

"Ross, I apologize for sharing these remarks as they are not what you hoped for, but I needed to put my charitable thought into some context. I hope even priests are allowed to take a short political step over the line, on occasion."

Ross Anderson simply nodded at Father Woods. Anderson's issue was with the President's policies and his lack of transparency, not whether he was religious. Anderson thought to himself: *Well that was pretty darn interesting. I couldn't care less if the President worshipped his garage door or believes in a sun god. I just hope FatherWoods hasn't screwed this up for anyone else. I guess we all come at this from really different directions. I had no idea this was what was really eating at my friend when we were discussing putting this event together. Now, I know.*

The priest continued: "As to what Ross Anderson and his friends thought I would chat about, the church and this election are caught between two different methods of taking your money; both will cause it to be nearly impossible to build any facilities for the church. None, nada, no new churches. Lovely Reesa here chatted about the increasing tax cost of her donations under the President's plan and the lack of benefit to her contributions under the Tea Party's plan. For church charities, this may be an insurmountable problem. Even our friends in the Mormon faith might have a bit more trouble getting their ten percent fee to be loved by God if it suddenly costs twenty percent to give that ten percent." This caused an uncomfortable squirming and scattered laughter as the audience assumed that the room was not Mormon free. But, there were no Mormons in the room. Father Woods knew there were no Mormons in the room before he had uttered his last sentence, but would have made the comment regardless. The reality for Father Woods was that he wished the Catholic Church had mandatory tithing too. *What a great business plan!*

"Of course, I would never have said that if there were any Mormons here, but this is such a serious group and that was a joke." Very little response. "Maybe I will just apologize and move on. By the way, the President could have said, *I am sorry* to that Cambridge policeman, but apparently, the man never makes a mistake, so he need not apologize, ever. And if I sound a bit worried and bitter in that comment, it is only because I am."

The Priest's green eyes seemed to dominate his ultra white complexion. "The church in America, all churches, will face serious financial issues if our major donors are taxed on their donations. You can see the decline of the church in Europe and a great part of that decline is the over-arching disinclination to give money away as charity. Our current tax system encourages our charitable culture. Our charitable culture is a foundational block of our society.

"Reesa has it right. Under the President's plan, people will pay a tax, in addition to their contributions. This is not good for many non-church charities because their members will lose these deductions. It is a nightmare for the Federal government because if the Red Cross, for example, loses its major donors, if the government determines that the Red Cross is perform-ing an important duty, it will either need to perform that duty or give the Red Cross the money. In that world, if Reesa does not make her gift of $1 million to the Red Cross, the Red Cross loses $1 million at day one. But, if the government wants the Red Cross to perform its role, it will give them the money or have the Federal government do the task. Either the Red Cross will get the money from the government and perform the task or the gov-ernment will spend the million dollars, although we all know the govern-ment will find a way to spend more than $1 million to accomplish the same $1 million level of work. If it falls to the government, the work gets done, but it costs the government twice or three times as much to do the job. I know Reesa said this, but I thought it was worth repeating.

"The church is different. We cannot get money from the Federal gov-ernment because this country rightfully has a separation of church and state. We have a secular government. So, if Reesa does not give her $1 million to the church, there is no one to fund the church. Our church in America funds its operations from the collection plate, small donors who love God and whom God loves in return; our facilities are funded by large donors like Reesa and donations from them over time will either be reduced or will cease. This will kill churches in the United States, not immediately, but over time. Just like France. The church will bleed to death. And that is my message to you; this election is about the survival of the church." The Father handed back the microphone to Anderson who placed it on the tablecloth on the table in front of him.

Anderson spoke a bit more loudly to the audience than before. "Two things. Our friend Mr. Roland does not want a FairTax. The Tea Party does. And I suspect the Tea Party will drive Roland crazy on this issue. When Father Woods and I talked about that, I explained that a FairTax would essen-tially put the entire tax burden on the middle class and that was enough for the good Father to understand that while this might free up money from the wealthy for contributions, it would do great harm to most of the people in the pews. Father Woods dismissed the FairTax out of hand. Second, I asked Father Woods not to make any comments about the international arena. We left that job to Beth Midlands."

Virtually, no one in the room knew who Beth Midlands was three years before today. Still most did not know who she was now. She had become one of the few female presidents of a New York Stock Exchange traded company, but she had little interest in self-promotion. She had guided her company to significant earnings through a worldwide strategy of placing her operations all around the world in a manner that produced a superior product at a lower cost to the consumer. While she was not the only female president of a New York Stock Exchange company, she was virtually the only black female president of any major company in the United States. Had she wanted to be visible, she would have been as visible as she chose.

"No, Ross. I definitely do not need a microphone. Midlands' natural voice was significantly louder than the amplified voice of Father Woods or the unamplified voice of Anderson." She walked into the audience with the style and grace of an evangelical minister. At close to six feet and well over two hundred pounds, none of it muscle, one had to conclude that this woman's success was based on her skill set, not her appearance. And her skill set was more than a bit formidable with an engineering degree from MIT, a master's degree in quantum mathematics and a PhD in industrial psychology. Both of the latter degrees were received during her three years at Stanford. After four years teaching and consulting at the University of Washington after receiving her final degree, she threw away the cap and gown and entered the business world as a senior vice president at Soroly Corporation and as they say, the rest is history. Actually, the rest was magical as it turned out that this person was a charismatic business leader for whom people loved to work while she was also a genius at both engineering and marketing.

"I too supported the President in his campaign." Beth Midlands roared to the audience. With Midlands, there was more of a Southern accent than one might have expected given her educational background. The *I* was *Ahhh* and the cadence was significantly slower than whatever the norm was for Southern California. The cadence might have been slow, but the volume was more than sufficient. "I thought that our ability to grow our little business around the world would instantly be enhanced by electing anyone except another white Republican male. I thought that the President would open up areas of communication around the world. And I was wrong." Wrong seemed to have an *awn* instead of an *ong* as Midlands pronounced it. She was speaking without so much as a three-by-five card and slowly walking from table to table in much the same way as a cocktail singer in a 1940s black and white movie or Jean Simmons in *Elmer Gantry*. And just like in the movies, every individual in the room was hanging on her every word. When they handed out charisma, the woman received her share and that of several others. When she stood by a table, every head was turned to her and each was attentive; no one was staring at their feet.

"Today, so far, we have been unable to bid on a single opportunity in Iraq, which I thought was the nation that George Boone saved from the wrath of Saddam Hussein and his henchmen. All this administration will tell me on this is that we need to be patient and the President is not going to get involved in internal Iraqi politics. My people in Iraq tell me that other countries are paying the Iraqi ministers bribes that are illegal for us and we do nothing. Nothing!" With her grey shirt outside the pants suit outfit, Midlands looked both enormous and intimidating, but her words, not her attire were resonating with those assembled. Other businessmen in the room were nodding. "And in the rest of the Muslim world, we do not even have the opportunity to lose in an unfair bid. We are uninvited and unwanted in the bidding process and there is no smokescreen around the discussion. Our new international goodie-two-shoes approach has made the Muslim world feel insulated from any ramifications for their actions, particularly from the United States. Our new approach is the walk softly, carry-no-stick approach.

"My Saudi friends tell me that buying from the United States imperils them if Iran decides to use its army or its nuclear weapons to conquer their nation. Imperils them on a human being level. That means, folks," she said, now standing in the very back of the room with her booming voice slowly speaking her words in that Southern Georgian accent she had picked up as a child, "that they do not believe that if push comes to shove, this administration will react to a war in the Middle East with any more than a call to the United Nations. They think we are, to use a phrase that was used in the 1950s, believe we are a paper tiger. They think they will be abandoned,

abandoned in such a complete way, they fear for their lives. They are afraid to do business with us. Rightfully so, perhaps.

"My gosh, the French who put up about two dollars and fifty cents in aid, openly accused the United States of occupying Haiti on day seven of our relief effort after the earthquake. President Boone, who is extremely far from my favorite president, would have been on the telephone to Sarkozy in about two seconds asking him what that was about. Our current president was campaigning in Massachusetts and far too focused on his own domestic issues to take time to offer a response. Why did he run for office if he only wanted to campaign? He could have campaigned to his heart's delight as chairman of the Democratic Party.

"When we talk about individuals who talk big and don't deliver, mah friends from Texas use the expression: Big hat, no horse!" Midland just stopped and waited for the light laughter to stop, but instead the laughter seemed to be a release and it rose to a crescendo and died down like a wave at a football game making its third pass around the stadium.

"Big hat, no horse. Ah guess this urban audience doesn't hear our Southern expressions very often. Hits home, does it not?" Midlands had a huge grin at this point. "Mah friends, it only gets worse. The Israelis believe the President hates Jews, while the South Americans just ignore us, move left and expropriate American companies. The negotiations with North Korea, who for God's sake actually fired a nuclear weapon at South Korea, are going nowhere except to a repeat of sending them food for their promise to not launch another nuclear weapon. Japan and China are respected and feared by North Korea. We, the supposed leader of the free world are a joke to them. Big hat, no horse. That should scare everyone in the free world."

"We pander to dictators who find us naïve and powerless. We either lecture our allies or ignore our allies when we do not need them. What is it about the United States of America that this president dislikes so much?

"Mah friends, we are truly a paper tiger, and because of that, business cannot get traction in world markets and, Father, forgive my choice of words, American business is just plain screwed!" Here another long pause and seemingly the finale rested with the next sentence: "Higher taxes, higher union costs, less access to world markets, distrust in the USA as an ally, this is a formula that could have been designed by a combination of Herbert Hoover and Neville Chamberlin."

By now, Beth Midlands' two-hundred-pound body was back in the front of the room. She just looked at the folks in the room and almost as one they again stood and applauded. No one really knew whether they were applauding the woman, her ideas or if they thought she was done speaking, but it was unlikely to be the latter."

Midlands began speaking again: "Is it any wonder that the nations of the Middle East, including Israel, have lost faith in the United States of America and our, yes *our*, commitments to protect them? Is there any surprise to the massive arms build-up throughout the Middle East as Iran continues to pursue a more and more significant nuclear arsenal? These are rhetorical questions because we can all read the newspapers, or the electronic versions on our Kindles.

"And Paul Roland, that skinny little man from the eighteenth century, he wants us to go and hide. I don't know which is worse: Talk softly and carry no stick or hide in an isolationist mode like an unborn child in the womb, while knowing that the oceans provide insufficient protection for the United States in the world of 2012.

"I only know that the positive change the country bought into four years ago has been a complete negative change internationally and the world is a darker place for it. We need new leadership to protect and honor this great nation. We need new leadership to make us feel like Americans. While the President of the United Sates may not believe in American exceptionalism, I believe in our country, I believe in American exceptionalism and I am committed, checkbook in hand, to support Senator Vincent in his quest to return our country to greatness. And yes, I mean *return* as I believe we have already lost our status as world leader." She looked at Ross Anderson, stared again at the audience and sat down. A second standing O.

After a moment, Ross Anderson's surprise, Beth Midlands stood again. "I forgot. You know, there is all of this talk and all these lawsuits with respect to immigration. Let me tell you what it is doing to our country. First, if the Federal government does not rigorously enforce the borders, who does this benefit? Oh, don't think about cheap wages. The poor folks crossing the border, many carrying drugs for the Coyotes, are not sufficiently educated to work in most of our technology businesses. By not defending the borders, this lack of enforcement is benefitting the drug lords, foreign and domestic. The Federal government is aiding and abetting the drug smugglers and their minions in their distribution systems throughout the United States. And this hurts everyone. Remember the rave event in Los Angeles a few years ago? How is it possible that half of an underage audience could be stoned unless the Federal government is turning a blind eye to drugs? And in the international arena, our drug addiction is killing our neighbor to the South. If it was not so easy to get drugs on our side of the border, the Mexican border cities would not have the drug lords fighting over turf on their side of the border and there wouldn't be the thousands of dead Mexicans on their side of the border. And in my humble opinion, this is entirely on the President's administration at this point. And if you think the border violence will stay on that side of the border..." Midlands' voice trailed off and she sat down again.

Ross Anderson again walked to the left side of the room, stage right. This time, he spoke into the microphone, again showing his accent-free Southern California upbringing. "So, that is our pitch. Reesa, Father Woods, Beth and I have spoken about areas of our interest. I set the stage. I know we could bash the President on other issues like the gulf or much more on immigration. We have not beaten you to death on all of the issues. No need for this group. I do believe that most of the business people in the room will agree that, obviously, the President had no idea about the difference between stimulus and deficit financing. Equally obvious, the President and at least until November 2010, the Congress, used the nation's wealth to repay political favors to individuals, entities and political cronies who helped them with the election and to accomplish purely political goals instead of focusing on the economy. Even today, I don't think the President remotely knows or cares about the states' pension crises.

"I would argue that the election results since New Jersey, Virginia and Massachusetts were the result of his behind the scenes deal making, particularly the favors granted in the health care legislation. The lack of transparency when full transparency was promised has united so many voters against this president. I do not think the Democrats have yet grasped the reasons for their defeat in 2010.

"In defense of those who would stand here and say it was the same under the Republicans, I could not disagree, it was bad. But this...this President has brought cronyism and unionism to a new level. F–ing spendthrift! And if we are honest in this room, some of us were recipients of that political largess. Certainly, my support of the President in the campaign was repaid through access and a few wonderful contracts with the Federal government.

And believe me, if a guy in my businesses can profit from Federal contracts, anyone can get to the front of the line with the right contributions.

"And honestly, all of this being said with the number of Tea Party candidates on the right and Paul Roland as the Republican standard bearer, none of the four of us are comfortable with a Republican Party mandate including the House, the Senate and the presidency. The current political leadership of both parties scares us to death.

"I think we all now recognize what a disaster this president has been and it is the bigger picture that has us terrified. Both political parties, in my opinion, have been aiders and abettors. We cannot have a Federal government that is being run exclusively to benefit its supporters and we cannot have a government that has become a bully. I would argue that no matter what side of the argument you were on with respect to health care, the actions of the Congress and this president embarrassed your view of what government was supposed to be. We just cannot have the key discussions taking place behind closed doors with deal-a-minute marathons. It makes the government of the United States look corrupt. Both look and..." He did not finish this sentence.

"Sadly, the Federal government is so big now that the employees of the Federal government can independently influence elections, Federal and State. This is just crazy and the impacts can be seen at every level in terms of their pensions and health plans. The difference between the pensions being paid to government employees and the private sector is staggering from an economic and from a fairness prospective. How is it managers with no entrepreneurial risk are paid more than the private sector?

"Can you imagine four years ago, talking about the Federal government bringing in union bullies to a political rally to stymie debate? Oh my God, what has happened to my country?" This was followed by a few moments of silence and Ross Anderson walking back to the head table to take a brief look at his notes.

"Let me remind you that this is the last meeting of this group. There will be no lunch, no minutes to review and our expectation, and frankly our prayer, is that most of you will either sign up to contribute to issue campaigns or open your own independent expenditure campaigns for the American Exceptionalism Party for its presidential and vice presidential candidates, George Vincent and Jordon Scotch, the economist from UCLA, up the street here. We are hopeful that the majority of money will be spent on independent campaigns.

"We have done nothing this morning to keep you from having your own independent campaign, but rest assured, if you so much as coordinate your independent spending with your favorite server at Starbucks who also has her own independent campaign fund, you are violating the law! Let me repeat this admonition, if you so much as coordinate your spending with your favorite server at Starbucks, you are violating the law. If you go forward with our ideas, you will need legal help to make sure you remain a virgin with the legal system *AFTER* the election.

"Three things left and we will be done, forever, with this group. One, we will take a few questions, two, we will ask you to anonymously enter the amount you intend to spend in this effort and, lastly, if you choose, the independent issue expenditure signature/sign-up lists are in the back. I believe that the overhead on the other side of the room has the list of issues to be addressed by the committees, if they can be funded. When was the last time anyone in this room saw an overhead projector? Wow. Questions?" Anderson was incredibly pleased that since the initial exodus, not another soul had headed for the door.

Several attendees got up and expressed their appreciation of the effort it took to get the group together and the importance of the meeting. Mercifully, no one in the room gave a passionate defense of the President, or a speech on behalf of Paul Roland. These people had to be in the room, but each one determined that there was nothing to be gained, and maybe a bit to be lost by expressing either of these opinions.

Anderson continued to take questions for ten minutes and was determined to keep the questions coming until the elephant in the room was finally sighted and discussed. He knew that everyone else knew there was a huge elephant in the room and he was not ending this discussion until the question was asked. He had formulated his answer; he just needed the question and he could go home, or go surfing.

Finally, a business mogul from Chicago stood up and asked the question: "Ross, you know the kind of hardball politics these boys play. I represent shareholders who may or may not be in agreement with what is happening. Obviously, the polls don't have the President at a single digit percent approval rating and he is still certainly the favorite to be re-elected. Don't you think that if we play this particular game, they will punish our individual businesses and industries? It certainly seems to me that this group in Washington has a with-me-or-against-me mentality and they have the tools to make our lives miserable!"

Be careful what you wish for was the first thought that went through Ross Anderson's mind. The second thought was classic rethink: *Shit, am I personally going to lose everything by doing what I think is the right thing?*

Ross Anderson stood as tall as he was able, his full six-foot-four-inches, paused, then lowered his head and said: "Chuck, that is the major personal concern the four of us discussed. Of course, Father Woods will always have a job. What if we lose and what if we suddenly find our businesses facing some ridiculous new regulatory rules or Federal investigations? What if we become the designated bad guy of the month? Can you imagine a Federal hotel tax confined to certain locations and a special tax on surfwear because of concerns with skin cancer? Hell, is that any different than punishing the banks for the actions of Fannie Mae?" Ross Anderson paused and moved to stage right, and a few feet closer to the audience, as he now wanted to drive home why this was so important in his mind.

"What if we become Governor Bertha Aplin after the 2008 election with whatever phony number of ethics violations in Alaska that were intended to crush her? Everyone knows that this involved just a few democratic activists trying to break her financially as she was forced to defend those accusations in court. It wasn't the Democratic Party, but it happened. Many of us believe the reason she left the governorship was that she could no longer fund her personal litigation. She was looking at bankruptcy. Those same jerks could attack our businesses.

"Well, at least it is neither Virginia in 1776, Valley Forge in 1778 nor Berlin in 1935. We don't have and don't need a Thomas Paine, a Von Steuben or a Diedrich Bonheoffer. We will not be risking our lives. Our fortunes, yes, but we will not be making the kinds of sacrifices that men and women have made for the United States and around the world for democracy for well over two hundred years. While Newt Gingrich may or may not be this room's hero, read his book, *Valley Forge*, from 2010. Those patriots suffered and died for our freedom. The four of us have decided to do what we see as the right thing and take the risks associated with that right thing.

"We cannot tell you there are no risks if we are unsuccessful and that is simply the way it is." Anderson put the microphone, which he had picked up

35

after Midlands' presentation, to his side for a moment and then lifted it back up and strolled to the middle of the room.

With a force of conviction which radiated throughout Max's Place, Ross Anderson proclaimed: "I for one have committed $25 million to this effort and that is a more significant piece of my net worth than makes any intellectual sense. But, I suspect that my relatives who died fighting the British back in the 1770s would be pretty proud of me, maybe a bit disappointed that I have not stepped to the plate sooner, but that at least I had finally arrived at the ballpark and brought my equipment with me." This was intended to draw applause and it did, significant applause and not just a few people standing. Sometimes the carefully scripted was as powerful in delivery as in expectation.

From behind him, Beth Midlands stood up and offered: "Well, Ah think I can match Mr. Anderson's commitment. Who was it, *Horton the Elephant* who said, 'I meant what I said, I said what I meant, an elephant is faithful one hundred percent?'" With that she sat down having admitted to herself that she was giving up a third of her net worth and about $25 million more than her total net worth only fifteen years before.

A San Diego businessman stood up, started to speak, and Ross Anderson offered into the microphone—"Folks, we are not a committee, we are not a group, we are not an evangelistic gang of believers and we don't want to have any other individuals making verbal commitments. That sounds a bit like a conspiracy to me." A wink at the lawyer. "We wanted you to know the extent of our individual commitments as we asked you to come a long way to hear our pitch. Of course the good Father Woods has already committed all of his worldly goods to an even higher calling." This took a bit of the tension out of the room with the laughter it produced.

"So, that is it. Less than two hours, thank you for coming. I only ask that you pick up those little machines and tell us what you intend to do; this is an honor system. Please, if you do not intend to spend any money, don't enter any amount. We will give you a minute to enter your commitment and then we will announce the number and then off to our homes and businesses. This is not a charitable auction, we will not come back at you and ask you to commit more money; we believed everyone would find this information interesting and useful."

The crowd did not applaud as every member of the audience picked up the tiny battery powered devices and many entered numbers. More than a few just pretended. After five minutes, Ross Anderson picked up the microphone one last time as most of the gathering was shaking hands, milling around and just chatting. "My friends, the commitments are for $1.68 billion. Yes, one point six eight billion dollars." There were no rounds of applause, gasps, or any level of surprise. The audience knew who was there and that Anderson and his friends had made their case. They also knew that some, probably many, commitments would not be kept, but also that word would leak out and more than a few other financial giants would join with their own independent campaigns. They also knew word would leak out and that players from other teams would also step up taller to the donation table; that was the way the world worked.

One last comment from Ross Anderson: "We are all honest people, we will fix this country for all of the right reasons. We will keep our commitments and we will obey the Federal laws on campaign contributions. Finally, the sign-up sheets for issues are in the back of the room. Thank you for coming." And that was it.

The crowd left fairly quickly and the only level of confusion that resulted on the way out was that so many of the people had arrived in black Chrysler Town Cars. People were looking for their drivers rather than going directly to where they had parked. A pretty funny scene. The possibility that with all of the private security and all of the weapons in the various cars that something would go woefully wrong was not fulfilled. Not a single person even tripped on the uneven asphalt. The parking lot was completely empty within fifteen minutes. Max's Place collected their modest fee, the wait staff returned to the restaurant to clean up the room and wait for the lunch crowd, and Max's lone security guard returned to his post to finish out his regular Friday shift. In Anderson's mind, the birds were singing. In that real world place, the world had changed, permanently.

~

TUESDAY, AUGUST 7, 2012

North-South Polling Service:

The President	50%
Congressman Paul Roland	45%
George Vincent	5%

~

From the day's *Washington Post* editorial page by Randy Kraus:

AMERICAN EXCEPTIONALISM PARTY CONVENTION
STARTS AND ENDS TODAY

Like many well-financed plays, the American Exceptionalism Party will have its premiere performance in Cleveland, Ohio. This evening, like most plays that open in Cleveland, this play will close in Cleveland. Broadway will never have to suffer through an evening watching the cast of this play self-destruct.

Armed with more early money and organization than anyone could have ever imagined and financed in a manner that probably skirted election laws around the nation, the American Exceptionalism Party, known to many in the beltway as the American Empty Party, rolls into Cleveland today for its one night stand.

The AEP comes to Cleveland with virtually no political support from anyone or anywhere. Senator Vincent will be nominated as their first and final presidential candidate and some fellow named Jordon Scotch will be nominated as their first and final vice-presidential candidate. Vincent is a senator from Ohio who, although he has served in the Senate for two plus terms, is virtually unknown nationally and Scotch, an economist from the West Coast, is completely unknown beyond his cubicle at UCLA.

The television networks, except RBC, have determined—or at least felt obligated—to cover the convention this evening. RBC is showing Casablanca, ensuring an entire new generation will see the beauty of a black and white love story in which no one removes so much as a single piece of clothing. The good news is that the best part of Casablanca will not be missed if one turns into the first ten minutes of the AEP Convention and then switches to RBC. The convention will be history, a short history, but history nonetheless, and one might wish to see the initial moments of the event.

The two of us who will actually watch the entire convention will see a third party making its debut and having its going-out-of-business sale in a single night. Mercifully, Senator Vincent must have decided a one-night stand was all the country could take of his attempt to destroy the two-party system and oust the only minority president in the history of our nation. Hence, the entire AEP Convention will take place beginning at 8:00 p.m. and, hopefully, end before 11:00 p.m. this evening.

Bottom line, the AEP stands for Empty. Their party platform, if it were written down, would be the equivalent of a benign cyst. The reality of this convention is that the delegates are at least ninety percent Caucasian and that is all one needs to know about tonight's event.

In states that had open primaries, the AEP had some modest success with protest votes being cast for Vincent; in all of the other states, George Vincent received his nomination with but a tiny, tiny fraction of the actual voters as virtually no one is registered as a member of the American Exceptionalism Party. In many states, only the minimum number of voters were registered to allow the AEP on the ballot and then only a small percentage of that minimum actually took time to vote.

If you are into the celebrity sighting part of politics, tonight will offer nothing whatsoever. The agenda that has been given to the press shows no star power, a few speeches and then, if the American public is lucky, an early concession speech by Senator Vincent. Again, the key to remember this evening is that Casablanca has a reasonably easy plot to follow with great acting, so missing the first few minutes would not be a disaster.

~

Senator George Vincent sat quietly with his wife Marge and his long-time advisor, Stanley Martin Wade, in a private and very Spartan room in the Q. The Cleveland convention center has been known almost exclusively as the Q since it opened with a Billy Joel concert on October 17, 1994. Its given name is the Quicken Loans Arena and, tonight, it was the location of the American Exceptionalism Party's political convention. The letter Q was being widely used to criticize, satirize and generally attack everything about Senator Vincent's third-party candidacy to be elected President of the United States:

>Vincent Plans **Q**uick Exit From Political Stage After Convention In the Q
>
>Did **Q**uicken Loan Vincent Money For a Convention at the Q or Did They Require the Money In Advance?"
>
>The Cleveland **Q**uicken Arena, All That Needs To Be Said About the Vincent Campaign
>
>The Cleveland Browns Have a Better Chance Than the Senator From Cleveland
>
>Even the Cleveland Cavaliers Have a Better Chance Than the Senator From Cleveland And They Have No Chance
>
>Tonight, a **Q**uick Exit for Vincent At The **Q**

The senator and his wife sat next to each other on a small couch while Stanley Wade, his campaign treasurer, sat on a grey folding chair, the only other option in the room. A mirror opposite the couch saw Marge Vincent fiddling continuously with her curly hair and checking every thirty seconds to see if her makeup was in place. The senator was deep in thought while Wade was trolling through computer runs on his lap. Wade's folding chair was in extremis from his three hundred pounds.

Senator Vincent broke from his own thoughts and lifted his now only somewhat tubby, but still unsculpted, body off the couch. He also could not resist looking in the mirror. In anticipation of a presidential campaign, he had peeled almost twenty pounds from his waistline, yet he still looked quite a bit overweight. The mirror did not lie. He thought to himself: *Well, you over-educated farm boy, if you could grow a few more strands of hair and another four inches, you wouldn't look too bad for fifty-three years old. Of course, given those two knee surgeries, if you were in perfect shape it would take you about forty minutes to get from one end of the Q's basketball court to the other. What the heck happened to you? It's not that you were ever the most handsome guy at the party. Or second most, but...*

Such were the thoughts of a politician who had never played a quarter of a basketball game or a single down of football in his life, yet he dearly loved sports, particularly football. Basketball he liked, football, he loved. The knee surgeries were from carrying too much weight most of his life. Vincent was, however, one of those rare somewhat overweight individuals with near perfect health and one who would rarely sleep more than four hours in any twenty-four hour period. This he knew was a God-given blessing and one which would play to his advantage if his campaign actually got off the ground.

George Vincent had been thinking about the prospects of his imminent ninety-day whirlwind presidential campaign with the normal accompanying family and personal concerns. He looked at his wife and then nodded to Stanley Wade. Both wistfully and rhetorically, he asked: "Do either of you guys believe that someone can really look down and see a political convention from heaven?" Marge did a bit of a double take because, absent the senator's regular appearance in church, he was not one to talk about religion very often and she had never heard a single remark about either heaven or hell from her partner of almost thirty years.

"I hope so, because I am sitting here thinking about my grandfather— my mother's father—and everything he taught me as a boy. It is really his values that brought all of us here tonight. That *never lie, never overstate, always over deliver, once a friend always a friend*...that stuff he believed and he taught me to believe. God, I hope it is always in vogue and it is in vogue with the people we have here tonight. I hope my philosophy does not make me a relic and just an historical footnote. One really has to wonder if we still believe that a handshake is as good as a forty-page contract. Pop was a goody two-shoes in so many ways and I guess, actually I hope, he trained me the same way." Senator Vincent never seemed to move when he talked. Even this soliloquy was being delivered seated on the tiny couch. The senator had his arms folded and was steady as could be.

"Stan, you don't know the story. My mom's dad literally walked out of Russia in the late 1800s. He and his brother decided to go East instead of West because he thought that in going away from Europe, they had a better chance of surviving their travel from Russia to the United States. He was less worried about the distance and the Siberian cold then the pogroms of the czars. In the late 1880s, it was still dangerous being the proverbial stranger. Maybe it still should be.

43

"He lived with us when I was in high school. He was not exactly sure how old he was, but the guess was that by then he was in his late nineties or early hundreds. Strong as an ox. Even at that age, he still had a head of hair that had only receded from his eyebrows about half an inch. Obviously, I missed that gene. He was brilliant, yet, could barely read or write.

"This was a guy that was well over six foot and two hundred pounds and when I was a little kid, I watched him get in a fight when he was probably in his late eighties. Tough guy. In his day, his size made him a literal giant, and yet he was sufficiently afraid of the pogroms that they went East to get out of Russia. When they reached Alaska, he stayed there to build a fishing business while his brother continued to Philadelphia to do the same. Apparently, he stayed on Kodiak Island for almost a decade. He always said that it was when he was living with the Eskimos that he developed the set of values that sustained him for his entire life. Of interest Stan, he told us many stories about Alaska and we believed about a quarter of what he had to say…old man telling stories, etc. Well, my cousin—you know, the one with the PhD in chemistry from Penn—she decided to research our grandfather and, low and behold, everything he said and claimed to have done is fairly well documented. There is even an inlet named for him on Kodiak Island; he owned a company there, the whole nine yards. As I always say to Marge, that Internet is some tool.

"Pop had values that could not be easily surpassed by a head Rabbi or a Catholic Archbishop. As I said, I don't think he could hardly read, but when he shook hands with you, you never needed to think about it again. Actually pretty funny, I doubt he ever applied for citizenship, which would make this current president laugh pretty hard given those crazy birthers and all of the immigration issues we have. My question is how can I convey that this is a country that could use a few million William Sklaroffs. This is a country that needs an injection of ethics and work ethic."

Marge looked at her husband and wished with all of her heart that she had not felt obligated to support this quest to become the President of the United States. Marge was the same age as her husband, fifty-three, but had not been blessed with his robust health and unbelievable genetics. George Vincent's father and mother were still alive as well as most of his uncles. Vincent regularly said that if you did not smoke in his family, you had a better-than-even chance of making it to one hundred years old, and he had never smoked.

Twenty-five years of smoking for Marge, now ten years behind her, had done nothing for her long-term health and she sensed that her unfortunate Parkinson's disease genes were going to torture her as they had both of her parents. No one in her family had seen their early seventies; many had not seen their early fifties. It seemed her genetics were the polar opposite of her husband. She had kept the bit of shakes she recently started having in the morning a secret from her George, but believed the press would begin to sense something over the next few months. He would never notice. He loved his wife, but seeing a minor change in her health was not in his makeup.

It seemed that the diet Marge Vincent had started with her husband the moment it became clear they were going to begin this journey had not been at all good for her symptoms. While he seemed to look so much better from the diet when fully and smartly attired, she was looking a bit frail in the mirror in the morning and the only cosmetic steps she was willing to take were appropriate makeup and coloring her hair. The rigors of this campaign scared her. Nowhere was it written that two spouses would age at the same pace and in her case, it was not working out the way she might have hoped. *If only I can get through these ninety days without anyone noticing. Don't have to worry about George, he might not notice if I began dressing in a mini-skirt and wearing a peace button. Paying attention to 'small' things is not my George Vincent. A million big things, but not very many small things.*

A bit earthy, when asked publically a few years back about her looks, Marge Vincent responded that she had seen the senator from California and the Speaker of the House and she preferred that her friends from college not need a nametag on her blouse to recognize her. The press had been merciless for a few days, but the comment had made her an instant hero with the late night television and cable crowd. Thereafter, every time the Speaker of the House arrived with a bit more Botox, yet another face-lift, or California's junior senator had arrived with the hairdo of a sixteen-year-old, the television picture was preceded or succeeded by Marge Vincent's offhand comment.

Other than her regular video on television, Marge had, mercifully, been completely forgotten for a few years by the media. She liked that the print media had forgotten all about her and the Saturday late night television guys primarily used her as an occasional prop to hurt a couple of women for whom she had no respect. She thought to herself: *Golly, all I ever wanted to be for the last ten years was to be a grandmother and now this; not very fair. George is*

45

going to be pretty disappointed when he has to call Cleveland and ask for a date with his wife of twenty-nine years, because while it might appear to the public that I will be living in the White House, the chances of my not seeing my two grandchildren a couple of times a week, are slim to none. The presidency is one thing, Caleb and Sozzette, they are the only thing that my life is about. God, how many times am I going to have to explain the spelling of Sozzette's name, which I will never understand myself; it was the creation of my daughter-in-law. Ah me, only a little less than one hundred days of being the perfect wife. Georgee, I may have married you for better or worse, but dinner in the damn White House every night rather than hot dogs and beans with Caleb and Sozzette; my dear, you come in a distant third! I guess the good news is that you are betting your political career on this election idea and if you win, you get your White House and if you lose, you get Cleveland every weekend. Senators don't stay in Washington D.C. during the weekend. Either way, my time is going to be spent with my grandkids and they are in Cleveland. Keep your mouth shut, Kid!

Marge got control of her thoughts and smiled, having honestly wished she had met William Sklaroff. He must have been the real deal. "George, let's get a bit more makeup on you and then go visit your guests. I looked in the holding room an hour ago and then a half hour ago; I swear that the egos in that room have raised the ceiling a couple of inches. There is only so much room. Good news, a couple of your 'big boys and girls' said not having a separate waiting room was okay or you would have needed to partition the entire building into small cubicles."

Without another word and without any more makeup (which was virtually none), the senator started towards the door. Wade smiled and continued to look at his computer runs. He wasn't leaving his folding chair or this room and neither the senator nor his wife ventured a syllable asking him to join them. Stanley Martin Wade was a political strategy and numbers guy. His presence with the assembled mass of *friends* was not going to add anything to the mix. He could be in the room for an hour and not utter a single word. He would leave only to find food or wander down after the show started.

As Senator Vincent turned the handle of the door to walk down the hallway, the Secret Service men and women formed around the candidate couple and created a little protective pocket. Vincent was not sure what to make of this new world, famous for its prophylactic of protection, as one of the old line agents postured to his friends.

The Q is Cleveland's best location and perhaps the only possible location in Ohio for a political convention. Aside from being the former home of LeBron James and the continuing home of the Cleveland Cavaliers, the Q was both in Vincent's home state and it was available this evening. For a building approaching twenty years old, it still looked brand new as the 310 pane glass canopy entrance was designed to be ageless, giving the building that sense of dignity and power that its designers had attempted to create.

The hallway the President and his wife currently travelled down required perfect identification to enter. It appeared that the Q's architects had considered security when they built the convention center and therefore, the access to the various hallways was, in fact, very easy to control. The State of Arizona could have been in charge of the security in this hallway and it would have been secure without help from the Federal government.

~

The inside portion of the arena had been set up as if the convention was an educational seminar or business meeting with semi-circular seating for the delegates at fairly small tables on the arena floor. The television viewers were going to see people sitting who looked like they were at a meeting rather than a rock concert. There were pads of paper and pencils for every delegate. The colors in the arena were locally popular and the furnishings were intentionally a couple of levels below other conventions. This was all planned to send a message. And the message would hopefully be obvious to the viewer. Senator Vincent and his advisors wanted to sell the public that his American Exceptionalism Party was a serious, frugal, taxpayer-friendly entity. The money thing was in the senator's foremost thoughts. The senator's team was terrified that money would be an insurmountable problem over the next few months, regardless of Federal financing, a fear that would prove completely unfounded. (He had called every political marker and spent most of his moderate wealth to raise sufficient dollars to gain access for the American Exceptionalism Party on every state ballot, so in his mind, his campaign would become a function of fundraising efforts.) While *frugal* was the way he intended to run the government, the organization of the convention was pure staging and when seen by the viewers, the staging delivered the desired and appropriate message.

One of the concerns of the senator was that a ticket to the Q tonight was not one of the coveted tickets of the decade, or even a Tuesday during the week of August 7, 2012, or even in Cleveland. Not very many people in Cleveland or anywhere else were very interested in this convention. A near empty arena was not a good thing for a political convention with full television coverage. While he knew (or hoped) that people would wish they had attended after the convention, it was not going to happen tonight. Besides the delegates, the audience was going to be mostly television viewers and reporters and the television reporters were always a problem for any party other than the Democratic Party. All were especially unhappy to be in Cleveland.

Senator Vincent assumed that the television cameras would singularly focus on the many empty seats in the arena. As a result, he had thousands of seats covered by what might look like the tarps that cover seats at a sports stadium because from these particular seats, the fans cannot see the field. Across the tarps were painted signs in very large print that read: *Elect George Vincent*. The senator was fairly comfortable that this was not what the television networks would want to show to their audiences and, therefore, the emptiness of the building would not be easily exposed. Having watched more than a few Indy car races on television where there were almost no occupied seats, yet no television viewer would know it, the senator was quite proud of his idea. Of course, in his fertile and often cynical mind, he had known that if he had the signs painted with *Re-Elect The President*, no one would see any portion of the convention on the floor as the cameras would have continuously focused on those signs and those signs alone. *The role of the underdog. And in the minds of the media, the role of a non-liberal, underdog bad guy.*

The conversation of what else could be written on the empty seat signs had been a hoot with creativity, humor and cynicism all rolled into a great fifteen minutes of a meeting that needed a relaxing break. Vincent's favorite was, *Go Buckeyes!* Senator Vincent's fervent hope was that millions of Americans who were not in the building would years later be bragging that they had actually been in one of the thousands of empty seats.

With the Democrats and Republicans somehow claiming red and blue, one of the interesting questions for the AEP was color. When the suggestion to use white was offered, Senator Vincent laughed out loud and responded with a "Oh, that should play well in the minority communities!" making the employee offering the suggestion seem a bit silly, but not quite dumb. Some research was performed and there was no good answer. As a result, everything that had a color in this convention hall was colored in scarlet and grey, the colors of The Ohio State University. This was a safe bet in Cleveland and as an Ohio State alumnus, a serious Ohio State alumnus, this was a great decision in the mind of the senator. He had not missed an Ohio State football game since he left school. Most of the time, he sat in the press box, but when it was cold, he would often put on a very bulky jacket and hat and go sit in the stands. That was how he preferred to watch his football, sitting next to some stranger who loved football and did not have some project he wanted the Federal government to build in his home state. Bottom line: let the networks figure out what color to put up on election eve, by then, who would even care?

The senator and his tiny team had given a great deal of thought to the political optics of the convention and the timing. He knew that the American Exceptionalism Party's Convention needed to be first and here they were on August 7, 2012, on a random Tuesday evening as the first political convention of this cycle. This would give the AEP a chance to define itself. This definition was crucial and had not previously occurred only because no one was deeply interested in either him or his political party. Tonight, the American Exceptionalism Party would move from the midway into the main tent.

Senator Vincent had watched the press try to destroy Bertha Aplin and define her within an hour of her nomination for vice president in 2008. A couple of reporters had tried to do that to him in the primaries, but there was such a lack of interest in the American Exceptionalism Party that viewers simply turned to another station when the talking heads mentioned him or this new political party. Since there was no party to speak of and there were no contested primaries, George Vincent and the AEP had flown significantly below the radar screen. To remain non-controversial, he and a few trusted allies had developed a platform that was as milk toast as possible.

The agenda that was distributed for the convention had nothing to write home to Mom about, but of more importance prior to the convention, there was not much included to be criticized, unless there was a politically caloric problem with milk and apple pie. He would set his hook and deliver the real political agenda tonight. His colleagues and the TV viewers would see something that would knock them off their chairs. At least that was the theory. The senator hoped that this convention would result in the United States of America being very interested in the AEP and George Vincent as a presidential candidate by tomorrow morning.

Senator Vincent understood that the average citizen would only be interested in the convention if it was entertaining and surprising. He had guaranteed both and he knew it would grab the viewers' attention within the first ten minutes. Thank you to the *Washington Post* for an editorial that suggested watching the first ten minutes. In the Washington beltway, mouths would open and voices would be silent for more than a few minutes after they got a whiff of what he was brewing. Hopefully, this convention would be the senator's version of shock and awe. The senator's youngest advisor had provided a single piece of technological advice that he guaranteed would instantly and continually expand the viewership once the show started. Vincent did not have a clear understanding of the idea, but he trusted the idea's author.

The newspapers around the country had given the American Exceptionalism Party Convention less coverage than a manhunt for a serial killer in the Ural Mountains. When not completely ignored, the editorial pages had been blasting the AEP since its formation as an attack on the two-party system and an attack on race. Vincent knew that the big newspapers believed that the op-ed section is where the opinion of the voters began and ended. He also knew that this had become complete hooey years ago as virtually no one read more than the first couple words of any newspaper editorial and that ninety percent of Americans read not so much as a single newspaper editorial in a single year. He also knew that after tonight, the editorial pages would take notice of him and his plans to become the President of the United States. Of course, he knew that notice would again take the form of attacks on him and his new political party. But again, who reads newspaper editorials anymore?

The blogs had been exceptionally harsh to Vincent and the AEP. He knew this was a real problem. Senator Vincent had become convinced that productivity in the United States was melting because office workers were spending time surfing the net to the tune of almost twenty percent of their average workday. He also knew that blogs changed on a dime and that after tonight, the non-far left and non-far right blogs could become big supporters. He also knew that the far right and the far left would be vicious, but might hold most of their anger for the other far side view once the other conventions passed. Plus, they were such jerks on the far sides of each party and there was nothing he could do to impact their blogging, good or bad.

In actuality, late night television had been the only serious continuing nightmare for the nascent campaign. The contest seemed to be whether the idea of Senator George Vincent wanting to be the president was indeed funnier than the creation of an American Exceptionalism Party. His campaign was perfect for opening monologues where there was a nightly, seemingly repetitive, thirty seconds of making fun of anything and everything about Vincent and his political party. The senator had wondered when storytelling had ended and mocking had become the primary statement of humor in the United States. The young voters who watched late night television had yet to hear a positive note on his candidacy and knowing tonight was the first moment of truth, he had considered and rejected the idea of appearing on these television shows during the primary season. That would have been a high-risk maneuver. He had recognized that his campaign depended upon this single night. The next few days would determine whether this was good strateegery or not.

The senator believed that virtually no one inside the Washington beltway could see that the AEP was a reaction to a president who had ventured far, far off course and had offended Middle America. He also believed that the AEP was a reaction to the Republicans who had done so little to distinguish themselves that their party was no longer seen as a viable alternative to the Democratic Party.

George Vincent believed that people who wanted to be left alone and have a stable government with a stable financial picture were angry, very angry, based on his reading of the polling data. A student of European history, Vincent was not completely sure that the thinking and actions of the elite and the average American were that different than moments before the French Revolution. The only major difference he could see was that the French were impoverished and hungry while the American public was fat, dumb and very unhappy with their government.

Vincent believed that the people of the United States wanted their nation to be a world leader, not a follower or, worse yet, a laggard with a "peace at all costs" philosophy. The senator believed that the Democrats and the Republicans had been taken over by career politicians who goosestepped to their own ideologies and their party leadership in the extreme. This was a tragedy that the senator blamed almost solely on computers and gerrymandering, where state officials carved out safe districts for their parties and therefore the most interested, powerful and extreme side of each party seemed to be Members of the House of Representatives. If someone needed a dinner speaker with some extreme left or extreme right philosophy, it was far too easy to find that speaker among the Members of the House of Representatives.

The senator had spoken and written about this widely for a number of years and was always well received by everyone, except other elected officials. It was this WIFM (what's in it for me?) philosophy that created these extreme political parties with no one capturing the middle ground. He also blamed flawed term limits legislation in most states, where it had become acceptable for a career politician to work his way up the political hierarchy and then work his or her way down so that, once elected, there was always effectively an elected official's job available for life. He had done some research and found that this phenomenon had resulted in an average age of elected politicians skyrocketing around the country. The same people were always elected, only changing positions regularly. Before 2000, whoever would have expected a former state representative to suddenly appear as the mayor of a small city?

What truly confused and angered the senator in the short run was the tone-deaf attitude of the leadership in his Democratic Party. This was his party and this was the party that had regained the White House in 2008 in great part because of their advanced understanding of melding communication technology with national elections. It had become clear to Senator Vincent that the party was politically lost and tone-deaf to the voters. Losing election after election since 2008 had cost the Democratic Party almost all of the moderate Democratic voices and instead of conceding to the reality that the party was far left of the electorate and the average Democrat, the party was greeting the losses in Congress as an opportunity to move even further left rather than toward the center. *How could we lose sixty-three votes in the House of Representatives and re-elect the same leadership?* Senator Vincent's answer, which he offered when he announced his own candidacy for the Presidency under the banner of the American Exceptionalism Party, was that his own Democratic Party's moving continually towards the left "was just nuts."

The senator was certain the nation's view of the American Exceptionalism Party would change tonight or, at a minimum, they would at least have a new view. The Party and he would both go from unknown to a significant presence in the span of thirty or forty minutes. He would awe the television audience with a major step towards turning their collective backs on the two existing political parties. Or so Senator George Vincent had convinced himself.

~

The television media was having a grand evening of diminishing the newly formed party literally before the first ever speaker of the AEP gaveled its meeting to order. For most of the media, this was their first real chance to spend any significant period of time discussing a subject they thought was a sideshow, the two-headed teenager at the fair. And for the first time, there was a viewer audience with all, or almost all of the television stations and cable networks covering this first convention. In each of the many press booths above the convention floor, no one in the mainstream media was sitting bolt upright in their chairs with expectations for an exciting evening. Not a single member of the media intended to vote for this clown and each knew that a debunking of everything Vincent and his party had to say would benefit the re-election campaign of the President or the election campaign of Paul Roland (for Fox News). The management of the major news organizations and its newscasters and many of the cable networks were jealous of RBC and its decision to telecast Casablanca rather than this American Exceptionalism Party Convention. Not even the highly paid production staffs earning excessive overtime wanted to spend this Tuesday night in Cleveland, Ohio.

The destruction of every non-left wing candidate continued to be the unwritten business/political plan of every mainstream television station, except Fox News. The non-Fox News media was not Democratic in its political persuasion, it was Progressive. However, Fox News was every bit as nonplussed as the rest of the media in their expectations for the American Exceptionalism Party. It was not lost on Fox News that George Vincent had been a lifelong Democrat. Fox News was merely there to report on an event which they also believed would have no impact on the election and which they believed was a side show similar to the Carnival Midway's continued exhibition of that two headed teenager.

There were a few bets in the booths as to whether Senator Vincent could obtain a sufficient number of votes in any state except, perhaps, his home state of Ohio, to impact that state's electoral votes going to the President or Congressman Roland.

The red light went on. Bob Colony's last thought before talking to the audience was: *Well, they are paying me for covering this nonsense and I am here, I will just do my best to make these guys look like the complete fools they really are.*

"This is Bob Colony with Marylou McBride from the Quicken Loan Arena, the Q, in Cleveland, Ohio. We are here tonight to cover the first and probably last convention of the American Exceptionalism Party. Marylou, what do you think about tonight?"

"Oh, Bob, I am guessing that this quote, unquote, I guess, political party, this American Exceptionalism Party, is a mile wide and an inch deep. Maybe an inch wide and an inch deep. Honestly, I can't believe anyone is watching and my guess is that most of our viewers are with us tonight because there are virtually no other programming choices. And wow, are Bob and I glad that you chose to be with us tonight. We do hate to be alone. We are going to give you the best coverage possible." Marylou McBride always tried to talk to the audience rather than to her co-anchor.

"Most of us had assumed that by now, someone we had actually heard of would have endorsed the candidacy of Senator Vincent or this convention would have been cancelled." Marylou McBride, one of OBC network's younger members of the news team loved to take shots at everyone and anyone, but she could change directions in a nanosecond. While she was anyone's definition of a good person, her personal business goals were personal recognition, wealth and little else.

Marylou McBride was with her co-anchor, Robert "Bob" Colony. Colony was one of the grey hairs who the networks believed were necessary as news anchors and for political conventions. Marylou always paid appropriate respect to Colony, but was certain that he was old enough to have fought at Gettysburg during the Civil War. Why he was covering a political convention in 2012, she had no idea. In her own mind, she paid Colony the lowest level of high respect. She believed she was a sharp-edged reporter who gave the viewing audience what they wanted and he was simply a skeletal reflection of another era. Worse yet, while Marylou admitted that she was often a bit one-sided in her analysis, this guy thought that the President was the only person in the world who did not put his pants on one leg at a time. Colony was a shameless Liberal, maybe really a shameless Progressive.

"Yes, Marylou, I am a bit mystified. We all know the Massachusetts stories of now Senator Scott Brown, we all know about the Republican successes in the 2010 midterm elections, but these newbies are on the national stage for God's sake. Four committed senators and four Members of House of Representatives do not make much of a political party."

"I believe that most of these senators in George Vincent's corner have already announced their retirement from the Senate." As was often the case with Colony at this point in his career, there was neither research nor accuracy behind this comment. "We received the agenda for this evening and including these precious few endorsers, there isn't a single surprise or moment of excitement planned for this evening." Colony looked at Marylou. Colony enjoyed working with Marylou because of her long, red hair and exceptionally long legs, in his mind, disproportionately long legs. It was as if her legs started about seven inches from her neck. He often thought to himself that there was barely room for all of the vital organs between her waist and her neck. He had also noted that this tiny part of her anatomy between her neck and her legs did contain two very large, but not too large, likely silicone enhanced breasts. Why she had forsaken modeling stockings and the like for the newsroom was something Colony never understood, but he had understood her clear disinterest in him as a friend or colleague. Robert Colony assumed Marylou's disinterest to be professional jealousy. Regardless, he did enjoy being able to sit on the set and appreciate the beauty of this young woman—a perquisite of the job. It would never dawn on Bob Colony that Marylou looked at him as a grandfather type while he looked at her as your average lust filled male looks at every attractive woman. The time for anything more than looking at pretty young women had past its warranty period for Colony, but his ego would never get to that reality. Colony had referred to Marylou privately as Big Red since meeting her for the first time. The name had easily escaped his private meetings and everyone at OBC referred to her as Big Red outside her hearing range. It described her perfectly; a compliment to describe a remarkably attractive young newscaster.

"Well, here is their first speaker, let's let the show speak for itself, Bob."

The television camera focused on the stage. "Good Evening and welcome to the first annual convention of the American Exceptionalism Party. I am honored to be in front of you tonight and frankly, I am mortified that we needed to form this third political party to save the United States of America.

"I want to make it clear tonight to everyone and anyone listening, I did not leave the Democratic Party, the Democratic Party, it left me!" exalted Senator Robert Jefferson Wayne. Each television network and cable put both his name and title—*Senator, North Carolina*—on the screen. "I want to make it equally clear that my Republican colleagues, each one who is here tonight would venture virtually the same statement, they did not leave the Republican Party, the Republican Party has left them. To that end, all of us have maintained our traditional party affiliations, be that Republican or

Democrat, with the hope that sanity will return and our parties will return to their more historical centrist philosophies. And by historical centrist positions, I do not mean the historical centrist position between the two parties, but centrist within their individual parties. Because this has not happened, tonight, we have come together as a group of Americans that represents the United States of America, not the extremes of the right and the left."

The convention crowd responded with an immediate standing ovation. With the small tables in front of the delegates, the convention had the appearance of a professional organization participating in a training seminar as opposed to a group of crazy convention delegates enjoying the silliness of a national political convention. There was not a single delegate wearing something designed to get them an appearance on television. A handful had arrived at the Q in traditional, *Yes, I am an idiot and I want to be seen on television attire*. They were asked to clean up their act before they were admitted. If a viewer was looking for the hat with the pins of forty-two straight state conventions or the hat with the state bird of Alabama, this was the wrong crowd. It was also not a coat and tie group for the most part, just folks attired in what the business world would generally describe as business casual.

At fifty-one years old, Senator Wayne, the five-foot-eleven-inch, former Green Beret Captain looked every bit the retired military officer that he was, ramrod tall in his posture, conventionally short hair (not a buzz cut) and sporting small, circular, somewhat old-fashioned, brown reading glasses. He had what might be mistaken for a briefing book on a bare wooden podium with a single metal stand. The teleprompter was not turned on for Senator Wayne.

"Tonight, we gather as Democrats who have seen our party taken over by zealots who see no exceptionalism in America and Republicans who, while they believe in American exceptionalism, also believe we need to be Samaritans while protecting each of our individual freedoms." More applause from the assembled delegates.

Most of the delegates knew Senator Wayne merely as a senator from North Carolina who had been elected fourteen years ago without any support from his Democratic Party. In his initial primary, he had faced a candidate from what the voters viewed as the left wing of the Democratic Party and he had decisively whipped that individual. He then achieved a fairly close victory against a Republican incumbent who Wayne thought was a pretty good guy. To his amazement, Wayne again was not supported six years later by the Democratic Party in his quest for re-election. In that primary, the Democratic Party this time supported a more liberal/progressive candidate than the previous election for the US Senate. In North Carolina, no progressive Democrat and no Republican had a chance against Wayne after his first senatorial victory.

Before his first Senate primary fourteen years ago, few knew of Wayne's six generation led passion for the United States. He was a many-greats grandson of Revolutionary war hero Mad Anthony Wayne, and a distant relative of Robert E. Lee. Before that first primary, it would have been easy to find this information with but a quick look at the West Point records from his class of 1980, but no one had bothered or had been sufficiently interested to look. Wayne graduated second in his class, but had served only eight years in the US Army following his graduation from West Point as the result of what he still believed was a minor injury to his right ankle in the Gulf War. While he rarely, if ever, discussed the issue, he never believed the injury sufficient to keep him off the battlefield. His military career was followed almost immediately by his election to the US Senate.

This particular Green Beret was an amateur historian as well as an expert in computer science and a decorated combat veteran. While recovering from those minor wounds received during the Gulf War, he had written a well-read work of historical fiction which highlighted his aversion to war as the first solution to any problem and established his disgust with the then current approach of the United States to international issues. In another time, he might have been described as an isolationist; an isolationist who wanted the strongest possible military to prevent any nation, group or individual from even thinking about doing minor harm to America or any living, breathing American, regardless of where in the world that individual was at any particular moment. Of some interest, during the intervening years since authoring his novel, Senator Wayne had made a rather significant intellectual move towards being willing to swing the big stick earlier than one might of thought from reading his book. His reading and personal writings in recent years included journals that discussed the lack of security that was provided in the current century from the oceans bordering the United States. Today, he would not mind swinging the stick, but he did not want any US Army overseas very long or very often. He did not believe that, in the long run, any nation could be successful in changing the culture of another nation or another society.

"We stand here tonight as Americans. We stand here tonight to establish ourselves as the real party of real Americans and willing successors to FDR, John F. Kennedy and Ronald Reagan." Applause; long lasting applause. "FDR, John Kennedy and Ronald Reagan, recent American presidents who believed that the United States of America was an exceptional nation made up of exceptional individuals." While the former Green Beret soldier certainly did not sound like he had spent his entire life in the South, there was no mistaking his origins. He would describe his regular speaking voice as *Southern light*. He would also tell close friends that when commanding troops in battle, he sounded like a modern day Lester Maddox with a choice of words that would have only seemed unremarkably offensive on an eighteenth century sailing vessel.

"The American Exceptionalism Party welcomes any American who believes in American exceptionalism, who believes in democracy, anyone who believes in helping his fellow man or woman, and who believes in individual work ethic. We welcome anyone who believes in the rule of law. We welcome you if you understand that there is a difference between protecting our borders and having a coherent immigration policy. The American Exceptionalism Party welcomes anyone who believes in democracy with a capital D.

"If you believe that government should be conducted behind closed doors with cash changing hands directly and indirectly, man, are you in the wrong building. If you believe that it is okay for a Member of Congress to use their office to avoid paying taxes or protect their spouse's business, man, you are in the wrong building! If you believe that a president should promise complete transparency and deliver total darkness, man, you are in the wrong building!" Wild and sustained applause.

"We want and need you to join us in this American Exceptionalism Party if you believe in America, if you believe in transparency, if you believe in the Constitution of the United States, and if you believe in a body of free people voting for honest people to serve the public, yes, serve the public interest!" Suddenly and truly suddenly, a political convention broke out in Cleveland, Ohio. This was red meat to this assembled group of Americans.

"Our party's name evolved from the President's remarks in 2009 when he effectively said Americans were no better than Brits, Greeks or anyone else. We believe in American exceptionalism. We believe that Americans are exceptional. We believe the United States of America is exceptional.

We believe that Americans have demonstrated their exceptionalism now for two centuries. We are the American Exceptionalism Party, proud of it and proud of our name and our country." The convention reacted as anyone might expect.

"We welcome Democrats, we welcome Republicans, we welcome Independents, we welcome anyone and everyone who believes in the America of our forefathers! We welcome anyone who does not believe that socialism, under the guise of either some European or Russian definition of fairness, is the American way! We are Americans, we are capitalists and we are proud of both. We want a country that is fair to all and equal to all regardless of race, creed, religion or financial wherewithal. We want a country where the government helps when there is an emergency and otherwise stays out of the way of our daily lives. We want a country where we do not have to choose between abortion on demand and no opportunity for abortion no matter the health of the mother or the extreme condition that created the pregnancy. We want a reasonable America." The convention stood and applauded these words, which they believed would propel them as a political party. The delegates knew their convention was being carried on every major television network save one, and hoped, although they knew better, that it was being watched by hundreds of millions of American voters. They also knew that—protest as he might—most Americans were beginning to see the current president as both a Socialist and an individual who was not representing the majority of Americans. They saw this president as intransient, unwilling to listen to other honestly held opinions. More than a few of these delegates thought worse.

"Let me pause here. Our friends at the *Washington Post* advised in an editorial this morning that those of you watching at home, our television audience should only give us ten minutes to see what we are made of and then switch networks to watch *Casablanca*. I have used a precious six or seven minutes already." This was followed by a few boos and catcalls. The Senator/ Green Beret Captain put up his hands, smiled and effectively commanded the catcalling to stop.

"Well, I suggest to the *Washington Post* that the next few minutes of this convention will even get your attention!"

"You may have noticed the fairly unusual organization of this stage and our delegate's convention floor. On the convention floor, we have working tables for our delegates who are from every state and every territory."

Senator Wayne knew that the television cameras would follow his travelogue of the arena area of the Q and then return to him. "On the stage, we have the same set-up." Wayne ignored for a moment, the flotilla of empty folding chairs around the small tables on the stage. "Of course, you have read in the *Washington Post* and other newspapers, heard on the television and been beaten to death by it on the Internet, that Senator Wayne and Jordon Scotch have not successfully attracted any major elected officials, so-called celebrities or social figures to commit to support his run for the presidency. Tonight, many of our quote, unquote special friends, individuals who have committed their support to Senator Vincent and Jordon Scotch, are indeed with us.

The camera of OBC panned the audience and many in the crowd had wrinkled brows with their forehead elevens showing as they had no idea where Senator Wayne was going with his comments. The only good news was that the delegates were listening. And as the crowd quieted, Senator Wayne spoke gently into the microphone. "As you know, our convention is planned for a single night. There is unity and unanimity in our presidential and vice presidential selections, there is unanimity in support of our platform and we want to get working towards electing a President of the United States who represents the people of the United States." Applause began again on the convention floor.

"While the media has driven us crazy over the past few weeks, we have not told anyone of our real plan for this evening. Oh, we gave them an agenda. Wayne speaks, someone else speaks, we nominate George and Jordon, blah, blah, blah, blah, blah, blah." Some nervous laughter from the delegates who had no idea what Wayne was leading up to and were therefore as deeply in the dark as anyone else. "All we really have said is that we will start at 8:00 p.m., check that box, and we will be done in the early evening, check that box.

"While I have had a wonderful life and a great career, I will admit that looking at these media moguls and telling them they will see the details and read or hear the speeches at the same time as the delegates has been a life highlight." Laughter from the convention floor. Senator Wayne had never worried very much about what anyone thought of him; he was comfortable in his own skin and that confidence was evident in his conduct and bearing. "As you know, the media has this entitlement mentality and tonight we just let them be one of the guys (or gals) and if they chose to broadcast the convention, they would see it unfold as our delegates and friends will see it unfold." Wayne looked around, focusing on the empty tables and chairs. "My friends, I don't think the media likes surprises." More laughter and some realization that something special must be on tap. "So, for our delegates and you media moguls in the mezzanine deck, we have asked a few of our friends to join us on stage.

"Folks, come on out if you would!"

Immediately, from the convention attendees' stage left, the other three founding senators supporting the American Exceptionalism Party nominees walked onto the stage accompanied by their four comrades from the United States House of Representatives. Not a hint of a surprise here. A standing ovation was expected and dutifully fulfilled. The delegates performed their task willingly. Some of the edginess was quickly disappearing from the delegates after listening to Wayne's presentation as they were beginning to expect something a great deal more spectacular than the seven elected officials that had already committed to the AEP. Maybe, at least a talking horse would come to the microphone or something or someone of true interest to them, not a few elected officials who had already committed to George Vincent. The senators and Members of Congress took only seven of the eighty or ninety folding chairs on the stage.

Bob Colony spoke two more sentences into his microphone from his spot high in the arena: "Nothing new or exciting so far as these are the few individual Members of Congress who have already committed to Senator Vincent. None of these individuals is considered to be a very important cog in the wheels of Congress. Maybe the *Washington Post* asked us to spend too much time watching this convention."

Almost seductively, Big Red spoke into her electronic noise machine and offered: "Oh Bob, let's give them a chance. Heck, maybe the former President and the former Secretary of State, Mallory Cloud, will appear on stage after being dropped through the roof with parachutes." Colony laughed out loud and Big Red laughed at her own joke. Each had the same identical thought: *This could be a very long evening with these clowns on stage.*

After shaking hands with each of the seven individuals again, this North Carolina senator with his military posture intact, walked back to his bare wooden podium with its steel stand and spoke another single sentence towards the rear of the stage and said: "What about the rest of you guys?"

Slowly, more bodies began to appear, all again, stage left.

Bob Colony and Big Red, along with millions and millions of television viewers looked at the stage as America heard an audible gasp from the delegates at what was only the beginning of a shocking procession.

"Holy shit!" Colony uttered into his microphone after perhaps as long as two full minutes had passed while the camera was speaking for itself. "Oh, I am so sorry, that has never happened in my career and I promise it will never happen again.

"There are now almost seventy individuals on the stage, maybe a few more than that, almost every one of them is or has been a United States senator, congressman or is famous in some specific line or vocation, some athletes, some movie people, a couple of business people, and they appear to represent both parties, both genders, all races and I will admit, a great variety of views. Like I said, there are also a few very famous athletes and celebrities on that stage as well. Marylou, this just may prove interesting."

"Interesting, Bob? Am I seeing half a dozen former Cabinet members and three former chairmen of the Joint Chiefs? Bob, this may be the most unprecedented moment in the history of the nation!" Big Red was standing and trying to capture precisely what was happening on stage. In a bare moment, she had gone from bored, cynical reporter to interested spectator. She recognized that this might be a moment to change reporting direction. Nimble, she was always nimble on the air. This might become a huge personal opportunity assuming her colleague would continue missing the massive change in the facts and, therefore, the story.

"Certainly in the history of the two major political parties, this is unprecedented." Big Red was beginning to grasp the moment and like many superior newscasters before her, she let the past die with a thud and instantly embraced what was happening on the stage. "Bob, I knew we should be here tonight; I cannot believe we don't have a scorecard, because honestly, Bob, I cannot identify each of the Members of Congress and each of these athletes, but I know the best athlete in the world when I see him and Bob, there he is, Efrin Holt, the running back for the National Football League's Super Bowl champions. I thought he was in training camp"

"Marylou, how could these people have not informed the networks and the American public that they were going to pull this kind of a stunt this evening? This shows a complete disregard for the voters. It shows an even bigger disregard for the media." Colony could never let go of his partisanship and was beginning to spin this unprecedented collection of very important Americans into an assault on the voters and the media by the American Exceptionalism Party.

The third person in the booth was a conservative radio talk show host from the Midwest. He was supposed to be there exclusively to sit on a panel and answer political questions when and if asked. The garrulous Thaddeus Milken laughed out loud in his highest pitched voice and embedded his uninvited voice into the microphone and said: "Great try, Bob. Not to be obnoxious, but good golly, what you are looking at is a sea change in American politics and you sound like a man whose wife forgot to get the BBQ sauce to go with your ribs!"

The television camera had switched from its rolling back and forth across the stage and began trying to pick up individually, who exactly was on the stage.

Colony and Big Red had assumed that Milken was only in the press box so that later in the evening when they needed to kill some time, this conservative commentator could and would provide an opinion from a different zip code. By the time they expected to ask his opinion, they expected to be alone in terms of a television audience. His participation this early was unexpected and unwanted by Colony and Big Red, particularly Colony.

Milken, in traditional white shirt and bow tie with his gold locks closely trimmed and a tiny almost yellow mustache had a huge smile. As a young man, he must have been the ultimate ladies man. When he was younger, he had had that Prince Valiant haircut which is always fashionable on the thin, handsome, blond boys. The closely trimmed gold locks today reflected the reality that he was in his mid-forties.

"Kinda makes you yearn for the good old days when you could spin the story because you knew what was going to happen before the audience did, right Bob? This is my turf, a live performance on stage and no idea what is next, huh?"

In that real world, the live television audience was exploding. Thank you, Twitter. Thank you, Facebook. Thank you, technology. Thank you, Milton Woo.

What one youngster on the campaign team had figured out was that if the convention produced a major surprise on air, the Twitter and Facebook world could add an extra twenty-, maybe thirty million, or who knows how many Americans watching the show in virtually a nanosecond. So Milton Woo, the twenty-four-year-old youngster, the computer guru from MIT, pushed a few buttons and broadcast what would become a viral message to one hundred and sixty-five million Americans within just a few seconds. Pure genius.

One hundred and sixty-five million people throughout the United States and in fact, the world, were instantly being twittered. Instantly, through the ability of Woo to access directly and indirectly, legally and maybe not legally, one hundred and sixty five million individuals. He or she who was twittered, twittered back and twittered others and the news of the convention became a Twitter virus. Within seconds, literally tens of millions of those Twitterers read something like *Now, amaz TV, OBC,* using the short wordage of social media messaging. E-mails were flowing and the viewership of this "ten minute convention" was increased by tens of millions within three minutes. Shockingly, because of the incoming tweets, producers sitting in the studios of the cable networks that had chosen cooking shows and whatever else for this evening were connecting to this live feed as "breaking news," if it was possible to do so without violating meaningful advertising contracts. At these cable stations, what they wanted for their advertisers were eyeballs focused on their advertising so more than a few actually made a guess that their advertisers would want them to switch to the convention.

If one could imagine, ESPN began to cover the convention, split screen, along with its baseball coverage. (The genius of getting Milton Woo to work his magic and having Efrin Holt on the stage produced additional magic.)

Thaddeus Milken was almost giddy at what he was watching and completely unaware that he now had an audience thirty fold his prior highest rated moment. He continued to a silent Colony and McBride along with this sudden national audience: "So, I think, the *Washington Post* gave the American Exceptionalism Party and George Vincent the ten minute opportunity of a lifetime and my goodness, are they taking advantage of it. I do wonder what the remaining Members of Congress are thinking. I would bet one hundred percent of these folks on stage are actively campaigning for re-election as Democrats and Republicans. Oh, I guess a few senators have no election this year, they only elect a third of them every two years. Now that I think of it, they must all be campaigning as Democrats and Republicans because those primaries were all months ago and there were no candidates for Congress running under the banner of the American Exceptionalism Party. Fascinating!" Milken was a bit nasal sounding for television. As a radio show host, his nasal was easy to identify by the millions of drivers changing radio stations as they drove to work every morning. On radio, it was a good thing. For television, it was open for debate.

Milken now realized that the next ninety days of talk radio would be as easy as putting his feet up on the desk and listening to callers. He also instinctively, having no idea about Milton Woo, knew that the audience for this extravaganza was exploding and he was not going to miss a personal plug. "You know Marylou, on my national radio show on Thursday, a caller predicted this very event. Maybe he was an insider, but he told me that this would be the show that it is becoming." Of course, nothing like that had occurred, but nobody listened to his entire three hour radio talk show and he could tell anyone who asked that his people had not put the caller on the air. In a final throw away thought, Milken offered: "I wonder if this is it, just the people on the stage, or as they say, there may be room in that clown car for just one more clown?"

Bob Colony was already tired of listening to both Thaddeus Milken and Senator Wayne. "Come on, Thaddeus, this is just a bit of theatre. Those people on stage are pretty much the lower tier of Congress and this is their opportunity to get some airtime. This is their Andy Warhol moment. They probably know there are no more than eleven people watching this thing." Little did Colony know.

"What the shit do you think you are doing?" This thundering angry voice came seemingly from the sky and pounded into Colony's earpiece. It was Merritt Goodman, the producer of the OBC's convention coverage. "Your damn job is to increase the number of viewers Bob, not diminish it. No more of this shit."

Bob Colony, the icon, pushed the button that transmitted only to Merritt Goodman and retorted: "Sorry Bob, but this is such a bullshit convention and such a bullshit gimmick." Colony thinking, but not saying, *Asshole*.

Senator Wayne walked to the microphone again. Ten minutes of wild applause had finally reached its crescendo and it was about time to get back to business. Again, this time, very quietly like a high school principal trying to get control of an assembly hall gathering rather than the Green Beret Captain that he would always be, Wayne spoke into his microphone: "Thank you so much, please take your seats folks, we have a lot of work to do."

The on-stage group obediently stopped waving, shaking hands and hugging. It was a curious late twentieth century change in American culture that American men actually hugged other men in public.

The superstars on stage had been together for close to two hours and although the excitement was at a very high level, they knew they were props

66

for the show. Many of them had already gotten a lot of business done backstage. Each would be checking with their people to see how much airtime they received on stage. As they sat down, it was very noticeable that at each of two tables at the front, there were two empty seats.

"Friends," Wayne asked, "Did a couple of our guests forget to come out?

"I know when I was back stage that the number of you who committed to Senator Vincent and Jordon Scotch matched the number of chairs. That is not the kind of mistake either the American Exceptionalism Party or Senator Vincent would make. And I know I did not miscount. The press would eat me alive if we had empty seats, especially up front." Now he effectively screamed into the microphone, "Come on guys, time is a wasting, we have some work to get done, if there is anyone else back there or do I need to ask four delegates to fill these seats? We need to get along with our business of electing a new President of the United States!"

"Marylou, I have the feeling that these guys are toying with us. What happened to the days when we were treated with some respect and someone told us what was going to happen. This is really unfair to our audience." Colony was whining. This was not show for the media; he believed that he and his media friends were the client, not the television audience.

The television cameras showed every head on the floor suddenly turn to the back of the room. They turned not to the stage, but to the back of the convention floor. Four more dignitaries were entering the room with a flourish. Instantly, not a delegate was in his or her seat and the people on stage had risen from their seats and were applauding long before they could see what was happening. Some were standing on their seats to get a better view. The applause had started both in the back and moved to the front of the room almost simultaneously. It seemed to form a crescendo in the middle. Many in the press box were standing trying to see who was coming in, but, in the rarest of moments, many of their teams had seen what was going on and were individually standing and applauding like human beings, despite their press credentials.

Before another word from the commentators, the television camera picked up two former presidents of the United States and two former first ladies in the very back of the convention hall. One of the former first ladies was the current secretary of state and had been a Democratic senator a few years previous. This foursome was walking into the convention hall together. Their pace was fairly brisk. They were not there to meet and greet like candidates, they were there to show support for George Vincent. Surprisingly, given the age of the oldest former president and his wife, each with a cane, they were able to keep a fairly good pace in traversing the required fifty or sixty yards.

There were a large number of high fives from this august foursome to the delegates and even more high fives between audience members. Even on stage, the celebrities began to understand what they were a part of and high fives were occurring on the stage too. Three of these four *celebrities* were not stopping to chat with any individual delegates. The current secretary of state needed to push her husband along because, given the chance, he would have worked the room like a first time candidate for city council.

The audience was making the sound of tens of thousands rather than their actual number. It was as if the delegates were witnessing the simultaneous combination of a grand slam home run to win the World Series and the discovery of the Fountain of Youth. Often said, but rarely delivered, it was a once in a life time moment.

In homes around the country, there were tears in the eyes of older Americans who were worried about their individual political party's choices for president, worried about their country in general, and especially worried about their health care being dissembled and reorganized as if they were cattle instead of American citizens. These legions of voters were desperate in their view of domestic policy and simultaneously perceived weakness in the foreign policy of their country.

Younger Americans watching were enthralled at the diversity and youth of the politicians on stage. Younger Americans were more excited at seeing the athletes and a few movie stars on the stage, but they fully understood that a sea change in American politics was taking place in Cleveland. It was impossible not to see this as a magic moment and the viewing audience continued to grow as the result of Milton Woo's technical genius.

It was clear to the keen observer that the Members of Congress on the stage were generally the younger Members of Congress. These men and women were risking their careers and their congressional power to support George Vincent. Not only were they risking issues at home in their own parties, but with their colleagues in the Senate and House of Representatives who would attempt to hurt them in terms of seniority, committee assignments and fundraising. Damn, this was exciting.

~

In the offices at 1600 Pennsylvania Avenue, Herman Sackman watched the performance with increasing concern. Herman, known only to himself as the Wizard out of his love and appreciation for the Wizard of Oz, was known to the rest of the world as the Enforcer because of his hardball, Chicago approach to politics. Not since Ehrlichman and Haldeman had any keeper of the President's door been better known and more disliked. Polls showed that only one-in-five Americans believed that the President should not fire Herman Sackman immediately. The division of four-to-one held through political party, race and every other demographic. Blacks favored the President literally twenty-to-one, and even blacks wanted to see Sackman fired. (Occasionally, a *Sack Sackman* sign would appear outside a presidential event.) No polls were taken, but there was certainly a fraction of the American public that believed he should be drawn and quartered for his controlling theory of government. He called it Chicago hardball politics.

Sackman had not expected anything meaningful from Senator Vincent or anyone else at the American Exceptionalism Party Convention. He was in shock watching this exhibition from his office television. He was in deeper shock that he had heard nothing about who the traitors were in his own party or the two supportive former presidents. When he saw the sitting Secretary of State walking to the stage, he went ballistic. With his curtains closed, no one could see this five-foot-two-inch, one-hundred-and-eleven-pound career politician literally standing on a couch in sweat pants and Dartmouth University sweatshirt screaming obscenities.

There would be hell to pay in a number of places, not least of all the Secret Service, who knew the schedules of many of the attendees. Secretaries of State and former presidents do not wake up one morning and fly to Cleveland without the Secret Service being informed and travelling with them. In Herman Sackman's world, keeping a secret that could hurt him (and he guessed that meant the President as well), was not keeping a secret, it was treason to his White House. There would be more than a few Secret Service personnel with new assignments in places that no one would wish upon a friend, or in some cases, even an enemy. The head of the Secret Service was suddenly in the sights of this powerful little man.

Sackman was taking a hard look at the stage when the television cameras allowed and already was beginning to compile a written list of the attendees. More than a few Democratic candidates would see their political clout and money trains in freefall. This performance was totally unacceptable and neither informing him before the event, nor telling the Democratic Party of their plans was going to be one huge mistake if he had anything to do with it, and he would have everything to do with it. 2012 was now and 2014 was not that many years away; new Democratic candidates could and would be found.

When angry, Sackman struck out wildly and ruthlessly; he was angry, very angry. The Democratic leadership in congress was going to be on the receiving end of an obscenity-laced conference call in the morning. It was their job to keep their people in tow.

The fact that the audience had not yet heard virtually a single word about the administration's failures and was already incredibly engaged in the convention was a very, very bad sign from Herman Sackman's perspective. It might be worse at the moment on television where starstruck announcers often forgot who was boss. When the speeches began—and there were now some of the best political speakers in the world on that damn stage—people would listen to the attacks on his president.

"Helen, get my team together and for God's sake, keep the President away from the press tonight and keep the Pillsbury Doughboy out of the press room!" he screamed this into his telephone. I want every member of my team in my office exactly fifteen minutes after George Vincent finishes his acceptance speech. I don't care if they are at home, in bed with their girlfriends, or in fucking Connecticut—fifteen minutes after Vincent finishes. And I want the A-team in here as soon as possible; some of them should be in the building."

The telephone made a less than gentle landing on its cradle as Sackman thought to himself: *This problem cannot be handled with any of that warm and toasty stuff the press likes. This will take an iron fist. Either you are with us or against us, no middle of the road crap.* Months later, as the election played on and on, he would realize that one had better know what is in every hand at the table before deciding to make that all-in bet.

With his internal calls made, he regained some measure of composure and began calling his media friends. It had not taken the Enforcer more than ten minutes to create talking points for the media. He expected to be hearing these points on every station, save for Fox News, within the next few minutes. Providing or not providing access to the President was a useful tool of his trade.

~

70

With silence again from Colony and McBride and the television picture seemingly speaking for itself, Milken sought more airtime: "Well, this is as good a show as we have ever seen at an American political convention. This American Exceptionalism Party has demonstrated in fifteen minutes that they will be a viable contender in the fall. George Vincent has demonstrated that he has the ability to bind people of different beliefs together. I suspect, at the White House, at this very moment, conversations have already turned to arguments as the size of this surprise dwarfs anything I have seen in my career."

Colony was having none of this. "Oh Thaddeus, let us not get carried away. While this is pretty interesting, perhaps not substantive, but pretty interesting, I can remember Scranton walking through the Republican convention trying to stop Nixon, in what, 1968? I have seen pictures of someone looking at Dewey and saying something to the effect that Dewey wasn't going to lead them down the road to defeat for a third time. Conventions occasionally strike a moment—but only a moment—of excitement."

Milken made no attempt to contain himself and barked: "Bob, that is the most biased piece of thinking, clearly not reporting, I have ever heard. This is damn unprecedented and you know it. And by the way, that was Everett Dirksen and the quote was: 'Don't take us down the path to defeat again.' He was also the senator that said, 'A billion here, a billion there, pretty soon it adds up to real money.' What a combination; prejudiced and unknowledgeable garbage!"

Mercifully, but not mercifully fast enough for a now fuming Colony, the four superstars had reached the stage and were standing next to Senator Wayne. When the crowd quieted, Senator Wayne looked at each former president and each spouse: "Mr. Presidents, Madam Secretary and Barbara, thank you for being here and thank you for everything you have done for your country." The four superstars walked to the middle of the stage and raised arms with hands touching, the two presidents in the middle with their spouses on the outside.

Another five minutes of wild applause. For the delegates, this moment was a confirmation of their foresight in abandoning friends and party and being in Cleveland. The camera popping looked like the first play of a BCS championship game. For George Vincent, the visuals were exactly how he had seen them months ago when the former presidents had agreed to join his campaign. The staging and timing had all been Vincent's idea.

71

None of this moment's celebration was being interrupted on OBC while Thaddeus Milken was literally being physically escorted out of the OBC booth by security personnel.

Mr. Robert "Bob" Colony was not going to be insulted or have to listen to this man again. No one was going to quote ancient politicians in his booth and make Bob Colony look ignorant. No way, no how. In what would quickly become more than a serious controversy for Colony, he was having Milken removed without so much as asking the permission of anyone, including his director/producer, Merritt Goodwin.

Bob Colony would find out in the morning that he was completing his own career on live television for OBC on this Tuesday, August 7, 2012, as the result of what would become well over three hundred thousand e-mails pouring into the station from people who were upset with his commentary, not Milken's commentary, but his. No one would find leadership or a ringmaster for the e-mails, because there wasn't a ringmaster. People were furious on their own and as the convention progressed, many of these tweet and e-mail recipients who had no intention of even watching the convention found Colony's presentation totally unacceptable.

On stage, Wayne seized the moment, went off script and again looked at the older former president and offered: "Sir, as the four of you agreed earlier, the young kid here is going to make a few remarks. Before that, Mr. President, would you mind leading us in the Pledge of Allegiance?"

President Boone walked to the microphone and looked at his wife of all of those years and said: "Barbara, why don't you join me and we will lead the Pledge together?"

None of this was scripted and Barbara emotionally hugged her husband, tears running down her cheeks, and joined with him. After the second word, the entire arena joined in and by the fifth word, most of the entire nation: *"I pledge allegiance to the flag of the United States of America, and to the republic for which it stands, one nation under God, indivisible, with liberty and justice for all..."*

A chant of *U-S-A, U-S-A, U-S-A* broke out in the arena. The chant was buoyed by the people on stage joining in and mugging a bit for the camera.

Bob Colony offered up that this was about as corny as anything he had ever watched.

Time had passed Bob Colony by in an instant. His politics and intuition, which had served him well on the air for almost forty years, were now poisoning that career, cyanide quick. At warp speed, his career was moving towards the I-need-to-write-a-memoir stage.

First, Big Red decided to let the tragedy in Colony's career take place without her help and then almost as quickly decided there was nothing wrong with her helping him travel closer to the great former media unknown. She instinctively acknowledged to herself the possibility that she could be OBC's anchor by the following week at the Democratic Convention.

Big Red thought to herself: *Well, maybe I can serve up a few questions that will help Colony implode on the air. If that works, tomorrow I might need to tell the brass that I tried to get him out of this, but he was just stubbornly marching to the beat of his own drum. They won't concentrate on my part of the tape.*

~

One of the many things that had not dawned on Bob Colony was that Thaddeus Milken had solid press credentials and that security had not escorted him out of the arena, only out of the OBC booth. Milken was still in the Q. Within minutes, Milken closed a one evening deal with Fox News. No one at OBC could or would give a thought to suing him for moving networks during the evening as his contract to broadcast for OBC was only for that night and that contract had clearly been broken by OBC. This was regardless of whether Bob Colony had any right to throw Milken out of the press box or not. There might be an argument that OBC need not pay him the contractual amount, but tonight was now about opportunity and the lawyers could figure out the financial and legal piece of his being escorted from his workplace at another time.

Thaddeus Milken's new gig would put him on the air in just a few minutes. How amazing would it be to a viewer who saw Thaddeus Milken on OBC at 8:30 p.m. and then on Fox News at 9:00 p.m.? For Fox News, this would be very sweet in an *inside baseball* sense. Fox News thought and hoped that Milken would take a few shots at OBC in the manner of a Leno or Conan O'Brien.

On stage, after what would best be described as a group hug, the four planetary heavyweights took up the remaining four folding chairs. It was great television and tens of millions of Americans were watching.

Woo, the young technical guru was not paying the slightest attention to the television, he had the script. He kept sending massive tweets, most of which he had written several days before, to millions and millions of twitterers. He took great pleasure in knowing that his tweets were hitting the iPods in the White House. Woo's mind went to how much fun it was to be the smartest guy in the room. *Super Nerd strikes! And Super Nerd has placed cookies in a ton of machines.* He now had e-mail and twitter addresses for millions and millions of potential donors.

Woo received a tweet that Thaddeus Milken was for some reason moving from OBC to Fox News for the evening and tweets and e-mails to that effect zipped out immediately. Something else newsworthy to send was an additional gift. It did not matter that outside of a small minority, almost none of the twitterers knew who Milken was. As a result of this event and brilliant editing by Super Nerd, a significant part of the now zillions of television viewers either turned on or moved with Milken to Fox News. The combination of the audience being mostly created via Twitter and then the audience moving from station to station as the result of Twitter would be discussed in communication and marketing classes in every university in the country for the next decade.

It made Woo giggle out loud that he was sitting in his small apartment in Cleveland in a pair of board shorts and a T-shirt. While not interested in sports, Woo filled the T-shirt out fairly well as a result of great genetics and a very regular exercise program. Often his best ideas occurred while he was completing a twenty or thirty mile bike ride.

Both presidents had returned to their seats, but the husband of the Secretary of State was still standing in front of his seat. Regardless, Wayne went to the microphone and began his own fairly short speech: "The first battle for the American Exceptionalism Party was to qualify as a political party in each of the fifty states and we have been successful. The utterly remarkable thousands of Internet donations we received to make this possible were unprecedented and assured the men and women on this platform that we, the American Exceptionalism Party, represent the citizens of the United States of America." Huge applause for Wayne's only major fabrication of the evening. If they had needed to rely on Internet contributions to get the AEP certified in every state, the American Exceptionalism Party might currently be registered only in South Dakota. Wayne made no mention of the serious money that had been received from their special friends. The good news was that these were not people who wanted power from their contributions; they wanted to get rid of the Chicago mob and not replace it with someone they viewed as a right-wing nutcase. They wanted a pragmatic, balanced president. Extremes were bad for business.

"The fifty separate battles we had to fight, literally a legal battle in every state, to represent you in the White House were demonstrative of everything that is wrong with our country. Democracy is not well served by trying to limit the choices of the voters. If we are perfectly candid, the Republican Party made this difficult in a few states, but my Democratic colleagues made them look like small time players. *My* Democratic Party." Wayne's inflection here was significant and obvious; this was not *my* Democratic Party any more, this was *MY* Democratic party. "How can any political party unleash the dogs of war to keep people from having honest political choice?" Wayne decided to rope the audience back into the presentation and repeated his question and waited: "How can any political party unleash the dogs of war to keep people from having honest political choice? This is now the same party that refuses to prosecute Black Panthers for voter fraud. A bit slow, but the audience repeated his key word, *how*, and Wayne made his pitch a third time with the audience literally shouting at him: *How?*

Wayne gave the audience a pastoral nod with his lips pursed tightly and then began again: "In my opinion, both political parties have forgotten that they are a part of the democratic process, they are not *THE* Democratic process, but the democratic process with a small *d*! How could this have happened?" Another *How?* From the audience and this became Wayne's first serious standing ovation for the content of what he had to say this evening. This was an audience that felt disenfranchised and Wayne had carefully squeezed that nerve.

Never a fan of the President, Fox News' Sean Hannity zipped in a single sentence: "Senator Wayne is being kind not to remind the audience that the President used the Courts to keep an opponent off the ballot in his first state primary race in Chicago."

"The presidency of the United States is not a race for the Chicago State Senate! Mr. President, you, individually, and the Party which you and your left-wing cohorts took away from mainstream Democrats, should be ashamed of the law suits and hysteria generated to stop us from exercising our rights to form a political party and have our voices heard as Americans!" The lid went off the roof of the convention. The applause went on for a full five minutes. This was the desired commentary for these delegates, and perhaps surprisingly, the two former presidents and then everyone else on stage rose to applaud the senator. The Secretary of State's husband, not missing another opportunity for camera time, actually walked up to the podium while the audience cheered, shared a word in Senator Wayne's left ear, slapped him hard on the back, turned and returned to his seat, and finally sat down.

Bob Colony, on camera, asked: "Marylou, Senator Wayne seems to be hitting the hot buttons here with these folks and as you would expect, they are buying in. Just pure politics, makes you a bit ill. I cannot see any substance here whatsoever. What do you think?"

Time for Big Red to strike: "Bob, I know—let me repeat—I know this is going well, better than well, and I suspect that tomorrow morning you are going to see changes in the poll numbers that will be unprecedented. Many, many people have great confidence in the men and women on that stage. We are reporters, we have to report what we are seeing."

With the camera on him, Colony did a visible double take to Big Red's comment and stammered that he was just reporting what he was seeing and he did not believe that the AEP would be around in ten days. As Big Red planned, his comment demonstrated that through the viewing lens, Bob Colony had badly faded with age.

Wayne put his hands up to quiet the audience and looked at the two former presidents and made the very briefest of introductions: "Ladies and gentlemen, let's hear from our distinguished former presidents." This was not in concert with what Wayne had decided earlier and was not in his script. He was supposed to introduce only the most recent president. Oops.

Quickly, the two former presidents stepped to the microphone. If there is such a thing as unprecedented applause at a political convention that rings true with excitement, the American Exceptionalism Party had just achieved what might have previously been thought of as impossible. The applause, the cheering, and the emotion were unparalleled. Everyone in the room loved at least one of the two men. Everyone loved one spouse and many in the room also loved the other. Those that did not love the current Secretary of State applauded only the three of them, but who would know or care? All realized the political risk the Secretary of State was taking on behalf of the American Exceptionalism Party, a risk this group of politicos understood better than most and appreciated.

~

Upstairs, at 1600 Pennsylvania Avenue, the President had no inkling what was going to happen at the American Exceptionalism Party Convention. He had expected the entire experience to be an unfortunate circus. He was certain that while this new party would take a few votes away from him, he was equally certain that it would only enhance his win in the Electoral College, as the Republican candidate, in his mind, was just too conservative for a large segment of the Republican faithful and unacceptable to Independents. Where it might matter, the President saw Vincent drawing votes from Roland, not him. In some ways, he felt sorry for the four senators and four Members of the House of Representatives that had committed to Senator Vincent. He assumed that first their seniority would be taken away by their colleagues in the Congress, and then they would lose their next primary to new, carefully selected candidates that supported either himself or the Republican nominee, dependent upon party.

As the President believed (in his mind, knew) that he was doing a fabulous job on the issues he could control and with the polls running in his personal favor, his instincts were to feel sorry for the carnage that this AEP would cause for a few sitting Senators and Congressmen. The President never fully grasped that the losses his Party had experienced in 2009, 2010 and 2011 were the result of his policies and his ruthless pursuit of those policies with his White House team. For a reasonably smart person, it was surprising that the only poll he paid any serious attention to was whether the American public liked him, not the polls indicating that his job approval had waned so substantially, or the polling results for the members of his own political party. Neither the election in Virginia, nor the election in New Jersey, nor the election of Scott Brown in Massachusetts had changed his view of himself. The losses in the midterm election had the same non-event impact on his self-vision, none.

What the President did not grasp was that outside of the black community, his political support had so significantly eroded elsewhere that he was seen as only a slightly better alternative to the Republicans, but not as the perfect person to be the President of the United States. George Vincent had grasped this not from polling, but from meeting with the political elites around the country and occasionally donning a pair of levis and a flannel shirt and going into a random restaurant, airport or mall and asking a few questions. Outside of Ohio, he was rarely recognized and this was essential for getting honest answers. Really, one only had to see or be a part of a

Townhall meeting—a legitimate Townhall meeting—to realize that the public was beginning to despise both of the existing political parties.

The Democrats he expected to see at the American Exceptionalism Party Convention were not his problem; his team would take care of anyone who strayed from the Party line. These idiots that had moved to the American Exceptionalism Party would certainly not be at his convention. This was actually good as there should be no tension from the moderates at the convention if these folks were gone. As a result of this thinking, the President was not watching the AEP Convention and was just beginning a meeting with his advisors on national financial issues in his private quarters. They were discussing the combination of continuing falling tax revenues and the unprecedented increase in spending from his stimulus packages and the resulting national debt. These were difficult meetings for the President as balancing his personal checkbook was beyond his financial knowledge. His wife ran the family finances.

When his family was on vacation, the President preferred staying out of the Oval Office in the evenings and stayed in the private residence portion of the White House. Tonight's meeting was unusual. The truth was that he rarely worked in the evening and preferred watching ESPN, spending the public's money on a dinner or a concert at the White House, or on maintaining the White House grounds. It was nice to be king.

A moment after the two former presidents and his Secretary of State entered the American Exceptionalism Party's convention, the President's evening secretary had sprinted upstairs with a note and the President had immediately reached for the remote control and switched on RBC, his favorite television network. The screen showed Humphrey Bogart and Paul Henreid in *Casablanca* and with a shrug, the President clicked to OBC.

As the LCD screen filled again and the sound ricocheted a bit off the walls of the room, the President stood away from his chair, open mouthed, and stared at the screen. The screen showed the two former presidents and he could also see the Secretary of State in the background. "You have got to be fucking kidding me. Those…those ungrateful…those…those traitors…" The stammering stopped and he crossed the room to his bookcase and opened a book entitled *The History of Norway*. It was carefully placed on the top shelf next to a never opened book on Federal Taxation. From what normally would be the pages of the book, he produced a menthol cigarette. Two deep puffs on the cigarette and the remote was hurled at the wall next to the television. With the cigarette in his mouth, he relaxed a bit, but only a bit. "You have got to be fucking kidding me," he repeated over and over, each time a bit more quietly. "Guys, can we continue this meeting another time? I need to watch this."

Saint Saline (her real name) was the administration's new economic Miss Fix It. An honors graduate of the Chicago Business School who had studied at the London School of Economics and had been exclusively studying and writing about macroeconomics in her cubicle at Harvard for almost twenty years, this tiny little woman with skin so white it had probably never seen the beach, had joined the administration only days before. This was the administration's first outreach effort to a completely non-political economic genius. She was thought to be the only one at Harvard who might be able to stop the economic ice cream cone from melting. Saint Saline was an economist's economist. She was replacing a small handful of economists who could not seem to get the President to focus on an economic policy that was coherent.

Saline was no touchy-feely academic; she wanted to use this evening to carefully explain to the President and his advisors her view of the economy. This was her first bite at this apple, an apple she had very reluctantly agreed to eat and she was intent on not losing this first opportunity. She was uncertain that the economic ice cream cone had not already melted. "With all due respect, Sir, the Treasury…"

"Not now, Ms. Saline," was all she heard from the President and all that was offered after she watched everyone else instantly stand up. She lifted her briefing book and headed toward the door. *Politicians*, she thought to herself, *maybe I'll find a television and see if those clowns in that new political party have any idea what to do; I am not committed to going down with this ship. I should have taken a picture, because I am out of here. Doesn't this guy know it is his job to fix the economy and someone else can tell him what happened in some stupid political convention?* And Saint Saline was not kidding herself. She had not wanted to take this position and Harvard had told her they would keep her cubicle warm.

Saint Saline went to her hotel (as she had not had time yet to rent an apartment), packed her clothing, got in her car and began the drive back to the safety of Harvard. This at 8:00 p.m. at night. A short political career indeed. Four days.

~

In Cleveland, Ohio, finally, after nearly ten minutes of wild applause and excitement, the younger of the two former presidents put his one good arm in the air and began to gain some level of control of the convention audience. While not the healthiest man in the room, he still had those intense, charismatic blue eyes that had entranced political leaders and the rest of the planet for the eight years of his Presidency. In pure Arkansas Southern form, he offered, "Don't you just love a surprise?" Another few minutes of craziness.

~

Now armed with a new, one page, one night contract with Fox News, one that had started only a few minutes ago and would end at 2:00 a.m., Thaddeus Milken was back on television. A smart guy, Milken was being compensated at an hourly rate that would have made a Washington D.C. lobbyist blush. The Fox News producer decided to put Milken instantly on a panel and let him begin without so much as a tiny, tiny introduction. That, Milken suspected, he would read about in the trades over the next few days. *How did Thaddeus Milken manage to find himself on both OBC and Fox News last night?*

Thaddeus Milken began his Fox News career with: "Good to be here. As you know, I was escorted out of the OBC news booth but ten minutes ago, but that is a story about me and a story for another day. Let's just say that Fox News is committed to being fair and balanced, not something else." This single sentence was his sop to Fox News and to him, worth every penny he was being paid for the evening. He knew they had escorted the wrong guy out of the booth. *Someday, I will be sitting in that booth and it will be just me and Big Red. Robert 'Bob' Colony, once a reporter, currently a jerk, would be in the retirement home. Since everyone knows I am a seriously religious Catholic and married, I suspect Big Red will be more comfortable with someone next to her who doesn't try to look down her blouse every time she looks away.*

"What is happening on that convention floor is exactly what we drone on and on about on what some call right-wing radio. We talk about what could, should or would happen if a third political party caught the attention of the American public. In this case, it appears to be the party of the middle and it has caught the attention of the American public. The Tea Party movement must be wondering tonight where they would be if they had accepted serious political leadership like that given to the AEP by George Vincent. This is a wonder.

"While we will need to see the polls tomorrow, actually probably Thursday or Friday, this has to be a galvanizing moment. If all of these politicians and former politicians, including two former presidents and what appears to be a rainbow of American thought, gender and consciousness, does not give you reason to think there will be political consequences from this evening, then I am missing something. The public will need to see and hear ideas from Senator Vincent and Jordon Scotch, but if they can convey what Americans wish to hear, the American Exceptionalism Party will be a big player in this election. Maybe the dominant player." Milken leaned back in his chair. *Magnifico*, he thought, *what an evening!* Thaddeus Milken was of course still attired in his definition of trademark casual, blue sport coat, white shirt and his Cornell University red-colored bow tie. Only his mother would have noticed that the coat was a bit dirty on the left collar as the security personnel had literally thrown his coat at him and it landed on the Q's not so pristine floor. As usual, his trademark gold locks were in place; moving fifty yards down to the hallway did not change his aura.

Over at OBC, Bob Colony was looking for traction. Merritt Goodman, his producer, was certain, his instincts being accurate to the max, that they were losing viewer share and losing it fast. He found out that Colony had dispensed Thaddeus Milken when his boss in New York, who was channel surfing, saw Milken on Fox News. The conversation between Merritt Goodman and his boss was brief and only fairly cordial, but the long-term implications for Bob Colony were fairly clear. *Exactly who decided Bob Colony made these types of decisions? Dumb ass!*

Goodman had screamed at Colony that he, *Colony*, had gone well over the line and that he, *Colony*, was going to begin positing a positive spin on his conversation with viewers over the next few hours on what was happening or he, Merritt Goodman, was going to appear on live TV and throw him, with his chair, over the balcony. While Merritt Goodman weighed well over two hundred and fifty pounds, he did not have the look of someone who could or would throw so much as an ice cream wrapper over the balcony and onto the delegates, his point was well taken.

Bob Colony tried to leap into the action as he was directed, but became instantly introspective to the media angle which he was playing over in his own mind: "Marylou, on that stage down there is a very significant amount of raw political power and experience. Let's talk about the media aspects of this. While the surprise of the moment is astonishing and clearly has our undivided attention, the viewership cannot be half of what it would have been if we had been able to tell the viewers what was going to happen tonight. Whoever is making the media calls for this so-called political party missed this one, big." Goodman again started screaming in both Colony and now McBride's earpieces that he wanted something positive, he repeated *POSITIVE!*

Big Red again had more than a fleeting thought that the center chair might not be as secure for Bob Colony as she would have thought thirty or even fifteen minutes ago. Looking at him, she was astonished. Classically confident attire, natty in his pink shirt and reddish tie, thinning grey hair parted in the same place as thirty years ago. The Botox had been pretty effective at eliminating the eleven as well as the wrinkles in his forehead without making this guy look like he had just been given a choice of his money or his life by a thief wearing a ski mask.

"Bob, I have to think that with the element of surprise coupled with the death of the eleven o'clock news and the advent of YouTube, we may have seen the end of politicians cowtailing to us in the mainstream media. This is brilliant. And as to our audience, during the past thirty minutes, I have gotten a couple of dozen e-mails and I can't count how many tweets telling anyone and everyone to turn on their television. Someone out there really wants everyone to see this convention. I suspect our ratings are totally though the roof. Surprising to us, but maybe that is no big deal in the world of instant communication." Big Red hoped that this arrow would give rise to a bit higher blood pressure for this soon to be passing icon.

The overnight Nielsen ratings would show that the convention was receiving ratings generally in tune with an NFL playoff game but that the OBC crew was running fifth, which meant it was behind two cable networks. The ratings would also show that as the evening progressed, the audience was moving faster and faster to Fox News. Every demographic seemed to be gravitating to Fox News. Viewers actually did believe Fox News was fair and balanced. (The Beltway might believe that Fox News was out of step, but the viewers are the viewers. As to the buying public's demographic, Fox News had, at that moment, captured both genders' key 25-54 demographic. This was a huge win for Fox News.)

It had always interested Big Red, and many viewers, that Fox News never had Bill O'Brien on for the election night coverage. O'Brien claimed he was not good at election coverage, but most in the business actually believed he did not want to seem happy or sad based on the results. First, it would kill his self-image. Second, as outspoken and ornery as O'Brien was, he had a personal view of ethics that he never violated. The truth was that when O'Brien was on, Fox News was fair and balanced if one looked at a full month rather than an individual segment. Since O'Brien was paid to have a firm position on all issues, he managed to anger about fifty percent of his audience in every segment. Sometimes O'Brien seemed to lean over backwards to make it fair and balanced, but longtime viewers had come to understand that this usually occurred when the subject was intellectually over his head. The viewers also understood that as O'Brien aged, he did seem to talk over his guests more and more, but they tolerated this.

As Big Red predicted, Colony did not back off one bit: "Oh Marylou, the audience has to be tiny. No one ever heard of these guys ten weeks ago and no one knew what we would be seeing tonight. This has been a major, I repeat, major error in strategy. Maybe, just maybe, that will cost them any opportunity to garner votes as the election progresses. Remember that by the time of the Republican Convention, most of tonight will be forgotten by the general public." *Merritt Goodman is not going to tell me what to say or think; I am the anchor of this show and this network. I am the star, always have been, always will be.*

On stage, the younger former President of the United States had gained control over the convention delegates. He wondered to himself, *If I told them all to buy stock in Accelet tonight, I wonder if they would do it. I could make a killing. OK, Mr. President, it doesn't work that way and you know it!* He offered a smile to both the audience and himself. *God, how I love this!*

The elder former president, President Boone, the one who had a son in the White House for eight years, just a few years before, had returned to his seat and watched the proceedings with great interest and enjoyment. Try as he might, he could not dislike his successor. There was something magical about him. Of course the woman sitting next to him, with whom he had spent the last sixty years of his life, did not have similar thoughts. *If my husband had done some of the things that man had done in the White House...*

The former president drew a breath and in his most folksy style language began again: "Y'all know I supported the President's 2008 election campaign." As usual, he was speaking in soprano as he had the highest-octave voice in the history of the presidency and *you all* was pronounced as a single word. "So did my wife and y'all know she continues to serve in the administration, although I suspect that may all come to an end fairly quickly." A roar of laughter. "Honey, have you checked your Blackberry in the last few minutes?" Great laughter from the delegates; the former president seemed especially relaxed and a couple of the congressman were howling thinking of the Secretary of State receiving an e-mail from the President in the last or next few minutes. Each had his or her own mental version of the next e-mail or telephone call she would receive from the President. "As I am sure you know, my wife is mortified at the approach the President is taking in Korea, and there was, as you may know, the appointment of Czar Rosent to oversee activities in the Korean Peninsula before the nuclear bomb effectively put her on the sidelines. And, well Honey, why don't you finish this story…"

With her former president husband standing two steps to her right, the Secretary of State, wearing what had become her trademark dark blue pants suit, stepped next to her husband at the small wooden podium. The teleprompter was still not turned on and her comments were to be without notes, much less a teleprompter. The teleprompter was nothing more than a prop and the audience would understand this later in the evening. She received a nice round of applause and successfully kept her game face on for this serious conversation. She waited a bit too long and then began: "The series of miscalculations in Korea could have cost millions of lives. Honestly, there is nothing I can do in my current role to make America stronger. Every time I try to use the power of the United States, I get undercut by the White House. My title may be Secretary of State, but this president believes he is President, Secretary of State, Treasury Secretary, Secretary of Commerce and probably is looking to cook his own dinner in the White House kitchen. The man cannot ask for advice, he cannot delegate. He believes he is the Oracle of Delphi."

While the delegates hooted and hollered, the gang on stage was a bit taken back by the strength of the language being used. There would never be any reconciliation or perhaps more than an impolite shrug in a reception line between she and the President after this last sentence. Thanksgiving dinner was definitely out. This was anything except a president who could accept criticism, tiny or as this was, huge. This was both a resignation speech and a call to war.

"Now, I know the President would be furious if I made this statement in private and more so in front of millions of Americans, but the truth needs telling. Maybe furious does not quite get to the right level of his personality." The Secretary of State gave a knowing smile and the delegates roared *furious, furious, furious.* "And I think you know what happens in this president's administration if you disagree with the boss, you find yourself looking at a czar who has been appointed by the President and vetted by no one. I already have seven czars and czarinas ruling over various aspects of the United States' international relations around the world. These unknown and unvetted individuals have taken to calling presidents around the world without so much as a thought about the State Department. Not one of them has appeared before Congress. I received a telephone call from the administrative assistant of a NATO ally last week asking me who a certain czar was and announcing that her boss was fairly convinced this czar was sufficiently ignorant of world politics to think Arizona did not have a border with Mexico." This brought laughter to the audience and constituted a zinger at the President's immigration policy and some poor Wisconsin politician who had been given a geography lesson on live television a couple years prior.

"The czarina of the Korean Peninsula was and is a complete disaster, was not qualified for the assignment, and the results literally could not have been worse. I think the czar of the Middle East actually believes that having a single nation for Palestine and Israel would solve the conflict." The Secretary of State paused here as she changed subjects a bit.

"Maybe, just maybe, this president will ultimately determine that talking weak is being weak. Teddy Roosevelt talked about walking softly and carrying a big stick; he would not have understood this president. My friends, we are weak-kneed and it is hurting the United States all over the world. It is hurting the entire world. We are weak in Iraq. We are weak in Afghanistan. We are weak in the Middle East. We are weak at our own border. We are adopting military policies that could make us weak compared to Tahiti. It is sad that blame for all of this can and should be placed at 1600 Pennsylvania Avenue." Wild applause and a few more chants of *U-S-A, U-S-A, U-S-A*.

"The man believes he is a transforming figure and all he is, is a non-transparent know-it-all. The man believes he is a transforming figure and all he is, is a non-transparent know-it-all." This was followed by more chants of *U-S-A, U-S-A*...

Madame Secretary made a show of going back to her chair and looking into her purse and pulling out her Blackberry. She looked at the Blackberry and then looked at the audience, smiled, shook her head up and down, and returned to the podium. The smile was phony and she did not care. In fact she hoped it would appear phony. She was angry. And she believed if she had let this anger escape four and a half years ago during the Iowa primary, she would be working in the Oval Office tonight, there would be no American Exceptionalism Party and the world would be a safer place. She continued: "There appear to be a few messages,"—looking at her husband—"and I think he can wait for a few minutes. What exactly is the severance arrangement for a Secretary of State?" Significant laughter from her husband and the other former president was holding his sides. In actuality, there was no e-mail from the President or anyone else at the White House.

"The combination of absolutely no experience and nearly unlimited power in this White House is beginning to scare me. Congress has fulfilled none of its duties under the Constitution. Congress needs to be reminded that it is supposed to be an active part of policy making.

"As you all know, I could have challenged the President in the Democratic primaries this year and the polling data gave me a very good chance of winning. But, and I am certain that I was right, I believed and still believe that the United States of America needs a fresh political start. We need a political party that is not tainted with either the far right or the far left. We need a political party that represents the eighty percent of Americans that do not have some crazy agenda. And because of that, I have forsaken what would obviously have been my last chance to become President of the United States. I have forsaken that opportunity to order up support for George Vincent in his quest to become our president." She looked at her husband and stood just a bit away from him to gain her own well-deserved applause and the applause was over the top. Inadvertently, she had effectively nominated George Vincent for the presidency and the convention reacted with unbridled enthusiasm.

After a full three minutes, Madame Secretary's husband took two steps back to the microphone and spoke: "Somehow, the Congress has followed the wrong leader up too many wrong hills and we need new leadership. Somehow the Congress has allowed the President to have a shadow government in the form of czars. This is not Russia; our government needs to be structured under the Constitution of the United States, not the Constitution of the old Soviet Union! We need to get rid of his czars, his czarinas and this ultimate American Czar, now!" To this, the delegates went effectively nuts. What was being said was something that millions and millions of Americans had been sensing for three and a half years and no one had had the nerve to step up to a microphone and say it in such straightforward, un-couched language.

After some time, the former president completed his exceptional remarks: "We cannot let historic political party affiliations get in the way of preserving our nation. We need to lead; we need to follow this American Exceptionalism Party to a new presidency in November." Applause. "This is not my night, this is your night, this is not my wife's night, this is your night, this is America's night and this is the night of OUR nominees, George

Vincent and Jordon Scotch." Again the chants of *U-S-A, U-S-A* rebounded across the arena.

Hannity zipped in a crisp rhetorical question on Fox News: "I wonder how anyone could possibly manage all of the czars? I wonder if he knows all of the names?"

The Secretary of State, a bit chagrinned that her husband had taken away more than a bit of her moment yet again took the microphone and added, "As my husband said earlier, his predecessor in the White House graciously allowed him to speak for both of them and we both agreed to be brief and take nothing away from future Vice President Jordon and future President Vincent. Thank you." The ovation was incredibly strong and the former first couple held hands like little kids. Then, former President Boone appeared between them and they joined hands with upraised arms. Everyone on stage spontaneously joined in standing and lifting up raised arms. A few of the athletes gave it a solid fist pump before joining in the raised arms. The convention went silly with animated pride and encouragement.

~

The President was on cigarette number three and dialed his nighttime secretary. "Three things, Betty. Would you make sure that the Secretary of State is at Camp David at exactly 1:00 p.m. tomorrow? I do not care what is on her schedule or my schedule for 1:00 p.m.; that is when I want her there. Then, at 2:00 p.m., I want to see Al Gore. Please tell him it is urgent. Oh and at 10:00 a.m., I'll start with Sackman and Matta. That means the helicopter at 9:30; I will travel alone. Finally, can you have someone bring up a cheeseburger, fries and a Coca-Cola, and if my wife finds out about this there will be a death in the kingdom. And Betty, you will need to air out the room tomorrow morning, you know, and there might be just a bit of a problem with the paint on the West wall. Can you help me with that?" He was only semi-kidding about the death in the kingdom line; Mrs. President would not take kindly to any of his current responses to the American Exceptionalism Party Convention: not the cigarettes, hamburgers, fries or the Coca-Cola.

~

"Wasn't your hero eloquent, Bob?" asked Big Red, again trying to light Colony up. Colony was now on his second Alka-Seltzer in less than an hour. He ducked the question and answered a different question entirely: "Marylou, it's been quite a show so far. Heck it is only 8:25 and these folks have played every trick in the book. How are they ever going to fill up the rest of the night? And Marylou, did you notice who was absent on that stage? Weren't there several members of the Cloud administration you would have expected to be on stage? This American Exceptionalism Party may still be somewhat of a sophisticated joke. Their absence speaks volumes, doesn't it?"

Both OBC commentators' ear phones yet again heard the blasting voice of Merritt Goodman: "Colony, I told you that if you make one more God damn nasty remark about this convention, I was going to throw you over the fucking balcony. I'd throw you both off the air if I had so much as an intern to put on this stupid convention. Marylou, stop baiting him for God's sake."

Marylou decided that being an actual television reporter for a moment might be the best thing for her career. She folded her long precious legs under her chair and took control of the show. Speaking only to her audience, she began: "What we are seeing tonight is unprecedented. In a way, we are witnessing a revolution. The two-party system may be permanently gone by the first Tuesday of this November or one of the existing parties may ultimately be forced to fold into this American Exceptionalism Party, not vice versa. There is absolutely no way to know. This happened to the Whigs one hundred plus years ago. By tomorrow morning, we will have an initial idea of how many senators and congressmen are jumping on this bandwagon and by the end of the week, I cannot imagine that their numbers will not increase dramatically. If the polling data is good, the American Exceptionalism Party will be a destination resort for Members of Congress up for re-election this fall.

"There is enough charisma on that stage to change a number of political equations. I do see at least seven senators on that stage who are running for re-election and have already been nominated by political parties of which they may or may not be continuing members." The OBC cameras were now focused on Big Red. She was wearing a fairly short skirt, which the cameras kept drifting further away from her face to show along with her exceptionally long legs. Her amply-filled, plain white blouse buttoned up to her neck with her red hair flowing down her back gave her a homespun and clean cut look that older viewers loved. To the older viewers, she had the "my other daughter, the pretty one" look and this was not very far from the truth. To the younger viewers, she was just hot.

Big Red was involved in a long, long-term monogamous relationship with a New York lawyer that she knew would turn into marriage the moment she was willing to have a bevy of new Big Reds at home. There was never a hint of scandal because there was never a hint of foul play. She was ambitious because that was the way she was raised in her Pennsylvania, middle-class home. Big Red was a class act when one got past her naked job ambition. While she lived with her lawyer boyfriend, she was otherwise personally pretty conservative. She was very much a creature of the new century.

Big Red continued: "The same can be said of every congressman on the stage. It is as if the stage has fifty or sixty Senator Leventhals. I think Senator Leventhal has the distinction of being the only member of his own political party. I think he is officially a member of the Independent Democratic Party of Connecticut, having left the Democratic Party and here he is on the stage with the American Exceptionalism Party, pretty interesting stuff. Oh, I cannot wait for the polling data."

Big Red wasn't going to give a moment to her soon to be former colleague as she continued: "What does this do to the 2012 presidential election? What does this do to the 2012 congressional and senatorial elections? No one, literally no one, could have any idea. All we know is that we do not know. I believe that the initial reaction of the public will be wildly positive. The Democrats have historically low positive ratings, and while the Republican Party has benefitted some, it remains an unacceptable alternative to many. The final Boone years have not been forgotten.

"So, on stage, we have Senator Wayne again, I guess he is the master of ceremonies, returning to the rostrum."

Colony launched into a few poorly chosen words attacking America's *other daughter*. "Marylou, you are not experienced enough to understand the allegiance that people have to their political parties. Most Americans would never abandon their political party. The Democrats are generally the party of choice, that is what the polling data always shows."

The cameras were back on the podium. Senator Wayne had begun to look like a war hero at a Veteran Day's parade. He appeared exceptionally proud and honored simply to be on the stage with the assembled group. His appearance reflected his mood. Nothing in his look differed from his feelings. As he waited for the attention of the audience, he thought to himself:

Well Mom, I am doing the 'right thing' as you told me so many times; it has always been good advice before, let's hope it remains good advice. Honor, a hard and dangerous strategy! The audience grew still.

"We are here to do the right thing for our country. We are not here to listen to ourselves or bore a national television audience to death." Applause, strong applause. "The American Exceptionalism Party has held its primaries and its candidates have been travelling the country for a couple months telling the American people that it is time for a new beginning. No video presentation, no great introduction is going to change anyone in this room's minds that we have the best two possible candidates.

"Tonight, we will have only the three originally planned additional speakers, our two candidates, Senator Vincent and Jordon Scotch, and Caleb Smith who will nominate both George Vincent and Jordon Scotch. President Boone also asked me if he could have five minutes and who could possibly say no to President Boone? Of course, President Boone needs no introduction, ladies and gentlemen, President Boone!" Senator Wayne had not known what to do when the former president asked him if he could speak and said *of course* before he gave it any rational thought. The convention did not need another speech, but what could he do?

Well loved, well respected and effectively forgotten as a president that had served a single term almost twenty-five years before, President Boone returned to the little wooden podium. At eighty-seven, he did not bother trying to give it a slow walk to the podium to gain attention. He knew the polite applause that awaited a bland speech when he heard it and that he was almost the only thing between the convention delegates and their two candidates. Most everyone in the audience had heard some version of his disappointment with the current president and his concern that old values were being pushed aside along with health care for senior citizens. He generally believed that former presidents should just stay out of the way except when specifically asked to help by the sitting president and had professed this belief widely since he was voted out of office in 1992.

While his right knee and artificial right hip betrayed his age and forced a slight limp requiring a cane, President Boone had not lost a mental step from his Ivy League days at Yale. He continued to read four newspapers a day and found time to read several books a week. Over the past three years, virtually every picture of the former president showed him Amazon Kindle in hand and it certainly appeared, and it was true, that he spent every available moment reading current information from what he considered an "amazing little machine." He had become a walking, unpaid advertisement for intellectual growth through Amazon. Amazon had tried to pay him a fee to do advertisements, but he just laughed and said he wasn't ever going to play Jack Lemon to James Garner in *My Fellow Americans* and embarrass the presidency. Plus, it just galled President Boone to see the current president on television every day, often in commercials for some non-profit government sponsored program. This seemed so unsightly and of course, he could not understand the absence of press conferences. This was his view of dictatorships, not his view of the United States of America. He often questioned: *When did this guy work?*

Until two minutes before, President Boone did not want to give any speech, especially an impromptu speech. It wasn't his style to steal the stage, it wasn't his style to deviate from the program, but in the minutes before he started to the podium he heard from the young fellow who was distributing water to the guests on stage about what was being said about Senator Wayne's speech and/or the American Exceptionalism Party by the television panelmysters as he thought of them and he became angry. He hardly knew Senator Wayne and frankly did not agree with some of his speech. But, he thought the speech resonated with the delegates and the thought of talking heads attacking Senator Wayne was distressing to him. In the former president's mind, twenty-five years of hearing nasty, uninformed partisan talking heads manifested itself in an explosion of ideas and thoughts. He heard all of the nightly commentary and unless it was on Fox News it always seemed as if it had come from a single source and he believed that source was that Herman Sackman guy at the White House. No doubt, Sackman had already e-mailed talking points to every network as this convention was taking place. What had the media come to when they were given talking points from the White House as opposed to doing just a bit of independent thinking? His final thought as the polite applause wound down: *I just may replace Spencer Tracy in the Last Hurrah, but what the heck, the only time I make headlines these days is if I jump out of an airplane.*

"Thank you, thank you. It is great to be here this evening. Frankly, at my age, it is just great being anywhere." Polite laughter and light applause.

"I need a favor here and I don't know who to ask. Could someone remove the teleprompters from the stage?" President Boone knew that neither Caleb Smith nor Senator Vincent would use the teleprompters. He had asked Jordon Scotch earlier about teleprompters and Scotch indicated he always kept his notes on his lap and rarely used them. He also knew Senator Vincent rarely used one. Therefore, this former president had no idea that the teleprompters were intended to be a prop for later. If he had given it a thought, he would have decided that if Caleb Smith needed them he could have them replaced.

The former president stepped back from the microphone expecting someone to leap into action; nothing happened. "I'm sorry, I would like to have the teleprompters removed before I begin to share a few thoughts." He stepped back again and looked in every possible direction while the audience murmured with little interest. "No, I don't want the things turned off, they are not on. I would like them removed. The President of the United States should be able to speak in his own words and not just read a damn speech off a stupid machine!"

Both Big Red and Bob Colony sat bolt upright in their chairs. Every news commentator turned almost violently toward the little wooden podium and the talking heads stopped talking, and for just a bare moment, there was pure silence on every television screen in the country. One could have heard a pin drop on the convention floor. The delegates were virtually frozen in their current positions. "Did I just hear what I thought I heard, Bob? Was that a zinger at the President," offered Big Red to her still frozen co-anchor.

"I think so, Marylou, and I am pretty sure that in his entire life, President Boone has never used that language in public; I do not believe I have ever heard him swear or curse. Like him or hate him, and you know I am no fan, this man has always been a class act. Maybe he is showing his age." More silence as an astonished media watched men in work clothes appear from nowhere and lay down the three teleprompters.

President Boone turned red and looked a bit sheepish and stepped back to the microphone. The audience, who moments before seemed about as interested in what he was about to say as a college senior in the last fifteen minutes of a 4:30 p.m. lecture, had every eye staring at him with total attention.

"Thank you for getting rid of those *darn* teleprompters." When he said *darn*, his time spent in the Northeast reverberated from the microphone. A smile from the former president and a laugh from the audience, then serious applause for this former president because everyone hated to see politicians using teleprompters. "Friends, don't you just wonder if the President ever read one of his speeches before reading it off a teleprompter? Doesn't it bother you to have all of the commentators repeating the same spin as someone includes for him on the teleprompters?"

President Boone then took off his coat and dropped it to the ground. Then, he loosened his tie and rolled up his sleeves. This was a pose never seen during his presidency. There wasn't an anchor, talking head or convention delegate who did not know when something special, good or bad, was about to unfold.

~

In the White House, the office of the President's Wizard was filling with members of the "A" team and Herman Sackman was reaching for his bottle of Tums. This was not good. For the second time, he telephoned Bob Colony's assistant on her private, unlisted cell phone and fed her a few more talking points. Colony, like most of his competitors and colleagues, had parroted Sackman's talking points word for word after Senator Wayne's speech. This time, Big Red was sitting close enough to hear Sackman's side of the conversation.

Off microphone, Marylou called at Colony: "Tell Herman Sackman he has to be kidding. Boone just outed you and he has his coat off, has thrown his jacket to the ground and Sackman wants us to cut to a panelist and for a second time regurgitate remarks from him; we may all be sluts over here, but we are not stupid!" Similar comments were being passed along to Herman Sackman by every television station; the anchor at Fox News was the only one to not respond, but this was because he was also the only one to not receive the talking points. This time virtually no one was going to prove the former president right by parroting a phrase that could be simultaneously uttered from another network anchor's mouth. For most anchors, this just might be one of the fun moments of the century where their viewers weren't going to miss a millisecond. That being said, Colony managed to quickly rattle through a few of Herman Sackman's talking points.

When Sackman heard Big Red in the background, he committed her name to his special list. There would be no special leaks to her or OBC's nightly newscast for some period of time. *People are, individually and collectively, either with me or against me. I am the Wizard and Enforcer.*

~

97

The former president gathered himself and wondered if the next few minutes would be his legacy or whether someone might look at the totality of his career beginning with his time in the United States Navy. *Ah well, might as well start before I lose my nerve; I just hope I remember all those thoughts from all of those times when I was completely alone—some of 'em were pretty good.*

"Friends, by now the press usually has a copy of a wonderful fifteen page speech so that if they knew I would be speaking tonight they would be expecting me to deliver to your polite applause. But, I told Senator Wayne that I was not going to give that speech tonight. What, no applause?" Light applause and laughter. "Well, I am sure if you want a copy of an old Boone number one speech, there is a way to get it, but you are not going to have to listen to it tonight." More applause.

"If you choose, you are going to get to listen to an old man who is angry. I am angry at the so-called mainstream media and, frankly, I am angry with everyone who listens to it and permits our nation to dwell in the gutter with respect to every public figure and every important issue. I am equally angry with the White House spinners. Herman Sackman, this speech from this old man is for you."

On Fox News, Hannity quickly told the audience that Sackman was the President's assistant and enforcer.

"We are the most blessed people in the history of the world and we seem to be on a level playing field with Lindsey Lohan. We don't have a clue what is important, we don't care a whit about anything but ourselves and we are destroying a nation that may be the world's last hope for decency."

Silence in the convention hall. Silence on the television sets. Silence in Herman Sackman's office. Silence in the President's private quarters. Terror in the mainstream media from the possibility that there might be no way to fight off this former president's assault. Who was going to call President Boone a bad guy and drag his unimpeachable life through the gutter to defend themselves? Maybe the blogs could get away with such heresy, but certainly no one was going to attack George H. W. Boone as a person. That would be the end of a great career or the end of just about any length of career.

"How in God's name can we tolerate a president who seems to have but a single talent? Chief finger pointer! I predict that his speech to the Democratic Convention will be only about blaming anything that is wrong on the prior administration and mocking both the convention and the candidates of the Republican Party. If he talks policy, it will be in generalities, and frankly, overstatements and half-truths.

"Why do we tolerate a president who graduated from Harvard Law School and doesn't have the international political sense of a sixth grader? Give me a break! Was there and is there no one in his entire administration that didn't know that the president of North Korea is a few cents short of a dollar?" Applause started and as it was building, former President Boone put his hands up and yelled: "No applause, darn it, this is not a political point, we are talking about a nutcase who used a nuclear weapon and a president that wants to just talk about it. Talk, talk, talk, talk, talk!

"My boy warned our country about an axis of evil. He warned the world. Three countries that could destroy our country, three countries that could, in fact, destroy the world. The press corps made my son out to be a madman, a warmonger, a fool. Some fool. Saddam Hussein had killed millions of his own people and threatened the world. Does anyone possibly think that Saddam Hussein would not have had nuclear weapons by now and would not be threatening to use them again? Probably would have already used them. If you don't believe that, let's be honest, you are a fool." This time he did not stop the applause.

"This is a dangerous and serious world. It is not a place for some naïve Ivy League kid with no experience to flit around the world in Air Force One and think that his rhetoric is changing minds and cultures. I am old enough to remember Neville Chamberlain flying in an old British transport airplane to meet with Hitler. He also thought that a ruthless dictator could be treated like an honest man. He also believed that he was so special that he could convince pure evil to become a respected member of the international community. One hundred million deaths later, Hitler was gone." The former president paused for a long time.

"And why can't this man put on a tie and show proper respect for the office to which he was elected. I don't want to see my president in blue jeans and sandals representing the United States of America in that costume. He just does not get it. I don't want my president to be bowing to anyone, let alone some foreign dictator. It is not about the president, everything is about the presidency and what it means." Applause.

"When you are eighty-seven years old, maybe you do not have to pull a punch. We stopped a dangerous man in Iraq at a steep price of blood and treasure, and this administration seems willing to remove itself from Iraq and position Iraq to have the Taliban and/or Al Qaeda in control of a tenth of the world's oil reserves. We stopped a dangerous man who was murdering his own people and had sons who made him look like a peace activist at Woodstock. This administration seems to believe that a Taliban or Al Qaeda controlled Middle East is just something we may need to accept as a reality. Stupid, stupid, stupid!" There was no stopping the applause.

"I mean stupid. These Taliban people are misreading the literature of a wonderful religion and using that misinterpretation to launch a continuous attack to destroy any portion of modern civilization they can impact. They are training their children to believe their own heresies. And make no mistake; they are successful. Is there a single meaningful Islamic leader who ever speaks out against Islamic violence? No!

"As to the amount of oil in Iraq, oh, I am not sure whether it is a tenth or an eleventh or even a fortieth, Mr. Newscaster, so please don't correct me if my math is a bit off, just get the point. We cannot abandon the people of Iraq or else no one, *no one*, will ever trust us again! There is a lot more riding on our actions than a few barrels of oil. Riding on our policies is the question of whether anyone can trust the United States. Who would trust a nation that abandoned another country's leaders after they risked their lives to attempt to be a democracy?" Applause, overwhelming applause! The former president seemed to be thirty years younger than eighty-seven.

Barely over the applause, Bob Colony spoke into his microphone: "Folks, while the convention hall may like this speech, it cannot be registering very well with the rest of America." Before the President spoke again, Lance Amplington (not the last name given him by his parents), the networks' OBC pollster and focus group guru, jumped on the air and reported: "Bob, Marylou, the three focus groups we have tonight, one Republican, one Democrat and one Independent are eating this speech up. The positive responses in every group are well over two-to-one and..."—the producer, Merritt Goodwin, cut him off as the former president began again.

The former president slowed the applause again and spoke: "The Iranian people rose up against a crooked election and our president voted *present*. It took him ten days to find a message and while he was looking for a message, the politically elite of Iran murdered and imprisoned the leaders of the Iranian democracy movement. The President and Vice President decided instead of doing anything, they would get together for hamburgers and probably sent the Ayatollahs a list of their favorite burger joints near Washington

D.C." The applause was deafening. "Now, Iran is a nuclear power, including a delivery system.

"Like millions of Americans over the past two hundred plus years, I put on a uniform and proudly served my nation. I was shot down over the Pacific during World War II defending a nation I believed in, a concept of democracy that was and is unique in the world. Now I hear this president talk about Greek exceptionalism or Zimbabwe exceptionalism, as if he never read a history book." Again, deafening applause.

Oh, I wonder if I am making an old fool of myself, thought President Boone.

"For my entire life, I have been proud to talk about American exceptionalism. I am proud of what America has done and while I am interested in what other nations think of themselves and of us, I know that it is the United States of America that has led this planet since World War II and it is American exceptionalism that has led the scientific community during that period. American exceptionalism, you are darn right Senator Vincent." Standing ovation on and off the stage.

President Boone continued: "I read somewhere the President of the United States is somewhat embarrassed that we dropped two atom bombs on Japan. Has he read nothing? Nothing? The United States of America was attacked on a Sunday afternoon when we were at peace. Thousands died on December 7, 1941, and around the world, millions more died trying to defeat the attacking armies of the Nazis and the Japanese during World War II. The experts expected the United States to have one million casualties if we would have invaded Japan to finish the war. Or we could drop those two bombs. Those two atom bombs saved those million American lives and the lives of who knows how many Japanese. I read not so long ago that ten percent of the population in the United States is here today only, yes, only because we used the atom bomb. The forefathers of my son's generation would be buried in overseas' graves if we had not used the atom bomb.

"It is a pretty good bet that I am here because we used the atom bomb, as I was poised to be part of the invasion of Japan in 1945. Remaking history and getting to the wrong answer is historically wrong, morally wrong and sends a plain stupid message to the next generation." Now, the convention went crazy. One couldn't hear; one couldn't speak. The former president was speaking for tens of millions of older Americans and he also hit home for younger viewers with the reality of the number of listeners who would

101

not otherwise be listening if their fathers and grandfathers had died on the shores of Japan.

"While I will be criticized for this next sentence, this President would probably be here because his father was not an American citizen. His father was a young man in Africa and probably could not have cared less if one million American men died attacking Japan. Well, I would have been one of those men attacking Japan and I would have cared. Both for myself and for my wartime colleagues." Huge applause, for some Democrats on the stage, a bit muted.

Bob Colony took just a moment to again speak over the former president and added: "President Boone is showing his age a bit here and is more than a bit over the line."

"But, my friends," the former president began as the delegates quieted down, "nothing I have just said is a surprise to any of you. You have all thought about it, you have all begun to wonder what is happening to truth and you all know the answer. And I have shamefully remained quiet since the day I left office because that is what I believed good former presidents did when they retired. Other than President Carter, every former president has gone about his life, contributed when asked and kept quiet the rest of the time. President Carter knows how I feel about his comments about my son and many other political issues, but he is an adult and can make his own bad decisions.

"What caused me to speak tonight? First, before the convention I decided to throw away my wonderfully benign speech that would have been on those wonderfully silly teleprompters. I decided to let President Cloud speak for both of us. Then I heard Senator Wayne and what was being said about his speech and about the convention in the mezzanine level. Except Fox News, you could hear the silent voice of the White House talking points behind those identical spontaneous thoughts." With that, he pointed at the mezzanine level, which was reserved exclusively for the press corps, the television teams, the talking heads and the occasional Internet reporters. "It was those folks." He pointed again and within a few seconds, the crowd was pointing at the mezzanine level and chanting: *You folks, you folks, you folks...* and the former president, now only encouraging the convention audience, let it go. *Well, this is pretty fulfilling,* the former president conceded to himself. *Let's drive home the truth.*

"I listened to Senator Wayne this evening and by golly, I liked most of what he had to say. The senator presented a few facts about what has been happening these past three and a half years and by golly, he gave his opinion." *Darn, stop using that 'by golly' phrase, you sound ancient when you do that!* "Was he one hundred percent right? Was he one hundred percent accurate?" The crowd shouted, *Yes! Yes! Yes!* "Well, honestly, maybe he was a bit over the top, but his remarks were straightforward, substantive and worthy of an American senator. And what happened within five minutes of his speech? Within five minutes of his speech, just by accident, a matter of surprise, a coincidence, almost every one of those folks had the same talking points attacking Senator Wayne." The former president pointed at the mezzanine level. "All but one, go figure? What an upset! What a coincidence?" his distain showing in every word from the former president.

"Well, I say shame on the media. Shame on the media!" The crowd took this up and as one, again, pointed to the mezzanine level: *Shame! Shame!* The former president, again, did nothing to stop the crowd. After a few minutes the old warrior put his arms in the air and after a bit he regained control. It was not only a blunt attack on the media; it was also a velvet attack on the White House and its political team.

"I am just plain tired of a White House that is controlling the commentary of our historically independent media. We all know that the media's talking points come directly from 1600 Pennsylvania Avenue. Shameful, just shameful!"—and the chant of *Shame!* Again took over the arena. In an interesting turn of events, virtually everyone on the stage had become just members of the audience and they too pointed and chanted. Even the former Cabinet members and former President Cloud.

"A White House e-mailing, talking point propaganda, yes, propaganda, and a president who needs a teleprompter to say, 'Good morning.' This is all very, very bad.

"I look back four years and I see a young, attractive politician come forth to represent my Republican party. Perhaps a bit naïve, perhaps a bit too early, but she was a person of spunk and honesty. And the media tried to destroy her and destroy her family. Shame on that media." Pointing again followed by the chant *Shame! Shame! Shame!*

"Is this national media simply an organization without honor? Has politics become a participating blood sport? Do those weasels on television have no bosses, no ethics, no ombudsman, no class? Does this national media actually think or do they just parrot what is given to them by Herman Sack-man representing the President of the United States?" If one did not see an eighty-seven-year-old man on stage, one would have thought there was a young man at the microphone. The former president's voice remained strong.

"Four years ago, I was awake late one night hearing a talk show host—a buffoon who married the mother of his son four or five years after he was born—attacking the fourteen-year-old daughter of a political candidate. A day later he apologized, kind of, and said he meant the eighteen-year-old daughter. That mean spirited buffoon is still on the air. This blood sport was permitted by his bosses—those corporate guys who wear two thousand dol-lar suits and represent that their networks are supposed to be unbiased while they should be requiring their networks to show some dignity. How can this be? How can this be in the United States of America? We have no independ-ent media, we have a media without class and they all know they are guilty. Guilty, Guilty, Guilty!" The crowd now picked up the chant of *Guilty!* And pointed at press row. It was loud, it was long and to the media, it was just a bit frightening on the mezzanine level.

The television cameras picked up former President Cloud and the Sec-retary of State and one could see that they empathized with this part of the speech. The Clouds also felt a special bond with the former vice presiden-tial nominee who had been mentioned without the use of her name. While politically they could not have been farther apart, they knew the press had mercifully left their daughter alone and they were mortified at the treat-ment of their rival's family. *There but for the grace of God went we,* thought the Secretary of State.

Bob Colony injected into the conversation: "The former president has now gone completely over the top and..." The producer cut Colony and his microphone off as fast as possible and yelled: "You foolish SOB, he calls you an idiot and your first damn sentence is to try to prove him right. Shut up and take your medicine! The media will have twenty-four hours to spin this how we, or it, wants." Colony screamed a few obscenities at his producer, but his airtime was over, at least for a few minutes.

"I challenge the White House, I challenge the media, to tell us where those talking points came from tonight and why those damn talking heads all suddenly had the same thoughts, every station but one, and all the same.

Shame, shame, shame." Another few minutes of pure theatre with the convention enraptured, engaged and chanting.

"My friends, I have exceeded my time. I perhaps have exceeded my welcome, but I feel better and"— smiling—"that is important, at least to me."

A shout came from the audience: "We love you President Boone." The former president blushed and the delegates cheered. The former president blushed even more visibly.

"I have watched this country be led astray by unelected, uninformed, vicious and violently prejudiced media characters for too long. I have watched a media that has fawned over undeserving people of dubious character, attacked men and women of good character with whom they disagree, and brought the tone and quality of the debate to the gutter. I have watched the media heighten small events to make the Republicans look bad and bury major errors by the Democrats. I am just mad as hell and I am not going to take it anymore!"

The crowd took up the chant *I am mad as Hell and I am not going to take it anymore!* As the former president calmly picked up his coat and walked back to his chair. Nothing the crowd could say or do could bring him back. Next to him, this former president's wife had an expression of awe and it reflected her deepest thoughts and a lifetime of love for her husband. She hugged him and kissed him on the forehead. From the stage, President Boone received a standing ovation from everyone. Not a single folding chair had a single occupant.

Senator Wayne returned to the microphone. "Thank you, President Boone. And that woman was right, we all do love you so much!" Great applause.

~

Senator Wayne continued: "My good friends, oh goodness, don't you hate those three words *my good friends*. In the United States Senate, we use those three words to describe colleagues that we would prefer to introduce as,"—he paused on the line which he had been thinking about for about two weeks and his wife had urged him to leave on his desk in D.C.—"we talk to and about people as *my good friend* who, frankly, we believe are no better than a wolf dressed as a mouse, people who would mislead one hundred thousand people around the country on an important piece of legislation to garner three votes in their district." The television again focused in on President Cloud who was doubled over laughing at Senator Wayne's remark. This was something everyone who had ever participated in a Congressional hearing knew to be absolutely accurate.

"But, that being said, Caleb Smith is actually my good friend. It is no secret, I think, most Sunday afternoons after church we sneak out and play golf together; we play right until dark. The man must have a putting green in his den; good gosh, he is one good putter. He is also one of the great Members of the United States Senate and could not lie if you put a gun to his head. Caleb?" Great applause for this next speaker, Caleb Smith, who would, in his own unique way, nominate the first presidential and vice presidential candidates of the American Exceptionalism Party.

Slowly, almost too slowly, the six-foot-four-inch, two-hundred-forty-pound Republican senator from Nebraska walked to the podium from his folding chair. Unlike every previous speaker, he had on neither a suit nor a sports jacket or tie; Caleb Smith came to the podium wearing a black, button-down, collared shirt and grey slacks. Still lifting weights at age fifty-two, the Nebraskan farm boy could probably still comfortably play a few series at center for the University of Nebraska. It always seemed a bit odd that the Republican Party seemed to attract big, athletic men to run for office and the Democratic Party did not.

If Smith's chair had a voice, it would have released a sigh of relief as Smith stood and walked to the podium. The American Exceptionalism Party newbie was welcomed with moderate enthusiasm. After twenty plus years in the Senate, the party faithfully knew Senator Caleb Smith could be counted on to be down to earth, but neither remotely entertaining nor meaningful. More important than anything else, Smith was probably the most conserva-tive man in the room and his early endorsement of Senator Vincent was a great shock to the conservative voices of the Republican Party and a concern to some of the more liberal delegates at this convention.

While President Boone had kept the delegates on their feet, there was no such anticipation for Senator Smith. Of course, there had been no anticipation of President Boone's speech. Smith's down home style may have been effective in the farm belt, but he was only occasionally interesting. Brilliant, yes; interesting, no; charismatic, not a chance.

Senator Smith's immediate personal thoughts would have surprised even Senator Smith just a few months ago. *Okay big guy, this is either your Andy Warhol nightmare moment or your opportunity to lead this screwed up democracy back to the Promised Land. Think Moses! Don't blow it!*

Senator Smith's size was both part of his self-image and a significant part of his public image. The former center of a national championship football team, acknowledging his foot speed to be a bit disappointing, had turned his back on a professional contract that he believed would have left him on a cold bench in the fall of his first season. Instead, he had accepted a Rhodes Scholarship upon graduation from Nebraska. Every Division I football program had a couple of guys, at a minimum, who were academic superstars. These guys were all that was left of the student athlete image that all of the universities promoted but now only regularly existed in Division III. Smith thought of himself in the same mirror as a couple other Rhodes Scholar athletes and a UCLA football player named Cormac Carney, who is now a brilliant Federal judge in Southern California.

After a feckless year studying Greek philosophy at Oxford, he had returned to the University of Nebraska where he garnered simultaneous masters' degrees in agriculture and business. Of course, also simultaneously, he was the graduate assistant coach for yet another national championship football team. He married a young, attractive sophomore who was studying political science.

No one could deny that Caleb Smith lived the good life, even as a graduate student. Following the conferral of his advanced degrees, he and his pregnant, now junior wife, joined Dad on the family farm. Coaching was over as a profession. The family farm was already twenty thousand acres and Caleb used his education and homespun charisma to begin to grow the family farm into one of the great farming fortunes of the Midwest.

Ultimately, Caleb was convinced by his friends to run for the United States Senate. They told him, and they were right, that he could manage his farm managers from Washington, D.C. His constituents wanted a representative in the Senate who was as honest as the day is long and a supporter of everything and anything to enhance the lives of farmers. Neither in his first primary nor in subsequent elections, did either party ever produce a serious opponent. This former center of the Nebraska football team, this Rhodes Scholar, and this successful farmer was an untouchable Member of the United States Senate.

After making a show of his great size while adjusting the microphone to a position where it worked for him and getting his body comfortable, Senator Smith waived to the crowd; he knew he looked good up there. He then took a personal moment, knowing it would look good on television, to waive to Mrs. Smith and their five handsome children—all very tall, somewhat broad shouldered, boys and girls alike—in the guest box.

He laughed to himself wishing someone would have told him that the teleprompters would be taken down. He opened his three-leaf binder, relieved that he had brought it with him, and looked down at his speech. There was no chance he would ask for the teleprompters to be replaced. That would be a decision reserved for an idiot and he was not an idiot.

As Senator Smith took his time at his microphone, the mega-television anchors focused their disdainful coverage of the AEP Convention.

"Mercy me, Marylou, how could these guys have decided on Senator Smith as their nominating speaker or whatever he is? Maybe I am wrong, but hasn't the senator already indicated that this is his last term in the Senate? And has he ever been known to get anyone to applaud after a speech? Can Caleb Smith get them engaged and involved?

"With two living ex-presidents and several congressmen who can pound through some of the popular positions, whatever those are—and we know every political speech will find some red meat for the audience—why anyone would have picked Senator Caleb Smith to speak at this point in the convention is a mystery to me? Maybe they simply selected the biggest senator they could find to speak and as he is a conservative Republican, so he does provide some balance. Yes, George Vincent is a Democrat, maybe he does add balance. And, Marylou, my guess is that he will give a lackluster speech.

"Marylou, do you think Senator Vincent is still registered as a Democrat or did he need to change parties to run for president? Well, Smith may not be the best the Republicans have to offer the AEP, but he is surely the one who is the biggest. Again, clearly not the sharpest tack in the drawer, but one easily found." Of course, Colony said not a word about the educational background of Senator Smith; that would have ruined the attack and he would have none of that.

Goodman did not yell at either commentator at this point. He was a bit worn down and he had personally suffered through a few Caleb Smith speeches before. The commentary was fair to a point. Hopefully, the guy would be brief.

Big Red again tried to bait Bob Colony: "Bob, yours is a pretty harsh assessment, but I will admit, pretty funny. I guess it would be funnier if I didn't know the guy was a Rhodes Scholar and has a handful of advanced degrees. Caleb Smith is not known as, one would say, a stemwinder, more of a just-a-lot-of-words guy. But, he is one smart puppy. Let's see what he has to say."

Colony could not let it go: "Marylou, the man is a mental lightweight, Rhodes Scholarship or not."

~

The speech by Senator Smith was on the agenda given to the press. The truth was that virtually everyone had the same thoughts as Bob Colony: *If this clown speaks for more than ten minutes, it will be sleepy time in the Eastern time zone and George Vincent will give his acceptance speech to a television audience that is either sound asleep or an audience that had finally turned to RBC to watch Humphrey Bogart turn his back on Ingrid Bergman in the final scene of Casablanca.*

"Thank you, thank you. I am honored to be here tonight and honored to be able to speak honestly and frankly to you all." The applause was tepid and the senator thought about going to plan B, using his traditional stump speech. *Aw hell,* he thought, *President Boone was great, maybe I am too. One great block and I get another championship ring.*

"President Boone, you were magnificent. Sorry about not having a coat and tie, I must have missed the memo. Actually, Mr. President, you are stone cold right and I apologize to Senator Vincent, Jordon Scotch and our delegates for not paying sufficient, visible respect for our country by not having a coat and tie on this evening.

"I stand here so angry at what the President of this United States has done to our economy and to our middle class that I wish we could step into the ring and, as they used to say, "Settle this like men!" Applause, lots of applause, surprising length and a bit of cheering. *Maybe they are listening, a good start; best remind them of my intellect.*

"Oh, I bet that last sentence would have lit them up at Oxford. They never could understand how this old giant football player could have been awarded a Rhodes Scholarship and how he could be studying Greek philosophy. Something about not being able to dress him up and take him to the annual dinner dance." Laughter, deep, long laughter. *This is kind of fun. Time for a serious line and then hit 'em with the homespun humor.*

"Sadly, there is more truth to my anger than I wish. I worry for my country, I worry for my family, I really worry for my grandkids and I worry for each of you. Can you imagine Thomas Paine seeing more than half of his income being taken for taxes, taxes that are causing our economy to collapse? Expenditures that are making us a financial nightmare." He repeated the question relying on the response to previous speakers in hopes of getting an answer from the crowd. A pause and suddenly a truly spontaneous *No!* from the convention floor.

Without any thought, Big Red looked at Bob Colony and spoke quickly into her microphone: "Bob, Where did this come from? Senator Smith has the full attention of the convention floor and I am alert as well."

"Or, for God's sake, a tax on not buying health insurance! Would those patriots in Boston have accepted a tax on not buying health care insurance? Does anything that has been done on health insurance make sense? Didn't the President tell us we could keep our existing insurance? Did he forget to tell us that if we kept our existing insurance, because we wanted our families to have access to the best doctors, that we would have to pay a tax on that insurance? And did he forget to tell us that our employers would be forced to change their insurance plans and therefore, since we would not have our old plans, he couldn't deliver on that promise that we could keep our existing insurance? Oh, sorry guys!" Long pause. "Is that fair?" A huge *No!* from the convention floor.

"Did anyone understand what I just said? Did this president really both agree and propose something crazy like that? How could any sane system tax someone for not carrying health insurance?" Serious applause and Senator Smith put both arms in the air in an attempt to go on with his speech. Even more applause. "I mean, really? A penalty if one does not carry health insurance? Maybe we should set up a collection booth at the border for illegal immigrants! Who is kidding whom? What's next, a penalty for not eating broccoli?" It may not have been perfectly reasoned, but the audience loved it.

Fox News' anchor, Arthur Ninoah, whispered into his microphone: "Senator Smith not only seems to have struck a chord with this audience, but our undecided sample group in our studio is also buying into this presentation, almost with unanimity."

Thaddeus Malkin leaped in to add: "These are issues that people never think about when they write legislation, great stuff."

Lance Amplington at OBC was having the identical response from his three focus groups.

Smith: "And Cap and Trade, this proposed tax on our electricity, which is presented as essential to climate change. Terrific, if you don't happen to use electricity. And I don't need talk about the fruitless stimulus package, not a job builder but a government work continuation program. Well folks, when the government takes my money, I don't call it Cap and Trade, I don't call it stimulus, I call it a damn tax! When the government prints money, I call it stealing, stealing from our grandchildren." Now the applause was over the top, minutes elapsed before the senator could speak again.

"And couldn't this clown have used a stinking billion dollars of stimulus money to build a wall at the border?" This lit the convention up even more. "Isn't it interesting how he spent a trillion dollars? He spent a fortune to change the windows on an abandoned building, but he couldn't find the money to protect our borders. This would be funny if it was not so sad!

"This president promised no taxes on the middle class and he is now taxing them to death and calls the taxes fees, sin costs, climate saving costs, puppy love, whatever! Let me make this as clear as it can be: when the government takes your money, you can call it anything you want, hell, you could call it apple strudel, but it's a damn tax!"

Now, slow 'em up big boy, this is your moment. "I see the Democrats trying to repeal Republican tax cuts that have been in place for twelve years. I see the Democrats calling tax increases tax cuts for the wealthy. I see the health care tax, I see this phony Cap and Trade tax stuff, and I see the end of the middle class. I see an economy in collapse. I heard a president promise no new taxes on the middle class a bazillion times and then he says he is agnostic on taxes to the 2010 Deficit Commission. I don't get it. I don't even know what agnostic means in that context, but I am pretty sure it is really bad. I do know that Democrats are going to leave the Democratic Party and join us in the American Exceptionalism Party for the presidential election. I know Republicans are going to do the same thing. I know, at first, they are just going to vote for George Vincent in the fall, but many, many of us are going to rally to the middle, the place most Americans want America to be, in the middle." More applause, lots more applause. "I am pretty sure that is where the independent members of the Tea Party want to be, in the reasonable middle.

"I am just a big, old, Nebraskan farm boy with one wife and five wonderful children, but when I see this nonsense from this president, I am reminded of the big city newspaper man driving down the country road. Seems the man was looking out his window and he saw a pig working his way towards the pasture on crutches. He drives on a bit and begins to dwell on that pig. Finally, he turns around and drives back to the farmhouse, parks on the road and walks up to the farmhouse door. The farmer comes to the door and the newspaperman introduces himself. It's Nebraska, so the farmer asks the newspaperman how he can help him and if he needs a glass of water." Gentle laughter. "The big city newspaperman declines the water, tells the farmer he saw his pig and asks the farmer why the pig is on crutches. The farmer responds by telling the man that he has just seen the best pig in the history of the planet. It seems that several months before, this pig was in his pen when the farmer's youngest daughter decided to use her inner tube to get to the middle of the lake. The daughter slipped out of the inner tube and, unable to swim, began screaming for help. *And that there pig*, the farmer told him, *somehow he knocked the lower log off the pen and ran to the lake*. As the daughter continued to scream and began to swallow water, the pig swam into the middle of the lake and pushed the inner tube under his girl. Then he swam behind her and pushed her to the edge of the lake. Best darn pig in the history of the planet!" Curiosity, a bit of giggling and then silence as the senator took a long pause. "*That is a fabulous story and obviously the pig is headed for the pig hall of fame,* offered the newspaperman, *but with all due respect it does not explain why the pig is on crutches, was he hurt while he saved your daughter?*" Smith paused. "*Oh gosh no,* said the farmer, *the only way we decided we could reward that there pig was to eat him slowly.*" Silence, realization, laughter, more laughter, and a standing ovation. President Cloud, a notoriously easy audience, laughed loudest. The Secretary of State, not an easy audience, also laughed loudly.

Senator Smith grinned from ear to ear and again put his arms in the air and thought: *You got 'em Bubba; now take 'em home and get off the stage.*

"The American people are no longer willing to be the pig who is being eaten slowly. We cannot be taxed to death. *We cannot be taxed to death!* We cannot let this president undo almost two hundred and fifty years of true democracy." The applause and screaming were building, the senator went on: "We cannot let this president turn us into the old Soviet Union; it is time to take our nation back! *It is time to take our nation back!*" Now the applause was deafening, not a person in the convention hall was sitting. In the history of American politics, no candidates had ever followed a speech that so honestly lit up the delegates as much as Smith's words. The audience began to shout *Take our nation back!* And the folks on stage were spontaneously up and cheering with them. Every soul on the floor of the arena was completely enthralled with the senator, the evening, the American Exceptionalism Party and everything else. In the cocoon of the Q, life was perfect.

Caleb Smith was satisfied with himself, more than satisfied. *Winner, winner, winner! Let's set the boys up and get out of the way.*

"This president is destroying the America we received from our parents? Is this the America we want to leave to our kids and grandkids? Do we have to mortgage their future?" A resounding *No!* from the audience. "Or are we going to leave this convention united in an effort to take back our country, to defend the principles of our founding fathers and reestablish this democracy?"

Yes! Yes! Yes! Hollered the audience. No one was in his or her chair. With great skill, the senator milked the moment and then brought the convention hall to near silence with the forefinger on his right hand to his lips.

~

Trying to turn down the volume on the audience, Colony spoke to Big Red on microphone: "Not very professional in his delivery, but do you think the convention seems to be buying what Senator Smith is selling?

"Yes," he responded to his own question, "but I suspect the people at home are out getting a Coca-Cola and wondering about his choice of words and stories. A bit immature for my taste." Yet again, Colony could not have been more wrong, the Twitters were doing their thing and the television audience had super bowl type numbers. Political conventions in 2012 were supposed to be impossible to make surprising and funny, yet these people were pulling it off. Amplington's focus groups were essentially confirming positive responses from almost one hundred percent of their subjects.

At Fox News, Ninoah tried to let the picture speak for itself. He remained quiet and allowed the crowd to speak for him. His only thoughts were of where the convention was going and whether the convention would be early ripe, early rot or middle right, middle rot or whether the American Exceptionalism Party would grasp that they had hit the right nerve and finish the evening with the same scheme. *If they grasp the exasperation of the electorate and campaign to that exasperation rather than to the far left or the far right philosophies*, he thought, *this might be the most interesting election in history.* The two parties he had seen for his entire life had been disenfranchising the more moderate wings of their parties for years and might be suddenly realizing that each of the two politically active wings could be smaller than the middle. *Heck, that's the way it works with a chicken, why not politics?* He liked that and followed that line of thinking for a few minutes with his panel of political geniuses including Thaddeus Milken who was ready to name George Vincent's Cabinet.

~

Smith elected to finish his remarks: "My friends, if we are brutally honest, as bad as it has been within the United States, including all of the rights that the current president is trying to take away; the current President of the United States has been more successful domestically than internationally. No one in this room could believe that weakness by our president did not cause the North Koreans to attack South Korea. For all we know, if the Chinese and Japanese had not intervened, the President might still be voting *present* as to what action needed to be taken. I will leave the issues of the world to the next President of the United States, Senator Vincent, and the next Vice President of the United States, Jordon Scotch, but let me acknowledge that we will not exist as the nation that every one of us loves if we do not elect Senator Vincent and Jordon Scotch this November!" The audience became nearly out of control as the senator accepted their applause. At that moment, without any further introduction whatsoever, Senator George Vincent and economist Jordon Scotch were stage right.

When the audience saw them the enthusiasm started all over. It went on and on and on. It was the real thing and it would be seen as the real thing by honest observers, of which there were virtually none in the mezzanine section of the arena. On the floor, no balloons, few banners, only excited delegates.

Senator Smith walked to the two men, shook hands with Scotch, who he had never met, and hugged George Vincent as if they had not seen each other in years. Vincent hugged back, hard, as the reality of the success of this political show, so far, had been very emotional for him.

The audience was already standing and pandemonium broke out for the umpteenth time.

~

"Marylou, we may have a few minutes and our panel is ready to comment on Senator Smith's assault on the President. With only Jordon Scotch and Senator Vincent on the dais the rest of the night, we should be able to squeeze in a few comments before they begin to bore us to death." Bob Colony removed his earphone as he handed the show off to Marylou and her panel for a few minutes and headed down the hallway, first to hit the head, and then to quickly chat with Merritt Goodman who said he wanted them to spend a minute together. *Goodman is such a pain in the ass!* Colony was hopeful that Goodman had found a third voice for the booth as he was not enthralled with Marylou having as much viewing time as she was getting. *Best to keep number two as close to number three as possible* had been his personal motto over the years and it had worked pretty well for him.

Big Red was full head-to-toe with legs featured sitting in her executive chair in front of three talking heads. An above average student at Miami University, Ohio, Big Red had not slept her way to the co-anchor role. She had gotten there with hard work; being beautiful did not hurt either. Her work ethic combined with a level of ambition generally only known to great ice skaters and swimmers was a powerful package. She could easily manage her panel.

~

The President of the United States sat alone and silently in his chair in his private quarters. The room smelled as if there had been a convention of smokers rather than only the President of the United States, a man who wanted all Americans to stop smoking and eat healthy foods. He had smoked nearly a pack of cigarettes over the past hour. During his term, he added taxes to cigarettes and yet denied he had raised taxes for those earning under $250,000. At a pack of cigarettes an hour when he had told Mrs. President he had completely quit, that was a bit much, even under stress, and not good.

Before becoming president, as a community organizer, he was virtually never challenged in anything that he did, whatever that was, and certainly he was never challenged or confronted by anyone with an IQ in his zip code. Since the financial, Korean, gulf spill, immigration, and who knows what other fiascoes, there had been regular and sufficient intellectual challenges and because of his inexperience with adversity, the pressure was difficult for him emotionally and physically.

The President could not acknowledge that his lack of managerial experience was hurting his policies, the economy, the seeming forever continuing clean up in the Gulf and really, just everything. In street terms of a foregone day, he was rattled. This was the reason he had ceased having press conferences. The questions were easy; it was the answers that were hard. In his mind, he still had absolutely never failed at anything and if press conferences were a struggle, he would not have press conferences.

Not being one to go to sleep early, or during, or even after a difficult evening, he also was not one to lose himself in a good book and not remotely interested in anyone else's company right now. He just sat by himself in front of the television. He was despondent at both what was being said and who was saying it. His despondency would lead to anger and then he would calm down and go through the same process again and again.

~

At OBC, Merritt Goodman had had it. He was a career producer and had watched uncomfortably as news had become editorial and editorial had become unreserved enthusiasm for Democratic candidates on his network. There was a difference between sycophant and news, and Bob Colony had crossed the line too many times in too many comments for too many years. Tonight was the worst yet, by far. He had asked Colony to come over to see him for a minute. Colony would open the conversation by asking for something; he always did. Again, he tried to convince himself: *It was not Colony's last on-air statements; it was his body of work over the past couple of hours that was causing this meeting.*

Mercifully, Merritt did not have to deal with the former prima donna at MSNBC who was capable of bringing the level of discussion down to the second grade level. Merritt could still quote Keith Olbermann's rant on Scott Brown, the senator from Massachusetts: "In Scott Brown we have an irresponsible, homophobic, racist, reactionary, ex-nude model, tea bagging supporter of violence against woman and against politicians with whom he disagrees."

Maybe it was just that Merritt Goodman had reached the end of his patience with Colony. They had never been friends and Colony's arrogance was just too much for a man not drawing the appropriate percentage of the viewing audience to maintain that arrogance. In truth, his time had passed a few years ago in Goodman's mind as his ratings had been slipping for half a decade. Not knowing how Colony was going to react, he had a two-person security team outside the door.

Before Colony could sit down, get comfortable and ask for something, Goodman took off his headphones, looked at him and said: "Bob, we are going to let Marylou finish the show tonight. Why don't you take the rest of the evening off and we'll get together the day after tomorrow in New York and replay this one." Goodwin delivered these thoughts very calmly and without any emotion in his voice. A confrontation was the last thing he needed at this moment and he certainly did not want the other networks seeing a big fight in a glass-enclosed cubicle.

"Pardon me?" was all Bob Colony could muster. He was one of the deans of the network, in fact, in his mind, the dean of television news and he was not one hundred percent sure what he had just heard.

"Bob, I said I want Marylou to finish up alone tonight."

Colony's color changed at this point and his reddening face contrasted sharply with his $525 perfectly fitted pink shirt and perfectly tied solid reddish tie. He knew he was in a glass cage and knew he needed to keep control of himself, otherwise he might become the story and that would not be good for him.

"Merritt, that is not going to happen. I don't know what you are talking about, but I am going back to the booth to finish my broadcast." He was near whispering to Goodman in an effort to stay in control and was already up and turning toward the glass door.

"No, Bob. I wanted to do this thirty minutes ago and decided I needed to talk to New York first. Sometimes one just needs to know the exact powers of being the director/producer." Again, Goodman was keeping his voice even and trying, with some success, to make this sound like a very normal business decision, which it was not. "Bob, I tried to warn you, what, six times this evening? I think, tonight, that you were not the commentator, you were not the newsman, you were a Democratic cheerleader. All you needed was a skirt, a tight blouse and a pom-pom. You were a hack. Sad to say, but you were quite honestly, a hack. If you think I am mad at you over your commentary, you should have heard Dr. Alemerck. Remember, Alemerck can fire me!

"If it had been his choice, I think he would have left Thaddeus Milken in the booth and let you make a deal with Fox News, if they would have taken you!" Goodman had somehow lost control of his emotions even though Colony had been near silent and he paused to let this overstatement seep in.

Goodwin knew that the top news people were, in some form, artists, and he had wanted to make sure he was on firm ground. After talking to Alemerck, he knew that what he was doing was what another somewhat impartial observer would do and this impartial observer signed his paychecks. "Bob, you far overstepped your bounds tonight and we need to bring in a relief pitcher. Let's decide you don't feel well and pick this up again Thursday." He looked squarely at Bob Colony, looked back at his console and stated what, for him, was the obvious. "It sounds so obnoxious, Bob, but I have a show to direct and this decision has already been made."

"You are right, Merritt. I don't feel well, because you make me fucking sick. But I suspect I will feel better after we all get together with our lawyers." Colony opened the door and turned...

"Bob, this would be a good time to quietly walk to your car. Anything you say to anyone, I repeat, *anyone* on the way to your car will probably be one big, huge fucking mistake. Sorry about this, Bob, it is just business. Tomas, why don't you and Ruben walk with Bob and make sure the paparazzi don't bother him." Merritt Goodman put his headphones back on with his fat, little fingers and went back to work. Doing the right thing was not as hard as he thought it would be. *Just business, that sounded pretty good,* he thought to himself.

~

"Glenn, what did we just witness on that grand stage? The audience seemed pretty fired up." Big Red was continuing her panel without any idea that she was now the lead anchor.

While the camera moved to Big Red and the panel, Bob Colony was opening the door to his rental car and heading for his hotel room. He had not flown into Cleveland on the corporate airplane and there were no airplanes back to New York until a scheduled American Airlines flight at 8:45 a.m. He would be on his cell phone long before the first airplane took off. He had already e-mailed both his legal counsel and Dr. Alemerck. His e-mails were less than politically correct.

"Ooh, Marylou, this is exactly what we could have expected if we had really given this very much thought. Here we have a fairly senior, but unknown, Republican senator—at least unknown outside of Nebraska—attacking a president that is trying to clean up a mess made by the prior administration and is adored by the great majority of Americans. Give me a break." This from panelist and former Democratic Congressman of New York Glenn Duneaberg. "A story about a pig! This guy hasn't seen the barn on his forty thousand, or five hundred thousand, or whatever acre farm for decades. This is a man who opposed Cap and Trade because he thought he should be able to drive an SUV from his home in Nebraska to his vacation home in Colorado. This is a man who truly doesn't care about health care for the poor. It was a sad performance. Forgive me for saying this, but he's just a big, friendly, dumb ex-football player." Former Congressman Duneaberg wondered if Senator Smith even had a vacation home or an SUV, but it was a great point he was making to benefit mankind and to keep him in the limelight. All he could think of was his own vacation home that was being paid for by these silly panels discussing political speeches for television audiences. *What a joke and it pays me so handsomely.*

"Wait a minute here, those are some pretty serious allegations, the man was a Rhodes Scholar..." started Luke Stratman, the designated conservative on the panel who was found wandering around the spin rooms when Thaddeus Milken had moved down the hallway.

"Oh don't start, Luke," interrupted Duneaberg who had started the trio's analysis. "This is a guy who has no right to be on any national stage. He actually believes that climate change is a good thing. Probably thinks that if New York is covered over by the Atlantic Ocean, it is a good thing. How can we..."

"Thank you, guys. It looks like Jordon Scotch, the completely unknown economist from UCLA, and American Exceptionalism Party nominee for the vice presidency is ready to speak. Let's give him a minute and then we will go back to Luke."

~

Dr. Jordon Scotch was the first vice presidential candidate who was rolled onto a dais and then rolled to the podium. And with all probability, he was also the smartest vice presidential candidate in well over two hundred years. The full scholarship at MIT followed by graduate school at both the London School of Economics and Berkeley had nothing to do with the wheelchair. The wheelchair was the result of a horrible bus accident returning from a high school track meet.

Jordon Scotch was world-class smart. He was destined to be one of the most respected economists in the world after catching the attention of senior faculty at MIT during his second week on campus. His Nobel Prize in 2004 was no surprise to anyone. It seemed there was no area of economics where he was not arguably the most knowledgeable in the world. His PhD thesis had been a comparison of the different welfare plans in Europe in the 1950s and in essence was a discussion of the ultimate impact of welfare on the lives of its recipients over the ensuing thirty years. Jordon Scotch knew where the European culture and economy were going long before the Europeans and he knew where the American culture and economy were going if there was not a hard turn at the helm.

Ayn Rand would have thought Scotch the smartest man on the planet. In this room, there was a lot of empathy for this man who had been in a wheelchair for forty years. Ayn Rand would not have appreciated or understood that empathy.

Scotch was not and had never been an elected politician. He had never so much as run for class treasurer in high school. He was a well-respected economist who had predicted the collapse of the housing market and the underlying reasons almost three years before the bubble began bursting. He had also begun writing about many political issues in very technical journals from an economic standpoint many years previous, while quietly doing the kind of research done at many think tanks and other universities around the country. He was currently a full-time professor at UCLA, a place he had come to love. His work in economics in concert with his studies on taxation, were the reason he was selected to be the vice presidential candidate. Scotch had an extraordinary record of being able to predict behavioral changes resulting from tax law changes and the resulting increase or decrease in tax revenues from such changes. This had become the focus of his research in recent years. His behavioral predictions were uncanny, as he had developed models that could determine the amount of research and development, or the success, of the American tool and die business by simply inserting different tax rates and other researched tax and economic data from around the world into his model.

On the UCLA campus, it was never a surprise to see a couple of limousines arrive in front of the John Anderson Graduate School of Business and world famous businessmen exit the vehicles. Most of them were headed for a conference room and hopeful to get as many of Dr. Scotch's two-grand-an-hour conversations as Dr. Scotch would allow. There was never a shortage of visitors to Dr. Scotch and along with the hourly fee, no one was ever granted a second visit without making a meaningful contribution to the John Anderson School of Business at UCLA and a second contribution equal to half of whatever they gave to the business school to the athletic department. Dr. Scotch would do anything for his close friend Dan Guerrero, the longtime athletic director at UCLA.

The delegates to the American Exceptionalism Party Convention had no idea what to expect from Dr. Scotch. The media had already decided to frame his character as a pencil-necked, intellectual geek. This had occurred while Dr. Scotch had been campaigning around the country as he was still learning to keep the number of syllables in his words to less than six. It was amazing to him how the media could get his persona so wrong in such an incredibly short period of time. The liberal press wanted the economic genius in the wheelchair to be a geek.

As Jordon Scotch was not a household name to the media until a few weeks before, it was certain that no one had, or had taken, the opportunity to get to understand the man. Decidedly, no one had taken the time or thought to check ratemyprofessors.com where Dr. Scotch had received almost perfect scores from his students since the inception of the website. This was unheard of as the website was generally used to assault professors on an anonymous basis. The comment, "Best and funniest lecturer on campus," would have been a bit of help to a diligent reporter trying to frame Dr. Scotch's personality. But, as always, the reporters were focused on what was possibly wrong with Scotch and they assumed that an economics professor in a wheelchair would be the ultimate geek. Only in the eyes of the media could being a brilliant economist, a successful professor and an all around good guy be a bad thing. Then again, if Dr. Scotch had been pulled from obscurity by the President, then...

There were still no teleprompters; Dr. Scotch was in his wheelchair next to the podium. Dr. Scotch had a hands free microphone in front of his mouth like a rock star. He had not left his ever-present briefcase in the briefing room. He put it down next to his wheelchair. After the applause ceased, the professor reached down into his briefcase and pulled out a newspaper. He then carefully reached into his jacket and pulled out a pair of reading glasses. Without so much as a thank you to Senator Wayne for his kind introduction or to the audience for their applause, the professor looked into the newspaper and began reading: "Dr. Scotch is a PhD in economics and a Nobel Prize winner in economics. He is an economics professor and has no experience in national politics or local politics, and apparently is equally indifferent to the arts. It is utterly amazing that the American Exceptionalism Party would pick a vice presidential candidate who is virtually unknown, even in his own state. This one is not even known on a citywide basis. We have not even found a record of Dr. Scotch ever visiting Washington D.C."

"OK, let me make this one issue as clear as can be, I have been to Washington D.C."—a very long pause —"once. It was very hot and it rained." He deadpanned; the audience laughed. "The newspapers are completely wrong." He pointed at the mezzanine level. "When I was in the third grade, my parents took my brother and me to Washington D.C., Philadelphia and Gettysburg. It was a grand trip and I learned a great deal about our country and its history. My late Dad was a history teacher at Hamilton High School in Los Angeles and I suspect my brother and I knew more about those three historical places before we arrived than any other third or seventh graders that summer, or the combined media today. I learned a lot about our country and I learned that the humidity in Washington D.C. could be higher than the temperature. Hence, I have never been back. I was invited to the White House after I received my Nobel Prize, but I declined.

"Even today, I continue to try to conduct my consulting business on the UCLA campus and while every summer I go on a lecture tour across the country or around the world, I find most of the people interested in listening are in cities other than Washington D.C. There are a lot of talkers in that Washington D.C. but few listeners." His presentation, very slow and deliberate and a bit squeaky, made one instantly think of Ben Stein. The audience was eating it up. "Hence, I always lecture elsewhere. Rest assured, I have been teaching a long time and I have found that whether I lecture or I teach using the Socratic method, when there are no listeners there is no learning.

And in Washington D.C., it is really hard to find someone who is listening." He flashed a perfect smile and the audience applauded. He smiled again and stated: "I take it many of you have been to Washington D.C." A great laugh. His charm would be evident throughout his short speech.

Dr. Scotch paused and looked at the audience: "And perhaps the real first question for tonight will be asked by a conspiracist and the question will be: *Was that really Dr. Scotch or is it his evil twin brother masquerading as a professor and not really needing a wheelchair?*" Sounding like the deep-voiced pitchman for most previews in the theatres, he again asked: "*Could this really be Jordon Scotch or is it his evil brother masquerading as someone who needs a wheelchair? At night, does he slide down the rain spout behind his house and train for the Boston Marathon?*" Laughter. A bit uncomfortable, but laughter.

"Well, let me empty my old briefcase here," and he literally emptied his briefcase onto the floor next to the podium and his wheelchair. Papers flew in all directions. "Okay, it is all there, my grades from grammar school, college, various academic scholarship offers and whatever, my birth certificate, marriage license, pictures of the kids, pictures confirming that I am, in fact, in a wheelchair, an MRI showing the complete tear in my spine, receipts for my season tickets to watch both the UCLA Bruin's basketball team and the Santa Monica Community College basketball team as well. I think there is an article about the Nobel Prize there somewhere. Also, I think there is a copy of my pass to use the recreational swimming pool at UCLA so that I do not become the largest American in a wheelchair."

Professor Scotch pointed to a picture on the floor. "There is a picture of my wife Maria who went to Smith College in Indiana. We met at Berkeley when I was studying for my PhD and she was studying for her PhD in nursing." His speech was now comfortably slow and almost in travel show mode. "My floor library here includes her diploma and her work address where she continues to teach nursing to aspiring young registered nurses. If it comes up, I suspect she is a really great professor because her graduates seem to continue to contact her even decades after they become registered nurses.

"There are pictures of the two of us with our four children. All four are by the grace of God. Three are ours naturally and one is the daughter of my wife's sister. Her parents both died on September 11, 2001. And again, yes, the other three are ours, people in wheelchairs actually can have children." He looked at the private box with the whole family and said: "Guys, give the television folks a wave. Media people, please take a long and wonderful

127

look and then leave my kids alone, they will be in school during this election and after Senator Vincent and I are elected, please do not make them part of your media blood sport."

Pointing back to the floor, "All this stuff and more are up on my website, lots more. The website is Jordon Scotch boy professor dot com, no blanks.

"I am giving you all of this stuff as I don't want to have you bothering the hospital where I was born looking for a birth certificate or MIT to get my grades, which classes I took or anything. Rest assured, I was not admitted to MIT or anywhere else because I am a minority and the scholarships were purely academic, nothing else. If you want to know anything about my history, just ask. Send me an e-mail. I've got a pretty good memory and while everything in my life has not gone perfectly, it is what it is.

"George Vincent looked up the definition of transparent and we are going to use the textbook definition thereof. Others may just use the word, George and I will walk the talk." Long pause with almost dead silence in the arena as the delegates focused on that last sentence. "Okay, George will walk the talk and I will roll the talk." Hands up, big smile and within seconds, Dr. Scotch owned not only the delegates but everyone watching who was not so partisan that they could not recognize a pretty terrific guy without permission. Charm was clearly encapsulated in the body of this UCLA professor of economics.

Big Red, now the solitary queen of the air, spoke over the laughter and applause: "This election just could turn out to be a great deal of fun."

Over at Fox News, anchor Arthur Ninoah remarked: "This guy must have charmed a lot of graduate students in his career. I already wish he had been my college mentor. One of our guys did check him out on ratemyprofessor.com a minute ago and he really does have dozens and dozens of perfect scores. Our guy said he scrolled down the list of other UCLA professors and no one had scores even close to those of Dr. Scotch. Some of these professor evaluations are brutally negative. Ugh."

Big Red offered a quick thought to one of Scotch's remarks: "I wonder if Dr. Scotch's comment about not being a minority admit was a challenge to the President to disclose his college records?"

Scotch: "Transparency is having press conferences, regularly, not once or twice a year. Transparency is not having some unelected press spokesman try to hide the ball.

128

"So who is this guy that has been nominated for the Vice President of the United States? Well, you may have noticed I am a bit shorter than our current vice president and I have quite a bit more hair, every strand original and in its original location." Laughter, great laughter from the delegates, each thinking of the hair plugs on the VP's head. "So let's get the easy questions out of the way, just in case you have not yet read the documents I have just supplied,"—laughter—"I am a professor of economics at UCLA in Los Angeles. It is the greatest job one could ever have and frankly, it is only with great reluctance that I am willing to go to Washington D.C. and live in that humidity. Some would call me a fool, but I would prefer to be listed as a patriot for being willing to run for the vice presidency. A patriot, but not a politician, and given the general definition of a politician I do not intend to become a politician, ever.

"Sooooo, who am I? Well, you may have noticed that I do not walk anymore. That stopped one sunny afternoon in high school when my track team's school bus had a very unfortunate meeting with a semi-trailer. The good news is that while there were a plethora of broken bones on that bus, I was the only one with a lasting injury. A lot of plans changed that day; I am not the first or the last person to be put in a wheelchair. And I am not the first or the last person who has had a certain level of success in a seated position." Applause.

"No applause, it is not as if I am going to be the first person to climb Mount Everest naked," Long, long pause. More deadpan. "I remain afraid of heights.

"I am married and again, we have four wonderful children, which answers another large handful of questions, I suspect." Nervous laughter. "And all of that information is on the floor here some place. My kids are terrific and we have had some pretty interesting political discussions over the past four months. Let me again speak to the press and the dark side of the blogosphere; my kids are kids. They do things right; they make mistakes. They dress like kids; they are kids. LEAVE THEM ALONE!" Huge applause.

"Let's talk about the negatives first. God only knows that the media will hit all of the negatives first and make up more than a few extras. By the way, if my least favorite late night television host is listening, start making fun of me tonight, because until there is a very public and complete apology to the last Republican vice presidential nominee and her daughters, I will make a point of being available to every reporter and talk show host in

North America, except you!" Standing ovation. "I find it kind of interesting that both President Boone and I feel that the attitude exhibited by that man is so harmful to our American culture. I remain appalled at that attack on a young girl who had nothing to do with the 2004 campaign except to have a parent that wanted to serve the United States of America." Another standing ovation. "I have never met the governor and I honestly do not think she was ready to be the vice president, but her kids had nothing to do with any of that and, Sir, I therefore hold you in what the Brits refer to as the lowest level of high esteem. No, actually, I think you are an embarrassment to American culture and a jerk.

"Why am I bringing this up right now on this stage at this moment? Because other than the enemy I have just created, I don't think I have an enemy in the entire world and now everyone knows the rules. Pick on the guy in the wheelchair; leave my family alone. I want to do this job because I love my country, but I love my family more and that is the way I believe it should be." Another standing ovation for the professor.

"Thank you for the standing ovations. So you know, a regular ovation from me is like this,"—clapping his hands in front of him—"and a standing ovation is like this"—clapping his hands above his head. Uproarious applause.

~

Big Red commented from her booth into the live microphone: "This is pretty unusual. Le Secousse is a big player and his comments on the former VP candidate's daughters seem to be a theme tonight. I am not sure what to make of that. But this man looks like he can defend himself pretty well and, frankly, no matter how one feels about the former candidate or the talk show host, what was said was very inappropriate and he should have immediately and graciously apologized, not tried to ignore and then dodge his error. If you are listening, David, I think the economist on the stage is telling you it is never too late to apologize."

In Big Red's ear was Merritt Goodwin: "Marylou, that was absolutely perfect. Now leave it alone, no reason for my number one to go into the enemy creation business herself."

~

Scotch continued: "My guess is that those guys up in the mezzanine level are already a bit surprised that I would start out my political life by blasting the media about leaving my kids alone and bringing up comments made by a stupid talk show host several years ago. But it may not be a surprise that future President George Vincent must have asked a lot of people about being the next VP before he got to me. And probably most of them would just not risk putting their families into this, what I call, media mix master. Finally, he came up with this guy in a wheelchair. But this guy in a wheelchair has four kids and a wife and, to the best of my ability, I want to set limits now. My kids will not be a part of this campaign after tonight, they will not make appearances in support of my candidacy—and hopefully will not make appearances opposed to my candidacy—and they are, therefore, not a fair target. I have asked for my wife's vote and she told me based upon what she knows today," he slowly delivered, "at this point in the campaign, I have her commitment." Great laughter and as Rebecca Scotch was forewarned, this was a moment where the cameras would fall on her and their children. They smiled, laughed and waved.

"Well, that's the way it will be from Jordon Scotch. You are going to get candor, complete candor. Oh yes, I will dance around a question designed to anger some ally of the United States, but if it is a question I can answer without doing potential harm to the United States of America, that answer is going to be without any holds barred. And if there is a reason I cannot answer a question, I will tell you that I am not going to answer that specific question and if I can tell you why, I will; I will not dance"—pause—"In so many ways, I just don't dance." Laughter and applause.

"If you ask me whether we are appropriately securing our borders, I will answer the question. To that question, the answer is *no*. It is not that hard of a question and I don't know why the President of the United States cannot be remotely so concise. I know, you know, we all know he wants some form of amnesty for illegal aliens. I know, you know, we all know that he masks that desire in an amazing choice of words: comprehensive immigration reform. And we all know he is holding border security hostage to comprehensive... border...security. The economist made comprehensive border security into a phrase that took a full four seconds to say and the sarcasm was not hidden from the audience. "Why not say it, if you believe it, say it. If I believe it, I will say it. I believe we need to clean up our immigration system. I also believe that we cannot reward people who came into this country illegally and then allow them to use other laws to bring entire families, millions of families into the United States legally. We cannot afford it. That's what I think. Like it, dislike it, your choice. Clearly stated, I think, no terms designed to let the listener think I said what they wanted to hear. That's the way it is going to be.

"As to my background—different rules than with my family—if you cannot read what is on the floor, I am an open book. Actually, everything that is on the floor has been copied and in about three hours will be up on the web. I teach at UCLA and have learned that if it was up on the web right now, my better students would be tuning me out and looking at the web rather than listening to my lecture." Laughter. "So, it is set to go up in three hours. It angers me that our current president has released thousands of pages of what the prior administration believed must remain highly confidential while refusing to release so much as his college transcripts. He talks about transparency, but he does not walk the talk. His life is apparently a secret and apparently, he thinks that should be okay with us. Well, it is not acceptable, at least to me. Myself? Walk the talk, no; roll the talk, yes. And let me be as clear on this point as I can: I challenge this president, the President of the United States to be equally transparent. I penalize my students at UCLA for being late on a project, but I don't fail them for it. Come on, Mr. President, give us a break and step to the plate.

"I wanted to speak to you tonight briefly and narrowly—and I mean briefly and narrowly—about three subjects: taxes, domestic policies and foreign policy. But, I am the vice presidential candidate and George has told me that he would cover domestic policy and foreign policy for you tonight. Unlike that guy currently residing in Washington D.C. as the Vice President of the United States of America, George Vincent and I will speak with one voice and since he is the boss, I guess I'll talk just about taxes tonight.

"There will be time for lengthy position papers and lengthy debates at another time. I will not take up your entire evening, but I will take a few minutes.

"First and foremost, that quote that the current president would not raise taxes on the middle class; well, if George and I say something, you can believe that we will do everything we can to keep our word. And if for some reason we cannot keep a commitment and God forbid we have to go in another direction, we will be honest and candid about what happened. We will not, let me repeat, we will *not* dance with you. We will not hide behind a committee or panel and tell you we are *agnostic* as the President described his view on the Deficit Commission with respect to taxes. If as a candidate, the President said that he would not raise taxes on people making less than $250,000 a year, then he cannot be agnostic on taxes unless his word is just a word. With respect to George Vincent and myself, our word is not just a word. My word is my promise, not just a word. George Vincent's word is his promise. One's word is important.

"If we had told you that we would not raise taxes for people making less than $250,000 a year, we would not have proposed policies like Cap and Trade, which would raise your electric bill and would, in reality, be a tax. We would not have raised excise taxes on cigarettes. We would not have baited and switched you on the cost of health care reform. Let me be clear here, if we put in policies that directly increase your costs and the money ultimately shows up in the Federal coffers, that is a tax. You can call it a fee, you can call it environmentally the right answer, you can call it a health care bill, you can call it a baseball bat, but it's a tax and we won't dance you around the room with words like fee or deposit or whatever. You will not need a poet and a dictionary to interpret what we have to say.

"The most important thing we can do to change the nature of the political debate is to be straightforward and honest." This statement, which was delivered exceptionally slowly with a slow cadence, drew a standing ovation. While applauding, those paying careful attention realized they were listening to a person who spent every day giving lectures to brilliant young UCLA students. The national scene and television would be a bit different for him, but a lecture was a speech and only the audience had changed.

He repeated for effect: "If we put in place policies that directly increase your costs and the money ultimately shows up in the Federal coffers, that is a tax. You can call it a fee, you can call it environmentally the right answer, you can call it a health care bill, you can call it a damn baseball bat, but it's a tax and we won't dance like that.

"And the same with cigarettes. Ignoring the benefits of not smoking— and I urge everyone who is listening to stop smoking this evening or never begin—a tax on cigarettes is a tax, short and simple.

"And taxes are already too high and too difficult to compute." Strong applause. "But that is the easy part and the part that politicians of all parties and, frankly, in all countries and all planets always say. I have studied the issue and of course that is clearly what makes me so, so boring." Laughter.

"We have this Internal Revenue Code. Our current president said during his campaign that everyone should be able to prepare their tax return on a three-by-five card and then he immediately requested tax credits and a disallowance of a portion of tax deductions that would have taken one of my colleagues in the mathematics department three years to create a calculation that actually resulted in the right answer." Laughter and the recognition of more than a glint of humor in the eyes of Professor Scotch. "Then, he proposed a health care bill that put a requirement to either show proof of health care insurance with your Federal income tax return or pay additional taxes, which required another Orwellian presentation. Well, maybe the President had in mind a three-by-five card that was a bit different than the three-by-five cards many of us use at home and school, maybe his card is three-by-five-feet." Scotch held his hands as far apart as possible to demonstrate the size of the tax return required. The man's presence was so powerful that this might have been the first time that no one noticed that Dr. Scotch did not have a suit coat over his white shirt and UCLA blue and gold tie.

"What we need to do is remake the Internal Revenue Code into a tool for collecting taxes, not a tool for social policy. That was the original intent of the Internal Revenue Code. If it is not too burdensome, we can use the Code to give incentives to a few, only a few, good behaviors such as home ownership.

"What we do not need however, and this will not resonate well with some of our current supporters, is to change our entire system to something crazy like the FairTax. Let me speak to the FairTax proposal for just one minute or so. It is not fair, it will not collect sufficient taxes unless the rate is confiscatory, and the administrative burden and costs to the Federal and State governments would be excessive. This changes nothing except it makes preparing a tax return something that does not requires the calculation of a simultaneous equation. If you need more than that, there is a book out there called *The FairTax Fantasy, An Honest Look at a Very, Very Bad Idea* written by my friends at Chapman University in Orange, California. Read it. Buy it and read it, my friends get a royalty.

"So, how do you fix the Internal Revenue Code? The first thing you do is expand the rate tables and reduce tax rates to eliminate the exemptions, the standard deduction, the three percent reduction in deductions for high earners and anything else where the rate tables can make the desired calculation rather than the taxpayer. The next thing you do is eliminate the state and local tax deductions and throw that into a reduction in the tax in the rate tables too. Next, you eliminate most of the miscellaneous deductions and let the employees work that out with their employers. Next, you eliminate all special tax rates for capital gains and dividends. If Congress wants to reduce taxes on any item, through a percentage times the item. At that point, we have not changed virtually anything except a bit of tax reallocation state-by-state because of the elimination of the tax deduction and your tax return preparation time was just reduced by two-thirds. Really, for ninety percent of us, simple and really, non-political change would reduce tax preparation time by at least two-thirds without making an impact on the amount of taxes." Applause. "OK, that was a bit fast, so it will be up on the website tonight as well. And what I did not say is that with those modest changes, the number of people paying the alternative minimum tax will be down to several thousand who would not be paying taxes without the AMT. This will happen too.

"Of course, my colleagues and I wrote an article about this along with a discussion of eliminating and combining certain tax credits and we were not even asked to appear before the Democratic tax-writing committee. This should tell you a great deal about politicians' promises on tax reform; the promises are pretty easy to ignore because they are generally not promises made to keep, only promises meant to attain votes.

George Vincent and I will propose legislation in the first thirty days of our administration to accomplish the following goals: One, we will propose legislation that will make filing tax returns easier for ninety percent of the American taxpayers and not a bit easier for the remaining ten percent. We know that if we propose a tax code that is easy for everyone, the wealthy will easily avoid paying his or her taxes and that is not what we want to accomplish. So, easy for ninety percent, difficult for ten percent. Two, our proposal will not significantly change the allocation of the tax burden between economic classes. Our goal is not to make any political group happy, it is to simplify the Internal Revenue Code." Modest applause.

"Now, let me talk to the allocation of Federal taxes between economic classes. Senator Vincent and I believe everyone should pay some Federal taxes, even if it is only one dollar—*everyone*. It shows commitment to our country. We have far too many Americans not paying taxes, not serving in the military and not performing public service; we view that as a long-term systemic and cultural problem. Now, George and I will be pilloried for these comments, but we believe that everyone should pull a portion of the boat, not simply the rich. We also believe that welfare or relief should be taken out of the tax code and delivered as welfare or relief. These two issues, taxes and aid, should be considered separately.

"I want to give you an example of what I am talking about. Today, we have both a minimum wage and an earned tax credit. The earned tax credit effectively raises the minimum wage for the employee, but the cost is in our taxes and shared by everyone instead of the employer. We would rather increase the minimum wage and eliminate the credit. Simple as that.

"Folks, I am not a spellbinding speaker and I am not going to become a spellbinding speaker. It just isn't me. I think you will find out as the campaign unfolds that I am a pretty good fellow. I hope. This being said, I think the vice president should be a working, thinking machine. And that would be my plan, early to work, hard at work and the evening for our family. It should be fairly clear that I am not, and will not, be a song and dance man and looking for me on the golf course would be a waste of time. That being said, trust me, I will find a local college basketball team to root for and I will attend games to the extent I will not hurt the traffic or fun for the other fans. If it will be a security problem or a traffic problem, the ESPN complete college basketball package will be on my television, actually, it will be either way. Got to see my UCLA.

"We want our administration to represent substance, not appearances. We, frankly, have had enough of the great speech followed by behind-the-scenes intimidation and power lust. Chicago politics has to be the politics of yesterday. By the way, it should be old news in Chicago, too. That just isn't about George Vincent or Jordon Scotch. It is about serving voters. So, one promise, if elected to this august office, I will work hard for you, the citizens of the United States." The delegates gave Jordon Scotch a healthy ovation, nothing like what had been seen earlier in the convention, but a healthy ovation. A presentation of substance was rarely a positive with the delegates at a political convention.

~

Big Red was alone in her little broadcasting cubicle with her panel next door. She sat fairly quiet for a moment trying to do the political calculus. There would probably be time for only a thought or two and she wanted to get this one right. This was not the strongest moment for this convention, but was it meaningful?

On the air: "Jordon Scotch has been entered onto the public stage. Was he a dynamic speaker? Actually, I think he was and I suspect he connected with the voters. He was entertaining and his wit seems pretty strong. It does not take but a few sentences to realize how smart the man is and I have to admit, I rather liked him.

"Was he featured during the primaries? Not at all. Even after almost fifty primaries, this was probably the first time almost any American has seen or heard Dr. Scotch at a microphone. It remains to be seen whether Jordon Scotch will be a drag on the ticket or whether his plethora of positive individual characteristics will galvanize important segments of the voters. Clearly, a minority male in a wheelchair is a unique political figure. I found it fascinating that he did not give the audience so much of a hint as to his racial minority except when he threw down the gauntlet to the President with respect to his grades. That minority comment had to be a challenge to the President. I wonder if George Vincent will work this minority piece into his presentation.

"Scotch certainly did not seem nervous before the national audience, but he clearly did not give a speech intended to electrify the delegates. This one was a bit complicated from a political perspective, but the one thing I can say, based upon his use of the English language and his academic credentials, we are going to find out that Senator George Vincent did not select an intellectual lightweight for his running mate."

At Fox News, Arthur Ninoah was equally cautious and offered that the speech was clearly substantive with an occasional shot at the President and his administration. He did suggest that the current vice president would need to avoid a debate with this economics professor in any way possible since they clearly were not in the same intellectual zip code.

At MSNBC one of the commentators chortled: "He hates the Internal Revenue Code and hates the FairTax, oh I bet the FairTaxers and Tea Baggers will try to swallow him whole."

~

When the audience concluded its appreciation of Jordon Scotch's remarks, Senator Vincent moved to the podium without any introduction.

Senator Vincent did not want to come onto the stage with the typical political convention introduction and response. He had chosen to sit in a folding chair on the far left side of the stage with the rest of his supporters actively listening to Jordon Scotch's speech. His sitting on the folding chair had a folksy look. As he made his way from stage right, he either hugged or shook hands with literally every person he passed. Some of the men were hugged; several of the women shook his hand. It was all perfectly natural. Many at home noticed that he hugged the former presidents and shook hands with the Secretary of State.

There was great thought given to not having but a moment of time between Jordon Scotch's speech and Vincent's acceptance speech. The senator knew that if he gave the talking heads two minutes, they would instantly churn a discussion about taxes going up for the poor, which would be intellectually inaccurate, but they would not care. He knew exactly what Dr. Scotch had in mind, he agreed with it precisely, but he also knew that he would need to expand and explain that taxes would not be increased for the poor. His decision, made weeks earlier, was to hurry to the microphone just like a college football team trying to beat instant replay. More importantly, he wanted to be different and not have some stupid introduction that wasted everyone's time.

When he arrived at the little wooden podium with the steel base, he had his vice presidential candidate a few feet away from him as well as all of the previous speakers. He had asked Scotch not to move into the background. There was no teleprompter. His three-hole binder with his speech was waiting for him on the podium. As Senator Vincent made his quick round of hellos, a young man raced on the stage to pick up all of the papers Dr. Scotch had thrown onto the floor and returned them to Dr. Scotch's briefcase. The young man also placed George Vincent's speech on the podium.

The viewers could see that Senator Vincent was not a handsome man. In fact, when one looked at him, one could not help but laugh if he thought of a combination of Churchill and the comedian Dennis Miller. Vincent was rather short for the times, had rounded shoulders and his new suit could not hide that he was still a bit tubby. The senator was fairly close to bald and had perfectly clear, grey eyes. He always looked a bit disheveled. The impact of his various parts made him look more like the classic college professor than

139

Dr. Scotch. All he would have needed was the tweed sports coat with the patches on the arms.

George Vincent had that unique ability to make an audience of five or five thousand people feel that he was speaking directly to them. He was a gifted speaker and he could look at an audience and connect instantly; call it charm, charisma, standing, whatever it was, he had it. The closer the camera and the audience, the better his grey eyes.

As he was walking to the podium, it was obvious that along with the traditional pinstriped suit and red tie he had put on two different colored gloves. On his right hand, he was wearing a red glove and on his left hand, he was wearing a blue glove.

"Good evening," he ventured at the assembled mass. "Friends, I need your attention because we have an incredible task on our hands and if we do not achieve our objectives, the United States of America as it has been thought of for more than two hundred years could be nothing but a footnote in an unread history text." The applause exploded as Senator Vincent was relying on those same speaking talents that had made him the president of the student body when he studied at The Ohio State University.

"We cannot fail! This will be a serious speech, brief, but serious. Very brief in comparison to most speeches at political conventions. I ask that you take your seats and if you must, occasionally provide some applause, but let us not get carried away with show and let us talk about how we got to where we are tonight and how to get the country to where it should be." The delegates began to take their seats. The air was electric with expectation. He was a great speaker, but never moved an inch from the podium.

"Let me set the stage visually." He did not have a microphone similar to a singer at a concert. He held up his hands. As he took off his red glove, he offered: "If elected, I will not venture too far to the right." And then he took off his blue glove and said: "And, if elected, I will not venture too far to the left." The crowd roared its approval. He produced a small American flag, which he very slowly unfurled and placed in a clear flag holder on the podium, one that previously had gone unnoticed. "If elected, I will attempt to govern as a citizen of our nation, the United States of America!" Again, the roar was loud and sincere.

From the OBC booth, Big Red gave it the verbal high five: "Senator Vincent has, in less than sixty seconds, delivered the message he wanted to deliver. He wants the middle of American voters to support him. I think this is brilliant and the rest of his speech, I suspect, will mirror this position."

"The past three plus years have been the most painful of my career. I supported the President in his run for the Presidency. As you know, I spent months going from city to city speaking in support of the Democratic Party, the President's campaign and against the policies of one of the son's of a gentlemen sitting behind me on this stage. I wanted change.

"But the change I wanted was different than the change that we have experienced or the change promised. I wanted us to raise the level of health care for all Americans; I did not want the level of health care to collapse so that we could cover more citizens, but cover everyone poorly. I wanted to raise the bar on health care for everyone, not lower it for some and raise it for others. I didn't want to cover people who were illegally in the United States. I wanted to keep those who were happy with their health care happy with their health care and figure out a way to provide for everyone else at the same time. I certainly did not want health care to bankrupt the United States of America because, at the end of the day, a bankrupt United States of America won't be able to provide health care to anyone. The only way to have done this was to increase—dramatically increase—over time, the number of doctors, nurses and related practitioners. What the President and Congress have done is a disaster. All words, no actions.

"I wanted the United States to be a leader in the world and I thought *leadership* meant leading towards a world where all who sought democracy had a fair chance to obtain democracy. The United States was not supposed to be the heavy-handed implementer of some form of democracy in other countries that did not want democracy. I did not want to embrace the dictators of the left in some crazy effort to get them to be friends of the United States. I wanted more allies; I did not want our old allies to be abandoned. I wanted the United States of America to retain its honor."

Turning to look at former President Boone, he said: "Honestly George, I thought we lost some of that honor during your son's term. You and I have talked about that issue and I know we disagree on that, but I assuredly did not think of the United States as the bad guys, just the good guys on steroids." The former president nodded and smiled as the delegates gave him an ovation. Of course, the former president knew exactly what Senator Vincent was going to say before he flew to Cleveland.

"Sometimes, we need to use the power of the United States and then simply get out of the way after things have calmed down. That model worked in Japan and Germany after World War II. It works in a world that has different cultures and different values than our own."

"I want the United States to exhibit strength so that petty dictators do not feel emboldened. I shivered at our position in Honduras where the President backed the bad guy instead of democracy and I cringed while watching the dictator in Venezuela upstage the President. I cringed every time the President bowed to another head of state. Maybe the first time was a mistake, but, my goodness, how many times has he demeaned our country with his bowing? I knew that the wrong message was being delivered by this president: The United States' current president would rather be liked by what I will honestly characterize as the bad guys than have his country respected." Vincent's style was one of speaking in long bursts without much time between sentences. He felt that this kept the audience attentive, and it was working this evening.

"I knew the danger of this president's style of governing. I studied World War II. I went to the President in the Oval Office in March of 2009 with a copy of Churchill's *The Gathering Storm* and I read to him a single paragraph:

> Mr. Chamberlain continued to believe that he had only to form a personal contact with the Dictators to effect a marked improvement in the world situation. He little knew that their decisions were taken. In a hopeful spirit he proposed that he and Lord Halifax should visit Italy in January. After some delay an invitation was extended, and on January 11 the meeting took place. It makes one flush to read in Ciano's diary the comments which were made behind the Italian scene about our country and its representatives. Essentially, writes Ciano, the visit was kept in a minor key...Effective contact has not been made. How far apart we are from these people! It is another world.

The Fox News anchor broke in to offer an interesting comment: "Senator Vincent seems to be speaking at a much higher plane than the President in talking to a national audience. I do not know how it is being received, but personally, I find it very refreshing and I suspect that many Americans believe that the senator is talking to them as if they were educated adults as opposed to speaking in glittering sixth grade generalities. Again, I—for one—find it refreshing."

Senator Vincent went on: "I begged the President to stop appearing weak. He laughed at me, literally laughed at me, and told me that time had passed me by and that his form of friendship and logical diplomacy was the answer. I reminded him that the tech bubble was created by people who wanted to ignore the rules of business and that he was ignoring history by trying to negotiate from any position except strength. I told him that the way to avoid our destruction and a world in chaos was to be strong and become stronger.

"When I began to speak out and vote against certain president supported programs, my state began to see less Federal money and I found problems getting some of my telephone calls returned from the administration. This was change I could not be a part of or it would have undone my entire self-image and what I have told the people of my state since I was a freshman senator. Heck, this was contrary to the way I conducted myself as the student body president at The Ohio State University. In my world, you continue to work with people with whom you disagree. In elected office, your job is to focus on issues and serve your constituents. A president who plays power politics, Chicago style, is no better than a thug. I wish I did not believe that or feel it necessary to discuss.

"I saw a House of Representatives where a Republican—and God knows I am no lifelong Republican—was given the same opportunity to participate in the making of laws in the United States as a leper had to participate in society in the 1500s. The Republicans are representatives of the people, not enemies of the state. A president cannot talk of transparency and nonpartisanship and then hide in his office making deals with every interest group on the planet and refuse to meet with Republicans. That is not in tune with our American democracy. This is what happened with health care. The President should not encourage or tolerate a Congress that is so partisan. Partisanship against Republicans and in favor of the special interests is repugnant. This is not the America that I know and it is not the America that I believe ninety-five percent of Americans want it to be. We are a democracy and in a democracy, both sides are heard." Here, as he knew he would, the senator lost control of his audience and the response was strong.

"Now you may laugh, but the moment I knew that something was totally wrong with this administration was not when the world, as we knew it, changed on that one small island in Korea, not when Iran announced it had nuclear weapons, or when some of the monumental and socialist programs were passed by our Congress, but when I was watching the All-Star baseball game in St. Louis three years ago. Yes, I am serious and if the guys will turn down the lights for a minute, I will show you." The lights went down.

"You know I am a football guy. I did not play football in college like Senator Smith, I just love to watch the game and see the discipline and team-work required by all eleven players to be successful on every play. If you graduated from The Ohio State University and you are not a lifetime foot-ball fan, you are—as they say—in a very, very small minority. But, I watch baseball because what else is there to watch in the middle of the summer?" Vincent offered the smug smile of a lifetime Ohio State football fan. "So I am watching the All-Star Game and out comes the President. I thought this was interesting particularly since, to the best of my knowledge, the President loves basketball and apparently has discovered a great gym program but, like me, there is nothing in his history to indicate that he was a successful athlete of any kind in high school or college. So, I am watching this and thinking about former President George W. Boone when he threw out the first pitch at an All Star game." The screen above and behind the senator showed former President Boone zipping the ball from the pitcher's mound to home plate. "George W. played baseball at Yale. And then I watched the current presi-dent try to do the same. He throws and his delivery is clearly not someone who had ever thrown a baseball. At a different time, we would have said he throws like a girl, which is fine. We did not hire him to be Sandy Koufax.

After the President throws, we don't really see the ball as it reaches the plate. What we do see is his fist pump after the throw and we therefore assume that it was a perfect pitch." The screen showed the picture that the television audience saw. "Pretty good, great pitch and a fist pump, what a guy? So the next day, I get this YouTube video from a friend." Up pops the YouTube video on the screen showing the picture from centerfield with the President standing closer to home plate than the pitching mound and the ball apparently bouncing, or near bouncing, before it even gets close to home plate. The catcher moved forward to keep it from hitting the ground and the President gives the fist pump. "Friends, quite honestly, if we have a president who needs to orchestrate throwing out the first pitch at an All-Star Game in such a way that it appears to the United States citizens, boys and girls, or whoever, that he burned a strike when he virtually bounced the ball to home plate, we have a man in the White House who cannot be trusted with the presidency. The President of the United States must be honest with himself and the American people. To me, the inability to laugh at himself and the obvious plan to make him look like the athlete he never was is scary. Scary in terms of seeing into one's values." And the place went wild. For television viewers, this analogy of the President's image over reality struck home, again including the people on the stage that stood and applauded for the first time in this speech. Efrin Holt high fived a retired Hall of Fame pitcher standing next to him on stage.

"I want to bring to America a presidency that is honest in big things and little things. I don't want an imperial presidency; I want a presidency that reflects truth, justice and an America that sees what actually occurs. I want Americans to know what I can and can't do as a president and as a person. To think that the President of the United States would attempt to delude the American public with something as trivial as a pitch to home plate gives an insight to the man that scares me. It is like some of the far fetched braggadocio that we saw from Comrade Mao in China forty years ago, just silly stuff. Didn't Mao claim he surfed from China to Hawaii or something like that? Maybe Mao invented the Internet." More applause, some shouting and some laughter.

"As time went on, I was struck by the speeches from this president. He uses the word *I* in a manner that *this* American does not associate with democracy. It seems to me that the President is the CEO and that the Congress still has a role and that in a representative democracy, it is always what we"—*we* was spoken in a manner that it leapt from the podium—"did as a country, not I, as this president seems to see it. The American presidency is about *we the people*, not *I the president!*" The audience was smitten by Senator Vincent.

"When the President told us that we could keep our health insurance and a few days later, it turned out that the plan in the House of Representatives said, *yes, we could keep our existing insurance, but we could never, never move to a new plan,* I knew we had the wrong person in the White House. Of course, it turned out far worse than that as Jordon talked about earlier. The House of Representatives' plan was a hoax and the President knew or should have known that. Under this health care plan, we may be able to keep our insurer, but the plan will completely change and be much more expensive. We need a President of the United States who is better than that. We need a president who is more than a great speech giver" pause, long pause—"or great speech"—long pause—"reader!" The delegates went crazy. "We need a President of the United States who is a hard worker and garners success for 'We the People.'"

"And I have to talk about this teleprompter stuff." A picture of the President speaking to a sixth grade classroom from behind a teleprompter went up behind Senator Vincent. We have a president that speaks to sixth graders with a teleprompter. A teleprompter!" George Vincent slowly shook his head back and forth. "What is that about?" The audience shouted back *No teleprompter, no teleprompter.*

"Now it is one thing to give a speech at the United Nations and be afraid to have so much as a misplaced comma, but to always, always have a teleprompter, my golly, in front of twenty sixth graders, give me a break! To virtually never hold press conferences, to virtually never meet with Republicans, to never do interviews with any media that does not tow the Democratic boat, give me a break! Answering questions at a press conference with a teleprompter!" The senator just shook his head.

"I remain unconvinced today that the President has ever read or even remotely understands the health care legislation that was passed, which he promoted and he signed. I think he was just put in front of a teleprompter and told to read carefully. I think this is fully evident any time he is in a position to speak without a speech written by some bright, young person in the White House staffing room." The delegates were wild in their acceptance of these extremely harsh remarks.

At Fox News, Arthur Ninoah, again leaned into his microphone and offered: "The President must be about as upset as a human being could be about these last few remarks. When you cut through it, the President is being accused of being a phony in fairly clear language and in the political business, that is nearly unheard of."

In the residential suite at the White House, another missile—actually a plate that had moments before been the final resting place of a cheeseburger and fries—streamed across the smoke-filled room and bumped beneath a pre-Civil War Cabinet. The floor was the winner.

"Let me change direction for a minute, we are a new political party. Officially, we do not have a single senator, or congressman, or congresswoman. Many of the people up here with me are running as Republicans or Democrats in November. We support them and we look for a new start, a start where Americans come first and party comes in a very distant second or, really, way behind a distant second!"

The speech went on to discuss the politics of his supporters and Senator Vincent's reliance on the basic goodness of his supporters and a strong desire to receive proposed legislation from a bipartisan legislature; the theme was one of unity and moderate political activity. It was all very well received; the occasional negative comments from the network anchors were without any significant merit.

The speech went on to criticize the President for not realizing that he had actually been elected in 2008 and, therefore, he had continued to campaign for four years rather than work. Vincent made a point that no one could manage the White House if they were giving four hundred fifty plus speeches a year and travelling virtually every day of his Presidency. "At some point, a president needs to actually work."

George Vincent came back to actual events when he paused for perhaps a few seconds too long and stayed behind the podium: "I blame the evisceration of that island in Korea on the President. His weakness, his lack of historical prospective, and his inability to seek advice from experienced ambassadors and foreign service personnel probably led to that use of a nuclear weapon." This comment was greeted with silence. So many people believed this, but few on center stage in American politics had had the nerve to say it. "Yes, I believe this to be true. I am certain the Secretary of State here believes it to be true. I do not like saying it, but I believe it to be true. I know that many commentators will report to you that I should not have said it and a few will talk about foreign policy being beyond politics, but essentially, this was the President putting his crazy left-wing philosophy in front of foreign policy that caused this catastrophe."

A glass followed the plate; this one actually reached the cabinet and the crash was instantly followed by a Secret Service agent entering the room to ask the President if he was okay. The Agent received a simple nod in return and abandoned the playing field leaving what was left of the plate and glass on the floor. Both had been purchased through donations made to the White House when Jacqueline Kennedy was the First Lady.

Senator Vincent continued: "We need to get the Harvard dormitory discussions out of the White House and replace them with mature and balanced policy. We have fifty states and 300 million Americans and it seems if you do not work in a Chicago zip code, you cannot be a member of the President's inner circle. If you are in the private sector, even if you live in Chicago, unless your brother and dad were Chicago mayors, there are no seats available to you at this president's table. That is nuts.

"The use of force is far less necessary by those who hold the biggest stick if there is even the remotest thought that the holder of the stick is not terrified to use it. In physics, there are laws and theorems. That is a law, not a Harvard dormitory late night discussion theory." A huge ovation was the response to Senator Vincent's remark.

On domestic issues, George Vincent talked in the generalities of the moment and discussed the over-reaching polices of the President's administration. He showed great concern with many Federal agencies that were exceeding the authority given to them by Congress. He wanted Congress to regain control of its own legislation. He expressed his concerns about Social Security and crazy health care laws destroying the economics of the country. He explained how small business was being decimated by the policies emanating out of Washington D.C. He exploded at the President about a worthless, intellectually worthless, stimulus package and the national debt. He explained that real stimulus created private sector jobs and the President's stimulus package only kept government workers employed and that this type of stimulus only increased the deficit and devalued the dollar. He made it clear that he agreed with Jordon Scotch's thoughts on cleaning up the Internal Revenue Code, in part, by making the Code oriented to collecting taxes and letting agencies be responsible for any public programs approved by the legislature. They would work together so that the Internal Revenue Code was cleaned up without hurting the working poor.

The speech was less than twenty minutes and concluded with the traditional balloon drop. In the minds of the delegates, it was no less than perfect.

As the speech concluded, onto the stage walked three of America's best-known performers. One from Country and Western and the other two from pop culture. All genders and races as well as more than forty number one songs were on the AEP Convention stage. No introductions, nothing from any microphone in the way of identifying the three household names.

Fifteen words into the National Anthem, everyone in the Q, all except for a few members of the national media, was standing and singing along. Strikingly, both the Fox News anchor, actually on microphone and not very well in tune, and one other anchor joined in the singing.

The cameras showed a few faces in the crowd. These faces showed the same passion that someone a bit older could remember from *Casablanca* when the entertainer sang the Marseilles over the German's singing of a German drinking song. (By sheer coincidence, this was just an hour after this took place in the actual movie being shown on RBC.) More than a few tears went down the eyes of the delegates. The cameras found the emotional Senator Wayne, who appeared to both singing and crying. Thaddeus Malkin, all five-foot-eight of him and golden locks, looked at his companions, stood, put his hand over his heart and sang like he was in the church choir.

Senator Wayne, with handkerchief wiping his eyes, walked to the microphone and shouted: "The First Annual Convention of the American Exceptionalism Party has nominated George Vincent and Jordon Scotch to be the President and Vice President of the United States. There are only a few months until November 6, 2012. Let's go to work and make the United States of America the United States of America!"

GAME ON!

~

In Washington D.C., at the home of a prestigious Democratic fundraiser, the fundraiser and three prominent elected Democrats had been watching the Convention. There was an open bar and a white-coated waiter bringing in continuous canopies and cocktails. Democratic Congressman Grable of New York, had been four Cutty Sarks and waters into the evening festivities and had lost a bit of his studied calm exterior and notice of exactly where he was when he belted out an, "Attaboy," during Senator Vincent's speech. After his outburst, he was just sober enough to become a silent Sam in this cabal. Grable, at fifty-two years old and more than a touch overweight knew that his political career would go no further than the United States House of Representatives but that if he chose, he could retain his seat forever, unless he did something really stupid. New York was for the President and he would be for whoever New York was for—right, wrong or indifferent. He believed that was how one stayed in office and he loved, as he thought of it, his knighthood or was it actually still called a seat in the House of Representatives?

Senator Elevlyn Grace of Illinois, the newly elected black senator from Illinois saw trouble in all directions. Senator Grace was, and knew, she was the real deal. The unmarried daughter of a North Chicago Minister, she had gone through college on one scholarship after another and her minority status never appeared on a single piece of paper. She was world-class smart, a hard worker and tough as nails. As a double major in economics and African American studies, her guiding philosophy was of a government that provided help, yet expected a return on its investment. This sold well to both Democrats and Republicans. She often wished that she had been born a couple of decades earlier as she would have been easily aligned with President Kennedy. Today, she was quite a bit right of her Democratic Party on domestic issues and a bit left on foreign affairs as she found the very thought of any weaponry repugnant. Comfortable in her own skin, Elevlyn Grace was under-dressed for the occasion in designer blue jeans and an old crew cut sweater. Wearing the same glasses she had worn in graduate school, she assessed her appeal as purely intellectual. The other individuals in the room would have been shocked to know that if she had been asked to be on that stage, she would have been there. While she would acknowledge later that a black president was obviously a great thing, she would have preferred an individual who walked the campaign talk and worked hard rather than spending his time giving speeches, playing golf and being a groupie to so many athletes and entertainers. She believed that this president's persona was bad for the black culture. She would have preferred a president who had a daily routine similar to past presidents rather than that of a small business where the son was running the store. Given a little attention by the American Exceptionalism Party and an arrogant display by the President at the Democratic convention, she thought: *this young senator might surprise a few folks.*

Senator Grace understood that Senator Smith had captured a certain rage in the taxpayers. She knew the President had been badly over-estimated in his intellectual capabilities before he took office. Individually, she wondered about the classes and his grades. After a couple White House meetings, she guessed Harvard Law School had more than a few affirmative action admits with soft grade points or weak entrance examinations. Maybe both. Even worse, to Senator Grace, the President honestly believed that a speech by him was a game changer and that he could convince the Hatfields to love the McCoys. She knew the bitter truth that the President had only two overwhelming gifts, speech giving and the ability to employ a level of political ruthlessness that had previously been reserved for local politicians in places like Chicago and cult-like presidents in South America. She believed that these were his only gifts and that after that he was a pawn for those who could gain access to his kingdom. She also knew that three years into his presidency, he had worn out his domestic welcome with the voters. Grace believed the President made the old British Prime Minister Neville Chamberlain look like a realist in dealing with foreign leaders; she thought the President to be the perfect intellectual fool for believing that foreign leaders were and are more interested in doing the right thing than in preserving their personal power, naïve about far too many things.

Senator Grace knew that the President had never had an entrepreneurial moment in his life, assumed he had never had so much as a semester of economics and could not follow the presentations by his economic advisors. She was unsure whether the President had ever had a summer job before or during college. She had attended a meeting at the White House where his questions would have made a freshman economics professor blanch.

Senator Grace had become very concerned that the President had walled himself away from the private sector. Weeks could go by without him encountering an entrepreneur. It had become painstakingly obvious to Senator Grace that he made his economic judgments based on listening to presentations that he did not understand and placing his faith in the best sounding presenter. Worse yet, whenever he was off-script and off camera, he sounded like a twelve-year-old in his economic analogies. He would come to events armed with a teleprompter and four or five lines that made him seem as if he knew something about economics and then, God help him if he was trapped with a question. Did he always need that teleprompter and, good God, was President Boone visibly taking down the teleprompters at the convention a scary moment? Her thought process was straightforward: *I am going to have to be very careful for the next few months. My re-election is a few years away and I may need to be a team player, but distance from this president may be the key to my long-term survival. I think that the flu is the best answer to the Democratic Convention and then I can go give a number of speeches to friendly groups and raise a bit of money for the President. Or…*

Congressman Gibbling of Vermont had not uttered a word during the entire evening. With Congressman Grable also playing Silent Sam, this made the evening a bit awkward for the small group. His math was that the liberal underpinnings of Vermont's political establishment could be changing fast— *think Scott Brown.* This AEP gang might present a long-term problem. When faced with a liberal/conservative choice, Vermont came down squarely on the side of liberal. But, this middle ground might be a place that Vermont found more comfortable. Fox News had been beating Vermont up for years and it had begun to have an impact on the electorate.

At seventy-four years old, Congressman Gibbling was the classic Vermont congressman. He was a Princeton graduate with a law degree from Georgetown and had labored in the union defense area of law before chasing a congressional seat almost thirty years ago. His congressional seat followed a scandal involving the prior congressman and a young intern. This made Congressman Gibbling very careful in dealing with any female in his office and, except in the most rare of circumstances, he was never alone with any woman. (The irony of this was that his predecessor had ultimately divorced his wife, married his intern and they had settled into a very comfortable Vermont lifestyle and at age seventy-five, he and his intern second wife now had three grown children and two grandchildren.) Gibbling knew that he looked and walked like a man of his own age and this was never good when the voters were interested in the country's political situation. He considered his seventy-four-year-old body and realized he was grey haired and that was how it was supposed to be at this moment of his life, but this was not good politics. He knew he was not going out a loser in 2012 and if the polls looked bad in 2014, he would not run for another term. Maybe Congressman Gibbling was a free agent at this point.

The last of this esteemed group and the owner of this fine Northern Virginia mansion was Elmer Tyler, an old Harvard Law School friend of the President. Actually, the President would describe Tyler as a friend. Tyler thought that the President was a very, very useful acquaintance. The President was someone he had never really figured out and was certainly not intellectually in the top half of Harvard Law School graduates like himself. He would have never guessed that this man would end up as President of the United States.

Elmer Tyler was a highly paid advisor, lobbyist and confidant of the President and could, on occasion, calm down this privately combustible president. "Let's just see what is up with the President tomorrow, gentlemen. I cannot remember a single speech this man Vincent has ever given before this; there is no reason to think that will change. Within fifteen minutes of this convention, we will set loose the dogs of war on this clown. Let's hope the twenty-minute news cycle makes this evening all but go away." Tyler thought about his personal power and net worth. While he had had great success as a lawyer and a third-tier lobbyist, these past three years had helped build his mansion. The President was the key to his current success.

What was meaningful was not what was said, but what was not said. Immediately after Senator Vincent finished his speech, all three electeds gathered their stuff, left their chairs with polite good-byes and headed to the door. The quick exits and the exceptionally quiet evening more closely resembled the quick exits made by friends of a comedian after a dreadful opening night. Tyler would report to the President that this American Exceptionalism Party *gang* was a serious, serious problem and that problem could quickly metastasize into his own political base. He was certain at least two of his visitors would bolt if the cards began to fall the wrong way, maybe all three. Perception was one of Tyler's great strengths. He was a great listener and not hearing anything positive, actually not hearing anything at all, was a terrible message. If the the-every-Democrat-for-himself flag went up, he thought these electeds would agree to help anyone to keep their own political careers on line. There would need to be some harsh realities brought to their egos.

~

As the convention ended, the President stood and walked to his door. He eyed the Secret Service agent and without a word, delivered the message that the room needed a bit of work in the next few minutes. (At a minimum, the Secret Service agent was expected, again without a word to the President, to have someone clean up the dish and the glass remnants and get some air freshener in the room, a significant amount of air freshener.) It would have enraged the President even more than his current state if he realized the Secret Service agent would gather a couple pieces of the plate as a keepsake and that a few years out, this episode would help the agent's book sales and provide a few bucks on eBay.

By the time the President hit the first floor, he knew that a cadre of people would be on their way upstairs and that his room would be in perfect condition when he came back upstairs. No first-class cruise ship penthouse offered the service rendered for the President of the United States in the White House. He knew that the smell of the cigarettes would magically be gone and the book with his cigarettes would be both back in place and restocked. He briefly wondered who paid for those cigarettes and if there was a manner in which his wife could find out how many he smoked when she was gone.

The President began walking the White House hallways and again wishing that he had taken a few business management classes during his academic career. While perhaps there was a bit of hyperbole by his critics, he really did not grasp how to effectively manage his team, what made the stock market go up or down, and certainly could not relate his policies to unemployment. How could he know, he had no experience in the private sector. And before becoming president, he had never fired an individual in his life. The White House was a tough place to learn how to manage.

It seemed as if he often needed to add the word *not* in front of many of the conclusions of his economic advisors to make them right. This president had no idea which ideas were great and which ideas needed the word *not* inserted therein.

Wow, this job seemed so much easier in the dormitory in college or on the streets of Chicago.

More importantly, he had that feeling in his stomach that he was going to wish he had done something or not done something else on the international front over the past three years, he just didn't know what. The Korean debacle had been just that, a debacle. The actions of the North Koreans con-

154

tinued to make no sense. The President could not have been clearer in his quest for dialogue and improved relations. *How can they be so stupid? I really do want to bring about transformative change! I want to help them! I just don't get it.*

As the President considered the Korean issue, for a bare moment, he considered how lucky he was that of the fifteen thousand US soldiers that were in South Korea, all were safe. He worried and knew that more than a few would ultimately show signs of radiation issues, as would a large percentage of the South Korean population, and perhaps a few Alaskans as the result of an unfortunate wind pattern, but his understanding was that this would be years away.

The President thought about the Mexican border for a nanosecond. *How bad could it really be?*

The President took a few laps around the building and looked into the Oval Office and the attached study. He always giggled when he looked into the study and thought about events that occurred in there a couple of half decades ago. *Not a mistake I will ever make. I married over my head and that is a good thing. Thank God for my wife and the girls.*

He walked through the White House offices and as usual, there were lights on in more than a few offices and cubicles. The world was flat for the White House; it was always morning someplace and someone was always doing something. Somewhere around the globe there was something happening that required a White House understanding of events, or at least, that had been the culture of the White House since World War II.

The President looked into Herman Sackman's office and saw a handful of staffers with him. He opened the door and said: "Tomorrow, 6:15 a.m. at Camp David, just figure out how to get there. Bring your resignation letter and we will decide what to do with it." He paused to see the effect on the staff, knowing that given the age of the people in the room—a nation run by recent college graduates—most would hardly understand that he was pulling Sackman's chain. "Okay, I already have that undated resignation letter, I think that one is on the green tinted paper with the red border. How about a new one on white bond? That will be sufficient." The young staff now laughed when they understood it was a joke, but the laughter was far from pure; this was a White House without great humor. To the best of anyone's knowledge, there was no court jester.

"Let's meet in my office after the CIA and economic briefings and figure an hour or so. We will be cancelling most of the rest of the day and heading for Camp David. I will meet the Secretary of State there at 1:00 p.m. Some meetings should force the attendees to be inconvenienced and out of touch. Interesting evening. I need to think on it." He turned and left as he heard Sackman say: "Thanks, Boss. Do you think my book will get me a ten million dollar advance?" The President did not acknowledge that he heard the remark.

The President continued his slow walk around the White House. The President decided on discretion and called no one after the American Exceptionalism Party Convention closed. He visited with no one other than his minute with Herman Sackman. He knew that his people and the nation were reeling. He was caught completely off guard as well. Mercifully, his wife and the kids were on yet another excursion overseas and he would not have to face mortal combat in the bedroom or bathroom. While he prided himself on clear and compact reasoning, his wife, although a great deal smarter on paper and in the classroom, was far more emotional and the last thing he needed were her emotions added to his at this hour of the still fairly early evening.

The world just wasn't fair and the President could see why President Boone had kept to himself during his last four years in the White House. The President knew he was positioning the United States and its citizens to survive the twenty-first century as a nation. He believed that his actions would make its citizens stronger and happier and yet, every step of the way, there were barriers being set up impeding his progress. Alone, very alone, he began a replay of the tougher moments: *What kind of a nation would ration health care by monetary rationing rather than by what was age appropriate? Who could possibly not see the wisdom of spending our revenues on those contributing to the working society? Don't we love our kids the most? What kind of a president would have expected the Korean Peninsula to explode into ashes based upon the whims of a psychotic ruler? Does the American public want a warmonger as president? Do they want me to respond eye for an eye and nuke the entire peninsula as a reaction to their stupidity? What good would that have done? How could the leaders of the Middle East not have some reasonable level of tolerance for other religions? I respect all religions. Not too interested in any of them, but tolerant. How could a modern and scientific nation like Israel or any nation in 2012 be following a Middle Ages religion based on the Bible? What a crazy world. Can't they see what a great job I have done and if they let me, what an even better world I could create?*

~

156

At Fox News, OBC and every station except RBC, the talking heads were on the air within seconds of the final gavel. RBC ran its normal news broadcasts and normal late night talk show host. On all of the other networks and cable stations, it was all spin with panels and panelists of left and right taking positions that they would forget within hours. As no one had known the number of supporters that George Vincent would be able to attract, the panelists' comments and thoughts could not have been more than an hour old and therefore most of the television audience would have been able to provide analysis on an intellectual and knowledge level equal to the talking heads, but without the assured arrogance. The commentators served their two special roles: Always certain, not often correct, time fillers.

The only meaningful or useful comments were by Lance Amplington, OBC's pollster, and similar comments by the Fox News pollster who responded to questions about political impacts with a fairly concise and interesting analysis: "There was an air of confidence on display tonight. This American Exceptionalism Party seems to know what direction it wants to take this campaign. What I want to see in my polling is what influence the presidential election will have on other congressional races. Are the people who were on that stage tonight heroes in their local districts or piranhas? If they are heroes, there will be more heroes, if they are piranhas, there will be few additional supporters. And folks, the task of sorting this out will take more than a few days. Tonight, they celebrate, tomorrow…?"

One person turned off his television and was giddy as he pulled up his covers. Milton Woo thought to himself: *Super Nerd!*

~

"Mr. Sackman, we have Vincent already, some of those statistics are clearly wrong. His numbers sound like he has Alzheimer's."

"Get out of here. All of you. Get out of here now! A room full of fools is the last thing I need when I need to think. These assholes have hit a series of fucking home runs and I have no idea how to respond! You are no help!" screamed an infuriated Herman Sackman. *For God's sake, some of the networks did not use my talking points.* Sackman always needed someone to yell at when he was at a loss for his next step. *I need some time,* he thought. *I need some serious time to figure out how to make these guys seem silly and out of touch. The Korean thing I think I can deal with, the deficit, the Gulf and health care, God, they are hard to explain when the Republicans are so philosophically full of shit. Rich bastards! And I need to figure out who is stupid enough to try to deliver the message and attack Senator Vincent or Jordon Scotch. Where is the damn Vice President? I have to find some use for him. Tomorrow is going to be a long, long day. We will need to have a long list of blamees for this fiasco.*

~

WEDNESDAY, AUGUST 8, 2012

From the day's *Washington Post* editorial page by Randy Kraus:

AMERICAN EXCEPTIONALISM PARTY
CONVENTION ON ITS WAY TO BROADWAY

No one told the media, certainly no one told the *Washington Post*, but the American Exceptionalism Party is apparently the real deal. At least it is the real deal for the next three and a half months.

Let us make a rare apology. If you took my advice last night and watched Casablanca on RBC, you saw one of the greatest movies of all time. But if you did not take our advice and watched the American Exceptionalism Party Convention, you saw one of the greatest one night political openings in history. Of course, the good news is that this show has only begun its three-and-a-half-month run on the national stage and likely will not change much during that period. You will be able to see it again, and again, and again.

Whoever said that there are no secrets in 2012 did not know the leadership of the AEP. Without so much as a whisper from anyone in the campaign or the offices of the dozens of current senators and congressmen, athletes and what appeared to be every major retired politicians in the United Sates, all appeared on stage at one time, without a leak—if one can imagine—in Cleveland. Yes, *that* Cleveland, the one in Ohio.

It turns out that two former presidents are supporting George Vincent in what before yesterday appeared to be only a silly, ego-filled independent campaign to be the President of the United States. Both ex-presidents made magnificent speeches in favor of Senator Vincent. The current Secretary of State (as of this printing) was part of the show as well, making fun that her Blackberry had not yet produced a good-bye message from the President. You can bet your house that tomorrow's *Washington Post* will report that she has resigned from her position as Secretary of State.

Whether keeping all of his support a secret and unveiling it all on one night was a good idea or a bad idea is subject to speculation. It certainly made for great theatre, and antidotal reports are that the entire Twitter crowd was watching by minute twenty-five of the convention. This writer counted twenty-two tweets during the first hour of the convention. Maybe there are more surprises to come; everyone loves a winner.

Where o' where were some of the more formidable former Republican and Democratic leaders is a question being asked on the blogs. Our best guess is that some from the last administration remain toxic and the last Republican vice presidential nominee will be even deeper in the Republican mix very quickly. Those missing from either party are not centrists and would appear to have no interest in becoming centrists. As to our most recent former president, this writer speculates that he will sit this one out. However, there is not one chance in one hundred that his dad would have been on that stage if his son did not want him there.

Well, they fooled us yesterday, but *Casablanca* is a great movie, isn't it?

~

The President confirmed that the day after the American Exceptionalism Party Convention would be spent at Camp David. For more than a single sound bite, he would not have to deal with the press; he could leave that to his press spokesman Peter Portman, aka the Pillsbury Doughboy, which was one hundred percent of the description anyone ever needed, except, add glasses. He may have been the shining example of everything that was wrong with Washington, but he was this president's shining example of everything that was wrong with Washington and therefore his guy. When the President thought about Peter Portman he always thought the man had been bred as a cross between *Bagdad Bob* and the character Dustin Hoffman played in *Wag the Dog*. Fiction was his reality. A political whore—no more, no less—but an effective political whore.

Getting to Camp David, even for the right people was always an interesting nightmare from a logistical sense. For the President, loading his political team into a helicopter with the cameras rolling was never a good thing, so the President always exited the White House alone, walked quickly to his Air Force One helicopter and climbed the stairs after a very quick salute to the military guard. This president generally eschewed the dog, which he truly disliked, photo ops to the contrary. You either are or are not a dog person and this president was not. On the way to the helicopter, he yelled back that he had been reading last night and that represented his entire response to the American Exceptionalism Party Convention. He thought that a level of disinterest was the best face he could put on the new guys' convention.

The President took his seat, divested himself of his coat and watched the earth below and his squadron of other identical helicopters as he made his way to Camp David, where he would plot his second term election run and if he had his way, direct the drawing and quartering of a former rival for the presidency. At least a drawing and quartering would eliminate a current rival for the support of the American public, whether she was running for office or merely supporting the AEP candidate. Her dismissal would not be in the general character of regular White House or administration departures. *Sneak up on me and pay the price, woman.*

His thirty-minute helicopter ride to Camp David was non-eventful. The President was far from a frequent user of the facility, but he was aware that arriving late mid-morning during the summer and leaving after dark avoided the thermals and rough air in both the early mornings and the late afternoons. His arrival was precisely at 9:22 a.m. and his plan was to meet with Herman Sackman and Ray Matta by 9:30. They had a great deal to consider.

Herman Sackman and the President's other doorkeeper, Ray Matta (officially White House Counsel), had driven to Reagan National Airport at 8:15 a.m. where another helicopter was waiting. They would be the President's political team for today and his only meeting, not counting what they expected to be a remarkably interesting meeting with the former senator and current Secretary of State. In their minds, she was already the former Secretary of State. *Why had I ever listened to my campaign team and not jettisoned the former president and his politician wife from any political involvement?* Was Sackman's thought as the door to his flying machine closed. *These people were and are just trouble. It would have been so much easier to let the ex-pres make his ten million dollars a year from speeches and have her in the Senate.* Having this woman in the Senate had been such an ugly thought for Sackman. He had thought, and to some great extent he was correct, that making the senator the Secretary of State would eliminate her ability to challenge the President in 2012.

Sackman would have to tell the President that Al Gore was out of the country and would not be at Camp David today. He had no idea why the President wanted to see the former vice president.

~

Super Nerd Milton Woo had not arrived at his office in Cleveland until after 10:00 a.m. Today, in his office uniform of khaki pants, a flowered shirt and sandals, he immediately sat down at his computer to see if he had achieved the unachievable during the middle of the night. On instinct, at about midnight, he had sent an unauthorized Twitter and e-mail to everyone he had touched using the spyware program he had attached to all of the evening's missiles. The message was: *Hlp.Vincent.com, $! Desp Vincent.com.*

Now the dark-haired MIT educated computer genius smiled and fist pumped as he looked at the incoming e-mails on Vincent.com and a couple of cumulative totals from the money pit before he sent his next e-mail:

> Senator / Mr. Dankberg / Mr. Wade: I forgot to tell you that I was going to ask last night's Twitterers and e-mail recipients for contributions through the website. Sorry. Software is a little overloaded, but it appears that sixteen million people donated a total of about $75M dollars. Will confirm by the end of the day. Assume that is good news.

Woo laughed. He knew that if his work added $75 million to the campaign fund that would bring the total campaign fund to about $75 million. *Yes, I am the great one, maybe another new nickname: Woo-Man the Magnificent to go along with Super Nerd. I need to change my e-mail address and call sign.*

~

163

Peter Portman, aka The Pillsbury Doughboy, walked to the microphone for his morning press conference knowing that, as always, this would be an interesting morning. As the President's spokesman, this Pillsbury Doughboy was a combination of diplomat, politician and Herman Goebbels. Exclusive of the fact that pressure was only a word to Peter Portman, he was the American poster boy for how not to take care of your body as one aged. Thinning grey hair presiding over a body that had not seen a gymnasium since required physical education classes ended in junior high school and a nose that presumed more than an occasional cocktail at the end of the day, which, for him, usually occurred around 9:00 p.m. Even if he was home with his family, who had effectively written him off as a participating family member, Portman was attached to his Blackberry and the family television twenty-four-seven. The down payment on the price he would pay with his wife and family was already partially in place as one high school student was beginning to simply ignore him in totality while letting light drugs become a part of her daily life. His wife had finally moved his bed into the attic and put a flat screen television next to it. The other son was beginning to show serious physiological signs resulting from what was effectively abandonment by his inattentive father. Portman had not noticed any problem with his kids. As to his wife, he had never treated her as an equal partner, so it was same o', same o'.

Portman went through the normal litany of what was taking place around the world and that the President was on his way to Camp David for a day of meetings with his staff. As the President was *off-campus*, the press was unscripted and all newspapers and television stations would have their chance to fire questions at him. While the President had assertively decided to eliminate presidential press conferences and pretend to stage *open* town hall meetings, Portman had to deal with the press every day. This, he knew, would change in his second term. They would just ignore the press, just like President Boone, unless a constitutional amendment was passed allowing the President's team to stay in the White House, forever.

OBC was always first and asked the expected (requested) question about the President's reaction to seeing the former presidents on the dais the prior evening. Portman responded by pillaring the former presidents because they had not contacted the White House to inform them of their plans. This, according to Portman, was inappropriate and showed a lack of respect for the electorate. Their follow-up question, harsh for OBC, isolated the Secretary of State as a member of the administration and asked whether this was a sign of disloyalty, which would be punished by firing. Portman indicated the President's disappointment was that he was unaware of her decision to support George Vincent and that the President would be meeting with her in the afternoon. She was an American and free to offer her opinion. No decisions had been made. Portman almost laughed out loud at his own response, *no decisions, still wonder whether it will be a hanging or a firing squad.*

Fox News pursued the election angle and Portman offered a comment that he would be forced to relive, as polls being taken as he spoke showed that the idea of a third party had instantly begun to resonate among the voters: "Third parties in America have rarely had any meaningful influence on the American elections. The usual is that they garner a couple of percent from each side and confuse the electorate a bit. In this case, the American Exceptionalism Party, or whatever they call it, will undoubtedly take the moderates away from the Republican Party and that will be about the only impact. It should significantly help the Democratic Party in this year's election." The press corps did not ask him whether that was a sound answer after watching Scott Brown's polling data move some thirty-five points in less than thirty-five days in 2010, or how the AEP could impact congressional elections without any American Exceptionalism Party candidates. The press corps was sufficiently slow as to not recall that Ross Perot had probably elected Bill Cloud. *Wonderful press corps.*

Portman allowed one question from Fox News. Fox News' White House correspondent questioned Portman: "It sounded to me as if Jordon Scotch was challenging the President's college admissions with his comment that he was not a minority admit to the colleges he attended. What did the President think of that and how will he respond?"

Portman fielded the question with one of his classic double steps. He responded that the President had a law degree received with honors from Harvard, and that he believed Dr. Scotch was having a little skirmish with respect to the value of his degree from MIT versus Harvard. Portman indicated the President thought the whole discussion a bit beneath the AEP nominee.

As usual, the remainder of the questions were fended off with long, windy and meaningless answers. The press conference was followed by a quick luncheon of pastries left over from another White House meeting.

~

Camp David is an interesting place. It is officially named the Naval Support Facility Thurmont and is located in Maryland. Presidents have used it since Franklin Delano Roosevelt was in office. It is probably significantly safer from a security standpoint than the White House as the result of its middle-of-nowhere location and its elite Marine contingent in charge of security. It is the ultimate retreat for a president that chooses to be alone, or not so alone, for any period of time. During this administration, it was also the home of the President's church, the Camp David Chapel. The chapel was never used, but often referred to by the President as his church for his period of time in Washington D.C. Who went to church alone in 2012?

Whether the President would return to the White House or stay the night in Aspen Lodge, the designated cabin for the President was unclear. He guessed that he would return to the White House after dark, but it was not very important with his family away; he hated the late afternoon thermals so he would absolutely stay through nightfall, which in August was not particularly early. The President planned to conduct his meetings in and around Aspen Lodge and at least shoot a few hoops before returning to Washington D.C.

As the President's helicopter landed, his team of lookalike helicopters hovered near the property and then flew to a holding location. Sackman and Matta were waiting outside the Aspen Lodge. Outsiders would always wonder which one was playing the role of Halderman and which was playing the role of Ehrlichman. It was fascinating how a very liberal president could have his two key players imitating the guardians of the Nixon era. Matta actually did look like he could have been Ehrlichman's brother or son. No one looked at Ray Matta and concluded this was a man with whom it would be easy to become friends.

The President landed, skipped his salute to any member of the military crew—as there were no cameras—and headed for his two-man political team. As he approached them he gave their appearances a quick thought: *Here I am promoting good eating habits to reduce health care costs and I find myself meeting with two guys who live on coffee and one who lives on doughnuts. If I ever want to change political advisors, I should grab a couple of Marines and insist that they can play a quick game of half-court. The overs and unders for the first heart attack for Matta could not be fifteen minutes! In casual clothes, Sackman looks like he just left Dachau, a tiny man in so many ways. I would think that they would care about how they look. Obviously not.*

The President was all business. He strode past them towards the cabin, entered the Cabinet, sat at the head of an old oak table where two Coca-Colas on ice were already waiting and began talking before the two politicos had so much as sat down. Sackman and Matta both knew that there was a lengthy soliloquy in their future.

"I cannot believe that you did not know what was going to happen last night. No excuses, no discussion. I want a report back from you next week that explains how this could have been kept a secret from me. In that report, I need to understand why the Secret Service did not say so much as word one about the movement of so many important public officials to Cleveland, particularly the former presidents. Understood?"

Two nods.

"Next," and next led to a twenty-minute diatribe on treasonous Democrats and the Secretary of State in particular. The language was harsh, the President's eyes nearly bulging in anger and the two politicos fiercely jotting down notes that they would throw away soon after the meeting. This was a president giving orders that would be ignored for his own good. Matta always wondered whether the President knew how hilarious he sounded when he was angry. Matta always laughed at the President's instructions as this president never looked at the detail, never asked if an order had been accomplished, and tried to manage about seventy-five different direct reports, which effectively made him impotent with respect to his own administration.

Matta was a student of organizational theory, a graduate of the Kellogg School at Northwestern University, and that theory demanded a span of control (management) of no more than six to eight people; the President had only seventy more than recommended. He was totally inexperienced about how to manage and that was fine with Matta and Sackman as they effectively were co-presidents and would continue to be so as long as they did not let the President understand that reality—ignorant, good. While he loved his job, Matta loved the power more and the fact that the President of the United States had never managed anything, not so much as a taco stand, made manipulating the President into trying to implement the Matta economic and international strategies fairly easy. Matta knew his policy power came from the President's complete inability to lead or manage.

Matta's view of Sackman was not significantly different than his view of the President, except that he knew Sackman was especially bright and his powers of retention were spectacular. That Mensa thing was real. Sackman had shared his personal view that having the world think of him as the Enforcer and believing he was the Wizard behind the screen explained everything Matta needed to know. Sackman was a man he would scale buildings to avoid if there was any disagreement. Sackman got off on winning conflicts; winning was far more important than governing. Matta understood that Sackman would be a bad enemy and that was not something he had and was not going to let happen.

Sackman had unintentionally given Matta enough leeway to impact legislation more than himself. When things were not going in the direction that Matta wanted, he would create some direct friction between Sackman and whoever the problem was at that moment, but never between the two of them. Sackman was *always* more interested in showing his power than in anything else, so if Matta described winning to Sackman, Sackman would destroy anything or anyone in his path to get to winning. While a man to be feared, Matta thought the foul-languaged Sackman to be the dumbest smart man he had ever met. Also the meanest person Matta had ever met. While Matta was walking across the street or scaling buildings to avoid a fight, Sackman was a guy who would walk across the street to get into a fight.

Finally, his rage expended, the President slurped down his second Coca-Cola, found his special Camp David book on the shelf, *The History of Sweden*, and pulled out a cigarette. Both Sackman and Matta knew this was when the meeting part of the meeting actually would begin. Both non-smokers, Sackman and Matta instinctively moved a few more inches down the table away from the President. Neither Sackman nor Matta had the tools and people available to the President and knew that if they got home before their wives went to bed, each spouse would remark that the President was again smoking heavily. Matta's wife, who thought she was a walking joke machine, would ask Matta if she had the name of the hotel where Mrs. President and the kids were so she could call and tell her that her man was smoking heavily again.

"OK, so what do I do with the Vice President? It really has been a good couple of weeks. I guess he has been on vacation, because I cannot recall any incredibly stupid remarks during the past two or three weeks." The President's sarcasm kicked into gear when he said: "Ray, didn't he get the name of the decedent correct in Brazil a few weeks ago? Should have sent him flowers! The VP, not the late Vice President Ramirez."

Sackman now engaged: "There is nothing you can do about him. You are going to get a political platform at the convention that will be so far left, you will need to visit Greece a half dozen times to find out whether socialism without state owned oil reserves can work financially over the long term. We need to cover all of the issues we will have politically with the platform. But we cannot lose anyone approaching moderate leaving for the AEP. I don't trust that S.O.B. one inch. If we drop him, he will support Vincent.

"We do not have the juice to change what will be done on the platform committee. We need a white, former senator as a prop for a few months and our beloved VP is the guy for this task. His political instincts will kick in and he will not go off the reservation. Beloved, as I call the guy, is only close to the dullest tack in this drawer."

Matta entered the fray: "Isn't there some former senator who is bored to death that we can put in place for him. The guy is next in line to be president."

"Hold on guys, this president—that would be me—has the best assassination insurance of any president since Theodore Roosevelt. Who would be crazy enough to want to have Beloved or the Speaker of the House as President of the United States?" Both Sackman and Matta laughed as they always did when the President discussed his assassination insurance. If anyone had been counting, they had heard this line well over one hundred times in the past three years. They believed the President might have said this to get them to laugh, but in reality, they thought he believed what he was saying. No one of any intelligence, no ally, no enemy, either foreign or domestic, would want to deal with the United States with Beloved as the President.

Leaning back in his chair, the President quickly lit up cigarette number three and tried to do the calculation. "What I really need is a woman." He paused and continued, "If one of you mentions the Secretary of State…that is why the Marines are outside.

"What am I looking at? George Vincent is an amiable guy who will not debate well. And Paul Roland, well, he is Paul Roland. I cannot imagine that he is going to be a player in this game. Congressman Roland will start and finish his Republican run for the presidency with the same constituency. He has not secured a vice president. Certainly, if Cheney were alive and healthy, he would have loved to do it, but that is not going to happen and no one is going to give up a Senate seat or a House seat to be his running mate. The man I really worry about is this Hispanic economist in a fucking wheelchair. Ray, what do we really know about him?"

Matta: "Jordon Scotch is the real deal in business and economics. Apparently, he was one heck of a high school athlete and that really did all end in a bus accident. The scuttlebutt is that he was going to go to Michigan, run track and graduate in three years. His goal was a Rhodes Scholarship followed by a PhD from the London School of Economics. Ultimately, he settled for Berkeley for the PhD, where there are, what, forty Nobel Prize economists on their faculty. He is a tenured professor and teaches and consults at UCLA. Even among the most liberal faculty, he is thought of as some kind of God. Apparently, his classes fill up instantly and he is a very, very hard grader, so there is a message in that. At one point, we contacted him to see if he had any interest in coming to Washington and while polite, he had no interest in what we were selling.

"I have had both CBO—I know I am not allowed, but I did—Treasury and Commerce review his writings and we should be able to label him as too conservative, but I suspect the press will run pictures of him working with the French, the British and the President of Chile. A conservative Hispanic is not a contradiction in terms regardless of media comments to the contrary. Years ago, he consulted for the Federal Reserve and they said that senior economists at the Fed had begun asking his opinion when he was in his late twenties. The man is rocket smart and from last night, it is abundantly clear that he is a charming speaker."

"Family?"

"Apparently dotes on his kids and wife. Met his wife while they were at Berkeley and unlike you, she has been an athlete her entire life, not some pretend basketball star." Matta sometimes heard what he was going to say at the same time as his audience and if he had had the ability, he would have grabbed that sentence back out of the air.

The President screamed at him and threw *The History of Sweden* across the room. A few packages of cigarettes left the book and landed on the table. The President was standing when the two Marine guards entered the room and he offered an embarrassed smile.

"Can't decide if I should have you kill him or not. Is there a guillotine on the property? We are okay."

Without a smile, the Marines left. "Ray, you are wearing very, very thin. You know damn well that I was not just a joiner in high school. Could have been captain of the basketball team if I had wanted. What else about him?"

WEDNESDAY, AUGUST 8, 2012

"We have found absolutely nothing about him that can be used for attack purposes. Obviously, he has no professional political experience, but again, there is not a Secretary of the Treasury in the past four administrations that has not called for his advice. That does include us although there are no fingerprints. We never listened to him; a mistake I suspect we will hear about. Pretty amazing that none of the three of us really know very much about him, but I did a little internal personal review of where he was when we were picking economic advisors. As I said before, we are not his guys. His views on stimulus made him anything except our guy. In his writings, there are pages and pages of reasons why our spending did not stimulate the economy. Maybe we should have kidnapped him and forced him to be the Secretary of the Treasury."

"How would Beloved do in a debate with Jordon Scotch?"

Matta jumped back into the discussion, scratching his limited hair a bit. "Jordon Scotch would make Beloved look weak intellectually at levels that would be extraordinary, even for him; he would also appear to be a nicer guy which may or may not be extraordinary. Can you imagine the pre-debate build up when they bring out the pictures of Beloved asking the other guy in a wheelchair to stand up? Let's remember, he actually did that. There simply cannot be a mano a mano debate with Jordon Scotch, but a three way would be okay if Paul Roland selects anything except an economist. Either way, it has to be fairly brief. We can orchestrate Beloved's comments to be singularly aimed at the Republican Party and the Republican vice presidential candidate. No one will be able to attack a guy in a wheelchair. I would guess that they will field someone that is slightly to the right of Himmler, given the number of more moderate Republicans that have already pulled out of the Republican Party for purposes of the presidential race."

"I don't want him on the ticket, I don't like him. I don't trust him and he makes me look like a buffoon for selecting him. The only thing he is good at is appearing next to me when I make appointments. Even then, as we know, he can screw up an announcement."

Matta effectively closed the discussion: "Mr. President," he only used this traditional expression when he was being insistent upon a conclusion and making sure the President knew he was dead serious. "This should be a dead issue. The public knows he is not a great vice president, but you need to consider two things. One, he is very white and two, you may not be able to control this convention and you certainly cannot control him if you sack

171

him. With the gaggle of morons from California on the convention floor, you could find yourself with a Barbara Boxer or a Nancy Pelosi. At that point, you become George McGovern or Jimmy Carter and I think we all like this gig."

"OK, OK, we can move his offices to another city after the election. Actually, I am serious about that, you guys can figure out a way to move him to Kansas City or Boulder, Colorado for security purposes. Maybe a continuity issue; I bet you can put him two thousand miles away for four years and then eliminate his budget and activities. Find out where Hoffa is and let him guard the body. Someone at home should know. My second term is going to be a blockbuster as I get the final touches on total wealth distribution and fairness for everyone. And, we may revisit this decision before the convention. Not concrete yet in my mind.

"So, what did those traitors do to me last night?"

This was Sackman's area and he would be in a guessing game for a few days, but he wanted to stay a bit in front of the game. "I don't think we will have any definitive polling for a few days. The impact of this American Exceptionalism Party is going to put a focus on certain states far more than last time. For example, I think in New York, Vincent guarantees us a huge victory, a really huge victory, as I don't think you will lose many votes to Vincent, and Paul Roland will lose a large number of votes to him. But in Florida, you could instantly lose the Jewish vote—but *how* they could be voting for us all along? That, I could never understand. Overall, I think Vincent absolutely guarantees us the popular vote, but the electoral vote could be pretty interesting. What we do not understand is how they used the Internet to engage such a large audience last night. Either the AEP has some computer guy who is light years ahead of us or word of mouth was significant last night—maybe a bit of both."

The conversation and the cigarettes went on for a few hours with the presidential staff bringing in cheeseburgers and fries for lunch. When the cigarettes were in evidence and the wife was elsewhere, the burgers and fries were a given. Nothing except the VP choice was resolved regarding the campaign, which would ultimately fall on Sackman. Beloved was given a new four year, no cut contract to warm the bench, if he could find it, again subject to the President rethinking this decision.

The President had already given a lot of thought to how he could ruin the Secretary of State's day and had decided where he would have dinner at Camp David after a brief, one-man workout on the basketball court. He also thought about making sure his clothing was clean and smoke free when Mrs. President returned from vacation tomorrow. *Here I am giving speeches on eating healthy to be healthy and I seem to be smoking more than ever. The burgers are probably okay, but the cigarettes and the fries! Not good.*

~

As she was getting off the helicopter, the Secretary of State was particularly amused.

The President had moved the meeting to Camp David to have complete control of her day. She knew that. She had never been fired from any job in her entire life and since she was not going to resign, this was going to be a first. *What great payback? While I was the Secretary of State, any time there was an important task there was a czar, a czarina, or a special envoy. What bullshit was that? I gave up a seat in the United States Senate that I could have kept for the rest of my life while Bill was earning a fortune giving speeches; big mistake, I knew better. This president is going to know exactly what I think in a few minutes. OK, don't trip on the stairs, either now or on the return flight. Can this guy make me walk home?*

The President drove to the helicopter to meet his Secretary of State in a golf cart. He was now wearing a pair of light blue jeans, which hung fairly loose on his exceptionally thin frame and a tight golf shirt, which showed the impacts of some fairly serious weight training and a good trainer. It also showed him as seriously underweight. The golf shirt was a gift from the South Carolina 2010 national championship baseball team and was too tight.

It was still midday in terms of the sun and heat, always a delight in the mid-South in August. Humidity and temperature were both about ninety-four and sweat was the order of the afternoon. The Secretary of State was in her standard blue pants suit, the official uniform of the soon to be former Secretary of State. The President shook her hand, looked at her and said: "No need to talk about this. Resign or be fired, which is it?"

"Good to see you too, Mr. President. I will not resign; everything I have been asked…"

The President, who had been thinking and waiting for this moment for almost twenty hours turned his back to the Secretary of State and called out: "Herman, send the press release that says I fired her ass for incompetence." Ten steps later, he returned to his golf cart and was off to the working cabin. After the short ride, the door closed behind him.

The Secretary of State had her cell phone out almost before the door closed behind the President. And next to her, before the door closed, was a Marine. "I am truly sorry, the President would prefer that you wait until you leave Camp David and return to Reagan to make any calls. It is our protocol." The Marine did not think to ask her if she had taped her conversation with the President.

There are places in the world where if asked not to make any cellular calls, one could or would simply ignore the rules. Almost anywhere, if fired, an individual can follow the boss into any doorway and continue the conversation. Almost anywhere, a fired employee can call his or her spouse immediately. Camp David is not one of those places where normal rules apply. The Secretary of State neither made her call nor followed the President into the cabin. *I guess I am not on the short list for VP!*

"OK, am I allowed to return to the helicopter and go back to Reagan, or do I have to walk home, or has he arranged for a firing squad? I saw a movie once where the government blew up a Cabinet member in a helicopter. Do you feel safe? What an asshole!"

"Yes, or I mean no." The Marine was a bit out of his element. "I have been instructed to direct the helicopter back to Reagan, Washington, D.C. Sorry, Madam."

~

Long before the helicopter had risen six inches over the cemented heli-copter pad at Camp David, the following was released:

From the *White House*:

FOR IMMEDIATE RELEASE

SECRETARY OF STATE FIRED

WASHINGTON D.C., August 8, 2012, 1:45 p.m. — After a meet-ing and extensive discussion this afternoon with the Secretary of State, the President of the United States determined that they had different visions for the role of the United States in the interna-tional community. The President believes the State Department has not been sufficiently supportive of the goals and objectives of the White House during her tenure and that this lack of support has hurt the United States throughout the world. When asked for her resignation, the Secretary of State refused to resign and the Presi-dent informed her that she was no longer a Member of his Cabinet. He instructed the deputy Secretary of State to have her personal effects delivered to her home as soon as possible and informed her that she was no longer an employee of the government of the United States.

Obvious to any White House advisor, the President had instructed Sack-man to draft a harsh press release. This job Sackman performed with enthu-siasm. He hated the woman.

~

The bellicose William (Bill) Patrick O'Brien had spent the better part of a day trying to think through a three-party election with a vibrant third party. It had all of the complexity of launching a mission to the moon guided by some clown with a slide rule. Of course, that worked for Apollo 13.

Bright to beat the band and more knowledgeable about history than most or perhaps all of his competitors combined, O'Brien struggled a bit with numbers and the chart he was reviewing was beyond his analytical mathematical capabilities. "Jenn, can you come look at this with me? I have got to interview this guy in a few hours and I am struggling where to start."

Jennifer Cho walked into O'Brien's office. Jennifer Cho was now a fixture on cable news. Her general resume and appearance was a model for cable news and commentary; jet black hair, very, very attractive, perfectly circular face, high cheek bones, tiny from the neck down, reasonable law school, clerked for a Federal Court judge, exceptionally innocent looking and about as charming as any human being on the planet. Jennifer Cho was single, a US citizen born in Taiwan and just a shade over thirty years old. "What's up?"

"Well, I think this research is telling me that this election will end up in the House of Representatives."

Cho and O'Brien had become fast friends. While O'Brien was about as abrasive as a seventh grade boy at his first dance, he was a complete prude and had been married to the same woman since before Cho had been born. While Cho thought he would love to bed her down, she knew his fear of hurting his reputation, Catholic upbringing and terror of his wife and daughter finding out outweighed anything he would consider without about fourteen drinks, a habit he did not have. This made working with O'Brien about perfect. And God, his wit was so quick, it was always fun when the studio lights were not lit to one hundred degrees for a live show. He really had become a good friend and in some ways, a partner.

In her own world, Jennifer Cho ultimately wanted to be Mrs. Right. Working with someone who she could work with and not worry about his trying to grope her in an elevator or try to meet her in a midtown $800 per night hotel room was a wonderful change from every previous job. Jenn's near perfect face on top of her tiny body gave her an angelic look. A definite stick figure, but angelic. Usually, the men who found her attractive did not match up with her preference for finding a muscled up, brilliant guy. She kept hoping this man would show up on a white horse wrapped in a Chinese body. Any ultimate spouse would need to appreciate very highly spiced Cantonese foods and a woman with a family eight thousand miles away.

"Bill, when you read the Constitution, you always need to remember a few specific things. One, it was 1790. Two, Jefferson was the man of the people. Three, Hamilton was literally a poor bastard who didn't trust anyone. Four, Virginia had about as many people as the rest of the country combined, a bit of an exaggeration, but you get the point. Thirteen states, virtually no one was allowed to vote: only men who were property owners and no Native Americans, slaves, etc., and there were not all that many white men who owned property. The Constitution is littered with what would appear to be odd ideas two hundred years later. Think slavery, which was already either outlawed or economically unworkable in great swaths of the colonies. It took huge compromises to get rid of the Articles of Confederation and get to the Constitution."

"I know all of the history. It always shocks me when Ms. Taiwan here knows. My question is why will this election end up in the House of Representatives? Isn't the President going to destroy the GOP and win in at least two-thirds of the states? The GOP needed a man of the middle who was acceptable to the right. That is not what they have."

Cho either nodded or shrugged. No verbal response was needed while O'Brien was thinking out loud.

"Well, this guy says no one can predict what is going to happen in the House of Representatives and he says it could get there. In 2004, the Republicans had a majority of congressmen, by 2008 you were beginning to need a microscope to find a Republican and now, in 2012, the place is essentially fifty-fifty after the Congress and the President lost their minds on everything. And of course, redistricting moves a few House seats between states for 2012. What is the deficit, $149 billion, zillion? But what has my attention is that there are no American Exponential Party congresspersons or senators, no its not exponential, what is it Jenn?"

"Can't take you anywhere, Bill. American Exceptionalism Party." Cho was amazingly quick-witted in English and had a spooky knowledge of the political system for a young woman who had only been in the United States since her freshman year in high school. Taiwan was home and the location of her parents and sister. When she fully understood every word delivered to her, she was funny and quick. Somehow, she had run the immigration gauntlet while in law school and became a US citizen. O'Brien had never asked exactly how she managed that trick.

"What, about thirty or forty senators and Congress Members have committed to Senator Vincent? And, I suspect, if George Vincent has done this right that number will grow significantly. So, how do those people vote if the election goes to the House? I feel like I am getting ready to interview the guy that wrote the Wizard of Oz."

"That would be Victor Fleming, Bill."

"Thank you, Miss Smarty Pants, little Chinese woman, know-it-all I work with. A really useful piece of information, what, crossword puzzles at night since there is no boyfriend?"

Cho blanched a bit at his accurate description of her last few weeks and months, but responded: "Bill, look, your audience will not understand how screwed up this is unless you spend an entire week taking them through it. My Constitutional law professor was never certain the country and the Constitution could handle a serious third party. There are all kinds of things that can go wrong, including the electors voting for whoever they want."

"Huh?"

"Don't you remember that there was an elector in 2004 or 2008 who voted for the other candidate because she thought it was the right thing to do. Shoot, let me think, Barbara Simmons from the District of Columbia cast a blank vote rather than vote for Gore. I don't know what that was all about."

"Jenn, how could you know that?" O'Brien just stared at her and again wondered how she could know so many obscure facts.

"I am a Harvard educated journalist, not some constitutional scholar. I've got this memo I don't follow and I have to meet with this professor type. I think we listen to this guy and then put him on the shelf for a few months." When just a bit agitated, O'Brien sounded like an annoyed father. "No one in my audience wants to listen to some geek talk about the possibilities of something that will probably not happen."

William Patrick O'Brien was the real American original. While another radio talk show guy claimed that mantle, it properly belonged to O'Brien and Fox News scheduled their evening platform around his ability to bring in huge audiences. Straight talking with an ego that just exploded on the screen, the traditional television executives could not understand how or why people watched. But they did watch, measured in millions.

"So Jenn, what do I do with this geek and his five minutes tonight?"

Cho thought this sounded pretty funny. O'Brien's show featured a couple of political giants plus his regular cadre of beauty queen smarties and a couple of women who had been, at best, modest looking women who, after six or seven different hair styles and completely different clothing, began to look like babes. One had never quite gotten to actually being attractive; she was now always shown from the side to show a mammoth set of breasts, which had been stapled on in the past few months. Of course, this drove the eighty-pound Cho to distraction, but she knew if she ever said word one, O'Brien would work her comment into every third sentence. Cho always appeared so nice and so uniquely attractive in an ultimate clean-cut way. That is what the viewers saw; she wore her heart on her sleeve. She knew she did not need breast augmentation to help her remain a viable television personality.

Jenn Cho often thought that she had not seen the station try to take an unattractive man and make him handsome. The closest they had come was to rip a bow tie off one young reporter and try to make him look like an adult. "Well, what does Geekhead look like and what does he know?"

"Geekhead, I like that. Apparently, he knows more about elections and mathematics than Einstein and I have no idea what he looks like, why? Looking for a new man in your life?" O'Brien could never resist.

"Yes, that's it; a man named Geekhead is precisely what I am looking for. Bill, I can see this guy, five-foot-three, my weight, brown shoes with grey slacks. This election is going to get crazy. Why don't I size up Geekhead tonight, turn the guy into Prince Charming like you do with those women you sleep with and keep him around for a few months. We can use him when you need him."

O'Brien's coffee had nearly escaped from his mouth with the *women you sleep with* comment and there was no way that was racing by him. He knew Cho thought he found her incredibly attractive; he actually saw her as part additional daughter and part good buddy. There were many people he would go out of his way to help quite a bit, but he really loved this kid and would do anything for her. *Maybe a different time and a different place?* "Remember, this good Catholic boy and remember, I see everyone pre-make-up. Those women have about the same chance with me as Geekhead will have with you, or with me for that matter! I see your picture of Geekhead and I am certain you forgot the acne. Just don't start fantasizing about Geekhead tonight, strictly business my little newsperson. But that is one heck of a good idea, I think I'll just get the flavor of the man and then we will decide what to do with the subject and Geekhead. I'll wing it on the technical stuff and see what the post game show gives us on audience interest levels."

O'Brien looked at his notes and asked Cho for an easy favor: "Jenn, I have the feeling I am really going to get lucky with the Secretary of State." Cho's eyes lit up with that kind of smile that starts with the eyes and radiates down to the mouth. "Stop it, you and your ever dirty mind. She is teed up with us for Monday night. We have that press release that says she is no longer the Secretary of State. This smells like a dog eats man event and I am guessing that she has her own press release in the mill.

"The President's press release was pretty harsh, actually, incredibly harsh and unprecedented in the modern era. I am guessing she will not like that at all. Maybe she will issue something before we go off air tonight. Let's make sure we don't miss that. I think I will promo Madame Secretary in my opening comments tonight and express the possibility of competing press releases. If I am wrong, no one will think about it and if I am right, it will give us another opening segment for Thursday. Jenn, the next few months are going to be really easy. I think we could start sneaking up on six million viewers."

~

The defrocked Secretary of State had returned to the helicopter and quickly realized she was facing the four-corner offense. Everything went into slow motion as a part was replaced in the door, a complete check of the machine took place and finally the helicopter took a route from Camp David to Reagan National Airport that would have made a great travelogue for The Discovery Channel. Knowing she would quit or be fired from the get-go, this entire process should have amused her. However, not being given an appropriate opportunity to say her piece angered her, a lot. She knew that the travelogue experience was designed so that she would miss the press cycle this afternoon and she guessed this was to be expected, although she missed it in her thinking and planning the prior evening. She was also fairly certain that when she arrived at the airport, her driver would inform her that the Federal government would return her personal effects to her home by the end of tomorrow, August 9. The keys to the State Department Building, which were really an ID card, would no longer be operable for her.

When they—she, her husband and George Vincent—had game played this scenario, the facts of the day (firing) came in number one (unanimous) in their forecast. This, they believed, they would ultimately use to their advantage. The Secretary's game plan was perfectly organized. She would now avoid the press through Sunday evening. During that period, the President's administration would defend the undefendable (his campaign was far more important than any Secretary of State in his mind). George Vincent and his people would reiterate his convention comments and she would only issue her press release, which was drafted and awaiting her decision to release it to the media. She only needed to read the President's press release and then, with the concurrence of George Vincent, reread and perhaps edit her statement. Then, she would release it. When she saw the harshness and the President's misleading remarks, her press release would need some serious changes. If things worked as she hoped, by December 1, she would be part of the Vincent transition team and her major hope was that her successor would not have time to change her desk; she liked that particular desk.

Oh, I wish I had a copy of that press release and a parachute so I could get out of this machine. And the thermals! Ugh!

The former Secretary of State was already booked on the O'Brien show for Monday, August 13 for almost twenty minutes. She had been interviewed by O'Brien during the primaries in 2008 and believed the interview had gone fairly well. She and O'Brien would have a common purpose: create news from the AEP Convention and from her firing. O'Brien had been less critical of the President than many of the other Fox News commentators, but the rupture between the parties was good business for him and Fox News.

~

Geekhead arrived timely at 2:00 p.m. to videotape his portion of the evening show with Bill O'Brien. He had no idea what to expect. While he was waiting in the lobby, at least half of the women administrators and executives found a moment to walk through the lobby on the way to some important meeting. Certain types of news travel through any office in seconds.

Geekhead looked like he came out of central casting for one of those 1940s movies where the lead character was sculpted from marble. While only about five-foot-ten-inches tall, Geekhead had those Steve Garvey, Popeye arms and looked like he could wrestle a bear. He was clean-shaven with short side burns and had fairly long locks of curly, dark colored hair. Geekhead was concentrating on his notes and appeared to hardly notice the women employees taking a long, long look at him in the lobby. At the moment, he was girlfriend free. He had always been bemused when he sat in a lobby and the company's women all made their way through, sometimes checking to see if they had locked their cars or their car trunks were securely closed. One got used to good looks. Geekhead knew that most of the women walking through the lobby would find his interests in life to be way too boring after or, far more often, far too early during the first date.

Into the lobby came Bill O'Brien's top administrator and when she saw Horace Cicerone, she just laughed out loud. "Mr. Cicerone, I am Ginny Manning, Mr. O'Brien's administrative assistant. I'll need to take you back to makeup and let them get started, although I think you know that you won't need much work."

Horace Cicerone blushed. This would be an interesting experience. He had never been on television and the closest he could remember to being on a stage was when his sisters and three hula dancers had tried to drag him up to dance at a Luau when they were in Hawaii during his junior year in college. The hula girls had begged him, and then his sisters had begged him, to come up on stage, which he did not do and later that evening they had all partied late into the night (or early into the Hawaiian morning).

This academic did not think of his classroom as a stage, which made him ever more effective with his students. "Thank you, Ms. Manning, I think. This is a bit out of character for me, I pretty much prefer to hide in front of my computer and think about the Constitution of the United States."

Ginny Manning had Geekhead out of his chair and going down the hallway when she asked him if he was a lawyer.

184

"Hah, Ms. Manning, I never had very much interest in the law in the sense of using it to anyone's advantage. I have always been interested in the law and particularly the Constitution as a political tool, more interested in the past than the future. I wouldn't be a particularly good ambulance chaser."

"Call me, Ginny."

They walked into the makeup room and Manning introduced Horace Cicerone to the makeup master. "Lilly, this is Horace Cicerone, but we call him Geekhead up on the twelfth floor; it's a long story." Manning giggled and told Geekhead she would be back in a few minutes and then they would get together with Bill O'Brien.

A moment later, Ginny looked into O'Brien's office: "Bill, Geekhead is here. There cannot be a woman in the building who isn't going to think of having you run over by a train if you don't have him on every night."

"Really?" Bill responded, not really hearing exactly what had been said. "So, can Geekhead string two sentences together or am I going to have to both ask and answer my own questions?"

"Bill, you do that every night with almost every guest."

"Cute, what do you think?"

"He seems pretty modest, but assuming he does actually teach a few classes every semester, I am guessing he should be fine."

"Well, bring him in when you are ready. Give us ten minutes and we will do the taping immediately after. Get Jenn to listen to the taping; I'll want her input as to whether we find a legal beagle or stick with this guy over the next few months as we finish up our every four-year battle between the big money candidates and the folks."

"Bill, you are going to have a revolt if you don't hire this guy. I spent five minutes with him and decided that if he asked me to marry him on the way to your office, I was going to leave Walter and our four sons." This caught O'Brien's attention.

Geekhead arrived in Bill O'Brien's office and like most men, O'Brien looked at him, saw Geekhead was six inches shorter than he was and maybe a couple dozen pounds lighter and didn't give Manning's comments another thought. Geekhead quickly briefed O'Brien about the Electoral College and the House of Representatives and they set out to the taping room.

O'Brien did the taping in a single sitting. Geekhead was a little over O'Brien's head and most of his audience, but between them, they set the hook fairly securely with the audience that there were constitutional issues out there with three viable political parties.

After the interview, Bill asked Geekhead if he could wait in the lobby.

Jenn and Bill got back together in O'Brien's paper filled office to decide what to do with Geekhead. "Keep him," offered Cho. "Bill, he is the most handsome man I have ever seen and articulate, wow! Did you see those forearms?" *Hold on, Kid, he will give you a hard time about this for months if you give him the chance. But, wow, what a stud!* Rolled around in her mind. *And smart!*

"Jenn, keep your blouse on here, the interview was fine, but as smart as the guy seems to be, there was nothing sensational here. I need him to help me develop some themes that I can pound on for the viewers. They need controversy. Let's do this, but I don't want to guarantee him too many shows until I see the feedback, but I want to keep him on the hook. If he really turns on the women viewers, and you and Ginny seem to think he will do that, we'll find a place for him like some of the other folks we have on occasionally. Take him over to legal and tie him up for ten weeks in some way that keeps him off of the other shows and makes him available. Don't let Willie overpay because you think the guy is cute."

"Stop it."

"Seriously, if you think this guy will be good for us and the viewers react positively; help him figure out how he can be controversial, interesting and right about the way this election is going to go down. That little guy is attractive?"

Jenn ignored O'Brien's last question. All big men seemed to think attractive was a function exclusively of size. "I'm on it, Bill. What time are we taping the review of that Supreme Court decision on that condemnation of a portion of a high school campus? Are they going to put in a transmitter for a cell phone company?"

"In about an hour, we'll call you. Go make our deal with this guy."

As she walked down the hallway, Bill sat at his desk and wondered whether this guy would be worth an eighth of a point in the ratings. He'd been on top a very long time and being on top meant lots and lots of what he loved most, not fame, money.

"Mr. Cicerone, I am Jennifer Cho." *Not very creative Bozo,* thought Cho after spending fifteen minutes in the bathroom fixing her hair and makeup before finding Geekhead. She had brought Ginny Manning with her as she had thought through how she was going to get to know this man without making it appear that there was such an immediate and intense attraction. *This is really odd*, she thought.

"Hi. I have seen you on Mr. O'Brien's shows, I enjoy your commentary."

"Thanks, Bill thinks that we should be able to do a series of interviews over the next few weeks. Do you have any interest?"

"I guess so, but I thought we were pretty bland and Mr. O'Brien did not seem very interested or very pleased."

"So that sounds like we have a deal. Bill needs to understand the topic before he can become the public know-it-all people see on television. It's funny, I have never figured out how a guy that would run over a bed of nails with a small foreign car strapped to his back for someone he considered a marginal friend could be hated by so many millions of people who never watch his show. He is a very good guy and trust me, a very quick study. Well, a quick study on everything but business issues, where he seems determined not to let the facts interfere with his conclusion. Anyway, let Ginny take you to the guy with the four-hundred-page contracts and we'll figure out a way to make you a national heartthrob." *Brilliant*, she thought, *just brilliant. He probably doesn't even know your name and you call him a national heartthrob.* Cho, now a bit red, turned around and left stage right, *right out of his thoughts.*

"OK, Mr. Geekhead, let's go see Willie." Ginny took Geekhead by his Popeye arm.

The little one that left is really attractive, really attractive. Cute, thought Geekhead, *very cute.*

"What is this Geekhead stuff?"

"Just a twelfth floor joke. We saw your resume and we all expected a little guy with glasses and a bow tie. Let's go get your contract signed. Then you need to understand television a whole lot better than you did during the taping. You will need to get together with Jenn to, shall we say, spice up your style. She said the only time she is open is for a quick dinner after the show tomorrow night. Does that work for you?" Ginny thought to herself that Cho's schedule for these kinds of meetings was never for dinner. She might have told her a dozen times to never, ever schedule a dinner meeting with anyone, particularly men. *Very interesting.*

This all sounds like fun, thought Geekhead. *That Cho girl is cute. I wonder what her deal is—probably best to keep some distance between my world and the entertainment field. These people eat their young from everything I have ever read.*

~

187

Back from Camp David after a drive from Reagan National to the White House, Sackman and Matta were at the conference table with a few staffers ready to go to work to re-elect their president. How silly it was that they could not use the White House lawn for the helicopter instead of wasting time flying to Reagan for appearances. The ride to the White House was always painfully slow.

Now, decisions loomed. The President had to formally move quickly on the Vice President to make sure speculation stopped and the convention delegates did not feel empowered to enter the discussion. They needed to develop a compelling story as to why the President was going to have Beloved again as his running mate. In the minds of the assembled team, this was a story that belonged on the New York Times best-seller list, as fiction.

The team also needed to move quickly to develop a strategy that would marginalize the American Exceptionalism Party. They had to move quickly to undo whatever the AEP had accomplished and Sackman's people needed to create a carefully crafted message that defined the AEP and recreated their message to one of fear, as opposed to hope. They would need surrogates on the television stations this coming Sunday. They also needed to develop a Mallory Cloud story. She still had a great following in the Democratic Party and she definitely needed to be marginalized; this might prove very difficult. Her press release contradicting the President's press release would have wheels.

Herman Sackman, self-appointed Wizard, matched up a handful of Tums with three successive swallows of flavored coffee. Once a hard drinker, the Wizard had begun to worry about his drinking habits a few years before and virtually overnight became a very occasional social drinker. What a wonderful thing was the White House mess that could create coffee drinks that easily rivaled Starbucks and with no cost to the consumer. A great perquisite. That being said, Sackman was skinny as can be and neither his health nor his demeanor was helped by all of the caffeine included in these drinks that tasted so good. *Weird,* he thought, *my weight never changes, but I have become flabby and hyperactive. Being skinny and being in great shape were not necessarily a certain combination.* Tonight, he was thinking, very rare for him, that a smooth glass of Jamison accompanied by a thousand-dollar prostitute would be a great deal more fun than spinning away a brilliant presentation by a guy who days before he had wondered why he was running for president. (Unlike President Carter, Sackman felt absolutely no guilt when he wished for the

Jamison or the thousand-dollar hooker. As he might have the occasional glass of scotch, he knew he would not have the remotest idea what to do with the thousand-dollar hooker. He was married, and in his mind he equated sex with love and simply could not understand the whole prostitute thing.)

"Ideas, ideas, quickly. We have to create several plans here. You guys know the drill: attack, attack, attack, unless the target would be viewed as a victim. I need to know how to classify Jordon Scotch. Scotch looks like he could fight any of us to the death if he got his arms around us and he seemed like a pretty good guy, so I need to know how we undress him. In particular, is there a health angle to pursue? Can we find a blogger to question if he is the father of his children? How can we marginalize this guy?"

Karen Kirby was neither new to the team nor enamored with the American Exceptionalism Party. Her background made her an integral part of the team. As a graduate of the ultra liberal Columbia School of Journalism who wrote the first draft of nearly half of the President's speeches, she was intellectually the key to his successful teleprompter experiences. Her friends called her Ms. Teleprompter and she physically fit the bill with a curveless, five-foot-seven-inch frame topped by a frizzy hairdo that reached about half way to her shoulders. Without a doubt, one of the skinniest non-anorexic people on the planet. Karen Kirby could consume four thousand calories a day and not gain an ounce. She was the most, or second most, outspoken liberal in this conference room and probably walked that talk more than anyone else as well. She took the Metro to work, was generally annoyed that the building was not too hot or too cold, and therefore using too much energy, and it drove her absolutely crazy when the President used the 747 as Air Force One rather than a smaller, more fuel efficient airplane when going on one day ventures throughout the country. She offered a rebuttal to the American Exceptionalism Party Convention in liberaleese: "Herman, this convention was a joke and we all know it. They pounded on the President without offering a single idea or plan. They don't have an answer for health care, they don't have an answer for the economy, they offer nothing. I would…"

"OK, we have heard from the village idiot," the Wizard/Enforcer interrupted Kirby. "Karen, this is not about issues, it is about perceptions. Governing is about issues; politics is about images and perceptions. You know that better than anyone in the entire damn building. Let's put the policy crap in a sock here and focus on images."

Kirby folded her legs under her bottom and sulked like a little girl. She reached into her purse for a Snickers and consumed it mindlessly. The only thing she could have added to the picture was to begin sucking her thumb. Sackman had seen this behavior many times before and knew she would re-enter the debate with the best ideas. Usually, the time span between sulking and great ideas was about fifteen minutes.

Ray Matta entered the discussion. Putting down his omnipresent presidential coffee cup, he tried to review the turf in fairly stark terms: "Let's go through the players: Vincent, we should already have the research and what he voted for and against. We need something to push on him. We need to have someone read all of his political writings and campaign statements, there should be something in there to cause people to be concerned. I need to know how often he voted, both in the Senate and in the voting booth, whether he has ever joined any organization that is right wing, all that stuff. When did he vote with and when did he vote against the President's programs? I want to know who all of his political clients are and whether we can make him into something awful. Mallory, let's leave the former first couple to Herman and me. Smith, I think, is a non-player. His five minutes are over and we can ignore him. I suspect Scotch is going to be the hard one. See if we can scare up something that would indicate that he does not care about the Hispanic community, you know the drill, the guy who walked away from the ghetto when he had five dollars in his pocket. Anyone else?"

Robbie Awazin, dressed as always in dark slacks, an orange shirt, blue sport coat and bizarre tie actually stood up from his chair and offered his thoughts: "We should be immediately attacking George Vincent and Smith as a rich Republican businessman, men who haven't done anything in their entire lives worth mentioning except make money and gain power." Awazin walked while he talked. "Let's define them as climate change deniers and against anything that will put working people back to work. Don't forget about the fact that Smith is one really rich dude. We…"

Matta cut him off: "Too much powder, we need to save that characterization for Paul Roland and his gang. We cannot label former Democrats as suddenly becoming Republicans and being soundly against things that the record will show they voted for and voted with the President. We need to finesse the attacks on the AEP and use your words for the Republicans. Remember, Vincent said in his speech that he stumped for the President and

190

that is the truth. We do need to know where they have parted company, or maybe if they have parted company and this is only about power."

Next in this line of idea people was Rula Wast. She was the youngest person at the table. This African American studies major from UCLA made Karen Kirby look like Rush Limbaugh. Wast offered that the President should run on his record: health care, comprehensive immigration reform and economic stimulus. Sackman was polite as Wast had access to the President's wife. "No Rula, we need to sell ourselves to the middle. We already own our base."

Kirby had her feet back on the floor and provided her thoughts: "Incumbents need to be for something and need to embrace what they have accomplished. We need to run with and for what we believe in rather than attack everyone. We cannot fall into the defensive strategy that undid the Republicans." This was viewed as equally unhelpful by Sackman. But her next comment had the two door guards listening: "My research and my instincts tell me that Vincent trumps Roland right out of contention. The focus has to be Vincent. And my best guess is we need to make them twins. It is going to turn out that Vincent is pretty conservative."

Herman Sackman put a sheet of paper in front of the seven people at the table. It had come from one of their private polling companies and was still wet from last night's polling. In the voice of a man that had worked with the President for almost eight years in the stress-filled environment of the Presidency: "Read this!" The team complied.

"OK, what are you trying to tell me?" asked Matta.

"Well, we are getting fucking killed in the Electoral College polling. And..." started Sackman.

Matta: "God damn it, we are something like ten points ahead in the polls! Don't tell me we are getting killed!"

"Ray, we are winning California, New York and Illinois by percentages never seen in a presidential election. Not too damn amazing considering the amount of money we send to those states. Not too damn surprising as that is where all of the stimulus money went and where there are the three largest cities in the country. But winning by thirty percent in an uncontested New York ain't going to do you too much good in Ohio if you lose by a dozen votes. With ninety days left until this the election, there is about zero chance we are going to be the leader in electoral votes in this election."

191

"OK, foul mouthed Harry, I know, I know. That is what this data says. Now, no one is going to be here unless you have some ideas. Let's get with it."

"Sorry," Sackman emitted with no feeling. "The good news is I think we—he—is going to come in first and achieve this fifty percent margin in the Electoral College. This is not in the bag, but if we can reasonably, and they can quietly, enhance the Black vote in a couple of Southern states, those Independent Democrats, aka the AEP, are actually going to help us convert a few Reds to Blues. Our strategy has to be pointed out. Vincent and Roland are the same conservative assholes, just two different names.

"Now, look at this press release by Mallory, this ain't good either," offered Sackman.

~

From the desk of Mallory Cloud:

FOR IMMEDIATE RELEASE

MALLORY CLOUD, A WOMAN AT PEACE

WASHINGTON D.C., August 8, 2012, 9:15 p.m. — Earlier today, I was summoned to Camp David for a thirty second meeting with the President. The entire conversation, and I apologize for the language used by the President, is outlined below.

President: "No need to talk about this. Resign or be fired, which is it?"

Cloud: "Good to see you too, Mr. President. I will not resign; everything I have been asked..."

"Herman, send the press release that said I fired her ass."

At that moment, the President of the United States turned his back on me and returned to his office at Camp David. The President did not thank me for my service or provide me the opportunity to offer a single full sentence. A tape of the "discussion" will be made available on my website later this evening.

Many Americans may wonder why I determined to support the American Exceptionalism Party's candidate for the Presidency. So much of what is wrong with this Presidency can be gleaned from this experience. So many of the reasons for my decision to support another candidate and not resign from either my position as Secretary of State or the Democratic Party can also be gleamed from this experience.

We need to elect a President who is more interested in competence and the United States of America than he is in politics and his own ego. It is a shame that this is the case, but it is the reality.

The press release missed the night's O'Brien show except on the West Coast repeat where the press release would be showing on the bottom of the screen while O'Brien was speculating about the nature of Mallory's press release.

~

193

THURSDAY, AUGUST 9, 2012

The conversation that was taking place between Rhonda Peterson from *Absolute Mortgage* and Reid McAllister, a television packager, was fairly heated.

"What do you mean the price has quadrupled for September, October and the first week of November? You are not talking about just the major networks Reid, you are talking about cable, not even big time cable; we are talking about reruns of *Father Knows Best* for goodness sakes. It cannot be the damn election, four years ago there was hardly a blip on the radar screen from the election and it sure as hell isn't the economy? Do I need to go price your services after all of these years, Reid?"

McAllister was not surprised by this conversation. He had been having this same conversation all day, just with different people. The networks and the cable networks had instantly gone from beggars to choosers and his monthly game of waiting until the last minute to buy time, which had been magic for three years, was now a catastrophe for the next ninety plus days. He had been frozen out, which meant that his customers had been frozen out. McAllister was afraid that both he and his customers were screwed.

Suddenly, there was virtually no media space available from Labor Day through the election and it had happened within a period of about three days. Oh, there were some buy-out clauses available, but the cost of the buy-outs plus the advertising costs were way too rich. The buyers were apparently all political guys—despite the protestations of his clients—and they were pre-paying, so there was not going to be any fallout for anyone to buy in the secondary market. His sources said a great deal of the buying was being done without any realistic price discussions and by people apparently unfamiliar with the business. When he opened *The International Journal*, he noticed that all of the media companies had increased their profit estimates for the third quarter. This had required them to file special notices with the Securities and Exchange Commission and they had all appeared within a few days of each other.

Rhonda started into the same conversation that McAllister had memorized from both sides of the telephone. A cigar smoker, at this point, McAllister was certain he could have coughed his way through both sides of the conversation for twenty minutes at the *Comedy Store*. But, Rhonda was a great client and had to be listened to. "Reid, I need these ads to sell my insurance products. I cannot be out of business for three months because an election is taking place. What is really available?"

"Nothing, nada, nothing that makes sense for your business. And don't ask me about radio, unless you have a need for something in a foreign language which is not Mexican or Japanese, it is all sold out. Happened in seventy-two hours. I don't have a clue where the money is coming from, but if you hit Yahoo financial, you will see that the stocks of Comcast, Disney and all of the others are each up about ten percent based on high third quarter earnings expectations. I actually bought some options on Disney a few days ago and Thomas and I will use the profits to offset our lost profits from our business. Here is a tidbit for you, both the Democrat and the Republican parties are screaming too. Apparently they were playing a little Russian roulette and there is no space available for those guys either."

"What do I do?"

"The only opportunity is magazines and newspapers. We know newspapers do not work for your business, maybe any business, but magazines are pretty good."

"Are they loaded up?"

"Yes, that is the downside. Whoever is buying the time on television is also buying magazine space, but you know magazines, they can deliver as much magazine space as they can sell. There just may be pages and pages of advertising between stories."

"Well," getting seriously frustrated and annoyed, "I don't know what to do. Direct mail has not worked very well in the past few years. What do you think about e-mail lists?"

"Rhonda, anyone that is considering using direct mail is out of their minds. I think a number of traditional advertising campaigns are going to be S.O.L. for television and radio and their only way to spend money is going to be direct mail. This will mean postal workers trying to carry extra loads and squeezing that stuff into mailboxes. I cannot believe that an insurance brochure will not go the way of the political mailers, right into the old green canister for recycled paper, the famous three foot drop, without having been read. E-mail too may be worse. Just hit that old delete button."

"No one is going to read it. And let me finish the thought pattern, Kid. I cannot imagine that anyone, I mean anyone, is going to be answering the telephone after the first of September. Those political boiler rooms are going to be going crazy and I understand that the pollsters from Rasmussen to Bob from Accounttemps are absolutely sold out for getting survey data to the political guys."

"Oh, Twitter and the Internet—maybe some banner advertising—gone."

"Oh my God, Reid, why?"

"Like I said, there is more money chasing this election than there is media. We are not sure where the money is coming from; it is really odd. Nothing like it has ever happened before. Might even keep the newspapers in business for an extra week. Kid, we have been doing business together for a long time, I suggest that the best use of your advertising dollars is to contact your existing clients directly and hunker down for three months. Send them personally typed letters and try getting them to answer the telephone as a customer, not a prospect. Then let's bulk up for the winter. As they—whoever they are—say, it is what it is!

"Thanks, Reid, I think. Talk to you soon."

While it would become apparent to the rest of the world fairly quickly, the folks who had been at Max's Place had kept their word. The media buy had been almost instantaneous and had surprised the marketplace as well as the Democratic and Republican experts. The prepayment, which each multimillionaire could provide, was an instant hit in both network and cable. A few purchased paid programming half hours on the late night air. Crazy. The radio shows were putting their regular customers on limited advertising and bilking the political types at price levels that were both unprecedented and apparently, unnoticed.

~

Delf Spooner was pure capitalist. He was the CEO of a monstrously large and complicated international conglomerate that included one national television network (RBC), dozens and dozens of local television stations and four talk show stations. The talk show stations all presented the view from the right. Spooner prided himself in going with the flow and often thought to himself how smart he was to be the purveyor of the most ardent right-wing radio along with newspapers and television stations that had occasionally been referred to as left of left. The conglomerate was also into every manufacturing industry in the world. The business made money, lots and lots of money for both Spooner and his shareholders. An administration happy with its coverage could dole out favors, which were not understandable to the local guy on the street. With right-wing radio and left-wing television, Spooner had it all and he had it both ways.

His empire had long since given up the coat, the tie and the dress. Spooner always found this to be a stupid decision and he continued to wear a traditional suit and tie. Apparently, his staff thought of him as eccentric and did not see this as leadership; no one seemed to follow his lead. Today, as always, his was the only coat or tie in the room. He was convinced that the cost of business casual was significantly more expensive than just throwing on a white shirt, tie and yesterday's suit. He was also convinced that a forty-year-old woman looked a damn sight better from behind in a dress than in a pants suit with a forty-year-old soft bottom seemingly filling up a necessarily over-sized bottom section. Ah well, comments he could surely never share. He sat at the head of the table and looked at his team of business gurus.

"OK, I am worried." He looked down at his key executives. There was not one of them that Spooner thought was anything but exceptional. He had a business plan that seemed to work for him and his companies. Good times, bad times, his executives rated their subordinates. In every division, there were always eleven different possible results. One through ten, and other. The rules were as simple as they were unusual. Two of the top ten individuals had to be terminated, with honor, every year. Of the rest, two new executives had to be inserted into the top ten from the next category and the remaining eleventh category was subject to the vagaries of the market. The eleventh category included more than ninety percent of the employees of the media empire. Some employees spent decades doing their job without any interest of being promoted from the bottom part of the top ten; this made them more comfortable in their jobs and lives, despite their market-place risk. Others remained successfully and happily in the eleventh category and the small remaining group at the very top who were the aggressive decision makers either succeeded or failed based on their nimbleness.

In this room, each executive had an annual contract, renewal based solely upon the whims of Delf Spooner. In many ways, they had no more job security than a professional football player who could be cut during the exhibition season, thereby making his contract null and void, or Juan, the car dryer at the car wash, who had no union, no access to legal help and only wished that whoever was president would create an immigration policy that would include him.

Despite his rules for the rest of RBC, Spooner rarely made changes to his elite ten in corporate. These men and women had survived his system and they were good, exceptionally good. Spooner expected no loyalty, but gave his employees enormous loyalty from his end. When a top ten executive took a CEO position with another company, Spooner often gave that person a significant bonus for his past contributions. The rules on new job opportunities were simple. If offered, Spooner expected to know immediately and if unhappy, Spooner expected to be told that as well. Violation of that policy meant instant evisceration, but it was so explicit and so embedded in the culture, it had been a very long time since Spooner found out someone was looking for a new job from anyone except the job seeker.

He looked directly at Samantha Whitspon, the president of all media operations. "Samantha, how are we doing in the ratings?" Whitspon was dressed in 2012 business casual for women. Spooner, if asked, would have told her to figure out a way to see herself from behind and then either go to a gym more often or find a new style of dressing, maybe a dress.

Whitspon, no kid at forty-eight, looked down for a moment, thought carefully and responded: "Weird, Boss. I would be lying to tell you I have my finger on the whys, but the results are fine, actually as you know, this quarter will be significantly better than fine. These new political buyers will turn these next three months into windfall profit territory, although I hope to receive all of the credit for the windfall. But, I really worry about the next four years. And trying to marry that concern up with the political perks that are attached to the stations that support the presidential winner for the rest of the business is a riddle at the moment. Understanding how good coverage for the President ties to other corporate areas is, as the President says, *beyond my pay grade.*"

Samantha continued, "Our national television strategy on personnel has seemed okay on the news side: old white male anchor, big-titted, young weather ladies, and an ex-jock for the little bit of sports we throw at the viewers. Focus our news attention on what the President is saying and doing and turn a blind eye to virtually anything and everything that makes the President look bad. I do feel pretty guilty about not providing more coverage to our courageous troops in Afghanistan for a host of reasons I will save for a lunch meeting one day. After listening to George Vincent last night, I feel even guiltier about not attacking the President flat out for his lack of leadership in the Koreas or, frankly, a hundred other issues.

"We have those two clowns late at night and remind them daily that we at RBC only make enemies of people who cannot hurt us. God, they have made a number of enemies, but no one of consequence. I have been unable to find that slightly left of center black personality to take over one of the two late spots, but I see enough of the Comedy Shop that I more than occasionally get a free rum and coke. I wish Cosby had a son or daughter in the industry. We are a solid number two here. It may actually be the correct place to be, but I'd like to have a spin as number one. The advertising revenues are okay, but not outstanding, ignoring this crazy election spending. By the way, the political advertising is coming from ultra wealthy individuals and they seem paranoid about not breaking any law and absolutely we can find no price point. Like I said, weird.

"In radio, although I get hits regularly from the White House, we capture those same six to eight million conservative listeners every day. This is the most loyal listening demographic in the history of the industry. The only issue here is that they do not buy anything and too often the advertising proceeds do not match up with the number of ears. We have doubled down on the accompanying websites and these sites get the same eyes whose ears we already have on radio. They do not buy very much here either. It is a fairly interesting dynamic in that they only buy what they agree with. We had that anti-FairTax book a year ago and that book sold bupkis. Since our main guy wrote it, I read it and if you read that book, you wouldn't have the word FairTax on your spell check. Yet, a few thousand copies against his book on Christianity, which sold in the hundreds of thousands, go figure? The book has to be the most boring, over arching discussion of Christian thinking ever written. But, a lesson learned. I would change nothing on the radio as we make a little money and virtually no one else makes any money. As to the web in its purest sense, we are experimenting with a couple of websites, one very far right and the other very far left. These get traffic, but the ability not to have some posting that recommends that we either assassinate the Pope or the President is awfully expensive. And stuff gets by us and when it does, we get criticized to death. Still an experiment.

"As I think we have discussed, the liberal talk show hosts cannot hold an audience. I have always guessed there are fewer liberals driving around all morning. Not sure why, but that is what I think. Maybe they like music more, but there is just no loyal audience out there for the picking.

"The newspapers would be the eight-million-pound elephant in the room if we were not trimming them down to produce something similar to what Thomas Paine probably handed out in 1773, pamphlets, just a few pages. This business is dead and its only hope is Kindle, iPad and the other electronic delivery devices. Unfortunately, with the Internet and the banner advertising that drives the Internet sites, paying for a newspaper as opposed to looking on the net for no cost news will probably just make the business close at a slower rate. With all due respect to Murdoch, people don't know quality from no quality and as long as they can get what they think is news from the free Internet sites, they will do it. I think it was Newsday that offered *for pay* Internet newspaper service and received thirty-five customers in its first four months. We won't go in that direction.

"There is a surprisingly strong market for solid, two-sided opinion, but most editorial pages, ours included, are as one sided as fly paper. We will introduce a daily Internet opinion newspaper right after the election and I suspect that we will get some traction there. Banner advertising will be our revenue source. No news, just opinion and responses from Internet users. We will see. The rest of the industry will just chew up paper and lose union jobs until the business is just an historical footnote. I will add here that absent some significant crisis or change in our schools, the answer here is some type of device that can deliver news by voice, but in some presentation format that works for a different generation. Something more than radio and less than talk show conversation. That is an area we are beginning to think about at the moment, but in the long run, it might be the future of news. Something the listener agrees with that is available instantly." Samantha finished her newspaper eulogy.

Spooner, as usual, had listened intently and asked the following: "What is going to happen to us if the President is sautéed in this election?"

"Well, there are two possibilities, I think. If Congressman Roland does it for the Republicans, that is bad news on all fronts. No surprise here, the Republicans honestly believe we have sold them out on TV and with the newspapers with our positive coverage of this president after we savaged his Republican predecessor every day for eight years. Guilty as charged, Boss, but our television ratings in the last Republican administration were off the charts. I suspect the non-media side of the business will also pay a price. On the radio side, a real conservative would kill us. Who would listen if our boys have only positive things to say? We'll probably have to go to music a few more hours of the day as our boys can attack anyone but a conservative. On the newspaper level, doesn't matter, dead man walking.

"Now if the American Exceptionalism Party were to pull this off, that is a winner. Just the great unknown of where everyone would land after the election, what would happen in every state, how the House of Representatives would be led and managed, worse in the Senate. If these guys win, the all is forgiven banner will not be hoisted by anyone. Pure leadership chaos. I think Pelosi, as you know, I call her Hands because"—there were a few knowing guffaws and serious laughter at the *Hands* comment—"there is no Botox cure for hands. She could be out of the picture with an American Exceptionalism Party win. I think that is coming regardless. I am too young to know if she was ever a great Democratic leader in the House of Representatives, but no one could believe that there is not someone in the Democratic Party who could do a better job after the past two years since she lost the Speakership. I continue to recall her comment that unemployment insurance is the best possible stimulus. Sorry, but she is brain-dead. On radio, this AEP is a wow, and maybe for quite a while a significant increase in listeners. Everyone will want to follow the growth of a new party. The conservatives would hate her and that would be good news for radio. This country has never had three truly viable parties and…"

"Actually, Samantha, in the early middle 1800s we had three relatively viable parties. Think Whigs," corrected Bobby Joe Smolden, the CFO, without any malice, but trying to keep her correctly on course.

"Whatever, Bobby Joe. Our right-wing nuts would be able to talk a stone to death on these issues and their audience will be interested. Our boys can continue to attack everyone. That is a very good thing." Whitspon was not taken back a bit by Smolden's comment. That was the way RBC and Delf Spooner operated. It was ok.

"To answer the unasked question, the President would be a same o' same o' for us. We are currently best positioned for him to serve another four years, but we would be more profitable with Vincent. I, we, would be unready for Roland."

Spooner looked at his assembled group: "Guys, I think it is time to make a calculated bet. Samantha, let's expose the President for what he is and to do that, we need to find out what he really is."

"Oh Boss," jumped in Regina Goldman, the president of retail sales... but this part of the discussion was about to be quickly over.

Spooner snapped: "Regina, you have been blaming this guy's economic plan—or lack thereof—for the continuing fall in your sales for exactly thirty-one months. I don't think the guy can add, subtract multiply and divide, or understands anything about economics. Hell, I'd take my high school senior in that debate. Of course, he will be attending Notre Dame on a full scholarship in the fall." Ten people laughing out loud was not unusual at RBC. In this case, there was no one at the table who did not know that Hank Spooner was the top tight end football recruit in the country and that Spooner had been sweating out the results of his son's entrance tests for months. Putting Hank up against the President in an economic debate was the ultimate intellectual insult to the President.

"Samantha, I try to stay out of your way in media, but I do want you to put a team on the comments of the Secretary of State this week, both her press release and her Monday interview with O'Brien on Fox News.

"More important, I want to see a full ten minutes on the news, let's say one week from Monday, on what information has not been released on the President after four years of asking. Test scores, entrance exams, but not the birth certificate; you name it, we talk about it. If the accusations are real and my stomach tells me they are with respect to his grades, let's chew him up, a coordinated mission, radio, television and newspapers and see if we get any reaction. Hell, the last time someone did something like this, we found out the senior senator from Massachusetts had about the worst grades in the history of his university." He paused, looked at his president of aerospace, Troop Rasmer, and received a comforting pastoral nod that he did not think this was crazy. They were having lunch later, but if Troop sensed trouble, he would have immediately positioned Spooner to think this over more carefully and suggest the group meet again the following morning. "Sam, I want this in three pieces following the inquiry piece and then let our network guys and radio guys run with it. Let's make ourselves a story here and milk it everywhere we can.

"Troopster, let's you and I make sure I am out of town the morning after Samantha's first report. Once we do this report, everyone will feel obligated to pile on. After a couple of days, we'll just be another of those overpaid investigative news organizations.

Spooner rose, he had never taken off his grey suit coat, and headed for the door. It was nice to be king.

Samantha did not give her personal misgivings a second thought. If this direction were a mistake, Delf Spooner would admit his mistake and acknowledge his ownership of the idea. That was Delf Spooner and RBC. Before Delf closed the door on the way out, Samantha Whitspon was working on her operational strategy.

~

FRIDAY, AUGUST 10, 2012

The multiple roles of the political talk show hosts are to find viewers, keep viewers listening for prolonged periods and keep them listening day after day. There is some math involved in creating and sustaining the audience. It takes unique abilities to maintain the audience and finally, the financial value of the audience is very much dependent upon the demographic of the listeners.

The platform presented by the American Exceptionalism Party was the grist of political radio. Change and fear drive people to listen and the possibility of a massive change in the American electorate was confirmed by the appearance of the two former Presidents of the United States on the AEP stage. The appearance of Mallory Cloud gave the added element of drama. That drama was enhanced by the exchange of blunt press releases. This was all talk radio needed to be interesting for a few days.

What would be best for the United States was not a factor in the decisions on how to couch the message and the discussion. What was best for the talk show hosts themselves was the meaningful question in couching the discussion.

Treason to the country? Treason to the Democratic Party? Treason to the Republican Party? Destruction of the two-party system? A conspiracy to elect the Republican candidate? A conspiracy to elect a Democratic candidate? All had appeared on the radio beginning at 6:00 a.m. EDT on Wednesday morning, August 8, and it easily continued into Friday.

The political elite were all listening to the message. And the message was mixed. Perfect for talk radio.

The right-wing radio hosts blasted the American Exceptionalism Party as a party with a lack of political consciousness. Theirs was an attack against the values of the right: anti-abortion, anti-deficit, strong conservative cultural issues. For the talk show hosts that offered daily, three-hour speeches, this was pretty good radio, but not terrific. For the shows that featured call-ins, it was just perfect radio and by afternoon, the focus was on Mallory Cloud and her rift with the President. The possibility of the American Exceptionalism Party being a meaningful player was not a part of their conversation. The conversation was moving towards Mallory.

The few remaining left wing radio hosts that had viable audiences, and there were only very few, talked about race and the sell out by the white middle class voter. The race issue was displayed in the same manner as the political appointments of President George W. Boone. That Jordon Scotch was not an authentic minority person, which came as just as big a surprise to Jordon Scotch it did as to Judge Thomas and others when it was their turn in the barrel. Apparently, race was not a component of race.

The sell out of the white, middle-class voter argument used Mallory Cloud as the poster child. This was great radio for the truly committed. The possibility of the AEP being a meaningful player was not a part of their conversation.

A few middle right talk radio show hosts talked about the politics of a third party. These shows featured guests with an historical perspective and queried whether their listeners found the AEP position compelling. These radio shows were giving and getting a completely different view of the AEP Convention. The country's middle seemed very interested in moving away from each existing political parties and the issues appeared to be two-fold, nut cakes and trust. In some sense the listeners were voicing their concern that the nut cakes of each party—and some appointed czars—were so far away from the mainstream that they did not represent the country and that neither party was honoring their election rhetoric.

As the polling data appeared, the conversations would undoubtedly move in different directions. While there was extreme disappointment in the AEP camp and some elation in the Democratic and Republican camps, outside of the middle right talk shows, talk radio had it wrong, very, very wrong. The one thing talk radio had going for itself was that it was rarely wrong for very long and flexible like a female, twelve-year-old German gymnast. The discussions would quickly move to match the hot buttons of their audiences.

The four networks and the big cable television networks covered the AEP Convention like a news event and therefore their instant interest was on Mallory Cloud as much as anything else. Television did not see the potential impact of a third party, forgetting Ross Perot and not knowing so much of what was happening around them. They too would be quickly influenced by the polls.

~

Throughout the United States, in every major city, the American Exceptionalism Party Convention caused deeper thinking and more handwringing
within one special business community than any other. The political consulting business is one of the largest consulting businesses in the country. By
2012, a school board race in a city of 30,000 people generally had six candidates, six consulting firms, six election strategies, mailers, meetings and
as most of the public referred to it, all of the normal bullshit. The national
races made the school board candidate's political consultants look like little
boys and girls.

Before the convention, the reality of the American Exceptionalism Party
had not set in within either of the major parties at the national level, more
so the consultants at the local level. While the national level of the American political system garners the most attention, all politics is essentially and
eventually local and local still somewhat describes congressional races.

The AEP Convention made every consultant edgy, very edgy. And it
caused each to consider the reality of this sea change of national political
activity in the context of their specific campaigns; *WIFMC, What's in it for my
candidate? And WIFM, What's in it for me?* At the state and local level, the questions were fairly straightforward:

1. What would the AEP do to fundraising for my candidate? Will it
   matter at all? Will it be a drain on the campaign? Are the people
   funding my candidate's campaign going to take sides in the AEP
   game?
2. Should, must, can my candidate take a position or change a position
   with respect to the national campaign? Is this a positive? Can I talk
   the candidate out of standing up and taking a position at least for a
   while, as any position will cost my candidate votes?
3. What does our individual, our micro-electorate, in my tiny community think about this and how do I need to change our message?
   Do I change my message?
4. Will this event energize the total electorate toward the election in
   general or take away from the interest, if there was any to begin
   with, in my candidate's campaign?
5. What about money and this rumor that someone had come in and
   done an unprecedented media buy?

The questions were endless, the meetings over the next few days would
be endless and depending upon the consulting contracts, there would be

little, if any, financial gain to the local political consultant. At the national level and in reality, only senators knowledgeably saw themselves in national races and not all of them. The questions were the same, but the ramifications were entirely different for Senate candidates. *Would support for the AEP or lack of support help or hurt my candidate?* While the primary for the AEP had proven interesting, unless the state was an open primary state, of which there are very few, the AEP primary provided very little tangible information as to the voter interest in the AEP because there were so few registered AEP voters. Primaries themselves are generally not worth very much to begin with because they are of interest only to those most politically interested and everyone else is focusing on the beginning of baseball season or what to do with the kids during the summer when schools are not in session.

Was the AEP Convention a once-in-a-lifetime movement in American politics? Was the convention a sea change in the American political vision with a sudden shift to the middle? Was it a single moment with impacts for a single election or was it a one-night story? An endorsement, the lack of an endorsement, or a dodge could suddenly impact the career of the candidate and equally important, the career of the consultant.

On a national level, those candidates who were not on the stage with Senator Vincent and not extremely conservative or extremely liberal generally were told to be very unavailable to the press while the other rail of the political industry went to work, the pollsters. Polls would need to be analyzed from both a national and local vent. While an endorsement of the AEP might present a political risk inside the House of Representatives after the election, voters might be currently lost locally or vice versa. Backtracking on existing commitments was also a problem, or an advantage. Candidates taking on sitting congressmen were developing the mathematics of their constituency. It was a given that the people who had propelled the congressional candidate through the primary election were the exact people who would have been appalled by the AEP Convention, regardless of party affiliation. However, the candidate pursuing an existing congressman's seat, by definition, had to reach into that candidate's constituency. *Who really understood the Scott Brown effect, if there really was one? And this? Was the AEP most meaningful in the close races?*

The scenario that had many a House of Representative consultant worried was in districts that had not been gerrymandered in a manner where seventy percent of the voters were Democratic or Republican. There was the possibility that the Republican candidate who was going to poll forty percent of the vote yesterday, was going to poll fifty-one percent if the Democrats split between the Democratic Party and the AEP. A few previously determined sure losers were already beginning to think about whether they were going to have to move to Washington D.C. because they were silly enough to put their hat in the ring for a congressional seat they never could have won when the music stopped. Conversely, that Republican candidate who had fifty-two percent in a district that was generally Democratic might lose an important sliver to the AEP in the sense that if he took a position in favor of the AEP candidate, his voters might just stay home or skip over his box in the voter booth. *Decisions!*

There is an old Yiddish expression that was being repeated over and over in the minds of campaign consultants throughout the country: *Oy vey!*

Careers of consultants could turn on their next major piece of advice to their clients. Those who guessed right were always in demand for the next election, often moving up the food chain to bigger elections and bigger fees; those who guessed wrong were often doing consumer research for food companies during the next cycle.

The two monsters of the midway, the National Democratic and Republican Committees were apoplectic in terms of what to do next and e-mails were more than numerous in the first forty-eight hours after the AEP Convention. The messages being received by Republican and Democratic candidates were not subtle in terms of requesting funds from their national committees.

The political consultants were, in total, individually and collectively, taken back by what they saw on television at the convention. Political contributors were also in the never, never land of complete change. Candidates—*their* candidates—candidates they had given money to or those who had promised to give money to other Democratic or Republican candidates were on the stage endorsing a candidate for president, a candidate not of their party. *How was this going to work? How were they going to be able to conduct a state-by-state campaign where the elected primary candidate of their party was endorsing the candidate of another party?* This was not the incredibly well respected and very senior Joe Lieberman in 2004 endorsing another candidate who was both a friend and had similar political views on an unpopular war. This was a new party, which had grown out of the old parties, Zeus to the second power.

Early morning meetings were taking place in both national party headquarters. To say initial opinions were varied would be one of the greatest understatements of all time. *If my greatest fundraising asset was a former President of the United States, how do I use him if he is supporting the AEP candidate? Can I send him out to raise money for a senator supporting the President? How do I allocate the money in the bank? How do I raise money?*

The immediate political positions of most of the candidates of both parties was summarized by the response a major donor received on calling a sitting senator who had recently won a hotly contested primary in a swing state: "The senator will be in congressional meetings all day and will be returning calls tomorrow or early next week." Whether there were funerals to attend, meetings to invent, or foreign travel to complete, as the political consultants thought their way through their specific issues, the elected officials of the United States were unavailable for the next couple of news cycles. Political heroism was not in full bloom.

And all of the grinding of teeth was before any of the consultants saw any reputable polling or fully realized that the television and radio time they had not yet purchased was unavailable.

~

Throughout the weekend, a radio advertisement was playing on stations that played oldies but goodies twenty-four hours a day. It was a simple commercial with a woman's voice:

> *How did your congressman vote on the health care bill? Is your medical insurance better and less expensive than it was two years ago or are your benefits being cut and your co-pay increasing? Does your employer sound like he is going to be able to keep your existing plan?*
>
> *This radio commercial was paid for by the National American Healthcare Alliance*—a group no one had ever heard of previously.

~

"Who are *you* going to vote for?" This was the first sound from Professor Hirschel in almost twenty minutes. For the entire meeting, he sat quietly listening at his desk, occasionally rudely glancing at his e-mails.

Professor Hirschel was Molly Tom's mentor. She had a pretty rough time her first few years at the university, but he was always there to encourage her to pick herself up and mentor her to use her almost criminally superior brainpower to succeed. She had matured at least ten years in the four years she had been at the university. This summer, she was on campus doing research for one of the university's Nobel Prize winners on certain auction-type relationships to ultimate price. The Professor loved to watch his students grow as people. This student had gone from timid, unattractive and shy to almost bold and much more attractive. In some ways, actually many ways, she was Eliza Doolittle from *My Fair Lady*.

Hirschel, sixty-four years old and showing every year of it in his well-lined face, was still able to do an hour on the stair climber every morning and then lift considerable poundage of stationary metal. As a result of good genetics and his daily exercise program, not too many of his friends or students could work his consistent eighty hour weeks. He did everything in his power to appear to be a Renaissance man, seemingly knowledgeable on virtually everything. (Of course he knew better about the silliness of the Renaissance man stuff, particularly since his view of a Renaissance man was the ability to speak several languages and he could hardly say hello in any language except English.)

The Professor was teaching two summer school classes. As always, the classes were filled and the textbook was only the beginning. The lectures piled working knowledge on top of textbook knowledge. As always, even in the middle of a one hundred plus degree summer, the classes were filled and the students attended every class.

An accounting professor with rich experience outside the university, The Professor's students were encouraged to know everything that was going on in the world and to read the daily newspaper cover to cover. By everything, he meant *everything*, including the sports page, as he knew that his students' future clients read the sports page every morning. Professor Hirschel would occasionally begin class by asking who had replaced who at third base of some sports team, a part of his teaching methodology that Molly Tom could have done without.

"What does who I am going to vote for have to do with what we just discussed?" offered Tom. The Professor looked across his desk and over his shoes, smiled his all-knowing grin and replied, "Kid, we haven't discussed anything. You have been making a presentation." Long pause and he grinned again. "A good presentation, perhaps, but no discussion yet. Who are you going to vote for?"

"H., to be honest, that is none of your business. I want your opinion on my research!" Tom wasn't the only student on campus who might call Professor Morton Hirschel by his campus nickname, H., as he asked them to do. But in truth there were not more than two students and a couple of professors on campus who had enough self-esteem to talk to The Professor like this. The Professor loved everyone on campus and told anyone who would listen that leaving the world of public accounting and coming to the university was the best decision he had ever made. That being said, as his wife reminded him, far too often in her opinion, he was a pretty intimidating figure.

"OK, let's take a step back. What is the value of research?"

"This yet again? I hate when you do this. The value of research is not on the table." Tom fired back. Greeted by dead silence, another glance at his e-mails and that grin, Tom knew this was getting her nowhere.

"The value of research is to improve future decision-making and I am going to vote for Congressman Roland because I have decided Professors Turk and Booth were right and the President is, in actuality, a socialist. And yes, I hate to be wrong just as much as you do, maybe more and especially in front of you."

Molly Tom gave Hirschel a great deal more credit than he deserved for her future success in the business world. Hirschel loved his students. This one he was certain would remove him more slowly from her radar screen after graduation, but one like the rest, who ultimately would figure out that all he really offered to his students was sound listening skills.

"OK, so what are you going to do with your research? As we have said over and over, good research is supposed to impact decision-making. Just knowing or publishing in an obscure journal is not successful research. You have spent a great deal of time thinking about this, what are you going to do with your research?"

"I don't know."

"So why did you waste your time on the subject matter?"

"Only because some stupid professor told me that I should read the newspaper cover to cover. I realize he did not say I should think about what I read, but I thought that this was implied. I did and then I thought about it some more. It is really weird, but I have become a bit paranoid on this subject and my natural compulsiveness has taken over. People should be alarmed by what I have found."

"OK, let's summarize your thoughts:

If the Electoral College does not select a President, the determination goes to the House of Representatives.

If the House of Representatives gets involved, it gets until January 20 to decide who the President is before the Vice President becomes Acting President. After that, until and if the House ever gets to a decision, the Vice President is the Acting President."

Molly Tom quickly realized that this accounting professor, who she knew had a great interest in politics, was not repeating what she had just told him, he was telling her a process that he clearly knew by heart. She had spent six hours in the library and The Professor apparently could have provided her this information off the top of his head if she had asked. Not one of her political science professors had had a clue what she was talking about and this stupid accounting professor seemed to have written a thesis on the subject.

"The Senate in this situation selects the Vice President from the two highest vote getters for Vice President. Molly, I think that you forgot the piece about each state only getting a single vote in the House of Representatives and their only being allowed to select from the top three vote getters from the Electoral College.

"I miss anything? I assume you looked at the Truman era Succession Act and all of its amendments. What did you think of those?"

"Well, I did not and I don't think I heard you right on the one vote per state thing. I stopped where the Constitution stops and focused on the possibility that the Senate could not get a quorum to select the Vice President and it appeared to me that the Speaker of the House would become President, or using your words, Acting President."

Molly Tom was completely engaged in the conversation. Twenty-one years old, she was excited by The Professor's brainpower. He was excited by her maturation over four years at the university. During those four years, The Professor had watched her grow into an attractive young woman. Now, always attired in tight-fitting blue jeans and either a brightly colored T-shirt, sometimes loose, sometimes tight, with her long dark hair, Molly now always got a good look in the hallway from the male students. If they got to know her, her brainpower was intimidating to most of her colleagues, but she now had that kind of pretty that would last long past her college years. Anorexic teenager to babe in four not so short years.

"The Speaker of the House thing cannot happen. Look, Molly," Molly looked up when she heard the magic word *look*. While The Professor did not know it, every student on campus knew that when he used that specific word, *look*, at the beginning of a sentence, he was going to say something useful and you needed to listen. In poker, they call it a tell. *Look* meant the item was going to be on the next examination and in a private meeting meant that you were talking about something that interested The Professor, or on occasion, simply amused him. Hirschel's approval was exceptionally important to Molly Tom and she knew this was only the beginning of a discussion.

"I will be here tomorrow, why don't you look at a few things and the Succession Act, then we can talk. Read the Senate's quorum rules, but my memory tells me that the Senate can do everything, including hire a foreign army to produce a quorum and therefore, the rules with respect to the Speaker of the House are only useful in cases of classic succession, death or impeachment. The US Senate's rules are quite different than those in Wisconsin where apparently, a state senator can simply cross state lines to avoid voting. That being said, it wouldn't hurt to read the rules of succession, the Succession Act. The Constitution, in one of the amendments, gave Congress permission to create succession rules and I believe this has been done and they have been revised a couple of times.

"At one point, when I was a kid, I think the Postmaster General was in the succession line; I don't even know if we have such a position today. Like I said, when I was a kid, I think the Postmaster General was in line because I remember that my father had either met or knew him.

"And finally, if your research, as you said, is designed to help people make decisions, do some more reading about the Electoral College. The ghosts of both Jefferson and Hamilton haunt both the rules regarding the selection of the President by the House of Representatives as well as the specific actions of the Electoral College. Think about the term *unfaithful elector* and what that means in a three-party race. Oh, and look at how many votes the President needs to get in the House to become President. Then come see me as a fully knowledgeable researcher. Now, let me spend a few minutes trying to think about SAS 70, so as to torture you in your class at 4:30."

Molly Tom was dumbstruck. The Professor seemed to have already done this research himself. Her thoughts were repeated: *He is only an accounting professor after all, all I wanted to know was whether I was right on the Electoral College, which it appears I wasn't.*

And now, she was committed to research the Electoral College and more, who knew what else. Another night lost, maybe more. Without a word, she abandoned his office and closed the door behind her.

The Professor laughed out loud the moment the door closed. Maybe the reason he liked this particular student so much was that she seemed to find topics to talk about that he himself found fascinating. The Professor had read all of this stuff twenty or thirty years before when there was a third-party effort that turned out to be serious only in the eyes of the third-party candidate. He then read the same materials again when Ross Perot made his zigzag effort to become president and unintentionally, or intentionally, elected William Cloud to the office by swaying votes away from President G. W. Boone. He ruminated to himself: *The answers were amazing, maybe even a threat to the United States of America, but the time before last, the candidate was, if he remembered correctly, some guy named Anderson, the only thing he was sure about the vice presidential candidate was that it was not him. Or was it Perot? Well SAS 70 this afternoon and I would guess the Electoral College in a few days.* Even Molly Tom was going to be overwhelmed by the Electoral College and the rules in the House of Representatives, which he always thought of as something schemed up by Groucho and Harpo rather than those so-called genius Founding Fathers.

~

"George, were you involved in that advertisement campaign piece on O'Brien tonight?"

"Honey. I was nominated for president three nights ago and if I guess right, our campaign fund had less than $10,000 before all of that money that came in from that Woo kid's idea. We are just trying to fire up a real fund-raising arm and begin mounting a campaign. What ad?"

Running her right hand through her curls, Mrs. George Vincent looked hard at her husband and asked again: "You really don't know what I am talking about?"

"No, dear, I have no idea."

"Well…first there was a picture of the vice president and the voice on the screen said something like," Marge Vincent attempted to capture the deep voice of the actor that read the advertisement, "The President's first important choice as the Democratic nominee for president was to select a vice president and this was his choice. Then it showed the vice president saying something like there was a three letter word that described what the country needed, J-O-B-S, then the voice asked if there was anything else the country needed to know about the President's decision-making capabilities."

George Vincent laughed out loud. "That is pretty funny. We've known the VP for a long time and I am still trying to figure out how anyone could picture him as a Vice President of the United States. He is still the kind of guy that will go out of his way to find someone who will tape a really stupid remark. Nice enough guy, but Vice President of the United States? Who did the ad? Pretty funny stuff."

"It said it was paid for by some woman I have never heard of and I don't remember her name. Is it some kind of independent campaign?"

"Now that is interesting, really interesting, Honey." Vincent picked up his Blackberry and sent an e-mail to Stanley Martin Wade and asked him to find out what was going on.

"I'm doing talk shows all day and night and someone else is running an independent campaign? I cannot imagine. Boy, I bet that was an expensive joke."

~

SATURDAY, AUGUST 11, 2012

"Even for me, and I am wealthy at levels most people cannot understand, we are talking about an extraordinary amount of money." Isadore Yergler was sitting in his icebox of an office in his specially designed high-backed executive chair. Because his desk was sitting on a small platform, he seemed like a normal size person instead of his five-foot-one-inch. He picked at the ever present full bowl of peanut M&Ms that rested at his left elbow. Yergler was an exercise nut and the M&Ms never seemed to add an extra ounce to his tiny but very well conditioned frame.

"This is really tricky. As you know, we decided that going back in 2012 to the 2008 phony credit card scheme was not going to work and was potentially very dangerous. In retrospect, it was pure luck the Feds never figured out that so many of those credit card donations to the campaign were from people our boiler room either made up or took from telephone lists, a single credit card for a single contribution and then killed off. Hell, there were tens of thousands of contributors who never knew they were contributors. Ah, the magic of technology…"

Sam Dehning was interrupted mid-sentence by Isadore Yergler. "Yeah, pure luck, not as I recall your description at the time," his voice reeking with cynicism. "My God, all the steps we went through to launder the money. All the *fees* we paid to people all over the world to protect the source of my money. Hell, I would have thought only an idiot would not have known there was fraud, yet I don't think the President's people or the regulators ever had a clue as to what happened. Maybe, maybe more likely, no one wanted to know. Thank God we also ran against someone who thought we were as honest as he was. Naïve!"

"Anyway, as I was saying," Dehning continued, "I believe you have to focus on electoral votes. And this is a monster in so many ways. With the President's policies in his first two years, it is amazing that Democrats have a majority in any state, yet we still control some of the major state legislatures. Gerrymandering is such a wonderful thing, or an equally horrible thing.

"We warned this president to take it slow. Hell, we made him and yet he thought he knew everything about being president and that he could gut his way through anything. Rhetoric has limits, I told him. The moment he began talking down to the people about health care, awful. He has begun to sound like Cliff from Cheers, a remarkable, but empty-headed know-it-all. I knew we were going to take a pretty good beating in 2010. The *silly* description of that police officer, that cost us a block of voters we will never get back. Candidly, off script, he apparently cannot hold his own against the VP and that is really saying something."

"Gee," the next word Yergler offered, "when I was at Colorado, we had an alumni head cheerleader who was just a complete embarrassment and frankly, in my opinion, an idiot. I always used to say, he may be an idiot, but he was our idiot!" Yergler laughed at his own joke.

"We only need four more years before the actions of this president and the 111th Congress will become virtually impossible to undo. People are not going to give back their health care, they are not going to reduce tax rates on the rich and God knows, they won't be able or willing to increase taxes on themselves. The EPA rules are impossible to undo and they have already killed dirty energy. Not my problem, but half of West Virginia is unemployed. With debt at all time high levels for the Federal government, by the end of his second term the United States will have no alternatives to becoming a fourth rate financial power. There won't be a dime available for investment in anything. With our investment strategy of leveraged investments in other currencies and our quiet takeover of the clean energy business in the United States, in four years, I will have more money than Crassus."

"What are your real goals, Isadore? You already have more money than Midas or Crassus, whoever he is."

"Crassus…Rome…read a book some day. Oh, I don't know, I guess I may just be trying to undo a wrong committed to my family almost sixty years ago. Most of our family was on the Saint Louis when FDR wouldn't let the ship dock in the United States. The family voyage ended back in Germany and that was that.

"We are all tribal, Sammy, and when the *elite* in the United States of America are feeling just a bit more pain, I will figure that we are even." Yergler raised his hands and continued: "Don't tell me that all of the people involved in that decision are dead and this would be as dumb as paying reparations to the families of slaves. Some things are just not logical and we had this conversation four years ago. My rules were simple, help me elect this idiot and keep me out of jail. Those rules have not changed.

"This Congress is not going to destroy the United States without a re-elected president, it is just going to make the people feel a bit more pain and maybe, just maybe, cause all of those old school politicians to leave office. God knows nothing really changed when the Republicans took over the House of Representatives. God love that odd little man from Nevada. OK, enough history, where do you want me to put my money?"

"Isadore, the only way we can play this is through an independent personal campaign. And frankly, I think you are going to have to be out front as the funding source; it might even be easier for you to be the sole contributor. This means not seeing the President or even talking to him for several months."

"That's pretty funny. Four years ago, you had me orchestrate the fraud of the century with those credit card contributions and now, instead of a potential felon, you seem to want me to be Simon Pure."

"Well, no one ever doubted my clarity of speech," responded Sam Dehning. Dehning could never decide whether he hated himself for this kind of consulting, but supporting a wife and five kids along with a fairly young and needy mistress was killing his checkbook. At thirty-four years old, he was beginning, perhaps more than beginning, to show the strain of what had become a double life. His wife believed he was just a wonderful person, not Tiger Woods. She thought he was all over the world working when he was usually less than two hundred miles away trying to spend as much time as possible in his mistress's bedroom. His wife had significant problems after the birth of their fifth child in less than seven years and he was unwilling, and in his mind unable, to remain anything close to celibate regardless of whether she really could or could not regain her sex drive. He continued to tell himself he was neither a Catholic clergyman nor gay and his sex need was a fact of life.

Dehning would have had no problem if he had not decided to get involved with a young woman who had absolutely nothing to lose if their relationship was discovered. Big error. At some point, he was going to have to find Little Sheba—as he thought of her—a new boyfriend, even if he had to pay someone to begin sleeping with her so he could catch them in bed. But, boy, she was great fun at the moment. *What a life?*

"You will need to come up with about $10 million to seal the deal. Yup, $10 million because we need to tilt about seven separate states and while we will need to campaign generally around one campaign issue, the advertisements will need to target different candidates in successful human connection mechanisms." Dehning thankfully knew that Yergler would not have a clue what *successful human connection mechanisms* meant but would be too arrogant and/or embarrassed to ask. A good thing, because making up a definition for something this silly might have been a bit difficult. It sounded pretty deep. Far more important, Yergler would never figure out that combined with his fee and his kickbacks, he would not have any problem maintaining his social situation for at least a few more years. Yergler would never know that $10 million would not have any real impact, certainly not after he skimmed at least the first $3 million. *Dear God, don't let the IRS come knocking.*

Yergler never stood up behind his desk once he sat down. If he needed to leave the room, he would call a break in a meeting to take some mythical call and ask whomever he was with to come back in a few minutes. He had it all worked out with his secretary. There was no way he was stepping off that platform. "I guess we are going to do this. So get me a budget and let's use Carl McKitterick for our lawyer. I'll continue to feed Billy some work so he doesn't go state's evidence on our last venture, but I think a new lawyer who thinks you and I are the Pristine Twosome of Hope is a pretty good idea."

"We're now the what, Pristine Twosome of Hope? Wow, I didn't know." Dehning was up, out of his chair and headed toward the door. "Isadore, this is not a sure thing." And as he closed the door, "None of us have ever seen a ménage à trios, at least in national politics. I will get a budget together tomorrow and e-mail you asking for the check. This time we will document everything… everything. And never, ever forget, that delete button is misnamed; it should say *hide*. The FBI can find anything in that machine if they are interested."

~

Paul Roland viewed himself as a proper politician. While a member of the Republican Party for most of his career, that was in name only. He was truly a Libertarian, which could be considered the right wing of the Republican Party or could be considered a deeply held philosophy underpinning his decision-making. He was not remotely uncomfortable with the Tea Party. He preferred being described as a highly principled conservative and had earned the right to that description during his two stretches in Congress as a Member of the House of Representatives.

The mainstream press preferred to describe Paul Roland as a right-winger. That description included a host of individuals the congressman would have refused to allow inside his home. But, he was stuck with the image that the press had provided him. *Maybe I should have just continued to practice medicine. Nothing wrong with the old family doctor or obstetrician, whatever.*

With a family situation that would have more closely resembled *Ozzie and Harriett* when the boys were younger, Roland perceived himself as an old-fashioned religious man. He lived his life the way his father would have expected him to live it. He had worked hard in and out of school during high school, attended the University of Texas and then went to the University of Texas medical school. The last efforts required working as a security guard at night and attending medical school by day. The medical school prepared him for his future on many levels, including his career as a congressman and now as a potential President of the United States.

A Southern radio host, an economist and the congressman sat quietly together in a booth in the back of a bar in Red Oak, Georgia, outside of Atlanta. Classic Southern food was on the table: fried chicken, mashed potatoes, Coca-Cola and beer. The discussion, as would surprise no one who saw the talk show host enter the restaurant, revolved less around the third-party effort of George Vincent and his new friends and more about the FairTax.

"Paul, this is just a nightmare for you guys," started the radio show host. "Without bold ideas, the moderate and liberal Republican vote is going to flow right into the toilet of the American Exceptionalism Party or whatever they call it. You could become the least successful Republican candidate for president since before the civil war."

"Gentlemen, you know who I am and what I stand for. I am in favor of good ideas that are articulated in the Constitution and I am against good and bad ideas that are not permitted by the Constitution. That is a pretty simple philosophy and that is who I am."

The Southern radio host leaned forward and spoke in the manner that one might expect from a bully rather than a talk show host talking to a presidential candidate. The talk show host was a condescending bully on the radio and that was not too far from his real self; he could never get too far from his true self. While holding a law degree, the truth was he had never been successful until he tried radio on a lark. Here, his legal training—such as it was from a non-accredited law school—gave him a framework from which he could lecture an uneducated audience from his chair in an empty radio studio.

"Paul, you don't get it. The FairTax is the only chance you have. Without it and without me, you are going to lose at levels that you will find incredible. Those middle-of-the-road Democrats and those damn moderate Republicans are going to swarm the American Exceptionalism Party. All you represent when the lights go off is a bit of honest philosophy. With that, you might just as soon turn out the lights and go home. I will forget you and when that happens, the public is going to forget you." The radio talk show host was broad, but not a big man attired in one of those loose, blue collared shirts that men do not tuck into their pants. With his bald head, oversized belly and glasses, he looked like most of the other people in this cholesterol-laced restaurant.

"Thanks, now I suspect you will start the name calling. Let me be perfectly clear here, I still love that expression, I was elected by a bunch of wonderful Texans, so don't try to or even give any more thought to bullying me. That is not going to happen. As to the FairTax, I met Hugh Hewitt a month ago and he gave me a copy of a book he wrote…"

"The real author of that damn book is a bookkeeper named Hank Adler; Hewitt doesn't know squat and Hewitt was no more than an editor and political consultant."

"Well, that's not the way Hugh remembers it and I also had a cocktail with Adler. He sure made sense to me, and that Hewitt, he understands this stuff from A to Z. Why do you need to demonize and insult everyone, especially when you don't have a clue? Anyway, your baseless attacks are not worth much at this table. I read your book. I read their book and they seem to undress the FairTax pretty effectively."

The economist jumped in and explained: "Yes, they really did throw a few bowling balls at us and we have carefully not responded. They are right on quite a few of their issues, but each of those issues can be corrected in any serious legislative proposal." The economist had found the FairTax a bonanza. The secret club that had thought up the idea had paid him a fortune to document its functionality. What he found as the idea played out over time was that he could get very rich touting something that really was pretty silly.

"So where are they right and where are they wrong? Roland reached into his pocket and pulled out a list. Here is what Hewitt said he would ask if he ever got you on live TV:

1.   The Prebate doesn't actually equal the FairTax, so destitute people would actually pay some amount of FairTax and therefore the poor are not exempt. Right or wrong?

2.   The administration costs would be ghastly. No one could control 113 million checks or deposits a month. Right or wrong?

3.   The administration would have to write checks or make more than a billion deposits a year. Right or wrong?

4.   Most of the tax would fall on those that don't have rather than those that already have. Right or wrong?

5.   At twenty-three percent, everything that has happened in the last decade is totally ignored in you calculations. Right or wrong?

6.   It is really a thirty percent tax rate to a layman—and Hewitt was careful to make sure I asked you what the tax would be if the seller got $100; he says $30. Right or wrong?

7.   And the promised rate is a joke, right? Probably twice that amount unless spending is cut almost by sixty percent given the interest now due on the national debt. Right or wrong?

His list has a few more parts, but I think that covers the ones I wrote down. What about it?"

The discomfort in the radio host was obvious. There was a little sweat in what was left of a once full head of very dark hair. His stomach muscles were tensed and he was now holding his glasses in his left hand. No one wanted to debate or play poker with Paul Roland, this obstetrician turned politician, he apparently read people like it was the third time through a book he particularly enjoyed and he had done his homework. And in some fairly gentle fashion, he came straight at you.

"Guilty on all counts, Paul. We have never responded to those clowns because this is all easily repairable, but admitting to the errors at this point would kill the movement. Plus, we don't believe that anyone would believe us at this point if we started to make the corrections. The FairTax puppets have bought into what we already told them, hook, line and sinker. The issue isn't about the details; it is about a new form of taxation. All of those things, we can work them out.

The economist knew he had to speak, but he was fully aware that this congressman from Texas understood the issues; he needed a new track to get him where he needed to get him. "Sir, the most important thing here is that our tax rate would work with your spending goals. If you think about it, we have successfully found a tax rate that would work with your goals and objectives in reducing spending. On that basis, there is plenty of room."

"Fellows, I think, but am frankly not sure you are well intended. But rest assured, you can sauté me on your show, but I would never support a proposal that you already know doesn't work. Game, set, match. I may well be in favor of a flat tax like Steve Forbes or a VAT, but this thing is just a monstrosity. I just wanted you to hear that directly from me. Call it old-fashioned values. And by the way, I don't have a clue who you could support in this election if you do not support me. I am thinking that supporting Vincent or the President would be pretty much the end of your radio career." The tall, narrow Texan put a few dollars on the table and walked to the exit. His Secret Service detail jumped lockstep in line with him as he exited the bar.

"Well, we will have a bit of fun at his expense next week. We will miss him," shouted the talk show host to the economist. The economist was someone the radio host could bully, after all, the economist knew that his published papers on the FairTax were academically flawed and he never gave any thought to retractions or corrections. A weak man selected because he was both smart and weak.

To his credit, the economist looked at the radio host and disagreed: "I think you are jumping to a bad decision here. While I would prefer a Fair-Tax, a VAT is the next best idea out there. The goal is a national sales tax instead of the income tax."

The talk show host responded quickly: "The goal is also to have something to talk about on the radio. We have long ago picked our horse and I fully intend to trample this asshole with our horse."

~

SUNDAY, AUGUST 12, 2012

Reesa Jonathon knew that her commitment to an independent campaign would attract an amazing amount of attention and had steeled herself to a few immediate television and radio interviews. This was not her battlefield of choice as she was somewhat shy, but a commitment to do X almost always involved Y. She had known her life in anonymity was behind her and something far more intrusive than her days as an Olympic swimmer was upon her. She had left her prior life of swimming, self-torture, liquor, and infidelity behind her for decades; how hard could this be?

She decided that her first interview would be with Chris Matts on the first Sunday morning after church. Reesa had a fundamental dislike for Matts as she believed his role on television should either be as a partisan or as a newsperson. She believed that he was a partisan pretending to be a newsperson, pretending to himself as much as pretending to his audience. Self-delusion was simply self-delusion; she believed his audience for the most part knew exactly what the score was.

She knew that he would be the most aggressive of the interviewers she would undoubtedly face, but her stomach also told her he would go for the cheap shots and she could make him look the fool. More important, if she could get him stammering, she knew she would have a YouTube moment or two from the interview. This would be a victory for George Vincent. She was also absolutely certain that if he did not want to chat with her before the interview that he would underestimate her and wear this interview around his neck for the rest of his career. And his people had done nothing to try to arrange any kind of preshow meeting.

Reesa shook hands with Matts sixty seconds before the interview began. Unbelievably, that was their only mano a mano event before the interview. The lack of any clarity for the interview and lack of any meaningful pregame discussion was sufficient proof to Reesa that this would be an interview designed to demean her. *You know, this might actually be a bit of fun.*

She had wheeled herself to the conference table about fifteen minutes before the lights were to come on. She sensed that the crew did not know she was arriving in a wheelchair. They had asked about makeup and she had declined. She believed it would be to her advantage not to look her best. Reesa presumed that a few hundred thousand people were pouring their Sunday morning coffee in hopes of a television mugging. Reesa presumed that no one realized the amount of forethought she had put into this interview and that she would, at a minimum, have the possibility of a great sound bite. She intended to be the mugger, not the mugee.

As Matts had arrived only seconds before, Reesa took great comfort that he barely looked at her as they shook hands and that he had a sheaf of notes in his hands. Reesa had been briefed by her staff on the small handful of questions they had received the week before from Matt's staff and she had instructed them to speak only off the record as if they were in fear of her whip if they said something wrong. Her staff was informed that Matts was not to find out about her charitable inclinations from the calls to her people. This was fairly safe as only three people outside of her attorneys were involved in what she called her personal income redistribution plan. There was the risk that Matts would have heard about this from someone at Max's Place, but she hoped that was not likely, as the featured stories she had seen all concerned politics and her promised independent campaign. Plus, his people had not asked for confirmation of her philanthropy. If someone had talked about her charitable giving, the questions and the press coverage would have been different.

"This evening we are interviewing Reesa Jonathon. As you may have heard on the news in the past few days, Ms. Jonathon is part of a group of multi-millionaires or multi-multi-millionaires that met secretly a few weeks ago to attempt to raise hundreds of millions of dollars to force the President from the White House." Matts was already two octaves above average and using his strange ability to enunciate every syllable of every word. "Ms. Jonathon, what say you to the facts? And can I call you Reesa?"

228

Reesa smiled and paused in an attempt to provoke another question before she had a chance to posit so much as a word to the public. It worked like a charm.

"Reesa, is America to anticipate that a small group of exceptionally wealthy Americans are going to try to buy this election?"

Reesa smiled again, rolled her wheelchair back just enough so that anyone watching knew that Chris Matts had begun to attack a woman in a wheelchair on live television this early Sunday morning. She had hired a professional to help her with this interview and while she balked at this first suggestion to make her first statement by showing the wheelchair, she knew it would be very effective and accepted the advice. She had further accepted that her goal for the interview was first to win a touch of sympathy and understanding for herself and what she was doing, and then make it sound like a perfectly logical and patriotic thing to do.

"Mr. Matts, as you know, I have never appeared on a national news television show before and the last time I was on national television is when I finished third in the butterfly in the 1976 Olympics qualifying championship. And obviously, a lot has happened since, so please forgive me if this is impolite, I would like to answer your questions rather than have you answer them for me. So, if I may, let's go back to question one."

Matts was taken back and started to stammer, *perfect*, but Reesa talked over his stammer. "Mr. Matts, you know there are no secrets in politics. When one stands up—and I use that as a matter of speech—and announces you are going to spend $100 million in a political campaign, asking people to keep it a secret is really asking them not to open up their cell phones and iPads and broadcast that information to their friends before the end of a meeting. You know that. It just doesn't happen that way. Had I wanted to keep what I was doing a secret, I would not have told anyone."

"Well, Reesa…"

"Mr. Matts," not giving him a chance to articulate another soprano syllable, " you know, you never so much as came out of your office to meet me and spend a few minutes chatting before this interview, so I think we can stick with Mrs. Jonathon. I am pretty proud of that name and equally proud of my husband."

Now, Chris Matts was a bit stunned and was suddenly wishing this was not live television and quietly wishing he and his staff had not underestimated this interview, maybe by quite a bit. Her response that a first name was not acceptable had never happened before. This was far from a good start to the evisceration he had had in mind. He had the sense he was being undressed by someone that he had intended to easily humiliate. And Reesa did not miss a beat: "Mr. Matts, no one can buy an American election. Our voters are uniquely able to get all of the information they want and they have the capability to understand and interpret the message. And please, Sir, I am intending to spend my own money as an American citizen. I have no politician or television producer so much as suggesting how I spend it or what I say. My sole purpose, and that is it, my sole purpose, is to use my money to educate as many Americans as possible as to why George Vincent is an excellent choice to be the next President of the United States and"—she waited a full five seconds before finishing her sentence—"and the current President of the United States does not deserve an extra hour in the White House." The total statement was fairly close to accurate, but many would consider most of her advisors as politicians, regardless of the titles on their business cards.

Matts spent his next couple of questions letting the viewers know that Reesa was very, very wealthy; she let him proceed on this track with near certainty in her mind that he would again slash into her on the money issue. She hoped her personal story was going to make him shrink nearly under the desk. He did not let her down.

"Mrs. Jonathon, would it not be better to take this money and spend it in charitable ways rather than just run political advertisements. Wouldn't that be better for the country? You are apparently one of the wealthiest women in the United States and you are not connected with any major charities." Matts savored this last sentence as he had personally double checked Google when his staff told him that after reading a few articles about her swimming and an apparent problem with alcohol, which he decided to save for a closing flourish, they discovered she had spent her life in near complete seclusion. Reesa Jonathon had not had a single entry in Google for well over twenty years. There was not so much as a picture or mention of her at some $500 charity ball or a single political contribution. Matts would fire one research assistant later in the day when he found out after a few telephone calls that her charity had been mentioned at Max's Place.

"Wow, Mr. Matts, that seems a bit harsh. Wrong, terribly wrong, but more hash than wrong. And frankly, none of your business. A viewer might think that the purpose of this interview was to hurt me as a person. Maybe I should just fall out of this wheelchair and you can kick me around the floor."

This, Chris Matts had also never experienced and he quickly retreated to the information about her drinking thinking truth might bail him out. "Reesa, frankly, when we looked on Google and made inquiries about you, all we were able to find out is that you rarely leave your home, you have struggled with alcohol since your accident and now suddenly, you appear with a bag of money earned entirely by your grandfather and you want to try to help steal an election for a political party that did not exist six months ago."

"Mrs. Jonathon," she stated flatly. "Mr. Matts, have you ever heard of the Hepsen Foundation or the Lost Lives Foundation?"

"No, I do not believe so."

"How about the Statin or Afable Foundations?"

"No, I don't think so, what are you getting to here? We want to talk this morning about that $100 million that you have admitted to be giving to Senator George Vincent and…"

"Stop it, Mr. Matts, please give me a minute to respond and stop trying to spin this old, crippled woman into a witch." She paused here and carefully moved both hands to her legs and rubbed them. The consultant told her that if she did this whenever she felt Matts had overstepped, he would look like he was picking on her. *This is great; maybe I should have been an actress.*

"Again, you seem to thrive on asking me a question and before I can draw a breath, you ask a second question. I asked you about those foundations because I have formed well over one hundred foundations to hide my charitable giving over the past twenty or thirty years. Yes, hide it, because I really never intended that anyone know about it. Maybe you think that anonymous charity is some form of crime?" Reesa paused, but gave him no chance to speak. "It should not be important to the discussion," she was pretending so hard to be totally miffed and taken back at the accusations, as opposed to fist pumping her success in making Chris Matts appear to be the bad guy. She had bated him magnificently. "But if you need to know, last year I gave, through these foundations, $175 million to charity and I think over some period of years, I have given over $2 billion dollars to charity. Frankly, again, I thought my charity was my own business; but I guess without charity, I am meaningless to you. How much money did you give to charity last year, Mr. Matts?"

She did not even think about giving Chris Matts a chance to respond to that rhetorical flourish. "And until right now, when it became clear that you

231

had invited me on to your television station to judge me rather than inter-view me, I really did not think it was anyone's business what I did with my money. And by the way, the President and his wife were making well over $300,000 a year before he was thinking about running for president and they were giving less than $6,000 to charity two years before his election. And the Vice President, his tax returns showed the same two or three hun-dred dollars in contributions for every year for almost a decade. I personally suspect he never really ever gave a dollar to charity."

If the purpose of live television was to occasionally have a riveting moment, live television was producing such a moment. Chris Matts was on the edge of speechless, sweating profusely and looking for a commercial break, which mercifully arrived. "We will be back with our interview with Reesa Jonathon in just a moment."

The red light went out and Chris Matts quickly got a grip on himself and more quickly threw his staff under the bus. "I am so sorry, Reesa. I had no idea of what you have been doing. I asked for everything we could find on you and no one had any idea. Your staff offered us nothing."

Reesa sat quietly in her chair. Not a word for a moment and then said simply, "Mrs. Jonathon...Mr. Matts, I have watched your show every Sunday for years. You think you have the only view a smart person could consider on every subject and that those that disagree are fools." And she could not resist, even knowing she had a few minutes to go, for which she was perfectly pre-pared. She looked Matts up and down and said: "Sometimes, your arrogance just makes you appear to be a sad, mean little man. Such a shame."

"Sixty seconds."

Matts fumed for the full sixty seconds and when the green light went on, he leaped back into the fray; "I am interviewing Ms. Reesa Jonathon and she was just filling us in on her background which we were unable to obtain from her people." His voice was back at the highest octaves and every syl-lable was again being enunciated as if he was teaching English to an Italian family at a Berlitz school.

"Mrs. Jonathon, was it the alcoholism after the accident that started you on this mission of philanthropy?"

"Still going for the cheap score, Mr. Matts? Yes and No. Unfortunately, I did not handle moving from potential Olympic champion to wheelchair lady very well. But after a few sad years, I joined Alcoholics Anonymous and at their meetings then and now, I arrive in a small, old Honda. I have

232

wonderful friends at AA and they could not care less that I am wealthy. I have remained true to my friends at AA. To them I am just someone up the street who formerly abused alcohol, wants to make sure she doesn't regress and wants to help others deal with this disease. And you should know, I love that little group of ours and that is who I really am. We have done pretty well as a group and every one of us knows that it is a day-to-day battle, never won, always fought.

"After AA began to take hold, and you cannot imagine what a long and difficult pathway a journey back from alcoholism can be, as that journey is never completed, my husband suggested that I could gain some life satisfaction in charitable giving as a donor, not as a seeker of fame or publicity."

Matts was now a helium balloon that had lost far too much helium. He weakly asked, knowing he had only a few more seconds before a Midwestern governor would save him from the worst show of his life, "Mrs. Jonathon, we only have a few seconds, what are your goals with your money in this election?"

"Pretty simple goals, I am going to invest a great deal of money in this election with the sole purpose of giving the American people the opportunity to understand why Senator Vincent would make a great President of the United States and what policies he would try to have passed in Congress to undo the disaster of these past four years. I certainly do not trust the media to treat the election fairly and I feel more strongly about this now than I did when I entered your studios."

"Thank you, Mrs. Reesa Jonathon."

Reesa could not wait to get out of the studio and without a word, rolled her chair around and began her exit. Then, Reesa's sense of humor and a bit of her ego got the best of her and she looked over her shoulder and said: "Let's do lunch some time." Matts breathed not a word, knowing that he had been had.

On her way out, Governor Forstein saw her coming the other way. He leaned very close to her and whispered: "That was the most magnificent thing I have ever seen. Thank you on behalf of millions of Americans." He paused. "Could we get together and talk about the University of Iowa, they are really suffering financially in their agriculture school?"

Reesa looked up and said: "Thank you, Governor. Have to laugh, the world hasn't known about my philanthropy for ten minutes and I have already heard from the governor of Iowa, who obviously attended the University of Iowa. Sir, I have read about you and your policies in Iowa and I would be honored to help. Just tell my assistant, Sheila, that I agreed we would get together. Be aware Sheila could tell the Pope I was not taking calls, so be a bit pushy." They both laughed and he knew that his interview with Chris Matts would not be too tough this Sunday morning.

Reesa had played her cards perfectly in her first national appearance and would quickly become the darling of the right and the enemy of the left.

The interviews would come in a flurry for Reesa over the next several weeks. In what could not be a surprise, she was toxic to CNBC, RBC, and others, but there was a love fest for her on Fox News and talk radio. OBC also found a soft spot for her because of her human story and focused on her many years of sobriety and her decision to go the philanthropy route. On OBC, there was never a question asking her about her acceptance of God in her personal growth process. She did manage to ask one question on the OBC Sunday morning show which became a blog favorite for forty-eight hours: "Why is it acceptable and apparently a positive thing for a baseball or football player to point to the heavens after a homerun or touchdown, and that same God has no meaning for me when it helps direct me to give over $2 billion to charity or help conduct a political campaign?" She loved the church channels on cable and now they loved her.

Reesa found the entire experience to be life changing. She had never been certain that her mental rehabilitation was complete and that it was okay to be rich and equally okay to be in a wheelchair. She loved being on television and trying to focus the debate on the importance of having a charitable man in the White House and expanding the nonprofit community instead of relying on government and therefore taxes to accomplish great things. While she thought she would hate the exposure, the literally thousands of letters she was now receiving from the recipients of her philanthropy over the past years was like drinking a dozen energy drinks. The letters from thousands and thousands of members of AA were heartwarming as well. Her husband, with whom she had shared a great life and whom she adored continually and enthusiastically, told her how good she looked and how much fun he was having watching her on television. He was beginning to suggest that she consider running for office, something local, and she was warming to the idea. Maybe not exactly local either.

While she hated the moment on a personal level, one moment Americans would remember was when a television cable interviewer asked Reesa Jonathon if she was attracted to the American Exceptionalism Party because they had nominated a vice presidential candidate who was also in a wheelchair. Her response was instant television legend: "Sir, I take it that if I was the interviewer and you were the supporter of a candidate that had an IQ of less than fifty, I could have rightfully and respectfully asked you if you supported him because neither of you was very bright?" This YouTube footage went viral.

The interviews for Ross Anderson, Beth Midlands and Father Woods were generally positive, but Ross Anderson was unable to convey the message that the purpose of the meeting at Max's Place was to tell other moderates what opportunities and responsibilities were out there. The far left had immediately branded them conspiracists and it seemed to stick to him. In hindsight, he wished that he had issued a press release after the meeting. He needn't have disclosed the name of a single attendee, but he could have shaped his own message.

Anderson also realized that his generalized message of government incompetence was a hard sell when he was interviewed by liberal reporters and newscasters. These interviewers were in the *gotcha* business and made him seem as if he thought that Glenn Beck was a moderate. It became obvious to Anderson that while he made a great sale at Max's Place, he needed to stay off camera and focus on his television and radio campaign. The campaign strategy part was great fun and he began to expand both the message and the targets.

Father Woods was never invited on a mainstream media television station. His view that the President of the United States was involved in developing a policy that would kill the church in the United States was a discussion the secular media wanted no part of; no part at all. They also did not want to hear about the President's two-step on abortion or what Woods described as his abandonment of his own church. However, the priest was travelling the country like a rock star with a different city every two days. His message was well received by every diocese in the country because it focused on the capital needs of the Catholic Church and because the leadership of the Catholic community believed his message to be true. And, conservative radio loved him.

There had been a very angry telephone call placed to the Vatican by the administration about Father Woods and the response had been shocking to the President. "Would the President like to meet with *Cardinal* Woods before the election?" That message was not subtle and had been unmistakable; no second call had been made to the Vatican or was there a mention of Father Woods from the White House at any time thereafter. The Pillsbury

Doughboy was asked about Father Woods and he responded about the separation of church and state and the President's belief that he should never comment on the activities of the church or its leadership.

Father Woods worked his way through every day with a combination of talk radio shows and speaking to special meetings at most dioceses. While the church realized that Father Woods was causing some long-term issues with the United States' view of separation of church and state, leadership decided to organize a meeting to discuss the issue in July 2013 and responded to the press on this issue with the announcement of their plan for discussions *soon*. This gave Father Woods the ability to move confidently around the country, talking to at least a few hundred people every day, more often than not in a religious setting or before a quarterly or monthly dinner group.

One of the local pastors of another church in Southern California had been fairly deeply involved in the 2008 campaign for the presidency. That pastor had faced the candidates on television and realized that he had never asked the correct follow-up question on abortions. In his own mind, this was one of the great failures of his life. While the community continued to love the good pastor who, in all things, tried to do the right thing, he knew that his congregation believed he had fumbled the major important religious issue of the current century while on national television. Father Woods represented the closest thing he was going to get in terms of a second chance, because scheduling would make it impossible for the President to do a live interview with the pastor despite the pastor's insistence that he could arrange with a local Washington D.C. church to do the interview in Washington D.C. (At least, the pastor was informed it was *scheduling*.)

Asked about the comments of Father Woods, the pastor responded easily by again offering to host a debate between Senator Vincent, the President and Congressman Roland. They would exclusively discuss religion, separation of church and state and other human issues. The President's people again indicated he was too busy for that event and that discussion quickly moved to both the abortion issue and the President's reluctance to address the issue in a complete and unfettered way.

As the President's people rejected the pastor's debate ideas, a debate was ultimately *scheduled*, with or without the President for late October with the pastor, Vincent and Roland. Father Woods thought: *An empty chair should be pretty effective.*

~

After Reesa Jonathon's pasting of Chris Matts, Sunday morning's television was filled with interviews of both George Vincent and Jordon Scotch, as well as political spokespersons for both the Democratic and Republican Parties. The President never did these shows as he believed he needed to stay away from the difficult members of the media. For him, there would never again be what was referred to as a "police acted stupidly moment."

Both Vincent and Scotch provided information about what they believed and focused on what was wrong with the existing president's policies. Mostly, they focused on the President's mistakes. Vincent and Scotch both attempted to test market a few campaign issues; they had already paid for focus groups to watch their performances. What they found was very, very useful. The American people, at least based on their focus groups, wanted to be left alone and wanted Congress and its legislation to become background noise. It was okay to be in favor of this or that, but their highest marks were in condemning government flowing out of its banks and intrusively into the public's lives. Deficits were also near the top of the list. They found that the words shadow government and providing descriptions of the histories of some of the appointed czars in the White House raised eyebrows among likely voters of both parties.

George Vincent quickly found out that an accurate description of his views placed him far closer to Paul Roland than the President. It wasn't that he was that close to Roland, it was more that he was that far from the President. This surprised Vincent, but complimented his belief that the Democratic Party, not him, had moved dramatically to the left.

Jordon Scotch eviscerated Congress over giving the stimulus package money to the President as a trillion dollar slush fund. When reminded that Senator Vincent had voted for the stimulus package, Jordon Scotch responded that, "the difference between people and chipmunks is that they learn from their mistakes. No one had understood that the President was going to use the stimulus package as his personal political pocketbook. He thought the President would use it for economic stimulus. Silly him."

Both the Democratic and Republican spinners spent as much of every Sunday as they could discrediting the American Exceptionalism Party and the people on the stage of the convention as traitors to their parties. Vincent had been certain to keep some of his focus groups watching these spinners and the reactions were heartwarming. Americans were not buying into the traitor concept when the stage included the former presidents. Apparently,

237

George Vincent and his small cadre of speakers at the convention had successfully focused the debate on issues like democracy and overly expanded government.

Paul Roland and his advisors tried to watch all of the Sunday shows and reach some consensus of where to go with their convention. Congressman Roland saw several positive signs for conservatism. In his mind, the AEP, as he was starting to remind himself to call it, was a reaction to liberalism not a call for a new party. He believed that if the AEP supporters really understood the Constitution, they would be supporting his candidacy. He would move his presentations to the right and focus on government intrusiveness. He would also take note of the czar discussions and the inability of the Democrats to shoot significant holes in any claims made by the AEP. With this, he was becoming aware of a seemingly new issue. Based on the sudden increase in media costs, he was worried that there might be so much money chasing this election that he could quickly get moneyed out. Running third was daily becoming more than a significant possibility in his mind.

~

The President thought of nothing except the AEP and their attacks on him. He watched, often on TiVo, some of the Sunday shows, but also, with the family still away, took the opportunity to play thirty-six holes of golf. He had neither figured out why he had started to play golf or whether he actually enjoyed the experience. He was certain that it did not take a great athlete to master golf, but he also found that when he had something on his mind, it was tough to focus his attention on every shot. Golf was mind-numbingly punitive.

The President could not get it out of his mind that his successes were being described as failures and his failures were being described as debacles. Not launching a nuclear attack after the Korean nightmare seemed a positive to him and his people continued to tell him that he could use this as a positive. But, on talk radio, one might think that not killing millions of poor North Korean peasants was a high crime. All he really needed was for the Congress and the people to get out of the way and let him institute the changes that the country needed. The President was in poor spirits and his golf game reflected his spirits.

~

MONDAY, AUGUST 13, 2012

North-South Polling Service:

The President	30%
Congressman Paul Roland	35%
George Vincent	35%

~

From the day's *Washington Post editorial page by Randy Kraus*:

AMERICAN EXCEPTIONALISM PARTY CONVENTION
TURNAROUND POLLING

Who would have thunk it? A week after the American Exceptionalism Party Convention, George Vincent has picked up almost one-half of the President's support. Yes, a week ago, North-South Polling Service had the President with fifty percent of likely voters, Paul Roland with forty-five percent and George Vincent with five percent, which was probably a rounding error in Vincent's favor. One convention and one week later, George Vincent has overtaken the President and is tied with Paul Roland.

We suspect the polling data includes a short-term convention bounce, but this was the bounce of a super ball. We certainly do not know what will happen between today and the election, but we are certain that Senator Vincent will have an impact.

What a difference a week makes! We cannot wait for the next two conventions. We will not be recommending any old, black and white movies rather than watching the remaining two political conventions.

~

Molly Tom again appeared at The Professor's door. Today's attire was the standard brightly colored T-shirt, a full size too big—and apparently not accompanied by a bra—tight jeans, sandals, with her long dark hair, clean, but in no particular style. The Professor's big grin greeted her and he waved her in. "Been a few days, I am guessing that Constitution thing threw you for a loop!"

"A loop. You have to be kidding! You would need six weeks and the Rosetta Stone to be able to know what would happen if there were no winner and an effective three-way tie in the regular election. The Rosetta Stone might not be enough. Did the Founders ever read through the Constitution and game play it?"

"Really?" The Professor responded. He could not help himself and just started to laugh. "The Rosetta Stone, eh?"

"Don't laugh at me! This is important and you think because you already know the rules that this is funny. This is important."

"OK, I'm sorry," snorted The Professor. "Back to the basics. What do we do with good research?"

"We use it to make good decisions and I need to go see Paul Roland's people. They need to be ready to deal with a three-party race."

"That's easy to arrange. But, Congressman Roland has the same chance of becoming president as you and me, and last time I looked, you were too young and I am not interested. Our horse is going to be George Vincent and I guarantee you a great ride if you are willing to participate in the race. Let's talk about what you found."

"Are you telling me that I need to support Vincent George or George Vincent, whoever he is?"

"Yes, and you need to trust me on this. He and Jordon Scotch are really good guys and they may have a chance to bring together a sufficient number of people to put this country back in the center where the American voters live. This president is an incompetent lefty and Roland is an ideologue who could not change his bet if the horse race was already completed. Nimble, he is not."

"How do you know?"

"I know them all, Molly. I don't know this president as well as the other two, but I have sat down with all three of them over the past year to explain the relationships of tax policy to tax collections. Frankly, the only one of the three who wanted to understand at more than a surface level was George. Of course, that might be because I have known the S.O.B. forever. And Molly, all of this becomes confidential at this point. My whole world changes if my colleagues understand I can pick up the telephone and get a return call from all three of these guys." *And a significant number of other senators and Congress people, but you don't need to know that.* "I need to be able to count on you for this."

"Do you know everyone?"

"Nah, but getting to people with important information is usually pretty easy. You just need a small network of friends."

"Sure, just a small network of friends. Here is what I found. First, the electors…"

"Come on, Molly, let's start with the bottom line. What do you need to communicate? How meaningful is the Electoral College likely to be? What is the purpose of your research? And will you buy into George Vincent, who is the only one I am willing to help?" The Professor seemed to be somewhat frustrated and this both surprised Molly Tom a bit and began to scare her based on the tone of his voice.

"I don't know."

"Enough, this is a yes or no—your call; you know I will hold you in equally high level of respect if you decide to follow up with Roland on your own."

Taking a full and long five seconds to compose herself, Molly learned forward and nearly whispered: "I say, yes." Now completely attentive and in academic high gear, "The presidency can be decided in three possible places if there is no electoral majority in the election. One, the electors can decide to follow their own conscience rather than listen to their voters in most states, so they could decide the election. Very unlikely; number two, the House of Representatives could chose a President; or three, the Senate could chose a Vice President who would be the Acting President if the House cannot decide on someone. Lots of other rules like what it takes to get elected, quorum rules and how they vote—very odd stuff."

"OK, sounds like you know the rules, Kiddo. Now, the only meaningful question, how can what you have learned impact decisions?"

"Professor, the fact that you seem to know this stuff scares me to death, but I think if someone else was reading this stuff as closely as I have, they would realize that this election is probably going to be determined between the election night and January 20; the national vote is only a prelude."

"Stop using the words *this stuff*; it's not professional. So, what is your point?"

"Huh?"

"Don't let me down here. What will you recommend to our boy, George?" The Professor was now standing and at his full six-foot-one he looked like a giant to the diminutive and seated senior accounting major. *What have I gotten into?* She wondered to herself.

"I would be doing several things. I would be compiling lists of delegates, doing research on every one of them like they were trying to get a seat on the Supreme Court and gathering all of the legal power I could get. I might have some legal briefs written both challenging and defending the votes of the Electoral College. I would be doing research on every congressional district, I would..."

"Why focus on the Electoral College?"

"Just in case the Electoral College was within ten or fifteen votes."

"OK, what else?"

"I guess I would start trying to figure out how the individual states would vote in the House of Representatives. How can it be that a single congressman from North Dakota has the same power as the entire State of California?"

"That's the key, Molly. That's also easy to understand if you remember that nearly half of the population of the United States lived in Virginia in 1790. The other states were not going to give all of the electoral power to Virginia. Now, what else?"

"Gosh, Professor, I think that is about it."

"Not a chance, Kid, but we'll cover that next week when we meet Senator Vincent. What are your class hours next week? Write them down." She pulled out her schedule and handed it to The Professor. "OK, now get out of here, I need to make a few telephone calls! No, sit down and listen. Damn, you are smart."

"Professor, I don't have the money to go some place to meet the senator and I need to go to my classes."

"No problem, he will come to see us. Maybe, we will have to drive up the freeway a bit, but that would be it."

"He will come to see us? How do you know that?"

"Just close the door and listen. We need to scare a few old friends. Should be fun. Your questions will have to wait."

The Professor just shrugged as the door closed. He had not thought there were two or three people in the entire country that had or could think through the dilemma of a successful third party before the problem hit the nation with a thud. How lucky she was. You cannot teach brilliant. Of course, he knew that it was solely his ego that asked her to sit and listen to this call. *Ah, well, some things never change.*

If she had intended to vote for the President or Paul Roland, he would have asked a few questions and minimized the issue. But, he guessed, just sitting back and enjoying the show was now out of the question. Maybe it would be a little bit of fun, but he wasn't moving to D.C. when it was over. That part of his life was long since over. He might not feel any loyalty to a group of politicians who he believed had, as a group, forgotten their roles, but his loyalty to his students was total. Again he thought: *Good God, I don't want to be in the next administration and this young kid is going to put me out front again. Hell, she is younger than some of my shirts. And Mrs. Hirschel has about as much interest in moving to Washington D.C. to watch me work sixteen hours a day in Treasury as I have in having the skin peeled from my back. Ah well, no good deed goes unpunished.*

The Professor reached for his computer and found the number for the Vincent campaign, dialed and began to talk before the person on the other end of the squawk box said a word: "Is Skeeter in?"

"Senator Vincent's campaign office," answered a male administrator.

"Is Skeeter in?" asked The Professor with his best grin being nearly wasted in his near empty office. *Molly Tom is going to get the full show.*

She watched her mentor closely. *Really, who is this guy?* She thought.

"Skeeter, Sir?"

"Is Skeeter in?"

"Skeeter?"

"Yes, Skeeter, that senator who is, I am told, apparently running for President of the United States."

"Yes, Sir, but Senator Vincent is in a conference. Can I tell him who called?

"What is your name, son?"

"My name is Joshua Ybarra, Sir. I am sorry, Sir. I have no idea who Skeeter is. Is this a prank of some kind?"

"Joshua, my boy, this is no prank, but that is a fair question. Same with the Skeeter part. Skeeter is your boss, Senator George R. Vincent, senior senator from Ohio. Good hands, no speed, that would be Skeeter."

"Who is calling please?"

"Tell Skeeter, The Professor is on the line." He emphasized the *T* in *The*.

"Again, Mr. Professor, he is in a meeting and cannot be disturbed."

"Well, Jonathon, can you slip Skeeter a note and tell him The Professor, capital *T*, capital *P*, is on the line? Not Mr. Professor, just The Professor. And again, put a capital *T* on it like *The* Ohio State."

"No, I cannot do that and Marshall Dankberg is in the meeting. Mr. Dankberg is actually my direct boss. I think the senator knows my name though. I can leave them a message, Sir."

"Hum, how about we do this, Jonathon? Would you slip a note to Mr. Dankberg and tell him The Professor is on the telephone for Skeeter and maybe the three of us should chat right now. I know you don't know me, son, but really, has anyone asked you to do anything like this since you have been sitting outside Skeeter's office? If I didn't know the son of a bitch better than you know your own brother, I wouldn't be asking you to do this. Now, I have to teach class in forty-five minutes, are you going to take that note in?"

"Joshua, Sir, not Jonathon. Sir, they told me they did not want to be disturbed."

"Jonathon, I mean Joshua, I am sure you are a wonderful son to your mom and dad and you are polite to beat the band. Just trust me on this. If I called and said the building was on fire, you would deliver the note, right? Just trust me on this."

"Well, no, uh okay, but can I have a real name, Sir. This is a little bizarre and I have the feeling I may be risking my job for either someone really important or for a real jerk."

This last comment made Molly Tom laugh out loud which clearly did not help the conversation move to the right answer.

"No, they know who The Professor is"—again emphasizing the T in *the*—"and they might say yes to both the important and the real jerk categories. By the way, while they are talking to me, get started on determining where in Southern California they can be this Friday or the following Monday. I should be able to make a meeting anywhere in Southern California around noon, either day."

"You have got to be kidding, they are booked end to end for the next three months. They can't possibly meet with you this week, particularly in Southern California, but I am beginning to believe you are the real deal."

"Joshua," The Professor said a bit sternly, "please put either Skeeter or Dankberg on the telephone, now. I need to go teach a class."

"OK, Sir, I am going to do this, but please be the real deal. Hold on."

Twenty-two-year-old Joshua Ybarra got up to interrupt the senator and his top political advisor and tell them some guy who referred to himself as *The Professor* wanted to talk him, now. *I have lost my mind!*

Having made his decision, Joshua Ybarra all but ran to and opened the conference room door with the note for Marshall Dankberg. He knocked as he opened the door and walked into two glaring faces, Senator Vincent asked, "What's up, Joshua?"

"Uh," completely forgetting the note, "I am really sorry, Sir, but I have a man on the telephone who insists on speaking to you right now and keeps referring to you as Skeeter. I am really sorry..."

"The Professor, Marshall," huge smile on the senator's face, one of relief, "I knew that asshole could not miss a good fight. I told you we would hear from him and we would be better off waiting for him to come to us. He is about three weeks late based on my prediction, but that bastard is the best political analyst in North America. Joshua, would you do me a favor?"

"Yes, Sir."

"Pick up this telephone for me and tell The Professor that, and quote me here, Senator Vincent says that you have told the world that you have already worked on your last campaign and since everyone knows that the good professor never lies, Skeeter wonders why you are calling. And then hand me the telephone. Joshua, if this guy actually comes around, just try to stand next to him and hope that maybe something will rub off. He is absolutely a piece of work, but he is the smartest person I have ever known."

Joshua pushed the connect button and repeated exactly as he was told. He handed the telephone to the senator and all he could hear was laughter. The senator hit the conference call button.

As soon as the senator hit the conference call button, he spoke into the air: "I'll bet you $1000 that Marcia doesn't know you made this call! Joshua, the language from this guy may be a little rich for your pay grade, but if you want to listen to one of the true jerks in the United States, close the door, pull up a chair and we'll let voice mail get the calls until The Professor is done. You are worth listening to, aren't you, Professor?"

"So I am told. Ah Skeeter, you always make me feel so loved. Hey, I have Molly Tom in my office. Molly may be the best student I have had in decades, smart and aggressive, seems to understand this election, which given who you are with—not you, Jonathon—puts our end of the call one up on you. And, Skeeter, Molly would be perfect for Jonathon, you are single, aren't you, Jonathon?"

Molly Tom was instantly a burnt orange and if her face could have been turned into cloth, it could have made its way into a University of Texas T-shirt. But, she grasped that she had been admitted to an inner circle that few ever entered.

"Professor, don't scare the boy. Hi, Molly. Wish the school could have given you better instructors. Nice to meet you. Professor, always a pleasure to have you and Marshall together. And, Professor, the kid is Joshua, not Jonathon. What's up?"

"Joshua, I am struggling with that. We need to meet, Skeeter. I think you have opened up a Pandora's box with this third political party thing. And by the way, the newspaper said that was quite a show last week."

"Of course, you didn't watch, did you?" Marshall Dankberg's first words to The Professor, who he detested. The Professor was just an arrogant know-it-all to Dankberg and of course the problem was that the guy actually was a legitimate know-it-all. While he could not stand Professor Hirschel, he knew that the guy thought about politics at a level that was unheard of in the business. Always three steps ahead, the ultimate political chess player.

"I don't do TV. Just read Drudge and Breitbart on the web. Best to have a properly biased account of what is happening."

Dankberg: "Professor, we are really busy for a few weeks. How about a couple of hours when we get to Southern California in early October?"

Joshua got a huge smile on his face because he had fairly quickly figured out that whatever The Professor wanted, he would get and the sparring was only that, sparring. Joshua instinctively knew that he would be changing schedules within a few minutes.

"Not a chance, Marshall. By then, you will have already lost the election for Skeeter. You are already so far behind on the key political issues, it is criminal. Skeeter, you should have hired a smart consultant or at least someone who is literate. We need to get together by a week from Friday, out here because Molly needs to go to class." Molly had slowly turned to her regular pale face, but quickly returned to burnt orange.

"Seriously, Professor, can you give me a clue and come on, don't pick on Marshall?"

249

"Seriously, Skeeter, the chances of this election beginning on November 6 instead of ending on November 6 are about one hundred percent and you need to start getting ready for the real election today."

Dankberg: "Electoral College? I have been thinking about that, but we have not spent a moment on it."

"The Electoral College is only the beginning and probably just a side show, I can conjure up a reasonable scenario where the whole thing gets to a pretty bizarre result."

"OK, Joshua is our guy, we will be in touch. Probably late Friday, so I can have a few meetings as I work myself West. Thanks, my friend, I know you are showing off for Molly and Joshua, but I also know you wouldn't make this call unless you wanted to help."

"Enough of that shit, Skeeter. See you on Friday afternoon. Joshua, bring flowers for Molly," and the call was terminated.

Joshua had his mouth open on the Vincent side of the conversation. Dankberg had his annoyed look on and Vincent was amused. The senator trusted The Professor with a lot more than an election strategy. "Joshua, arrange Friday for us, maybe we can leave here at 6:00 a.m. and see some donors in Denver on the way. Let's take the Hawker to Orange County so we can get back here by midnight or so. I don't think there are any nighttime takeoff restrictions in Orange County if we leave in a private plane.

"Joshua, sounds like you are part of the away team. Hire a new receptionist and knowing The Professor, bring flowers for whatever her name was or he will slowly eat you alive as Friday afternoon progresses. And dress like an adult. You will find out why.

"Since you are now a political consultant, cancel your dinner plans for the next week so you can tell us what the hell The Professor is talking about as we fly across the country. You will find his name and all that stuff in that old Rolodex out front. Google him. He used to have a website. See if he has written anything on this. Knowing him, we will be better off grabbing a conference room at one of the hotels across the street from the Orange County airport. Joshua, I think there is a Hilton or a Sheraton across the street."

"Sir, who is this guy? With all due respect, I have never heard you talked to like that and I didn't particularly like it. And I don't exactly need a matchmaker to meet a co-ed."

"Joshua, I'll let you make your own judgment about him; I know Marshall here cannot stand him because of his style. Me, I am just into having the smartest and most honest guys in the room helping me win this election and serve my country. And believe me, The Professor is one of those guys. You have to understand this guy. He would have been a great Roundhead in the eleventh century. What is that damn quote he is always reciting: 'I'd rather be right and repulsive than wrong and wromantic?' Yup, that's my Professor! To say he is one of a kind is the ultimate understatement. And by the way, the guy is sixty-four or five and still has the stomach muscles of an eighteen-year-old swimmer. That is about the exact point where my envy turns to hate."

"Right! Flowers?" he asked.

"Your call, but you heard my advice."

"Flowers..." as he exited the room shaking his head, and he could cancel his plans to *cocktail* with the guys after work for a few days, but certainly not the weekend. Joshua Ybarra was one of those young men who thought buying two beers for any woman he talked to in a bar entitled him to a full evening of sex and his personal experience seemed to validate his thinking. What he never understood was that while a significant portion of his success was based upon his natural good looks, most of it was the result of what type of woman was inclined to be interested in a stranger who would buy her a couple of drinks.

On The Professor's side of the call, Molly had just finished telling The Professor that he had embarrassed her. She had finished by mentioning the Scott Brown victory speech where he said his daughters "were available."

"Only the beginning, Kid. This will be great fun, now get out of here. You will make the presentation, so e-mail me a first draft the first chance you get. You will be great."

"I will be what?" Out she went and again closed the door behind her. Somehow in just a few days, she went from simply curious about the Electoral College to making a presentation to a presidential candidate. And she knew she could not tell anyone.

~

Mallory Cloud had appeared on the Bill O'Brien show when she was running for the presidency. She had not appeared until after her quest for the presidency had begun its incredible fall from leader and anointed candidate to follower. By that time, the momentum of her campaign had flagged so significantly that there was little or no hope.

Bill O'Brien had the biggest audience on cable television. His show was watched every evening by multiples of the other networks. He was the king of cable and his audience spilled over in both time slots before and after his show for Fox News. He had developed the show quickly and it continued to dominate in its time slot for over a decade and regularly beat many of the major television shows in its ratings. O'Brien believed himself to be completely fair with his guests and in truth, often, but far from always, he lived up to his self-held view. When the very top political personalities appeared on his show, he was generally not nearly as tough as he believed, not even in the same zip code as tough. Of interest, and sadly so, if one of his guest colleagues began to gain too much traction, he would mock them on live television.

The business mystery to Bill O'Brien was that the other cable networks apparently believed that he owned the middle, middle right and the right side of the political spectrum. This made him a very, very rich man and the combination mystified him and some business analysts. In the entire history of television, success was and has always been followed immediately by mimicry. For a half decade, television provided westerns day and night on all channels. (There were only three major networks at the time.) As westerns ran their course, the nation was treated to spy shows on every channel, then, there were situation comedies and more recently lawyer mysteries, and currently, crime and reality shows. For O'Brien, the middle, middle right and right evening viewers were his and his alone. The other cable networks responded to his success by offering essentially the same format but with left and far left moderators. There was no equivalent in television history. On one hand, it was as if the networks thought it was the format or the host and therefore the content was immaterial. On the other hand, it was as if O'Brien had an exclusive on his audience. In fact, the politics of groupthink gave him a monopoly.

The other cable networks were all directly or indirectly owned by organizations that either had business dealings with the existing Democratic administration (businesses having nothing to do with television) and/or were either afraid to broadcast a single more conservative show to compete with O'Brien or believed that what the conservatives had to say was wrong. Either way, O'Brien had his monopoly. O'Brien had felt for a decade that if any network had a brain, they would find a pretty or handsome person of the right to compete with him every night at his same time. Mercifully, from his perspective, it never happened. Beyond that, Fox News surrounded his show on both sides with conservatives. The closest he ever had to competition came from Fox News affiliates.

Mallory had a good interview with O'Brien during the Democratic primary of 2008. It was far too little and far too late and O'Brien's audience could only have helped her in a general election as opposed to a primary. The often-referenced fact that O'Brien had a balanced viewership was accurate that evening, but that meant there were only a million or so Democrats nightly, not enough for Mallory at that point in the election. But, she had held her own and O'Brien had been quite professional in the interview.

On this late Monday afternoon in New York, the former senator and former Secretary of State came to the New York studios where the O'Brien show was filmed. She was on time and the interview was scheduled live. Manning greeted Mallory Cloud at the door and ushered her into makeup. Their conversation was extremely cordial and Ginny explained that O'Brien thought it appropriate that they not meet before their interview, but that he wanted her to know that he was going to focus on the administration's actions and how that influenced her to leave the administration and support Senator George Vincent for president. She also indicated that this would be intertwined into a conversation about her role in the administration and the key events over the past several years. Mrs. Cloud interpreted this to mean that she was going to be pilloried because she remained in the administration for such a long period of time. She spent a full twenty minutes with the makeup guru. Young, Mrs. Cloud had not been seen for a serious period of time.

Mallory, as always, in traditional dark blue pants suit, arrived to the other side of O'Brien's table just moments before the interview began. O'Brien was in a grey suit with conservative white shirt and yellow tie. His ensemble balanced his pale complexion and made him look particularly healthy. The seats were arranged to show his extreme height. In this interview, he would tower over Ms. Cloud. Each cordially said hello before question one.

O'Brien and Mallory Cloud began the interview with a quick review of their last interview in 2008 with O'Brien reminding her that he had been absolutely fair and she gave her concurrence—as if she had a choice. O'Brien had decided that in this interview, he would give Cloud the opportunity to tell her story and maybe, but maybe not, ask a few tough questions. So, after the self-flagellating *what a great guy I am*, he asked her the first of what turned out to be many softball questions.

"Senator," O'Brien used the title that Ms. Cloud would hold for her remaining life despite the fact that she had not been in that office for almost four years, "Was it a series of incidents that caused you to make this decision to resign as Secretary of State or was there something that put you over the edge?"

"Bill, I did not resign as Secretary of State. I was fired because of a decision not to support the President in his re-election campaign. I was fired without any discussion and without so much as a thank you for my service. I was fired and never consulted, not for a second, about anything I was currently doing and I was not asked or permitted to work on the transition. Bill, when I took over at state, I talked at great length with George W's Secretary of State when I took over in 2005. Say what you want about George W. Boone, but he cared first and foremost about the country, not first and foremost about his ego. That may tell you everything about this president." Cloud was seated on the front quadrant of her chair. Under her eyes were bags that makeup could only impact marginally and these were beginning to portray her age.

Questions on the meeting between the President and Mallory lasted until the third advertisement, about twenty-one minutes of face time on the air. It was that rare O'Brien interview that was both interesting and not remotely offensive.

"Senator, let's come back to your endorsement of Senator Vincent. I am going to assume that when you walked onto the platform at the American Exceptionalism Party Convention, you knew you were not going to be the Secretary of State for very long. What caused you to make this decision?"

"Bill, actually, I thought that the President and I would have a meeting to discuss why I had made my decision and that after the meeting, he would give me a courtesy and the opportunity to resign. I should have known that this was not going to happen because the President virtually never met with me while I was Secretary of State. Instead, he was disinterested in my thinking, allocated less than a minute to meeting with me last week and just wanted to try to humiliate me. And, I don't know if you know it, but my return helicopter trip to Washington from Camp David, I think, was via

Florida. The normal few minutes trip, just by chance,"—cynicism dripping from her lips—"took virtually an hour and forty-five minutes and of course, I missed all of the East Coast news deadlines. This is not a nice man!

"To your specific question, it was ultimately a mistake for me to join this administration. I thought that I was going to be a decision maker and in fact, I was pushed out of the way. This is a classic political trick and I fell for it. I was given a prestigious title and sent to small countries to discuss small matters while the world hurdled itself in many horrible directions.

"I knew I was going to leave when the North Koreans began to seriously threaten South Korea and the President appointed a Korean czar. I should have resigned at that moment, but you know, Bill, you are in the position of Secretary of State of the United States of America and you believe you are doing something important, you convince yourself that if you resign, the country will be hurt. As you know, I think, I called the President immediately after that Korean czar decision and we argued over my role. I expressed the view that the very naming of a czar would empower the North Koreans to believe that the USA was not prepared to honor its treaty obligations. Bill had gone to Korea to free those kids from that newspaper that had wandered over the border three years ago because he owed Al Gore a favor. I, and we, had some serious credibility with the North Koreans. Anyway, the horrible result in Korea was the result of our showing our weakness to that devil.

"And, as you know, we never honored our treaty obligations and the Japanese and Chinese did our job. We are now no longer viewed in Asia as one of the world's leaders. I stayed in office thereafter because I thought the President would need my help. He never asked. When Senator Vincent came to me a few weeks ago and asked me for my support, I made what I thought was the right decision for the country. I guess that means I simply gave up on this president."

O'Brien knew he had the right guest on the right night. He also knew he had the widest audience in terms of political philosophy he would ever have and that his ratings would be over the top, maybe seven million viewers. What he did not know then, but would know almost immediately, they were at that moment in time—absent a world crisis being watched live—speaking to the largest cable audience in the history of cable.

"Mallory, if I may call you that, what about your husband's support. It is nearly unheard of for a former senator and her husband, the former president, to join a new political party. What gives with that?"

255

"Bill, we did not join a new political party. We are Democrats. The reality here is that I do not believe that today's Democratic Party or the President are Democrats. They are left wing nuts, as you would say; Progressives."

Laughing: "Mallory, I would be afraid to use those specific words."

"No, you wouldn't," and O'Brien laughed for the second time in a single minute during the interview.

Although originally scheduled for a third of his show, the interview went on for yet another twenty minutes, the entire show, albeit interspersed with a few too many commercials, but Mallory Cloud's admonition that the Democratic Party had been hijacked was the only news that would be covered on the major networks and the cable networks. The blogs would, in general, see Mrs. Cloud's comments as politically motivated. There were no judgments made for the correct reasons on the blogs, only cynical political steps and conspiracies. The mainstream media would see her as a traitor. Talk show radio would forgive her for being a Democrat. She would continue to believe she was a patriot.

~

Of the thousands of restaurants in New York City, Jenn Cho had been to a greater number of them than most and they all represented the same problem. People liked to come to her table and tell her or ask her something. It might be just to thank her for her reporting, something they wanted O'Brien to know, or just to get an autograph. Both her natural personality and her quest to be well known and well loved caused her to be gracious one hundred percent of the time to one hundred percent of the people who would and could inadvertently ruin a wonderful evening. Nice was in her DNA. For tonight, she wanted someplace special, someplace intimate. She also wanted a location that looked like a business meal to Geekhead and to anyone else that spotted them during the evening. In New York City, with cell phones and maître d' on the payroll of columnists, the possibility of a picture in the newspaper or a note in a magazine was about fifty percent for a television personality having a casual or business dinner. With Geekhead being on the show, that would not be good.

Jenn gave some significant thought to where they should have dinner. This was crazy as she had hardly exchanged fifty words with this man and other than a valueless Internet search, she had never had time to find out if he had a wife or girlfriend, or as O'Brien probably said, a boyfriend for that matter. Regardless, she could feel a very unusual attraction. She initially gave some thought to having a meal catered to her condo, but that brought with it the possibility that the evening could end up somewhere other than the dining room and with this man, that was not going to happen on the first date or whatever this was. In current dating etiquette, Jenn was a prude because she did not sleep with anyone until she actually knew them, trusted them, and thought there was a real possibility of a long-term relationship. Her mother would have used a word other than prude as Mom continued to believe that a woman's first sexual experience should be following the wedding party, or so Jenn believed. Despite all of her conservative personal history in one basket, there was something about this man that made her extremely cautious, not of him, but of her.

So, here they sat at John Lee's Chinese Gourmet in a booth where they were far enough away from each other that it would not look like a date to anyone that recognized her. Of course, she reminded herself that it was not a date and Geekhead was there to discuss business. The side benefit of John Lee's was she could find out if he liked his food on fire. As she looked at him,

257

she thought: *This must be the most attractive non-Chinese man on the planet. Being with him is wonderful. And red pepper seems to be his thing.*

The evening ended about two hours later with her arms bolted around Geekhead's shoulders in front of her door. *If this man is within fifty feet of this door again, I am going to drag him inside and keep him forever. Wow!*

~

TUESDAY, AUGUST 14, 2012

Molly Tom sat in front of her computer and began to realize that The Professor did understand the Constitution, but he might not have a full understanding of the mathematics of that arena into which this third party and he had thrown her. She was looking at the Electoral College and not yet looking at the House of Representatives. (She would discover this to be a near waste of her time.) She also now understood that the United States Senate would ultimately become a player under the Constitution, maybe the ultimate player, but perhaps not in the manner The Professor was thinking.

The thought of telling The Professor that he had not thought through the issue was something that in some ways Molly looked forward to with an eagerness that would be hard to describe, almost a physical thing. If she wasn't forty years younger than The Professor, she might have found him attractive, particularly because he could talk to a presidential candidate like he was a naughty twelve-year-old and yet treated his students with the highest degree of respect. Sometimes that high degree of respect that Molly held The Professor to on a personal level was undoubtedly mutual, as he asked the hardest questions on the planet in the classroom. There was always a Madam or a Sir in the front of his questions. Sometimes he toyed with her in class, but she really felt he was educating her by making it tough. She quickly let her mind go back to the subject at hand, because no matter what he thought when he looked at her, he was over sixty years old and there was not even a hint of a rumor about his fidelity to his wife.

Molly knew what The Professor also knew: that the Electoral College was a mess. Her research told her that it was more of a mess than he ever dreamed. The electors, for the most part, did not seem beholden to the voters in any significant way. Not all of the states required that their electors do anything other than vote. Many required their delegates to follow the will of their party, but did not have any teeth in their requirement and only one or two made it a felony to vote except as instructed by the voters. In no case did it appear that regardless of the penalty imposed on the elector after the elector cast his or her vote, the elector's vote would not count as cast. Generally, the penalty for voting for Mickey Mouse rather than the presidential candidate selected by the voters carried less of a penalty than crossing against a red light at two o'clock in the morning. (In Los Angeles, a jaywalking ticket now cost $191.) Perhaps the single most important reason there had been so few unfaithful electoral votes over two hundred years was that each unfaithful vote was an individual, there had never been a group decision.

The elector rules allowed for a challenge to an entire delegation only if the delegation was not confirmed by the state of origin. What that meant was that if a state confirmed the outcome of the electoral voting from their state, there was no opportunity to challenge the electoral vote from that state before they cast their electoral votes. This rule was in place to prevent the Congress from destroying the electoral system by challenging every delegation. It appeared that the only way the Congress could challenge a delegation was if there were two or more delegations from a single state. In that case, it would take both the House and the Senate to agree on a delegation or the governor of the state in question could decide which electoral state would be accepted by the House of Representatives and if the governor of that state took action, then Congress's decision making was abrogated. The governor's decision was final. How odd was that? Bottom line, if there was no winner in the Electoral College, there might be a great deal of smoke, but likely no fire in the actions of the Electoral College unless the electoral result was incredibly close, maybe a delta of two or three votes. Then, and only then, would an unfaithful elector or two make a difference.

In any event, Molly could not find a realistic scenario where the electors would have any final impact on who would become president in 2012. She suspected the Electoral College would create a great deal of attention and debate, but no meaningful result. Maybe five minutes of fame for a couple of electors, but no meaningful result.

Molly and The Professor had talked about this, but she now realized that it was in game three at the House of Representatives and in the Senate that the presidential game would be played. She sensed The Professor knew this but she wondered whether he had a grasp of the particulars. In this rare case, she guessed against.

In the House of Representatives, if there was not a majority of states for a President, there was no President. There was only an Acting President selected by the United States Senate. Molly Tom found out that the election in the House of Representatives was by state and the presidential candidate needed to achieve a majority of the states, twenty-six. This seemed bizarre to Molly and she began thinking through how it might be possible or impossible to achieve a majority as many states might be split fifty-fifty, Democrat to Republican, in their number of seats in the House of Representatives. *What if Members of the House of Representatives might never support another party's presidential candidate?*

Molly Tom also began to think about the public and the possibility they might believe they had been cheated if their candidate was not inaugurated as president if he won the popular vote or if he won the most electoral votes. What if the candidate who was third in each category became the president? What if the president and the vice president were from different parties? That was one of the original reasons the current system was in place via the Constitution in the early 1800s, to keep the possibility of having a president from one political party and a vice president from a different political party. The public's ignorance—that would more precisely be the public's incredible ignorance—could not be ignored. Combine that with the spinners on television and radio, Molly Tom began to wonder if she should be storing food under her bed. *Terrific,* a cynical, but accurate response.

All would be discussed with The Professor on the way to the meeting with Senator Vincent. The Professor indicated that he would be writing until they left the meeting and did not wish to be disturbed.

~

"We have money, we have lots and lots of money; we have bullets and we have brave young men willing to die for the cause. I do not understand this nonsensical and complicated election process that you are describing. Do they not simply vote for their president and be done with it? Infidels! You could make a dog fight confusing! Don't even tell me what you need to do, just do it, be successful and get out. The check will be in your account by the end of the day today assuming you are still using the same bank in the Cayman Islands." Somewhat harsh—but more so dismissive—words as always from Sheik Maardi. The Sheik believed that all Americans and all infidels were corrupt and that this dark-haired, black-eyed heathen was someone he simply had to deal with, for now.

Sheik Maardi's consultant claimed far more credit than the Mullah knew he deserved for the election of the current American president. But the Mullah believed he had helped remove the infidel cowboys and replaced them with a man of words, just words, nothing else. *The perfect American president, for me,* thought Sheik Maardi. Since the President's election, this man in front of him had almost single-handedly caused the confrontation between the two Koreas and had it escalated as they had expected; the assorted actors could have bombed both Koreas back into the Stone Age. It was the action of the Japanese that came as the biggest surprise. *Who knew the Japs were players? The Chinese would never have acted if they did not suddenly have to deal with a nuclear Japan.*

The Sheik knew that most Americans would be shocked to understand his personal financial involvement in fueling and financing the psychosis of the North Korean dictator and the involvement of his consultant. Maybe it would have been best if this consultant had been on the South Korean island. Fairly well educated and a compulsive Internet user, the Mullah was still trying to figure out how the Japanese could have developed a nuclear arsenal and delivery mechanism without any fingerprints around the globe and without a single nuclear test. Smart little men. A shame they only threatened to use their weapons.

Sheik Maardi was certain, with a little help, that given another four years, this President of the United States would perform magic between Iran and Israel, total war. Sheik Maardi could see the ultimate result was that he could become the ruler of most of the remaining Middle East. He had an advanced army and air force and had no intention of spilling the blood of his warriors to kill off the Israelis. Iran would do his dirty work and then receive the ultimate payback from Israel. Losing Iran would be a plus as well; after all, there are no Arabs in Iran.

Robert Smith (his real name) never turned his back on the Sheik, even as he went to the door. He had no feeling either way about the Sheik; his feelings were for money and what it would buy for him. This freelance mercenary from Belgium cared about no one except himself; there was no meaningful *other* in his life, not so much as a dog. His home was on the edge of the Amazon; he loved the game and the money. He selected the Amazon after reading a Grisham book. Like Grisham's character, he found the Amazon and its isolation to his liking. Smith could hardly distinguish the difference between himself and a pirate in the Caribbean in the 1700s. In fact, there was no difference; he would do whatever was necessary to earn his bounty.

Robert Smith would use the money very carefully and in ways that would not occur to other political consultants. The suicide bombers and the third party stuff would take a little thinking, but money always talked, particularly cash.

"On second thought," he looked at the Maardi and offered: "I do not know yet if I want to meet either of the operatives and I might need four instead of two. When they die, they will gain their reward in the hereafter. The key is that their delivery to me in Phoenix be in this specific box." He handed the Sheik a briefcase with the initials STE on the handle. "If I do this right, I will not need to kill anyone else. We'll use our same prepaid telephone card communications and materials delivery system as last time. Just make sure they deliver exactly what I asked for and that they expect something in return for you." With that, Smith opened the door, and was gone.

~

WEDNESDAY, AUGUST 15, 2012

George Vincent was at the podium at a dinner raising money for the Multiple Sclerosis Foundation in nearby Springfield, Illinois. He was the featured speaker and was at the podium with his wife seated next to him. The evening was an opportunity to lay out the reasons for his seeking the presidency as a third-party candidate. During the afternoon, he had been playing with his grandchildren and noticed a bit of shaking in his wife's hands. He had asked her about it as he knew about her family history with MS and she had indicated she was just a bit tired. The coincidence was too strong to ignore. Unusual for him, after his introduction, he had leaned over and hugged and kissed his wife in front of about five hundred people.

"Thank you. Thank you very much. It is a great honor to be here this evening and to help you raise funds for MS research. This is a very personal issue for Marge and me as MS runs in her family. Please do not ever forget that we are available to help you raise money, any place any time." He took just a moment to wink at his wife. This was not staged, it was real.

"As I suspect you all know, I have decided to run for President of the United States of America." Laughter. "This was not an easy decision. And if we are honest, I don't think Marge will ever forgive me. She thinks I don't know, but if I win, I am going to need to come to Cleveland to see her. At least I was smart enough not to ask her if she would choose to be with me or the grandkids." More laughter, another wink and a wife having trouble not spitting out the swallow of water that she had taken right before this remark. *I guess he really does know me pretty well after all of these years.*

"This was the toughest decision I have ever made. I have been a Democrat my entire life and I spent countless hours campaigning for the President four years ago. Unfortunately, I was wrong about the President and wrong about the leadership of the Democratic Party. Sadly, and I mean this, sadly, the combination of the leadership of my former party and the President produced a toxic brew of legislation that I could not and cannot support. This president is out of touch with everyone except the mainstream media and the far left of the Democratic Party. I don't believe that outside of a few significant urban areas that the President could carry twenty-five percent of the population of the United States. In this, we have a president and a Congress—at least the Democratic side of Congress—that is out of step with most Americans.

"And here is where I was caught by surprise, I did not realize how far left the House of Representatives leadership was until the President was elected. Oh, my God.

"I felt I needed to step into the arena. I felt that America needed a candidate that represented the eighty percent not currently represented by the Democrats or Republicans." Applause.

"What also began to trouble me during the past four years was that both parties were beginning to tolerate no dissent on any issues. It was as if the parties were being elected and the individual senator or congressman was immaterial once they were elected. There appeared to be this oddity that the candidate would campaign on a variety of issues important to his or her constituents and then upon arriving in Washington, he or she was expected to vote exactly as directed by their party leadership. Well, rest assured, a Democrat from Ohio—that would be me—is not going to be walking lockstep with a Democrat from Berkeley and maintaining his honor code. The big tent is becoming a straightjacket and the American people are not served very well by this.

"What do I want to accomplish? I want the Congress to address and solve, yes *solve*, the key domestic items of our time: Social Security, immigration—but after we secure our borders—and the deficit. I want to fix health care without destroying the American economy. I want to rebuild our relationships with our traditional allies and reach out to our non-traditional allies. But, and this is an important but, I don't want to bow to anyone. We are the finest nation in the world, we are the freest nation in the world and we are the most powerful nation in the world, and I want to maintain all of the above. I don't want the citizens of our elected officials to delegate duties to a president, to czars, or to nameless, faceless regulators." Applause, significant applause.

Vincent went on to lay out an agenda that he believed most of the non-activists of both parties would embrace.

~

THURSDAY, AUGUST 16, 2012

Even though seemingly made twice already, the hardest formal political decision still facing the President was his vice president. Not young any more, the Vice President had to be one of the nicest individuals the President had ever met. If the President asked him to run into a building that was on fire, was in danger of collapse and the purpose of the trip was to retrieve a favorite fountain pen, the Vice President would have raced into the building without a second thought. In private, he was occasionally—but very, very occasionally—helpful. The President did believe the Vice President had great political instincts for a man with average intellectual power.

There were two things the Vice President could not do. He could not walk by a microphone or a news reporter without engaging it or them in conversation. And, in that conversation, it was virtually impossible that at some point during his comments he would not say something so entirely stupid that he would make the evening news. With an assortment of just horrible comments to choose from, the President's favorite was the Vice President suggesting that flying commercially or perhaps leaving one's house on day one of the swine flu contagion was a mistake. He was going to keep his family at home. Special—remarkably dumb—but special.

"What can I do with the Vice President? Legally?" asked the President. The President was concerned. He was beginning to get slaughtered in the polls; anything would be an improvement. "Herman, let's be honest here and go over it again, Beloved is likeable, loyal, a wonderful guy. The Vice President would make a great pet.

"To be honest, he is not that dumb, maybe not the sharpest tack in the drawer either, but not that dumb. But, set him loose and he becomes the village idiot. For the last two years, I have been afraid to send him to the funeral of a foreign leader lest he get the name of the deceased or the country wrong. A walking, ahh, what was the name of that Jewish comic, Norm Crosby? Some nights I wake up in the middle of the night wondering whether the entire intelligence system was in disarray when I was first elected because the Vice President had sat on the Senate intelligence committee."

Sackman just sat in his chair wordless and bemused because he knew the President would eventually finish this conversation with himself. If this continued its normal pattern, Sackman would get his secret high five from himself just for knowing the President's approach to issues so perfectly.

"I just wish you had told me this man was such a loose cannon when you insisted I nominate him." The president paused. "Just kidding, I think you said he was fourteenth on your list and looking back on it, you had him overrated." Sackman got an additional personal high five as he very rarely got even a nod. A mea culpa was the highest possible score. "So here I am with a seventy-five percent minority convention…"

"Twenty-five percent men, and I am guessing that the committees will chase some more elected white boys and girls home," offered Sackman to guide the President to the only possible answer.

"Pardon me," offered the President, "what do you mean chase the elected white boys and girls home?"

"Mr. President, I know we sent you the draft convention platform. This platform is going to scare the hell out of many white congressman and many delegates. What we have not had time to personally discuss is the credentials committee proposals." The President was up and headed to the cigarette book. Sackman thought to himself: *Good God, I am going to die of secondhand smoke if Mrs. President doesn't get back to this White House soon and stay here for more than a night at a time. I know she hates the place and intends to meet him in Chicago, but maybe she should come back to D.C. for my health. Maybe, just maybe, she will sneak in for a quick conjugal visit before long.* "I am pretty sure that Congressman Schreiber is going to require delegates to sign a loyalty oath to the Democratic Party. You and everyone else will need to sign it to enter the convention."

"You have got to be kidding. Why haven't you told me about this?"

"I sent you the info. I haven't said a word because the guy is going to do it even if we cut off all Federal aid for his state and district. Somehow, this is important to him and I suspect he believes it will help him fend off any arguments that he is not close enough to the left wing of our party. I know that his decision is not subject to threats because I have threatened everything but beheading. Dead he might get sixty percent of the votes in his district so long as he pays homage to the left. Safe district. Gerrymandering, it cuts both ways. I haven't gotten you involved because he effectively told me if you called, he might decide to move to the Progressive Party, the DFL. Those guys have had the real power in Minnesota for some time and that is a conversation I do not think would be in your best interest. Remember, this is a guy who couldn't get a job selling peanuts at the ballpark. It's crazy out there."

"Terrific" taking a very deep drag on the cigarette and he thought about times long ago when there were better and stronger alternatives available than a cigarette. He was back in his chair. *Time to move away from filters to real cigarettes.*

"So, you are going to tell me that I am stuck with my VP because he is white, aren't you?" Just a nod from Sackman. "And they will beat on him like a drum. Ugh. I guess Mallory isn't on the short list!" Grumbling to himself, the President lifted his skinny body out of his chair, took a stance like a soccer player and softly kicked the Oval Office's two-hundred-fifty-year-old copper wastebasket. It rolled across the floor. Even around Herman Sackman, the President was always attempting to appear to be the athlete he wished he was, but was not. The weight lifting and the well-documented basketball demonstrated interest, not ability. This president had never played organized ball and while he loved having the appearance of an athlete, he knew better. There would be no more All-Star Game first pitches in this president's future.

"So, I get this walking mistake up in front of the convention and make him the vice president. Well, it provides the best assassination insurance since Teddy Roosevelt. Wasn't he the one who was instructed by Congress that if he wanted to go in a submarine, he had to take his vice president, or something like that?"

"Pretty good, Boss, wasn't that Charles Fairbanks?" *How many times?*

"How would I know? OK, it's a redo. Don't make a formal announcement; just tell the convention powers, Beloved and the Pillsbury Dough Boy. You tell Beloved. I don't want to tell him. And figure out a way to move him to Colorado to ensure continuity."

~

271

The Mullahs met in a small room in a small Mosque in Qom. There were seven of them and they were the seven most important people in Iran. The President of Iran and other elected officials might occasionally pretend publically that they were important, but the power in Iran was and is concentrated with the clerics in the religious sector of the country.

Mullah Annihiab spoke after the appropriate prayers had been offered: "What can we do to keep the infidel's president in office? We are poised to be the most powerful nation on the earth and return the Islamic Empire to its previous glory. We need only for the Americans to follow their pacifism and cowardness for another three, maybe four years and there will be nothing they can do without endangering their own population."

Mullah Banahm offered a rather odd response: "Perhaps we could point out that the man is half white. I have not understood the entire process of how this man proclaimed himself black instead of half white or white. He was raised by a white woman. Didn't her white parents really raise him? Isn't that what he is, half white? Wouldn't this increase his standing with the white population?"

The most powerful Mullah, Mullah Seecaaj laughed at Mullah Banahm: "Do not think that we can understand the infidels. White, black or whatever, we will not play that game. My reading says that your thoughts are correct logically and wrong in US political terms. We would be better off ensuring that the blacks vote, acknowledging they may have gotten nothing of what they wanted from the President, they would rather have this man over any white man. But, it is not in our culture to understand how a man is two colors and declares himself one color. I have read a few comments on this in Western newspapers and apparently it is something they cannot discuss. Free press, political correctness, it is very, very odd. Another reason we will control the earth.

"Let us talk in two different veins," offered Seecaaj. "First the easy part, we agree that the President is the best choice for us. I believe that it is a closer decision than others because I believe Congressman Roland is what the Americans call an isolationist and I believe he would withdraw from the rest of the world. That would be good in terms of more quickly creating a bigger Islamic State, but a United States that understands that it has sufficient energy sources within the United States, if it makes but tiny changes in its living standards is also a dangerous United States. I also worry about his thought processes and he may be a person who would move precipitously with American air and sea power if appropriately motivated. He appears not to struggle with decisions, as does this current president. He could be a dangerous man in the long run, but in the short run, he would be wonderful.

"It is Senator Vincent who loves the world's status quo and might be willing to engage us militarily when we move against the Saudis or the Israelis. Defending the status quo is not good. That is dangerous to us.

"We will support voter registration quietly but with many, many dollars. There are non-profit groups who will recognize that it is the poor who need to be registered. Whether they are what they call legal, we do not care. We don't understand how these uneducated, thoughtless, jobless people can be allowed to cast meaningful votes regardless of where they live; we will simply ride their ignorance. We will launder money through our friends in Mexico and Ireland. Our friends in Mexico will also once again slow the drug trade and their so-called drug war will cease until after the election. It need only last ninety days. Pay them; pay them whatever it takes. We will send our president to Columbia and make energy commitments for his help over the next ninety days. That is the easy part—does anyone differ?"

The looks around the room said everything. When Mullah Seecaaj offered an idea, it was more than an idea.

Hearing no objection, Mullah Seecaaj continued, "Use the same man as last time for both the cash that needs to be moved for voter registration and the cash that needs to be paid to the drug cartels."

No one in the room knew of the actions of Saudi Arabia's Sheik Maadi or had ever heard of Robert Smith's activities with the Saudis. If they knew of those activities, he would not have been their conduit and consultant to move funds in the United States.

~

FRIDAY, AUGUST 17, 2012

On page three of each of the thirty major newspapers in the country was a full-page advertisement paid for by Isadore Yergler.

Below a giant picture of the President there was a single line:

CHANGE WE BELIEVED IN FOUR YEARS AGO AND BELIEVE IN TODAY. FOUR MORE YEARS OF MAKING AMERCIA INTO THE DREAM IT CAN BE.

The actual bills received from the thirty newspapers were close to $400,000 short of what Sam Dehning charged Yergler. (This took a bit of work with the invoicing system, but was not that hard for Dehning as this was how he funded his multiple personal relationships and he had been at it for a while.) In what would be a three-month hosing of Yergler, Dehning was beginning to realize that using Yergler's name in the advertisements was a huge positive to getting his bills paid timely. It turned out that Yergler absolutely loved seeing his name in the newspapers, and hearing it on the radio told him that he was a player. Dehning had known Yergler enjoyed the skullduggery of the last campaign and the money hiding, but the public aspect apparently was even better for him.

~

Throughout the weekend, a radio advertisement was playing on stations throughout the entire radio spectrum, twenty-four hours a day. It was again another commercial with a woman's voice:

> *Mr. President, we have been thinking about that transparent thing again. How was it that the health care bill was about two bazillion pages that neither you nor we had time to read and now we find out it will have about ten bazillion pages of regulations?*
>
> *Mr. President, we have been thinking about that stimulus package again. How was it that the stimulus bill was about two bazillion pages that neither you nor we had time to read and now we find out it did not produce more than about a dozen jobs? And after spending a bazillion dollars on shovel ready projects, you tell us there is no such thing as a shovel ready job?*
>
> *This radio commercial was paid for by the Americans for Truth and Transparency*—another group no one had ever heard of previously.

~

In Dallas, Texas there are some of the most famous luncheon and evening clubs in the world. These clubs all seem to have been created, designed and decorated based upon a television show from the 1970s, *Dallas*.

When one approaches the front door of the Peter Cambron Building in Dallas, one is also approaching the outside elevator of Dallas's New Century Club. When using this private elevator, which requires a key card plus an identification number to use, one gets an entire view of Dallas towards the airport. From inside the elevators, it is not rare to see an airplane taking off from the Dallas/Fort Worth International Airport, just under twenty miles away.

Dallas was a free architectural zone in the 1960s and 1970s and this particular building, the Cambron Building, looks as if someone stole the bottom third of several floors on its North side. When it was first built, the building was nicknamed Sideswipe as a reporter cynically offered during construction that it appeared as if a large truck carrying a huge load had crashed into the building and taken away a part of the first several floors. As it was still standing, the architects apparently had the last laugh, as the angular front of the building continued to cause havoc with short skirts, as when the wind whipped through the open area it created the world's smallest wind tunnel.

Anyone that enters the private elevator, completes the verification process correctly, and rides to the forty-third floor of Sideswipe exits into a bland entry area highlighted by an oak door resting ten feet tall. Normally, in front of the door resides one of the prettiest women in Dallas. Her job is to review membership cards for entry. These receptionists were always four of the prettiest women in Dallas, each trusted with this assignment and each expected to be able to name, or at least recognize, most of the five hundred club members. Each receptionist could also generally speak at least two languages fluently and had graduated from an elite American university. These women were carefully selected, overpaid and forbidden from dating any member or relative of a member's family. Most of them used the receptionist position to attain an entry-level position at a major Dallas company. Everyone knew that the receptionists at the New Century Club were the smartest and most attractive young college graduates in town, so corporate CEOs would not take any grief from hiring one of these beautiful young women for their companies. The dating rule was generally obeyed although there were two members' wives who at one time had been receptionists for

277

the Dallas New Century Club. Rules were rules, but occasionally rules were broken when physical attraction on one side of the reception desk was recognized as a significant monetary opportunity on the other side of the desk.

Today, there was a visible gentleman sitting in the reception area a few feet from the statuesque, black, honors graduate receptionist from Yale. He was half of the security team for Congressman Roland, and the earpiece along with the oversized sport coat were clues as to his job duties. His security partner was on the other side of the door.

Inside the mahogany laced rooms of this Dallas men's club were several private rooms for meetings and lunches. In one room this early afternoon was Paul Roland and his four closest friends and advisors. Their lunch plates were clean and they had just completed both their lunch and their dissection of the Dallas Cowboys and University of Texas football teams at levels that would make anyone think the group was far too immature to run the government of a small city in Texas, let alone the United States of America. Of course, this standard would have eliminated seventy percent of the men around the world from participating in any form of democracy.

The winner of every Republican primary was a sixty-one-year-old, six-term congressman, who had continued to be an obstetrician between his terms in the House of Representatives. He had served a series of terms in Congress, became disenchanted and returned to his medical practice. After practicing for a few more years, he became so disappointed in his political party, that he decided to run for office again and try to get more done on a deeply philosophical basis on his second try. His views were very straightforward as he now only had two steps in determining whether he would support legislation. First, was it constitutional and second was it something he thought was a good idea and fiscally prudent. It needed to pass both tests. His reading of the Constitution of the United States was exceptionally narrow, which he believed to be appropriate. Some of the expansionary readings of the Constitution, especially the expansionary readings of the commerce clause, enraged him.

The Republican primaries had been a long and difficult battle. While Roland won every primary, each one had been a struggle. It had begun with Iowa and what seemed to be well over one hundred candidates. One wag had written that there were more candidates for the Iowa Republican caucus victory than there were voters. He was not too far off. Ultimately, the congressman had won the caucuses with less than twenty-five percent of the votes cast. His success was tempered by the former governor of Arkansas being the solid Tea party candidate. Fortunately, the governor spent all of his political and financial capital on Connecticut and Connecticut was more interested in jobs than Tea Party philosophy. After Connecticut, Congressman Roland faced the Republican stopper of the week or month. As these individually crashed and burned, new rivals continued to appear. At the end, Roland managed to win every primary, but he had both run out of money and failed to develop a constituency beyond his conservative roots.

Rail thin with a lifetime history of morning exercise, the congressman was in far better physical shape than any of his advisors. He had never smoked and effectively did not tolerate anyone who did. His view was that smoking was fine if done in the confines of one's own automobile alone, but if you smoked near him, he viewed that as an intrusion into his space. He unmercifully teased and prodded everyone around him to stop smoking and if he smelled tobacco on an individual, he would always say something about the dreaded lung cancer opportunity they were creating. In his fairly young patient base, he had seen his share of brain cancers that had moved from cancerous lungs. It drove him nuts. Even with his philosophical stridency, smoking drove him to distraction because of the damage that it caused.

"So, my friends, where do we take this campaign and what the heck has happened over the last few weeks. Please, I want to hear your thoughts and I want you to know that this American Exceptionalism Party Convention caught me completely by surprise and I am not sure whether it is good news or bad news. What do you think?" With Congressman Roland, the questions were always truly questions, he wanted opinions and if he asked, he had not made up his mind.

William Ulmstead was the oldest of the group and usually spoke first. He was born and raised in Texas, earned a degree in physics at the University of Texas, served in the navy during Vietnam, and came home to manage the family ranch. Unlike any of his friends, his first marriage had only lasted a few years and he never remarried. He managed to stay close to both of his children and his son was the one who was running the family ranch today. Ulmstead's spare time, which was most of the time, was spent fishing and hunting with a preference for trying to find the world's largest small mouth bass. His only other hobby was the local hospital where he had been a board member seemingly forever and where rumor had it, he wrote an annual check to make up the difference between the expenses and the income.

At the hospital, the only thing he ever asked was that his name never, ever appear on so much as a broom handle in recognition of his contributions; he thought charity was from the heart.

"Well, Paul, I think the first thing you need to do is step back and decide whether you are running to win or running to defeat this left-wing nutcase we have in the White House."

"What do you mean?"

"Well, the way I see it, if you run a truly honest campaign, there cannot be but eight states that would want you to be the president rather than that Vincent guy or the President. You are too old and too grey and too white, not to mention being a serious conservative. Oh, you can run to the middle like those politicians you have complained about your entire life and make an honest run to be the president, maybe, and then decide whether you want to lie to yourself and govern from the middle or lie to the poor bastards that believed you and govern as a conservative. And, even then, I think you are still a long shot if you run to the middle." Ulmstead, as always, spoke with his slow Texas twang.

"OK, that is one point of view, but help me with the whether I want to defeat the President part or not. I did not get any clarity on that." Roland asked the question in a purely conversational voice; these men were his friends and he trusted each one of them with his life.

"Well," It seemed that Ulmstead started every paragraph with the same word; he could not say hello without first working *well* into the greeting. "I think you know what I mean and you are not ready to step into that position. This president is a generation younger than we all are, hell, maybe I am a generation older than you, Paul. His definition of ethics is different than yours, Tommy's, Pastor John's or mine. It is cultural and he doesn't believe he is lying when he says things, although the four of us would consider his speeches to be lies."

The congressman interrupted: "Give me an example, I still don't follow."

"Well, Paulie, remember he gave that health care speech on Labor Day before his speech to the joint session of Congress. He said in that speech that the Republicans had offered no solutions to the health care problem. He knew that wasn't true, but some speech writer put it on his teleprompter. Senator Virchick was talking about this three weeks ago; this SOB president just read it like it was true. Didn't bother him at all. Same with that keep your old insurance plan stuff, just a bunch of crap."

"Well, got it. But, okay, go on about running to beat the President without winning myself."

"Well, I think if you ran only against the President in an absolutely honest, two-man, but no holds barred manner, and simultaneously you both voiced what you believe, you might beat him into submission. But in this game, while you were winning on points against the President, for the most part, you would be driving votes away from the President and to Vincent. And understand, I think that is a worthy goal. Vincent has a reputation for being a pretty honest guy and maybe that would be the best possible result this time around. One thing for sure, Vincent is not the President."

"Immeresting as my oldest kid says. Not sure what you say all fits together, but I've got your point. Tommy, what do you think?"

"First, I think Marc should be here. Not to sound obsequious, but he is smarter than any of us—sorry Pastor—and he is much more in tune with the generations in their twenties and thirties and could give us a pretty good idea from a different perspective."

"Tommy, Marc will be here in a few minutes and he is bringing his girl-friend with him. God, I hate this living together thing, but she is an honors graduate from Rice in political science and while she doesn't agree with anything I believe, I think she likes me and she is honest as the day is long."

"Good. So, I tend to believe that I have about as much chance to become President of the United States as you do, Paul. Seriously. We may all believe in the Constitution, but these voters for the most part have not studied the Constitution and its history in the classroom and think it is just old men who think what was written down two hundred years ago is worth looking at. And don't tell me about the history of the law, and whatever else, that isn't the point. You lose all of the minorities at moment one and maybe you lose the black vote by more than one hundred percent of the legal voters if the President gets his way on registration in a few states. Maybe if the third candidate had been a liberal, a traditional liberal, not like the President, you might have had a chance. Same thing with moveon.org, but George Vincent has cut off your left nut as it were. He gets the middle, period."

"Nice analogy, Tommy. That is why Marc and Crystal are coming in a little while. Pastor?"

"Congressman, for the church, the President is worse than someone advertently trying to destroy the church. I don't know how smart he is, although my guess is that he is a lot smarter than most conservatives give him credit…"

Tommy interrupted: "Pastor, I am not believing the guy is anything but a minority admit to Harvard Law School. There ain't no way that isn't the reason he won't release his college grades." For Tommy, a sentence with a triple negative was not all that unusual. When annoyed, Tommy Carnevale talked as if he had been and remained an uneducated poor kid from the hills outside of Austin. Only the first half was true. This nondescript gentleman owned more than two dozen small shopping centers in various suburban locations in Texas. He got there through street smarts alone. "And as far as the Editor of Law Review part, from what I have read, no one has yet to find a single journal article that guy ever wrote. Appears to have created a resume out of nothing. The press treats him as an academic, a professor. My right wing buddies at UT seem to think calling him an academic as an insult to academics. They say the guy was nothing more than an adjunct professor who filled in classes when the real professors were too busy with research. I guess that is the norm in most graduate schools and law schools as well.

"Smart, no; savvy, probably; brilliant, not a chance. And catch him needing to formulate an idea which he was not prepped on, his serve and volley skills are very poor, if—and it is a big if—the other side of the conversation is allowed to serve and volley. Add to that, I don't think there is a soul in that administration who could help him with business and economic advice. They are all academicians and not a one of them has ever hired someone they needed to pay for as an employee in their lives. More importantly, there isn't anyone in the whole Cabinet that has ever needed to meet a payroll or fire someone. Other than that, I think this president is the most brilliant SOB on the planet! Make a pretty good intern, we could train him to be a professional and give him some management experience."

The pastor listened closely. He had gone to Vietnam as a Marine lieutenant and returned to attend divinity school. In the crush of the jungle, this super star, West Point trained soldier had found God and that was it. He had also found humility, of all things, in Vietnam and had never quite come to grips with his survival while friends and other servicemen he served with had died. His use of the firepower he controlled in Vietnam resulted in many deaths of the enemy and yet he seemed to be able to deal with this better than the loss of his own team. All of this left him with a gift for direct conversation. He explained: "Congressman, you have an obligation to tell the people what you think. If you cannot do that, I couldn't support you myself. If that helps the President or the other guy, that is irrelevant. You need only two goals: be honest with yourself and be honest with those around you."

"Well, Kid, no one in this group ever holds back, do they?" responded Ulmstead.

"No, and not me either. I would really like to be the President of the United States, but I agree that it is a long shot. Not the hand I expected to be dealt, but the hand I will have to play. There isn't any chance I can run against my principles. So, I judge my job is to represent my principles and the principles of the individuals that will be delegates to the Republican convention. If that helps the President or Vincent, so be it.

"I am going to have to speak out against the past four years and against a man I believe misrepresented himself to the American people. And I think he misrepresented himself in many, many ways, not just health care. I have never forgiven him for some of those czar appointments. We don't know how he managed to find these guys, whether they were friends or friends of friends, but oh my God, what a collection of neophytes and un-American types. I have not forgiven him for all the closed door stuff on health care. And a recess appointment for this left-wing academician on health care, he should be put over someone's knee and spanked."

Pastor John Smith, a classic American name, looked Paul Roland right in the eye and asked: "Congressman, are you sure you want to do this. It will be tortuous and the press will attempt to destroy you and your family. They will turn you into the country's most powerful bigot and some of your friends will inadvertently help them when they defend you."

"Yes, Pastor, what's the worst that can happen? Based on what you have told me during the past decades, I am headed to heaven, so how bad could this be? Besides, I did win every primary and every caucus and if I lose this gig, it isn't as if I do not garner pleasure from saving an occasional life in the operating room."

The Pastor responded: "People save themselves for the life after life, you extend life, Ron."

"Well, great job. Who exactly did you defeat in those uncontested primaries?" son number one entered the room trying to comment on what he just thought he heard. "Dad," smiling and obviously happy to be there, he was wearing the brightest burnt orange shirt ever made along with casual brown pants and sandals. "No one is going to give you the last rights or anything, are they?"

Paul Roland hugged his son and reminded him if he was still hoping for his last rights in his church, he should be attending a bit more often. They both laughed, but the point, as always, was made on Robert Roland, a good kid by virtually any standard. Paul Roland thought back to the Scott Brown interview after his election to the US Senate. While Brown was significantly left of Paul Roland, Roland appreciated the obviously close relationship between Brown and his older daughter. Family first. He hugged the girlfriend as well and after a couple of years, she had managed to learn to trust the famous, old conservative and hug back.

"Oh, Dr. Roland, we were not invited down here to discuss that living together thing again, were we?" Crystal could never resist, even with strangers at the table. Paul Roland always wondered what his boy saw in this young woman. Modest looking, today attired in a golden blouse, Levi's and sandals, but articulate to beat the band and one knew exactly where she stood, even if disinterested. Given that Roland believed his son could be with any woman he wished, Paul generally concluded that this young lady must be very special, a real pain, but very special. *I wonder how she got past the front door in Levi's?*

"No, Crystal, but I still have that fund in the bank for the wedding and the honeymoon. We'd all have a great time and the Pastor here would make it a beautiful ceremony. Pastor, could we do it right now?"

"Oh, Dr. Paul, we'll make you happy some day. Maybe early next week during the convention if that's okay with you?" Crystal took absolutely no guff from the congressman or his son and that was one of the reasons why the congressman really did want them to get married. She also took great pleasure in rotating the names she called him: Dr. Roland, Dr. Paul, Dr. Congressman, etc. From her prospective, he would learn to understand why she was special when he needed to understand. And of course, fathers really never understand why their sons are attracted to different women.

She would be good for my baby boy.

"Well, Kids, enough of that. I love you and we'll do anything that makes the congressman happy, we need your help. Your Dad here is dealing with a dilemma and I don't think the three of us are providing him with any twenty-first century input. We think that the only way he can win the election is to move to the center and he seems unwilling to do that. While we admire this, that will assure a loss in our opinion. So the question is, should we be advising him to move to the center or simply be a blocking back for Vincent? If your dad runs as a true conservative, every vote he loses will be a vote for George Vincent, but every vote he gets will be a vote for the President." Ulmstead had summed up the prior discussion in just a few sentences.

The congressman's son and his girlfriend laughed and laughed hard.

"Well, what am I missing?"

Crystal spoke first: "We talked about this with great specificity driving over here. We knew that this group would come to the same conclusion and, Mr. Ulmstead, you would work into the issue an analogy to football. Oh, blocking back, that is sweet. Men!"

Crystal continued: "You have to confess that there would be a standing room only crowd to see Dr. Congressman say something he did not believe to be true. It really is remarkable that he ever got elected to anything in the first place, given his ethics, straightforwardness and ability to articulate and defend ideas no one else wants to hear."

"Crystal, that's a bit hard on my colleagues and the voters. They aren't all Charlie Rangel, but far too many are."

Crystal blanched at the response. "Sure, but you are what you are, Dr. Paul. We think the only issue is whether given the new facts of a serious third party is whether you should get the convention to pick someone else and allow you to withdraw." She smiled and paused. "Seriously, there is no way you cannot be you and no way, with George Vincent drawing from the more moderate Republicans and moderate Democrats, that you have any chance at all."

"Crystal, you really should marry Robert right now. He won't ever find anyone better. Your candor qualifies you as a member of our family. And I think you are partly right. I do believe I was nominated in the primaries because I am where the Party faithful wants to go and I think the majority of them would rather lose doing the right thing. What I did not hear from you or my old friends here is that you thought I would hurt Vincent to the point of giving the President another four years and that is the question I am thinking about. If I can go out to this country and have them listen to me while electing George Vincent by my rhetoric, that is probably the best I am going to do in this election. I think many of my constituents would see that as a win. But, what if I run and the opposite occurs?

He did not wait for a response. "OK, so I will do this crazy thing with that reality; I will run a brutally honest campaign and lose. But, we will run as hard and honest as we can and who knows?"

"You know, Dad," Robert entered the discussion in a serious manner for the first time. "I am not sure you have thought through the impact of having three candidates. What if no one gets a majority of the Electoral College?"

"Son, that is a bridge we will cross if we get there. At that point, it is up to the House of Representatives and someone will broker a deal. That may be a bad spot for old Dr. Paul Roland, Mr. Inflexible Ethics. So, son, what about a VP?"

"Dad, if you intend to lose, why don't you have some fun and nominate Mom. It will cut down on the costs."

"That would be a great idea if it were legal. But, as you *should* have learned in high school," Paul loved to toy with his son's historical knowledge, "the nominees cannot be from the same state. Seriously, what would you recommend?"

"You know, Dad, I would go with the former governor same as last time. Her negatives and her positives are high and her philosophy is really right on point."

"Can't do that one, Son. I know she is the most unfairly treated person in the history of American politics, but she would take away from the message. And honestly, I have not figured the woman out yet. I am old-fashioned and what scared me about the President scares me about the former governor. I want a president who has accomplished something in some non-political field. Other than being a successful mayor of, what, some small town in the middle of nowhere, I don't think she has done anything. She wasn't a governor any longer than the President pretended to be a senator. Smart enough, I don't know, but I think so. She is off the table."

"Given what you have talked about for the last hour, I think you go with the most conservative man you can find. You won't be taking any votes away from Vincent and you will be representing your honestly held views. The man part is because you don't want to have the only woman in this contest. It would hurt Vincent." Tommy Carnevale was the political guru in the room and he only spoke when he had thought an issue through from *A* to *Z*. Tommy had served on the Plano Board of Education for almost a decade, decided not to run for re-election for a third term and refused to look at higher office because he had hated the school board job and knew that his lack of a college education would kill him. He believed he was doing more good for more people by showing up at work every morning and making significant annual contributions to charities that helped kids. Plus, he really liked seeing his wife every morning and evening.

Crystal: "Mr. Carnevale, is that really fair? Should Dr. Paul really be excluding women?'

"Absolutely not fair, but the right decision, Crystal. Don't you think, Paul? This is about not re-electing the President and a woman in our camp could hurt Vincent."

"Guys, I have a meeting to go to and need to raise a bit of money, actually a lot of money, I think I'll actually work the convention a bit before I pick a vice president. There must be a young Ronald Reagan out there someplace. Thanks for your help. I love you all." And, with that, he popped out of the room, joined his security number one, picked up security number two in the lobby and rode the elevator down to his waiting SUV. He loved the view from this forty-one story outside elevator.

~

MONDAY, AUGUST 20, 2012

North-South Polling Service:

The President	32%
Congressman Paul Roland	34%
George Vincent	34%

~

Throughout the day, a radio advertisement was playing on stations over the entire radio spectrum twenty-four hours a day. This was not a simple advertisement; it was a challenge to the President. The first message was in Spanish with a voice the consultants hoped people would accept as the voice of a Mexican peasant. When finished, the entire message was repeated in English with the same voice.

> *Mr. President, the gangs are in our cities in Northern Mexico. We are afraid for our lives and we know that if you secured your borders, we would be safe again from the drug cartels. We are a peaceful people and we have been overtaken by a war which is being fought exclusively to supply illegal drugs to an American marketplace."*

The second message was a voice the consultants hoped would sound like a ten-year-old Phoenix resident.

> *Mr. President, we are afraid to go camping in the desert because of the Mexican gangs. Our desert is only thirty miles East of Phoenix and the Department of Homeland Security has put up signs that say we risk our lives in our American desert because of drug smugglers.*

The last voice was the traditional, deep voice of a professional political advertisement announcer.

> *We need a new president and a new border policy. This radio commercial was paid for by Beth Midlands.*

~

290

Geekhead was completely focused on their early Tuesday morning flight to Chicago and his role on Tuesday, Wednesday and Thursday night when O'Brien wanted a comprehensive idea of where the election was going from a theoretical standpoint. After watching Jennifer Cho stare at Geekhead at the studio, Ginny Manning at Fox News would not have laughed out loud that Jenn was actually having another business meeting dinner despite that it had seemed so odd to Manning when it first came up. Jenn was very busy, it seemed, playing coach.

Yet another stranger, the fifth or sixth person actually, came over to the table to ask for Jenn's autograph. He was only the second to recognize Geekhead and the first to ask for his autograph. The man was trying so hard to be nice, but *couldn't they just leave us alone?* Jenn thought.

This evening was not going at all like Jenn had planned or expected. Every time she started to move the conversation towards something personal, someone approached the table or a waiter delivered yet another course. John Lee of John Lee's Gourmet Restaurant was in the restaurant tonight and everything he did right was wrong from Jenn's prospective. Having Mr. Lee sit with them for almost fifteen minutes was never a consideration in Cho's planning for the evening. It was simply painful for her.

As they were leaving the restaurant, Geekhead grasped Jenn's left hand tightly in his right. Jenn was about to suggest a glass of wine at her place as he leaned his mouth into her left ear and told her: "God, I love being with you. In a different situation, I would suggest going into the bar for another glass of wine. Tonight, I think I had better go home and review all of my notes for the week. Don't want to let you down."

Jenn looked up, her body suddenly taught, and told Geekhead that sounded like a smart idea, but to make sure they only shook hands when he put her into her cab. One never knew who was watching or if there was a camera outside the restaurant. After getting into her cab with her handshake completed, Jenn cried all the way to her apartment. *Every moment I spend with Geekhead is wonderful and it isn't working out. Maybe he does not want a Chinese woman in his bed.*

Geekhead decided to walk back to his apartment. *I wonder if I am playing my cards too fast with Jenn. She is the first woman I have ever met that I wanted to take home to my parents and say: 'Look what your baby boy found. Isn't she perfect? She is nicer than she is beautiful and she is the prettiest woman I have ever met.' At some point, I need to change this relationship from business to personal. I thought we crossed that bridge in front of her apartment. Maybe she is reluctant to get involved with a Caucasian. That would kill me. Maybe this woman is too special for me.*

~

TUESDAY, AUGUST 21, 2012

From the day's *Washington Post* editorial page by Randy Kraus:

DEMOCRATS TRY TO STOP THE
BLEEDING CONVENTION STARTS TODAY, ENDS THURSDAY

At dawn, sixteen days ago, we believed that we were about to watch a traditional November election for the President of the United States. We believed that this would be another titanic battle between the Democrats and Republicans to see which political party could drag the nation to the far end of its individual political spectrum. Before their convention, we believed that the American Exceptionalism Party would drain a few votes from each party and the game, in historical terms, would be interesting, important and unexceptional.

At 8:15 p.m., August 7, 2012, when former President Bill Cloud and wife, Mallory Cloud, along with former President George Boone and wife Barbara Boone walked onto the stage in Cleveland, the world changed. Who said nothing of any importance ever happened in Cleveland? Actually, that was me.

The polls tell us that this election is now a three horse race. The polls tell us that there is no leader and no follower. We think the polls are correct. We believe the voters will race toward and then back from this AEP. When voters realize that if George Vincent is elected President he will not have a single reliable ally in the United

States Congress, they will find this very troubling. He would not be able to shepherd any legislation through Congress and that gang in Congress could and would run rough shod over his presidency.

While we applaud the excitement, we urge and expect the Democrats this week and the Republicans next week to lay out a cohesive and successful case against the American Exceptionalism Party. Early ripe, early rot.

~

The President sat in his study at his Chicago home and contemplated his convention. The convention was in his town and here, he remained the most popular candidate and person. Unfortunately, by being in his own home, he had to read about and watch the cable news moderators re-review his purchase of this home with the help of his friend, a convicted and still jailed felon. Would this story ever die? Then, he had to relive the pontifications of his local pastor who had been more of an ally than a friend or pastor to the President. He also had to relive his affiliation with a known urban terrorist. That was never fun. *God, if I had only attended church a bit more often after the girls were born, I would have seen enough to realize I had to get out of that church and stay away from some of the high profile hanger-ons.*

As a television spectator, he quietly witnessed Congressman Schreiber position him on the loyalty pledge to the convention; he concluded that he was going to have to sign the pledge. He could later ignore it, but he knew it would chase him around the country with the assurance that storms move from West to East in the Northern Hemisphere.

Well, he was not appearing at the convention until Thursday night, the stage had been properly organized (with teleprompters) and he would be ready to go. The delegates would warmly support him and all would be fine. Golf today. A private course with limited access; no cameras today.

He would indirectly need to address the television commercials. *Odd. That should not be that hard.*

~

On Tuesday night television at 7:30 p.m., virtually on every traditional and every news and entertainment cable station, an advertisement appeared for the entire country to view simultaneously. It was a sequential advertisement, simple, inexpensive to produce, and easy to understand.

With no sound, the advertisement first showed a single, simple sentence:

MR. PRESIDENT, IT IS TIME TO EXPLAIN YOURSELF.

Then a series of statements with well-spoken voices from many obviously different races and backgrounds asked questions with just the words and simultaneous pictures:

WHY WOULD YOU SUPPORT A HEALTH CARE BILL THAT WOULD DESTROY MEDICARE?

(Picture of an old man in a wheelchair.)

WHY DID YOU PLACATE NORTH KOREA?

(Picture of the Korean island after the nuclear bomb.)

(Second Picture – Sunken South Korean War Ship.)

WHY DID YOU DISHONOR AMERICA BY NOT HONORING OUR TREATY WITH SOUTH KOREA?

(Picture of an American flag obviously taken during action of World War II.)

WHY DID YOU WASTE A TRILLION DOLLARS ON A STIMULUS PACKAGE THAT ONLY STIMULATED THE POCKET BOOKS OF YOUR POLITICAL SUPPORTERS?

(Picture of an unemployment line.)

WHY DID YOU APPOINT INDIVIDUALS TO SERVE IN YOUR ADMINISTRATION THAT REPRESENTED COMMUNIST VIEWPOINTS?

(Picture of a White House appointee who resigned.)

(Second Picture – Vladimir Lenin.)

PAID FOR BY REESA JONATHON, AMERICAN
Someone needed to speak up!

(Picture of Reesa Jonathon as a competitive swimmer.)

(Second Picture – Reesa in her wheelchair seated in front of a group of children.)

~

The platform committee of the Democratic Party was two hours into completing their work and all pretenses were gone. The Democratic Party was putting together a political platform that represented a move so far to the left that it was unprecedented in any previous Democratic platforms. The members of the platform committee were Progressives with a capital *P*, not traditional Democrats.

With one prior President supporting the American Exceptionalism Party's candidate and most of the senior non-urban area senators following suit, the now most powerful members of the Democratic Party intellect were not John Fitzgerald Kennedy Democrats. The platform was sneaking up on completion and contained a series of positions that would make any traditional Democratic candidate seek medical advice before advancing it to a crowd of individuals over the age of thirty in at least forty states. It would be okay if the platform was presented on the campus of a large state university or an elitist Ivy League campus, but nowhere else. The President was going to be asked/told to sell:

1. Abortion on demand and by demand (specifically disallowing a Catholic hospital or Catholic health practitioner from refusing to provide third trimester abortion services).
2. Closing of all foreign military bases and the immediate return of all US troops from foreign soil. The language of the provision included the elimination of the naval base and the prison at Guantanamo and the US base in Diego Garcia as well as the return of the entire naval fleet to US ports. This apparently also meant bringing home all troops now assigned to NATO.
3. Free health care with the nationalization of all health care activities including doctor's offices and privately owned and charitable hospitals. In an effort to provide the same level of care to all Americans, the platform specifically made illegal the delivery of any health care services unauthorized by the Federal government.
4. Gasoline rationing to limit automobile emissions.
5. Requiring a labor union in any business with greater than ten employees or $100,000 of revenues.
6. Federally supplied pensions for all Americans with the surrender of all existing retirement accounts into one Federal department to fund and administer payments.

7. Equal pay for equal work for all Americans. Equal pay for equal work boards to be organized in every state under the direction of the Federal government.

8. Taxation of all land and activities of all tax-exempt entities including churches.

9. Individual tax rates of sixty percent on income over $250,000 and ninety percent over $2 million.

10. Reparations to blacks and Native Americans.

11. Identifying sugar as a drug and therefore giving the FDA the ability to regulate sugar in food products.

12. More of the same through #50.

After the platform proposal presentation, Congressman Homer from Western Pennsylvania asked at his microphone whether any of the platform was negotiable or whether it had been worked out privately and the preceding two hours' presentations had been for show. The congressman was booed by almost everyone in the arena and he suddenly found himself standing next to a union member who was of sufficient size to block the sun.

The union member swiped the microphone from Congressman Homer's hand and asked the room's attendees: "Do we need any more discussion on the basic principles of democracy and fairness?" The delegates roared *No*, and he moved for approval by acclamation and the chair asked the question. The congressman simply looked at the union member and shook his head.

On the way out of the Platform Committee meeting, one member of the press saw Congressman Homer and asked him what was happening. The congressman, surprisingly poised, looked at the media member and replied: "Off to my hotel room to pack and go home. If there is now no room for debate in this Democratic Party, I guess if I win re-election this year, then in November 2014 I will be either an Independent or a new member of the American Exceptionalism Party. I'll have to figure that out, but I clearly do not belong in the same political party as these people. I do not know how long it has been since someone was tarred and feathered in Western Pennsylvania, but I do not want it to be Congressman Justice Homer and signing up to this platform, give me a break! What a tragedy."

What would be surprising to the hoteliers of Chicago, along with the Democratic leadership but not the President—who was not in control of this platform committee—was that about fifteen percent of the delegates would leave Chicago by nightfall. The Platform Committee was like all of the delegate meetings, far left leadership protected by union members who were intimidating to any average human being and delegate.

Several of the President's top financial donors also left Chicago. Richardson Vogel, the chief executive officer of the largest retailer in the country remarked that the convention reminded him of a scene from James Clavell's book *Whirlwind*. He offered a short burst to his wife on the telephone as he headed for the airport: "Claire, remember when we read *Whirlwind*, once the revolution starts, everyone is in danger. I am coming home, now."

~

The formal main room at the Democratic Convention was beginning its featured sessions. The convention was now beginning to look like a meeting of minorities with a sprinkling of 1960 radicals. As Congressman Homer and old-school Democrats began to quietly, but quickly, exit the city, the convention was beginning to look Spartan in terms of Caucasian delegates. It was difficult to find a straight Caucasian male delegate on the convention floor who was not running for re-election. Some candidates running for re-election needed to be on the convention floor regardless of how they felt about the platform.

As every delegate that had taken the place of a Democratic delegate that had officially moved to the American Exceptionalism Party was a minority, and as the substitute delegates who were taking the place of the departing delegates were exclusively minorities, the convention floor became the polar opposite of Democratic conventions in the 1940s and 1950s. Cameras would have to search for an elderly white schoolteacher in a suit or a dress. The Credentials Committee, under direction of Congressman Schreiber, had completed its contract for each delegate:

> I herewith agree to support and endorse the Presidential and Vice Presidential candidates of the Democratic Party in the Presidential election of 2012. I endorse the Democratic Party platform and if I am a candidate for any political office, I agree to campaign to support such platform and will include the following sentence in all campaign literature: *I support the Democratic party, all candidates of the Democratic Party and the Platform approved at the Democratic Convention of 2012.*

This loyalty oath was a requirement of entry into the convention hall on this Tuesday evening and every subsequent session of the convention. It was going to be enforced at the entrances and there was adequate security and technology for enforcement.

The loyalty oath was a two-edged sword for candidates, both edges pointed at the candidate. Without signing the oath, the candidate was not going to get into the Democratic Convention and was assuredly going to lose the financial support of the Democratic Party. And with signing, the candidate was going to be painted during the campaign as the world's foremost supporter of whichever platform plank, or planks, would most anger the voters of his or her district.

Congressman Schreiber of Chicago had started the Credentials Committee meetings on Monday with the statement: "This is the Democratic Party of today. We are one Party with a single message of hope and promise for all Americans, not some or most Americans, but all Americans. We believe that we need to level the playing field for all Americans with respect to all things. While some will be hurt in their wallets and they might see equality as an occasional line for some essential services, most will benefit in the short run and all will be equal under the law in the long run. As Americans, we will all pull a single oar in the same direction in this race!"

Unlike a traditional candidate who could run away from a platform created by his or her party's elite, this was not a platform one could run away from if they signed an oath supporting the platform. While security might ensure that every individual on the convention floor signed the oath supporting the Democratic platform, the President could enter free of this requirement. He could decide himself whether to sign the pledge.

~

With the convention in progress, the former Speaker of the House of Representatives was back in her element. While her power on a national basis had diminished dramatically with the Republicans becoming the majority in the House in 2010, in her role as minority leader, if anything, she had become more powerful. She was ruthless if anyone crossed her and as she was no longer the Speaker, she had more time to be visible and ruthless. With the continuing accession of the Tea Party, the Democrats were looking to become the majority again in the House. With that, she saw her opportunity to control all of the chairmanship appointments and this would make her the most powerful person in the House once again.

The Speaker had been given her moniker by the Secret Service and she was known to her security team as Hands. Behind her back, very far behind her back, the security team joked about what they *kind of* believed was the Speaker's search for some product that would make her hands look younger. They kidded about sending teams of scientists to Scandinavia in hopes of finding the elixir that would make her hands look like they were twenty years old. The most senior of her security detail regularly remarked that his thirty-five-year-old daughter had more signs of age above her neck than the seventy-plus-year-old Speaker. He was fairly certain that the Republicans were searching for the Dorian Grey picture in her attic.

While the former Speaker lost her Secret Service protection in January 2011 when the Republican majority took control of the House, there had been an agreement that the political conventions would all have significant Secret Service protection. Hence, the former Speaker had her Secret Service entourage back for what she hoped would not be a one-week only return engagement.

One of the true concerns for the Secret Service was that a significant element in maintaining the security of an individual is to watch their eyes and the area around their eyes. The experienced Secret Service agent knows that more than fifty percent of the time the individual being protected recognizes the danger first. With the Speaker, she now looked permanently startled and this made her protection ever so much more difficult.

The former Speaker of the House was tone-deaf to anything other than the far left side of her political party. Despite the independent campaign against her, given one of the safest seats in the history of the Republic, the Speaker's agenda was always to increase her power and the power of the left. She had waited a lifetime in her quest to move the country to the left and this convention was going to be the fulfillment of her quest. Nothing less, nothing more. Always one to try to force the President to her viewpoint, she had expressed her desire to have the President of the United States sign the loyalty oath, uttering a short response when asked by the press: "Of course the President will sign the loyalty oath, he is a Democrat."

The former Speaker sat in a private room awaiting her chance to address the convention. A part of her power was in the President's fear of confronting her at the national convention of their party and she was going to use her full power this evening to set the platform committee's agenda as the President's agenda. As she got to the podium a full day before the President, how hard could this be?

~

The convention podium, if it were the wood it appeared to be, would have weighed ten thousand pounds. The Democratic Convention was being orchestrated as the polar opposite of the AEP Convention: three full days, the opulent United Center in Chicago, and thousands of people surrounding the United Center in support of these Democratic candidates. This was a convention given by the party that controlled the Presidency. Perfectly prepared signs with the equally perfectly prepared hand-made signs were available for all. As the key nights of the convention took place, there would be televised pictures of Hollywood celebrities in the opulent and private bar areas within the building. The Democrats were the party of celebrity.

The powerful state unions had promised that there would be thousands of pro-President voters in front of the United, as the arena is called in Chicago; they promised these minions for every minute that the convention was on television. Despite ninety-degree heat and ninety percent humidity, they would meet that commitment for the best friend of unions in the history of the United States presidency. None of these demonstrators would be having a very good time given the heat and the humidity, but the compensation for their efforts made their time worthwhile. The unions were paying union wages for these efforts. Union wages were not always the case with protesters holding signs attacking employees in front of non-union construction sites; often these *protestors* were minimum wage independent contractors.

The audience was both seated and standing on the floor, which featured theatre style seating with blue cloth coverings. The floor coverings were also blue and when the convention hall was empty, the arena looked like someone had either spilled a giant pail of blue ink from the top of the arena or the Boise State band was going to entertain at halftime. But, with a full crowd on hand—and that is when the television cameras were on—it had a royal look. There were wide aisles and ample numbers of microphones throughout, although other than the official state-by-state vote for the president and vice president, there was no expectation or possibility that these microphones would be used. The microphones were there to give the viewers the appearance that there was some form of democracy with a small *d* taking place on the floor. The truth was that it had been a very long time, since that had been the aroma lifting from the floor of a Democratic or Republican national convention. Certainly no one would recall so much as a discussion of a single issue from the recent American Exceptionalism Party Convention and for these long memories, there remained only memories of true debate in black and white television coverage. This was a show, not a debating society.

Far from the United Center, there were a few thousand protesters who were every bit as angry as the anti-Vietnam protestors in 1964. It was hard to display their anger given the distance from the United that the antis were required to be and with the hordes of union members milling about every part of the city. The union members could put a very effective cap on the exuberance of the protesters. Many of these protesters came to Chicago to let the President know that they blamed him for what took place in Korea. More came to protest policies they believed were going to destroy them and the US economically. These demonstrators came to protest a president who also seemed to love every culture and country he visited more than that of the United States of America. Others came because of the jobless rate. These protesters came to voice protest, no more.

Along for the ride were the now usual gang of anarchists who came to Chicago to do damage to the Democratic Convention, damage to the President and damage to the country. This group learned from the European protests of the G8. They were masked, armed with tools of destruction and more than willing to get arrested if caught. About two thousand of them thought of facemasks as a tool. One masked demonstrator was asked about his mask and responded curtly: "The Democrats may believe that we all look alike, but we fear the cameras." These protesters felt they had missed the American Exceptionalism Party Convention not because they did not hate the AEP (they hated any and all political parties), but because they did not think the AEP was a big deal.

Fires, broken windows, a burned police car and any other car on the streets, the two thousand chanting angry demonstrators marched but could not get near the United Center. In the beginning, there were no arrests. In the beginning, there was a clear decision—as much as any decision can be made by two thousand demonstrators—that there would be no violence towards the police, but property was another matter. The violence decision lasted right until the first water cannon was used against the demonstrators. Those not still in jail in Chicago after the Democratic Convention had plans to get to the Republican Convention. Like the line in the Kingston Trio song, they: *don't like anybody very much!*

Television barely covered the anarchists, but informed viewers knew that their actions at the Republican Convention would be covered as it were

305

gavel-to-gavel. The police had learned an incredible amount about how to handle a convention riot over the intervening forty years since the riots outside the 1968 Democratic Convention in Chicago. They isolated the problems, then crowded and further isolated the demonstrators to the extent possible. They gave the television networks reason not to provide coverage and the networks responded as if it were an order not a request.

~

The Democratic Convention's first night featured two speakers. The first speaker was Congressman Alteran Jones, a former Black Panther, who had become a California congressman in 2006. As a graduate of Berkeley with a law degree from the University of California at Davis, Jones was no one's intellectual underling. He was brilliant and about as far left as one could be without picking up arms for an insurrection. The keynote speaker was Ethel Toomany, a Native American who had studied at Northwestern before doing Peace Corps work in Africa and then working for the President as a czar, focusing on education.

Alteran Jones was a spellbinder. He was tall, he was elegant and he spoke as if he had an IQ in the Mensa range, which he did. The voice was deep, very deep and the cadence was crisp like a Southern preacher. His message was clear and crisp. He wanted a better America for those he described as punished by experience and heredity. His audience hung on every word. His speech started with a somewhat inflated discussion of the Middle Passage where far too many slaves died in route to the United States. It did not matter to either Jones or his audience that he exaggerated the number of likely deaths by a factor of a thousand. What did matter is that he described a situation that embarrassed any thinking American over the past almost two hundred years since the last slave boat crossed the Atlantic on its way to America.

Alteran's presentation went on for almost thirty minutes and was essentially an assault on America's past. He easily held the attention of his convention viewers. At home, the audience was as one might have expected, interested based on age, race and financial demographic. But anyone who was really listening began to pay close attention as Jones came to his final few minutes: "And I submit to you that it is time to understand and admit that the efforts to cure race as an issue in the United States have failed. Our black teens and black children are not being well educated and they are not being trained to succeed in our society. They recognize that they are not being trained and not being given a chance and as they recognize this reality; they are dropping out. Today, we need to commit to helping the black community, not with loans for education, but with grants, scholarships and tuition. And not just at traditional colleges, we need to educate our population in all aspects of life in this country. We need to give grants, not loans, to provide training for technical and trade jobs, jobs where a man or woman can earn a fair living and not be changing sheets in a Ramada Inn for their livelihood. And we need to close the borders and send the illegals home." The audience went silent.

"I know that this is not popular with our Hispanic friends, but we all know that if the illegals go home, wages will increase and Black Americans will get the opportunity for higher wages. And the United States has to be first about protecting its own citizens and first about bringing my people into the greater community with dignity and through fair wages." The stunner was that the audience of convention insiders agreed with Jones. There was a roar of approval and television cameras panned the audience to see the response was nearly universal. Universal did not include the Hispanic delegates.

Big Red looked at her assembled panel and asked the question that was on the mind of anyone watching: "Did the opening speaker of the Democratic Convention just take a shot across the bow of the President's position on immigration?"

Thaddeus Milken, who had returned to OBC network after Bob Colony had "decided to write his memoirs before he got too old," could not wait to respond: "Yes, Marylou, that is exactly what Alteran Jones did. And he will be verbally assaulted for this on the liberal networks. But," Milken paused a bit too long between words, "he said exactly what I have always thought was on the minds of black voters. How can we be embracing immigrants who will be taking our jobs, the only jobs that significant segments of our population can perform given their lack of education from the state which did not care about doing anything but paying the teachers."

"Wow," responded Big Red, "that sounded like a very strong response to me. Glenn, what do you think?"

"Marylou, you know I hate to agree with Thaddeus on anything, but there is a sprinkling of truth in what he says and as to Jones's remarks on education, I could not agree more. You know that I am as liberal as one can be, but the teachers' unions have been all about teacher compensation and teacher union power for far too long. The results truly do not marry up to the teacher success stories they throw at us."

Big Red continued into her thoughts: "I just cannot imagine a Democratic speaker at a Democratic Convention getting off on sending Hispanics home to free up jobs for blacks. Ignoring for a moment that I have no idea if the thought process is rational from a job prospective, this will not play well in the Hispanic community. It may also not play well in the black community where there have been some significant achievements in terms of black/brown relationships over the past decade. What could they have been thinking when they reviewed Jones's speech?

Milken again: "Maybe no one saw the speech before it was delivered. The only good news here is that if the speech had been given at the Republican Convention, there would have been riots in the streets. Confused riots, I might add, because few see the Republicans as the protectors of the unemployed black male. The underlying question is who will this help if it resonates as badly in the Hispanic community as all three of us seem to think?"

The cameras went directly to Duneaberg and for a full two seconds, he sat in his chair and stared back at the viewing audience. "I don't get it. Trust me, I don't get it. I am glad I am not sitting with the President watching this evening. This hurt! As to your question, I guess there are three possibilities. One, the President walks the comments back, although challenging Jones could really hurt him in the black community. Two, it helps both Vincent and Roland because the Hispanic voters will sit this one out, or three, it helps Vincent because he becomes the only place the Hispanic community can go. No, I just don't get it."

"I guess that is the reason we show up at these conventions and report what we see and hear," returned Big Red. "Maybe the keynote speaker, Ethel Toomany will shed some light on the subject. She is at the podium. Again, that is really an interesting perspective from any viewpoint. I truly do not know what to think. Let's listen to tonight's keynote speaker. About ready to speak is Ethel Toomany, the President's czar in charge of education.

Ethel Toomany was a beautiful, tall, dark Sioux Indian. She walked to the podium with the grace of a prima ballerina. She was dressed in Washington D.C. standard black pants suit with a white blouse. Some may have expected complete Indian attire and war paint after Jones's remarks, but what they got was a classically attired career civil servant and doer of good deeds.

She began her presentation with a sentence equally shocking to what the delegates had just heard: "Alteran, from your mouth to God's ears." The applause returned. "We need to find a way to educate our black and Native American communities. If in ten years, we can educate that community, the United States of America will achieve the President's dream. It will be a country of fairness. At that point, maybe our unemployment rate among young blacks and Native Americans will go away. And we all know as the number of available job seekers diminishes, wages rise. After all of this hap-

FROM THREE TO FIVE

pens, then we can talk about needing immigrants to do some jobs." And it went on from there.

From Toomany's view at the podium, she could see she was losing more than a small number from her audience as Hispanic delegates began to get up and leave the floor. It was not an organized exodus, but an exodus it was.

~

The President looked across the room to the Pillsbury Doughboy and quietly asked him: "Are they trying to kill us? What was your role in this?"

"I have no idea," and he did not have any idea. "These two sounded like a couple of right-wing nuts and they are our people. The damage they have done to our campaign in the last few minutes has got to be catastrophic. Let me get on the phones."

"Too damn late for that. I'll have to deal with the issue in my speech." And the President left and went into another room to think. The President couldn't believe what he had heard. In but one hour, he had watched the leadership of his party squander the Hispanic vote, or so he thought. *How could this be so difficult? The idea was to use the convention as a tool to increase the number of friends and demonize the opposition. Why wasn't all of this carefully scripted?*

~

Ethel Toomany closed the evening with a Native American prayer blessing the earth and all of the creatures that inhabit it. The spin that followed would have been fascinating to anyone. In apparently unplanned and certainly uncoordinated presentations, Jones and Toomany had probably driven hundreds of thousands of Hispanics away from the Democratic Party. The question was how many actual votes the Democratic Party had lost among registered voters. This was a question made for television and radio audiences clambering for controversy and the instant experts made this a very interesting evening aftermath.

~

Jenn Cho and her panel were mystified at what they had just watched. "That was quite an evening, certainly unexpected. Horace, I mean Dr. Cicerone, what did this mean in terms of your analysis of the election itself?"

"Jenn, I will have to read the polling over the next week or so. My expertise is in the Constitution and its practical interworkings, this is at best a little beyond my level of expertise."

Jenn needed him here to balance out what the liberal Blake X. McCaffrey would have to say, so she followed up with Geekhead before turning to McCaffrey. Tilting her head a bit and effectively flirting with Geekhead, Cho asked: "Dr Cicerone, you are one of the smartest people I know, what would you think if you were a member of the Hispanic Caucus or the Hispanic community?"

Geekhead paused, realized he had to respond and offered: "Jenn, I would be livid. What else could you be? Here you have the keynote speaker of the Democratic Convention calling for large parts of your community to be mailed back to Mexico and parts of South America. That cannot be the message you expected to hear when you arrived here this evening. The quiet walkout was certainly warranted from my perspective. I also believe the President will remedy this in his remarks. There is nothing here that is consistent with his politics."

"Oh, let's not overreact. We know that the President does not believe what we heard and the Hispanic community knows that this is not what the President believes. His actions over the past four years have certainly not been considered to be anything except pro-Hispanic and pro-black. This is just an aberration." So spoke McCaffrey although his unspoken response was: *Where the shit did that come from? This is the Speaker's convention and her job is to make sure nothing like this happens. Should throw her under the bus by tomorrow afternoon, but it won't happen. Too damn powerful.*

~

WEDNESDAY, AUGUST 22, 2012

It was an unusual evening when Fox News had both William O'Brien and Arthur Ninoah in the booth together. With them were Jennifer Cho and Geekhead.

O'Brien had deferred to Ninoah as the leader of the panel. Given his ego, people who did not know O'Brien would have guessed that this would have been unthinkable for him, but O'Brien was fully conscious of who the senior member of the team was and had both self-confidence and a belief in that seniority.

Ninoah opened: "Good evening from Chicago. I am here tonight with my colleagues Bill O'Brien, Horace Cicerone and Jennifer Cho. Bill is my old friend and the good Doctor along with Jenn will lend us two old war dogs a bit of brains and perspective. So, Bill, given last night, where do you think the former Speaker will take us. As I understand, after a few speakers who will be no more than an introduction, the former Speaker will nominate the Vice President for a second term."

"This should prove interesting, Arthur. The Speaker and the Vice President are old-style lefties and both are getting pretty old. I know everyone expects that the former Speaker of the House will get her position back if the Republicans lose the House, but I think she is sour milk and Democrats will reject her. As to the Vice President, I continue to shudder thinking he could be the President of the United States if this president passed away."

Tonight was a night where Jenn could participate as an equal. "Bill, I think you have the story right, but you underestimate the power of the former Speaker and overestimate the country's feelings for the Vice President. He is only being renominated because the President is afraid to bring in a new man, or woman. The President doesn't want to have any competition in his vice president and you know the joke, a bad vice president is about the best life insurance policy a president can have."

Geekhead took his turn and caught both Ninoah's and O'Brien's attention. "The Vice President should be working hard tonight. If the national polls mean anything on an electoral basis, I think the US Senate will be selecting the next vice president and with twenty-three Democrats up for re-election, he should consider his audience a bit right of the people in this room."

Jenn responded first: "Horace, you may be right intellectually, you always are, but a Democratic vice president cannot give that kind of speech."

Ninoah: "We find out in a few moments what kind of moxie the Vice President can show tonight. That will be right after his nomination by the former Speaker of the House of Representatives."

~

The Speaker's nomination of the Vice President was fairly benign except for the remarks about the Hispanic community. She used a short video, which lauded the Vice President's career and service in the United States Senate. It also lauded the service of his son in the military of the United States in Iraq. She kept to the Democratic Party's traditional talking points, except she paid great attention to the remarks from the prior evening and then talked about the importance of coal to the United States. As this was contrary to the goals and objectives of the President and his clean air allies, the use of this stage for this part of the presentation was remarkable for its sense of trying to protect Senator Manchin of West Virginia. The convention floor produced little applause for her personal remarks and try as they might, the sounds of a few catcalls were heard on television with respect to her remarks on coal.

The coal discussion was the result of polling that indicated that the President's policies were undoing a lifetime of positive thoughts about the Democratic senator from West Virginia. (The President's coal policies and the junior senator being unavailable—attending Christmas parties—to vote on the START Treaty were being worked very hard by his Republican opponent in his West Virginia senatorial campaign and Virginia was key to holding the Senate for the Democrats.)

The Speakers remarks about the Hispanic Community were lengthy and displayed her horror at the remarks the prior evening. Her theme was that the Democratic Party had always and would always be the party of the people. The Democratic Party was for equal rights for all and against discrimination against any group, black, brown, etc. She was eloquent in her defense of the historical positions of the Democratic Party and adamant that with additional economic growth and government involvement, the jobs issue would vanish.

Finally, when she returned to her job of nominating the Vice President, the audience rallied to the side of the Vice President being renominated. When the name of the Vice President was placed into nomination, the convention floor erupted as was expected and perhaps, even required. As the Congo lines wound through the United's floor, the commentators went to work on the Speaker and her poorly received remarks about the coal industry. The Vice President's nomination was effectively ignored.

~

An older viewer at home might have thought that Spiro Agnew's little brother had been nominated for the vice presidency. The Vice President had begun to look like a slightly smaller version of the disgraced former vice president. Their fairly large heads, white mains and straight jaws were very similar at roughly the current age of the Vice President and they even seemed to sound alike. In what could be the oddity of comparison, neither one of them was ever at home reading from a script and neither was viewed as anything except a potential nightmare when left unscripted. The major difference between the two was that the current Vice President was not and could not possibly become a felon. Like him or hate him, this vice president was an honest man.

"Thank you, thank you. I will be honored to serve as the Vice President of the United States under the banner of the Democratic Party." The Vice President read from one of the three teleprompters. There would be no chances taken with his presentation. "The President and I intend to honor the commitments we made to the electorate four years ago. We are doing our best, but as you know, for four years, the Republican Party has delayed and delayed everything we have attempted to accomplish. They have ruthlessly stalled, they have ruthlessly delayed and even ensured that we have lower taxes for the rich. They have been representing the special interests." The speech became a Sunday morning press conference on MSNBC without the leading questions. The speech contained not an ounce of new news, but was well delivered and received well by the delegates. Despite the Vice President's vigorous arguments in favor of comprehensive immigration reform, the one obvious thing on the floor was that the Hispanic delegates had not returned and equally obvious, the specific immigration issue of the prior evening was unaddressed by the Vice President.

Jenn: "So far, the *send the immigrants home* statement is the only story of the convention, Ninoah. No press release from the President and no remarks by the Vice President. I do not know what to make of it, but I will make you a bet, I will bet you that the President begins, no not begins, but by the third sentence is speaking Spanish tomorrow night. Maybe the delegates will be back, maybe not, but the Hispanic voters will be watching the President so he will devote more of his speech to them then he might have two days ago. You can bet on that."

It was the same on three mainstream stations and every cable network. The only difference in the coverage was the mainstream media trying to block and tackle for the President by assuming he asked the Vice President to allow him to speak to the issue of the Hispanic voter, but was saving the issue for himself.

~

After the show, the producer, Ninoah, O'Brien, Cho, Geekhead and McCaffrey headed for a small conference room in the United to discuss the President's forthcoming acceptance speech. It was well past midnight when they broke up and their cars took them back to their hotel. Cho, Geekhead and the producer got into one SUV right behind O'Brien and McCaffrey.

As Geekhead and Cho exited from the left side of the car at the hotel, Cho grabbed Geekhead's hand and squeezed it. "Would you walk me to my room?" All Geekhead could do was take a very deep breath and nod. Cho had scripted this moment a few times during the day and it seemed to be working itself to perfection. Geekhead was caught a bit by surprise, but was quickly excited by the invitation.

"Hey, Geekhead," called O'Brien from next to his car. "Let's have one quick nightcap and you can explain to me where the Democrats are going to be on Election Day."

"Great, Bill," Geekhead reflexively responded. From excitement to distraught in ten seconds, Geekhead found himself holding no one's hand and watching Cho power through the revolving door. *Damn.*

Cho entered the elevator alone and feeling humiliated. *If that guy comes knocking tonight, there will be no one home. I have never come on to any man before and this...* tears again began rolling down the world's prettiest face.

~

THURSDAY, AUGUST 23, 2012

Throughout the day, a new radio advertisement was playing on stations throughout the radio spectrum twenty-four hours a day. It was again a simple commercial, this time with an older man's voice:

> *The President selected a man for vice president who thought jobs was a three-letter word. The President is going to do it again. He has to be kidding! This radio commercial was paid for by Ross Anderson.*

~

On Thursday night, on virtually every television station and on the cable station that sold advertising, at 7:30 p.m., yet another advertisement appeared for the entire country to see. It was a new advertisement and easy to understand.

With no sound, the advertisement first showed a simple sentence:

MR. PRESIDENT, IT IS TIME TO EXPLAIN YOURSELF AND THE DEMOCRATIC PARTY.

This time the first voice was one that was recognizable as William Jefferson Cloud:

WHY WOULD YOU SUPPORT A DEMOCRATIC LOYALTY OATH? THE UNITED STATES IS A NATION OF INDIVIDUALS, A NATION OF INDEPENDENT IDEAS!

(Picture of Independence Hall in Philadelphia followed by a picture of the signing of the Constitution of the United States.)

MR. PRESIDENT, WE NEED A PRESIDENT WHO SUPPORTS THE UNITED STATES OF AMERICA AS A REPUBLIC, NOT A NATION WITH A KING AND AN APPOINTED FEW PRINCES AND PRIN-CESSES.

MR. PRESIDENT, WE NEED A PRESIDENT WHO WANTS TO HELP PEOPLE FIND WORK AND SELF-RESPECT. WE DON'T NEED A PRESIDENT WHO BOWS TO FOREGN LEADERS, FRIEND AND FOE ALIKE.

(The first picture on the screen was of a Russian Czar.)

(The second picture was of the President bowing to a Saudi king.)

(The third picture was of the President bowing to the Japanese emperor.)

(The fourth picture was of the President bowing to the Chinese leader.)

PAID FOR BY WALKER SMILTON

Someone needed to speak up!

No one immediately could identify Walker Smilton. Perhaps five people at Max's Place shook hands with the reclusive businessman in early August. As it were, a new country heard from and one who could get the former president to record a voice message.

~

His entrance to the convention was perfect, the chorography magnificent, his suit perfectly fitted. The prelude, a twenty-minute video extolling his personal history, his family and his presidency was worthy of the
$850,000 spent to create and produce the film. The accompanying music
was a full step above the average overture currently being heard in top flight
movies and that came free from a Hollywood composer who was a true
believer.

The President did not enter the convention from the podium side of the
arena. The President had seen the American Exceptionalism Party Convention. He entered from the back, just as had been done at the AEP Convention. He was completely alone and without the appearance of any security.
(The security was throughout the hall and he was instructed that he needed
to follow, and did follow, a series of red dots on the floor in moving through
the crowd to the podium. It looked like he had not a care in the world
except to stop, chat with and hug the occasional delegate. The Secret Service was strewn throughout the convention floor, almost all without Secret
Service identification. For the delegates on the floor, a strip search would
have been less intrusive than what they endured getting into the convention
center and then the delegates faced the metal detector and explosive device
detector once they entered the building. The current Secret Service attention was nice; this was a very safe environment for the President.

It took the President a full thirty minutes to walk from the back of United
Center to the front. This was about thirty minutes longer than Michael Jordon took to cover the same distance during a championship basketball game.
For a viewer, while it took much too long, it was either like watching an
extremely popular president or a benevolent South American dictator greet
his flock, depending upon the political persuasion of the viewer. If one
looked past the possibly accurate analogy, it was great politics. Many watching on television, if not most, loved the show. One thing that could not be
lost on the television viewers was that the audience was virtually devoid of
Caucasian males and was definitively dominated by black women. Without
the invisible Secret Service team, it would have looked significantly more
towards a convention consisting almost exclusively of minority women.

The President of the United States made his way to the podium at his
own pace. This was his turf, his auditorium and his crowd. The reaction of
the crowd to his appearance was breathtaking. These were the true believers.
This group believed that this president was the Anointed One as television

personality Sean Hannity regularly informed his viewers. The absence of the Democrats who defected to the American Exceptionalism Party as well as those delegates who departed Chicago earlier in the week removed almost one hundred percent of the Democrats from this convention who believed the Party had moved too far left and was trying to enact its agenda far too fast for the American public. Those delegates that had left the Democratic Convention and were missing from the convention floor were generally liberal and while they believed in some, or in some cases most, of the platform, they believed that America was years from embracing the full scope of this Democratic platform.

Absent some commentary on Fox News, there was no sense in the audience or on television—again, unless one was watching on Fox News—that many of the initial delegates had switched allegiance to the American Exceptionalism Party at the moment these people bolted from the President's camp. For the most part, the issue was not discussed. These delegates were replaced with pro-president delegates. If anything, the crowd that the President faced this night was the friendliest crowd that he had ever encountered.

As the applause grew to an overwhelming crescendo, Arthur Ninoah offered his thoughts on the approaching presentation. "The President is being received by this convention at an unprecedented positive level. For him, this is the good news and the bad news. The audience in this room wants him to take on the American Exceptionalism Party, the Republican Party, and talk about more plans to move the country to the left. His audience on television is probably looking for an explanation of his policies, including some mention of the alleged failures of the administration in Korea, the administrative and regulatory debacle that appears to be the result of health care, and how he will deal with a Congress that has had him tied in knots over the past two years. There is evidence that the voters are now terrified about the deficits and I think he needs to deal with this issue as well. And his special audience, the Hispanic community, whose delegates have returned to the audience tonight, are very subdued. The Hispanic community needs to understand fully his views on immigration." Ninoah was doing his job as an anchor. As the senior Fox News anchorman, he had been at this business of covering conventions for a long, long time and that meant he was covering conventions before there was a Fox News. He saw his job as one to enhance the viewers' knowledge of what they were watching, not to influence their opinions. He was old school and looked the part in his pinstriped suit and conservative dark blue tie. Part of his deal with Fox News was that he would share the seat with another newsperson, but he would not moderate any panels, which he believed undermined his credibility. Tonight his co-anchor, actually assistant anchor, was Jennifer Cho, not Bill O'Brien. O'Brien might do some individual commentary and sit as a panel member, but Arthur wanted it to be clear that he was not in charge this evening.

On CNN, Chris Matts spoke about the beauty and pageantry of this Democratic Party and this united party: "I am looking down on the most unified Democratic Party in the history of the Republic, yes, probably the most unified party in the history of the Republic. It is a majestic event to see this President of the United States being greeted with the love for him and his policies that is being demonstrated on the floor of this convention. Conventional wisdom may be that the President is facing a declining level of popularity among independent voters, but the solidarity and enthusiasm of this convention must make every American proud of their president." Matts had long since lost any political breadth for his audience as he lost any shred of impartiality. His listeners were a demographic for him and they loved what they were seeing and hearing.

After close to twenty minutes more of applause and cheering, the President determined to speak to the assembled Democratic delegates and the television audience. The President was by now, exactly fifty minutes from his initial entry into the convention hall. He carefully checked both teleprompters and began to speak.

"Thank you, Chicago! Thank you, my fellow Democrats! Thank you, America!" The delegates then proceeded to use another five minutes of applause and while enjoying the adulation, a note flashed across the teleprompters that he needed to get started on his speech if he wanted to have anyone watching him tonight. The adulation was chewing into his television time. "Thank you, America. Let us give a shout out to the Mayor of Chicago and to the Speaker of the House of Representatives. Make no mistake, I love Chicago!" More adulation.

In Spanish, then in English: "And let's give a shout out to our Hispanic delegates who represent what is best about America." This did not play well. The response from the black delegates was polite applause and the Hispanic delegates cheered in Spanish. This was not what the President had in mind and from his side of the podium, since this was his only planned comment on the issue, his speechwriters had let him down.

325

"Let us talk about what we have accomplished in the past four years," thus beginning his clipped presentation, speaking in five to seven word segments and emphasizing the last word of each segment. This worked for the President on two levels, one being that it was natural for him in that his thought processes comported with bite size verbal segments, but even more so because it did not require any serious speech preparation time as there were only short phrases to be read off the teleprompter. He was the best and most effective speech giver the country had seen in years, maybe decades, maybe ever.

"After eight years of economic neglect of all but the Wall Street bankers and the very rich, we are beginning to see a positive response in the economy. While unemployment remains too high, the economy is slowly recovering from the excesses of the Boone administration.

"After eight years of responding only to the voices of the rich and extreme right wing of this country, the voices of the people have and are continuing to be heard. Make no mistake; what the Republicans did to us in the eight years of the Boone administration was catastrophic. And make no mistake, if the Republicans had not lied, yes lied, their way back into more seats in the House of Representatives, our recovery today would be far further along and far more robust." The final word, *robust*, was emphasized by the President and the convention floor erupted as he clearly and specifically placed the blame for the current economic mess squarely on the Republicans.

"I am criticized for blaming economic problems on the Boone administration. I am criticized for blaming problems on the Republicans for fighting everything I have tried to do for the people for the past four years. But, in fact, the Republicans have slowed the ship of state. I have tried to help those who are unemployed or do not have access to a doctor. I am criticized for trying to reduce global warming and save the planet. Who is doing the talking? It is the Republicans who got us into this mess and the Republicans who are trying to keep us in this mess by ignoring the average American and only trying to help the rich. Now, you know how it works, I put in health care to protect the weak and the poor, and the rich Republicans attack me because they are afraid they won't be able to get the government to pay for their acne treatments. They simply do not care about the health of the poor. They offer no plans, they criticize, they are the party of no." He repeated: "The party of no."

326

"I fixed the banking mess that the Boone administration caused. I fixed the mortgage crisis, which the Boone administration caused. We now protect banking customers, borrowers and homeowners and what do the Republicans want to do? They want to undo all of this and go back to the failed policies of the Boone administration." The audience was cheering and hollering. Unlike the American Exceptionalism Party, there was no chanting of slogans or words in response to the President's comments, but the audience gave the identical sense of agreement that had been achieved by the AEP.

"By not funding the health care passed by the Congress and signed by me, as your President, the Republicans are trying to take away your health care. Allen Grayson was correct. They don't care if you die!

"Let me talk to my Hispanic friends." This was extemporaneous, as the President's speechwriters had believed that the statements of the Speaker were sufficient. "The United States of America needs both comprehensive immigration reform and a secure border. Not one without the other. Not one without the other. We cannot disconnect families that have been on both sides of the border for generations. We cannot leave twelve million Hispanics in limbo. We need a plan that provides for a reasonable and reasonably quick path to citizenship for our undocumented workers.

"And be aware, the Republicans are trying every way they can think of to take this government away from the people! Anyone that does not believe this American Exponential Party, or whatever they call it, is not designed to help Republicans and hurt Democrats just does not get it." The incorrect name of the AEP was in the script and he delivered the intended blow by getting the name wrong. The President was barely in control of this expectedly friendly convention floor. At most points, he was speaking over the yelling and hollering. "We need to rally our supporters and support Democrats. Anyone that does not think that this third party will hurt the poor just does not get it."

"Look at these television advertisements and ask yourself if they are being paid for by rich Republicans. These rich Republicans want to steal away your government and we cannot let them do that!" The presentation was flawless. The President went on for nearly an hour and ten minutes. The entire speech was aimed at his success and his belief that the Republicans were trying to undo the America that he was changing.

~

Big Red was at the head of a table, which included Thaddeus Milken, former Congressman Duneaberg and Roberta Whates, a liberal radio show host. The viewpoints were, as usual, quite predictable.

Big Red had on a short, red skirt and white blouse, not low cut, but shear. Since the camera would see her at the end of the table from her left side, most of the audience would focus on her long, red hair, great upper body and long legs. Tonight, more than a few men would focus solely on the side view of the white blouse. Milken was with white shirt, bow tie and golden locks, still a bit too long. The former congressman was nattily attired in a grey suit with blue tie. Tonight he was trying a more cerebral look with reading glasses. It was late summer, and from his tan, it was apparent that he was getting ample time on the golf course. The newcomer, Roberta Whates, a tall, thin newcomer with short, dark hair wore a very bright red blouse. The rest of her was not visible. While she had on the other end of a nice pants outfit, she could have been stark nude from the waist down for all the viewing audience would know.

Watching from the back of the booth was Warren Talbot, corporate lawyer, and long-term boyfriend and roommate of Big Red. Talbot asked if he could join her at the convention, something he had never done before. Partly, he came to Chicago to see the show; partly, he came to Chicago to understand if Big Red's emotional attachment to the highs from her job were so powerful that he could not compete. Talbot was not going to wake up childless at age fifty; he wanted a family.

Big Red started: "I am here with our distinguished panel and you can see on the screen behind them, Lance Amplington is busy with his three focus groups. Before we get to Lance, Congressman, let me start with you. How would you define tonight's speech?

Congressman Duneaberg did his best to look thoughtful through his wire-rimmed glasses and offered: "I agree with everything he had to say about the legacy problems of the Boone administration and I believe that until the day the current House of Representatives showed up in Washington D.C., January 5, 2011, the President was successfully doing everything in his power to fix an ugly situation. I do think the President's speech was aimed at an audience that already intends to vote for him. I certainly agree that attacking Republicans is always a good idea publically, but I am not too sure about treating the American Exceptionalism Party as a spinoff of the

Republicans. That may hurt. It is a tough sell to me with a Democratic sena-tor heading the AEP ticket."

Whates could hardly contain herself: "This was a brilliant speech. Most important, he set the record straight with the Hispanic community in a way that should not cost him the black vote." This was Whate's first chance at a national television audience. Her radio audience in Minneapolis was reason-able, but not sustainable after the election unless she managed to convince management in other cities to pick up her show. She needed this exposure and had practiced her lines all morning in anticipation of the questions. "All the President needs to do is carve off a piece of the middle and he wins this election by thirty or forty electoral votes. I am only disappointed that he took no time to go after the Tea Party for…for…for being, what, the Tea Party?"

Milken could not let this love fest for the President continue. "The polls show that the President only has clear leads in the states with large urban centers, New York, California, etc. That's it. Only those states. A speech designed to encourage these voters in Chicago was no more than a waste of time for the President in an electoral sense. I do not believe that he did any-thing to help himself tonight, except I completely agree with Roberta that he probably righted the Hispanic ship. I always enjoy the speeches where he condemns a prior president who kept unemployment down for seven of his eight years in office and the economy only got screwed up because of Fannie Mae and Freddie Mac, the two great friends of the Democratic Congress. If the President cannot undo the American Exceptionalism Party on ideas and proposals, not rhetoric against the unknown and a past Republican presi-dent, he will be a one-term president. This speech might have been a terrific speech to the committed, but it was a nightmare for everyone else. And as to the Tea Party, I think we will find out where they are at the Republican convention next week."

Big Red was enjoying this much easier role at the head of the table. Keep-ing three ego laden, yet politically knowledgeable, individuals on course was not very challenging. She looked at the screen and asked Amplington: "So Lance, what say your focus groups?" As the camera focused on Amplington, Big Red winked at Talbot.

Lance Amplington, as usual, was dressed in a benign sport coat, white shirt and light colored tie. After being on television for several years now, he could still walk through most airports without ever being recognized.

"Marylou, this is incredibly interesting. I think Thaddeus must have a spy in our focus group rooms. The Republican room, no surprise here, started ten to one against the President, and probably is now ninety-five percent against the President. Republicans have tired of hearing the former president bashed. The Democratic room was split about eighty percent for the President and did not move a click. That surprised me a bit as I expected that the rhetoric was squarely aimed at this group and I would have expected some additional benefit to the President in this group. I don't have an answer for you here, but I am going to ask some follow-up questions in a little while.

"Our last room is Independents; there really is no AEP. Wow, this group was split about forty percent for the President, thirty percent Roland and thirty percent Vincent two hours ago. The moment the President indicated that the American Exceptionalism Group was a ploy by the Republicans and got the name wrong, this focus group turned against the President. And it never moved a bit after that remark. The group ended up almost sixty percent for Vincent with twenty percent for both the President and Roland. I need to think about this, but my visceral reaction is that the Independents found the argument against the prior administration somewhat compelling, but the comments about the American Exceptionalism Party unusually offensive. I may be wrong here, but my experience says the President had a bad night. A great speech in my opinion, but not effective for those not deeply committed to him already. This was certainly not a night where the Republicans gained any ground either. It is going to be an interesting year."

On Fox News, their pollster produced almost identical data to the data produced by Lance Amplington. Jennifer Cho had been trying for an entire evening to be impartial. Cho now sat at the head of a panel that included Geekhead, a Southern Country and Western star, Regina Harper, and former Pennsylvania Senator Blake X. McCaffrey.

"Dr. Cicerone, what is your take? Is the President on sound ground here with the American Exceptionalism Party?"

"Jenn, I don't think the President can get on sound ground with anyone who was instantly inspired by the AEP. Let's remember that the name itself is a reaction to comments made by the President, which implied there was no such thing as American exceptionalism. The President talked about exceptionalism in the Greek and a half dozen other cultures, I believe. No, if one believes that both parties are over the edge, the President may have no way to bring those people back into the fold unless he can somehow convince them they are wasting their vote. At the moment, that would be anything but a sound analysis as the polls keep moving to Senator Vincent.

As usual, Cho was seated in a manner that gave the viewer a look from the shoulders up with her collar-high blouse; she looked absolutely radiant. She and Geekhead had a very early dinner together at Spiaggia on North Central before heading to the United. Jenn had never been happier in her life than when she was with Geekhead. They had been careful to sit across from each other, not sharing a bottle of wine, and when anyone was within hearing or viewing range, talked about nothing except the upcoming presidential speech at the convention. When they thought they were alone, they talked like two people who wanted to get to know each other, not as public personalities. Celebrity was usually only a word when celebrities were in the beginnings of a new relationship. A careful observer would have noticed that Geekhead seemed to make Cho sparkle. In an abundance of gossip insurance, they took separate cabs to the United. In her cab, all Cho could think about was Geekhead and her inability to move the relationship along. In his cab, Horace Cicerone was beginning to believe their relationship was cursed.

~

FRIDAY, AUGUST 24, 2012

On Friday night television, again on virtually on every traditional and every news and entertainment cable station, at 7:30 p.m., an advertisement appeared for the entire country to see simultaneously. It was a sequential advertisement, simple, inexpensive to produce and easy to understand.

With no sound, the advertisement first showed a simple sentence:

MR. PRESIDENT, IT IS TIME TO EXPLAIN YOURSELF.

(Picture of the Vice President.)

IS THIS THE BEST THAT YOU COULD DO?

(Picture of the President in golfing attire.)

Someone needed to speak up!

(Picture of Reesa Jonathon as a competitive swimmer and a second picture of her in her wheelchair seated in front of a group of children.)

There was a second advertisement on the radio at almost the same moment:

> Mr. President, rest assured that I am running to become the President of the United States because I expect to be elected by people who believe I am the best person for the job. These voters will be people who believe the country has moved too far to the left under your leadership and people who believe that Republicans want to move the country too far to the right. These are the Americans that Jordon Scotch and I believe we represent.
>
> This is Senator George Vincent and I authorized this ad.

~

333

RBC did not do anything half way. Samantha Whitspon assigned her best investigative reporters in the quest for information on the President and used her two assistants to help with the work. They had divided the project into four separate components: college and law school, college friends, post college friends and birth certificate. While she was asked not to report on the birth certificate issue, Samantha knew this could still be a real story on a couple of levels and if something broke in that direction, she was going to be ready. *There are still some crazy bloggers out there trying to prove the long form birth certificate is a phony?* From day one, their instructions were that if her team found something, they would pay a visit to the CEO and let him decide what to do. It was expected that they would find something. It was 2012, not 1750, and therefore the three reporters started by spending a couple of days searching the Internet. In many ways, this was a research project that had already taken place four years before. The research had been conducted by many academics, bloggers and the politically active. Nothing had changed.

On the birther front, Samantha's team focused on a different twist: *Why would he have kept the birth certificate a secret? Before he finally released the birth certificate, some people wondered if it indicated the father was unknown or someone else other than previously reported? Others thought the birth certificate indicated he was a Muslim. What a weird duck? There was nothing there.* The only surprise to her and it was meaningless was that he was a II. As the research continued, there was nothing that did anything to change her opinion.

Rush Pfeiffer had laughed as he sat down on the Internet. Well over one million individual hits on the first issue. *Well, this will be a delight.*

Another researcher was looking at four thousand Internet hits on the President's grades. This was going to be pretty easy at the get-go, but then it was going to take a bit of time to find people he went to school with in college. Lucie Wiener immediately found that the President graduated with honors from Harvard law School, but then immediately determined that virtually everyone who graduated from Harvard Law School graduated with honors. *What a joke that must be, I can remember my accounting professor at Penn informing us that the average grade in his stupid basic accounting class would be a C. That SOB took ninety percent of his freshman and made them ineligible for magna cum laude after four months in college. Turned me into a journalism major. Should have gone to Harvard Law School, I guess.*

Rita Sanchez went to Google and searched the President's name and the term friends. The reality of twenty-eight thousand hits in front of her did get attention. After a few hits, the fact that, at first blush, Obama's friends were generally neither black nor white also got her attention. Also, there did not seem to be any longtime friend evident over the years of his life. *Maybe, I'll try girlfriends*, she thought.

~

As the closest advisors to the President filed into the Cabinet room, the President was already seated at the head of the table with a cigarette and an ashtray. Mrs. President had obviously stayed in Chicago with the girls to be with her relatives. Sackman and Matta glanced at each other and knew this was going to be a difficult meeting. Since being elected, it was almost unheard of for the President to be on time for a meeting, so the sight of him sitting and waiting for a meeting set the tone before anyone could so much as say good morning. The cigarette made the difficulty of the scene complete. The President did not get up as the group entered the room and after everyone was seated a near stony silence filled the room.

Matta noticed that the President was becoming so thin that absent his suit coat, he was beginning to look frail when one sat a few feet away.

No one spoke as the President took a deep drag on what was clearly not his first cigarette of the morning. While the sight of the cigarette was a sign that the First Lady was not on campus, it was not always a bad sign in terms of temperament of this president. The cigarettes usually had a calming effect. But, when one followed the cigarette to the ashtray, there were two cigarette butts waiting for the new one to join them. This meant the cigarettes were not having their desired effect.

After everyone was seated, the President spoke. "The coverage of the convention was unfair, uneven and against the public interest. What tools do we have so we can lean on the so-called independent voices during the next four months?" The clipped presentation focused precisely on tools and independent voices. The inference was clear that the President had watched Fox News upon returning to his Chicago home before turning to Air Force One and a very late night flight home.

~

Senator Vincent scheduled his meeting with The Professor knowing that he, the candidate, would be on time and The Professor—as he had been at every meeting since they first met—would be fifteen minutes late. The senator knew The Professor continued to consider his personal appearance, other than on campus before a class, something equating a Papal visit, so the senator knew he would be late just to satisfy his ego and to look more important to this student he was bringing with him. Maybe Vincent and The Professor went back too far; Vincent was absolutely certain that if he became President of the United States, he would one day find himself waiting in the Oval Office for The Professor. The Professor would be having a leisurely breakfast at the Willard, within walking distance of the Oval Office while he, the POTUS, was waiting. An interesting relationship.

The senator along with Stanley Wade and Marshall Dankberg were working on other issues in a small rented conference room at the Hilton across from the modern Orange County John Wayne Airport. The Hawker was parked on the other side of the airport and they needed to take a cab to the hotel. They had managed to enter the hotel from the back without being seen. As usual, one of the Secret Service Agents insisted on riding in Vincent's cab and the other transited in the second cab. Joshua had been sent to the reception desk to procure the keys to the conference room. They had brought along Joshua as instructed. The Professor and Molly Tom, timely, arrived exactly fifteen minutes late. Timely based on his expectations only. Joshua had been sure to arrange to have a blackboard and a large screen from the hotel as the senator knew that The Professor would make a very professional presentation and would bring one of those key ring things to put in the computer to make his presentation. When The Professor and Molly arrived, Joshua, who had been waiting in the hotel lobby, immediately bought them into the conference room. The Professor only noticed one of the two Secret Service agents on his way from the lobby to the conference room.

The Professor had immediately gone to work on Joshua. After introducing Molly to Joshua, The Professor got to about one inch of the young man and asked: "And?"

"Molly, I understood from The Professor that you were a lover of flowers and might be a bit nervous meeting Senator Vincent, so I brought flowers that are in the conference room for you."

Molly was speechless and a bit confused since she had no idea what was happening. While she remembered the flowers conversation, she thought everyone was joking. Of course, what was actually happening was that The Professor was giving her the flowers, but appearances and her mind calculated this differently. Her mind said: *What a dork.* Her mouth said: "Gee, that was really nice of you." And all three stood for an awkward moment that The Professor just loved. *Keep 'em all off balance, so much more fun.*

As they entered the hotel conference room, The Professor looked at the men he came to see and said: "Skeeter, good to see you. Marshall, you look unchanged, too bad, probably not any smarter, done your electoral homework? Stanley, you have got to lose some weight." The three men made their hellos and introduced themselves to Molly. Neither the senator nor Dankberg asked Joshua to stay. As Joshua started to leave the room, The Professor looked at him and started his routine: "Joshua, where are you going? You put on a nice sports coat and tie, flew across the country in a private airplane, probably a first for you, and I brought you the finest woman in Southern California. Take a seat." Joshua sat.

Before The Professor began to speak again, Stanley Martin Wade, the always silent one, asked: "What is this Skeeter stuff?"

Senator Vincent responded before The Professor had a chance: "A bad mistake on my part, Stanley. I attended a seminar with The Professor a long time ago, I think at Northwestern, and in his seemingly absent minded way, he told us all that we could put any name we wanted on our name cards and he would go with that. Then he said, 'If you ever wanted to be called Skeeter, that was fine with him.' What I did not know was that whatever name you wrote down, you would apparently be tagged with for the rest of your life. Just for fun, I wrote down *Skeeter.* Who would have thought I would ever see this clown again?

"When we had our first child, he sent us a small set of tools, go figure, and the tools were marked Skeeter's Tool Chest. When I was elected to the United States Senate, he had a damn skywriter fly over my home: *Congratulations, Skeeter.* Of course, he did not tell the skywriter what the message meant and no one, I mean *no one*, had any idea what was happening. I have always thought someone, somewhere, beneath the skywriting thought some young kid named Skeeter had gotten lucky for the first time. Oops, sorry Molly."

While the senator talked, Molly organized the computer set up, put in the Emulex memory stick and everything was ready to go. While there were only six of them in the room, The Professor had not sat down and apparently did not intend to do so.

With no introduction at all, The Professor started: "This is Molly Tom. She is far and away my best student, in fact the best student I have had for quite some time. Certainly smarter than anyone in your seminar, Skeeter.

"Molly has done virtually all of the leg work for today. What I ask for her is some credit and a position in your campaign, that is, if she is still interested after our meeting. I have not asked her about this, but I think the answer should be axiomatic. Let me repeat, Molly is a very, very good student, maybe, the best I have ever had, but she is not the smartest or most astute person in the United States and you need think about that as we go through her presentation, because someone else has done this analysis. If I had come up with this, you might think there was a ninety percent chance that I was the only one, but that cannot be the case. If Molly has figured this out without any prodding, no experience and as an accounting major, someone else has and therefore, this election will be a numbing multi-tiered fuzz ball. The only person who seems to be sneaking up on the issue is that Horace Cicerone guy, apparently an election expert being used by Fox News. I think he grasps the issue, but doesn't have a wit of an idea of the politics involved. The fact that no one else is talking should scare the heck out of you. Those independent ads we are seeing and hearing should scare the heck out of you, even if they are ads in your favor, my good Senator, something is going on out there and I don't think anyone knows what those people are thinking.

"Rasmussen has not touched the subject we are going to discuss. He will when it becomes public and on the public relations side, you need to develop an immediate response, which is, I think, we will let the election go to the people and worry about the Electoral College and the House of Representatives later. If, of course, that is actually your action plan, then Marshall is just dumber than I ever thought, and that is saying something."

"Professor, back off on Marshall. Today is a business meeting. He is my guy. You can pick on me to your heart's content, but let's leave everyone else alone today. Try for once just to be a good guy! And I tried to get a telephone call with that Reesa Jonathon, what a tough broad she must be, and her secretary said that her lawyer was not going to let her talk to me or any of the other candidates until after the election. I fought her a little bit, but that call is just not going to happen. I am kind of hoping the President calls her; that should be an interesting conversation with her secretary."

The Professor heard, did not acknowledge the slap about his picking on Dankberg, but decided not to step over the line for at least half an hour. "OK, Molly, talk." The Professor finally took a chair next to the door, directly behind Dankberg, assuming this would be incredibly uncomfortable for him, which it was. *Great fun.*

Molly had dressed in her interview uniform, business suit with pinstriped, dark blue slacks. Today, her long dark hair was neatly groomed and virtually straight down her back. When she dressed like this, she generally looked like she was entering her freshman year rather than a graduating senior. Young, and after four years at the University, cute—very cute—and a bit awkward in dress up clothes like most twenty-one year olds in 2012. Of course, she had not been one hundred percent certain she was the speaker, but she had considered it and assumed she would be the great enlightener and should be in her business best, heels and all. Why would The Professor treat this meeting as anything but another couple of hours in a Socratic classroom? *Out of my league this morning.*

Molly started without notes after flipping on the projector with its slide deck: "We believe that this election will not be conclusively decided by the voters of the United States of America. Our analysis of current polling, which is not very different from what you can get from the web or on cable, is that if the election were held today, the President would easily carry the three states with the largest urban centers, California, New York and Illinois. We think he will also carry Pennsylvania, Minnesota and Michigan. We also believe that the President will win the popular vote, perhaps by a very wide margin. This margin will be exacerbated by what we believe will be easy decisions by you and Paul Roland not to campaign in the urban centers. We believe, in a campaigning sense, you will concede these states." Both Wade and Dankberg nodded at Molly Tom's comments and agreed with the detailed information showing on the slides. This was all information they had before the meeting started. "We believe Congressman Roland will get to the same decision and this alone will give the President the national popular vote if, as we believe, he gets sixty-five percent of the popular vote in his states.

"We think that is about it and we believe that the other two candidates, you and Paul Roland will split up the remainder of the states with you, Sir, coming in third in the popular vote and first in the electoral count, but the electoral count could be very close among the three of you or you could

FRIDAY, AUGUST 24, 2012

run pretty far ahead electorally. You could run second in the popular vote, but we doubt it. Each of you, Vincent and Roland, will be benefitted by the redistricting as I don't think the President will pick up a single state where the number of delegates and electoral votes have increased." Molly had thought she would be very, very nervous if she was asked to make the presentation, but she was whipping through the slides like a fifty-year-old human resources guru. Regardless of her comfort level, she wasn't sure her last paragraph was as clear as it could have been, but assumed everyone got the major points. *Maybe a little nervous.*

With her first grin, Molly continued: "Sorry, Skeeter, that is how we see it, barring some eleventh hour surprise. That being said, we see the next President of the United States being either you or Jordon Scotch." Molly paused for a moment thinking she knew the response, but allowing sufficient time for it to happen.

George Vincent had almost spit out his coffee when this young kid called him Skeeter. This could be really tortuous. *Had Frankenstein created Student of Frankenstein?* He instantly now knew he needed both. The comment about Jordon Scotch left him sitting bolt upright in his seat.

"What in God's name are you thinking about, Professor?" asked Dankberg incredulously. He asked The Professor, not Molly, the question. Then, looking at the senator, "Is this guy and his student wasting our time, Senator? I could be doing something useful regarding the actual election. That is why we are here."

The senator and The Professor went back way too far and he barely nodded at The Professor. The Professor took this as a message to amplify, but before he could say a word, Vincent looked hard at Dankberg and allowed: "Marshall, relax. I don't know where Joshua is in the pecking order, but I am learning quite a bit here." Stanley, fat overflowing both arms of his chair, offered his comment that the projection presented thus far was eminently possible based on his analysis.

"Now, Professor, what is this senator or Jordon Scotch crap?" Dankberg not giving an inch.

The Professor smiled behind Dankberg: "Molly, why don't you tell this $1000 an hour so-called election guru, what every schoolgirl knows about the Constitution. And Marshall, Molly isn't any schoolgirl. Ask her the questions, I'll just jump in and amplify if you are having trouble with her four syllable words." The Professor leaned back in his chair, got his mercurial grin on his face and relied totally on Molly. She had expected, listening to The Professor, that he would make Marshall Dankberg look bad and that Dankberg would help them every step of the way. Who knew she would be the tool to make Dankberg look so stupid. Whatever there was between The Professor and Dankberg, it was not good. She was not sure she liked this new piece of politics.

Working over people he did not like was like finding a fourth food group for The Professor. Molly, as a student, had not really seen this in the classroom. He was sure she would not like it but would continue on with her presentation. While he fully intended to make Molly look like a genius and help her career, for the moment, she was a prop.

"Should I use the slides with the calculations?" she asked quietly. The Professor nodded and commented a bit about how Molly had raised this issue in the context of reading the newspaper and implied that everyone in this room should already know about that which she was going to enlighten them.

"As you know, the Founding Fathers devised what today could easily be perceived as a bizarre system of deciding who ultimately becomes the President of the United States. The peculiarities apparently had a lot to do with the differing views of Jefferson and Hamilton. Remember, the Constitution was prepared in secret and presented to the Constitutional Convention as a fait accompli. It was a classic take-it-or-leave-it presentation. It was done in a way that Harry Reid probably would have loved! Without going through a history lesson and assuming your generation learned all of this in high school, we all know that the citizens vote, then the electoral delegates vote and if there is no winner, the decision is made by the House of Representatives. Simple so far. What few people know is that the decision in the House of Representatives is made on a state-by-state basis. Let me repeat that, a state-by-state basis with each state receiving a single vote. The first thing that jumps off the page is that the single Member in the House of Representatives from North Dakota or Delaware has exactly the same voting power as all of the Members of the House of Representatives from the State of California." She was going through the slide deck as she spoke. "And with each state getting a single vote, to become President you will need twenty-six states, a majority of all of the states, not a majority of the states voting. As weird as that sounds, it gets more interesting, please remember that you, Senator Vincent, will not have a single member of the American Exceptionalism Party in the House of Representatives. That, of course, is because you did not form the American Exceptionalism Party in sufficient time to find candidates and, frankly, based upon my reading, probably could not have found very many qualified candidates. Today may be different, but this was a year ago. You may well have not wanted any American Exceptionalism Party candidates for all we know." Molly may not have been the arrogant and brilliant Professor, but she knew when to pause for effect.

The senator folded his hands together and leaned on his left elbow, which was on the table. He was trying to put this information into his mental computer and tie it to the Jordon Scotch comment, a connection he could not yet make. Certainly, this was not the presentation he was expecting. He had been expecting a presentation on the Electoral College, an organization that he thought he understood. He did not know the House of Representatives voted by state.

Dankberg was trying to see where all of this was going and was more than a bit annoyed that The Professor had given him no heads up on the discussion or that he would have a twelve-year-old make the presentation. He knew there was another oops in his equation, but he also had not gotten that the Jordon Scotch or George Vincent piece was what he had missed in terms of importance.

Dankberg knew, but ignored the state-by-state thing. He disliked The Professor far more than either the President or Paul Roland but, for the moment, he knew he needed this man.

Stanley Wade had immediately become a student of The Professor and Molly. He did not know that the House of Representatives voted state-by-state. His math stopped on Election Day.

Joshua was only looking at Molly's legs and thinking that she was becoming more attractive with each sentence. Joshua was one of those young men that found women became more attractive as they demonstrated their intellectual power. While he was not remotely interested in her intellectual power, brains made women more desirable. He had no good reason to think about any further adventures, or a first adventure with The Professor's student as Molly had barely smiled at him, but young men rarely allow intellectual thinking to impact their dating decisions. He was trying to determine exactly how many beers it would take to have her begin to beg him to take her to his apartment.

Joshua was wasting his fantasies. Molly was the typical female college senior of 2012. The fear of disease kept her from sleeping around and there-

fore she had had only a few sequential and meaningless monogamous relationships during the last couple years of her college education. She had been
a virgin until almost the end of her freshman year. She had given herself a
psychological characterization during her junior year: she decided she was a
serial monogamist. While her current relationship was not going to last until
moments past her graduation, both he and she fulfilled each other's physical
and social relationship needs and that was exactly what she wanted at the
moment. He was a pretty nice guy and smart enough to have real conversations about real issues.

No additional questions yet, as any question would be faced by a
response from The Professor if she missed the answer. Molly continued:
"The final and perhaps most important technical point about who becomes
President is that if the House of Representatives cannot get to a majority
decision—over fifty percent of the states, twenty-six states—the Vice President becomes the Acting President.

"Under these weird rules, given to us by the Founders, the House selects
between the top three electoral vote getters for President. If no decision can
be made in the House of Representatives, the Vice President—who has previously been selected by the Senate—becomes the Acting President. And,
Skeeter, we believe this could happen.

"In this weird set of rules, the Senate selects between the top two vote
getters for Vice President. The VP becomes the Acting President if the
House cannot elect a President. Of course the Senate is supposed to be only
focused on the Vice Presidential candidates as Vice Presidential candidates
when they make their vote. The Senate should easily be able to select one
from two based upon our read of the 2013 Senate but, in the House of Representatives, selecting a President from one of three with a fifty percent vote
requirement, with voting by each individual state, with each state getting a
single vote, is a totally different equation. Think about a state deciding that
the Acting President requires no compromise and is an easier choice than
you, the President or Paul Roland."

The Professor could not resist another punch in George Vincent's stomach. "Skeeter, your man Jordon is playing your Bertha Aplin to John McCain.
I hope you and he can weather the storm."

Molly picked it back up: "Let me go back to the House and expand just
a bit. To become President in that vote," Molly repeated, "the President in
that vote, the President must achieve twenty-six of the states. Think about

how difficult that will be considering that there are three candidates and many states will have equal numbers of Democrats and Republicans. And we do not know how obligated anyone will feel towards you even if their voters voted for you. You never served in the House and you are, for these purposes, the only official member of the American Exceptionalism Party."

Now you could see recognition in the eyes of the senator, Wade and Dankberg. Joshua could see the technical piece, but why this was remotely urgent or even important was still pretty far from his thought process. *I can get to this girl. I need to figure out how to have her e-mailed to Cleveland. Little bit of liquor or weed, whatever her choice of relaxation. This should be a pretty easy deal. Can't be that many guys who want to bed down Ms. Genius. Her pickings might be pretty small at school and maybe her passion for this politics stuff can be expressed in different forums.*

"Finally, on the technical side is the concept of the unfaithful voter in the Electoral College, although this is probably not at all that important.

"Apparently, Hamilton prevailed in the discussion of the necessity, or lack of necessity, of the electors voting for the candidate selected by the voters, rather than having the voters select the direction of their state. In 1800 or whatever, there may have been an expectation that the delegates would not always listen to the voters of their state; it was always *men* in those days. Hamilton probably saw the electors as a governor, a break, on the excitement and ignorance of the voters." Molly emphasized *men* in her presentation, stared for a moment at Joshua and he, not understanding that this was far less than a compliment, began yet another full assessment of the remainder of Molly's individual body parts. "Now, these are the two slides that are important..."

"Let me take it from here, Molly. Skeeter will latch onto this issue faster than you can imagine, so I want to take this along at his pace and he can explain it to Marshall later." The Professor flashed that grin again, the one that his best students lived to see and his lesser students complained about on websites. Marshall just stared at him. "This slide shows a map with the quote, unquote, states where it is illegal for the delegates to vote other than as the individual state votes. You can see that there are only a handful of states that do not require their delegates to vote for the candidates voted on by the voters. This slide shows the states where the legal penalties are the equivalent of a felony for not voting as directed by the people. That would be a total of two or three."

The senator sat bolt upright in his chair as he suddenly thought he mastered the issue. He broke in: "Professor, are you telling me that after the election, we are going to have a God damn three-ring circus with a set of rules which are completely unclear or are meaningless in the House of Representatives?" He paused and The Professor let him gather the rest of his thoughts just as he would have so many years ago in the seminar where they initially met. "Molly," the senator continued, "forgive my language, this is what this guy has always done to me. So you are going to tell me that step one is to get the electors to ignore their own state voters. I am supposed to cajole them into not allowing the House of Representatives to make the call and warn them that the Senate would have to choose between the current vice president who we would all agree is a walking empty suit and Scotch who is just another God damned economist?"

"Molly, he really was a pretty good student, not quite as good as you, but close. Skeeter, you have the big picture, but I think the elector battle will be all show and no go. The game will be played exclusively in the House of Representatives, where you do not have a single registered American Exceptionalism Party member, but you will have a number of Representatives who will only survive in Congress if you win. At the end of the day, I don't think, unless someone is a half dozen votes short of a majority of electoral votes, that the Electoral College will do any more than eliminate Roland's vice presidential candidate, whoever that is. That will happen because Roland will finish third in electoral votes. In this, I have a much higher level of confidence in my prediction than Molly. What neither of us knows is whether this is good news or bad news in the House of Representatives.

"I cannot imagine Paul asking an elector or electors to vote in a different manner than his state voters had voted. He is far too ethical. Now, perhaps this president thinks that is the way the game should be played. That may well be the Chicago politics thing. But he will be way too far off the necessary electoral votes to close the deal.

"There are lots more to both the rules and the next steps, but the House is the issue. Molly is still trying to figure out the role of the House with respect to challenging the votes of specific electoral delegates, both when they vote and when they do not vote with the voters, but I think it is more of an academic issue. It has happened so infrequently that there have never been any challenges.

"It should have dawned on some Member of the House years ago to challenge an unfaithful elector just to work out the rules. It has been a long time since we elected what one might call the best and the brightest to the House of Representatives, hasn't it? There is a bit here where the governor can ultimately decide which group of electors represented his or her state, right along with the mermaid dividing the votes of the coastal states; it is a bit much."

Molly went back to work. "These next slides break the game down into component parts. The first slide lists every delegate by state, if they are required by law to vote as directed and if there are meaningful penalties. Again, a delegate can apparently break his pledge on how to vote and simply be known as a person who breaks his word or have a small monetary fine. In only very few cases does voting for someone else impact the individual's life. Don't worry about this slide today. We can work that one later. I cannot see an electoral result where absent an entire state ignoring their votes, the actual election could make a difference.

"This next slide breaks down the House of Representatives by one vote per state based on Rasmussen's and Cook's projections. Small voter changes here could be very impactful, very impactful."

The Professor re-entered the conversation: "My conclusion is as follows: The House of Representatives will not be able to elect a president. The Members that hate you or the President along with the Democrats who hate anyone who is not a Democrat make this a game that should be very difficult, or impossible, to win. That is today, not a close call. You may find someone smart and with some congressional experience and a current Member of the House to review our data, but letting this cat out of this room right now would probably be a big mistake. I suggest you hire Molly and she can work out of her apartment on campus. We know Molly can keep a secret and if she came to Cleveland every weekend, this will give Molly and Joshua a chance to select a wedding location. She is your *guy* in my opinion, but I want her to get an hourly fee equal to a fifth of Marshall's, probably deserves double, I don't want to get into that conversation, Skeeter, because you will yell at me. I think since Molly got us started down this pathway, one-third is fair. Skeeter, you know my fee." All Joshua heard was *if she came to Cleveland every weekend*.

Both Joshua and Molly looked closely at The Professor. Molly was almost certain he was entirely kidding about everything and Joshua thought he was looking at a guy who was just really smart and always used all of his brainpower as a hammer. Just a jerk, but people would and always seemed to need to tolerate a jerk if they need what they are getting.

"My guess is, Marshall, you might try to develop a strategy to convince about two hundred electoral delegates that they vote for your guy. And it is my guess that there is absolutely no chance you can accomplish that goal and it will hurt you, perhaps kill you in the House. Word could easily get out. Besides, I cannot believe that there would be that many electors willing to crush their future political involvement in their local communities. Any state where you came in second and the Republicans came in third would be the primary target, but again…the game is in the House of Representatives right after the Senate makes Jordon Scotch Acting President. Of course, you will be effectively running against a guy in a wheelchair who is your vice presidential running mate when you begin begging the House of Representatives to make you the President of the United States! Of course, Scotch being a minority should really help. Right?" He said cynically. "But, why should that be a problem?

"I think this is something you need to think about, but after a while, I suspect even Marshall here could work out a strategy on where and how to campaign. It's a small campaign, limited to only the Members of the House of Representatives. What I will insist on is that you prepare a statement to the press immediately after the election that you believe it is inappropriate for anyone, and you will mean anyone, to try to tamper with the electors. Tamper may be the key word for public consumption. Make a note of it. You will need some horsepower to add to this equation. As a starting point, I would look to the former presidents, but I would also quickly reach out to Congressman Roland. He is a student of the Constitution if there ever was one and he would find a Chicago politics approach to this appalling. I don't think the President would sign on to this, but again, there will be no possibility he could get enough electoral votes no matter what he did.

"You are also going to need a strategy in the Senate. Your guy's opponent could be the VP or Roland's guy. I have no idea who Roland's guy will be. Just hope it isn't Bertha Aplin. That would be a nightmare. You will need two strategies assuming that you will be number one or two in the electoral vote category. One of them will need to be unleashed on the day after the election. My guess is that a Republican Senate would rather have Darth Vader than the Vice President. No waiting. Of course, if you are third, you will only need a strategy for the House of Representatives noting the Vice President will not by your guy.

"You need to fully understand the Constitution and the Electoral College, Skeeter. You need to understand its history; you will need to understand the law and in fact, you even need to understand your abilities to pardon those who commit Federal crimes. You need to be able to talk about this like a PhD in political science when the time is right. You need to decide how important this race is for you, because if it goes the direction I predict, it will be truly, truly ugly. You will need to appear the expert and not be remotely surprised at the consequences of the election. Here is a list of books you need to read. This will help you in the House of Representatives and with the public. The President won't spend the time, of that I have no question.

"You need to develop alternative strategies where the holder of the fewest or second fewest electoral votes, based on the current system can or should become President of the Unites States of America based on some reasonable premise. Great country, isn't that right?

"And Jordon Scotch, I have no idea what he will be thinking assuming you come in first or second. Being the Acting President for four years does not sound like bad duty to me and the one thing I think is true, as I think I said before, is that the United States Senate ain't going to want the current vice president as the vice president or Acting President of the United States."

The senator, Dankberg, Wade and Joshua were silent. The Professor showed that grin and finished by saying: "Well, I guess you guys need two new consulting contracts, Skeeter. I'm not doing anything without Molly."

The Professor knew that besides him, Molly Tom was now not the only person in this room who could think through the nightmare in the House and the awaiting three months more of the election and sixty days of positioning. Skeeter's guys were a career political consultant and a statistician. Both would have been surprised to learn in actuality that no other political consultant in the campaigns had so much as given these key issues a serious thought. While these paid consultants knew that the election could go to the House of Representatives, their jobs were to get votes from regular folks. Sometimes, it was the guys outside the game who could see the forest for the trees.

Senator Vincent began to think that his campaign should be directed to coming in second and spend most of his time helping moderate candidates of both parties that would vote for him in the House of Representatives. Of course, he knew that some of these candidates would absolutely not want his help. He was a very quick study.

Senator: "Molly, you are on the clock if you want to be. Actually, if you want to be on our team and be our extra genius, then you were on the clock the moment you broached this issue with The Professor. That means I want a bill for the hours you spent reading about this and getting us to where we are today. That is fair to you and to the campaign."

It did not get past Molly that she would be earning something like $100 per hour and had already earned over $6000 if she billed the time she had already spent. She was currently receiving $11 an hour as a tutor on campus. She would bill the campaign for fewer hours than she had already spent.

"Molly, as many hours as you need and in the next few days, I need you to write me a concise four-page memorandum. Less than four pages, if it works, four at the most. I want to see the various steps and what we need to do. I want it confidential and I want you to understand that someday, it is likely someone else will read it, probably some lawyer that wants to put us all in jail. I want more than a scientific piece, I want your thoughts, you are in the big game now and thoughts are more important than facts. Please also begin reading these books that The Professor said I should read. I am not going to have the time to do that, but I will need great, well-written and reasonable summaries, and some great quotes.

Molly nodded and Senator Vincent smiled and added: "I take it that was a yes." And Molly nodded again.

"Professor, you are so damn easy to dislike, but I love you and Marshall will learn that you are not a bad guy. Maybe.

"Yes, our regular deal will be fine. Professor, I do want you to supervise Molly and make sure that what she writes is what we need. Molly, don't let The Professor turn you into a miserable jerk, but listen to him. If he was interested, he could probably figure out if there really was a missing link between monkeys and standard poodles."

The meeting ended with a number of handshakes and George Vincent hugging a somewhat reluctant Molly. Dankberg was effectively moot. Joshua earned only a handshake from Molly, which in his world only made her more attractive as a future conquest.

As The Professor got to the door, Senator Vincent looked at him and asked: "Can we take a short walk?"

"Sure. Molly, can you wait for me for a minute?"

~

"So, what's up, Skeeter?"

"Morton, what am I doing? My party hates me and the Republicans think I am going to kill off the President and elect their guy."

"Look, Skeeter, we've known each other for a long, long time. You have not waivered an eighth of an inch in your principles and you understand that Congress has forgotten their job. The President is being given way too much power. That's why you are here, isn't it?"

"Yeah, I guess that about sums it up. I break it up into two parts, one part business and one part process. You've got the process pretty close. At some point in time, the Congress outsourced its job. And at another point, leadership seems to have put a hose in the ear of every Member and sucked out half their brains.

"Oh, I know how harsh that sounds, but golly, people vote for things or against things because leadership tells them what to do or promises them a partridge and a pear tree for their district. They don't think about anything except getting re-elected and making leadership happy. That has to be the last thing their voters want and the voters send them back to office because the party gives them the money to get re-elected. It's crazy.

"Now you have me started, leadership gives them legislation written by twelve year olds and that legislation delegates the important pieces, the damn regulations that become the operating law, to another group of twelve year olds. The second group of teeny boppers then writes regulations that are on the far edges of what anyone intended and there is no one in charge of making sure the regulations are in concert of what anyone intended. There is no regulatory oversight! Hell, the President sends over an appointed czar to Congress and Congress deals with another political nutcase. At the end of the day, the Congress has approved legislation that costs hundreds of thousands of jobs. It is just nuts. It is worse than the tail wagging the dog. The people have delegated governing to their legislatures, the legislatures have delegated their votes to their political leadership and the political leadership has delegated writing the laws and the regulations to kids that have never been out in the real world!"

"Well, Skeeter, what can the President do about the way Congress works?"

"It's all about the veto power. Congress does not want the President to veto legislation and explain to the voters that the legislation is not competently prepared or there is no oversight. I believe that this can be fixed in a single meeting with the Speaker and the Senate leadership. Just the threat should be enough. Either the legislation has to have precision or the Congress needs to approve the regulations with the ability to edit. Maybe, just maybe, I'll have to veto a piece of legislation like that, but the Congress doesn't have the self-confidence to allow that to happen more than once. They'll be just like a group of students trying to please a professor. Isn't that what you do?"

"I guess that is what I do, Skeeter."

"Morton, don't give me that bullshit. I've talked to too many of your old students, both at the university and at the leadership classes. They all know that after a couple of tries, they work hard to get your approval and avoid the whip of your tongue."

"Well, maybe, but Congress is a bit different...

"You really think so?"

"Well, actually no. Overall, they are usually the mildly successful attorneys in the neighborhood. The successful people are too busy making money. So, okay, I'll buy the process stuff, but that cannot be the only reason to want to be president?"

"No, although if I could get the Congress to do the job they were elected to, I would feel pretty good. It is not going to be any fun. Marge isn't ready for this. We've got grandkids in Cleveland and contrary to anything she might say to me or you, if she is in D.C. for more than two days a week, I would be amazed. And I worry about her. She looks pretty weak, she has that MS gene and sooner or later it is going to get out of the bottle. She won't talk about it with me and she absolutely refuses to see a competent doctor. I think she is scared and fully capable of going to see an acupuncturist for MS rather than go on serious drugs."

"So, why do it?"

"Come on Mort, you know that I am doing it because I have to do it. I'm a fixer. But, what I want to do is move away from the lockstep if you are a Republican, you believe *A, B, C,* and *D,* and if you are a Democrat, you believe *E, F, G* and *H.* This is crazy. I want to have a political party where you can have a varied view and you can compromise, not just run for the far right or far left. I want a party where someone can be against abortion, but be okay with abortion where the mom's life is at risk or there has been a rape. I want a party where it is okay to be grey, not black or white. Basic principles, but not applied like Stalin or Mao, does that make sense?"

"It may make sense to you and me, George, but the zealots are going to hate you. While they attack, you have to have precise positions and that will be hard. Every word will be reviewed and reviewed. Both sides will attack your view on abortion. And you are talking about forming a political party for real and for the long run. That might be tougher than getting elected president. Let's keep that idea a secret for the campaign."

"And that is exactly what I want. I want to be exposed as someone who can find the middle. You know I am pretty far right on foreign issues and pretty centrist on social issues. Shouldn't my views and I have a place at the table?"

"I think so, but I guess you have decided to ask the question on a national level."

"I sure have. But I'm not nuts, am I?"

"Skeeter, I wouldn't have called if I thought you were nuts. God forbid I should say something positive, George, but you are a fine human being, a little easy to tease, but a good person nonetheless. This three-party race is the only way a moderate can play in this game. You could never get nominated by either party, so here you are with a new toy. Mazel tov. Let's play it out and we'll see if it resonates. I think it will. Just remember, you need to follow my political advice carefully, because this is going to be one weird election."

"Thanks, I love ya, Morton. Don't let me screw this up. I wish there was someone else who would do it."

"Sure, Skeeter. Of interest and I really need to know, what kind of guy is Paul Roland. Not what does he think, but is he a good guy?"

"I don't know him very well, but if you put aside some of his honestly held views, I think he would be a pretty good guy to have as a friend, maybe even a president. From everything I have ever heard, you could put a gun to his head and he couldn't lie."

"Yep, that is what I heard and what I sensed when I met with him last year. Really, I think that is true with the President, but I think his problem is that he doesn't know when he is lying. I honestly believe he convinces himself of things that aren't true. He is a really odd duck, Skeeter."

"Morton, I have watched him pretty carefully. Odd duck, yes; smart, probably not, but certainly not dumb. Middle of the pack on most decent college campuses. If he were smart, he would have advisors who would tell him he is wrong when he is wrong.

"And, Morton, if we get this done, you and Marcia are going to be living in D.C. I will need you."

"Ugh."

~

SUNDAY, AUGUST 26, 2012

It was the kind of meeting every would-be politician, would-be political advisor, or political advisor would have wanted to attend; a meeting of three professional politicians plus a complete genius trying to determine how to allocate funds and what messages to disseminate to the voters. The attendees were George Vincent's political elite and The Professor. To this meeting, The Professor had not invited Molly Tom and from this meeting there would be no formal notes or minutes, just action items.

They were again at the Hilton in Orange County. Another small conference room had been rented and both Stanley Wade and Marshall Dankberg had quietly flown back in on the Hawker. This time, they had Milton Woo with them, but they did not need Joshua and this afternoon, he was nowhere to be found in Southern California. The Professor again drove across town and since there was no one to impress, he was on time arriving at 12:30. On the table was a small feast of cold cuts, soft drinks and pretzels. This was a working meeting. The environment was fairly relaxed, surprisingly so given that The Professor and Marshall Dankberg were within spitting distance of each other.

While the three experienced operators finished their sandwiches, Milton Woo tried to provide them with some of his election analysis and what he could do technically without causing a serious battle with the FTC or any other Federal agency with a set of initials rather than a name.

Woo was still only twenty-four years old. He attended the meeting in his professional attire, which for him was a short sleeve Hawaiian shirt, khaki slacks and topsiders. Today, he included brown socks in the ensemble;

most days he would have skipped the socks. His approach to everything was mathematical, which meant to his three collaborators, his comments were useful information for decision-making, but he would probably not be asked for policy advice.

"Gentlemen: Let me give you my summary and then if you want me to expand, I will. The polling data is fascinating to me because on a national basis the polls, like, are not worth, like, anything. I love Rasmussen, but, like, only if you pay for the underlying data. Like…"

The Professor was standing up. "Like, like, like, like, like, you sound like one of my fucking freshman business majors. Stop it! I don't care how smart you are, you sound like a fucking valley girl, now, talk as if you are an adult!"

"Oh, I am sorry." Woo went from sounding a bit like an over confident teenage poker player at the final table to a meek young man. Mission accomplished for The Professor. He had given this same presentation, with the same flowery language in his classes many times. It always had the same effect and based on The Professor's observations, the one-minute harangue usually had a lasting impact on the speaker.

Woo started again, carefully selecting his words and slowing his delivery pace: "Rasmussen has two fundamental presentations, strongly approves versus strongly disapproves and the general approval numbers. Then he provides the underlying data for the results.

"Picking a period at random, Rasmussen might report a seventeen percent net negative approval for the President and a fifty percent general disapproval. Applying some estimate of the value of the strong feelings in the approval/disapproval ratings, one would conclude that there is about a fifty-five to forty-five percent delta in likely voters. But when you look at the pieces of the puzzle, which Rasmussen sells for $19.95 a month, it turns out that black voters support the President about ninety percent to ten percent, and of that group, they almost unanimously strongly approve. This gives us an interesting bottom line. I would estimate that without the black voters, the strongly approve versus the strongly disapprove is almost forty-four percent versus twenty percent, a delta of almost twenty-four percent, and the general disapproval without blacks is closer to sixty-to-forty.

"Using standard voting analysis and standard political analysis that means we write off anything urban or black. The campaign should fundamentally focus on the remainder of the country. It is about ninety percent of the land and seventy-five percent of the voters."

The Professor, having made an identical assessment took the ball and ran with it. "Yes, Milton, this squares, with, like…" The Professor could never resist putting the needle in, "…like, like my thinking and understanding. We will get killed in urban areas as the black vote turns out in statistical terms in unanimity. But I think, and we don't have as much data on this, we also get killed in the solid Republican districts where there are no minorities. Anyone disagree?"

The Professor made a mental note to tell Molly to stay close to this Woo character. Once he stopped talking like a twelve-year-old valley girl, it was clear the guy was exceptionally smart and very well organized. Creative. He might be that rare stats/math type who could apply real world reasoning to his numbers.

Stanley Wade and Marshall Dankberg looked at each other and nodded. Wade added that his demographic got to exactly the same answer and that if the world went as he thought, Vincent could carry as many as thirty-two states or as few as twenty-two. The problem was that with all thirty-two states, he would not have 270 electoral votes. Dankberg had already seen Wade's numbers and with Woo and The Professor independently getting to the same place, the air went out of the room.

"OK, Marshall, this is why I got involved in this campaign and why I brow beat you guys on the telephone and in person. This election is not lost and not won. And it is not going to be won or lost in the damn election. Here is the strategy I want you to employ: One, make it appear that you are conducting a national campaign. But, we need to make two bets. The first bet is there is something going on that we cannot control, but it is good. Whoever these independent campaigners are, we need bet that they are going to continue to fund their campaigns and because they don't need to be politic, their ads will be more focused, more fun and more effective than ours. Two, we need spend our money helping a few well-placed friends, or new friends, win in key races where the specific race will determine the majority by political party in that specific state in the House of Representatives. Why, because as we will discuss in our next meeting with Skeeter and Molly, this election is going one hundred percent to the House of Representatives. We need to position ourselves to where we pick up two or three second level Democratic leaders in the House. We need friends in the House of Representatives; that is where our effort should be."

"OK, Professor, I think we actually agree on something. As usual, I assume you get all the credit and I get to do all the work."

"Absolutely, Marshall, you guys should have figured that out long ago. I want you to focus on Milton here and Molly as your resources. Milton, I am going to send Molly to you for the next few weekends. You can figure out whether you want her in Ohio or someplace else. When this is done, I want her to be the most knowledgeable politician under the age of twenty-one in the country. Work her to death. I'll make sure she keeps up in school.

"And, Milton, keep that Jonathon guy away from her. I don't like the way he looks at her."

Dankberg jumped in to help a bit. "He means Joshua, Milton. The Professor never misses a beat on relationships and I think he is right, all Joshua probably wants to do is pull her undies off and best as I can tell, all he ever wants to do is pull off any and every woman's undies. We are stuck with him. He is a big donor's son and that buddy is an old buddy of Vincent. You know the drill. Milton, you'll like her when you meet her. You can be her protector. At least she works hard."

Everyone laughed and a series of telephonic conferences were set up before The Professor headed home.

~

On Sunday night, on virtually every television station and on the cable station that sold advertising, at 7:00 p.m., another advertisement appeared for the entire country to see. It was a new advertisement, simple, inexpensive to produce and easy to understand.

With no sound, the advertisement first showed a simple sentence:

MR. PRESIDENT, YOU ARE RUNNING OUT OF TIME TO EXPLAIN YOURSELF, DIDN'T YOU WATCH THE AMERCIAN EXCEPTIONALISM CONVENTION?

(Picture of Jordon Scotch throwing his personal papers out of his briefcase.)

MR. PRESIDENT, WHAT CLASSES DID YOU TAKE AT OCCIDENTAL? WHAT CLASSES DID YOU TAKE AT COLUMBIA? HAVE YOU EVER HAD AN ECONOMICS CLASS?

(Picture of the President with a friend sitting on a couch.)

FOR GOODNESS SAKE, SIR, I WOULD NEED TO SUPPLY MORE INFORMATION TO GO TO WORK FOR THE POST OFFICE THAN YOU ARE WILLING TO SUPPLY TO THE AMERCIAN PEOPLE AS THE PRESIDENT.

(Picture of a postman.)

MR. PRESIDENT, YOUR LACK OF TRANSPARENCY IS JUST WRONG.

(Picture of Reesa Jonathon as a competitive swimmer and a second picture of her in her wheelchair seated in front of what was obviously a building on a college campus.)

I AM REESA JONATHON AND I RECORDED AND PAID FOR THIS AD. AND I WISH I DID NOT THINK IT WAS NECESSARY. THIS IS A SAD TIME IN OUR COUNTRY WHEN THE PRESIDENT'S PERSONAL HISTORY IS A SECRET.

~

The President, cigarette in hand, was staring at Peter Portman. The question of his grades and college admissions had been raised again. "Peter, why don't you tell the press that all is fine with my personal information and tell them again that I quit smoking because I love my two daughters? That should help." The President laughed at his own joke and continued. "Peter, just tell them again that this campaign is about issues and that the President is tired of covering the same ground over and over."

The Pillsbury Doughboy looked down and spoke to the table. "Mr. President, I am not sure where we go with these requests. At some point, people are really going to begin to wonder…"

The President responded with a curt, "It is not going to happen," and the Pillsbury Doughboy looked out the window of the Oval Office, sighed and began working his way through the other questions that might be raised at his daily press briefing.

This ain't going away.

~

MONDAY, AUGUST 27, 2012

North-South Polling Service:

The President	38%
Congressman Paul Roland	30%
George Vincent	32%

~

The RBC group again gathered together in their conference room. Delf Spooner presided over his team in his suit and tie. He decided he wanted his executive team to hear the presentation. No one else was sufficiently attired to join him for lunch today at his mid-town luncheon club. In addition to his management team, Samantha Whitspon brought her team of researchers with her. While not formally attired like Spooner, Rush Pfeiffer, Lucie Wiener and Rita Sanchez were fairly close to being professionally attired. At RBC, the entire team on any project was more than welcome at an executive committee meeting, but the presentation was always made by the executive team member. Questions were occasionally, but very occasionally, fielded by the team.

"Delf, our findings are almost laughable. My team has been unable to find anything significant in any of the areas researched. Anything." Samantha, clad today in a loose-fitting, flowered sundress made little effort to hide her disappointment in finding virtually nothing after expending the time of her able team. "It is not that the gang didn't do a credible job, there is nothing to find without breaking a few laws and the culture of this company continues to be that information found illegally will never be used. So, we didn't break any laws. Maybe group think, but here is what the four of us think: There is no information available to indicate that anything sinister happened, but he has very carefully eliminated his trail. You could only find this in a Clancy novel. And the character I play would be the bad guy, not the President of the United States.

"So, let me review the research in chronological order: First, we were not asked to look at the birth certificate issue, but we did anyway. May as well start at the start. The only thing unusual about the birth certificate is that it was unavailable for so long.

"Second, we found no newspaper or pictorial records of any kind with respect to the President from any grade school or other organization. We have determined that he went to the schools he has on his resume, but aside from attending, we cannot find so much as an attendance certificate. Our guess is that he was a decent student, but not an outstanding student or a failing student. He clearly was not an athlete, a joiner or a leader, pretty much an outsider.

"Delf, you and Trooper are the sports guys, we cannot determine for sure if he really did, or did not, play basketball in high school. If he did, he must have been a very minor cog in whatever wheel he was a part of.

You would have thought that this would be easy, but again, a blind alley. We should have been able to find the captain of his high school team, but to date, we have not accomplished that task.

"Lastly, we cannot get to either grades or classes taken at any level. Again, we can speculate to death, but we cannot get to the data. We believe this information has been scrubbed at every college or some geek would have hacked the information out of the systems. We speculate above average grades, no more, and African American studies as a major. We cannot find evidence of so much as an attendance award. This is highly inconsistent with what we generally know to be the academic results of most of the students in the schools he attended.

"Other than that, we found nothing unusual. My opinion is that there are issues at every step of the investigation. But, unless we are willing to break the law, we are not going to find out anything. Again, we found no whiff of anything sinister, but the whole thing is akin to a *Cold Case File* or something from *No Trace* on TV. The guy may have gotten along with everyone, but he did so very quietly."

Delf Spooner looked around the room. In his coat and tie, he looked a little bit like the guy who did not know the office policy was soft business casual. "Let's leave action steps on the table for half a second, does anyone have any idea how to get this information without tracking down the Wiki leaks people for help?"

The culture of RBC was to speak if you have an answer, speak if you have an opinion, and speak if asked a question. The room was silent.

"Samantha, last time we met, you indicated that the newspapers were, if I remember the quote, *dead man walking*, right?"

"Yes, Delf, I have not solved that business problem and am not sure there is a solution."

"OK, then hear me out. I have given this a great deal of thought and recognize that there is a considerable downside in this action plan, but I feel obligated to follow through on this. I feel obligated as, what did you call me, Troopster, a media magnate?" Troop Rasmer just nodded, but he was paying very careful attention. *The Boss might need a bit of bailing out in this discussion.*

"Samantha, here are the three steps I want you to follow: First, I want the Dallas paper to take this issue on with front page coverage Tuesday after the Republican convention, the day after Labor Day. Second, I want the coverage to start with a chart that shows each presidential candidate and

363

vice presidential candidate's personal information. Page one would begin the chart with each item you researched where you can get information for the other candidates. For the President, I want to see the paper reflect the language declines to state. You can figure out the rest. I want something in there about sports and friends. Maybe we can flush out, what, a friend or another ballplayer.

"And I don't want any of the candidates surprised. Third, ask them for lists by Saturday night and indicate that we will go to press within forty-eight hours, either way. We either get an exclusive on the facts within twenty-four hours or we go with the story. I suspect that we will lead with our chin. Got that, Samantha?"

Just a nod from Samantha.

"After this is published, I want it republished in every newspaper and I want our radio and television hosts to cover the story, as news and as opinion. Then we will just see what happens. Fox News will jump all over it and the other guys will just have to decide for themselves whether to get into the pool or hide in the shower room. Either way, we owe this to the American public. And let our outside lawyers know what is going on. At some point, we may need them."

The room was silent. Different area leaders had different concerns about the impact of this on their operations. As each of them hoped, Troop Rasmer asked the key question, in his own way.

"Delf, you know if we do this that we will have the regulator bees surrounding the hives, every hive. You know that if the President wins, his people will get even. They won't try to get even, they will fumigate the hive and kill the queen bee, that would be you. And you know, at least in the short run, it will kill the stock."

"Yup, anyone else?"

"Delf, how about we all see a preview of the newspaper article and then decide what to do?" Troop was looking for middle ground.

"Nope, I think we have made a decision here, unless someone wants us to take a vote. But remember, this would be one of those votes where at the end, I will look at you guys and say: 'That's the vote, ten to one against, and the one's win!'" Big smile. "I am a taxpayer here and I have reached my limit with this guy. I think I have a right to know if my President was the best or the worst scholar in high school or college. I have a right to know something about him. Frankly, I don't believe in massive conspiracies, but this is just so incredibly odd, I want to pursue it. If the Board of Directors makes me fall on my sword in a few weeks or months, so be it. Then you will find out if you are as good as I believe you are because the Board of Directors will have my head. If so, RBC will just march along with me spending one hundred percent of my time fishing, golfing and hunting."

~

TUESDAY, AUGUST 28, 2012

It looked like a Republican National Convention in 1956. There may have been a few more minorities in the audience, there may have been a few moderates, but this really looked like a traditional mid-twentieth century Republican convention crowd, not a twenty-first century Republican Convention. With the defections to the American Exceptionalism Party, the true, conservative Republican base made up nearly one hundred percent of the delegates. The average age of the delegates also reflected the conservative nature of the party. It was not a young crowd. It was hardly a middle-aged crowd.

The Scottrade Center had been a bit of an odd choice for a Republican National Convention. The good news was that after its controversial selection, the Republican senator from Missouri had stayed with the Republican Party, which had been a bit problematic for months.

The Scottrade Center was built on the site of the historical Kiel Auditorium in St. Louis. Until 1992, the Kiel Center had been the home of all things cultural in the city and this new building was now fulfilling that role for the city. The naming rights went to Scottrade in 2006, and based on Scottrade's success with $7 trades, it might be the Scottrade Center for a very long time.

Like the Democrats, and unlike the American Exceptionalism Party, the Republican leadership had many pre-game meetings. Also similar to the Democrats, but unlike recent Republican conventions, these meetings resulted in a platform that was perfect for the party faithful and exceptionally political, perhaps conservative to anyone that was not a political geek.

Many of the Tea Party movement's conservative positions were incorporated into the Republican platform. And also like the Democrats, the Republicans had replaced the delegates that had moved to the American Exceptionalism Party with more strident members of their own party. These replacements were conservative to the core. The Republicans did not have their delegates and leaders leave because of a loyalty oath issue, but the group behind the platform decisions was ruthlessly conservative and this was troubling to moderates.

The key political difference at the delegate level between the Democratic and Republican conventions—and it was a major difference—was that the Republicans had no loyalty oath to their platform and this allowed sitting moderate Republican elected officials the opportunity to be at the convention and not destroy their political futures. As was the historical norm for political platforms, anyone running for election or re-election could ignore any plank or all of the planks in the platform and continue as a Republican. While there were not that many high-profile moderate Republicans, the party needed the Scott Browns and Olympia Snows and their ilk in the Senate and the House of Representatives.

The only major political fight of the Republican Convention was fought at the platform level and that fight was over taxation. The FairTax movement was represented by Governor Huckabee and the talk show radio host, the ultra right and ultra obnoxious individual from Georgia. Paul Roland, who had rejected this position earlier in a luncheon with the radio show host was livid that this had been brought to the convention. He continued to see the FairTax as a threat that could both cost him votes and make him look like a nutcase. There was not a vote in the country that he would gain if he endorsed the FairTax and many that he would lose. This was simple math.

To the good fortune of his campaign, Hank Adler, the co-author of *A FairTax Fantasy, An Honest Look at a Very, Very Bad Idea* had been engaged early on to come to St. Louis to meet with the individual platform committee members days before the convention. While during the convention these members listened attentively to the governor and the radio show host, they firmly rejected the FairTax position based on Adler's presentation. The most telling points in Adler's presentation were his ability to explain that the proposed tax rate was really thirty percent, not the twenty-three percent purported and his explanation that he found it more than moderately surprising (amusing) that no matter what happened in the world—one dollar deficits or 1.5 trillion dollar deficits—the proposed tax rate stayed the same. His final point dealt the deciding blow. He described the 116 million monthly checks or deposits that the government was going to need to send to every family unit in the United States. That caused the committee to reject the plan without a dissenting vote. The Republican Party, with or without the Tea Party, was not going to suggest that the Federal government be responsible for sending out a billion checks a year. Not today, not ever.

The radio show host vilified Adler to the platform committee and his national radio audience, but no one cared about the vilification except Adler. He sold the 30,000 books he had thought he would sell when the book was published in 2010 solely because of the negative press he received from the talk radio host. It did not hurt that he managed to arrange a host of interviews on talk radio as well.

~

The Convention opened on Tuesday evening by the usual suspects. Nothing of note took place on the floor until Tuesday evening's speaker. Tuesday night's speaker was Governor Bertha Aplin. Ms. Aplin remained a rock star among most of the Republican Party's most ardent members. To the left wing of the Democratic Party, Bertha Aplin was now always the angry spouse after a few days of heated arguments. If she said it was too cold to go outside, the most liberal Democrats would have voiced an argument that it was too hot to go outside. The actual temperature would have been irrelevant to the discussion. Their response to Aplin was irrational four years after her introduction to the country. Once they blamed her for a political assassination of a politician in another state who she had never met or heard of before the assassination, all bets were off.

Bertha Aplin represented the Republican's core values: large family, anti-abortion, fiscal conservatism, self-made, self-reliant and personally strong.

Outside of Fox News, Aplin continued to feel the brunt of the lion's share of political commentary on late night television. She believed, "the whole thing was a sexist and a cultural issue." She believed that the Democrats actually believed an attractive woman could not be a meaningful political force. How this squared up with the National Organization for Women, she could never decipher. While there were many in the country that doubted her intellect, there was no reason to think, at least on a relative basis, that this was not a very smart woman. As Jenn Cho offered on Fox News, the current vice president certainly did not appear to have nearly the same intellectual horsepower as Bertha Aplin. As some right-based radio talk show hosts saw it, ditto for the President.

Regardless of all of the *noise*, Bertha Aplin was a hit inside of the Scottrade Center in St. Louis, Missouri.

The applause that greeted the former governor was over the top. The woman and her family had been unceasingly attacked for more than four years and yet, here she was, the ultimate survivor, the ultimate warrior, a family member.

At OBC, Big Red, now fairly comfortable as an anchor for a major television network, greeted Governor Aplin with a certain amount of positive passion and a certain amount of the media's disdain: "While the politically elite and the talk show hosts have continued four years later to make Bertha Aplin the signature victim of hate comedy, her refusal to hide and her ability to continue to participate in Republican politics made her a hero to everyone who believes in fairness and good taste. Those are the people on the floor of the convention tonight, and they are the ones giving her an ovation usually reserved for the candidate. While she might not be long on either policy or unscripted presentations, the Republicans love her for her irrepressible ability to continue on. With prepared remarks, she is always a sensational speaker; she is always on point. She has unlimited charisma.

"All of that being said, the fact that Bertha Aplin did not make a run for the 2012 presidential nomination and the fact that she has indicated that she has no interest in a vice presidential slot has been met by relief in the Republican Party's hierarchy."

Bertha Aplin looked radiant in her red suit, stockings and heels. This was a woman who was not ready for the over forty pants suit look. Bertha Aplin had the facial skin and legs of a twenty-five year old. She accepted the ovation, quieted the crowd and took her place at the podium: "Tonight, after four years of being the ultimate target of unfair, unvarnished and frankly, classless attacks on me and my family, I am going to take the gloves off for fifteen minutes." Applause, honest and sincere, not like the applause for a touchdown, more like greeting the graduating seniors on a football team. "I want to talk about what the cost of being an elected official is in today's world and what that cost is to your family. I want to talk about the blood sport of the press, the outright hostility of the press to Republican women and the harm it is doing to our nation."

"It's funny, I watched the former president cover some of the territory of my speech a couple of weeks ago at the American Exceptionalism Party Convention. For him, it was extemporaneous and for me, important in a political sense and yes, a bit cathartic as well.

"My husband was at home with most of our family when my youngest daughter was verbally assaulted by one of these late night so-called humorists. You may remember that I was visiting New York with our fourteen-year-old and David Le Secousse opined that my daughter, my *fourteen-year-old daughter*," she emphasized carefully and loudly, "had sex with a popular member of the New York Yankees during a game. He may have gotten a nervous laugh from his classless, baseless one liner, but my daughter was humiliated. Here we were in New York, just mother and daughter, and this clown goes after a fourteen-year-old. After some flack and frankly, not very much flack from the media, this jerk went on television not to apologize but to indicate he was referring to our other daughter. That daughter was eighteen. Apparently, eighteen is the age at which late night comedians think a young woman can be a target. Now that is class, isn't it?

"As you know, something similar happened with respect to one of Scott Brown's daughters in 2010. Let me ask a simple question, what would happen to a comedian who made similar comments about this president's children? The national media would go crazy. Resignations would be asked for and received. Regulations would be issued by some appointed czar. The NAACP would call out the idiot comedian or idiot late night host as a racist. Careers would end.

"But the national media has a different standard for white Republicans. This is not reverse racism. This is racism and elitist nonsense. It has to stop. If not, we are going to find, even more than today which is already a nightmare, prospective Republican candidates with families are going to be scared away from serving their nation. That's terrific isn't it? If you have a family, there is more reason not to be in politics than if you do not have a family."

The audience responded and not in the manner Bertha expected. One individual hollered: "Le Secousse is a jerk." And the audience picked up the chant. After just a minute or perhaps two minutes, she continued: "I talked to my husband and he was as livid as I suspected and we hoped ninety percent of parents around the nation were livid as well; we all love our children. He was just fuming and I always worry about a man his size who is fuming. You want to know what his first comment was?" Of course the convention hall shouted, *What?* "Todd wanted me to go on Le Secousse's television show the next night and just zip in a line about the timeline of the birth of his son and his wedding date. If I remember right, the son preceded the wedding date by about five years. He figured what was good enough for the goose was good enough for the gander. I actually think he wanted me to go on the show and get Le Secousse to throw a punch at me. He wanted me to duck the punch and humiliate his manhood.

"Now, of course, I could do none of what he suggested, but I understood. Frankly, I just wanted to wash the jerk's mouth out with soap." The chant of *Le Secousse is a jerk!* was again taken up in earnest by the convention.

Bill O'Brien offered from the Fox News booth: "I'm not sure that this rant is appropriate for a national political convention, but I have to admit, I pondered telling the country about Le Secousse's personal situation at the time four years ago and spending an evening talking about the hypocrisy of this man and the media in general. The American Exceptionalism Party did a pretty good job on this same subject at their convention. Maybe Aplin figures if she keeps the issue fresh, Le Secousse will suffer and we know she thinks that is okay. She definitely hit him where it hurts this evening.

"As I keep my family completely out of my public persona, I actually feared that one comment by me about Le Secousse would impact my wife and children. Was that selfish or was that my responsibility? I just left Le Secousse alone. At the moment, I am not quite sure if I did the right thing. There does seem to be a theme this year: Leave my family alone. Dr. Scotch was pretty clear about this at the AEP Convention." It was unusual for O'Brien to be in the role of newsman or convention commentator. Although he was a world-class newsman earlier in his career, he had walked away from the front line reporting for commentary almost fifteen years before. He was only there as a favor to the network to pump their ratings and he was going to try to play the role of unbiased newscaster rather than commentator. Arthur Ninoah had recently had surgery to remove his appendix and this was what O'Brien did for friends, he covered their backs.

Aplin continued: "The blogosphere is filled with brilliant commentators as well as some of the nastiest people in the history of the world. Given the First Amendment to the Constitution, that is a great place for anyone to gain the respect or disrespect of the readers. But, we need adult supervision of the mainstream media. This is big business and we should demand reasonable standards. Not any legal handcuffs for goodness sakes, not regulation, but owners and boards of directors should require their television stations and radio stations to act with class. Families should be off limits. Period!" Standing ovation.

"If a governor or president personally does something wrong, that is a different story. But, my golly, if my husband trips or one of my kids is not a Rhoades Scholar, someone should have the moral vision to shut down any coverage. It should not take moral courage, just homespun good taste. We cannot have candidates forsaking public office because the media sees their children as nothing more than political assets or in their minds, political liabilities.

"Trust me, because he gets a bazillion dollars a year on national television, Le Secousse does not curse on the air for a reason. If he understands he would be fired for bad language, he sure as heck could understand that families are off limits!" Greater applause.

"So let's talk together about the mainstream media. Let's start with the most basic questions, questions of family, faith and honesty, questions which should be fair game. Does anyone in this hall believe that if I misstated where I met my husband, it would have been ignored in the press?" A forceful *No* from the delegates. "The President did. Did we hear a single word after it occurred?" A forceful *No* from the delegates. "If I had attended church supposedly for more than a decade and suddenly stopped after I was elected president and said I was searching for the right church, would the press have remained silent or simply accepted I had elected to use the chapel at Camp David as my church?"—*No*—"Do you think they would have noticed that I was playing golf on Sundays, not after attending church, but instead of attending church? Don't you think someone would have noted that if he is raising his children as Christians, he is doing it without a pastor or a church? If I had said the stimulus package was working when the economy continued to be in near free fall, would the press have left me alone?"—*No*—"And if I said there would be transparency and everything was being done behind closed doors, do you think the press would have left me alone?" *No!*

"And the press knows so much about me and has done nothing to source this president. Not after four years. How can this be? How can we not know his college grades, how can we not know his college classes, how can we not know what classes he took in college? How can we not know what his social life was like in college? Should we just conclude that the President of the United States had no friends until he got married? Should we conclude he sat alone in his apartment for four years during college? We cannot even find anyone who knew him." There was a bit of stunned silence in the audience. These were questions generally only asked in the blogosphere, but they were questions that many millions of people really wished had answers. The convention had no idea what was coming on RBC, but Delf Spooner watching the convention at home knew he was moving RBC in the right direction. "And you know, the big one used to be the birth certificate. It was more secret than last month's testimony before the Intelligence Committee. I don't get it. Why in God's name did he decide to keep this a secret for almost half a decade? Doesn't that tell you something? Petulant child, arrogant politician, somewhere in between. I don't get it. I think that the game with the birth certificate and the continuing game with his college grades, etc., is just plain wrong. I think all of this has a meaning about the man that I don't like. I mean college without class schedules or college grades, and a plethora of things similar combined has meaning. The lack of a birth certificate for five years and still a president without interviews with lifetime friends, if there are any, produces an uncertainty of his past and that has meaning."

"And we have a media that seems to want to proclaim the President as some kind of great athlete. Remember, I was a pretty good high school basketball player myself; I am also that famous soccer mom. I know a host of business people and politicians who played ball in high school and/or college when I was in school. I found out when I was introduced to a national audience that there were literally hundreds of pictures of my high school basketball team and hundreds, actually dozens, of people who remember me scoring a winning shot in some ball game." The instant reduction from hundreds to dozens drew a laugh from the floor. "Of course, I don't recall all of those winning shots. Now, we have a president who wants us to believe he was a great athlete and yet, based on what is available, that would be nothing, it must have been on a different planet, another dimension, or in Indonesia, because there are no pictures, no newspaper articles and no friends that recall him so much as attending a high school basketball game.

"Of course, the media has given us an apparent great athlete who apparently never, ever so much as lettered on a high school freshman basketball team. Is basketball in high school or college important? Of course not." Aplin paused a bit. "But pretending to be something you are not. That really is important. And having the media be complicit in promoting that story, what garbage!" Now, a chant of *garbage...garbage...*broke out.

"I am really curious about all of the documents. It only matters because he does not want us to know these answers. The facts themselves are irrelevant. His reasoning matters. A baby is a baby. But, transparency is transparency."

The RBC anchor, Caleb Tyler, leaned into his microphone and offered: "Ms. Aplin seems to be applying the famous rule of political thumb. All of you jerks out there should stop calling me names. I wonder if this is working?" Tyler did not yet know what his company had going beginning Tuesday.

Aplin: "And what is news to this media? Why is it horrible front-page news when soldiers die in Iraq and Afghanistan under a Republican president and page fourteen under a Democratic president? Why, when Afghanistan is beginning to sound like Vietnam, does domestic policy dominate the news? Anyone seen Ms. Sheehan on television? While it is some time ago, why is a drugged and troubled singer talked about as nearly a religious icon and a four star general's death ignored? How does this work?" she rhetorically asked. "How can this be in a free country? How can we accept a shameless, one-sided press? I tell you, this is wrong." Significant applause.

"We need to talk seriously about the, quote, mainstream press in this country. I am not sure we have the free press that the Constitution says we need and assumes we have to protect democracy. I think we have a mainstream media, which is owned essentially by a few huge corporations, each of whom does business with the government and all but one of whom is a lapdog for this president." This comment brought the mainstream media to silence. They were listening to this woman who, in their hearts, they scorned. They knew she was correct. Her presentation, a bit Midwestern sounding, was rock solid. Charisma and confidence always created a sale for Bertha Aplin.

"In late 2009, Fox News started reporting about the President's czars. They started talking about an individual that was clearly so far left he belonged in the government of another nation, maybe China. Maybe too far left for China in 2012, but right in Mao's sweet spot. The individual ultimately resigned from the White House staff before the mainstream media mentioned word one. That was word one. When they finally covered the subject, the story was complete and they spun it so that the news reporters at Fox looked like bad guys.

"The same took place with other stories. The mess at Acorn was covered by Fox and ignored by the rest of the media until Beck and the rest of the Fox News gang demonstrated that there had been massive fraud. Even then, the mainstream media could have cared less. The mess with the Black Panthers scaring voters at the polling booth and the decision to walk away from their prosecution by the Attorney General of the United States, ibid. And I cannot think of a similar situation in reverse, a story covered by the mainstream media that was ignored by Fox News.

"And then there was Tucson. God love the congresswoman and the poor souls who were murdered, but what the mainstream media did to the notion of an unbiased free press was only one notch below the tragedy itself.

"Give me a break. I am not a regulator by nature; I am a Republican. But I believe we need to force these big, multinational corporations to divest themselves of their television and cable television networks. Maybe, just maybe, if one of these networks cannot trade good coverage for a new contract to build a submarine, we will get honest coverage. Teddy Roosevelt would have endorsed that piece of legislation." Applause.

376

"As you all know, I stepped aside in this political year. What is in my personal future, we will all witness together. I decided that a united Republican Party supporting Paul Roland was and is best for the United States of America. I appear tonight to support our Republican nominee for president." Classic political convention applause, marching and whatever.

Bertha Aplin's speech went on to extol the virtues of Congressman Roland and the issues included in the platform committee recommendations. No one remembered any of this. What they did remember, was her view of the press attacking her family, her strong comments about the President's missing documents, her first comments about Arizona, and that she believed in the regulation of the press in terms of ownership.

Following Aplin's presentation, the mainstream media went into overdrive to depreciate whatever value was left in the Aplin name. The most classic comment offered was that David Le Secousse's personal life should not have been mentioned by the former Republican office holder. It surprised no one, but the media could do nothing to blunt the force of Bertha Aplin's comments.

The focus groups hosted by Lance Amplington for OBC, produced some surprising results. Many non-conservative Americans were tiring of this personality from Alaska, yet they agreed with almost every word she had to say about the media. They saw the lapdog that the media had become.

One non-scientific poll on Fox News asked the question of whether the listener had the most respect for the mainstream media, the United States House of Representatives, or one of the characters in a recent animated cartoon. The animated character in the cartoon carried the day by over seventy percent. A joke, the poll may have been, but the message had been heard by the management teams of the media outlets and was being considered with that occasional level of humor produced in real life. A few in the Board of Directors seats of the multinational companies that owned the lion's share of television and cable industry heard the message as well.

Like most Tuesday nights at political conventions, there was more than a bit of rhetoric for the masses, but little else. The evening closed with a magnificent video extolling the administration and life of Ronald Reagan. No one at home saw the Reagan presentation unless they were watching public television, because like the Democratic Convention, the viewers saw but an hour or two on mainstream media television.

~

WEDNESDAY, AUGUST 29, 2012

Wednesday night was reserved for the keynote Speaker, the nomination speech for the Vice President and the speech of the vice presidential nominee. Paul Roland had decided to have the keynote speech and the nomination speech for vice president combined. Unlike everything else in politics in 2012, there had been no leakage on the vice presidential nomination. Paul Roland had been unable to think of a single reason for anyone to watch the convention on Wednesday night unless the evening led to a surprise and so be it, he was going to give them a surprise with his VP nominee. This was the same conclusion reached by John McCain four years earlier. The surprise would certainly not be as big as the Bertha Aplin surprise, but at least the nomination had remained a secret. In politics, that qualified as a surprise.

Based upon what Paul Roland had seen on television and read in the newspapers as well as on the web, the speculation was that at least two hundred people had turned him down for the VP nomination. Some of the individuals reputed to have turned down the nomination for Vice President of the United States were not even American citizens. It was crazy, but Congressman Roland knew speculation was great politics.

The lights went down and up popped former Senator Rolland Raptor. While the program committee would have preferred a younger keynote speaker on this night of the convention, the appearance of the former primary presidential candidate gave them the opportunity to present both the future and the past. Plus, Senator Raptor was well named. He could hold an audience based solely on his hands, which never stopped moving when he spoke and his articulation of clearly defined and aggressive positions. Not a word would be slurred or mispronounced. His speech pattern put the emphasis on the first syllable of every multi-syllable word. It was a bit odd for the first sentence or two, but more often than not, it made the listener hang on every word.

"My first role tonight is to talk about the past four years. My role is to tell you how concerned I was the day following the nomination of the President by that left-wing Democratic convention in 2008." Raptor pronounced president with emphasis on the *Pres*, which was unlike the way anyone else pronounced the word. The same with his name. Emphasis on the first syllable.

"My second role is to nominate a superior individual for the vice presidency. I do believe I will first discuss the last four years.

"Let us talk about mistake number one and mistake number one thousand and one by this president. Since they are the same mistake, we can look to Albert Einstein who once mused a definition of insanity: *Insanity*, he said, *is doing the same thing over and over again and expecting different results.*

"So, of course, we are talking about the Vice President." The audience heard the Vice President's name pronounced by emphasizing the first syllable of his name. This style of speaking began to draw them deeply to his presentation. It almost always worked. Plus, any mention of the Vice President was such an easy target for this audience. The audience laughed both at the pronunciation and the man.

"Think about it. You have spent your entire career in the United States Senate," Raptor paused here, "both months, getting ready for the moment when you are going to run for and be nominated for the presidency. The first decision is you get to determine your running mate. Now, of course, your entire working career in the United States Senate before you began your campaign for the presidency was actually not quite two months, it was only about fifteen days, not counting weekends." The senator hit a point that no one in the Scottrade Center this evening would disagree with, save perhaps a relative of the President who was working for a media concern.

"So, first big decision, this is your moment; I mean this is your moment to show the world that you have got what it takes to be the President of the United States, the most powerful person in the world. I mean, you are selecting a person that could become the President of the United States tomorrow morning, you hope not, but that is the responsibility of this first decision. And you pick, who?

"Who? Now, don't get me wrong, if I were going to go out and have a few beers, the VP would be at the top of my list. Actually, for several years, he was first on my list of calls to go have a beer. Heck, after the third beer, he is the most entertaining guy on the planet. Great storyteller, one of the greatest embellishers I have ever met, kind of guy that would pretend, just a *bit*, to make a story better..." Raptor had his arms spread to the max. Huge laughter and applause as everyone in the room was enough of a political geek to recall the Vice President telling a story about President Boone that apparently never happened, but made the VP seem to himself to be about twenty feet tall.

"Walking fish story. OK, maybe more than a bit of an embellisher. This is a guy who makes Senator Kerry's description of his war service seem understated. By the way, is it really Jennnngis Kahn or Genghis Kahn?

"This vice president as first in line to be President of the United States? Is this the same guy who can never stay on message? Is this the same guy who during the campaign against my friend John McCain said, and I quote: *Look, John's last-minute economic plan does nothing to tackle the number-one job facing the middle class, and it happens to be, as the President says, a three-letter word: jobs. J-O-B-S, jobs.* He's second in line?"...And the audience picked up the question: *Second in line?*

"Is this the same guy who thought the key to keeping the nation out of bankruptcy was to keep spending more and more?"

The VP quotes continued and the crowd's response went on for about ten more minutes. Raptor was particularly funny. How could he not be; the Vice President may have been a great guy, but he was a walking malapropos.

"But, you know, this isn't really all that funny around the world. The President sends this guy out to talk and then he has to have his press agent, excuse me, press spokesman, hold yet another press conference to just make a small change in what this guy had to say. Often the President's guy produces that perfect quote: *The President agrees with everything the VP had to say except,*" long pause, "except, please add the word *not* to a few key sentences." The convention delegates howled. "For example, in that first sentence where he said we will agree to that treaty, he almost had it exactly right, he meant to say *we will not agree to that treaty.* What's in a word?"...again chants of *Second in line!*

"And, yes, at that funeral a few years ago did he mean to mourn the death of the man standing next to him?

"So what did we find out last week? The president nominated this guy for a second term…" The audience participated at length.

"I am sorry, that is game, set, and match. If there is one thing I think all Americans can agree on it is that this was a bad decision four years ago and repeating that decision last week demonstrates that this president has learned absolutely nothing in four years.

"And how could that not be the case, if you give two speeches a day and travel from Washington D.C. to wherever and then from wherever to wherever and back to Washington D.C. every day," Raptor paused, "Yes, every day but Sunday when he plays golf, how could you learn anything because you are not working and learning, you are part of a five-year political campaign. You are not being a president; you are being an entertainer! And of course, if he is not campaigning, he is travelling, not working."

Raptor went on to discuss every perceived misstep by the President. After about fifteen minutes, he reached a climax.

"We need a *LEAD*-er who can create trust in the United States, we need a leader who does the right thing and does not shrink from responsibility, and we need a leader who does not blame others for his mistakes. We need to get that man out of the White House and elect Congressman Paul Roland to the Presidency of the United States of America." Pure bedlam followed.

While the audience went crazy, Senator Raptor leaned on the podium a bit longer than he had during most of his speech so far, as his tenacity and bravado were a bit more than his physical stamina. At seventy years old, he was in the twilight of his career and not in perfect health. He took off his coat and just waited for the audience to stop. For more than a second, he appeared physically uncomfortable. His wife, sitting in the special box for presenters, looked a bit concerned, but as Senator Raptor went back to the microphone the color seemed to return to his face. She thought to herself: *My man's patriotism is going to kill him some day, but not tonight. God, he looks pretty happy with himself.* "Thank you ladies and gentlemen, we are going to do the right thing this November and the world will be a safer place."

Senator Raptor went on to introduce the vice presidential candidate from the Republican Party, Senator Bobby Joe Blankly. The speed of the transition did not give the television commentators but a minute to discuss Raptor's offering or discuss whether Senator Blankly was a good or bad choice as the VP. Nothing was said of any special merit in the mezzanine level.

~

382

Senator Bobby Joe Blankly was both the definition of a reluctant vice presidential candidate and the ideal candidate. He was reluctant to be vice president because he believed he could be a United States senator for the remainder of his working life and that appealed to him. The hours were good, the work was interesting and he believed that he was helping the country. He was ideal because he had been elected to a term that did not end until 2016 and his constituents could forget this election episode, assuming it failed, before his next election campaign.

Blankley was a University of Oklahoma honors graduate. He continued his education after graduation at the London School of Economics. (With the nomination of Jordon Scotch, Congressman Roland believed he needed a candidate with impeccable academic credentials and Blankley fulfilled the role easily.) After college, Blankley moved to Tulsa, Oklahoma from Norman, Oklahoma—the location of his Boomer Sooner—to expand the family's oil business into the oil fields of Northeastern Oklahoma. Bobby Blankley was highly successful as an oilman; it was in his blood. A few years and a few dozen successful deep wells later, he succeeded a popular, many times elected Republican senator to office in Oklahoma. He relied on very little else than his personal fortune to win the Republican primary to propel him into office. It had not hurt that he was an heir to a significant Texas oil fortune before his personal successes outside of Tulsa.

Blankly had not an uncommon Oklahoma look about him. At six-feet-two-inches tall and not a pound over one hundred seventy-five with dark, dark black hair, razor thin lips, almost grey eyes, and an apparently permanent skin color that looked like he was George Hamilton, with two days growth of his beard, he would not have looked out of place on a drilling rig or at the end of a long bar near the University of Oklahoma. One could easily see that his body was all muscle and bones, the rock hard look of a manual laborer.

"My friends," sounded like *Ma friends* in his Oklahoman twang, a twang that he never tried or intended to change. He was one of those original born Oklahomans that would have been completely happy if Oklahoma was an independent nation and not a part of the United States of America. Oklahoma first.

"Ma friends," he repeated, "I see my role here to be somewhat akin to the role of the Ghost of Christmas Past in the famous Dickens novel *A Christmas Carol*. I am going to let Congressman Roland talk about the future while

I am going to dwell on the state of the Nation. I define the state of our nation today with a single question: What went wrong?…Yes, what went wrong? And I will be honest, at home—with the kids away—there might be a few adjectives or adverbs in front of wrong. Tonight will be the G-rated version made for everyone."

"You know, the President's wife complained about their law school loans as if their advanced educations should have been free. I grew up in a nation where if you wanted something the right thing to do was to pay for it. What went wrong?" Long pause. "This is the same woman in the White House who has twenty-two assistants and to the best of my knowledge hasn't yet cooked the President a home cooked meal. Just folks." Suddenly the vice presidential candidate was a comedian and the audience lapped it up. "You know, the President supported all that lending to people who could not afford those loans from Fannie Mae and Freddie Mac. He was sponsored by Fannie Mae through their election contributions to him. This has always seemed wrong to me. How can a quasi-government agency that is completely beholden to the government make direct and indirect political contributions? The same holds true for General Motors.

"Then the President wanted to forgive or reduce the Fannie Mae loans. I grew up in a nation where if you wanted something the right thing to do was to pay for it. What went wrong?" The convention picked up the cadence. *What went wrong, Bobby Joe?* "Those entities, supported and forced upon us by Democratic rascals have cost us trillions of dollars. What went wrong?" *What went wrong, Bobby Joe?*

"You know, I grew up in a nation that allowed one to pick his own health insurance or to fund it himself. What went wrong?" *What went wrong, Bobby Joe?*

"You know, I grew up in a nation that secured its borders." *What went wrong, Bobby Joe?*

"You know, this border security thing makes me so mad I could spit. We have a president who thinks he can fix global warming but seems to think the border is too vast to defend. What went wrong?" *What went wrong, Bobby Joe?*

"You know, I grew up in a nation that enforced all of its laws, not just the ones which did not offend constituencies of this president or his Attorney General! What went wrong?" *What went wrong, Bobby Joe?*

"Apparently, you can take a walk in the Arizona desert, take the risk of encountering the dangerously lethal drug cartels, and this president does not care." *What went wrong, Bobby Joe?*

Senator Blankley let the chanting stop, stepped away from the microphone for a moment and clearly hesitated. "I am going to get tarred and feathered for my next thought, so let me put it in context. I doubt there is a single Oklahoma voter who does not know that I am a direct descendent of Geronimo's family or that my mother is one hundred percent Apache Indian. Mom, stand up for a minute, would you?" The senator looked at the VIP box and his mother stood and waived. Blankley's mother was a short woman, and, as was her custom, she was dressed in very stylish grey clothing with a large Apache bracelet on her left arm, which was the arm with which she waved to her baby boy. The crowd gave her a very warm welcome.

"My mom taught me I was an American. I had Indian heritage, I had French heritage. I was not a white boy, I was not an Indian, I was not that term that no one in our home ever used for half Indian, half Caucasian. I was taught that I was an American. I was also taught that I was an Oklahoman. And ask me today, I will tell you I am an American, born and raised, proud. I am an Oklahoman, born and raised, proud." Huge applause broke into his speech for the first time. The audience could sense he was going into forbidden territory and given his ancestral background, he could.

"My dad is gone almost five years now, but in our house, we honored the Apache Indian, we honored his heritage from Tennessee, and a long time before his heritage from France, and we respected anyone and everyone. We honored our Native American history and we honored our Apache history. I studied the Bedonkohe band of Apache and my great, great uncle, Geronimo. Nothing has changed, my children are Americans and if any family member so much as utters a disparaging remark about any race, in my family, we still head for the soap and water. That soap and water was a good tool for my folks and while it would offend a lot of liberals, it was a great tool for us and I hope it will be used by the next generation of our family. Not too many children use the wrong wording in any sentence a second time after a few minutes spent with soap and water in their mouths. In my house, we call that parenting." Applause from this conservative audience.

"And now we have a president with a biological background not so terribly dissimilar to mine. Father from Kenya and mother, a Caucasian from the United States. He was essentially raised by his mother and her parents, as

I understand. Yet, he considers himself black. I guess a man can be anything he wants in the United States," long pause and a very serious look on this tall, thin, stern and muscular politician, "but I think we should all think it odd that the President considers himself white or black and far more important, it obviously matters to him. Let me repeat, it is only important because it matters to him!" This was delivered not with volume, but with a questioning passion. "This is the United States of America and I think," he elongated the think and it sounded Southern or Oklahoman, "I think that we should think of ourselves as Americans, not black, not white, not Apache. I actually both want and believe in a post-racial United States of America. I know that these thoughts about the President may not be politically correct in most places, but it is what I believe." A few shouts of *U-S-A* and then huge chants of *U-S-A*.

"Me, I am just a boy from Oklahoma who loves his home state and loves his country. I identify myself as an American." Now the applause was loud and sustained.

Big Red spoke over the noise and remarked: "These last words may really hurt Senator Vincent and Blankley in some parts of the country, but I have to admit, the President's apparent abandonment of anything white in his history is a question that has occurred to me occasionally over the past four years. Maybe I should not admit to that, but it is true. In a post-racial world, why does the President of the United States refer to himself as black, white, Indian or reddish green for that matter? He really isn't any particular color or background. What is wrong with American? It makes me proud to say that short sentence: I am an American and proud of it!" This was not what normally came from Big Red when she was on the microphone; the e-mails began to pour in. Perhaps, surprisingly, she had hit a positive note with eighty percent of her audience.

Merritt Goodman was on her ear piece as she paused: "Marylou, I don't disagree with a word you just said, but be careful here, there will be some race card pitching after this speech and you do not want to be either a pitcher or a catcher." Good advice, and received by Big Red exactly as it had been intended, as good advice.

On MSNBC, Megan Ybarra, the anchor, responded to Senator Blankley's remark over the crowd noise with: "In some states, this could be considered hate speech. I don't know where this presentation is going, but it is not going to play well in many communities across this nation. I myself, find it insulting." In what must have been a surprise to Ybarra, Erica Govaars, a pollster running yet another network's focus group, quickly noted: "You know, this may not be politically correct, but the questions are legitimate and my focus groups seem intrigued. All three groups, Republican, Democratic and Independent."

Over at OBC, Blankley had everyone's antennae up. Big Red again jumped into the fray and offered: "This is a very interesting tact. Blankley knows that with George Vincent in the mix, there cannot be very many black votes out there for the Republicans to get in 2012. These comments will get the attention of all of the voters and will not be instantly dismissed. One wonders whether these comments could resonate with some of the most liberal voters in this supposed post-racial society. Is the left sufficiently far left to truly be post racial? That is a question I would like to ask the President. Maybe, the question should be: Who is post racial?'"

Blankley looked up at the crowd and returned to his presentation: "Really, all of this is important, because it gets to the character of the President. I have never gotten over his response to that Orange County, California, pastor with respect to his question of when life begins. The President responded that the answer to that question was *above his pay grade*. Oh my God!" Blankley pulled back from the microphone knowing that his next comments were going to rip into the hearts of the anti-abortion crowd and probably more than a bit beyond that group. *What went wrong, Bobby Joe?*

"Above his damn pay grade? That was bull, plain and simple. He has a lifetime of votes and almost four years of a presidency that clearly demonstrates that he believes that abortion on demand is a woman's right, any time, any place. Actions trump words. This is America, he is entitled to that view. Yes, while I disagree, I respect that view. Of course my daddy and mommy would never speak to me if that was what I believed, but the President, as well as any other citizen, is allowed under our Constitution to believe whatever the hell he wants, even if he will rot in hell because of it!" A storm of applause and more than a few *Amens* following this thought. *What went wrong, Bobby Joe?*

"As I would never accuse the President of being a liar, I think he believes that life begins when the mother decides life begins, which might be hours or days after delivery. Guy would have made a heck of a Spartan." *What went wrong, Bobby Joe?*

Tyler: "That comment was over the top."

"All I know is that he does not believe life begins at conception and it appears to be a heck of a long time thereafter and he did not have the cajonies to share that thought with the American people. My gosh, he cloaks all of this under a woman's right to choose. Well, if you believe a woman can abort a child after the sixth month, I tell you that you that I believe you are in favor of murder. Call it what you want, he has the right to believe what he believes and I have a right to call him out on it!" Standing and lasting ovation. In this Republican Party Convention, his comments were golden. *What went wrong, Bobby Joe?*

"It gets to a matter of character. What does one believe? Who does one believe he is? What does one believe in his own set of core values?"

Blankley spent his remaining few minutes espousing the key values of the Republican Party. He focused in on religion as a Republican key value. And then the Wednesday night portion of the convention was over.

Bobby Joe Blankley made the rest of the evening very easy for the spin-meisters. The right positioned the conservative from Oklahoma as an honest, righteous man asking the hard questions. The left tried to define Blankley as a bigot of mixed race, the worst kind, whatever that meant.

~

The rioters in Saint Louis were the same rioters that were in Chicago. All had been released from jail if they had been arrested at the Democratic Convention and most had been charged with nothing. The Chicago authorities wanted to be done with these people and finding specific witnesses and evidence was extremely difficult.

The rioters were far from the Scottrade Center and while there was less violence than at the Democratic Convention, there were five times as many television cameras and reporters. During this week, the protestors were interviewed as if they were running for office as legitimate candidates rather than as scurrilous rioters planning to disrupt democracy and harass the legal system. Their every move was documented and critiques were made with respect to the Republican Convention for everything from failing to give the protestors a voice in the proceedings to not foreseeing a need for adequate temporary housing.

During Wednesday and Thursday night, the mainstream media was moving back and forth between the protests and the convention.

Fox News, who had the lion's share of the television audience, addressed their view of the coverage in *The Washington Times*: "The protestors were fewer at the Republican Convention than at the Democratic Convention. These fewer protestors apparently had a better press agent."

~

THURSDAY, AUGUST 30, 2012

This Thursday night of the Republican Convention was typical of the closing night of any Republican Convention. Like the Democratic Convention, the nominating speeches extolled the virtues of the candidate and the video was worthy on an Emmy Award. Congressman Paul Roland walked to the podium from stage left after the speech nominating him to be President of the United States.

"Thank you. I was born and raised in Texas. I learned my values in Texas and I believe in the values that I learned in my home, my school and my church. I make no apologies for my conservative values." Applause.

"My friend, Senator Bobby Joe Blankley, was born and raised in Oklahoma. He learned his values in his home, his school and his church. He makes no apologies for his conservative values. I make no apologies for his values. America, what you see is what you will get when we are working every day at the White House." Of course the convention floor responded with many minutes of celebration.

"We will be transparent in what we are asking the American people to support and what we support. Tonight, I want to spend a few minutes comparing and contrasting what we believe America needs with what is happening today. The differences between what we believe the government of the United States should be doing and what it is doing are stark. The differences between what we believe the government of the United States of America should not be doing and what it is actually not doing are equally stark."

A call came from the convention floor: "Don't hold back, Paul!"

Paul Roland paused, smiled and laughed. "Sir, I wrote this speech myself, y'all don't need to worry about Paul Roland holding back and you don't have to worry about a long current president-like speech.

"Let me explain where we are different than this president. Long-time Democratic Senator Robert Byrd and I disagreed on so many things philosophically, but we agreed on one thing without any measurement of difference. We believed we are a nation of laws and we believed the overall governing law was the Constitution of the United States. We both believed that we were experts on the subject, both in its history and its application." The congressman reached into his pocket and pulled out a small book. "This is my copy of the Constitution. If I am in Washington D.C., I carry this book in my pocket at all times. So did Senator Byrd. The only difference between my copy and his copy was that mine was signed by Senator Byrd and he included these words: "Paul, while we disagree on so many political things, so long as you continue to rely on a fair reading of the Constitution of the United States and it is the foundation of your phi-losophy, I will always be an admirer." Applause took hold of the Scottrade arena as it would regularly during the remainder of the congressman's short acceptance speech.

"Tonight, I will be far more brief than you expect. I am going to com-pare my view of the role of the President of the United States and the role of government of the United States. My view of these issues will be in a language that should not be subject to interpretation. Some of this will seem to be inside the beltway to you, some of it will seem axiomatic and some of it you may disagree with. It is what I believe.

"First, over the course of the next four years, I want the Congress of the United States to do its job and accept the responsibility that is granted to it within the Constitution. During the past twenty or so years, and dramati-cally more so within the past three and a half years, the Congress has given more and more power to the President. This is wrong, this is shameful and this is an abrogation of their duties and oaths of office. Fixing this will not be easy, but for starters, Congress needs to do a few things:

"First, Congress must begin to scrutinize the White House. It must pass legislation to reduce the number of appointments the White House can make without congressional approval. The wholesale appointment of czars and czarinas undermines the checks and balances of our system. Congress must take these powers away from the president. The president cannot be able to make appointments without congressional approval during recess. I will sign such a bill.

"Second, Congress must scrutinize the White House budget. When the President of the United States is using the White House budget so that the President of the United States can be on stage with famous entertainers every night, something is woefully wrong. The entertainment budget of this White House is right out of the Marie Antoinette playbook. The vacation schedule of this White House is also right out of the Marie Antoinette playbook. Between vacations, entertainment at the White House, and campaigning five days a week around the country rather than working at his job, this president has let the country down. We need a president who along with communications with the American public can sit at his or her desk and work.

"The White House budget must be explicitly approved by the Congress so that we don't have little princes or princesses in control. The current guy reminds me of a Czar from 1911 serving caviar to friends and listening to pop music festivals while the country is drowning in red ink. You can be assured that my family won't spend a million dollars of your money running off to Spain for a vacation. Ain't going to happen. And it is Congress's job to make sure it doesn't happen.

"Congress also needs to gain control of the regulation process. We cannot pass bills and have the Federal agencies writing regulations on the very edge of what Congress intended, if not beyond that edge. The only way to regain control of the process is through an active Congress.

"The president must enforce all of the laws of the Untied States of America. If the president believes the appropriate agency does not have the funds to enforce certain laws, he needs to ask Congress for the funds. If he does not believe a law is appropriate, he can ask the Congress to change the law. If Congress does not want to change the law, the president has two choices, direct the government to enforce the law or resign. This president disagrees with this theory. He believes he need only use the power of the government to enforce the laws with which he agrees. I would hope that if I don't try to enforce the borders, try to protect America and stop the drug trade that the Congress considers my impeachment. I really believe this. I want to be a president with a small P, not a president with a capital P.

"Again, the President must enforce our borders. As Senator Raptor said last night, this president wants to believe he can change the planet's climate, but claims our borders are too vast to protect. Is he kidding? Regardless of where we are on a comprehensive immigration bill, our borders are our borders and border enforcement is not a choice given to the president.

"We must undo much of what is in health care. The goal of the Untied States of America should be to enhance and expand care. When getting better care for one means a reduction of care for others, that is not the American way. We are better than that. We do not need to increase the administrative costs of health care by creating over one hundred new agencies. The goal of any involvement by the Federal government is to help provide better heath care, not expand the number of Federal employees. We should be smarter than that. And charging someone a fee for not having health insurance? That is flat out un-American. The first key to the health care mess is to increase the supply of doctors and nurses. This won't cost a trillion dollars.

"Next, we need not try to increase the scope of Constitutional law into areas previously not contemplated. If one can be forced to buy insurance only because one is alive, there is literally nothing the Federal government cannot mandate. When we end up with a two-thousand-page bill no one has read, we have an elected oligarchy bowing to an unelected oligarchy of Federal employees. That is not our America. I believe we will need a Constitutional amendment to narrow the Federal government's power under the Commerce Clause. The Supreme Court has allowed a huge expansion of the Commerce Clause and the way to fix that is through a Constitutional Amendment limiting the power of the Federal government as was interpreted by the Supreme Court for the first two hundred years of this republic. This should reduce the guesswork with respect to what the courts will determine.

"With respect to Cap and Trade, that should have always been a nonstarter. Any proposal that by its nature will make the United States less competitive and reduce employment will never have my support.

"As to deficits and taxes, this is the *Oh-my-God* problem. The Democratic Congress apparently did not understand that they were making the country insolvent. On this issue, I will add that I believe Congress and this president have been negligent, criminally negligent. These elected officials have properly railed at business people who have been irresponsible; but no one has been as irresponsible as Congress and this president. No one! And you have to layer the current level of Federal government employees and their pensions into the mix. How do you fix it? Congress must eliminate and reduce agencies where their efforts are not creating value to the public. Congress must eliminate agencies where their efforts are duplicative. Congress must hold Federal government employee's wages steady until we are in place to get control of our expenditures. That may not make Federal employees happy, but it is the right course of action. Like private sector employees, every employee can always test the job market."

While every statement was getting applause and hollering from the audience, this last statement brought such an overwhelming response that the Congressman needed to wait a full ninety seconds to go on to his next point.

"We need to eliminate Federal employee unions. The government cannot afford to have important pieces of our national fiber controlled by unions who would be willing to harm the country by going on strike. The results of Federal unions to date have been catastrophic. Just look at them as the biggest contributors to Federal election campaigns in the country. This is just wrong. This should be fixed legislatively.

"We should make our first major budget cut at the Department of Education. This may sound like heresy, but ask any local school board member if his school district can identify a single thing the Federal government does for them other than send money that is not redundant? The answer will be no. I would prefer to reduce federal taxes and let the states take full responsibility for education. If the state's citizens want to fund whatever the Federal government has been doing, terrific. If not, there is a message there.

"I used the Department of Education as my first draft pick for reduction and/or elimination, I think there are hundreds of billions of dollars that are being spent in the Federal government that we have no right spending. Mostly, these are issues the states are already dealing with and that is where the decision making and the funding should be. Congress needs to take corrective action, now. The Federal government needs to do less.

"We will lay all of this out with specifics as you would hope and should expect. But there is another major item this Congress needs to discuss. No one outside of a single Congressional District in Northern California elected Nancy Pelosi to the House of Representatives. We cannot have Ms. Pelosi or anyone else telling the individual Members of Congress how to vote. This may be the biggest scandal of the past few years. This has to stop. We need smart independent thinking in the House of Representatives and the Senate. We don't need one senior Member of those bodies calling every play for every Member. We need the voters not to tolerate, not to tolerate beyond one election cycle, a congressman or senator who does not reflect their constituencies' goals and objectives. We need to change the culture of our elected officials.

"A friend of mine used to be on a local school board in Southern California. He tells a great story that explains the duties of any government in terms of being involved in the decision making and not just a vote that someone else owns. As my friend tells the story, he was sitting at his desk working one day. He is an accountant by trade and his telephone rings. As I said, he is on his local school board, a part-time responsibility, and on the other end of the telephone is the mayor. This is the first telephone call he had ever received from the mayor and the mayor informed him that for reasons unrelated to the school board, a decision had been made to keep a parcel of land within the city that had previously been promised to another developing city. Several years before, the city had asked the school board to go along with a land transfer and the school board had gone along.

"My friend relates that he mentioned to the mayor that there were fourteen hundred houses being built on that strip of land and that the other city's school board had sufficient seats in their schools for the students, but that his school district had not expected the students and there was no way they could do anything except go on double session. He reminded her that she and her city council had asked that they give the land to the other city and when they had done so, the responsibility and planning for new schools had moved to the other city.

"My friend loves to tell this story because it gets to the finale. He relates that the mayor informed him he had to be a team player on this one. My friend responded and I want you folks to remember this response, he said: *My dear, I played football and I learned that the way to get a player to be a team player is to invite them into the huddle.*" That is the lesson the Congress must learn, they need to have their leadership lead by involving the Members in the decision making and not by threatening them with withholding appointments, earmarks or re-election campaign funds.

"And, my friends, my old buddy won the day, the houses stayed in the other city. He has never shared with me exactly what he did to change the mayor's mind and I suspect I do not want to know, but he got to the right answer. After that experience, the city and the schools seemed to learn how to work together, not sequentially. And, as he tells the story, the mayor, a decade later, will still go into a men's store at the local mall to avoid seeing or talking to him. Pretty funny. The moral to this story is that democracy only exists if the elected official is representing his local voters, not another politician."

Big Red leaned into her microphone: "The way to get a player to be a team player is to invite them into the huddle. That is a keeper. I like that. I think that Paul Roland is giving the kind of speech people really want to hear in this day and age. No theatrics, no generalizations, just what the man thinks."

Roland: "Most of what I just described has to begin in Congress. Congress has to restore its position and responsibilities as an equal third partner in government. It cannot be a rubber stamp for any president and certainly cannot continue to pass legislation that usurps its own important constitutional role. It is a shame Senator Byrd is not here to comment on these proposals. I cannot imagine that this man, with whom I shall ever and always be in disagreement philosophically, would not completely agree. He would also agree that we need judges who will enforce the law, rely on the Constitution and not generate their own new legal theories to support inappropriate decisions.

"Where does that leave the next president? Hopefully, it leaves the president as a leader in domestic and foreign issues. It makes he or she, a president, not a dictator. It eliminates these ridiculous powers we have granted the President and unelected regulators in the past few years. It makes us a democracy.

"Finally. Let me briefly talk about the oil spill in the Gulf of Mexico. This is where presidential leadership should and could have been useful. If the President had acted quickly, ignored the unions and represented the citizens of the gulf, he would have found someone like Jack Welsh to lead the government's efforts. The damage to the tidelands and the beaches would have been significantly less than occurred under this president's watch and it would have cost the government half of what it actually cost. A president must know how to lead. A president must know how to delegate, manage and lead.

"Tonight, we begin a movement to return to the things and ways that made and make the United States the most special nation in the world. We begin to return to a nation that represents the people of its nation, not the left-wing dreams of a small minority. Tonight, we begin the process of taking our nation back from those who deceived us four years ago.

"Tonight, we need to examine what makes America great. And what makes America great is our enduring respect for the rights of others, which is engendered in the Constitution of the United States. What makes America great is our love of our fellow citizens, which is demonstrated by equal opportunity and fulfilling our responsibilities to our less fortunate through that opportunity, equal to all, and through our charitable history.

"Four years ago, Americans wanted change. One candidate offered change and offered that change in a manner that whatever you had in your mind seemed like the change he was going to attempt to provide. And, wow, did we get change. We had a reduction in most everything Americans hold dear. We have been hurt more in four years than I had believed was possible in one hundred years.

"Tonight, we must begin the march to make the United States of America that independent minded, self-motivated, Wunderkind of mankind! Thank you and I accept your nomination to be your candidate for President of the United States of America."

The candidate looked at his audience and was finished with the shortest acceptance speech in recent memory. He believed he would have made both Senator Byrd and Lincoln proud.

~

Following the show, after a few quick casual sentences when they arrived at the pub nearest the Scottrade Center and ordered drinks, Bill O'Brien convinced his entire team to sit down at a single table, including himself, Ninoah, Cho, Milken and Geekhead.

"Thaddeus, what do you think?"

"Bill, I think Roland and Blankely are good men. I don't think they have a chance in the election, but good guys. I don't know whether Vincent and Scotch can win the election or if the President is going to skate into another term, but I do know that the American Exceptionalism Party has cut the legs out from Roland and Blakely. There will not be too many Independents who will fold in with the conservatives if there is a moderate party available. It is a shame because I think we have reached the time when we could have a great liberal/conservative face-off for the presidency."

Cho was next. "I think it will be a three-horse race. Looking at the polls, it looks to me like the race could be a popular vote three-horse-photo finish. How that will break out in the Electoral College, I look to Dr. Cicerone for that information."

Geekhead, wearing perhaps one of his now fifteen blue, button-down, collared shirts with the sleeves rolled up to show his massive forearms decided to hit the softball out of the park. "This election is very likely to end up in the House of Representatives. The general vote will not result in any candidate getting enough votes to be president. No more, no less." Geekhead had been one of the first individuals to know the election might go to the House of Representatives. As smart as he was, he was pretty far behind Molly Tom and The Professor in what would occur once the Electoral College voted.

Thaddeus Milken, golden hair flowing, laughed either with, or at, Geekhead. "Professor, I have been watching you for weeks here and I recognize how smart you are. I just disagree. I think the AEP will wallow in the process pretty quickly here and the voters will fall over themselves voting for Paul Roland. Without a real organization, I cannot see how the American Exceptionalism Party has a serious impact. If the Tea Party had split off, I would give you guys a different answer."

The conversation went on until closing time with all parties maintaining their positions. After they were done, O'Brien, Cho and Geekhead were picked up in a limo and taken directly to the airport and a waiting jet. NetJets made a certain amount of sense for celebrities and, when the convention ended at a late hour, gave them the opportunity to head to Newark immediately and not lose a day. O'Brien had arranged a second limo to take everyone home immediately upon landing.

During the flight home, Geekhead and Cho were as careful as possible not to appear to be a couple, which they effectively were not. While O'Brien was washing his hands, Geekhead had the opportunity to ask Cho if she was still interested in having dinner again soon. Her response was positive, but without any great enthusiasm. She had decided to appear to be a little harder to get. Something had to get this guy moving or she needed to spend the next six months trying to forget him, which she was unsure she was capable of accomplishing.

~

FRIDAY, AUGUST 31, 2012
FULL MOON

The Friday before Labor Day was a very, very busy day. This was the evening for everyone on cable to attempt to frame the election. In non-presidential cycle years, the evening would be filled with summer highlights and guest commentators no one had ever heard of (or would ever want to know). In presidential cycle years, if there was a late convention, this was a key date.

O'Brien had Jennifer Cho in his office at exactly 11:00 a.m. "Jenn, this is a crucial night for us. We need to lock our audience into a story that will carry us right through the election. Does Geekhead know what he is talking about? Will this election really end up in the House of Representatives? There seem to be some hints on this, but Perot ended up nothing but a loser who probably cost Boone One the election and Anderson was hardly strong enough to become as asterisk in the election history books. Nader, not even an asterisk, interesting guy, but hardly an asterisk. I need to make a bet here and if it is wrong, it is going to cost us viewers."

"Bill, I think the guy is brilliant. I think if he says the election will go to the House of Representatives, that is where it will go."

"Is that his forearms talking or your brain, Jenn? You guys aren't seeing each other, are you?"

From your mouth to God's ears. "Bill!"

"Just kidding, Jenn, but he might be a pretty good catch. God knows he appears to be a decent guy and all of the girls in the building seem ready to run through the lobby naked every time he walks through the building. With pretty technical commentary he has built a bit of a fan base. I need to know your thoughts here; my wife and I never discuss business. And since my second wife hasn't been born yet, you are my best backboard."

Oh, wouldn't you like to know what I really think. I feel like the ugly duckling who can't seem to ever get a second date, that is how I feel. "Bill, I would go with it. I would line up a couple of congressmen to assess the situation and see if they will let Geekhead ask the questions."

"Jenn, still my show, so I have to ask the questions. OK? I will let Geekhead have the floor for a few minutes with me asking him questions after we hear from a congressman. I always interview the electeds myself and I think most of my competitors are doing that as well. Good for me, good for the congressman. What do you think about the body language lady?"

"Her or the deal? You know I have never liked that whole deal, Bill."

"Oh, you just hate the fact that we have done so much to make her look attractive."

"You mean if there is a fire, she will melt? No, I think at this point, the conversation has nothing to do with what the candidates are saying. It all has to do with how the voters are reacting to them. If Geekhead is right, that is where this game is going to be played."

"OK, I agree. We'll go with the Republican former Speaker and then put you and Geekhead on a quick panel. I want you to press him on the electors. This is my decision, but I sure hope you are right. It might take half a year to get the viewers back if Geekhead is wrong."

~

At OBC, Big Red sat with Merritt Goodman. Tonight, they were going to do a ten-minute election feature on the nightly news and they were trying to determine which way to go. Big Red was news, not commentary, but Goodman's bosses were beginning to think that he might be able to rebuild their cable evening viewership if they put a great looking short skirt on opposite O'Brien. Nothing else seemed to work and it was not as if Fox News had not formulated most of their approach with blond law school graduates populating their shows. While Big Red wasn't blond, she was damn pretty and articulate. Anyway, this would be a great test to see if the idea made sense without needing to talk to her about it. This was a branding conversation and might involve the boyfriend lawyer if it went very far. Can't have her become the star and suddenly find her barefoot and pregnant.

"So, Marylou, I envision a full ten minutes of commentary with pictures tonight. I've got stuff from the writers, but we have six hours to tweak it and I think we want to proceed on the basis of where you think this thing is going. You have gone to all three conventions and listened to three dozen panels or so, what do you think?"

Amazing as it might be to viewers, this was the first time anyone had asked for Big Red's honest opinion since she had been at OBC. While they let her do the broadcast, her job was to ride the wave rather than create it.

"Merritt, unless our guys are just talking, it is a two-horse race, they just haven't told poor Paul Roland. While the polls show the three of them running virtually even, when push comes to shove, the voters are going to toss one of them under the bus in the next few weeks. The mainstream media—I guess that is us—will help that happen and I think the bus runs over Roland. His voters will be left with Vincent and then it will be up to the moderate left to determine whether the election goes to the President or Vincent."

"I am so glad I don't have to deal with Bob Colony any more, although that damn law suit may go on forever. Lawyers!"

"Hey, my boyfriend is a lawyer."

"Dumbest lawyer in New York City not to have put an engagement ring on your left hand." Goodman had never seen Big Red blush and it was a bit awkward for a moment. Then, it was just funny, as when a true red head blushes the colors are very different. She said not a word. "OK, none of my business. So, how would you play this? Is there an angle everyone else is missing?"

"Yes, I think that the President will win this election if it goes the direction we are looking at. I think he will win and win decisively because Vincent has no base from which to launch even a reasonable get-out-the-vote campaign."

"Brilliant, we will go with that. Let's go down and talk to the staff."

~

Friday evening had all of the appearance of a medieval joust to the professional directors and producers of the news media and political talk shows. Everyone had test marketed their plans on talk radio that afternoon and each was comfortable with their positions. It would be difficult to change these positions for the next few months unless the polls made some significant changes.

MSNBC went the easiest direction for them and their demographic. Their lead dog went after Roland as if he was a current member of the Ku Klux Klan and after Vincent as if he was a terrorist by going his own way rather than embracing his lifelong relationship with the Democratic Party.

At OBC, Big Red was sensational in finding an issue that no one else had considered. When she was doing a three-minute interview with Senator Robert Jefferson Wayne, the senator was caught absolutely flatfooted when Big Red asked: "Senator, where on earth is Senator Vincent going to find anyone to walk precincts and make telephone calls. By definition, his political base consists of those less interested in politics." Being right, polite and offering a new thought brought Big Red newfound respect in her media world. The right part set Wayne back on his heels and cell phones were buzzing around the country after her question, most of the cell phones were ringing in the hands of political consultants. What did Big Red's comments mean in terms of *my* candidate? Candidate for local offices around the country were trying to find firm ground for their candidates with respect to their positions on the national election.

Big Red's show was an hour before Bill O'Brien went on the air and in his business mimicry was the highest praise one could offer. After the former Republican Speaker of the House explained how the election could get to the House of Representatives and how important that made every congressional contest, O'Brien asked him about the get out the vote efforts by the three candidates. The former Speaker had been forewarned about the question. (That was one of the ways O'Brien managed to have his guests back over and over.) His answer was interesting at this point, before the spinners got in the way, everyone's answer to this question would be unique. The former Speaker indicated that the get out the vote campaigns for the other two candidates, no matter how sophisticated, would carry the Vincent voters to the polls for the most part.

O'Brien quizzed Geekhead about both the three-party race and if it was headed toward the House of Representatives and he handled the question magnificently. His best performance. After that, on the question of the get out the vote campaigns, Geekhead responded: "Bill, that is beyond my pay grade." On O'Brien's shows, often the highlight was when you could hear someone in the background laugh during the closing segment. Geekhead caught everyone by surprise; he had not displayed a hint of a sense of humor in the prior two months. Everyone laughed, O'Brien first and hardest, but you could hear a handful of individuals off stage laughing. It was a great moment. After laughing with himself for a moment, Geekhead readily agreed with the former Speaker.

~

As they walked off the set and down the hallway, Geekhead looked around and saw the hallway was empty. Walking on her left, he lightly put his right arm around Jenn's right shoulder, pulled her a bit toward him and intimately, and almost too quietly, asked her if she had time for a quiet dinner. Jenn had been hoping since last night's flight that Geekhead would say exactly these words at about exactly this moment. "Why don't we just do the leftover thing at my place? You can pick up a bottle of wine while I go home and get changed into something more comfortable."

With what now appeared to be soothsayer status, she had shopped extensively and carefully early that morning before she went to the studios. Tonight would include a fine meal with a second bottle of wine. Jenn had already called her personal trainer and informed her that she would not be at the gym Saturday morning.

Labor Day weekend, three days, perfect!

~

This time, very late Friday afternoon, The Professor and Molly Toms were picked up at John Wayne International Airport in Orange County, California, in the *Hawker* and were flown to Columbus, Ohio. The meeting was set around Molly's classes. They arrived late in the evening and were whisked off to the local DoubleTree Hotel. The Professor used the flight time to carefully read Molly's presentation and slides and then sat in his chair without saying a word for the remainder of the flight. His eyes never closed, he did not so much as hum a song; he just sat in his oversized private jet seat and thought about what they would tell the senator and his team.

Molly used most of her time on the airplane to study recent releases from the Financial Accounting Standards Board. This organization had nothing to do with the election, but everything to do with The Professor's advanced accounting class where, because she was spending so much time as a political consultant, for the first time in her college career she was not the top student in any class. The Professor did not give an inch on his grading because they were working on a political campaign together either. His grading integrity was much more important to him than the fact that she was working on the campaign with and for him.

When The Professor told the university's chancellor what was happening, the chancellor had insisted on some serious paperwork to protect the university. The Professor had her sign several documents before they got on the airplane confirming that this was a business trip and that the two of them had planned to have no social interplay. This was a new world and The Professor and the university were always careful with all of his students, even Molly Tom.

The Professor again said not a word in the Town Car that picked them up at the airport. Molly was hopeful that this was a walls-have-ears decision, but having been with him for over three hours and not hearing a word, her normal (and anyone's normal) insecurity began to take over. *What did I do wrong?*

As they checked in, The Professor asked Molly if she would come back down to the lobby after she got settled upstairs. They needed to chat a bit about her work. It took Molly about two minutes to place her bag in her room and she found herself pacing downstairs in the lobby for ten minutes waiting for The Professor. Of course, The Professor had not given a moment's thought to Molly Tom not realizing that all he had been doing was thinking.

In the hotel's small bar, the only public room available to them, The Professor explained to Molly that there would be a lot going on every weekend until election day. He wanted her to work for Milton Woo because, as he explained, this young man seemed to be using technology to accomplish great things for the campaign. She should be able to get a technological dump of knowledge that would be better than any three classes on campus. In her election related intellectual activities, he wanted her to focus on the House of Representatives. He would focus on George Vincent and the Senate. "The game will be played in the House of Representatives."

~

MONDAY, SEPTEMBER 3, 2012

North-South Polling Service:

The President	38%
Congressman Paul Roland	35%
George Vincent	27%

~

TUESDAY, SEPTEMBER 4, 2012

The Dallas Inquirer showed a chart on the front page. It was as devastating as it was simple. Under a headline that read *What We Don't Know*, were photos of each of the three candidates for president. Under two of the photos, it showed in line sequence:

High School GPA   Number

SAT Score   Number

College GPA   Number

List of College Classes Available   Yes or No

Graduate School Admissions Score   Number

Graduate School GPA   Number

Birth Certificate Available   Yes or No

The sequence was repeated for the three candidates for vice president.

Under the picture of the President, it said: "Declines to state."

The article would have been benign if both the sequence of information and the article had not focused on that one single response to each question: "Declines to state." The article was spiced up by anonymous quote after anonymous quote questioning and speculating about why the information was unavailable and what the information would reveal if it were available. One anonymous quote that was included on page one that would spark the most controversy was highlighted as a quote from a *source close to the President* stated: "I have been worried for four years that we would find out that the President was a minority or special admit to college and law school."

~

By 3:00 p.m., the President had his closest advisors in the Oval Office. He included Karen Kirby, his best speechwriter, in this cabal along with the Pillsbury Doughboy, Sackman and Matta. The President was livid and striking out at everyone. His sharpest fangs were reserved for RBC. "When we are done with RBC, I want them to be unable to gather a radio audience of fifteen if we find out there are aliens marching on Washington. I want their factories visited by every set of letters you can think of including EPA and the IRS. I want the God damn animal services people at their door, everyone."

In the Oval Office, the books on display included *A History of Bremen*, which was sitting on the President's desk opened to his cigarette stash. This was a high-risk maneuver as the President's entire family was in the White House this week. A system had been organized and if the President's wife was heading in the direction of the Oval Office, the President would have plenty of warning and the breath mint was sitting directly next to *A History of Bremen*. The only visitor to the Oval Office who had ever opened one of the President's cigarette books was the Swedish Ambassador who reached for the book when the President stepped out of the Oval Office for a moment during a meeting. He had replaced the book and uttered not a word of his discovery.

The President needed to close on the RBC piece immediately. The Pillsbury Doughboy had indicated that he could not gut this one out; he needed the President to come down to the pressroom spontaneously after Portman's remarks at the end of the day.

"What will I say? This information is not and cannot be released. Period, dot, end of sentence. It is not going to happen."

Sackman thought this was his job in terms of advising the President. "Mr. President, all they need to hear is that you want to focus on the issues and this is old news. Refer to the Aplin speech and indicate that there has to be a line between what is personal and what the public has a right to know. And then get the hell out of there."

And that was the strategy. The President took not a single question and while the press corps seemed to accept the President's explanation, this issue was not going to disappear in this campaign. The President would have to stay on message and demean the questioner when the personal issues arose.

~

RBC's questions and presentation were virtually the only news reported on RBC and most of the talk shows determined to pick up the issue. It was the best of talk show television because there was no research necessary, everyone had a position and no one's position was effectively right or wrong.

The best question and answer of the night was an exchange between Sean Hannity and Bertha Aplin. When asked what she thought, Aplin responded that reporters had visited every one of the five colleges she attended and interviewed virtually every professor of every class she had taken, they seemed to know that she favored a mechanical pencil. If they could do that, she wondered why the reporters had not had any interest in the President's college and law school experience. "What do we say? Picking on Bertha Aplin is in the national interest and asking difficult questions of the President is un-American. Something like that."

The shelf life of the controversy would be the entire week and the President did not give an inch. The other candidates, each with something they wished to keep hidden slowly rallied to a minor extent on the President's side. Their comments resulted from phrased questions about past girlfriends, etc.

~

This Tuesday night when people came up to their table at John Lee's Gourmet Restaurant to ask for autographs Jenn was as relaxed as could be. While she had not realized it, tonight, she was emotionally closer to showing Geekhead off than being angered and disappointed that people were approaching the table. Jenn was relaxed and happy, happier than she could remember. Geekhead on the other hand was hoping that everyone would leave them alone. He was also as relaxed and happy as he could remember; he just wanted to be alone with Jenn.

As Jenn was about to get up with Geekhead to leave the restaurant, they were sitting on opposite sides of the booth, she reminded him that this was a business dinner and they needed to have all appearances of a business meal. Then he smiled quickly and broadly when she asked him if he wanted to finish reviewing the charts and graphs at her apartment on the way home.

It's been almost twelve hours since we left my apartment. It seems like it has been a month since we have been alone. I am in love with this man, totally and completely in love.

~

WEDNESDAY, SEPTEMBER 12, 2012

Robert Smith was standing in a public warehouse in Elgin, Illinois, near Chicago claiming six individual boxes that had been shipped to Chicago from London. Each box contained twelve college-level, advanced French textbooks as well as six ounces of Semtex. The Semtex was disguised as bookbinders.

Today, he had a driver's license that had been issued in Marseille and a French passport. The warehouse agent spoke the same amount of French as Smith spoke Hebrew, but Smith did not speak to him in anything except French and some English with enough misplaced verbs and adjectives to leave no doubt as to his country of origin. While his disguise wouldn't make a secret agent proud, Smith would still be difficult to identify without the makeup and the hat, but this look matched his driver's license and passport perfectly.

The Semtex, an adequate explosive, which carried a non-generic marker, had been manufactured in the United States and purchased by Smith's colleagues from a now deceased US airman in Kabul. When the marker was ultimately discovered and traced, it would send exactly the message that Smith and his backers intended. The Semtex was well traveled before it arrived in Chicago on an airplane leased by FedEx. Smith assumed that initial blame would fall to Kabul, not his problem.

Smith had entered the United States from Brazil via Miami and had flown to Chicago. As always, he flew in and out of the United States under his own name and with round trip tickets. Even when the return date was open, the round trip tickets reduced the likelihood of close review upon entry or return. His personal passport was well stamped, but showed only trips to and from the United States and to and from London. All other travel was done exclusively under other names and with matching passports.

After completing all of the forms, Smith put a twenty-dollar bill in the hands of the warehouseman and asked if he could borrow a dolly. The warehouseman asked if he could help him to the car and Smith refused telling him that he was old, yet not dead. He did not want to have the license plate of his rental exposed even to a warehouseman who appeared to be paying attention only to making sure his paperwork was complete.

~

FRIDAY, SEPTEMBER 14, 2012

On Friday night, on virtually every television station and on the cable station that sold advertising, at 7:00 p.m., another advertisement appeared for the entire country to see. It was a new advertisement.

With no sound, the screen first showed a single sentence:

MR. PRESIDENT, HERE IS MY STUFF:

(Picture of Reesa Jonathon on a victory stand receiving a medal.)

HIGH SCHOOL GPA: 3.3

SAT SCORE: 1090

COLLEGE GPA: 2.7

**CLASSES AND SPECIFIC GRADES AVAILABLE UPON REQUEST.
SORRY, I HAD AN ACCIDENT AND DID NOT FINISH COLLEGE
OR ATTEND GRADUATE SCHOOL.
I AM REESA JONATHON AND I RECORDED AND PAID FOR
THIS AD.
I WISH I DID NOT THINK IT WAS NECESSARY. THIS IS A SAD
TIME IN OUR
COUNTRY WHEN THE PRESIDENT'S PERSONAL HISTORY IS A
SECRET.**

~

SATURDAY, SEPTEMBER 15, 2012

It was 9:00 p.m. and Molly Tom sat quietly in her hotel room reflecting on what she was doing with her fall. Sixteen units in school and she was leaving town every Thursday night to work, at a minimum, fifteen hour days in Cleveland on Friday and Saturday and eight hours on Sunday before catching a late airplane home Sunday night or early Monday morning. She found herself reading textbooks and writing papers in airport lounges and on airplanes. No social life. She had this boyfriend, but she was so busy and too tired for him. Beyond that, how could he compete with her life outside of school? Everyone at school seemed so boring. She was in the fast lane now.

The travel was very exciting until the first flight delay or the first three-hour airplane seat mate who had kissed his wife goodbye at curbside in front of the Chicago airport and immediately began looking for a new friend in Cleveland for the evening or weekend. This not only took away from the thrill of airplane travel but caused her to quickly leave the tight Levis and both the ultra loose and ultra tight T-shirts in the bag on travel days.

The political work at school and in Cleveland had been fascinating for Molly. The meetings where her technical expertise—specifically her now complete mastery of the Constitution—was needed, requested and acted upon were terrific. She believed she had helped George Vincent begin to understand that he needed to assess and work with current and future Members of Congress to ultimately become President of the United States. She was also monitoring the legal movement of funds into the various congressional campaigns.

Milton Woo had turned out to be the unexpected professor of the Internet. *Woo-Man the Magnificent, or SuperNerd, as he I've also heard him call himself, is performing magic for the campaign. He legitimately raised almost $175 million via the Internet and seems to be able to move polling data with a single stroke on his keyboard.What a great guy?*

When Molly thought about Milton, she thought about finding Milton a girlfriend. *What a great guy?* However, not knowing a sole in Cleveland, this was an idle thought. Three years older than Molly, at her age, this was the difference between old age and a schoolmate. Milton was…how did she think about him…cute and seemingly a bit naïve in his social skills. Maybe even a bit nerdy. But, Milton Woo seemed to be a very solid human being and more than always completely professional with everyone around him. If you handed him the materials passed around a meeting table on four million different occasions during a single meeting, he would thank you each and every time. That was Milton.

And what a great teacher Milton is and how open he is in sharing his knowledge. Given that there was usually a limited need for Molly Tom's constitutional knowledge and given The Professor's insistence that she be deeply involved in the campaign, she had been given to Milton as an assistant, a very highly paid intern. For Milton it was a great opportunity as he completely learned her skill set and he, as always, increased his knowledge levels by being able to teach. Milton was the type of teacher who learned more and more as he was teaching. It was the way his mind worked. His new intellectual sponge, as he thought about Molly, pushed back for more and more knowledge and this in turn increased his knowledge and abilities. In Milton and Molly's worlds, this was a win-win relationship.

The only downside to the trips to Cleveland was Joshua Ybarra. From the moment her airplane landed the first Thursday night, he had been obnoxiously hustling her. His costume at the airport that first night was classic. He had clothed himself in a clean T-shirt with the arms cut-off, which showed his meaty arms, shorts, a one-day growth of beard and flip-flops. It was as if he had been watching MTV to see what was cool.

He had picked her up late at the airport and was unsuccessfully insistent that they have a couple of cocktails or a little weed before he tucked her in. Not exactly what she had in mind with this hound. Then, that first Saturday night, he must have asked her four times if she wanted to go out with him and his friends and smoke a little dope. She remembered thinking: *smok-*

ing a little dope would be great fun, but not with this dope. She really could not figure out whether Joshua was interested in being with her because he was attracted to her or because she was there. He might have actually believed that for the price of the flowers he purchased in Orange County, he was entitled to physical payback.

By this weekend, Molly had stopped wearing any clothing in Cleveland that might have shown her nice figure and flattered her long, dark hair. She started wearing apparel more appropriate for a Quaker on the way to a meeting. Funny to her, in her mind, she was certainly not one who normally dressed in a manner that would result in being hustled at the super market. Now she was a Quaker. After three weeks, from Thursday through Monday, her entire time in Cleveland and travelling, for different reasons she found it incredibly easier not to look her best. She did not particularly like this, but given that outside of her hotel room, where she retreated every night to work to get some sleep and review the material for a few classes, there was no place where getting an additional glance as a woman was anything but a disadvantage.

The good news for Molly Tom was that there was enough intellectually challenging work that after fifteen hours at the office she was tired. Her natural interest and manner in being an intellectual sponge was completely satisfied after spending most of her time with Milton Woo, much more than it was in the classrooms of Orange County. If this was the price for this emersion course in politics, she had no trouble dressing like a Nun and reminding Joshua almost every evening she was in Cleveland that she had a boyfriend and needed to get a bit of studying done before she fell asleep.

~

SUNDAY, SEPTEMBER 16, 2012

George Vincent was casually dressed in tan pants and a red golf shirt. Six weeks ago, he probably could have gone into the McDonalds down the road in this outfit and if he had added a floppy hat, not a sole would have recognized their elected senator. "What I want to do is have this group meet Sunday at 1:00 p.m. every Sunday until the election. I have no idea where I am going to be, but in American politics, there are not too many Sunday afternoon political events. So, regardless of where I am, I will telephone in. Molly, this should give you a number of alternatives getting home timely Sunday night and if you want, there is no reason you cannot be on the telephone calls from the Cleveland airport if that is more convenient. Of course, everyone can call in. I am just not going to get a call from the chancellor of Chapman University regarding my keeping his student out of class. That would be really bad politics. Plus, Molly, I want you in class. I want to be able to write a recommendation as a part of your resume for graduate school.

"So Professor, what is your wisdom this afternoon?"

"For everyone else's benefit, Skeeter and I have had several conversations during the past few days. We are going to focus our discussion on these Sunday afternoons and I am going to focus my work, a great deal of which will be allocated to Molly and probably Milton, on the post-election game plan. Part of that post-election game plan will consist of developing relationships with the staffs of the campaign and office staffs of the moderate House of Representative candidates of both parties, ensuring that by the end of November, Skeeter has endorsed those he thinks, and they think, he can help their campaigns—Democrats and Republicans—and building Skeeter's political inside-the-beltway brand.

"This will need to be confidential and completely separate from the national campaign. Marshall, that means other than occasionally offering some solicited and unsolicited advice, I am going to stay out of your hair. That being said, I will need to know who you are talking to in order to be able to do my end of this project, and a project it is going to be.

"My hypothesis is that the race is going into the House of Representatives and the time to prepare for that eventuality is between now and the election, not between the election and the 113th Congress. I have prepared and distributed by e-mail a hyper-confidential memorandum about the process of the election after there is no apparent winner in the Electoral College. This must be kept confidential or all of this will be a waste of time. Share the memorandum, actually mostly prepared by Molly, with no one!

"Skeeter, let's get your appointment book up on some kind of platform that I can review. What I want you to be doing is to work quiet meetings with the local congressman into your everyday schedule. No one will be surprised at this, but your agenda will be to let that local congressman know that you understand his particular hot buttons. The tricky point will be also seeing his or her opponent and letting the competition know you know their hot points as well. Molly, your job will be to overlay the trips with individuals and hot points. Of course, where someone is far left or far right, a handshake will be more than sufficient."

"Professor, so you see my role as to meet and talk, not ask for any commitment?" this from George Vincent.

"Exactly," was the response and the meeting floated on for another hour.

~

MONDAY, SEPTEMBER 17, 2012

North-South Polling Service:

The President	32%
Congressman Paul Roland	32%
George Vincent	36%

~

On Monday evening, the following national advertisement began running on the three major television stations:

(Picture of the President in coat and tie.)

MR. PRESIDENT, THANK YOU FOR NOT GOING CRAZY WHEN NORTH KOREA RESPONDED TO SOUTH KOREAN PROVOCA-TION.

(Picture of the Korean island after the nuclear bomb.)

(Picture of Seattle on a clear day.)

WOULD ANY SANE PERSON HAVE LAUNCHED A NUCLEAR ATTACK ON NORTH KOREA AND RISKED A NUCLEAR RESPONSE TO SEATTLE?

Some sane person needed to speak up!

Paid for by Isadore Yergler, individual and supporter of the President.

~

TUESDAY, SEPTEMBER 25, 2012

The Washington Times ran the following article with one of those headlines that is usually reserved for October in American politics:

CIA WAS WARNING PRESIDENT OVER POTENTIAL NUCLEAR CONFLICT IN
KOREAN PENNINSULA

The Washington Times acquired today copies of computer disks that purport to show three separate meetings between the President, his key advisors and the CIA discussing the possibility of a nuclear war on the Korean Peninsula. These conversations were confirmed in off-the-record interviews with senior CIA officials.

Since the unprovoked attack on the South Korean island, the administration has denied that they had any advanced word or concerns about the possibility of North Korea launching a surprise nuclear attack on South Korea. The documents, which *The Washington Times* obtained, indicate that right up until hours before the attack, the CIA was warning the President that the possibility of an attack was imminent. The tapes discuss how the United States should respond to such an attack. The administration presented the argument that using American nuclear weapons in defense of anyone except the United States itself was not an acceptable response.

Upon requests for response from the White House, the President's spokesman, Peter Portman, indicated that the President is routinely told of imminent attacks around the world and that if he responded with force to each one there would be an American nuclear weapon exploding around the world daily. The spokesman indicated that there would be a special investigation into who leaked tapes of confidential conversations within the Oval Office. Portman made it crystal clear that there would ultimately be prosecutions. The spokesman also noted that there was no assurance that the tapes held by this newspaper were accurate or merely constructed to injure the President.

Presidential candidate Congressman Roland called for a congressional investigation. "I am a Member of the House of Representatives' Intelligence Committee and I was never informed of any CIA knowledge about a possible attack by North Korea on South Korea," said Roland, "In fact, just the opposite was the information we received from both the White House and the CIA. I would have to review my files, but I believe we heard from the CIA only a few days before the attack. I know the media will paint this as political theatre, but we need to understand precisely what happened here and that understanding should come from immediate hearings. We cannot have either, or both, the CIA and the President withholding information from the Congress. That is not the way it should work in a democracy."

Senator Vincent indicated that he hoped that the story was untrue and would make a further comment at a later date after he spoke to Members of the Senate Intelligence Committee. The senator did note that he was, "sick and tired of the White House continually and immediately threatening everyone and anyone who disagreed with the administration with lawsuits and prosecution."

Republican Congressman Offerin offered an un-postured response: "If this is true, we should be forwarding impeachment papers to the Speaker. I don't care how close we are to an election."

~

Outdoor advertising in some parts of the country had moved over the years from giant signs above the roadways to signs on trucks, billboard type signs on trailers, and the backs of busses. Through the end of October, the Valley Regional Transit System in Boise, Idaho, had signs on the backs of their busses with a picture of George Vincent that read:

TIME TO STRIKE OUT ON AN INDEPENDENT ROUTE.
– GEORGE VINCENT FOR PRESIDENT

Paid for by Beth Midlands, American

~

MONDAY, OCTOBER 1, 2012

North-South Polling Service:

The President	38%
Congressman Paul Roland	30%
George Vincent	32%

~

The President was near apoplectic as he stared at his briefing book and the data behind the poll numbers. "How can this be? We have raised and spent a fortune; I have been the best president in the past century. Despite being far ahead in the popular vote, these numbers tell me that I may win only a handful of states. The American Exceptionalism Party is no more than a group of ignorant and bigoted white people who do not want the minority populations of this country to have a chance. The Republicans are worse. They cannot have gained this kind of traction."

"Mr. President," Herman Sackman was rarely this respectful and equally rare was he dressed as professionally as he was this morning, with a grey suit, grey socks, a blue tie and black, wing-tipped shoes that tied rather than slipped on. The coat and tie statement by Sackman was never the sign of good news in this White House. Sometimes there was a foreign guest that warranted a coat and tie, so the suit was not a one hundred percent giveaway but on this date, there was no foreign guest. This Oval Office meeting was going to be difficult and career threatening to everyone in the room. Sackman had reached the point where career threatening was not an issue. He always delivered bad news well dressed.

Sackman had scheduled an off-the-record meeting in the afternoon with both a book publisher and CNN for next week. He decided he could finally obtain the wealth that he truly deserved for helping to create and advise this president. By the end of 2013, he would be a $1 million a year TV personality and a successful author.

Sackman had reached the final stage of his subservience. In his mind, he knew his client was insufficiently talented to accomplish the things for the United States that Sackman believed were necessary for a democracy—a liberal democracy, one by and for the people. He had tired of the President taking credit for the work of others, especially him. After four years in the Oval Office as an insider, but without the ability to put in place all of his ideas, the right ideas, like so many others before him, Sackman believed the only appropriate person to sit behind the desk in the Oval Office was Herman Sackman. And he knew this was not going to happen, ever.

He was now about to give advice to the President that would either catapult the President into another four years as the true second in charge, behind Sackman if he decided to stay, yet become the least loved president in history, or cause him to be just another one-term president. They both knew tomorrow would be a big deal for them.

The President was standing behind his desk, another heirloom from Lincoln that had been found in Illinois and transported to the White House only a year ago. The President believed it gave him an aura of power. In Sackman's mind, that aura of power was regularly destroyed by his insistence that blue jeans and tieless days connected him more closely to the people. Sackman always laughed to himself that the President's thoughts on what would make him loveable were those of an ignorance of history and arrogance in his personal lovability. There was a reason that over hundreds of years national leaders in all countries had worn costumes to show they were leaders, distinctive and more advanced than their citizens. All of these generals, kings, queens and politicians knew they needed to be different, not the same. He had once offered advice to the President using the powdered wigs of the seventeenth century as an example and quickly realized that history was a subject the President neither understood nor studied.

"You are going to need to play the race card, Mr. President," Sackman said slowly and precisely.

"Oh terrific, do you think I can get the cop in Cambridge to arrest another rich black man? Would that make you happy?"

~

Paul Roland was standing, microphone in hand, without a podium on a stage on Coronado Island in San Diego, California. In the background, one could easily see elements of the Naval Surface Force Pacific, one of thirty commands located on Coronado. He had a crowd of perhaps five hundred people and he had been speaking for about fifteen minutes.

"The United States of America must be extremely careful in how it uses its armed forces." The congressman/doctor was in a white shirt, no coat, and red tie. His straight posture and slim bone structure made him look a bit old, but he was perfectly conditioned. His looks comported with the facts. "Careful, but honest, honest in what we say and honest by ensuring that what we say is what we do. If we have treaties, we must use the tools at our disposal to honor those treaties." The background of the naval base and the two ships of the fleet said as much as Roland's words. "We now know that it was well known to the President that the North Koreans were planning to drop a nuclear bomb on South Korea before it happened. The United States neither did or said anything before or really after."

Roland moved to the front of the stage. If the stage had been a bit taller, the Secret Service might have been concerned that he was too close to the front edge. He looked down at the first row and slipped into a more Texas drawl and proclaimed: "In Texas, about the worst thing you can say about someone is *his word is just a word*. That is what happened next. The North Koreans launched a nuclear attack and the United States acted not like South Korea's treaty partner, it acted like the notes to those meetings. We did nothing. The word of the United States of America has become just a word."

The quote and message were repeated over the next twenty minutes and the message was well received by the audience.

~

"We need to immediately do something for the President. The proposal for Middle East peace was good, but not sufficient. There is no way he is going to win this election without more of our help. We were correct in our analysis and we were correct in deciding to set the stage quietly in meetings over the past two months. We are supporting a very naïve man in this effort. That man has never recovered from calling that white policeman stupid and he seems to have nothing positive happening in the United States."

Mullah Seecaaj continued, "We have followed our own advice precisely and we are ready to implement our, how do the infidels say, implement our strategy. We have spent tens of millions of dollars in the purchase of arms for our friends in Palestine in return for their inaction over the next three months. We have bribed the drug smugglers in Mexico and I think they will be still until after the election."

"Not always right, but always certain and this applies to this President of the United States." Mullah Annihiab entered the conversation. "The American president's veneer has worn off as Americans have discovered that, while he may or may not be very smart, there are few important areas where he actually knows what he is talking about. The problem is that he talks and talks and talks and by talking so much, his inability to get anything done has begun to overwhelm his incredible speaking skills. His attempt to mask his inability to accomplish what Americans want with insisting on nice language wore off quickly. But, this is why we want to keep him in office.

"Who can deny that his Chamberlain-esque belief that his Western culture based beliefs will be accepted by Middle Eastern leaders has not been a bonanza? Hamas is again rebuilt. Hezbollah continues to gain power. Nuclear programs are progressing well beyond the mere creation of a small nuclear weapon. The rich Israelis are fleeing because they are certain that they will slowly be destroyed by their neighbors or will be the loser in a nuclear war that destroys most every living organism in that part of Palestine. The President's incompetence with the Koreans has been yet another great opportunity for the Islamic movement. Americans are afraid that their nuclear umbrella is inviting a direct nuclear event in one of their major cities. Americans yearn to be left alone and the President believes he is protecting the cowardly fools by watching and not acting." Annihiab stopped, realizing that this was a meeting where Mullah Seecaaj should and would control the discussion.

"Yes, but while the President may be acting in a manner that is good for us and our friends, and while he is acting in a manner that reflects the isolationist tendencies of the United States, he is now thought of as ineffective in all domestic and foreign issues by the voters, except for the far left and the blacks. And while the Americans may have become a third world educational and moral cesspool, they will not tolerate an ineffective cesspool leader." Seecaaj seemed to be reading the daily reports of the far right in the United States.

Mullah Banaham, who had been educated in the United States, offered a bit of political history: "The polling is not odd from an historical viewpoint, but we need understand that the President's thirty-eight percent approval rating is not representative of the greater country. The black vote remains ninety percent for the President, so without the black vote, the President has only has a thirty-three percent or so approval rating. That is one in three. As black Americans tend to live together and their voting is more local than national, if the election were held today, either the Republican or the George Vincent person would come in first and maybe second as well."

"Yes, I understand." Mullah Seecaaj had begun fingering his beard, which was always a good sign for completing his thought processes. "Your plan is simple, but will not be seen as anything but weakness on the Arab street. But, on the day after the President of the United States is elected to his second term, we will have Hamas create an event and they can easily walk away from the plan. They have done this many times before.

"Syria and Hamas will announce that they want to have meetings before Ramadan to work out the details of a long-term peace plan with Israel. Syria and Hamas will announce that they need to focus on the clothing, housing and educational needs of the Syrians and Palestinians and if America will help in those areas, they would be more than willing to sit down with the Israelis and United Nations negotiators to complete a plan for both Palestinian and Israeli independence. They will cede Jerusalem to the Jews with a guarantee from the United Nations of an open city religiously. With our help, the President will take credit and the American press will give credit for this event to the President. This should move at least Florida to vote for the President and certainty add New York and California.

"And other than the bribes to the international media and the arms cost which we would have expended anyway, this plan is not very expensive. Of course, the moment the President is sworn in for his second term, they can launch a sufficient number of missiles from Palestine to get the Israelis to react and immediately cancel the meetings. Syria and Palestinian leadership need only appear weak for several weeks."

"Ah, that is very good, very good. It might work and either way, we need to inspire the Israelis to fight back against the Palestinians and a ninety-day break in Palestinian hostilities will have them fresh and ready to go. They need to be constantly reminded of the name and location of their enemies. They need to spend their resources on items that will provide them no economic benefit. They need always be afraid of our allies to their West.

"Mullah Annihiab, you are in charge of the final steps of this. Make it happen next week."

~

SUNDAY, OCTOBER 7, 2012

Father Woods appeared with the Pastor on a nationally broadcast Sunday afternoon show paid for by the Pastor's church after the receipt of an anonymous donation from a contributor who neither requested nor received a receipt. The check did not originate in the United States. The Pastor assumed that there was nothing wrong with the church receiving a check drawn on a bank in London. Actually, there was everything wrong with it, but the Pastor was not a lawyer and did not perceive that the check was an illegal and untraceable political contribution. The check had been laundered through many countries in the Caribbean and Europe before it got to London. The original source was a US businessman who did business with the White House before, but not after, the Democrats took office.

Several million people listened to the Pastor and Father Woods talk about the plight of lost and potential tax deductions and the church if the President had his way. Most of the commentary was far too technical for the audience although they caught the drift that the President was no friend of the church.

Once they finished with the donation part of the conversation, Father Woods moved onto the topic he wanted to get to in front of a national audience, albeit only a few million eyes. Father Woods' questioned the Pastor about not following up on his 2008 question to the President about when life began. The Pastor indicated that he wished he had asked a follow-up question and then remarked, "If you show me a man who said knowing when life began was above his pay grade, I will show you a man that believes in unrestricted abortion." This was a devastating accusation.

This Sunday show brought a firestorm of protest from the White House, directed only at the pastor, but both the pastor and Father Woods were ready for this firestorm. From the Pastor's standpoint, revenge was, in fact, a dish served ice cold.

~

MONDAY, OCTOBER 8, 2012

North-South Polling Service:

The President	38%
Congressman Paul Roland	29%
George Vincent	33%

~

Sam Dehning was tired and not in the mood to be in Isadore Yergler's icebox of an office. Dehning's plan for the campaign was not working and he was spending money for Yergler and on his personal situation like it was water. Dehning was beginning to realize that his mistress, Little Sheba, was more expensive than he could have imagined. At twenty-two years old, she seemed to be more and more demanding in terms of gifts and he could not get his arms around whether he was being played or if she really loved him. Regardless, she was becoming more and more of an addiction and her addictions to gifts—and now just a bit of heavy drugs—was proving a balancing act physically and mentally. To go along with everything else, Little Sheba had insisted on joining Dehning for a weekend in New York and during one telephone call home, Mrs. Dehning sounded different. Who knew what she knew?

"Isadore, we are going to need a great deal more money. I don't know for sure who is putting up the radio and television ads except for what you have also read, but they are spending a fortune. And Roland seems to be pulling the President's chain pretty hard."

Yergler was attired as if he planned to be on the golf course in a few hours, which was not something he ever did. Short sleeve, gold collared shirt with a monogram on the left sleeve that Dehning could not discern, but it clearly had the sun on it, and a sweater vest. As Yergler was seated at his desk, from Dehning's perspective, looking up just a bit under his desk, Yergler could have been wearing tuxedo pants or shorts for all he knew. He doubted it would be shorts because it must have been in the low forties in Yergler's office.

"This is bullshit Dehning. You have spent $10 million and there are no results? That doesn't make any sense. I have seen the ads; they were fine. What is going on? Has the President lost his mojo? I see thirty-eight percent of the votes going to him, what will it take to win?"

"I have got to think it is the American Exceptionalism Party and the opportunity for a racist country to move away from a minority and to a white boy from Ohio without having to vote Republican. We have a few angles we can play with the next $15 million, which I think will do the job. I sent you the creative files and I think we will be able to make Vincent look like a villain, to put it mildly."

"Dehning, it had better work. If I throw $25 million dollars into something I expect a return or I expect your ass." Yergler was attempting to sound menacing. Dehning heard the threat, but discounted it. Any time Dehning wanted, he could put Yergler into a jail cell for twenty plus years. He had kept plenty of evidence from the 2008 campaign. For again just a moment, Dehning considered the threat and discounted it completely.

"We have always got it done for you, Isadore." Dehning's mind was going a mile a minute. *This is not going to get it done for you. There is no way the President is going to win this election and $15 million is not going to impact the race a bit. Especially this $15 million because I am going to run a single advertisement and keep the rest of the money. Fuck him. With $13 million tax free I will be set and even Little Sheba can't bleed that kind of money out of me, but I do need to move on to something less expensive than her. But certainly not yet. From my end, her new and increasing drug addiction has increased the fun as the last of whatever her inhibitions once were have now completely disappeared. She will be flying into town tonight for a great mid-week holiday.*

Yergler and Dehning sparred for well over an hour, but Yergler wanted the President re-elected. Dehning left with a huge check drawn on a bank in the Cayman Islands.

~

TUESDAY, OCTOBER 9, 2012

Robert Smith was in Las Vegas and had been unable to determine a suitable new disguise, so he was wearing a cowboy hat and sunglasses along with very loose-fitting Levis and boots. He completed his attire with a cowboy shirt that would have embarrassed any real cowboy. It had a garish picture of Sitting Bull stitched into the front and an equally garish picture of a buffalo on the back. He had not shaved for several days.

Planet Hollywood has a Starbucks. It is not terribly big, but it does allow one to sit in a position where he can see quite a bit of the hotel gambling area without attracting any attention. For Smith, this was a reasonable tradeoff. He knew that he was going to be videotaped and photographed in the hotel, but made the calculation that these pictures would never get anyone's attention as his business plans were a month away and today's work might not be discovered for months, if not years.

Smith's two new Saudi friends arrived at Starbucks and, as previously instructed, waited in line and purchased two specialty coffee drinks and cookies. They were instructed to look for an idiot in a cowboy hat and walked over to Smith's table with their purchases.

Quietly, Smith said: "I don't want to know your names." He also smiled and shook hands with each of them as he stood up and motioned them towards the casino area. As they reached the casino area, Smith kept walking towards the parking lot and the Saudis followed while finishing their cookies and trying to drink a bit of their coffee. Smith's pace was brisk.

In the self-parking lot, Smith walked to his rented Toyota Celica and got in the driver's side, unlocked the other doors and the Saudis joined him.

After they were in the car, Smith informed them that he had rented them separate hotel rooms in separate hotels and that he had also rented a storage unit a few miles away where he had all of the necessary tools for them to complete their duties.

Smith turned on the radio and they drove in silence to the storage unit. The two Saudis, young men in their early twenties, did not know what to expect. Both were highly educated and spoke excellent English, but were prepared to attempt an assassination and probably give their lives up in the process. Such were their religious beliefs.

When they reached the storage unit, Smith drove the Toyota up to a key entry system, entered the code and drove to a unit in the back that approximated four hundred square feet. The garage door in front of the unit had a new Schlage combination lock and Smith exited the car, entered the lock's combination and pulled up the garage door. He motioned for the two to join him and after he turned on the overhead light, he closed the garage door.

Both of the Saudis removed their light jackets and looked around the space. There were two oversized metal barrels, several rows of chemical containers and a small desk. There were plastic tarps that covered most of the floor. Smith, still playing the role of a silent Sam, motioned to the two boys to follow him, walked to the desk, pulled out a black Walther CP99 Co2 with a silencer adapter in place and fired six bullets into the boys' bodies. He then walked to each of the boys' bodies and fired a single shot behind each ear. The event was sufficiently quick enough that there was not a sound from either of the decedents.

Smith moved the two barrels near the bodies, placed one body in each container along with the plastic tarps and his clothing and poured in the chemicals that were lined up on the garage floor. From his reading on the Internet, Smith determined that the barrels would emit no significant odors and that the bodies would be completely dissolved, save for the bones, within about six or seven months. The rent had been paid in advance for the next twenty-four months with cash.

Smith changed into an identical disguise to exit the storage lot, opened the garage door, affixed the Schlage lock and drove to his small hotel room on the outskirts of town. There, he changed back into his golf shirt and slacks, checked out of the hotel, threw the disguise in a non-descript plastic bag in the hotel's trash container in the rear of the facility and drove to the airport.

No one would care or ever ask about the two Saudi suicide bombers. They had some idea about what was planned and that was sufficient for their execution. They died for the cause.

Smith had asked for the two men before he had finalized his plans. By now, they were no more important to him or his patrons than the weather report for Prague this upcoming weekend.

~

WEDNESDAY, OCTOBER 10, 2012

On Wednesday morning, on virtually every television station and on the cable station that sold advertising, beginning at 7:00 a.m., another advertisement appeared for the entire country to see. It was a new advertisement, simple, inexpensive to produce and easy to understand.

With no sound, the advertisement first showed a simple sentence:

MR. PRESIDENT, WHY DOES A GOVERNMENT EMPLOYEE GET A PENSION EQUAL TO 90% OF THEIR FINAL SALARY?

(Picture of an older man sitting on the beach, fifty pounds overweight and enjoying a cocktail.)

MR. PRESIDENT, WITH THE PENSIONS BEING PAID BY THE GOVERNMENT TO GOVERNMENT WORKERS, THAT MEANS THEY NEVER HAVE TO SAVE?

(Picture of a younger man sitting on the beach, fifty pounds overweight and enjoying a cocktail.)

THAT IS NOT THE WAY IT IS FOR EVERYONE ELSE. WE ARE SAVING FOR OUR RETIREMENT.

(Picture of a woman sitting in front of her house in shorts.)

MR. PRESIDENT, YOU ARE ASKING THE WORKERS IN THE PRIVATE SECTOR TO PAY FOR GOVERNMENT WORKERS TO RETIRE AT A MUCH HIGHER STANDARD OF LIVING THAN WORKERS IN THE PRIVATE SECTOR. THAT IS NOT FAIR!

(Picture of Reesa Jonathon as a competitive swimmer and a second picture of her in her wheelchair seated in front of what was obviously a building on a college campus.)

I AM REESA JONATHON AND I RECORDED AND PAID FOR
THIS AD. I WISH I DID NOT
THINK IT WAS NECESSARY. THIS IS A SAD TIME IN OUR
COUNTRY WHEN THE PRESIDENT'S
PERSONAL HISTORY IS A SECRET.

~

The negotiations for the debate between the candidates to be the Vice President of the United States had been long and arduous. The Democrats wanted a format which would be effectively each of the candidates making a speech and responding to a few previously posed questions from a single interviewer and they wanted an interviewer with little grey matter between the ears. As benign as the event could be was the goal from the Democrats, that was the Democrats view. Bobby Joe Blankley could not have cared less. He knew he was bright enough and experienced enough to hold his own with Scotch, after all, he did have an advanced degree in economics from the London School of Economics and while he liked the current vice president, he knew he did not bring anything to the table. In reality, Dr. Scotch's people had very little to say except they wanted some physical space between the candidates.

When the negotiations were finalized, the candidate's representatives settled on Marylou McBride. The Democrats decided that she was only a pretty dress and the Republicans determined that not having someone from one of the three standard mainstream television networks was a huge win regardless of McBride's capabilities. The format included a five-minute opening speech by each candidate with the Vice President going first, Blankley next and Dr. Scotch last. After the introductory speeches, Big Red would ask questions and they could respond to each other.

The initial comments of the Vice President and Senator Blankley could have put a hungry fourteen-month-old child who had awakened from twelve hours of sleep back to sleep. The Vice President read a prepared speech off of a teleprompter and Blankley parroted Republican talking points. The Vice President had been given his speech and a set of instructions designed to put him in a straightjacket for the debate. Blankley only had a standard speech although without notes, he seemed more comfortable and confident that the Vice President.

Five minutes was a long time for a soliloquy and Dr. Scotch was ready. The Vincent team had decided to allow Dr. Jordon Scotch to demonstrate his intellectual underpinnings and they knew that working from glancing at an occasional three-by-five card, he would appear to be the Renaissance man.

After the quick thank you, Scotch began: "We tend to forget and take for granted the history that the so-called Founders of American democracy were educated in the classics and relied on a small cadre of books and lectures for their intellectual foundations. They took their cultural clues from the Greeks and studied Herodotus for a basis of the Greek social contract and relied upon Thucydides to understand the organization of the Roman government for a system to operate the United States. From these cultures, we as Americans got our feet wet and from these cultures come the key words to our precious Declaration of Independence and the Constitution. It was the Athenians that adopted the principles of direct democracy and, perhaps, the Athenians who first wrote about a social compact among all peoples of their nation. The Founders also read and studied Plato, Aristotle and Demosthenes. The concept of representative democracy was taken from the Romans remembering that the books read by the intellectual elite of the late 1700s included the works of Cicero and his like. From these historical studies, we were gifted the Constitution and this wonderful form of government.

"Our Founders should be treasured and events like reading the Constitution of the United States at the beginning of the 112th Congress are pure brilliance. Reading it as amended was a tribute to the Founders in that the original Constitution was organized so that the Constitution could be changed to grow with the times and correct wrongs of history. The goal, of course, was that if the Constitution was changed it would be changed by the voters, not the judges. OK, so I sound like an academic, which is what I am, but the history of this great nation can be great fun. We all attribute the postal motto of *neither snow, nor rain, nor sleet* to the Post Office, but the quote actually started in ancient times, probably not far after the Egyptians started a postal service probably 4000 years ago. Cyrus the Great of Iran operated a fairly sophisticated postal service 2500 years ago. The past is the basis for our future and we should both revel and understand from where our history emanates. This is how we should be able to avoid mistakes of the future."

In the UCLA Royce Hall auditorium where the debate was taking place, heads were turning. While this was home turf for Dr. Scotch, the audience had very few UCLA students or professors. It was the choice of subject matter that quickly gained everyone's attention.

"We need to see the past; we need not make the same mistakes of past civilizations. Even Rome fell to its successes. And we need to study carefully. One of the tidbits of history that I like to talk about with my students are the sequential mistakes of history. Most Americans over fifty know that Hitler's assault on Russia in June 1941 called Operation Barbarossa, repeated the military mistakes of Napoleon in 1812. What most of us did not learn in school was that Napoleon's 1812 venture was a repeat of King Charles of Sweden's invasion of the Russian heartland and ended in disaster at the Battle of Poltava in 1709. No one learned from history.

"While I am an economist by trade, any good economist knows that history is a great guide to future economic events. And today, we can learn that this president's economic policies are the same as policies that have led to the end of many great civilizations throughout history. We need change in our policies, or else our policies will be delivered to us by the Chinese and the Europeans, whoever holds our Treasury notes. And, Mr. Vice President, this has been on your watch." Jordon Scotch looked quietly across the stage. Scotch went on and built a long and dark history of what, in his view, was the Democrats seeming ability to ignore history while destroying the underlying economic strength of the United States.

"And there are other issues. These are issues of the heart and the brain, issues where the answers should be axiomatic, instinctive, not politically motivated. We heard a couple of years ago about Senator Kerry parking his new $10 million dollar yacht—I think it was $10 million—parking his yacht in Rhode Island instead of Massachusetts to save sales taxes. This was instinctively bad, but what the media should have been asking was why he had the yacht built in New Zealand. Here is a Democrat sitting in the United States Senate and he cannot figure out that it would help the United States to have his yacht built in the United States. It is the former Speaker of the House of Representatives talking green and flying a giant military airplane back and forth from Washington D.C. to San Francisco every couple of days. While it seems a strange line from a man in a wheelchair, the Democrats and the Republicans need to walk the talk."

Jordon Scotch took his entire five minutes to the very last second and after those five minutes, there was no question which candidate was the smartest. In demonstrating his brainpower, he did nothing to indicate he was anything except a regular guy. It was a perfect performance. While the Vice President was no intellectual giant, Senator Blankley was somewhere in that upper five percent of intellects and he was open mouthed at how smart this UCLA economist actually was.

Big Red asked the first question and under the rules decided upon, it had to be an issue raised in one of the opening three presentations. She asked a follow-up question on the history of the United States.

Marylou: "We just had an impressive historical presentation from Dr. Scotch. I think the only thing he left out of ancient history was the fall of the Pope in Rome in the early years after Christ. But what is important here is to understand the important changes and improvements that have been made in the Constitution since the Constitutional Convention. Take health care for everyone, what is the role of the Constitution today with respect to health care?"

Senator Blankley, without attribution, demonstrated that he had read McCullough's books on Truman and Adams. At least he was sufficiently verbose that it sounded to the audience as if he had read these books yesterday and he managed to do a great job. (This was not terribly far from accurate, as he had read both books on his 2011 Christmas holiday. He loved to read and his recall was excellent.)

Jordon Scotch's initial remarks in response to the question were priceless. He began by explaining to the Vice President that the Roman Empire had really not finally come to a conclusion until Constantine XI was defeated by Sultan Mehmed II, the leader of the Ottoman Empire. Scotch, for reasons not completely clear, rolled out a history of the Ottoman Empire, which concluded with an analysis of the problems created by the British after World War I where they created nations without understanding underlying cultures. Big Red should have stopped him a full three minutes before he completed the answer except she was mesmerized by Dr. Scotch's answer.

The Vice President talked only about the importance of health care.

The questions and answers rolled along without event until Big Red approached the end of her big moment. Her final question was to Senator Blankley with the Vice President second and Dr. Scotch last. "Please give us your view and comment on your own personal activities with respect to philanthropy."

Senator Blakely was widely known to have been an Eagle Scout and equally well know to have continued his involvement well into his adult life. Every year, he participated in summer Boy Scout camps and offered that he gave handsomely to the program.

The Vice President was wishing that the agreed program was over and that he would not have the opportunity to make final remarks. His track record had been well documented but little discussed. Charity was just not something that he participated in or made donations to. Before he was the Vice President when no one was looking at his annual tax returns, the Vice

President and his wife listed virtually the same amount of donations in their joint tax returns every year. The total was always significantly under $500 and the assumption was this estimate was always high. He spoke at length about his public service and his son's military commitment.

The Vice President's response was no match for Jordon Scotch's near encyclopedic memory. The economics professor began by reciting the Vice President's and his charitable contributions over the past ten years. The differences were very significant, but they were less remarkable than the lack of charitable activity by the Vice President. Scotch finished by indicating that his tax returns were on his website as promised and that words were words, actions were real.

A bad night for the Vice President, a good night for Senator Blankley and a great night for Jordon Scotch. A bad night for the President.

~

Those who thought they knew the Middle East knew that no one understood the Middle East. One could only observe and understand events that were transitory, all agreements were transitory and nothing was permanent. The leaders of Western civilization and their mostly liberal controlled media would and could never understand the Middle East because they believed that long-term agreements and long-term contracts were long-term agreements and long-term contracts. They also believed in the theory that all people yearned for democracy. Silly. The press, in particular, always seemed to believe their role was to embrace false hope. "The West was," as Mullah Seecaaj told his colleagues, "a civilization always looking for a new Hitler to negotiate with their ever-present Chancellor Chamberlains."

The simultaneous high-level government meetings in Tehran, Damascus and Riyadh were not witnessed or followed by the Western media. This was Mullah Seecaaj's goal. He wanted the nations participating to facilitate these ministers shuttling back and forth without notice. Their goal was a surprise announcement on October 10 that an agreement was reached to recognize the Israeli government if the Israeli government would conform to a set of reasonable requirements. Such agreement would be effective immediately and would occur without a formal treaty between any nations. There would be no other conditions requested and a host of trading mechanisms would be proposed along with a guarantee of financial aid from the oil rich nations of the Middle East to begin construction of schools and public infrastructure in the Palestinian territories. There would be a goal of statehood in twenty-four months. Jerusalem would be as before.

This agreement among the Middle Eastern nations and the Palestinians was only reached after an agreement was made to provide Hamas and Hezbollah with the rockets and other weaponry necessary to destroy the agreement and wage two parallel incursions/wars against Israel from Lebanon and the West Bank. Hamas promised to take action immediately following the US elections. The agreeing nations would withdraw their recognition of Israel at the moment of Israel's response to Hamas.

The announcement was made in Tehran and its impact on world news was immediate. To provide credibility to the announcement, it was made by both President Ahmadinejad and the Holy One, Mullah Seecaaj. It was also announced that the French would be making a similar announcement within twenty-four hours. There would be a ceremony in France within a few days. Thanks were offered to the United States and the President for their involvement and support of the preceding talks.

All world television, radio and Internet reporters made simultaneous breaking news announcements of the Middle East decision. Every foreign nation welcomed the proposal including the Israelis and every impacted Middle Eastern diplomat confirmed the agreement. On the record, all Middle Eastern delegates credited the President's determination to work with all countries of the world.

The White House exploded into action as this opportunity was a hand-made gift towards the President's election campaign. The beauty of the present was that no administration official was involved in the event and therefore no one could look back and attack a soul involved in the negotiations. The short-term advantage presented and being eagerly accepted by the White House was the underlying result the negotiation had produced. No one thought about this as a setup.

As the President sat with his speechwriters, the narcissism perceived by friends and foes alike took hold: "I have done it. My work in the Middle East is complete and peace has been established. I knew that if we continued to offer the opportunity of peace, years of conflict would be undone," offered a jubilant President, "I want the speech to focus on my four-year attempt to avoid war and its obvious result."

Herman Sackman had his most cynical face on and questioned, "What are the risks here? What if the Israelis ultimately disagree? What if we are being setup? Why would they give us credit?"

"Good God, Sackman, have you lost your mind? We will tell the Israelis that they can agree or be on their own. They have already indicated that this looks like a great opportunity. Those Arab dictators sure as hell don't want either Vincent or Roland to win this election. Either of those nutcases might bomb them back to the Stone Age if they reneged on their offer. If the Israelis say no, they won't have a friend on the planet, even here in the United States, and that about covers the table. The Chinese sure as heck don't give a shit!"

Sackman was not sure what he just heard was completely coherent, but gave in quickly. "I guess you are correct. It just seems a little bit too good to be true. The ability for you to go out and claim credit and claim that we have not so much as offered them the head of Bertha Aplin as part of the bargain is about as good as it gets." The laughter, as always, was limited, as even after almost four years with the same team this president never seemed to find his sense of humor. Sackman, neither for the first or last time, thought to himself: *This guy really does believe his own shit. Scary.*

"OK, I want this to be mine. Call Portman and let him know the White House will hold a press conference in an hour and address all issues. Herman, don't let the Pillsbury Doughboy near the microphone except to announce the press conference. Peter, get that imbecile from Fox News on the telephone and tell him he can have a ten-minute exclusive interview tomorrow, sometime in the morning, focusing only on this Middle East surprise. Let him know, the right way, that if he asks some snotty question or his boys make this sound like a bad idea, he can forget the exclusive and then he can be in New York for all I care when I give my speech in France. Karen, this is about my ideals and a key moment in world history, got it?"

Karen, a speech writer for the President, simply shook her head up and down and inquired: "How long will you speak?"

The President responded: "Let's go with a full fifteen minutes this afternoon and half an hour when we go to France in two weeks and find something I said during the campaign about pressing hard for peace with all peoples regardless of their historical thinking, a new beginning."

~

The press conference speech was elegant and the presentation crisp. The action by the Middle Eastern nations was the result of the President's philosophy and an example of the world beginning to understand that the planet was too small for any nation to act exclusively in its own self-interests. The President virtually glowed as he accepted a few softball questions from the White House press corp. As their hero took questions and credit for something that caught him absolutely by surprise, he was having a marvelous experience. The question by the RBC reporter took him a bit by surprise, not the question, but why RBC instead of Fox News: "Doesn't the timing of this announcement make you the slightest bit suspicious that the Arabs are casting a vote for you for president? Couldn't they walk away from their announcement the day after the election?"

The President stared at the RBC reporter for what seemed like a full minute. An observer might have thought the President was going to do an imitation of Marlon Brando in *Viva Zapata!* and was going to ask the reporter for his name. "You are old school cynical, you simply are a part of the old guard that cannot accept that this is a new world and that we have established a relationship with the rest of the world that is different than before. This is a world that wants peace and I am a president that wants to help that peace occur." The President smiled, looked around and turned back toward his office.

In the Middle East White House equivalents, there was laughter and hot tea; a perfect afternoon of entertainment. Perhaps a bit of a problem with the masses for a few days, but that would be easily handled. The money side for the press had not been shared with any of the players. They had found their Neville Chamberlain.

~

THURSDAY, OCTOBER 11, 2012

The former governor was about to conclude his time on the national stage. He had gone from citizen politician to politician to presidential candidate to television journalist to presidential candidate to television journalist. The television journalist gig had recently come to a conclusion because he was not gathering a sufficient number of eyeballs for his Saturday and Sunday time slots. While there could not have been a show on all of television less expensive to produce, people had stopped watching and without viewers, there are no advertisers and without advertisers, there are no profits for the network. So here he sat on a panel for OBC, a national network with millions of viewers giving a very straightforward and uninhibited interview that would shortly cause him to be labeled as a racist. His comments were made in such a way that he would be condemned by both political parties.

"Someone needs to address the race issue. Someone honest needs to address the race issue. I looked at our convention delegates on the Republican side and I did not see a reasonable number of minorities and it makes me very, very sad. I read some of the newspapers around the country and I heard the word racist. The party is not racist, but it is fair game because we represent a philosophy that apparently does not much appeal to the black community in the United States.

"Conversely, I looked at the Democratic convention and I believe that if you pulled the Secret Service off that floor, the percentage of Caucasians would have been less than fifteen percent. While it is not popular to say this, that convention was as racist as the Republican convention. No political party can believe it represents Americans if it only has a token of its membership being Caucasian when Caucasians represent about half of the population.

"So, what is a racist, today? Not yesterday, not after World War II, not after Brown v. Board of Education, but today. Apparently, the bar has been changed. If I heard the President correctly, it has been raised to a level that simple disagreement with the President of the United States' policies is racism. In a word, it is scary. And it is not raising the bar; it is using the bar as a sledgehammer. It is disgraceful and this president is more responsible for this than anyone in the country.

"For eight years, I was regularly mortified when President Boone bungled words and concepts. I was mortified by his fiscal policies and angered by his failure to ensure that our armed forces were prepared for victory in Iraq. Did this make me a racist?

"Six or seven months into this president's term of office, I was mortified virtually every time the President stepped away from his teleprompter. I find him unknowledgeable about policies that he is vigorously supporting and I listen to a view of America with which I totally disagree. His statements supporting and regarding health care were contrary to the bill's language. I am mortified by his fiscal policies and angered by his failure to understand the long history of failed armies in Afghanistan. Does this make me a racist?

"I would argue the answer to both questions is either yes or no; an ensemble of *nos* and *yeses* would be silly.

"These politicians need to raise the level of debate. They are as bad or worse than television commentators fighting for ratings. And they need to do it today, not tomorrow, not next week, today. This is not about using the words *cross hairs*. This is about policies.

"The health care debate would be handled better by a sixth grade honors class than by the House of Representatives, the Senate and the President. This *debate* was so bad one might consider removing the capital letters in the previous sentence."

Glenn Duneaberg watched and listened carefully during the governor's comments and was honestly horrified. "What I hear you saying is that the President is dumb and I can only conclude that as racist. I find those words hard to say, but that is in essence what I am hearing."

"And, Congressman, that is exactly my point. I don't think this president is gifted mentally and certainly think his policies get you to the same answer and your answer is that I am a racist. That is the tragedy of the left; indefensible positions by this president are indefensible. The critics are not racist and certainly I am not a racist."

Big Red was uncomfortable with the direction of the conversation. It was way too personal for her show; it might be great entertainment for some, but she wanted something else. "Thaddeus, what do you think?"

"My answer might surprise you," responded Thaddeus Milken, as usual with gold hair a bit too long and mustache untrimmed. "The element of racism is everywhere we turn and we refuse to look. One of my focuses the past four years has been watching the Rasmussen Reports' Daily Presidential Tracking Poll. What is obvious is that the President's poll numbers and issue related poll numbers go up and down in the every grouping except the black component. So, measure it how you wish; our responses to this president are very much racially based, at least in the black community.

Big Red offered, "Racism may be alive and well in many pockets of our community, but it is inconsistent within every race and every economic element of our society. Isolating it to the black community is simply not an acceptable position Thaddeus and with that, we will move on to another subject."

~

MONDAY, OCTOBER 15, 2012

North-South Polling Service:

The President	40%
Congressman Paul Roland	26%
George Vincent	34%

~

FRIDAY, OCTOBER 19, 2012

The airwaves became politics central.

Throughout the week, the following radio advertisement continued to play on stations that aired oldies but goodies twenty-four hours a day. It was a simple reading with a woman's voice:

How did your congressman vote on the health care bill? Is your medical insurance better and less expensive than it was two years ago or are your benefits being cut and your co-pays increasing?

Throughout the week, television saw yet another commercial from Reesa Jonathon:

(Picture of a West Point graduation.)

THE EXCLUSIVE UNIVERSITIES TOLD US THAT THERE WAS NO MILITARY RECRUITING ON THEIR CAMPUSES BECAUSE OF "DON'T ASK, DON'T TELL."

(Picture of a Naval Academy graduation.)

THE EXCLUSIVE UNIVERSITIES TOLD US THAT THERE WAS NO ROTC ON THEIR CAMPUSES BECAUSE OF "DON'T ASK, DON'T TELL."

(Picture of an Air Force Jet flying over an Air Force Academy graduation.)

"DON'T ASK, DON'T TELL" IS GONE AND YET THERE IS NO MILITARY RECRUITING ON ELITE UNIVERSITY CAMPSUSES. IT HAS NOT HAPPENED. WHY NOT, MR. PRESIDENT? I AM REESA JONATHON AND I RECORDED AND PAID FOR THIS AD.

~

SUNDAY, OCTOBER 21, 2012

Everyone was gathered on the telephone for the weekly meeting.

Marshall Dankberg spent the first fifteen minutes explaining exactly where the campaign stood and what the variables were for the next two weeks. He laid out the remaining strategy and the calendar of the candidate for the remainder of the election process.

Stanley Martin Wade took the group through the demographics and the expected election results in near excruciating detail. He lauded Milton Woo and his technology advances and the amount of money that Woo was able to raise through his Twitter/e-mail network. With that, Woo explained the technology based get-out-the-vote campaign. He expressed some concern that the get-out-the-vote campaign would not be as effective as the old call-them-on-the-telephone-and-bring-them-to-the-voting-booth   technique, but this was as good as they were going to do without a political party to carry the ball.

Vincent gave his thanks and his candid opinion that the election was unwinnable by anyone, but he believed there was a ten percent chance, if Texas flipped away from Roland, he could actually win the electoral vote. He called this a long shot and predicted he would win the most electoral votes and that the President would win the popular vote by a significant margin, but would be very far from fifty percent of the total vote.

The Professor weighed in with the facts and numbers with respect to the number of individual congressional candidates George Vincent had spoken to during the past sixty days. "George, I think you have done all of the right things and your list for the next two weeks is about right. Remember, the key to this strategy is to leave the congressmen alone after the reality of the situation takes hold. You have already done what you needed to do and the rest will play itself out over time. I am curious about one thing, which is outside my sphere of knowledge. Skeeter, this election has played out as if there was no Middle East and if there was one, perhaps the Romans were in such complete control that there has not been so much as a mugging in Jerusalem since August. Doesn't that seem odd to you?"

"Professor, it is no odder than the fact that there doesn't appear to be any illegal migration over the Southern border or any drug cartel action going on in Mexico. I talked to the Mexican folks about this last week and they have no idea what is going on. Apparently, there must be some level of truce among the gang members and in the Middle East, I don't have a clue; I certainly see this deal in France as a farce."

Vincent went on to thank everyone on the call and indicated he was off to a campaign rally in Dallas at 6:00 p.m. their time.

~

MONDAY, OCTOBER 22, 2012

North-South Polling Service:

The President	36%
Congressman Paul Roland	32%
George Vincent	32%

~

Throughout another week, the following radio advertisement played on stations that aired oldies but goodies twenty-four hours a day. It was a simple reading with a woman's voice:

How did your congressman vote on the health care bill? Is your medical insurance better and less expensive than it was two years ago or are your benefits being cut and your co-pays increasing?

~

It was Monday night and Bill O'Brien was concluding his opening statement for the viewers: "And so, with every organization on the planet doing polling in every state, city and maybe, house-by-house, it is becoming clear that absent some unexpected event, something even beyond what has been announced in the Middle East on Saturday, this election is going to end up in the House of Representatives. And in a moment, we have Horace Cicerone, our own Jenn Cho, and a new Fox News associate, Richard Dionisio, the former Republican senator from Pennsylvania to explain to us where this election is going."

It was unusual for O'Brien to have more than two commentators on at the same time. He was most comfortable sitting on one side of the table and having a twosome on the other side. However, he had begun to think that, on air, Jenn Cho seemed to be able to get Geekhead to loosen up a bit and provide value for his contract and Senator Dionisio was necessary to add context and experience to the situation in the House of Representatives. Before sitting in the Senate, he had served six terms in the House of Representatives.

The staging was important to O'Brien and what the viewers saw was carefully crafted. His table was set in the shape of a V with the open end of the V to the viewers. At the top of the V to the right was O'Brien with Jenn sitting to his left, closer to the camera. This would give the viewers the sense of O'Brien's size as he towered over Jenn and as the conversation continued, the television could focus on Jenn from the front and see, as always, her perfectly round face. On the left side of the V, the senator, a bit taller and significantly heavier than Geekhead would be nearly opposite O'Brien with Geekhead across from Jenn. As was their normal attire for their now weekly visits, Jenn was in her white blouse up to her neck costume and Geekhead was coatless with his blue, button-down, collared shirt, striped tie and sleeves rolled up. He had come to find the sleeves rolled up incredibly funny as he had never done this before in his entire life. He was most comfortable with the classic academic look, including patches on the coat sleeves. Dionisio was in classic dark suit, white collared shirt, no button-down, and light red tie.

The visual picture for the audience was exactly as O'Brien sculpted it. He was the senior player both in stature and position. Jenn was his cute, little assistant, Geekhead was the Steve Garvey armed academic and the senator was just an additional suit, effectively invisible.

"So, Dr. Cicerone, your scenarios seem to be playing out. All of the polls seem to indicate that this election will end up in the House of Representatives. What happens again in the House?"

"It is straightforward in concept, but perhaps not straightforward in what will be practice. The House will vote for the President with each state voting as a single entity with a president requiring twenty-six states voting in his favor to be elected. And as we have discussed, the only nominees will be the three top vote getters, the President, Senator Vincent and Congressman Roland."

"Dr. Cicerone, you have never mentioned the one vote per state rule. How does that work?"

The conversation would be a serve and volley conversation with O'Brien being the only questioner. "Dr. Cicerone, sounds to me like the election itself is irrelevant. You have looked at the data, can the House of Representatives get twenty-six states to vote for one of these three men?"

"First, it takes the results of the election to cause the election to go to the House of Representatives. No one knows what will happen in the House or what the exact composition will be in the House. Remember, every Member of the House of Representatives is elected every two years, so the individual state house compositions could change dramatically at the polls in two weeks or so. How many states will have ties? My best guess, based on the data I have seen, is that the Republicans will win in eighteen to twenty-five states and the Democrats will win in eighteen to twenty-five states. That leaves me in the position of telling you that neither political party will control the House of Representatives with at least three or four states having equal numbers of Democrats and Republicans. As you know, the House races across the country are incredibly competitive. Today, if it went to the House, the Republicans would have an almost two-to-one advantage. To that result, we do not know if a single Republican or Democrat would vote for Senator Vincent regardless of how their state voters voted. And if you will let me sneak in a single additional sentence, this is not like a convention where a fourth or fifth dark horse candidate can sneak into the contest. The House of Representatives will be limited to the three candidates. Of course, it is possible, not likely, that one of the candidates will not win a state. If that happens, we have only two who will get electoral votes unless there is an unfaithful elector. Think of that possibility, Paul Roland gets a single unfaithful voter and is vaulted into the House of Representatives top three."

O'Brien: "Jenn, you are a smart lady. How do we get to the finish line?"

Jenn, with the camera behind the former senator showing only her perfectly sculpted face responded, "Dr. Cicerone's analysis is brilliant, as always." She smiled at her lover. "We need to move from brilliant analysis to wisdom at this point. My father would say that a journey of one thousand miles starts with a single step. And my father would then ask: *What is the first step?* This is the difficult question. The first step is understanding whether a Republican or Democratic Member of Congress would cast a vote within his or her state delegation for George Vincent. Since Vincent is a Democrat, that question is especially interesting for the Democratic Members of Congress. The data does not help with whether George Vincent is a Democrat, a Republican, an Independent or just a jerk in the eyes of the Democratic Members of the House."

O'Brien looked frustrated which was the message he wanted to convey to the audience. "Senator, where are we going here? What will happen in the House of Representatives?"

Senator Richard Dionisio had been facing cameras for his entire political career, which was effectively his entire adult life. At sixty-eight years old, after so many years in Congress, he was extremely polished. Like so many senators of his era, he had graduated with honors from an Ivy League undergraduate program and attended Yale Law School. He had clerked for Justice Frankfurter, worked as a Philadelphia prosecutor and migrated to elective office. Visually, he was the aging former senator; he looked like Robert Young when he acted in *Father Knows Best* in the old, black and white television series.

"Bill, I am afraid we will be in the WIFM stage of this contest. *What's in it for me?* Anyone who is afraid of losing earmarks or seeing their congressman as an ambassador or as secretary of whatever is not going to like this process. I…"

O'Brien interrupted: "Are you telling me this is all going to take place outside of public scrutiny? I am shocked!" mimicking the policeman's cynicism in *Casablanca*. It seems like this election started and will end like an old, black and white movie—all intrigue, no action.

"And this should surprise you, why?" mocked Dionisio. "I don't know if you heard the political pieces on the radio over the weekend and continuing into today. They are fascinating and they ask the right question: *Who is my congressman going to support?* Think about it. Your state votes for George

Vincent and the Speaker or Minority Leader calls you and demands, let me repeat that, demands, that you vote for the party's standard bearer, either the President or Paul Roland. And that demand has committee selections, committee chairmanships, earmark opportunities, and future political contributions all over it. This will be ugly."

O'Brien blanched a bit at this incredibly honest, accurate and straightforward response. He looked directly at Jenn and asked: "Jenn, do you expect your congressman to tell you how he is going to vote in the House."

Jenn fired back: "He had better man up and tell me exactly how he will vote if he wants my vote."

The senator jumped back in uninvited: "Whoever the group is that is paying for that advertisement, they have the right first question. It is after the first vote that you need to understand. I think most voters expect and most congressmen will understand what their constituents want on the first vote and vote just as their state voted. But, I don't see that happening. George Vincent has nothing to offer; he is a pariah in the Democratic Party and worse in the Republican Party. I think the congressmen will vote for their party unless their congressional district voted overwhelmingly for George Vincent and there won't be too many of those. Remember, the Member of the House of Representatives does not represent the state; he represents his district. The Member wants to be re-elected in his district.

"My calcs tell me that George Vincent is going to win the most states and he would need virtually every one of those delegations to affirmatively vote for him on the first ballot to win the Presidency. I don't think that could possibly happen. And I think the media will weigh in. The mainstream media will pillar and make silly any notions that do not favor the President."

"Doctor, what do you think?"

"There is no history unless you go back to the 1800s and while I could speak for two hours on the Whigs, I don't think it is relevant. I think my job is to remind you that the Senate will pick a Vice President on January 7, either the current vice president or Jordon Scotch, unless something really odd happens. This means Roland finishes third in the Electoral College, which is an easy bet at this moment. My guess is that unless something crazy happens, the Senate will pick Jordon Scotch. On January 20 he will either become the Vice President or the Vice President and Acting President. While, it is outside my scope, I would bet you that at least for some period of time, and I have no idea how long, Jordon Scotch will be the Acting President of the

United States. Whether he ever actually moves into the Oval Office, your guess is as good as mine."

"Senator?"

"I don't know. For sure, Jordon will be the VP. Otherwise, my calcs say there are a handful of Vincent states that will have one Democratic and one Republican congressman. The pressure on those people will be enormous, *enormous*. The President will weigh in, the leadership will weigh in, every lobbying group on the planet will weigh in. WIFM! Absolutely."

O'Brien was mortified as a commentator and as a citizen. "This isn't how it is supposed to be. Jenn, you have studied this with Dr. Cicerone, what do you think?"

"The Constitution is not designed for a three-party race where the country is split in different ways for all three. But, we only have two political parties in the House. We literally could have a situation where the person third in the popular vote is first in the Electoral College, unlikely, but possible. While the Constitution was not setup for our fact pattern, the process that will result was probably intended by the Founders. Their faith was in the Electoral College, not the voters. If, or when, they don't provide an answer, it goes to the House. I think this will play out in the politics of the House of Representatives. It will not be pretty." As Jenn used the words *it will not be pretty*, this was an evening where Jennifer Cho looked especially beautiful. Whenever they were on the air and Geekhead began looking at her, he would lose his concentration and when she used this expression, Geekhead's active mind responded with: *Not pretty, Jenn, you are spectacularly pretty tonight.* This would have been considered cute if someone were writing a romance novel, but on live television, it was generally a disaster. Tonight was no exception.

O'Brien looked again at Geekhead and asked him if the Constitution could be fixed before the House of Representatives met.

Geekhead, still staring at Jenn, barely heard his name and then did hear *the Constitution*.

"As I said earlier, the Constitution provides…"

O'Brien interjected. He didn't become the top dog because he wasn't good at his job. "No, Doctor, not what it provides, what should it provide?"

Quickly realizing he had been daydreaming about Jenn, Geekhead regained his concentration and gave O'Brien and the audience a summary of what it took to change the Constitution and why that could never happen in time for the January session.

O'Brien: "More to come, but Jenn about summed it up: *not very pretty*. Thank you and we will reconvene when we know something."

The moment the cameras were off, O'Brien snapped at Jenn and Geekhead: "Damn it, Jenn, your job is to make Geekhead here a great commentator. Doctor, you cannot lose concentration with the camera rolling. God knows what, and I don't care what you were thinking about, but you are in the big leagues now and we expect and demand better. Jenn, damn it, spend some more time with the good doctor. He is smart enough, but we cannot have bad television, not ten seconds of it."

O'Brien took a deep breath; he hated to lean on Jenn and then apologized. "Jenn, I'm sorry, but that was a bad moment. Let's try to do better, Doctor." With Jenn, it was always like dealing with a daughter, he could only get mad for about fifteen seconds.

Off air, after he calmed down, O'Brien offered that the whole affair baffled him. He guessed that the President would pull off the election and have a contentious Congress. Senator Dionisio looked at Bill: "Bill, I don't think so. You can only go to the whip so often and then when a dog has the opportunity, he will either bolt or strike. I think bolting is in season. I can't say this on the air, but the majority of at least the Senate just hates the President. My old law firm taught me that you can only be arrogant if you have something to be arrogant about. The only thing this guy can be arrogant about is his ability to give a great political speech in front of a group of more than a few hundred friendly faces. He is, in my opinion, a walking disaster and I think at this point, while not very many in the Senate will talk about it, they all know the reality. I cannot imagine it is any different in the House of Representatives. His only hope is this Middle East thing and the polling data says the public is skeptical. I am as well."

Jenn and Geekhead left the studios about fifteen minutes apart. Right before she left, Jenn promised Geekhead a classic home cooked Chinese meal and the best dessert ever. He admitted to himself before the show that for the past month and a half, by about noon every day, he began to think exclusively about dessert after dinner. He was not exaggerating and for a moment tonight, it had made him look a bit foolish.

~

It was 2:00 a.m. in the morning and Robert Smith, through his binoculars, was watching a 2010 Chrysler Town & Country Minivan stop directly in front of The Beverly Hilton hotel. Smith was almost two thousand yards away on the roof of an office building about two blocks away. He had been waiting for nearly two hours for the van to arrive after disarming the alarm system to the office building's roof, establishing a proper position and organizing his equipment.

Ahmed Karzerine and Muhammad Aci were instructed to drive to the Beverly Hills hotel and put the vehicle in the self-parking lot on the first floor. Each was paid $150 even and given cab fare to return to their homes in South Central, Los Angeles after delivery. The two men were nobody and anybody. They worked in a car repair shop. Each lived in the United States for most of their lives. Both were citizens of the United States of America. Each had earned a high school diploma and attended a for-profit institution to learn their trade. Each was a devout Muslim; neither had the remotest interest in terrorism. Karzerine had a wife and two children.

Karzerine and Aci had performed a 36K-mile maintenance on the minivan earlier in the evening and were asked to drive the car to the Beverly Hills hotel after the late shift. Apparently, the van's owner was staying at The Beverly Hilton and would pick the car up in the morning. The car was purchased with cash by a well-disguised Robert Smith posing as James Kraft just a few hours before Kazerine and Aci took it to the repair shop. Nothing about the transaction was real except the one hundred dollar bills paid to close the deal.

Smith watched the car enter the self-parking lot and counted slowly to two hundred. He assumed that the two men would have parked the car by that time and would spend a moment deciding what they were supposed to do with the parking ticket and the keys at this hour. At two hundred, Smith pushed the enter button on his computer and the self-parking lot, along with the Chrysler Minivan, collapsed in their entirety after the huge Semtex-laden bomb in the back of the van exploded. Smith calculated that if the vehicle was parked anywhere on the first floor, the bomb would take down the parking lot, blow out several windows on the first floor, but likely only kill the two automobile mechanics. He was nearly correct. The only other person in the parking lot was a young community college co-ed who had spent the prior two hours making ends meet at a *business appointment* on the fourth floor of the hotel and was driving down to the first floor level to go home. She was just in the wrong place at the wrong time.

Smith, neither knowing about nor caring about the young co-ed, had not watched the explosion. He felt the blast just before he entered the door to go downstairs to the elevator and directly to the underground parking. Before going downstairs, Smith cleaned the roof with the intensity of a surgeon closing a wound in the operating room. This was his expertise and he was a top flight professional. The lookout building was carefully selected, as it did not have a guard after eleven o'clock at night and therefore he would not see a single person while there. His disguise for the cameras was not very clever, only effective. He wore a ski mask, Panama hat and combat fatigues. The only special effect was the padding under his long sleeve shirt that added the appearance of fifty pounds. He had been very hot on the roof, but the disguise would not have allowed his mother to recognize him and CSI would find nothing useful on the roof.

Smith was traveling to Chicago on non-connecting US Airways flights via Phoenix. His first flight would leave LAX at 9:55 a.m. and land in Phoenix at 11:16 a.m. After leaving the baggage area and returning as if he was a new passenger and changing his identification, he would take a second flight to Chicago from Phoenix and arrive in Chicago at 5:48 p.m. His return flight ticket from Chicago to Phoenix scheduled for Thursday morning would never be used. Neither he nor Mr. Brandon Lyon, the name under which he was travelling, would be on the return flight to Phoenix. His plan was to check into the Hilton within the Chicago Airport under his own name with his previously made reservation by 7:30 p.m., have dinner alone in the hotel's Andiamo restaurant and be in bed by 10:00 p.m. He would spend a leisurely morning in his room and be on his return trip to Rio via Atlanta on Delta's flight 2549 at 1:41 p.m. Delta was his favorite airline yet he dreaded the almost seventeen hour trip, regardless of his seating in business class. He was certain returning on the same airline that brought him into the United States was the safest course. This was the smartest possible travel solution, as he appeared to be a tourist or businessman. He was one hundred percent correct.

He would have laughed out loud had he ever known that exactly ten days after the bombing, the FBI had finally been given and reviewed the Beverly Hills office building security video. As he had been in the ski mask and military fatigues, the video had narrowed the potential number of assassins to about one hundred million people. He did laugh out loud when he thought of how he threw the combat fatigues and ski hat into the dumpster behind the Los Angeles Police Station at 1663 Butler Avenue, Los Angeles, CA 90025, one hundred feet from Santa Monica Boulevard. If there was one place on the earth no one would have looked for the disguise, it was behind a West Los Angeles police station. And with the trash being taken away several hours after he put his clothing into the dumpster, the clothing issue was a thing of the past. No one would ever know that they were currently being worn daily by Claude Clark, an employee at the recycling center. Claude had removed them from the recycle process for himself. Claude broke the rules by keeping the items for himself, but no one really paid very much attention to a minimum wage employee taking a pair of combat fatigues and a pair of combat boots home at the end of his shift.

Smith had taken the hard drive out of his computer, poured battery acid on it, and left it in a trash can behind the Hilton near LAX where he had breakfast before his flight to Phoenix. The computer would be compacted as fill in a landfill one hundred miles from Los Angeles for eternity.

~

TUESDAY, OCTOBER 23, 2012

Every newspaper, every news program and every talk show covered the bombing at the Beverly Hilton on Tuesday morning. The plan worked perfectly as the bomb had exploded outward in such a manner as to physically expose the driver and his friend. (It would be two days before the police found the local co-ed who had not yet been reported missing.) The men were easy to identify and their Muslim heritage was quickly determined. The programmed message from Al Qaeda, aka Robert Smith, was received by the Los Angeles Times. And Al Qaeda, while having no idea or understanding of what took place, took credit for the bombing. The President was scheduled to give a speech at the hotel on Thursday morning.

As the day progressed, the story became confused. Who would have thought that Ahmed Karzerine, auto repair expert, would have been a registered Democrat, have an *Only a True Democrat for President* sign on his apartment's front door, and have spent many summer Sunday mornings registering voters at the local mall?

When the fact that Karzerine was an outspoken Democrat hit the web, it went viral. Was this a Democratic stunt gone wrong?

By 6:00 p.m. EDT on Tuesday night, when Big Red sat behind her anchor desk and described the story, her take was pretty different from the manner the morning newspapers and web had reported the story earlier that morning.

Red hair in place, Big Red began: "Last night, two men drove into the parking lot of The Beverly Hilton hotel in Los Angeles and blew themselves and the parking lot into oblivion. The story is truly strange. Let me give

485

you the facts: Two Muslim men apparently drove into the hotel parking lot in the middle of the night and blew themselves and the parking lot up. The President of the United States was scheduled to speak at the hotel on Thursday morning. Upon the opening of the investigation, we find out that one of the Muslim men was a Democratic activist.

"It all seems so strange. Only an idiot would not know that the bomb sniffing dogs would have found the van long before the President arrived in Los Angeles. The good news is that it appears no one was hurt other than the two men in the van. In other news…"

The conservative talk show hosts launched into a conspiracy discussion the moment the identity of the Democratic Muslim became known. The less listened to liberal radio talk show hosts talked about a conspiracy to assassinate the President of the United States. Bill O'Brien did not cover the story. The President's speech was moved a few blocks and during the speech, he said not a word about the bombing. It was as if the potential story was so toxic, no one in the national media was comfortable talking about what happened and what might be the actual facts. Neither Smith nor his clients expected or could have expected this result. Very bad luck.

If they had known about the young co-ed, they would not have cared less.

~

WEDNESDAY, OCTOBER 24, 2012

Saturday Night Live would have determined that the actual negotiations for this presidential debate were so bizarre that they could not present them as comedy, only tragedy. The most important issue to the President's team was that his podium was in the middle of his two opponents. This was apparently a deal point until it leaked to the press. This was also a deal point to Roland and Vincent. They could not accept the President in the middle of them for the entire debate, as if he was in charge. This issue brought plans for any debate to a standstill. When the media intervened that there had to be a debate, a compromise was reached. As the President was unwilling to compromise on the issue in any reasonable manner, the debate was held with the oddest setting imaginable for three individuals running to be the President of the United States.

Senator Vincent's sense of humor was scaring him to death. Here he was standing behind a podium getting ready for a presidential debate, the only presidential debate, and his two debatees were standing behind identical podiums with identical backdrops in different locations. Three presidential candidates, three separate platforms, and three separate rooms—at least they were in the same building. *How could you possibly think this made sense?* In front of him, there was a fifty-five-inch screen showing Elizabeth Martin, the moderator and the senator's understanding was that the screen would show each of them when they were speaking. My God, what if I say something about how crazy this is or ask the President whether he is comfortable without his presidential seal on his podium? *Would people not know who he was?*

487

Elizabeth Martin was a well-known columnist who could write for the *Washington Post* and *The Washington Times*. Only the fringes of both parties could be upset with her being selected as the moderator. And of course, both fringes were upset with Elizabeth Martin as the moderator. As she had said: "You gotta love the Internet!"

Congressman Roland was annoyed at the whole debate thing. He knew that he was not going to win either the popular vote or the electoral vote. Tonight he would focus on issues and this format seemed to be the least conducive to asking or being asked hard questions. His strategy, mostly coming from his son, Crystal and his Dallas buddies was to ask the hard questions of his opponents and hope that they would either answer them honestly or not answer them at all. If he could demonstrate that neither of them had solutions or that either one of them would hide from an answer, maybe future conservatives would be more successful after the American Exceptionalism Party went away.

The President was standing behind his podium wondering what tonight had in store for him. He was without notes as were Congressman Roland and Senator Vincent. He did feel more than a bit naked. While he was constantly told that he was more eloquent without notes, and he realized that while his short opening speech would be the best of the three, his answers to hardball questions were often problematical.

Elizabeth Martin started the debate by setting general ground rules and indicating that they had each agreed to give a three-minute presentation and that the President would be first. This was yet another deal point that the networks and the candidates had finally succumbed to in order to have the debates. None of the three candidates underwhelmed or overwhelmed their audience with their comments. The only notable comment was from Senator Vincent who was attempting to position his two opponents as representing the extremes of their parties.

Martin refused to provide any of the candidates with her questions and for one night only, she decided that she would have a bit more fun than was perhaps appropriate in her choice of questions. Her first question, which was to be answered first by the President and then by Roland and finally by Vincent was in her mind, a whopper: "What about your opponents drives you crazy?"

The President cringed and furrowed his brow at the question and chose his pathway. "These are serious times and your question deserves a serious answer. My concern with Congressman Roland is that he is an extremist in his views and cares far too little about the average citizen and far too much about big business. My job as president is to protect the public from extremists like Congressman Roland. As to George Vincent, I remain appalled that he would abandon his Democratic principles in an effort to gain power." He answered crisply and in his distinctively clipped style and was wishing he could push the words back into his mouth as he finished his thought. The defending champion did not need to demean his opponents. It only made him look small. Virtually without pausing in this last sentence, he blurted out "But, do not misconstrue my thoughts here, you asked what drives me crazy about my opponents, they each bring good things to the table as well."

"Congressman Roland?"

The congressman stood as straight as he could and offered a fairly precise statement: "What drives me crazy about my opponents? Frankly, nothing drives me crazy about George Vincent. We disagree on many, many issues, but he is straightforward and honest. He is a good guy. As to the President, this president is petulant and I can't stand that in a leader. A leader needs to lead and decide what direction to lead based upon the best interest of the nation as a whole. Countries rise and fall on actions or non-actions of their leaders. This president is more interested in where he will sit in a debate with George and I than he is in governing. Petulant, so petulant, I am sitting in a small dark room instead of participating in a face-to-face debate."

"Senator Vincent?"

The senator gave up trying to look the part of a modern politician. Senator Vincent more resembled a frumpy college professor or Winston Churchill this evening wearing only a very light touch of makeup and a suit which was obviously worn a few days before. "You have to love Paul. He doesn't tolerate fools very easily. This of course is why I love him and why he drives me crazy as well. Paul will tell you exactly what he thinks, regardless of the setting and regardless of who is in the room. This can be good and bad. As to the President, I don't think the President is as interested in the job of being president as he is in being president. I have committed to being a twenty-four-seven president, which might mean an occasional speech away from Washington and an occasional round of golf to ensure that I remain sane, but I just don't think this president works hard enough. He knew what the job was going in and I think his lack of ever having had a real job before, one where people's lives are impacted by his efforts, makes him unable to work hard enough to be successful. I know that won't be a very popular statement among the members of my Democratic Party, my former Democratic Party, especially since I campaigned for the President, but it is what drives me crazy and it had a lot to do with my decision to run for President of the United States. Don't look for an ESPN special on my basketball picks for the NCAA tournament."

The President leaned into his microphone and began to speak: "Elizabeth, I need to respond to the comments of..."

Martin cut the President of the United States off without the blink of an eye. "Mr. President, the rules of this debate were very carefully agreed to before tonight. There will be neither follow-up answers nor follow-up questions. If a candidate begins to respond to a statement made in a prior question, I am to cut him off."

"No, that is not what I had in mind. I need to respond to these..."

"Mr. President, with all due respect, I sat in all of the tortuous meetings to ensure that this debate took place and these rules are as demanded by your representatives. I am sorry, Sir."

The cameras showed both Paul Roland and George Vincent. Both were watching the President on their televisions and they revealed nothing.

"That..."

"The next question goes to Congressman Roland. Congressman, what say you to the border and to immigration?"

The camera showed the President who appeared to be staring at someone in his room rather than watching the television. He was obviously very angry.

The congressman thought for a full fifteen seconds, which seemed like an hour to his wife, son and Crystal. They were concerned that he would be a politician rather than the conservative stalwart of his party. That would be the political thing to do. "Elizabeth, you will recall that we promised short, concise answers to these difficult questions. First, anyone who retreats to the call of full immigration reform is trying to hide from an answer. I hope you are listening, Mr. President. Second, we need to place the necessary assets on the border tomorrow to stop, not slow down, but stop illegal immigration through our effectively unguarded border. And I don't give a wit whether that is the National Guard or the 101st Airborne. Third, we need to retake, and retake is the right term, the land that has been occupied and controlled by the Mexican Cartels outside of Phoenix and inside a few major cities. We are beyond the ounce of prevention stage, but it is not too late to retake our country. When these actions are completed successfully, then we can talk about immigration reform in the context of the people who are left. In that context, we can talk about a program that will grant the children of some illegal immigrant's citizenship and contingent resident status to those who entered illegally. No one who entered this country illegally should be made a citizen, not today, not ever."

"Senator Vincent?"

The senator responded that he was disappointed that the President had not secured the borders and indicated that the first step was to control the borders and build an effective fence. If that fence needed to be eighty feet tall, that was fine, if fifty feet tall, that was fine. The key word was *effective*. He further indicated that he wanted to deport anyone convicted of any crime within the United States and that he would be willing to discuss a path to citizenship where there was a significant English language component. The senator indicated that without the United States securing its borders, Mexico, as a nation, was lost. Finally, Senator Vincent indicated that he would do everything possible to take away Federal funding from any city that represented itself and acted as a sanctuary city.

The President was last: "Any discussion of anything except comprehensive immigration reform is silly. There are twelve million undocumented individuals living in the United States and we need to start there. The Republicans will turn a blind eye to these individuals if we first close the border. We simply cannot do that. As to the border, we are already expending more funds and we have more boots on the ground at the Mexican border than we have ever had before. We are doing a great job."

Big Red was watching the debate along with her colleague Thaddeus Milken. While both of them had live microphones for the entire debate, neither of them said a word and for Big Red, she had forgotten the microphones were live. "Oh, my God, that could cost him the election, that single sentence."

Milken rushed to help: "Not really, Marylou, the President's support is closely identified with the immigrant community; let's just listen to the debate and comment later."

Big Red was flushed. Her hair color and her face color were the same. She turned her microphone off and leaned over to Milken and grasped his wrist: "Thanks, Thad. I forgot the mike was on and my role is not to do what I just did."

Milken smiled and nodded: "Yup, it just takes a while to learn. You are doing great, Kid."

The President wasn't flushed, he was just angry and over the next fifteen minutes, his answers were clipped and full of spin while both Vincent and Paul were trying their best to answer the questions completely. The President could tell the debate was going poorly for him, and he was not sure how the other two candidates were doing. He did know he could not serve and volley with them successfully in this format.

A question went to Senator Vincent and then to Congressman Roland. It was related to the stimulus package from 2009. Roland finished his exceptionally strident remarks with: "And we are left with three honest choices in terms of the President's actions, he either did not have the remotest idea what he was doing, or he relied on the worst set of advisors in American history, or he borrowed a trillion dollars to pay off his political allies."

"Mr. President?"

"As the President of the United States, I will not stand here and have my office and my staff attacked by this bigoted Texas congressman." The President walked away from his podium.

Thaddeus Milken looked at the screen and then looked at Big Red: "Marylou, you were just early, that stunt could have cost the President the election."

Elizabeth Martin coldly informed the audience, some forty million viewers, that the President left the stage and presumably was not returning. She indicated that she would continue the debate and she did, although all of the wind was out of the debate's sails.

The debate finished with Congressman Roland offering that his comment of the President being petulant and not interested in the hard part of governance was demonstrated an hour before. A bad night for the President.

~

492

FRIDAY, OCTOBER 26, 2012

Another radio advertisement and this advertisement played continuously on news stations and talk radio. This commercial was also simple and also had another woman's voice, except this woman was obviously over the age of forty:

> *If this election is decided in the House of Representatives, you need to know for whom your congressman or congresswoman is going to vote. Is that person going to vote for the same person you will for President of the United States, or is that person going to vote along political party lines. This is the most important election of our lifetimes. You need to know. Ask your Member of Congress today. You deserve to know!*

Another radio advertisement on different stations, this time with a man speaking:

> *This is an election about pensions. Why do government pensions equal one hundred percent of annual compensation and you only have a 401K? Why are government workers being made divas while we continue to work hard and pay our bills?*

Throughout the weekend, television saw a commercial from Beth Midlands:

(Film of the two Black Panthers in front on a polling booth in 2008.)

IF YOU HAVE A PROBLEM VOTING IN THE ELECTION OR YOU ARE WORRIED ABOUT VOTER FRAUD, SEND A PERSONAL NOTE TO THE ATTORNEY

**GENERAL OF THE UNITED STATES;
HE SAW NOTHING WRONG WITH THIS PICTURE.**
(Picture of Beth Midlands.)
**I AM BETH MIDLANDS AND I RECORDED AND PAID FOR
THIS AD.**

~

SATURDAY, OCTOBER 27, 2012

The President of the United States was wearing his grey suit, white shirt and red tie. He was standing at the podium with his teleprompters perfectly positioned. The other podium was sixteen feet away and identical save for the missing teleprompters and the presidential emblem. Behind the second podium stage left was President Mahmoud Ahmadinejad, the President of Iran. President Ahmadinejad was standing on a small, stable box so that while he was not the same height as the President of the United States, their difference in height was not evident.

The setting was dramatic with the ocean in the background. The location was striking, as there had never been a press conference on Normandy Beach, except to memorialize and honor the American and British invasion forces in 1944. The day started with the President landing at Caen, emerging from Air Force One and racing off to the cemetery at Normandy Beach in an American helicopter which had been flown in from a NATO base in Germany. The pilots for the flight from Caen to Normandy had flown to France with the President. The President had demanded his own helicopter pilots. Herman Sackman made it expressly clear that if the invasion site was to be used as the background for this momentous announcement, if the President did not, at the very least, stop and honor the fallen American soldiers before the presentation, the news story could and would revolve around his lack of respect for the Americans who died in Europe during World War II. This would have been catastrophic in the fifty and above voter category. Many veterans were still focused on the President's decision to play golf on June 4, 2010, D-Day, two years before this election cycle. This president was born late enough in the twentieth century and raised by a family liberal enough and living in Honolulu, that D-Day was not a subject ever discussed in his youth, but he understood the politics.

Following his obligatory visit to the cemetery, with the entire press corps in tow, the President returned to his vehicle and made his quick trip to the hilltop where the announcement was made. As was the norm, he would find out what he had to say as he said it. He had absolutely reached the point where he never reviewed his speeches before he read them from the teleprompter. (Occasionally, this resulted in a disaster such as referring to corpsmen as *corps men* pronouncing the silent *P* and *S*, but the press never made any meaningful fun of the President's gaffes.)

It was the oddest set of arrangements that any President of the United States had experienced. He was not cognizant that the event was one hundred percent show and would have absolutely no long-term impact. If the President of Iran was willing to help his campaign, the President was not going to stand in his way. That being said, it was without precedent that the President of the United States would travel to France, participate in a press conference with the head of one nation, sponsored by the nation upon who's ground they stood and agree not to have so much as a cappuccino with either foreign leader. What he did wonder a touch about was who was the prop in this equation. Who was the audience of the other two presidents? All he did know was that his people had read the prepared remarks of the French President and President Ahmadinejad and it all sounded great. He gave no thought as to why no one wanted to see his remarks beforehand.

The President assumed his speech would be good. Immediately after the presentation, the two other presidents were off to Paris and the President would return to the United States for urgent meetings, whatever that meant, maybe golf. Of course, there would be a campaign fundraiser. He marveled how certain Democratic candidates were thrilled to have him in town to raise money, but often now avoided any possibility of being in the same picture.

The Iranian and US presidents stood in front of a hastily put together group of US State Department and Embassy workers and Iranian diplomats, along with the world press. While hastily arranged, the security was visible and intense. There was not a single tourist within one half mile of Normandy Beach. Neither of the other two national leaders greeted the President, so he made his own way to the podium. When he arrived at his podium, the show was ready to begin.

The audience was literally silent; there was not a hint of collegiality in the air. The French president rose from his seat in the front row and spoke from the front row with a handheld microphone. His remarks were meant to puff up his standing in his country. Taking only four minutes and fifteen seconds, he thanked both presidents for coming, inferred that what was coming was solely the result of his personal diplomatic efforts, and introduced the two presidents only by title. There was absolutely no puffery in the introductions.

President Ahmadinejad spoke first, in French. He thanked President Sarkozy for arranging the news conference and thanked the President as the, "first President of the United States who understood the issues in the Middle East and the first President of the United States who did not have preconceived negative views of Islam in the entire two hundred year history of the United States." Ahmadinejad went on to provide a history of Iran for the past eight hundred years, emphasizing its historical acceptance of other religions within the context of what any listener would have concluded was his view of Muslim perfection. Like most of his speeches, the logic was compelling based upon a set of postulates, which were found in an imagination that might have been comfortable painting the Southern slaves in 1863 as the oppressors of Southern Slaveholders because of the cost of their care.

After about fifty minutes, Ahmadinejad finally arrived at the point of his trip and the news conference. In French he said, "Now I speak to the American people and speak to them in their own language." He switched to English and said, "Since World War I, the Middle East has been cursed with a mistake made by the British government in placing the Jews in Palestine. This has resulted in wars, the encirclement and effective imprisonment of the Palestinians, and countless unnecessary deaths of Palestinians. There has been no solution or reasonable solution ever offered to bring peace to Palestine. With the full consent of the legitimate governments of the Middle East, we are offering the following solution:

- We, and all of Israel's neighbors, will recognize Israel and its right to exist.
- Israel and Iran will immediately give up all nuclear weapons and submit to international weapons inspections.

- Jerusalem will become a city protected, at least in part, by the United Nations.
- Palestine will be broken into two independent nations, one of the West Bank and one being Gaza. These two nations will immediately have democratic elections, be admitted to the United Nations, and be recognized as nations by all nations of the Middle East and all Western powers.
- The Western nations will immediately provide funds for the development and construction of nuclear energy plants for power in each of these two new nations as well as funds for the creation of four new universities and industrial training for 750,000 Palestinians.

"With these modest conditions, the Iranian people believe there can be peace in the Middle East for millenniums."

With this, the President of Iran made a final salutation in Iranian and ceased speaking. He did not introduce the President of the United States. He only completed his remarks.

The President walked across to President Ahmadinejad, bowed and then with his right hand took Ahmadinejad's right hand and raised it high in the air in a victory salute. The box under Ahmadinejad's podium was of sufficient size that he had no issues with balance. Both men smiled broadly for the cameras and the assembled group greeted them with mild applause. The French president slowly rose from his chair and joined the three for pictures. As Ahmadinejad could not move two feet or he would be off his box, the pictures with the three presidents looked a bit odd as neither the French nor the American presidents could get very close to the President of Iran as he stood in the middle of his box.

Only Fox News would show the picture of the President bowing to yet another president of another nation despised by most Americans. (Mullah Seecaaj had filtered several hundred thousand dollars to an American advisor in an effort to remind the President of the United States that he had bowed to the leaders of Saudi Arabia and Japan and that a change of course would be taken as an insult to the people of Iran.)

After the President's thirty-minute speech giving almost the entire credit for this agreement to himself, he thanked the Iranian and French presidents and that completed his speech. There were no post speech conversations or pictures. It did not appear that either President Sarkozy or

SATURDAY, OCTOBER 27, 2012

President Ahmadinejad felt they needed to spend yet another second with the American president.

Noticeably absent from Normandy, France, on this October day was a single member of the government of Israel. There were two Palestinian ambassadors in the audience, but each had been instructed to keep a very low profile.

Since the President had left Herman Sackman in Washington D.C. and travelled with Ray Matta, with the exclusion of one member of the French military, a man who had been assigned guard duty at a small road leading into Normandy from the South, there was not a single Jewish person within ten miles of the ceremony, not counting the American dead buried in the background.

As the President's armored SUV roared toward his helicopter, parked almost two miles from his speech, he looked at Matta and exclaimed: "I hit a home run today. This is the first time since Jimmy Carter that we are headed for peace in the Middle East and I do not intend to let peace fail this time."

Matta had grown weary of his President and it did not take a cynic of his proportions to see something did not fit together perfectly in this story. Actually nothing fit together. *Why did they include the President of the United States? He was not involved in this deal for a minute and Sarkozy clearly does not like him. Ahmadinejad hates anyone who does not think he should be the president of a greater Ottoman Empire. The President of the United States was window dressing if I ever saw it. It was so obvious.*

"Mr. President, for the election this is huge, but I don't feel very good about the entire deal, the day or the fact that we are flying home and those clowns are going to Paris for dinner. I wish you had not bowed. I don't know if you heard, but the nuclear weapons line was a surprise."

The President was growing equally weary of Matta. "Ray, you couldn't say a nice thing if I put a gun to your head. As soon as we get on Air Force One, start telling the press what a great job I did and how our policy changes allowed and caused this momentous event." The President thought to himself: *The people that voted me the Nobel Prize knew I could accomplish great things.*

~

It was only 9:00 p.m. and Milton Woo and Molly Tom had already quickly made love two times.

The two-person team of Woo and Tom had run out of things to do around 6:30 p.m. and Molly had suggested they buy a bottle of vodka and get drunk. By Saturday evening, Milton and Molly had nothing else to do while everyone else was scattered throughout the United States. The two of them were stuck in Cleveland, Ohio, with the computer servers.

They retreated to Woo's apartment with the bottle of vodka and a huge can of tomato juice. The liquor was all Molly needed to desperately want to be intimate with someone. Her relationship at home had been exceptionally quiet and quite possibly lost as she had gotten deeper and deeper into the campaign and had been leaving campus early every Thursday evening and returning Monday morning, exhausted from working twenty-hour days.

Molly had enjoyed Milton Woo's company for the past several weeks and he had taught her everything he knew about computer technology and political surveys. She learned to enjoy being with him as a person and he was thrilled to have the working weekend company of a very smart and attractive young woman. Even in the dowdy clothing Molly had begun to wear, Milton found her very attractive. Molly was far and away the most attractive woman with whom Milton Woo had ever spent any significant time.

Although thoroughly feeling the vodka, when they first began touching Molly thought this was a bit different than her other experiences. While she had only had a small handful of partners, this was actually very different. After a few minutes, Molly had a pretty good idea of what was happening. Woo had been nervous, uncertain and a bit lost during their first breach and even with the haze of near terminal drunkenness, Molly realized that she was Woo's first woman.

Now, almost an hour later, he was quietly exploring her with his right hand and slowly gaining confidence as he experienced her reactions to different landing points. She smiled as she enjoyed his light, but uncertain touch. With Woo's hand in a very satisfactory place, Molly managed to sit up without moving his index finger more than a centimeter and swallowed a bit more than the equivalent of another drink and a half.

As Molly started to lie back down, she moved Woo's hand away and pushed him onto his back. At that point, her long hair flowing a bit behind and a bit beside her face on both sides, she began muttering something about his relaxing and she slowly started exploring his sculpted, hairless chest. For

SATURDAY, OCTOBER 27, 2012

the remainder of the evening, with unbridled enthusiasm, she started her new role as teacher with Milton Woo. Completely certain that he had not previously spent an evening in bed with a woman, a twenty-four-year-old virgin, she fully intended to simultaneously teach him how to be a competent lover and to use him to the point of his complete and theoretical maximum physical capabilities.

For Milton Woo, the change in the relationship from teacher/student at work to student/teacher in the confines of his small apartment was a life highlight, actually the life highlight. Milton's still drunken thought to himself was: *I kept my promise to The Professor; Joshua has never gotten near Molly.*

~

MONDAY, OCTOBER 29, 2012

North-South Polling Service:

The President	39%
Congressman Paul Roland	26%
George Vincent	35%

~

SATURDAY, NOVEMBER 3, 2012

Milton Woo had expected Molly Tom to say something during the day Friday and was surprised and disappointed when she offered that she was ready for an early night and would be catching up on a week's sleep at the end of a very long day. He spent the entire week thinking about and reliving the prior Saturday night. Now it was 6:30 p.m. the following Saturday, there was no one around, nothing to do and Milton had the hope and expectation of a kind of Groundhog Day for tonight. Thus far, this Saturday had been a replica of the prior Saturday with jobs to complete, e-mails to send and nothing pressing for the evening.

Finally, with the two of them alone in the office, he walked up behind her chair and put his hands on her shoulders, this being the first time they had touched each other in two days. "Molly, can I take you out to dinner tonight?"

Molly knew this was coming for a week and she knew she was going to hurt Milton Woo. He had sent her a few e-mails during the week and called her three times *just to see how her week was going*. Her decision was especially hard because Milton was so sweet and had been, in some ways, amazingly special last Sunday morning as they took a little more than an extra hour to get to the office. Her decision was also difficult because another evening in bed, given a sufficient supply of vodka, would be great fun and given his desire to please her at every step, physically very satisfying. But she did not believe Milton Woo was in Molly Tom's future and she did not think it would take a full second evening for him to start using words and having feelings that would be meaningful to him and unacceptable to her. The overriding problem she had with this plan was that she really, really liked him. He was so nice and such a sweet man.

Softly, Molly looked at Milton and told him: "Milton, last Saturday night was one of the most remarkable evenings of my life. You were wonderful and you are really, really sweet. But, Milton, I have a boyfriend at home and I never cheated on him before and I feel pretty bad about it." Nothing wrong with this complete lie. She had not checked, but she had stopped caring about him. He was history. "I just cannot be with you in that situation again, no matter how amazing it was. That just isn't me."

"Molly, you had mentioned that your relationship was a little rocky last week. We don't need to go to bed again, we could just have a nice dinner."

"No, Milton, it's just not the right thing to do. And we both know we would end up in bed; we were far too good together. Maybe, someday, Ted and I will finally break up, but until that happens I am going to go back to being the good girl I have always been. I am just going to have a quick bite at the hotel restaurant and take in a cable flick."

The conversation went on for a while with Milton Woo being a perfect gentleman and Molly fending him off verbally.

Ultimately, Molly headed off to her hotel room thinking, but very far from one hundred percent sure, that she made the right decision, particularly the right decision for Milton, but wishing mightily that she had taken a second bite at this particular apple rather than preparing to spend the approaching night lonely and sober. Once she got to her hotel room, it was difficult, but she managed to keep herself from reaching for her cell phone.

~

The President had played the race card and it made someone angry. No one would ever know who it made angry and everyone would blame everyone else. But what made whoever it was angry made for a powerful YouTube moment and that moment went viral at lightning speed.

The YouTube video was sequential and the background music was angry and highly sexual rap.

The first section of the video showed Michael Jordon racing down the basketball court and dunking the basketball over another player at the other end. As Jordon dunked the basketball, an obvious black voice quietly said: "Michael Jordon, an authentic, black basketball player."

The second section of the video showed Martin Luther King standing behind the podium in front of the Washington Monument. The same voice said: "Martin Luther King, an authentic, black leader."

The third section of the video showed a young president playing in the back yard with his white grandparents and his white mother. Whether these pictures were real or manufactured was unknown. They were probably manufactured, but it did not matter. The same voice asked: "Is the President an authentic, black leader?"

Condemnation ruled the airwaves. No one knew whether the video was designed to drive blacks to the polls or keep them at home. No one knew whether the producer of the video thought this would make blacks angry enough to vote or whether it would keep them from the polls. No one knew whether it was designed to appeal to white liberals.

The final day before the election had the media split fourteen different ways on this last and final election event. And no one would ever know to whom to give the blame (or the credit).

As it turned out, all election decisions had already been made, both as to the candidate and as to whether it was worth the time going to the voting booth.

~

MONDAY, NOVEMBER 5, 2012

North-South Polling Service:

The President	39%
Congressman Paul Roland	26%
George Vincent	35%

~

TUESDAY, NOVEMBER 6, 2012

Roger Walston, the dean of all newscasters in the United States was the only one on the screen. The dean was pulled out of either an ice locker or his retirement home for election night.

"Ladies and gentlemen, while Hawaii is not yet in, we have a winner. The winner is the House of Representatives of the United States of America. The President of the United States will be selected by the House of Representatives on January 7. Yes, for the first time in almost two hundred years, the United States has an election that will definitely be decided by the House of Representatives, unless something unprecedented happens in the Electoral College. The drama in the House of Representatives will be high.

"It appears that the sitting President of the United States has received the most popular votes, about forty percent of the total popular vote. In the popular vote, the President came in first, Vincent second and Roland last. The President received about six million more votes than Vincent. However, Vincent received 236 electoral votes carrying thirty-two states, far more than the President's 194 electoral votes carrying only twelve populous states plus the District of Columbia assuming Hawaii goes for the President, and Roland achieved 108 electoral votes carrying only six states: Texas, Florida, Arizona, Georgia, Mississippi and Louisiana. Will the President be re-elected to office? Let's ask our panel."

So it went on all three major networks and every radio station. At Fox News, the conversation was a bit different: Bill O'Brien did not do election night coverage for Fox News. Again, the man had the strangest view

511

of himself and as a result, he saw himself as a commentator and was home watching on television.

As expected, Fox News brought in Arthur Ninoah, its nighttime anchor, for election night and after providing the same basic details as the networks and the remainder of the cable news networks, Ninoah sat at a table with Jenn and Geekhead. The three of them were in the same picture as he introduced them, knowing that ninety percent of his audience had been watching the two of them analyze the election for months. Makeup aside, Jenn and Geekhead looked appropriately relaxed, but also exhausted. The exhausted part reflected their physical situation perfectly as around one o'clock the previous morning, Geekhead had found the nerve and the energy to give, and Jenn had accepted, an engagement ring, which set off yet another bout of serious love making. "Jenn, you and Horace Cicerone have been spending virtually one hundred percent of your time thinking through the possibility that this election would go to the House of Representatives. What happens now?"

"Thanks, Arthur," Jenn answered. "Maybe not one hundred percent of our time, but we think we finally used all our energy to get the right answer to this last night. We were exhausted. Right, Horace?"

Horace turned beet red. They had gone to great lengths at the station to hide a romance that had blossomed at a pace neither of them understood, but both treasured. At that moment, the great sense of humor that Jenn had discovered, and was trying to get Geekhead to display on television, finally escaped. "Yes," Geekhead responded, "we spent last night trying to think this through from every position." Two red beets behind the table.

"If Senator Vincent cannot scare up twenty-six unfaithful electors, this election goes to the House of Representatives. In the history of American elections, there have only been eight unfaithful electors and none of them have ever impacted the results of the Electoral College. But if, and it is a big if, Texas were to send its electoral votes to Vincent instead of Roland, Vincent becomes President of the United States.

"If that does not happen, there is no precedent for an electoral vote winner, who effectively has no political party, being placed before the House of Representatives. And what would be the reaction if the House selects Senator Roland with him winning only Texas and a few other Southern states. And the rules in the House of Representatives are pretty odd as each state only has a single vote in the election to become President. To become President, the candidate must win a majority of the States. This just might not be possible. So, if the House of Representatives cannot get to a conclusion, finally, if the House of Representatives does not conclude its work by January 20, 2013, the Vice President becomes the Acting President and begins to form his own Cabinet."

Jenn: "Horace, what about the unfaithful electoral voter? Given the harshness of this election, unfaithful has to be something that can be expected and anticipated. To me, despite that possibility, unfaithful has to be as far away from the right answer for an elector as unfaithfulness by someone who has only been engaged only a few hours."

Ninoah looked at Jenn quizzically as this was one of the strangest analogies he had ever heard. *What is going on here?*

Geekhead paused a moment too long and again turned unreasonably red. Ninoah broke in. "Horace, you have me taking notes here. It sounds to me like you don't think this election is even close to over. Why don't you give that a thought and we'll take a break and come right back. Well, we have something akin to a very odd three-way tie here and we'll break that down in a few minutes." Fox News went to commercial break.

Virtually never upset with anything, Ninoah began screaming at Jenn and Geekhead. "What is going on? It sounds to me like you two are having a personal conversation while discussing the most important issue of our time. Now, grow up or this is going to be the last show either of you ever do on this network, at least with me. Your guy O'Brien marches to the beat of his own drummer, so who knows if he wants to work with you two clowns!"

"EEEEEEE, I'm sorry Arthur," Jenn giggled, "Geekhead asked me to marry him last night!"

"You're kidding? Really? You must have said yes. Congratulations!"

"Wait a minute? You two look like a modern Ken and Barbie, a multiracial Ken and Barbie, but Ken and Barbie. If we blast this engagement out at the audience and work it right, we can triple our audience." This was coming from the show's producer Grant McConical. He never missed an opportunity and absolutely would have turned dog food into a gourmet meal for another two share. He did not offer congratulations or even consider saying something personal, he was as serious as a relief pitcher facing Alex Rodriguez with the bases loaded in the ninth inning of a tied game. "That's the way I am going to play it. Guys, get that press release onto the web right now and make sure everyone knows the love birds are breaking down this election on live TV.

"Jenn, put that ring on right now and don't you dare tell me you want your folks to know first or you want Geekhead there to ask your father if he can have your hand. If your dad is a traditionalist, just hope he is not watching, and wasn't watching for the last ten minutes."

"I can't do that. I need to call my mom."

"Do you think she is watching?"

"Of course."

"OK, you get two choices. You can either put that ring on and we'll see if anyone notices or I can just scroll the announcement below the two of you on the screen. There is no way you have time to call mom. You apparently had a whole day to do that already."

"EEEEE, please!"

Geekhead jumped into the conversation. "Jenn, it will be great. No one will notice and we can call your mom during a break and tease her that she did not notice." That sealed the deal and out, and on, came the ring.

"Let's rock and roll. We are live and going live in 5-4-3-2-1..."

"We are back. Horace and Jenn are here to break this election down for us. Horace, take us through this unfaithful voter thing first."

Both Jenn and Horace breathed a quick sigh of relief, as it appeared Arthur Ninoah was handing them the stage without embarrassing them at all.

"No, that's not right. Before you do that, Horace, why don't you get down on one knee and ask this woman to marry you like you are supposed to?" Laughter, from the stagehands, which could be heard on millions of television screens throughout the world as it rippled through the assembled crew as Jenn and Horace again turned into a pair of beets.

"Oh, this is going to be such a memorable election night on so many levels," offered Geekhead to fifteen million people. Almost robotically, Geekhead went down on one knee and offered the traditional, "Will you marry me?" In what was a complete shock to Jenn, Geekhead began to cry.

Jenn was flummoxed and could only manage a, "Yes, absolutely, yes." Then, as if someone had scripted the scene, she got out of her chair, pulled Geekhead to his feet and hugged him.

Ninoah: "Now, kiss her, invite everyone listening to your wedding and tell us who is going to be the next President of the United States." Ninoah knew he had just been involved in television history and that this scene would be viewed by almost 200 million Americans on YouTube and countless others over the next twenty-four hours. Pretty fun stuff. The two red beets merged into one for a little longer than appropriate, giggled meaningfully and Geekhead returned to his chair and turned to the camera.

"As I was saying," again laughter by the crew, "this is going to be a complicated process."

At that point, Ninoah started to laugh out loud. "Come on, Geekhead, leave the double entendres. Go and use that mega brain that Jenn apparently finds so attractive." This was the first time anyone had used the term *Geekhead* on the air and as everyone on the set knew that Horace Cicerone and Geekhead were one and the same, no explanation was offered.

The producer was having the moment of a lifetime. The station's website was exploding and at near capacity with almost one hundred percent of the e-mails wishing the couple best wishes. Not missing a beat, below Jenn and Geekhead on the screen were the scrolling words: *Cicerone asks Jennifer Cho to marry him as election results are announced.* This was so unusual that the other networks picked up the announcement before they realized it would cost them viewers.

Breaking every rule of television, Big Red wished the couple best wishes just moments before Merritt Goodman informed her that she should never, ever say anything nice about another show that was in progress. After the admonishment, Goodman couldn't resist and asked Big Red: "Here is your opportunity, Kid. Call that big time lawyer Talbot and have him come down to the studio right now and propose on live television. We can go for the who is the most beautiful television anchor who has gotten engaged in the last twenty-four hours contest."

Big Red just shrugged at Goodman. That being said, she could not help being a bit jealous of Jennifer Cho, who she did not know. *I can't let that birth time clock tick along too far. We need to talk about this at home.* Talbot had not joined her for the trip to the Republican Convention and he had begun to seem distant. *I can't lose him as the father of my children.*

Forty years of television told the producer, and this was confirmed a few days later, that at this moment in history, just a few moments after the announcement, the entire nation was watching Fox News and the three mainstream networks were alone. While each other network had an expert on the House of Representatives, Arthur Ninoah had the lovebirds and one of them appeared to be a genius. It did not get any better than this. Even if Geekhead really was light years behind The Professor, no one on stage or at home could have possibly known and as it turned out, Geekhead was ahead of everyone except The Professor.

At home in the Hamptons, Missy O'Brien snuggled in next to her husband. "Honey, you didn't tell me those two were dating, they are soooooo sweet."

Bill O'Brien looked at the screen and thought: *Well, you are one self-centered son of a bitch to find this out watching TV at home,* while he responded to Missy: "Missy, you know I can keep a secret better than anyone on the planet!" *Maybe I am going to get lucky tonight, myself.*

~

WEDNESDAY, NOVEMBER 7, 2012

From the day's *Washington Post*, a front page editorial by Randy Kraus:

FROM THREE TO FIVE

Two nights ago, the citizens of the United States went to bed thinking that they would elect one of three individuals to be the President of the United States on Tuesday, November 6, 2012. This morning, they have awakened to the reality that as the result of the election, there are now five realistic contenders to become the President or Acting President of the United States. Under the arcane rules of the Constitution of the United States, this decision will not be made by a vote of the people; that time is passed. The decision will be made by the people's representatives in the House of Representatives.

But who and where that decision will be made is not quite as precise as it could be. While it will likely go to the House of Representatives, nothing is certain. The ultimate selection may be made by the Electoral College, the House of Representatives or the United States Senate. And if the decision is made by the United States Senate and there is an Acting President, it can be changed by the House of Representatives at any time by their selecting a President until January 20, 2016.

The London bookies have established the odds on who will be the President of the United States or the Acting President of the United States on January 30, 2013:

1. The President   9-5
2. Senator Vincent 3-1
3. Professor Scotch   5-1
4. Congressman Roland   8-1
5. The Vice President   18-1

In the House of Representatives where the President is selected, each state receives a single vote. The states can vote for any of the three highest vote getters in the Electoral College, no one else. To become President, one of those three must obtain the affirmative votes of at least twenty-six states.

In the Senate where the Vice President is selected, each senator gets a single vote. The senators can vote only for one of the two highest Electoral College vote getters and the winner must receive a majority of the votes. If there is a tie, the current Vice President will have the opportunity to elect himself. Only the Republican Vice Presidential candidate, Bobby Joe Blankley has been eliminated. This should prove particularly interesting because the Republicans have a clear majority in the United States Senate. Will the Republicans vote en mass for a Democrat or a "Democrat?" Will the Republicans make a deal with the President?

If the House of Representatives is unable to get a majority of the States to select a President, the Vice President becomes the Acting President until a selection is made.

One needs to ask if any of this makes sense. What were the Founders thinking?

What do we know? Yesterday, we believed there was the possibility that any of three men could be President. Now the reality is that any of five men could be the President (or Acting President). From three to five!

~

In one of the strange moments of the fairly new century, an entire nation learned the rules of a political game at the same time. The rules that most thoughtful citizens thought they understood when they graduated from high school were not the reality. It did not matter whether they were a PhD in political science or a non-high school graduate working on the family farm, no one had fully understood the Pandora's Box of a competitive three-party system in 2012 if no one candidate received more than fifty percent of the electoral votes. It did not matter that Horace Cicerone had been talking about these rules for months; most of the country had assumed that election night would be the end of a presidential race. It was still a shock that once in the House of Representatives, the election was decided by a state-by-state vote. It was a major shock.

~

Molly Tom had stayed in Cleveland for the election. The Professor had cleared the missing of classes with her other three professors explaining that her consulting role would end immediately after the election and she would be on the stage in Cleveland with the future President of the United States when the counting ended. This was a once in a lifetime opportunity she should not miss. Who knew, she graduated in June and if, in fact, George Vincent was the President of the United States, she could likely find herself with a job inside the White House. He would certainly try to make that happen and based upon the reports he was getting from Wade and Woo, she was really very, very good.

While the result was not definitive Tuesday night, for a twenty-one-year-old student, the evening was magical. She had been invited to dinner with the insiders at the request of Senator Vincent. She sat next to Milton Woo and took a certain pleasure that Joshua Ybarra was not invited. During the evening, George Vincent had lauded everyone. Vincent had gone to great lengths to thank Milton Woo as the greatest fundraiser and technical guru in the history of modern elections. He had lauded Molly as a key expert in the Constitution and a fast rising star in political consulting. He went on to celebrate The Professor's advice and his insight into the entire election, but yet again mentioning Molly's anticipation.

The next morning, Molly found herself, for the second time, staring at a sleeping Milton Woo. Last night had been exciting politically and personally. Absolutely sober as the election results appeared, she found herself wanting to be with Milton in a full relationship, not as a one night sexual provider or recipient. Sometime between Saturday night and Tuesday night, she had figured out that this man was perfect for her. During that period, they had been feverishly working on polling and getting out the vote and he had been continuing to mentor her in what was then a twenty-four-hour-a-day finale. He was just so sweet, so innocent and such a good person. Regardless of her personal pulling back in their relationship, he had been wonderful, still the teacher.

For a while Tuesday night and very early Wednesday morning, she was unsure whether Milton was going to be a willing participant as the new boyfriend or maybe something more. He told her at one point in the evening that he was not sure he could trust her after their previous experience. She had hurt him deeply. Fairly late in the evening, she had literally chased him into the parking lot and sobbed into his shoulder about how unfair she had been and how she now thought, was certain, that she was in love with him. As Milton was still smitten with Molly, the only ally Molly needed now was time. The evening had been sufficiently long. They were still waiting this morning for the West Coast results and time was, in fact, her ally.

Momentarily, she decided she would wake him up and they would spend the rest of the morning refreshing their sexual relationship. Last night, he had shown that he was as quick a learner in the art of lovemaking as he was with all of his computer skills. For Molly, this was a morning different and better than any she had ever experienced. She needed to wake Milton up so she could make him happy, then happier and finally happiest; this was not an emotion she had previously encountered in her college relationships. Maybe this was the definition of love, the unbridled desire to make another person happy. Previously, it had been like it was at school, what could her companion do for her? For Milton, still asleep, he was right back where he was before, absolutely and totally enthralled with this West Coast genius, hopelessly committed. And when Milton awakened, his goal would be identical to hers; he wanted to make his new girlfriend as happy as possible.

After they enjoyed each other for a few hours, they went to lunch where they agreed that they *might* be in love and that although her role with the campaign was probably over, they would talk every day by telephone or Internet. He would find excuses to be in Southern California and she would work the campaign organization for more visits to Cleveland. "Love conquers all."

~

The story that should have been reported on every media exit point should have focused on the results of the election in terms of the lack of a winner in the presidential election from an electoral calculation. However, given that most of the media wanted the President to have a second four-year term, the mainstream media, their spinners and his spinners almost exclusively focused on the President winning the popular vote by almost six million votes over George Vincent and thirteen million votes over Paul Roland. While they understood the race was going to be decided in the Halls of Congress, the popular vote was easy and popular with the regular viewers of the left-wing cable shows and the mainstream media. It was an easy story and the story being promoted by the White House.

The focus by talk radio and Fox News was on the Electoral College and the popular vote.

The President received the largest number of actual voters. Senator Vincent received the largest number of states, the most electoral votes and was second in the popular vote. Congressman Paul Roland had successfully obtained six states and that sent the election into the beltway. What would happen in the beltway was anyone and everyone's guess.

Lost in that discussion was an important element towards ultimate resolution of the election. Not a single state was facing a recount in its presidential vote. Every state had a winner and two losers. There was neither a congressional race nor a senatorial race without a clear winner. This would be very important in that there would be no fight over whether the electoral delegates were legally constituted and no one would be arguing that the House of Representatives had some obligation to wait until some close election was decided by a recount.

Chaos might occur as the result of the presidential election, but chaos to the third power would not occur in the House of Representatives or the Senate with respect to who was permitted to vote in the Electoral College while an election languished in a state or Federal Court.

On a national basis, the Republicans found themselves with 214 House of Representatives seats and 57 seats in the Senate. The Democrats found themselves with 221 seats in the House and 43 seats in the Senate. The Democrats had reversed half of their 2010 losses in the House of Representatives. In the Senate where there were 33 seats in contention and 23 were Democratic, the Republicans picked up 10 seats. In a great oddity, the House of

Representatives went from Republican to Democrat and the Senate went from Democrat to Republican.

A CNN reporter interviewing the head of the Black Caucus in the House of Representatives was asking interesting questions on Wednesday morning. Reporter to black, New York Democratic Congressman Elijah Jones: "Well Congressman, in an effort not to plant any responses in your head. I will only ask: What do you think?"

Congressman Jones: "I believe that the people have spoken and that the President has received the highest number in the popular vote and he should be the President of the United States until January 2016. What other answer could one get in a democracy?"

Reporter: "It is clear, Sir, that none of the candidates have a sufficient number of votes to win in the Electoral College. Are you saying that the electors, or whatever they are called—I apologize for my uncertainty on the proper name—should be required to vote for the individual with the highest number of votes nationally?"

Jones: "I am saying that the President has won this election fair and square and he is the winner."

Reporter: "Respectfully, Sir, the President was second in the number of states won yesterday and second in the electoral vote, both by quite a bit. The president almost received fewer electoral votes than Senator McCain achieved in 2008 and that was considered a landslide by the President. While he won the..."

Jones: "That should just be an asterisk in the history books. This is 2012, not 1796 for God's sake. You cannot think that a White Congress would take an election away from a black man who received the highest number of votes? We are a nation still at war; we still have poverty and global climate change. The winner is the winner."

Reporter: "Congressman, are you aware that in the House of Representatives, each state receives a single vote? How will that impact the decision on who is President of the United States?"

Jones: "That cannot be. That would bury the black vote completely. There is not a single state where we comprise anything close to a majority. We will not stand for that, Mr. Reporter!"

Reporter: "Thank you, Congressman Jones. Back to you in headquarters. This should be one interesting experience. My sense is that my question about one state, one vote caught Congressman Jones by surprise."

Both Geekhead and Jenn had been up the entire night on television after virtually not sleeping at all the prior evening. They were exhausted. In Geekhead, the stirrings of a national crisis had for the moment replaced both his stirring for Jenn and his need for a couple of hours of serious sleep. For this interview, she was watching from the sidelines, as he and Bill O'Brien became the two talking heads on live television.

"Dr. Cicerone, there seems to be very little understanding of what happens at this point of the election process. Some are calling for the President to be the President of the United States because he has won the popular vote, some are calling for Senator Vincent to be president because he has won the highest number of states, and I assume some are calling for Congressman Paul Roland to be the president because he is, I don't know, the tallest of the three. Who is the President of the United States?"

"Not meaning to appear flippant, the only certainty is that the President will be the President of the United States until at least January 20, 2013. After that, all bets are off. What we do know is that any of the three presidential candidates can be elected president and either Jordon Scotch or the current VP will be the vice president. The only sure loser so far is Bobby Joe Blakely, Congressman Paul Roland's running mate. He is out of the game, but he will be a senator until at least January 2017." Geekhead had begun to be both polished and relaxed in front of the camera. It did not hurt that Jenn was sitting across the table and obviously hanging on her man's every word.

"Take me a bit through the details, Doctor."

"As a first step, the Electoral College will vote during December. I expect that there will be a great deal of haggling between here and there, but the Electoral College is—forgive my choice of words—mostly local politicians, political groupies and political hacks. There will be lots of discussions about these individuals voting for either the President because of his popular vote win or one of the other two candidates for whatever reason, but it is terribly unlikely any of this would occur in numbers sufficient to provide a winner. It is effectively a mathematical impossibility for the President or Congressman Roland. I guess, in theory, it could happen for Vincent. If the Texas delegation decided to vote entirely for George Vincent, he would become the president, but I just don't see it. Vincent is either a Democrat or a member of the American Exceptionalism Party and those Texas electoral delegates are Republicans from a state that voted overwhelmingly for Paul Roland. A change by an entire delegation would be unprecedented. But,

Texas has no constraints on their electors. No constraints, just as the Founders envisioned the system would work. I completely rule out the possibility that Vincent or Rolland could get multiple states to ignore their voters."

"Doctor, are you saying that the Electoral College is under no obligation to vote as directed by their state's voters?"

"Yes, Bill, that is exactly what I am saying, kind of. The Electoral College goes back to the 1700s and the thought was that the voters should only provide a preference and the more learned Americans who were the electors should make the final decision. This has all been lost to history and there have been virtually no electors that have ignored their constituencies in the past two hundred plus years of the Republic. Yes, every so often an elector did not follow his state's voters, but that has been very rare and never meaningful. Further, there are laws in many states to force the electors to vote this way or that, but, I note the penalties are quite small in most states if the elector goes out on his or her own and votes for someone else, the unfaithful elector. The state rules are after the fact and I don't think they would impact the result of the unfaithful voter's vote. I do not see this as a likely problem."

"You sound like you foresee a problem."

"Oh yes, Sir, I do."

"And what is that, Doctor?"

"Well, I don't know that the House of Representatives will be able to select a president and I don't know that the public understands the rules. Let me explain briefly: The Members of the House of Representatives do not each get a single vote. Each state gets a single vote and to win, a majority of states needs to vote for one of the three candidates. When you consider the fact that there are two political parties, three candidates and several states where there are an equal number of Democrats and Republicans, this could be a tough challenge. Remember, this is a House of Representatives that would have trouble agreeing that Wednesday followed Tuesday."

"Are you saying there will be no President of the United States? Would the President remain president until the House makes its decision?"

"No, Sir. The United States Senate will pick a Vice President between the current Vice President and Jordon Scotch. Their process should not take more than a few minutes and that person would become Acting President on January 20, 2012, and remain so until the House of Representatives selects a President. Should for some reason, if the Senate did not accomplish their task, the Acting President would become the new Speaker of the House assuming the Speaker was willing.

"The Speaker of the House will be selected before all of the other voting begins. But this will not happen. The Senate at fifty-seven votes for the Republicans is going to select Jordon Scotch. He is registered as a Republican and he is not the Vice President."

"I am afraid you are serious, Dr. Cicerone, aren't you?"

"Yes I am. I don't think the Founders had modern politics in mind when they decided on these rules."

"Thank you, Dr. Cicerone. I am certain that our viewers will be seeing a great deal of you during the next several months! And congratulations, I saw last night that you are engaged to our friend Jennifer Cho. What a catch! I assume that I will be giving the bride away."

The cameras went off Geekhead as he looked at Jenn off camera. Even without any makeup she was as radiant as any and every recently engaged woman.

Geekhead went back to their initial conversation and reminded O'Brien that there were more than a few technical issues that were not clear if things went in one direction or another. His specific prognosis had not been asked and therefore had not been answered.

On OBC, the focus was the same, but the presentations were less technical, more pronounced with talking heads taking more strident positions. The designated black intellect talked about the popular vote and the possibility that the black vote would effectively be negated by the rules under the Constitution. This undesignated and self-appointed religious leader of the black community talked about the popular vote and his lack of interest in rural America having a disproportionate representation in the Senate under these "silly rules." With respect to the House of Representatives, he asked how John Bronkin of North Dakota could have precisely the same vote as all of the Congressmen from the State of New York?

The conservative panel member with the black-rimmed glasses was one of talk radio's key conservative voices. He spoke to the solemn duty of all to perform according to the Constitution. His view was that everyone knew the rules or should have known the rules before the game began and no one changes the rules in the middle of the game.

The woman liberal on the panel was beside herself with the prospect that California and New York, with more than sixty-five percent of the vote going to the President, were being reduced to only two votes. This was crazy and she talked on and on about the National Voting Compact that would have handed the election to the President, as it should have done.

The host, Big Red, was in her glory. She made it through the past three weeks with flying colors. Her ratings were good. On a personal level, she had come to the conclusion overnight that it was time to marry Lawyer Talbot, her long-time lawyer boyfriend and his response was precisely what she had hoped. He was ready to get married in twenty-four hours or as soon as possible and ready to start a family immediately, so long as the first baby arrived after the wedding. She could become the most popular anchor newsperson on the planet or a stay-at-home mom, whichever she preferred. He simply wanted her on the condition that they would be a family and they would not become DINKS—double income, no kids. She had been right about him.

Big Red decided to bait the conservative. "So Thaddeus, why does it make sense that an entity like the House of Representatives, with its eleven percent popularity and confidence numbers, should be allowed to determine who becomes president?"

~

From Congressman Paul Roland:

FOR IMMEDIATE RELEASE
ELECTORAL COLLEGE MUST REPRESENT THEIR CONSTITUENTS

WASHINGTON D.C., November 7, 2012, 10:00 a.m. — Voting by the citizens of the United States of America was completed and tallied last night. Senator Blankley and I finished third in the Electoral College and third in the popular vote. Senator Vincent won the most states and the most electoral votes. The President had the highest number of actual votes in the popular vote.

The Founding Fathers, in drafting our Constitution, considered the possibility that the elections for President and Vice President of the United States of America might not produce a winner and in such a case as we have today, provided that the President would be selected in the House of Representatives and the Vice President in the United States Senate. Although Senator Blankley will not be eligible to be selected by the United States Senate, we both support the Constitution of the United States and will support the President and Vice President who will be selected by Congress. I hope that I am selected to be the President of the United States under the rules crafted by the Founders some two hundred plus years ago.

We have already read in the newspapers and the blogosphere and heard on the radio and television that there are individuals attempting to convince electoral voters to vote for whomever they please rather than the individuals selected by their individual states. While that might well be to the benefit of Senator Blankley or myself, we strongly urge all of the members of the Electoral College to vote as they were directed by their individual state's voters. Any other decision violates the spirit of elections and neither Senator Blankley nor I wishes to be elected in a manner that undermines individuals' voting decisions in their individual states. We believe that the members of the Electoral College have an obligation to their individual voters to affirm their voting decisions.

~

From Senator George Vincent:

FOR IMMEDIATE RELEASE
ELECTORAL COLLEGE MUST REPRESENT THEIR CONSTITUENTS

WASHINGTON D.C., November 7, 2012, 12:01 a.m. — We Americans voted in record numbers yesterday and when the voting was completed, we did not complete the process to determine the next President and Vice President of the United States of America. Our system requires the Electoral College to vote and then, assuming that no candidate receives the necessary 270 electoral votes, the Presidency will be decided by the United States House of Representatives and the Vice Presidency will be decided by the United States Senate. These rules were written more than two hundred years ago and provide a process whereby our elected representatives determine our executive leaders. I support the process.

While some ballots are still being counted in several states, Jordon Scotch and I have already read and heard that we should solicit the electors from Texas and several other states in an effort to become the President and Vice President of the United States through the Electoral College. With those States' electoral votes, we could achieve the necessary 270 electoral votes to be elected. While we understand that there is not a single member of the American Exceptionalism Party in the House of Representatives or the United States Senate and that makes our opportunity to be elected in those bodies difficult, we have no interest in making a deal to achieve the Presidency or Vice Presidency. That would be contrary to our values. We shared our values with the electorate during the campaign and we intend to continue to follow our values throughout this process and into the next four years if I am elected President of the United States in the House of Representative and Dr. Scotch is elected Vice President of the United States in the United States Senate.

Because we do not know and have not met with any electors and do not intend to do so, we ask every elector to vote as the voters of their states voted. Nothing could be less appropriate than for Jordon and I to be elected through a process that we would find personally repugnant.

~

There was no press release from the White House. The Pillsbury Dough Boy did not address the press on November 7, 2012.

~

This was an unusual political meeting in the Oval Office. Only the two key members of his team were in the Oval Office with the President. The President was wearing an open blue, collared shirt and Levis to go with his game face. He looked terribly underweight and tired. He sat behind his desk rather than on one of the long brown sofas where he usually met with staff visitors. Despite the fact that Mrs. President was upstairs, there was an ashtray full of cigarette butts and a cigarette carefully being held between two very tense fingers on his left hand. Both Herman Sackman and Ray Matta were coincidentally attired in nearly identical grey suits, Sackman with a blue tie and Matta with a yellow tie. Despite the time, there was neither lunch nor a cup of coffee in front of either guest. The President had a glass filled with Coca-Cola and an identical backup glass immediately to its left. The remnants of a burger and fries were off to the side with yet a third glass, empty, except for the ice, that likely had contained another soda a few minutes earlier.

Like most presidents, the President had redone the Oval Office in a style which he preferred and this president had been actively involved in every decision. He had his favorite furniture and a brown rug with his favorite quotations. Every time he looked at the rug, he became livid with his wife who had suggested a specific Martin Luther King quotation that King had used widely and the President had used in nearly every campaign speech during his career. Unfortunately, literally, the day he unveiled his new office digs, it had been pointed out to him that the quote had actually been a favorite quote *of*, not by, Martin Luther King. The author, Theodore Parker had been a bald, bespectacled white abolitionist who died shortly before the Civil War.

"What now?" started the President.

Sackman had settled into one of the two straight-backed yellow chairs expecting a morning dissertation on the campaign, the election results, his job, etc. The President was actually starting a meeting with a question, unusual.

"What now, Herman? This seems to be your turf."

"The numbers are stark. I know we all know them, but let's do a careful review of where we are: You decisively won the popular vote, but that being said, it looks like you will only have 194 electoral votes…"

The President interrupted Sackman. "Should that be it? I received the most votes. Why in 2012 is that not the end of it?"

"Mr. President, with all due respect, I am going to assume that the question is rhetorical and keep going."

"No, it is not rhetorical. That is the way it should be. I won!" The President was standing and almost hollering at Sackman, pointing with his left hand, the live cigarette again resting in the ashtray.

Sackman just stared at the President. For one of the first times in the years they had been together, Sackman wondered whether the President had a firm grip on himself. The guy taught Constitutional law; maybe he was just an adjunct professor, but every schoolgirl knew that the calculation was based on electoral votes. What was this about?

"This is just wrong. Continue."

"Restating from the top: You decisively won the popular vote, but that being said, it looks like you will only have 194 electoral votes, not many more than McCain in 2008. Second, George Vincent equally decisively won the electoral vote, but did not get to the necessary 270 votes to win."

Sackman paused and decided he was simply pissed at the President and expanded on the Vincent vote. "Vincent received 236 electoral votes and was, and is, only 34 electoral votes short of being President of the United States on January 20. And regardless of his press release, if somehow he gets Paul Roland to run interference for him with the Republicans and Texas casts their votes for him, he will be president on January 20.

The President interrupted again. Neither the tone of his voice nor the volume had changed. "They can't do that. Those delegates are committed to each candidate…"

"Dammit, no, get your head out of your ass," responded Sackman. It had been a long night and he was venting, something he had never done in the Oval Office previously.

"What did you say? This meeting is over. Get out. Get your coat and we will send you your stuff in twenty-four hours! Just like Mallory."

Matta decided to be the peacemaker: "Mr. President, Herman is just tired and he didn't mean anything by his choice of words." No one had moved and Matta guessed the moment had passed. "But, let's get to the heart of this. Both Vincent and Roland have issued press releases over the past few hours indicating that they do not want their electors, or any electors, taking it upon themselves to undermine the election as determined by the voters. I don't think this is a problem, but we will monitor Texas very carefully. The magic here is that if Vincent was a Republican, I think we might have a serious problem with the electors. But, I just do not picture the Republicans of Texas turning an election to a Democrat, even, I guess, a former Democrat."

By now, Sackman had calmed down and the President lit up yet another cigarette. Sackman, realizing the crisis was past, continued the conversation. "I see the game as making sure that Vincent does not get the necessary votes in the House on the first or second ballot. After that...

The President: "Wait, what do you mean after the second ballot. I was not kidding, I got the most votes and they should pick me in the first vote."

"Not going to happen, Mr. President. I think we will dodge the biggest bullet on the first ballot where the vote will either be on party lines or in concert with the election. Whichever way the first ballot goes, the second ballot will be the other of these two described ballots. Our job is to figure out how to get you elected after the third vote and long after Jordon Scotch is elected Vice President."

"Do you guys really think the Senate would pick an outsider?"

Matta: "With fifty-seven votes, that Republican Senate would pick Heidi Klum before they would re-elect the Vice President. Actually, I have watched her on television a couple of times, I think she is pretty smart, but no one is in Scotch's intellectual league. Beloved is gone.

"Again, the game as I see it is to start calling the Members, especially these new guys. I'll get them quickly whipped into shape. You may have to borrow a box at a Skin's game. You may have to make few promises you don't intend to keep. Same o', same o.'"

"OK, enough, I am going to go upstairs and get yelled at for smelling like tobacco. God, sometimes I hate this job." The President got up, security appeared and he was off to his residential quarters.

Not a thought was given to a press release, which was a mistake. It wasn't a big mistake, but a mistake just the same.

~

THURSDAY, NOVEMBER 8, 2012

The President allowed the Pillsbury Doughboy to effectively introduce him. The press secretary made a few introductory comments and then the President arrived. After a few meaningless remarks, the President made a few meaningful comments.

"There has been a great amount said and written about Tuesday's election. I am disappointed that the election will result in a decision made by politicians rather than the voters. I achieved a significant victory in the popular vote and expect to be elected president in the House of Representatives. Today, some two hundred years after the initial signing of the Constitution, it is difficult to imagine the candidate with the most votes is not immediately considered the winner. Again, while there is a procedure in place to look to the House of Representatives, and while there are more states with Republican representatives, I must assume they will do the right thing and elect the popular vote winner as president.

"I urge everyone to contact your Member of the House of Representatives and indicate that you believe that the winner of the popular vote, the winner of the popular vote by millions and millions of votes is the President. This is simply the right thing to do." The President was speaking in his staccato style as usual but was one half octave higher in presentation and looked exhausted.

"My staff tells me that there is a belief that the conservatives are going to try to purchase this election in the House of Representatives and try to eliminate your first minority president. We cannot let that happen."

The President's presentation went on for another fifteen minutes, but the premise remained unchanged. After he was done, he determined to take a few questions.

"Mr. President, Senator Vincent received forty more electoral votes than you in the Electoral College and if Texas should vote for him, he would become President of the United States. How does that calculation work into your comments that you should be president because you received the highest number of actual votes?"

"I think you answered your own question. I received the highest number of votes and, I think, any reasonable person would conclude that I should be the president."

"But, Sir, there have been elections where the highest vote getter did not become president and you received far less than half of the votes in the election. Don't…"

"This is 2012, not 1820. I received the most votes and anyone and everyone should expect that I have been re-elected."

"Doesn't talk like this increase the chance that your supporters, already aroused, will take to the streets?"

"No, that is insulting and bigoted. I have read the Republican's comments about my belief that I should already have been re-elected and I believe they are trying to provoke a reaction from the minority communities. They should be embarrassed."

~

FRIDAY, NOVEMBER 9, 2012

The riots that the President promised would not occur, did occur. They started following the President's speech on the night of the seventh. While turnout for the election was significantly less in the minority communities than in 2008, the minority communities had overwhelmingly voted for the President and he had won the states with huge urban minority communities: California, Illinois, Michigan, New York and Pennsylvania. (Los Angeles, Chicago, Detroit, New York City, and Philadelphia.) These states were won by overwhelming margins.

As there was a common belief by the minority communities in these cities that the President had done nothing or little special for them, the riots were a surprise to the leadership in these communities. However, a certain segment of social scientists saw the riots as a sign of general anger with the lack of visible improvement in these communities with unemployment and drug cabals worse rather than better after four years of this president. The excuse or opportunity for rioting was visible to anyone who looked. The words of these social scientists on cable and mainstream television seemed to provide fuel for the riots. The President easily won the popular vote and yet he was not president.

The President's success in achieving a popular vote victory and not winning the presidency was beyond the understanding, or the desire to understand, for most of the rioters. Of course, the percentage of rioters that actually voted was well below thirty percent. Greed had become a factor in any racially charged opportunity. More than a few saw a good race riot as an opportunity to pick up a free pair of Nikes or rape a grocery store. This was demonstrated so clearly previously in Oakland, California, in 2010. This, coupled with the President's vitriolic speech after the votes were counted resulted in a situation where anger plus greed equaled opportunity.

Two nights and three days of rioting occurred in most metropolitan minority communities. For the two nights and a bit of the second full day, the President was silent and this was seen as affirmation to the rioters, if they chose to see it as affirmation, and many did. Police forces around the nation were ready, but overwhelmed; most governors acted with dispatch and National Guard units were in place by the end of the second day.

The coverage of the rioting was a fascination unto itself. Within the confines of the national networks, there was a note of fulfilled expectation and a sense of this was what was to be expected. This did nothing to calm the streets. Full-time coverage on local television stations and the technology of the Internet, Blackberries and Twitter told the rioters exactly where the police were and where the opportunities were as well. On the cable news stations, the more liberal cable stations were presenting the view that, while not certain, the rejection of a minority president in the Electoral College was unacceptable to the American public. The view that the President should be re-elected based on the popular vote was covered without exception and occasionally to the exclusion of a complete discussion of the Electoral College and the thinking of the Founding Fathers. That the President might not stay in office was paramount in thinking and action. In these discussions, the argument that the Constitution of the United States was no more than a silly two-hundred-year-old piece of paper was presented over and over again until it seemed like a fact rather than an argument. This was not a testament to the education being given to successful newscasters or students in lower social economic categories over the past thirty years.

On Fox News, the discussion focused on why the President remained silent and was not fulfilling his obligation to lead the country. On talk radio, the talk was far worse than on Fox News television. The word *impeachment* was being used with surprising regularity and a few commentators quickly began to infer that the unsecured borders were mainly a test case for these riots. The possibility of Americans taking their rifles and pistols out of their garages and attics and defending their property was discussed in both historical and practical terms. It quickly became very scary.

On the morning following the second night of rioting, the President appeared on national television and demanded that the rioters return to their homes and families and declared Monday, November 12 a "Day of Reflection" for the American public. In four cities, he called out the regular army to regain control of the cities, but his request to end the riots was the most significant factor in the fires being put down and the communities returning to a resemblance of normal.

To the fury of the other candidates, the President declared again that he had won the popular vote and that he fully expected that the House of Representatives would elect him as president in early January. This mantra was immediately picked up by the national media, but at least the nation calmed for the moment.

Senator Suppling, a Democrat from the Midwest took to the floor of the US Senate on Monday, the National Day of Reflection, and made the following remarks: "Members of the US Senate, tonight I speak from the heart. I represent a small state and have chosen during my eight years in this body to represent that state and not attempt to become the President of the United States. I am not today, or was I yesterday, interested in holding that office.

"Today, I suggest the sitting President of the United States remind himself that he taught constitutional law as an adjunct at the University of Chicago and that the United States of America is bound by the Constitution of the United States and that his remarks regarding his popular vote victory were inaccurate, incorrect and unacceptable." The word *adjunct* was not heard as a compliment of any kind.

Two minutes before Senator Suppling began his remarks, there were but four senators on the floor. However, his reputation as a straight shooter who rarely made presentations on the floor and his reputation as one of the US Senate's more intelligent members began to bring more senators into the Chamber, almost before his first words were uttered.

"For four years, I have listened to an elected president speak to the world as if the United States had but a single leader, that being the President. As a Member of this body, I remember his presentation upon receiving the Nobel Prize and thinking that this man who started every sentence with the word *I*, believed he had become the sole owner of the United States of America, as if he had purchased a company. Never in either recent or long-term memory did a President of the United States appear to have less of an understanding of his leadership opportunities or his position. And in the past few days, his silence, and then the totality of his recent remarks, has brought disgrace to himself at levels that belong with the Huey Longs that have occasionally appeared in, yes, this body. But never before, no, never before, did such a man reside at One Pennsylvania Avenue."

Almost sixty senators were now in the Chamber and most were hushed in silence until Senator Hastings screamed, "Traitor," at the senator. This was followed by the sound of a hard gavel and the words, "Out of order," from the chair.

Senator Suppling was completely silent and stared long and hard at Senator Hastings. Waiting almost ten full seconds, Suppling looked even harder at the senator and began again: "No, Sir, perhaps I have been weak during the past four years in not commenting at the actions of this elected President of the United States. But I am no more a traitor today than I was as I trudged through the jungles of Vietnam so many years ago or when the people of my state first elected me to this office. You, on the other hand, have been no more than a jester in the court of a medieval king and for that, the people of your state should be embarrassed, my dear friend, as we say in this Chamber."

A pin-dropping silence resulted momentarily as these types of remarks were as infrequent in the United States Senate as snow in the valleys of Ecuador. Then hands and cries for an apology, points of order and responsive remarks. The gavel banged again and the chair reminded the senator to keep his remarks within the bounds of Senate decorum.

The senator smiled and continued without batting an eye: "To those who have not served in the United States military and use the word *traitor*, I say we find a place where it is legal and find a pair of dueling pistols!"

And now, a nearly full United States Senate Chamber heard this remark and again fell silent and again began to pay attention. Then shouts of anger, then another gavel, accompanied by a specific rebuke to the senator from the Chair.

"This is a call for senators to forget their damn party and remember why they wanted to come to this Chamber in the first place. We, and the President, represent the people of the United States within the framework of the Constitution of the United States." He repeated this last sentence.

Suddenly there was applause. First from the Republican side of the aisle, not his side, but then from both sides of the aisle. Several standing on both sides. No cheering, no boisterous remarks, simply applause as the senator's words rang true to many other senators.

"Let me repeat for a third time. This is a call for senators to forget their damn party and remember why they wanted to come to this Chamber in the first place. We, and the President, represent the people of the United States within the framework of the Constitution of the United States. Far too many of us have held our collective voices as this president and this Congress took actions beyond the scope of our Constitution. Worse, the courts, in some cases, went along. We, including me, all know this to be true. We all know that anyone who compared what was happening to the awful events of other nations moving away from their constitutional roots and general cultures were shouted down quickly.

"I believe that we have collectively wanted this president to succeed as a person, and frankly, as a minority to prove the success of our Democracy. While some may believe he has been a great president and others may not, since the election, I believe he has let us down, badly let us down.

"Neither anyone in this room nor the President of the United States have another vote in this presidential election. That decision now rests with our colleagues in the House of Representatives. They, not we, not the President, will do the people's business as has been our law since 1788 when the Constitution was ratified.

"I remind our colleagues in the House of Representatives that as a group, their popularity is in the teens. I remind them that the entire country will be watching and I repeat again, they need to represent the people of the United States of America and not themselves or their political parties. The very future of the United States depends upon their actions.

"As to the President's silence as portions of cities have been burned to the ground and more than a few deaths have occurred, were this any April or May instead of November of every fourth year, I would hope the House of Representatives would be taking out papers of impeachment. But, it is not April or May, it is November and that action would be both inappropriate and seen as a political stunt."

The remarks were not received kindly by the President's supporters, but not one stood to protest as there was no defending the President's silence.

"I will yield now, but let me unequivocally offer no apology for my remarks. The history of this great country and its Constitution are bigger and more important than any individual, including this president. Presidents come and go; the Constitution of the United States is forever. Let us support the House of Representatives in their deliberations for President of the United States."

Not all, but virtually every Member of the United States Senate stood and applauded Senator Suppling. Those that did not stand and applaud quickly left the Senate floor as those senators neither wanted to be part of the applause or a part of the audience sitting silently in their chairs.

No other senator stood in line to speak to the Chamber. That was the real message to the President.

~

SATURDAY, NOVEMBER 10, 2012

The dining room of Ross Anderson, overlooking the Pacific Ocean in the hills of Palos Verdes, California, was already decorated for Thanksgiving. It had the look of simplified elegance as one might expect of this multimillionaire maker of surfwear. At the table in casual attire with Ross Anderson were Beth Midlands, Reesa Jonathon and Father Miles Woods. Mrs. Anderson was out with the girls and there were no other living creatures in the house save for Pissy, Anderson's aging, miniature Australian sheepdog. Pissy was always a handful for guests in the Anderson household unless the guests made it immediately clear to her that they were strong people who were not afraid of a yapping dog. In this group, there was no weak link; Pissy was sleeping next to Anderson.

"So, what have we done?" offered Anderson after a review of the election, which he had prepared for them by a member of his office staff.

"First, a toast to our work and to our new found poverty," offered Reesa Jonathon, "and to the fact that the only communication between us over the past few months was tonight's dinner invitation from Ross." Glasses clicked and the discussion was on. Reesa's glass was filled to the brim with apple juice. The other glasses had a very expensive French wine, Pétrus.

Anderson continued: "I think we accomplished our mission of making Senator Vincent a viable candidate. I think he will become the president, but who knows, politics at its worst. I think where we missed was in those boys and girls who are going to put Vincent in the White House when they realize Roland just cannot get the votes."

Father Woods seemed a bit surprised and asked Reesa what she meant by the "boys and girls" who were going to put Senator Vincent in the White House.

Beth Midlands laughed out loud and jumped in: "Boys and girls, yes, I guess you could call me a little girl. While I did throw a great deal of money at the presidential race, I backed my bets up in any state where there were fewer than five electoral votes. My bet was that if the Republicans could control the smaller states, they could control the vote for president in the House of Representatives. That state-by-state vote in the House of Representatives thing seemed really odd to me, but once I understood the rules of the game, I backed my presidential money with House of Representatives money.

"I did not contribute a dollar to the big money Senate races as I could never imagine anyone wanting the current VP anywhere near the White House after his Saturday Night Live style for the past four years. I never guessed he was the stumblebum he actually is, but he is one dumb SOB. I wished during the last couple of months that I could have had you guys join in on some of my independent campaigns in such luxury spots as South Dakota and Alaska, but our agreement was that if we never so much as sent a tweet to each other, no one could come after us legally. And there were more than a couple of states where my money showed up in a single congressional race to elect a Republican majority or other states where the race ended up in a tie. I just hope they realize they should not elect a man who scored only six states in the general election."

Father Woods looked his age for a moment and then began laughing. "This is more complicated than trying to study the Bible or calculate pi. Beth, I had no idea. You really know what is going to happen in the House of Representatives?"

Ross Anderson gave the most straightforward answer possible: "Not a chance, Father. She can't possibly know. If the President needs to promise the people of South Dakota a deep-water port to stay in office, I think he would do it. And his team is good at politics; what I don't know is whether Senator Vincent has a taste for this game at this level. I don't think Congressman Roland would let his ego, ethics and conservative values slip to give away so much as an increased subsidy for the farm program in his own district."

Midlands: "So, we spent hundreds of millions of dollars to rid the country of a man far too liberal to be President of the United States and now we are just spectators.

"My current focus is on making sure that every dollar that I spent is properly accounted for and that I don't go near anyone with any influence until after this game plays out. The possibility of Republicans or Democrats voting in the House of Representatives for an independent candidate seems pretty difficult, but voting against the actions of your state's voters and voting for Roland where he ran third seems a preposterous result. Me, I am headed for my place in Maine and I'll just follow along on the Internet. Should be lots of snow on the ground in Southwest Harbor by the time there is a President of the United States."

At that point, Ross Anderson began enjoying the chili and beans he had his staff prepare before going off for the evening. "Nothing like a $1000 bottle of Pétrus with chili and beans." Nods followed from Beth Midlands and Father Woods.

After a while, Father Woods seemed a bit perplexed and offered that he was going to spend a few weeks in Washington D.C. helping aspiring congressional members define their values and ethics. No one at the table thought this was a bad idea.

~

SUNDAY, NOVEMBER 11, 2012

Everyone in attendance spent a few minutes before the meeting reading Molly's memorandum to The Professor:

To: Professor Morton Hirschel

From: Molly Tom

Re: Selection of the President

Date: November 8, 2012

THE RULES OF ENAGEMENT
ELECTORAL COLLEGE TO PRESIDENCY

1. Electoral College – Electors vote on December 15. Some state laws require the electors to vote in concert with their state's voter decision. Most laws are without significant penalties. There is generally no discussion period for the members of the Electoral College. The members of the Electoral College vote in their own state and the state provides the results to the House of Representatives. The single written vote is tallied in the House of Representatives and if there is no decision, the election goes to the House of Representatives.

2. House of Representatives – Each state gets one vote. (Yes, that is what the Constitution says. Each state gets one vote; the Congressman from South Dakota has precisely the same voting power as the Representatives of the 30 million California residents.) The Members are limited in their votes to the top three recipients of elector

votes. There is no process wherein the third place finisher is ever eliminated from the ballots of the Members of the House of Representatives. If the House of Representatives does not make a decision by January 20, 2013, the Vice President becomes Acting President. The Vice President remains Acting President until the House of Representatives selects a President. It appears this can occur anytime until the President's term expires in January 2017.

3. United States Senate – The United States Senate selects the Vice President if the Electoral College does not successfully elect a Vice President. The Vice President is selected by the senators from the top *two* vote getters for Vice President from the Electoral College. There are some fairly severe quorum rules for purposes of the Senatorial vote, but the rules of the United States Senate provide that the Senate can compel attendance for a quorum and therefore a vote.

4. If there is no President or Acting President from the above, it *appears* the Speaker of the House becomes the Acting President if he or she is willing to resign from the House of Representatives, with the President pro tempore of the US Senate next in line. (It only appears that the Speaker of the House and the President pro tempore of the US Senate are next in line because the Presidential Succession Act was written with the sole expectation that the rules would only come into play if there were multiple deaths in the line to become President. If you can imagine, while the Presidential Succession Act—which was passed during the Truman Presidency and amended a zillion times—goes no further in this crazy 2012 fact pattern as after the Speaker and the President pro tempore of the US Senate, all of the next in line are Cabinet members and effective January 20, none of these people hold office. Go figure.)

5. In a truly contentious election, there might be a handful of interpretations of the rules in every step of the process. I anticipate this outcome.

~

Mercifully, there had been no riots outside of Cleveland proper and the Sunday meeting was taking place with an ear to the radio, but no other changes in behavior.

The Professor, always the observer, noted that Molly was dressed a bit more provocatively than he had ever seen before. Plus, he noticed this change immediately because she had looked so homely the past two months in Cleveland and unchanged at home. The very light blue, shiny blouse covered everything, somehow clung to her in a way that exaggerated what was underneath. The Levis were a bit tighter and he had not seen her wearing black heals with the Levis before. Even her long hair seemed a bit more carefully placed than he could remember. She looked like a different person than he had been observing in Cleveland—trying harder. He looked at Joshua and tried to think back to last night. He could not remember seeing them together and was fairly certain that she said something about never drinking when there were important people around. He again looked at Joshua and thought to himself that Molly might be sending him a message about what he had missed over the past few months or, God forbid, what he had last night. This was the last meeting for Molly for a while, but The Professor still did not like what he saw.

The Professor looked at his watch and stood up. He indicated he was catching an evening airplane home and needed to get to the airport. He looked at Molly and asked her what time she was returning to Orange County.

"Professor, I don't have class until 4:30 tomorrow and decided that I would be better off getting to bed early tonight and catching the 8:30 tomorrow morning through Chicago. I'll be able to study on the plane. One of my friends sent me the material from today and by the time I land at John Wayne, I should be more than ready for class."

The Professor took another look at the way Molly was dressed and another look at Joshua. He was not leaving one of his kids with this brain-dead skirt chaser after the election was over and everyone was hyper-relaxed and hyper-tired. "Milton, I'll tell you what, if you'll take Molly to that steak house around the corner for dinner and drive her to the airport tomorrow morning, I'll pick up the tab for dinner."

Milton quickly responded: "Why sure, Professor, I would be honored. Molly, okay with you? I think I can think of a few ways to keep you entertained."

549

Molly smiled lightly and said: "Thank you, Professor. That will give me a chance to get to know a little more about Milton." *Ah, The Professor, always my protector.*

Handshakes all around as The Professor left, the meeting broke up and Milton Woo dutifully took Molly out to dinner. She would miss the first flight out of Cleveland.

~

TUESDAY, DECEMBER 4, 2012

The numbers were always clear to Paul Roland. With the American Exceptionalism Party having taken many of his Republican senators and Members of Congress away from him long before the election, he and Bobby Joe had absolutely no chance of winning in the Electoral College. He continued to believe, perhaps with some honest analysis behind his thoughts, that without Senator Vincent he might have given the President a heck of a run in the election. But, since Vincent was Vincent, it was pretty hard to hold a grudge. Roland knew he was the winner in philosophy and ideas, not either of his opponents. He knew this before the election, long before the election and nothing philosophically had changed. He also knew the future of the Republican Party and the United States of America rested on what happened with the election over. He was going home to practice medicine unless the House of Representatives voted along party lines and he got lucky. He did not even know if he thought electing someone who only won six states was a good idea.

The House of Representatives presented an interesting opportunity for Congressman Roland. The rules seemed to give some possibility that, being a Republican, he could garner a very significant number of votes on the first ballot. He also knew that there were Members in the House of Representatives that would have easily voted for Mussolini rather than Congressman Roland.

It did not seem impossible to Congressman Roland that he could get the requisite number of states. This, despite his collection of states in the election. But, if that happened, he, like the President, would have to deal with

Jordon Scotch as his vice president. Roland knew, if it happened, he could keep him busy on deeply intellectual projects and actually garner some benefit from his amazing brainpower.

Crystal Jackson, his son's girlfriend, entered the room with her normal level of confidence. The congressman had asked her to assess the political situation and this young, Texan woman would undoubtedly tell him exactly what she believed was the correct answer. The congressman had brought her into the campaign to get a viewpoint that was never impacted by circumstances. Crystal had opened a few eyes on so many levels in his campaign office. Here was a presidential candidate campaigning on everything traditional and everything conservative. Here was the potential daughter-in-law of potentially the next President of the United States. Here was a woman that this man hoped would marry his son, this black woman, the oldest daughter of a Houston pastor who was living out of wedlock with his own son.

As always, he asked her to sit down across from him on the aged, cloth chairs. As always, he thought about what a great son he and his wife had raised. Roland thought about his wife when he looked at Crystal. Roland's wife was a Presbyterian minister and there was no show in that woman. She believed in "everything that was right" and in the issue of morals, she actually believed that President Carter and his belief that thinking about a sin was as bad as committing the sin to be understating a moral life. Roland found this thought process to be bizarre, but found his wife to be one of the most wonderful people he had ever met. Despite being the world's biggest prude and dressing the part—in one portion of her life, in bed, for reasons he had never understood and certainly never wanted to understand—there were no limits, absolutely no limits.

The only time Dr. and Mrs. Roland had ever come close to discussing Crystal Jackson's color was when he asked his wife what she thought about Marc having a black girlfriend. Her response was expected by the doctor: "I think she is the best thing that ever happened to him." End of that discussion.

Right to business, Crystal leaned forward in her chair, placed her left hand on her right leg and began talking: "Here is what I see, Congressman. You are dead in the Electoral College. There is a prayer you could make it in the House of Representatives, but why not trade Texas to Vincent and you become Secretary of the Treasury. I think that deal can be made. Why not give the Texas Electoral delegation to Vincent? That would make him the

45th President of the United States. This would ensure that you have won the fight to change presidents.

Cynicism and annoyance were the proper verbs to describe Roland's next few sentences: "By God, I know why I want you in our family, Crystal. That is absolutely brilliant. I have been so focused on the presidency, I have lost all thought of W-I-F-M, what's in it for me, Secretary Roland. Would that frost the Democrats, not to mention Chris Matts? And I have already forgotten the President's cell phone number, so we don't need to spend another second on him. Secretary Roland, Crystal!" Roland paused and regained control, "Who are we? Who am I? I cannot make a deal for myself. That is everything I am not, everything that drives me crazy about politicians. Those Texas votes are not mine; they belong to the voters of Texas. This isn't you either; you are thinking about me, not you, not the country, not the ethics that we both represent." Roland sounded unusually frustrated with this young woman.

Crystal Jackson was ebullient. When she ran this past Marc, he told exactly how his dad would react. For her, it was a family test. Crystal laughed. She virtually skipped over to Rolland's chair and hugged him, embedding her head between his head and left shoulder.

"Congressman, you are the finest man I have ever met, except my dad, of course. This is exactly how Marc said you would react. It is how I knew you would react. You may be the one person who would still be in the Garden of Eden with an uneaten apple."

The congressman sat there with a silly expression on his face. He had been played and he loved it.

"I think we had a brief chat about the concept of the unfaithful elector. With the Electoral College split, the electors of Texas are only advised as to whom to vote for as president. They are free to do whatever they want. Tradition has kept the electors of Texas and the other forty-nine states voting in concert with their state's voters. The whole thing is a bit weird, but the bottom line is that under both the Constitution and Texas law, these electors are free agents. And you, Congressman, are the embodiment of the Constitution. I think you can argue that it is in the best interest of the United States of America and the State of Texas if the election is kept out of the House of Representatives. Here, you can couch your thoughts very carefully and indicate that you believe you would be the choice in the House of Representatives, but believe the actual voters, not congressmen should select the president. That is within the rules and if the Texas electors like it, you come home. That way, if it goes to the House, we can fight like the devil to get you to be president."

"I don't like it. I don't like it a bit. You may be right, but I don't like it. It's just not me. The Texas electors are not mine to give or trade. I can't stray from my ideals and try to break the Constitution. I have thought hard on this and suspect that history would give me a mixed review if I did as you suggest. I cannot get to the *right* answer for the wrong reasons.

"You know, Crystal, I may look at your idea, which I cannot do and not hate myself for doing it, but I guess I love the Constitution more than I fear this president. But, I do think we should meet with Senator Vincent. Can you arrange a quiet meeting?"

~

SUNDAY, DECEMBER 9, 2012

Senator Vincent had been hoping, but not expecting a call from Congressman Roland. Not surprisingly, the two men did not really know each other very well. Modern campaigns, even with their debates, presented no more time among the candidates than a handshake or a nod before the action began.

While Vincent and Paul would occasionally pass each other in a hallway in the Capital, to the best of Senator Vincent's memory, they had never had a meal together and had never worked mutually on a piece of legislation. One Democratic senator and one Republican congressman, ships passing in the night. This was one of the saddest parts of a modern democracy operating with modern transportation. Nearly one hundred percent of a senator's time was consumed with staying in office and if he was not meeting with a constituent or lobbyist in Washington, he was home acting like a candidate. Most Members of Congress were in the Washington D.C. area only about three days a week, thirty weeks a year. For many elected officials the reason he or she was elected to office, doing the country's business, was generally delegated to his staff.

So, here Senator Vincent sat, in the home of Rush Findley, a Republican donor from Norman, Oklahoma. Findley had a nice farm several miles from the interstate and the senator sat in Findley's den sucking down a second can of Red Bull. The ride down, in the back of yet another black SUV, with his seat belt fastened thanks to former Governor Corzine, seemed endless. A full year of campaigning and fundraising, probably not in that order, and here he was in this strange living room waiting for his opponent. This was worse than dialing for dollars to fund his operations through the end of the year.

Findley seemed like an affable man, but apparently the price for using his home for an hour was an obligation to discuss the different approaches to recruiting by the University of Oklahoma versus The Ohio State University. Vincent informed Findley that if the Buckeyes sent their dumbest six football players to Oklahoma, the grade point averages of both schools and the average IQ on campus at both schools would vault towards the ceiling. Even this did not cause Findley to change subjects.

Beginning to wonder whether it would have been better to hold his meeting with Congressman Roland at the nearest gas station, Vincent responded to yet another question: "We are never going to let our academics or facilities slip an inch. What we learned after Coach Hayes is that you need to be the best at everything, not just have the best coach or the best quarterback. At Ohio State, the players need to thrive in their difficult academic environment. The interesting issues we deal with now revolve around making the game experience a positive for both the spectator and the player. And trust me here, the average three-hundred-fifteen-pound offensive guard has almost nothing in common with the average fan."

The senator saw four black SUV's and enough dust to think about the Dust Bowl years as the vehicles came up the roadway. He breathed a sigh of relief and said: "Let's go meet with the congressman."

Findley: "Mimi, would you go fetch that camera phone, I need to get a picture with Paul and the senator."

"Mr. Findley," Vincent started—*darn, I wish I could remember first names for more than a tenth of a second*—"we could get some separate pictures, but this meeting is a secret, remember?"

"Sorry."

The foursome of SUVs made its way up the long farm road, which was entirely on Rush Findley's property. While Senator Vincent wasn't exactly sure, it appeared to him that Findley was growing almost exclusively corn, maybe for eating or maybe for feed, who knows? *Other than barren land waiting for the planting season, there is nothing to be seen at this time of the year. These farmers had a few great years before the energy industry figured out that ethanol was more polluting than coal on steroids. This is the quietest farm I have ever seen. Must be a story here that I have to be careful not to ask as this guy would take an hour to*

556

tell me. Something going on here I simply cannot figure out. Cost me another hour to find out and, I guess, I just don't care enough to spend the time with this character.

Both of the Findleys came out to greet Congressman Roland. The Findleys both had that wealthy farmer look with the pressed blue jeans and flannel shirts under their expensive leather jackets. Vincent walked out slowly, cold in his khakis and light sweater. As Vincent walked closer to the SUVs he looked at the farmer and thought: *Old guy is in pretty good shape. I got it. First farm I have ever been on where there were not any dogs, odd.*

The congressman was in the second car. The senator was more than a bit surprised when Roland stepped out of the car in a three thousand dollar suit, Oakley sunglasses and trademark cowboy boots. The senator had expected Sunday afternoon casual; there was a meaning here that Vincent needed to quickly get his arms around. Maybe a bit worse, and contradicting their discussion, Paul Roland had an aide with him. She looked like he may have picked her up at her home sixty seconds after calling her to tell her he was coming by for a long car ride. Although apparently attractive, after the long drive she was more than a bit disheveled and clearly attired for an event different than that which the congressman was attired. Probably a last minute thought to bring her. Well, he and this woman had apparently not dressed for the same parade.

The preliminaries were quick and deservedly so, as the sun was going down and it was now very cold instead of just cold. The congressman shook hands with Findley, hugged Mimi as if they actually knew each other and introduced his aide. The congressman then shook hands with the senator and suggested they go inside. He introduced Crystal in a manner that would have made one think that Senator Vincent knew she was coming and had met her several times before. Vincent had expected anything except perhaps an introduction of Crystal as Congressman Roland's aide as well as his son's girlfriend. *That Roland is the real deal.*

Paul called to his Secret Service agents: "I only see two of Senator Vincent's palace guards, so I am guessing they are in the pool room, why don't you guys join them?" The seven of them looked at each other and five moved in the direction of the house. Senator Vincent noticed that Roland had not asked if this was acceptable. He guessed it was fine as they were truly in the middle of nowhere.

As they entered the house, Mimi spoke to everyone in her down home Oklahoman accent: "Ah know y'all don't need Rush or me. I've got pork and beans on the stove and if it is fine, I'll just fill up some plates and deliver them hot. The agents downstairs have already eaten enough for about sixteen people, but we have plenty of food and unlimited soft drinks. As Congressman Roland knows and Senator Vincent found out a few minutes ago, the strongest thing we allow in our home is Red Bull. So, come on, Rush let's let these folks to do their important work." There seemed a touch of sarcasm in Mimi's tone, but everyone let it pass and everyone followed the directions given.

Roland took a seat on the couch while Senator Vincent leaned on the edge of a large coffee table and popped yet a third Red Bull. Crystal also took a seat on the couch.

"George, I hope I can call you George,"—the senator responded with a nod—"as you know, Crystal here is my brain trust and here to correct me if I fall off course in my analysis. Hopefully, my dumb son Marc will propose to this woman before I get too old to go to the wedding."

"Hi Crystal, boy, the Congressman would be one interesting father-in-law," offered the senator. He wasn't sure why, but he thought Roland might be trying to prove he was not a right-wing nut by bringing Crystal to the meeting.

Damn I wish The Professor were here thought the senator. *There is going to be some serious bullshit going on here and The Professor brings his own personal bullshit detector and, if he needs it, a separate bullshit maker to meetings like this. I am unarmed, at least I could have brought Molly.*

Crystal nodded and considered the senator carefully. Congressman Roland had made it pretty clear that she would speak when spoken to; she was there to provide data and emotional support to back up anything he said.

The senator offered to listen to the congressman in a fairly unusual way as he began to be seriously annoyed at the expensive suit and his bringing an assistant on a Sunday afternoon in the middle of nowhere: "Well, Paul, here we are under the cone of silence, three hundred miles from anywhere and probably on our way to the Wall Drug Store in the Dakotas. What's up that we could not talk about on the telephone?"

"Good to see you, George. So let's skip right ahead to where I think we are with our little quagmire. Our analysis is that, at the moment, neither of us can become the President of the United States. No Red Bull, no nothing, if we do not cooperate, either the President is going to serve another term or the next President of the United States is going to be your guy in the wheelchair.

"Jordon Scotch seems like a great guy, but, let's be clear here, as smart as he is, he has absolutely no political experience. Haven't we had enough of that? Schwarzenegger, Franken, the President, name your poison."

In a sense, Vincent was to have none of this. "First, Jordon Scotch's IQ is at least thirty points higher than this phony I helped elect to the White House. My guy writes and lectures about economics in a manner that brings visitors to his door by the hour and the guy in the White House became an adjunct professor as payback for some small favor done for a buddy.

"My guy has a Nobel Prize in economics and talks like a person you can spend time with and understand every word. The President has a Nobel Prize for, well, I don't have a clue why he has a Nobel Prize, and he pretends he was truly a professor of law, talks as if he knows everything about everything and no one knows what he really wants to do, or who's side he is really on, or who he really is. One of the amusing parts about the President is that when he campaigns as a law professor, the full-time, tenured law professors are livid. To them, he is no more than an imposter. My friends at the law school say his pretending to be an academic offends them and they are liberal to the extreme.

"So, I am not sure that we see this the same way on Jordon. If Jordon becomes the Acting President for four years and does a great job, I'll support him for the Presidency in 2016. And if you want a laugh, I am pretty sure the Constitution would allow him to serve two full terms as president after four years as Acting President. But let's assume you know these rules as well as I do; what is on your mind?"

"Crystal, why don't you give the senator a numerical view of what is going on here before I describe a plan which I believe will make one of us the president."

First Crystal explained that under the Constitution's Twelfth Amendment, if an Acting President served two years before he was first elected on his own, he would be limited to a single term as an elected president. Then, Crystal zipped through the analysis without notes. In the House of Representatives, Members who could vote for president were split 221 Democrats and 214 Republicans. The states were split 24 Republican, 18 Democratic and 8 with equal numbers of each. The Democrats made up a lot of ground in the House in 2012 and this would return the Former Speaker to the Speakership. In the House of Representatives, she would control the majority and she would control the rules. However, of the 33 seats up in the US Senate, the Democrats had 23 where they were either incumbents or defending an incumbent's seat and the result was 57 Republican senators.

In some ways, everyone was a free agent; in other ways, no one was a free agent.

Crystal's view was that Congressman Roland, her guy, could never get Texas to vote for Vincent to become president and that might sink both Paul and Vincent. She thought the President and the Democratic leadership would have the ability to hold their people, this despite the fact that Vincent was a Democrat until 2012. Therefore, she was certain Vincent could not hold his states without House Members who voted with the American Exceptionalism Party. And not all of them would be in line. She put the exclamation on the analysis by indicating that virtually all of the key tied states needed to have black Democratic congressmen and women vote for Congressman Roland and that this was not going to happen. This from a twenty-three-year-old black woman was hard to refute for Vincent.

Crystal concluded: "I do not see the House of Representatives being able to select a president. My analysis says that unless something dramatic happens in the first or second vote, Jordon Scotch will be the Acting President through 2016."

Congressman Roland jumped in at that point: "So, George, I wanted to know what you think. Crystal's comments to the side, I think I would be elected in the first round if you supported me. There are twenty Democratic Members in the eight states that are tied, Democrats and Republicans. If you could get just two of them to vote for me in the first ballot, I think I can pull this thing off. I would promise to work closely with Scotch."

"So I would have won thirty-two of the fifty states in the election and you would become President of the United States on the first House of Representative's ballot? That with you having only won six states?" replied Vincent.

"Yes, George, that is exactly right. I don't particularly like the entire mess. But, I think if you don't run for president, I am planning my inauguration speech right now. You run and somehow I finish third in electoral votes, third in popular vote and third in the number of states. We both come up short in different measurements. And, Crystal, tell the senator exactly what I will promise him in return for his support."

Crystal was a bit uncomfortable in her answer, but she went with the playbook and her knowledge of Paul Roland. "The congressman is stuck on the ethics thing and is not willing to make any promises to anyone. I disagree with him a bit on this, but not more than a smidgen. Frankly, Senator Vincent, I think the Senate needs you more and the congressman would make a great president."

Vincent was quiet again, for almost a full minute. "You know, Paul, in so many ways I wish I could do what you ask. I am not sure I could get it done, but it would be fun to try and it would so anger the President that I would get a huge charge out of it. But, first, it isn't the right thing to do and, second, we fundamentally differ on far too many issues. Intellectually, I think Scotch will do a great job. I think he will struggle with the politics, but maybe that is okay. Anyway, I just can't do it."

"George, that is what I expected and in some ways what I hoped for because it would be troublesome for anyone to become President of the United States based on a deal. But can we do this? Can we stay close? Can we coordinate a bit on press releases? I think it is important that the President be living in Chicago over the next four years and maybe we can just work together towards that objective."

The conversation went on for more than an hour and at the end of their time together, George Vincent and Paul Roland each decided the other guy had great ethics. That made the day useful and meaningful to each. They agreed to chat and keep the pressure on the delegates not to get rolled over by party leadership—leadership in either party.

~

MONDAY, DECEMBER 10, 2012

An interesting group arrived at the Anatole Hotel in Dallas; thirty-four Texas electors, two hundred people from every media outlet in the world, protesters of every possible size and description and every self-appointed mentor in the State of Texas.

In the lobby, there were also more than a few hotel guests who were trying to take advantage of the free coffee and bagels offered every morning. Unlike yesterday morning, getting to the coffee, which was a perquisite for guests of the hotel only, was more than a tad difficult given the number of people in the area.

The only major thing missing at the Anatole was adequate security for the delegates and their fairly small conference room. As there is no predetermined leadership for any electoral delegation, no one had thought to order security. In fact, all that had been planned with respect to the meeting was that one elector, Ralph Rohrer, a mayor from Plano, Texas, had sent out an e-mail suggesting they get together. He had fronted $300 for the room and forty chairs. He had not ordered coffee and doughnuts. With only thirty-four people, he had not so much as asked for a microphone.

For the most part, all of the electors were longtime, loyal Republicans. There were a sprinkling of mayors, former mayors, a couple of former congressman and a few contributors, but mostly the electors were individuals elected by Republican voters that, in most cases, had not the remotest idea who these people were. Who really cared? This was not supposed to be an important assignment. All an elector got as compensation was a reimbursement for gas if he drove to Austin to vote. The electors only got the reimbursement if someone told them to ask for it or if they asked the right person, and only a few on either side of the equation ever asked. As this was a non-job, at the time they decided to become electors, who won the University of Texas v. Oklahoma football game in the coming season had been far more important to most of the State of Texas than who the Republican electors would be in December.

The manager of the hotel, Reggie Roundtable, was at a meeting of hotel managers in Louisiana. The occupancy of the hotel was particularly low at this time of year. This was always a quiet week and a quiet week was always the right time for a hotel managers' meeting. The assistant manager lived on the other side of Dallas and because of a small dinner that evening for a very well-heeled Dallas dignitary, he had not planned on getting to work until about noon.

So, there stood Joe-Bob Willit, exactly eight weeks out of Florida International University's Graduate School of Hospitality Management. Joe-Bob had focused on hotel management in school. This was his very first job, unless one counted babysitting in junior high school. During college, he played football and was a national caliber thrower of the shot put. These activities were the time equivalent of a full-time job for all four years and he and his family were thrilled that he completed the college task in four years. He had effectively never worked a day in his life until joining the staff of the Anatole Hotel. Joe-Bob was six-foot-eight-inches in height and weighed one doughnut less than three hundred ninety-five pounds.

Mayor Ralph Rohrer approached Joe-Bob and asked him if he could clear out the little room he had rented so he could get started with their meeting. Joe-Bob looked down at the mayor and offered: "Mayor, there seem to be a few more people here than the room can hold, how about you take the ballroom and we'll whip up some BBQ for lunch—what, about three hundred folks at, say, $34 a head; I'll throw in the room for free."

Rohrer burst into laughter. "Terrific, Tiny, but I don't have ten grand. I'll tell you what, you get that room cleared and I'll get you a match against Hulk Hogan in the new stadium and we'll both be rich."

"Nice, you have me wrestling with a guy who is what, seventy-five years old? Well, how about we do this, I'm going to call the police, relax, not 911, and tell them we have a bit of a situation here. It will take them fifteen minutes to get here. While they are figuring out what the rules are for the media on the drive over, I'll get the boys to set up a microphone in your room for

$75 plus city tax, and you will ask the media to clear the room. I'd suggest you tell everyone that the delegates will be available after your meeting. And just because it's you, I'll stand next to you when you make your little presentation and I'll get one of our short order cooks to stand next to me. He isn't all that big, but he is one mean looking dude. Best as I can tell, Bart is as gentle as they come, but trust me, if it is all looking and no talking, he is one scary looking guy. I think that will work."

"Ok, Hulk, that brings our list of ideas to one, let's execute it and get that microphone set up. I would suggest you feed those television fools some coffee."

"Mike," Joe-Bob, initially ignoring the request for free coffee, called over to one of his employees. "Set up a microphone in there for Mr. Rohrer real quick, would you? And tell Bart I am going to need him up here for a few minutes. He won't have to do anything except stand next to me. And, Mr. Rohrer, I am going to walk over and introduce myself to that little news lady over by the South entrance and if she'll have a beer with me after work, the microphone is free, no free coffee." Joe-Bob smiled and just walked towards the news lady with his best smile. Joe-Bob had one thought: *Man, she is a pretty little one.*

After about fifteen minutes, Mayor Rohrer—with help from Joe-Bob and Bart—was ready, meaning Rohrer followed Joe-Bob and Bart to the microphone. The small town mayor quickly and loudly announced: "Ladies and gentlemen, this is not a public meeting. This is a meeting among the electors of the State of Texas; anyone who is not an elected elector must leave the room."

From the back of the room, a member of the media yelled back: "You have no right to exclude the press and we are not leaving." The media all voiced approval. Rohrer again stepped to the microphone and yelled back: "If you do not leave the room, I am going to ask my friends here to clear the room."

"You and he had better have great insurance, Buddy!"

About that time, a graying police officer entered the room with three other officers. Mayor Rohrer quickly moved to the back of the room and explained his problem. The police officer listened intently and profession-ally, but rather than help Rohrer, he moved to a corner of the room and called headquarters. After almost another full ten minutes (it felt like an hour to the mayor), he returned to Rohrer, Joe-Bob and Bart and told them that he was not authorized to clear the room. He was sorry, but his people were not going to take on that responsibility.

Mayor Rohrer thought to himself for a few seconds and walked to the microphone: "Ladies and gentlemen, this meeting was my idea and I paid the rent on the room and then paid this giant here to throw in a microphone. I guess it just wasn't such a good idea and I am headed home. I have informed the hotel that our meeting is over and I guess, at this point, you must be trespassing. The local gendarmes may be a whole lot more interested in trespassing then they were in my meeting. Y'all have a good day."

The press nearly suffocated Mayor Rohrer physically with questions. He snuggled in between Joe-Bob and Bart let them know he'd like to get the hell out of the room.

"Mr. Rohrer, I sure would appreciate it if you would meet with Lillian from RBC Network. She sure seems like a nice little woman."

"Joe-Bob, if you can get me out of this room and we can meet in your office, just the two of us, I'll talk to her for forty minutes. Just get me the hell out of here." With that, Joe-Bob replayed the last play of some 2011 football game and literally lifted one media member up off the floor, placed him out of the way, and got them through the crowd after that with ease. He put Mayor Rohrer in his boss's office and quickly found Lillian and nearly dragged her to meet the mayor.

When Joe-Bob returned to the foyer, he could see that virtually no one was happy. Thankfully, he had the foresight not to have the coffee urns replenished. One stray congressman clearly wanted to give a speech, most of the electors wanted to chat and the media wanted a piece of everything. Joe-Bob decided there was no winning hand available and directed his team to lock every vacant conference and banquet door in the building. In addition, he remembered something from Florida International and asked several of his crew to man vacuum cleaners. He remembered a professor saying something to the effect that if all else fails, get the vacuums going, and if that fails, put ammonia on the floors.

He figured that if the media and the remaining few electors had to stand in the foyer with vacuums as background noise, at some point everyone would get tired and leave.

Congressman Roland arrived as the drama was ending and requested a room on the first floor, a medium sized conference room. He came with four Secret Service agents surrounding him because he was one of three potential presidential candidates. Joe-Bob stood his ground and offered the congressman a room, any room from the Presidential Suite to a Banquet Room to a regular room on the third floor at a ten percent discount. If Paul Roland could have taken a pistol from a Secret Service agent and shot Joe-Bob, he would have. This was outrageous and he was not going to be accused of tampering with these electors in a private room upstairs. He couldn't rent a ballroom. How would that look? It would look like the whole thing was his idea, which it surely was not. He definitely did not want to do anything that was illegal, or immoral, or looked illegal or immoral. All he intended to do was to ask the electors to vote as directed by the voters, for him.

Joe-Bob learned a long time ago, maybe when he was fifteen, that his enormous size prevented most physical problems and the closer he got to who he was talking to, the less likely there would be any issues. Following that philosophy, every time the congressman took a step back to be able to look into his eyes, he took a step closer and responded, "I can't help you here, Sir! Do you want a room upstairs?"

Muttering under his breath, Congressman Roland began to head back to the parking lot with the media running behind. At this point, most of the electors had already fled and no one knew anything more than they did about anything than when they woke up that morning. Roland turned and looked at the reporters and their cameramen and spoke: "I do not know who is responsible for this mess, but I can assure you it is not me. I just came here to ask the electors to represent the voters of Texas as the voters of Texas expect to be represented." And, after patiently fielding a few questions, he and his team of Secret Service agents got into his SUV and left.

With the delegates gone and the press outside, Joe-Bob had his team lock a few more doors and put the vacuum cleaners away.

Almost thirty minutes later, Mayor Rohrer and Lillian emerged from Joe-Bob's boss's wallet-sized, windowless office. Joe-Bob saw Lillian thank the mayor, then she turned toward Joe-Bob, winked and off she went with her team.

"Thanks, Joe-Bob. Lillian seems like a good kid and the interview was fine. I suspect that some of her competitors will be a bit miffed that I only met with her, but really, at this point, I don't really care. You guys were great. Same time next year?" laughed an exhausted Ralph Rohrer. "Send me a bill for the microphone."

"You are welcome, Sir," offered Joe-Bob and then affected a huge smile and continued, "This has been one interesting morning. And, you know, maybe you don't remember, but you and I made a deal. After Lillian finishes her piece about you on the six o'clock news, I am taking that little lady out for BBQ. So, the microphone is free!" He gave Rohrer a thumbs-up and laughed as he walked off.

Yes, an interesting morning, Rohrer thought, *almost as interesting as the thought of Joe-Bob with that maybe one-hundred-four-pound news lady having dinner together. Great kids, both of them. Will have to learn more about Florida International University. That kid had great instincts and did really well. I need to send a note to his boss.*

Hours before Joe-Bob drove his pickup truck in front of the pretty little reporter's apartment, the possibility of Texas voting for George Vincent in the Electoral College was over.

~

TUESDAY, DECEMBER 11, 2012

The following article was featured as a guest column on Townhall.com. What were the chances that a dentist in Iowa would add yet another level of confusion to the 2012 presidential election? The dentist was not the most articulate or definitive writer in the fifty states, but he opened up yet another possibility as to who would become President or Acting President:

WHAT IF THERE IS NO PRESIDENT?

The talking heads have spewed forth for weeks about the five possibilities for President of the United States following this three political party election. They have missed the sixth possibility: No one! And the possibility is a real one.

When my kids were little and something would go wrong in the backyard, I always arrived with a single statement and a single question: "OK, let's start with the basics, don't tell me what you were thinking, tell me if you were thinking."—Apparently the question is appropriate for the United States Congress, past and present.

The Constitution provides:

Section 3 of the 20th Amendment of the Constitution of the United States provides that if the President-elect dies before his term begins, the Vice President-elect becomes President on Inauguration Day and serves for the full term to which the President-elect was elected. The section also provides that if, on Inauguration Day, a President has not been chosen or the President-elect does not qualify for the presidency, the Vice President-elect acts as President until a President is chosen or the President-elect qualifies. Finally, Section 3 allows the Congress to provide by law for cases in which neither a President-elect nor a Vice President-elect is eligible or available to serve.

The Presidential Succession Act provides:

(a)

(1) If, by reason of death, resignation, removal from office, inability, or failure to qualify, there is neither a President nor Vice President to discharge the powers and duties of the office of President, then the Speaker of the House of Representatives shall, upon his resignation as Speaker and as Representative in Congress, act as President.
(2) The same rule shall apply in the case of the death, resignation, removal from office, or inability of an individual acting as President under this subsection.

(b)

If, at the time when under subsection (a) of this section a Speaker is to begin the discharge of the powers and duties of the office of President, there is no Speaker, or the Speaker fails to qualify as Acting President, then the President pro tempore of the Senate shall, upon his resignation as President pro tempore and as Senator, act as President.

(c)

An individual acting as President under subsection (a) or subsection (b) of this section shall continue to act until the expiration of the then current Presidential term, except that -
(1) If his discharge of the powers and duties of the office is founded in whole or in part on the failure of both the President-elect and the Vice-President-elect to qualify, then he shall act only until a President or Vice President qualifies; and
(2) If his discharge of the powers and duties of the office is founded in whole or in part on the inability of the President or Vice President, then he shall act only until the removal of the disability of one of such individuals.

(d)

(1) If, by reason of death, resignation, removal from office, inability, or failure to qualify, there is no President pro tempore to act as

President under subsection (b) of this section, then the officer of the United States who is highest on the following list, and who is not under disability to discharge the powers and duties of the office of President shall act as President: Secretary of State, Secretary of the Treasury, Secretary of Defense, Attorney General, Secretary of the Interior, Secretary of Agriculture, Secretary of Commerce, Secretary of Labor, Secretary of Health and Human Services, Secretary of Housing and Urban Development, Secretary of Transportation, Secretary of Energy, Secretary of Education, Secretary of Veterans Affairs, Secretary of Homeland Security.

(2) An individual acting as President under this subsection shall continue so to do until the expiration of the then current Presidential term, but not after a qualified and prior-entitled individual is able to act, except that the removal of the disability of an individual higher on the list contained in paragraph (1) of this subsection or the ability to qualify on the part of an individual higher on such list shall not terminate his service.

(3) The taking of the oath of office by an individual specified in the list in paragraph (1) of this subsection shall be held to constitute his resignation from the office by virtue of the holding of which he qualifies to act as President.

(e)

Subsections (a), (b), and (d) of this section shall apply only to such officers as are eligible to the office of President under the Constitution. Subsection (d) of this section shall apply only to officers appointed, by and with the advice and consent of the Senate, prior to the time of the death, resignation, removal from office, inability, or failure to qualify, of the President pro tempore, and only to officers not under impeachment by the House of Representatives at the time the powers and duties of the office of President devolve upon them.

What does all this mean?
We think we know that the House of Representatives will have a very hard time electing a President. With states each getting a single vote and a third-party candidate in the mix, we think we know that selecting a President is going to be difficult to near impossible.

We think we know that the United States Senate will select a Vice President between the current Vice President and the economist, Jordon Scotch. We do know that if the House of Representatives, or more correctly, if and when the House of Representatives selects a President, the VP or Scotch would become Vice President. Until then, the newly elected Vice President would be Acting President.

The problem: What if the United States Senate cannot get sixty votes to stop debate on the selection of the Vice President?

At that point, the world as we know is unknown to us. There is no death, resignation, removal from office, inability, or failure to qualify event. There is only: nothing. Add to this, the inspired research of Yale Law School Professor Akhil Amar who has indicated that the current Presidential Succession Act is "a disastrous statute, an accident waiting to happen."

So there is our formula: If the Senate cannot get past a filibuster, there is no clear and convincing language that the Speaker of the House becomes Acting President or anyone else for that matter. And regardless thereof, there are Constitutional authorities who believe the Succession Act itself is unconstitutional.

Who would run the government while this was sorted out by the Supreme Court? And how long would it take?

Forty-eight hours later, the Townhall.com article was reprinted in the *New York Post* directly above one of Rich Lawry's weekly missiles. The dentist would ultimately receive a $250 check from the *New York Post* for the privilege of reprinting the story and scaring the heck out of more than 300 million Americans.

~

Geekhead had virtually run from the subway to Fox News' headquarters. Jenn had called to tell him that O'Brien wanted to tape a segment immediately in reaction to the dentist's epistle. No one at Fox News was happy that the dentist seemed to be the only person in the United States that saw the possibility that the country could, at least in theory, become leaderless.

Jenn was waiting for Geekhead in the lobby and after only a little more than a brief hug, she told him to expect a difficult live interview and that she, not Bill, would be asking most of the questions. He looked at her face and all he saw was the woman that he had fallen in love with; he did not see a newscaster or commentator. Every time he saw her, he was mystified at her perfect complexion; it never changed. He heard her, but did not respond.

"Remember, I am going to ask you a few very hard questions. It won't mean that I don't love you more than I believed I could love anyone. Bill told me that since everyone who watches Fox News knows that we are engaged, we have become great entertainment. Tonight we need to be the news."

"OK, not a problem," responded Geekhead. He finally considered the situation and thought: *This should be pretty interesting.*

Thirty minutes later, Geekhead was facing O'Brien, another grey suit and yellow tie and the love of his life in her neck-high, white blouse and a skirt of somewhat reasonable length. The television would pick up her perfect facial features surrounded by a smart, short, classic hairdo for her extremely dark hair. Skinny to beat the band in person, she was always radiant on television. Geekhead was in his uniform.

When they had finished the preliminaries of their future wedding on live television with O'Brien popping criticisms for a full forty seconds, O'Brien set the stage with the facts in a very rough form. Jenn asked Geekhead the expected question. "Why, Horace, haven't we talked about the possibility that the government will come to a standstill?"

"Jenn, I will admit this one caught me by surprise, but I do not think there is any possibility that this could get out of control. Speaking to the problem, I don't think Jefferson or Hamilton, or Franklin for that matter, gave any thought to either filibusters or Senate cloture rules. In the Constitution, the Senate was given the right to determine its own rules annually. As we know, the new United States Senate has fifty-seven Republicans; they control the Senate."

O'Brien could not wait for his trusted colleague: "But what about a filibuster? The Democrats could hold this thing up for everyone, forever. This could be a pure power grab for the Vice President. Remember, the Republicans are not the Democrats, they don't seem to hold together very well when challenged."

"Bill, you may be right there on the Republicans holding together, but that is really your and Jenn's turf. The filibuster opportunity is real, but the Republicans can, and I believe would, drop what is often referred to as the nuclear option if there was a filibuster. The nuclear option would allow the Republicans to have a simple majority to select a vice president."

Jenn again took her turn: "But wouldn't the nuclear option change the Senate for time eternal? Haven't both parties threatened to change the rules and then backed off when sanity returned to the arena?"

"Yes, Dear, I mean, Jenn." Geekhead and Jennifer Cho both turned their new regular color, beet red. "Jenn, I think this is what would happen. The Republicans would threaten to break any filibuster, the Democrats would look at their less than forty-five votes in the Senate and decide that losing on this issue would be better than facing a US Senate where only a simple majority was needed to push through an agenda. Add to that the famous *the whole world is watching* quote and the crisis is over as soon as it began."

O'Brien again: "But what would happen if there was no president?"

"I think, but remember that this is what *I think*, because the law is not as clear as it should be and of course, this issue has never been in the Supreme Court, I think the Speaker of the House would claim the presidency. There would be an immediate challenge, the Supreme Court would take the case and the Supreme Court would rule in favor of the Speaker. I don't believe the Supreme Court could allow themselves to determine that the United States of America did not have a President or Acting President. But remember, I am an academician, not a lawyer. But, Bill, the moment it was clear there would be a filibuster, the Senate would change the rules. The dentist reads everything right; he just doesn't understand the practicalities of the situation.

"Now, if you want a scary thought, what if in the next few years, the country keeps the American Exceptionalism Party and adds Progressive and Tea Party political parties on a national basis? Then, it is not crazy to say the House of Representatives and the Senate could not reach an election conclusion. And, as I said, that is truly scary. That needs to be fixed."

~

SATURDAY, DECEMBER 15, 2012

They were four of the more senior Democratic senators and each had enjoyed much of the first two years of the President's term, as they were able to force through liberal legislation that would have been unheard of even just a few years before. In fact, they loved every minute. All four of the senators believed that given their roles in the legislation that passed the Congress in 2010, they should each be eligible for inclusion in a sequel to *Profiles in Courage* (President Kennedy's Pulitzer Prize winning book describing politicians who took unpopular stances during their careers because they thought these views or actions were best for the country). Each had already risked their careers to support their liberal beliefs.

Thirty minutes before, they had completed a meeting with Herman Sackman over an early breakfast in the West Wing. They knew the meeting was complete when Sackman told the group to "go fuck themselves" and stormed out of the room.

Senator Booth looked at his colleagues and deadpanned: "He seems upset." There are some statements that are so understated they always draw guffaws and this was no different. Hearing the laughter, the waiter re-entered the room. Booth calmly asked the waiter if he could have a latte to take with him before they left. "Hold the hemlock." Booth was a full on Starbucks guy, but he found out over the years that the best specialty coffee drinks in the United States were to be found in this White House.

An hour later, the four senators stood in front of a microphone before the entire Washington press corps. On December 15, 2012, two days before the Electoral College voted, a press conference by four Democratic senators was news. The actual importance of the press conference was totally the result of the dentist's reprinted article in the *New York Post*. The dentist's article seemed to create a *Good God, what could happen now?* explosion in Washington.

Senator Booth was the lead dog for this brief press conference. "We are here for two distinct purposes; equally important purposes. First, we encourage every electoral voter to vote as directed by your states. While there is great uncertainty as to who will ultimately be our next president, we believe the electors owe fidelity to their state's voters. Maybe two hundred years ago, maybe not, the expectations of electors were different when we did not have great communications and our literacy rates were so low. Today, we believe you should vote as your state's voters directed. Anything less would tell your citizens you either don't trust or don't care and that would be flat wrong." The senator's New England accent effectively hid just the hint of a lisp. This red-faced senator could walk through a train terminal in Boston and rarely be recognized. By the time he got to Washington D.C., he looked unique and was always recognized with his red face, lack of tan and red hair.

Senator Booth went on: "For our second purpose, there is always a well or not so well-intended academician, author, or actually in this case a dentist who has some wild idea that there will be an election and no ultimate winner. Usually, but not in this case, the academic has a former president or the Commandant of the Marine Corps taking power. Today, we have what I refer to as another of the author Allen Drury's *Advise and Consent* moments. Three things: One, The dentist is not crazy. He raises an issue that could be a problem. Two, our four votes are not available for a filibuster, so the dentist's scenario will not happen and will not be a problem. We will not support a filibuster and therefore, there will be no filibuster. We are not going to play some political power game in our Constitutional role to select a vice president. Period. Three, we will endeavor with the House of Representatives to clean up the language in the Presidential Succession Act and perhaps the Constitution as well, as soon as we get a President."

It had not been the intent of the senators to take questions, but the member of the press corps from OBC fired off a question too quickly and too loudly to be ignored: "We heard that you had breakfast with Herman Sackman this morning. Is this what you agreed to do in concert with the President and his advisor?"

Booth had already turned and was a step away from the microphone as were his three colleagues. Booth could not resist and looked back toward the reporter: "Go to Blockbuster tonight and rent the first *Indiana Jones* movie. Watch the last ten or fifteen minutes. The answer to that question comes from the old knight, right after the villain chooses the silver chalice." With that, Booth and the other senators walked off laughing. Booth looked at the others and said: "You have to remember, the bad guy chose the silver chalice instead of the wooden chalice and immediately began aging at a mile a second. The audience screamed, but if you listened closely, the old knight looked at Indiana Jones and without any emotion said: *He chose poorly.*"

Among men, sometimes the term *asshole* is used as a compliment. It was not recorded which of the three senators paid Booth the compliment.

~

MONDAY, DECEMBER 17, 2012

By the end of the day, every governor had transmitted the names of the appointed electors and the numbers of votes cast for each candidate; one original and two copies with each state's seal were sent to the Federal Register.

The Founders would have been mortified at the state of the Electoral College in 2012. Probably, they would have argued that the entire current understanding of the Electoral College had been taken from a document other than either the Constitution of the United States or the Federalist Papers. The Founders had a vision that the voters would select the Electoral Delegates and these delegates would meet in their individual states and decide which candidates should be endorsed by their state. Hamilton had long ago proclaimed his pure contempt for individual voters:

> It was equally desirable, that the immediate election should be made by men most capable of analyzing the qualities adapted to the station, and acting under circumstances favorable to deliberation, and to a judicious combination of all the reasons and inducements which were proper to govern their choice. A small number of persons, selected by their fellow-citizens from the general mass, will be most likely to possess the information and discernment requisite to such complicated investigations.
>
> It was also peculiarly desirable to afford as little opportunity as possible to tumult and disorder. This evil was not least to be dreaded in the election of a magistrate, who was to have so important an agency in the administration of the government as the President of

the United States. But the precautions which have been so happily concerted in the system under consideration, promise an effectual security against this mischief.

Hamilton's concept was obviously foreign to elections in the twentieth and twenty-first centuries. The electors, as individuals, had become as invisible as the Maytag repairmen. If there was no true role for the electors in the current century, then there was nothing intrinsically good in having nameless, faceless electors in a time of crisis. If there was no role for them, nameless, faceless was probably best. In 2012, it would have been so much easier if human beings were left out of this part of the equation.

Article II, Section 1 of the Constitution gives the individual states the right to appoint their delegates in the manner in which they think is appropriate. Within this delegation of power to the states, many states had determined to ensure that their delegates voted in concert with the direction of the voters of their individual states. These active states passed laws to force electors to vote in concert with their state. Most of the penalties were no more than a requirement to sit in the town square with a dunce hat on, but a couple of states made not following the voters a felony. And many had not done a thing. That being the state of the various applicable laws, only eight voters in the past sixty-four years voted for someone other than the selection of their state's voters.

On December 15 and 17, there were fifty separate meetings of electors in the fifty separate states. Given all of the publicity and turmoil that surrounded the election and the electors, the results were a tribute to the laws of the states and the expectations of the electorate. Each state submitted the required documents to the archivist on December 17 with the votes, including their six copies of the Certificates of Vote along with the remaining six copies of the Certificates of Ascertainment previously transmitted to the Federal Register.

In his office in Orange, The Professor laughed at the process. He had so hoped someone would violate their states law and there would be a court action to test the constitutionality of the state laws. It had not happened.

~

THURSDAY, JANUARY 3, 2013

The meeting had been called by Martin Jakowitz, an entering freshman Democratic congressman from Texas. He indicated to the leadership of the Democratic Party in a letter dated December 30, 2012, that he represented seventeen Democratic congressmen and congresswomen. He was *demanding* this meeting on this date at this time. All he would say in response to the purpose of the meeting was that there would be significant consequences for the party if the meeting did not take place. His demand was without precedent, yet airplanes were flown across the country to San Francisco for the meeting.

The meeting was in the San Francisco offices of the former and presumed future Speaker of the House of Representatives and would include the presumed Majority Whip, Herman Sackman and Congressman Jakowitz.

The Speaker was attired in an Armani pants suit and flat heels while the Majority Whip elected to go with a sports coat and tie, a bit too tight fitting as the Washington life coupled with an election in limbo and his lack of eating discipline had run past his exercise program. Sackman was in Levis and his favorite Dartmouth sweatshirt. His new, slightly larger size was not lost on the Speaker or the Majority Leader.

Jakowitz arrived on time and was the last one to arrive. The Democratic leadership let Jakowitz wait in the reception area for a full thirty minutes while they tried to determine what a freshman congressman could be demanding. After accomplishing nothing in their guesswork, the Speaker got up, looked at her compadres and said: "Let's meet the young power broker and give him a lesson in Democratic politics."

In walked Jakowitz, average size, average weight, white shirt, striped tie, and grey suit. With perfect grace and confidence, he introduced himself to each of the three powerful Democrats. Without being asked, he quickly took the straight-backed seat that was obviously his with Sackman and the Whip taking their seats on the couch. The Speaker remained behind her over-sized, but perfectly clean desk. Jakowitz realized that the office was organized exactly like the Oval Office. The only difference was that it was a perfect square, but the furniture, chair, etc., were close to identical, including the rug.

Jakowitz pulled three sheets of paper from his old-fashioned and clearly long-used Hartman briefcase and handed one to everyone. Before he could begin a sentence, Sackman looked at him and said: "What the fuck is this?"

Jakowitz stood immediately and walked to the couch directly in front of Sackman. Softly and precisely: "Mr. Sackman, every Sunday morning, my wife, my children and I drive to the Second Baptist Church off the Katy Freeway. We don't drink or smoke and we certainly don't use foul language. I do not know what your role is in this meeting, Sir, but I can see from your attire that you do not hold me in a very high level of respect. I would very much appreciate it if you conducted yourself like an adult." He turned to walk back to his chair.

Sackman flung himself off the couch and screamed at Jakowitz: "Who the fuck do you think you are?" Sackman looked down at the paper in front of him again. "Don't you know this decision has already been made? What are you, the fucking village idiot?"

Jakowitz slowly sat back in his chair and stared at Sackman and there was a full twenty seconds (seemingly forever given the circumstances) before the Whip said: "Herman, sit down, now!" Sackman sat.

Apparently less intimidated than anyone might have expected, Jakowitz again stood up slowly and in a voice that was as frightening as it was soft in volume, looked directly at the Speaker, but responded to the President's emissary: "You know, Mr. Sackman, I led men into battle in Iraq and on one specific occasion had to send a patrol out to die. I read you are the kind of man who likes to bully people with threats and language. I would suggest to you that I do not bully very easily. And, additionally, I think this would be a good time to take a close look at the gold star I wear in my lapel and offer an apology."

Sackman stared at Jakowitz. As Jakowitz began to put his papers down on the straight-backed chair, Sackman assessed his situation and mumbled an apology.

Jakowitz picked up his papers and sat down yet again, still looking directly at the Speaker: "Ms. Speaker, the list of six names you have in front of you are the names that are acceptable to seventeen Democratic Members of the House of Representatives as the next Speaker of the House. The names on the list are not negotiable. The list of seventeen Members is not going to be made available to you, and you are going to be left with my word that there are seventeen of us who are going to vote for the Republican if the House leadership does not recommend one of the six names on this list to be Speaker of the House. No animus here on our side, you are way too liberal for us, and frankly, a bit too old. This is not to determine that we do not appreciate your career to date or what you have accomplished for the American people."

Sackman was up again. "Who do you think you are? We had not heard of you until you demanded this meeting. Do you know who you are in the room with? Don't you have the remotest idea what it is to be a team player?"

"Yes, I do understand team play. I suspect you, Sir, have no clue. As to who I am in the room with, two Members of the House of Representatives who I came to meet with and apparently someone who believes he is really, really important. So, please sit yourself down again. You are beginning to try my patience."

The Speaker jumped in at this point as she was beginning to believe that this guy must have come out of some war novel and she wanted no part of that. "Herman, sit down and shut up." Sackman sat.

"I am here because I could not care less if I am a one term congressman and certainly have no pride in where my office is and whether I get the blue sofa or the foot massage machine. That is not why I came to Washington. I really did come to represent my district.

"Mr. Sackman, that kind of changes the power curve doesn't it?" He did not wait for a reply and leaned back in his straight-backed chair taking the front legs up an inch or two as if he was the CEO and he was in front of three employees. "So, here is the deal. We do not believe that the House of Representatives is going to be able to select a President of the United States and we believe Jordon Scotch is a lock in the Senate. As a result of our thinking, we are unwilling to have you, Ms. Speaker, as next in line to be the President. Simple as that. So, again, here is the deal: we believe the Republican moderate who will be nominated for Speaker is more qualified, more represents the voters in our districts, and is closer to the right age than you are to be second in line to become President.

"We are informing you that if the party nominates anyone who is not on this list to be the Speaker, the Speaker will be a Republican. If you are professional in the way that this is handled, we will revisit the issue if and when the House of Representatives selects a President." *What a joke that would be, but it sounds good. There is no way this is not the end of the wicked witch.*

Sackman stood again and this time Jakowitz immediately stood up as well. With both standing, the ex-combat veteran towered over the President's guy. Jakowitz then turned to face the Speaker who had not said a word other than telling Sackman to sit down. "It was nice meeting you, Ms. Speaker. I wish it could have been a different subject. Nice to meet you gentlemen as well. And Herman, your reputation does you complete justice. Oh, and Herman, it would be one of the really smart decisions of your life to get out of my way as I leave this office because I have decided I really do not like you. Add to that my view of hardball politics might be a bit more earthy than yours." Sackman again sat.

To complete silence, Jakowitz picked up his old, brown Hartman briefcase, put his papers in one of the folder sections inside the lid side, closed the briefcase and walked to the door, opened it, paused for just a second and without hearing a word from the three power brokers, turned the door handle and left. All the remaining individuals heard was a brisk "Have a nice day" as the door closed. He walked through the reception area, winked at the receptionist, turned the next door handle and went to the elevator. In the elevator, he looked at himself in the mirror and laughed out loud. "Bet the next hour in that room is interesting."

In the Speaker's office, it was bedlam with all three politicians speaking at once. Finally, the Whip looked at the Speaker and asked: "OK, Kid, I believe him. Which from the list are you going to nominate? We are not going to have a Republican as Speaker of the House during the selection process for the election of the President of the United States."

Sackman gave them another "No fucking way."

Moments later, the threesome was joined telephonically by the President. The Whip and Sackman let the Speaker explain the situation after Sackman started the conversation and the Speaker told him again to "shut up." Two hours and thirty minutes later, the telephone conversation ended with number four on the list having agreed to become the Speaker of the House of Representatives on Tuesday, January 8, 2012. No one was happy, but politics trumped everything.

~

MONDAY, JANUARY 7, 2013

From the day's *Washington Post* editorial page by Randy Kraus:

CONGRESS MEETS THIS WEEK TO SELECT PRESIDENT LEAST POPULAR ORGANIZATION IN USA MUST REVERSE PERCEPTION

A significantly higher percentage of people in the United States believe that there really is a Loch Ness Monster than approve of the United States Congress. We could make many more and even more horrible comparisons of x, y, or z to the popularity of Congress. Let's leave it that the government of Cuba is also more highly thought of than the Congress of the United States. We finally note that the United States has not had relations with Cuba in so long that one needs to be on Social Security to have a clear memory of Cuba before the Cuban Revolution.

It does not take a great researcher to determine that Congress has never been very popular and we generally attribute that to the general human condition. Most of us would rather be the rule maker than the rule recipient. We understand that Congress's approval is rarely, if ever, at a mere fifty percent.

This week is Congress's opportunity to shine for the American people or to confirm their expectations. Can the House of Representatives rise to the opportunity?

We do not know the answer to our question. If Congress succeeds and looks professional, seriously considering the wishes of its constituents, politics will be benefited for generations. If not, perhaps Democracy with a capital D is in danger in the United States of America.

This newspaper is not in the habit of quoting President Ronald Reagan, but his quote on democracy is an appropriate reminder for Congress as it goes about electing a President of the United States: "Freedom is never more than one generation away from extinction. We didn't pass it to our children in the bloodstream. It must be fought for, protected, and handed on for them to do the same."

Our advice to the House of Representatives:

In the positive – Protect our freedom by being professional and representing the people and the country as if it were made of crystal.

In the negative – Don't look like a bunch of political hacks.

~

The Members of the House of Representatives had effectively represented only two different political parties for well over one hundred years. The occasional Independent or third-party member generally selects one of the two political parties with whom to caucus and for all intensive purposes, for leadership purposes, is a member of that party.

By noon on Monday, January 7, all of the Members of the House of Representatives were in Washington D.C. for their leadership meetings. The location of said meetings generally varies but all are in or near the capitol. The majority party controls all the meeting rooms so they get first pick. With the Democrats in power, they usually meet in HC-5, a room underneath the rotunda area or in one of the bigger rooms in the new Capitol Visitor's Center. The Republicans usually meet in a room in the Canon House office building or in a smaller room in the Capitol Visitor's Center. While this was not the case today, when the discussion is political of fundraising, both parties move the meetings to their respective clubs off-campus because elected officials cannot have fundraising discussions in a government building. (The Republicans usually retreat to the Capitol Hill Club.)

By the time the meeting of the Democratic Party was called to order, all, of course, knew that the House Democratic Conference had selected a freshman congressman from Pennsylvania, a former president of the Wharton School of Business at the University of Pennsylvania as the Speaker of the House of Representatives. All had heard that certain Democratic Members of Congress had made it explicitly clear to the existing leadership that they were no longer going to be the leadership of the House of Representatives' Democratic Party if the Democratic Party was to pick the woman from San Francisco as their nominee for Speaker of the House. No one knew whether this boded well or poorly for the House of Representatives. One wag did offer a bit too loudly before the meeting began: "The old bitch would have been far more comfortable representing the Czar than being the leader of the people's House. Never did get over the G5 or whatever the hell it was she needed to get home and back. Some Democrat."

The new Speaker of the House of Representatives would be a fifty-eight-year-old, former certified public accountant who had become an academic at age forty-eight. At age forty-seven, he was the managing partner of the second largest accounting firm in the world. It was agreed that there would be no discussion and there was no discussion with respect to his ascension to the Speakership. Politics was always more real and bizarre than fiction. In the midst of a crisis, an individual could be elected to the Speakership of the House of Representatives before he had spent a full day as an elected congressman. The vote in this caucus was unanimous. The assemblage moved directly into the Chambers of the House of Representatives.

The good news for all concerned was that Representative Gershwin Sarox had a lifelong interest in the Constitution and while the way this election had played out in the House was a surprise, and he had not yet quite grasped the deepest intricacies in the House of Representatives over the past few weeks, he understood the current issue and recognized that he was going to be the MC of one of the great moments in United States history.

The better news was that at fifty-eight years of age, Gershwin Sarox, Jewish and a foe of the death penalty, given his age and experience, would never have any higher opportunities for public office than the US House of Representatives. (This of course ignored the fact that until the House of Representatives elected a president, he would be second in line to be the President of the United States.) His experience as Dean of the Wharton School of Business gave him some sense of what it was to lead cats and this was therefore the perfect experience to lead the United States House of Representatives.

~

Big Red was wearing her new oversized diamond on her left hand. It was a New Year's Eve present from Lawyer Talbot; it had taken a few days to get it sized but it was now in place on the proper finger on the left hand. Big Red had actually asked Lawyer Talbot to marry her. Neither she nor Talbot would ever describe the exact circumstances surrounding the "Will you marry me?" and the "Yes, I will." A bit unconventional, but as he had told her years before that it was her decision to make and she had been the one dragging her feet.

There were a number of congratulatory hugs before the show. Everyone liked their newest anchor. Now, she sat opposite Isadore Yergler. It was not the easiest interview to arrange, and today there had been problems with respect to the organization of the set. So, actually, instead of sitting exactly opposite Yergler, Yergler was in the next room with the appearance that he was in Los Angeles with a Los Angeles city background. Yergler had insisted that he be shown only from the waist up and the demand had not come until he realized that the beautiful red headed anchorwoman was going to tower over him if they sat across from each other.

"Mr. Yergler, thank you for being our guest this evening. From our research and estimation, we believe your personal independent contributions to the President's campaign were approximately $7 million. Why would you spend that kind of money on a personal campaign?"

"I believe in this president and his policies. I can afford these expenditures and I think it was the right thing to do. I really did this in reaction to all of the crazy right-wing money I saw entering this campaign." *How could they only think $7 million? These guys are pretty good and I have written checks for a touch over $25 million. What is this all about?*

The interview was a bit benign and Big Red next interviewed Reesa Jonathon who refused to confirm or deny the amount of money she had spent on her campaign. Her disclosure documents, she said, would be timely and correctly filed. She forced the conversation to a discussion of the responsibilities of the Congress. She offered the opinion that Congress need follow their constituent's decisions and should elect George Vincent and "that should be that."

~

TUESDAY, JANUARY 8, 2013

All 221 Democratic Members of the House of Representatives were in the Chamber for the selection of the Speaker of the House of Representatives, the swearing in of the new Members of Congress, and the selection of committees.

Because the House of Representatives in the United States is not considered a continuing body, every two years, the Congress is considered a new Congress. This 113th Congress, perhaps well numbered, like all of the Congresses before it, was considered new. New in Congress means *new* and the rules of the House of Representatives need be agreed upon before any business can be done.

While the Constitution provides that the Congress convene on January 3 at noon, the prior Congress mandated that the date be January 8, 2013. This had everything to do with vacations and college football.

If the previous Clerk of the Congress gets re-elected, the Clerk calls the House of Representatives to order. The Honorable Lorraine C. Miller was re-elected and therefore called the House to order. The Chaplain of the House of Representatives offered a prayer after the meeting was called to order. The prayer was brief and maintained the relationship of God to the government of the United States without regard to the literally hundreds of Federal Court cases that would appear to make the offering of the daily prayer totally inappropriate and perhaps, illegal. To some in the Chambers, the daily prayer represented one of the major problems with the Federal government, not because of the religious aspects, but because far too many of the laws passed by the Congress exempted the Congress from those very laws that it was passing.

At that point in the proceedings, the Members-elect and their guests recited the Pledge of Allegiance. For the purpose of the organizational meeting, every Member of Congress is a Member-elect as the Congress is a new Congress. Before technology, a Reading Clerk called the role of the new Congress.

On this day, in 2013, each Member inserted an official voting card into the Chamber's electronic voting machine for the purpose of determining a quorum was present. It was rare for all 435 Members to be both healthy and present, but this was a very rare life experience for the Members and the remaining 300 plus million Americans who would watch or hear about the election of their President today.

Finally, in the perfect order used every two years, the Clerk announced the election of the Resident Commissioner from Puerto Rico, and the Delegates from the District of Columbia, Guam, the US Virgin Islands and American Samoa.

The first order of what most would consider business was for the House of Representatives to select its Speaker. As was tradition in the House of Representatives, both the Democrats and the Republicans nominated their candidates and the vote took place. The Clerk asked for nominations for the Speaker of the House. Congressman Arthur Lockard, a second-term congressman from Vermont rose to indicate that as chairman of the House Democratic Conference, he "was directed by the unanimous vote of that conference to present for election to the office of Speaker of the House of Representatives of the 113th Congress of the United States, the name of the Honorable Gershwin Sarox, a Representative of the State of Pennsylvania." This nomination, by yet another junior Democrat, sent other messages throughout the nation. The world had changed with the 2012 election.

With their nomination of Gershwin Sarox, a freshman Member, the Democrats had done something unprecedented. But all had been worked out previously. The Republicans made their nomination and there was a roll call vote electing Gershwin Sarox as the Speaker of the United States House of Representatives. The House elected Mr. Sarox, 221-to-214, strictly on party lines. This was the norm. At this point, the House of Representatives followed tradition with a few short statements by the leadership of each party, the administration of the oath of office for the Speaker, and the Speaker giving the oath of office to the remaining Members en masse.

Tradition now required, in order, announcement of party leadership, election of officers, notification of the Senate of same, and adoption of the rules of procedure. Generally, the House rules of procedure were carried over from the previous Congress with specific changes. The majority party determined the rules and the key rule addition for the 113th Congress was that if the House of Representatives was to elect the President of the United States, each state would be represented by the longest serving Member of the state's Delegation to Congress and that each time the state voted, he would identify, by name, the vote of each Member. These rules, also painstakingly worked out earlier, were passed unanimously without discussion.

The Rules Committee of the House of Representatives did an excellent job of determining the rules for the election of the President of the United States. *Excellent* in Congress was defined as completing the task. It was done in secret before the congressional session began and was released on the afternoon of January 7 after an entirely ceremonial meeting of the Rules Committee. The Republicans received a copy of the rules before the meeting and debate would have been nothing less than silly.

The private meeting to determine the rules consisted of Democrats only and was held in the home offices of the chairwoman of the Rules Committee in Rochester, New York. None of the Members or any of the congressional staff was happy about trudging to Rochester, New York in December, but the chairwoman broke her leg two weeks before and was convalescing at home. The December meeting included the six re-elected Rules Committee Democratic Members of the House of Representatives. Each assumed correctly that they would again serve on the Rules Committee and that the Democrats would control the House of Representatives and therefore the Rules Committee only need Democrats to complete their task. The meeting was polite, but strained. The contentious issues were how to organize the voting, how to allow the states to meet to determine their voting, and whether to have the individual states disclose their individual Member's votes.

They agreed that between the call for the vote and the voting, the Congress would be in recess for exactly forty-five minutes and that each state would then have its name called alphabetically with a paper transmission of the individual votes to the Speaker. Similar to the counting of electoral votes in the US Senate, the individual congressperson's vote would need to be offered after the individual state vote and before the next state vote. Objections would be handled on a majority vote of the states using a similar procedure. (It was hoped that there would be few, if any, objections to the state vote as the states with equal numbers of Democrats and Republicans would be a problem.)

There was a long and serious discussion regarding the states' individual votes. Article II, Section 1 provided only: *The Votes shall be taken by states, the Representation from each State having one Vote.* Article I, Section 5 provided: *Each House may determine the Rules of its Proceedings.* So the question was: When did a candidate have a sufficient number of votes in any state to determine the state's vote? The example was a state with nine Members of the House of Representatives where they voted four votes for candidate 1, three votes for candidate 2, and two votes for candidate 3. The next question was: Had the state voted for candidate 1 or had the state been unable to cast a vote?

The staff of the Rules Committee produced the limited history for the Committee. In 1800, the rules of the House of Representatives provided that to cast a vote for a candidate, a state needed to have a majority of its Members vote for the candidate, otherwise it cast a blank ballot. This was the reason that in 1800, it took until the thirty-sixth ballot before the House elected Jefferson after Federalist representatives in Vermont and Maryland broke the deadlock by switching their vote. In 1825, while there were no states that did not achieve a majority on the first ballot, the House of Representatives again required that to cast a vote for a candidate, a majority had to exist in a state. There had been no fact situation since 1825 which had arisen wherein the House of Representatives again needed to determine these rules in 188 years. The staff also noted that in 1825, the House of Representatives took a page out of the Vatican playbook and required that the House of Representatives continuously vote until a decision was made. Literally, the doors were blocked, no other business was done and only Members and a few others could enter or leave the Chamber.

This was the *Oh my God* moment and the Rules Committee sought the simultaneous advice of the woman they believed would become the Speaker of the House and the future Minority Leader. The situation could be challenged in the House of Representatives and no one on the Rules Committee wanted to have a revolution even before the first vote was cast. Upon this decision, perhaps, rested the ultimate identity of the next President of the

TUESDAY, JANUARY 8, 2013

United States. The only good news was that no one had the math and no one knew how the Members of the House would vote. No one knew whether the Members of the House of Representatives would feel any fidelity whatsoever to the voters of their state, whether they would feel obligated to follow the actions of the leaders of their party, whether they would follow their political instincts, or if they would just go for WIFM.

No one on the Rules Committee knew either Geekhead or The Professor, but an inquiry into either of these gurus would have found a definitive answer available from each. The only thing of interest would have been that both The Professor and Geekhead knew the history without research, something that was not the case for the young staffers working for the House of Representatives who had spent weeks writing their memorandum. The rules Committee itself was at a complete intellectual loss. Both The Professor and Geekhead independently assumed that precedent would be followed and they had not mentioned the issue either on television or to George Vincent.

The issue was solved by the Democratic Whip when he expressed the following: "It seems to me that if we stick with precedent, we won't find ourselves at the Supreme Court on the issue of whether we can set the rules for a state or they can set their own rules, which scares me to death. On the politics, we have eighteen states, the Republicans have twenty-four states and there are eight ties. Of the eight ties, we are split three Republican, three Democrat and two having voted for Vincent. I'm not smart enough to tell you how the vote will go, but I think Jordon Scotch is going to be the Vice President and my best guess is that the House is not going to want to have two guys from a political party with no backing in the Executive Branch. But, I have absolutely no idea what will happen once we convene."

The Rules chairwoman explained that each vote would be recorded by the individual Member, regardless of whether the states voted or had a non-vote in their plan, and no one objected. Another Democratic Rules Member opined that this might make it a bit more difficult to get to a conclusion, but that the voters would be well served to know what their Representative did in Congress. The committee then determined that they would follow precedent and require that each state have a majority vote for a single candidate or its vote would be considered a no vote.

The presumed Speaker of the House believed she could control her people far better than the Republicans and assumed with these rules she would wear them down and the Democratic President would be re-elected. The

Speaker solved the other issue: "And, we are not going to put other business aside and pretend we are in Rome. We will have two votes a day and only on the days where we are in session. I am going to be almost seventy-three years old when this starts and I don't do all nighters anymore."

All agreed. A single member of the Rules Committee guffawed at the Speaker's admission of her age. She was one of the very few Members who did not put their birth date on their website. The men did not much care about such vanities. To date, the closest thing to vanity on the male side had been the occasional wig and the Vice President's hair, and he would be an historical footnote within a few days.

The rules were distributed at the opening of the session and absent a sufficient amount of time to think about the rules, there was no objection from any Member. Since the rules were controlled by the party in power, any objection would serve only as a speaking opportunity for the Member, and the Members were very cautious on this opening day.

~

THURSDAY, JANUARY 10, 2013

At exactly 1:00 p.m., a joint session of Congress was gaveled into session by the Vice President. Sitting next to the Vice President was the new Speaker of the House. The likely soon-to-be former Vice President knew for weeks with reasonable certainty where and how he would be spending his time after January 20, 2013, and looked fairly relaxed in his favorite dark suit and white shirt with striped tie. The new Speaker of the House introduced himself to the Vice President as he arrived at the podium wearing his best dark blue suit, blue and gold striped tie and white button-down, collared shirt. The button-down, collared shirt, which his wife said befit an old fuddy-duddy accountant about as well as an old fuddy-duddy business school dean, was what he had worn since he graduated from college, regardless of current style. To anyone watching, the Speaker looked classically like he was still the dean of a business school. He was bald on top with a bit too much long, brown hair on the sides and back, with red cheeks and wire-rimmed glasses. There were four tellers, one Democrat and one Republican from each Chamber and they were positioned to count the ballots at the appropriate time.

Formally, Senate pages brought two mahogany boxes into the Chamber. The boxes contained each state's certified vote of the Electoral College. The Vice President's role was to open these envelopes holding the results of the Electoral College and read the salient part of each Certificate. The reading was in alphabetical order.

The Vice President performed his role loudly and clearly. Mercifully, there were no objections to any state's vote count. Upon conclusion of the voting, the Vice President, after waiting for the tellers to confirm, announced the final tally:

Votes for President of the United States:

The President	194
Senator George Vincent	236
Congressman Paul Roland	108

Votes for Vice President of the United States:

The Vice President	194
Dr. Jordon Scotch	236
Senator Robert Blankley	108

There being no winner in the Electoral College, The Vice President declared the election a Contingent Election, an historic term confirming what everyone already knew, that the President would be selected by the House of Representatives and the Vice President would be selected by the United States Senate.

The Vice President had only smiled when he announced his own name. He added: "Under the rules of the Constitution of the United States, pursuant specifically to the Twelfth Amendment, the House of Representatives is required to go into immediate session for the purpose of immediately electing the President of the United States."

The Vice President decided that it was appropriate to read the Twelfth Amendment of the Constitution, which in pertinent part provides as follows:

> The person having the greatest Number of votes for President, shall be the President, if such number be a majority of the whole number of electors appointed; and if no person have such majority, then from the persons having the highest numbers not exceeding three on the list of those voted for as President, the House of Representatives shall choose immediately, by ballot, the President. But in choosing the President, the votes shall be taken by states, the representation from each state having one vote; a quorum for this purpose shall consist of a Member or Members from two-thirds of the states, and a majority of all the states shall be necessary to a choice. And if the House of Representatives shall not choose a President whenever the right of choice shall devolve upon them, before the

fourth day of March next following, then the Vice President shall act as President, as in the case of the death or other constitutional disability of the President.

He indicated that the date was later changed to be January 20.

When he was finished, the Vice President got up from his chair, shook hands with everyone in sight and vacated the playing field. There were no frills, no conflict and nothing to injure his new position as Chief Paid Speech Giver.

~

The United States Senate has displayed the appearance of professionalism for over one hundred years. This was not the case when an occasional duel took place in the early nineteenth century, but today it is not uncommon for two men who literally hate each other at the same level as the presidents of North and South Korea, to refer to each other as *good friends*. This has been laughable for seemingly forever and is even more laughable in the twenty-first century.

Because of travel schedules and the creation of individual staffs numbering over one hundred, many of the senators needed to be introduced over and over to their own colleagues. While members of the US Senate who had been in the Senate for more than twelve years had developed close friendships, the newer members were more likely to be friendly with airplane attendants than each other. The nature of political fundraising, the availability of rapid transportation home and back along with Senate schedules being whittled to the middle of the week only, have been working away at both partisan and bi-partisanship relationships for a couple of decades and as the old guard retires or has died off, the likelihood of one hundred strangers, strangers to each other, being members of the US Senate is greater with each election cycle.

In the US Senate, the Vice President of the United States is the President of the US Senate and when he is in attendance, he acts as the chairman of the US Senate. The Vice President only votes if the votes of the Senate are equal, a tie. The oddity of this particular role is that the President pro tempore, who is the chairman when the Vice president is not in the Senate, is third in line to become President of the United States behind the Vice President and the Speaker of the House of Representatives. There has never been an event where the President pro tempore has become the President of the United States.

It is a tradition of the Senate to elect the senior Member of the US Senate's majority party to this seemingly ceremonial role as President pro tempore. After the death of Senator Byrd in 2010, Senator Daniel Inouye of Hawaii was sworn in as President pro tempore. Senator Inouye, a Medal of Honor winner during World War II, was eighty-five years old when he was sworn in as the President pro tempore of the United States Senate. And this was the oddity, third in line to become President of the United States at age eighty-five, almost a decade younger than his predecessor. Despite the fact that there had never been a Speaker of the House who had become President of the United States through succession and the fact that the holder of the title was often on life support, this ordering had annoyed every President pro tempore for well over two hundred years. Generally, the Senate felt superior to the House of Representatives in all ways, except through the language of succession in the Constitution of the United States and that they voted for the Vice President and the House of Representatives voted for the President.

Senator Inouye's term would end as the first item of the new Senate's agenda. As the Republican's held fifty-seven seats in the US Senate, he would not be re-elected as President pro tempore.

Every time an octogenarian or near octogenarian was sworn in as the President pro tempore of the United States Senate, at least a few freshman senators would look at the senator next to them and say: "Does anyone know that this guy is third in line to be President? Does anyone know that the President, Vice President and Speaker of the House of Representatives are together occasionally?"

On this Thursday morning, with the Vice President of the United States of America holding the gavel, the Senate quickly elected a member of the Republican majority as its President pro tempore. Senator Orrin Hatch had been in the Senate for thirty-six years, was very popular among his Republican colleagues and his support of Congressman Roland was not a concern among very many. He had that wonderful and unusual position of being respected by his colleagues on all counts. While Hatch led the Republican discussions regarding the election of a vice president, most saw the election of Jordon Scotch as a fait accompli as Scotch had been registered a Republican before becoming the nominee for the American Exceptionalism Party and perhaps more important, he was not the current vice president.

If there had been a ballot in the US Senate on the capabilities of the current vice president to be the President of the United States and the ballot had been secret, he would of have garnered only twenty votes. An old Democratic senator used the old expression: "A mile wide and an inch deep," meaning there was not sufficient brainpower or velocity of thought above his neck to trust him with any major decision, let alone the nuclear trigger. His many terms in the US Senate said nothing good about democracy or his home state in the minds of many. As vice president, he received coverage at a factor of twenty relative to his coverage as a senator from a very small state. With that coverage, he had become a caricature of himself with malapropos

601

after malapropos and several just plain stupid remarks. His only saving grace was that he was scandal free and a particularly nice guy.

The Vice President faced the daunting task of sitting in the role of chairman of the US Senate with the knowledge and reality that he would be effectively out of office before he left the room, which would be moments after the vote. (The term of the Vice President would officially end on January 20.)

On this day, the Vice President reviewed the rules and fully understood that there was no room for obfuscation, a slowdown in the procedures, or anything else that he could do to remain the Vice President of the United States. He might give it the old college try, but there was little in the way of meaningful action he could take. When the four Democratic senators announced they would not participate in a filibuster, the die was cast. This took the non-filibuster count to sixty-two including Senator Vincent. All the Vice President thought he could count on was that most of his Democratic colleagues would vote for him and he would achieve thirty-seven votes.

Under the Constitution, the Senate could only choose from the two top electoral vote getters for vice president and the only requirement was that a majority of the senators be in attendance. The Democrats could have had a bit of fun by not attending the meetings of the Senate, but it would have been an empty and a potentially embarrassing gesture. This was a game, which the Vice President was not remotely interested in playing. While his effective role in the United States government was going to end with this first meeting of the United States Senate in 2013, there was a great future for the former vice president as a lobbyist and over-priced dinner speaker. (Unlike the President, the Vice President was not wealthy. Somehow, he had managed to remain middle class economically throughout his long service in government, an unusual accomplishment.) If he was involved in even a momentary conspiracy to remain in office because of a technicality, his personal brand, as he saw it, would be destroyed. And to be fair, the Vice President wanted to do the right thing for the country.

The Vice President's conversation on the Senate vote and his explanation of his post-elected office strategy had not gone well at the White House. After four years of carrying the President's flag without hesitation, he was a bit taken back that he had become instantly old news along with the President's insistence that he fight the incredibly uphill battle for the vice presidency in the Senate. He had concluded his comments at his White

House meeting with his threat that "I too can write a book and it sure as hell won't be friction." (He meant fiction.) "And you know, people like me!" Delaware produced fairly unrecognizable accents. The emphasis on *me* was strong, but had no particularly noticeable accent attached to it. The Vice President was certain as he left the meeting that he was not on the President's, or either of his two key aides', Thanksgiving dinner invitation lists. He was also furious. *Narcissists!*

The Vice President called the session to order. With great ceremony, the new senators were introduced and all of the necessary parliamentary activities were executed to admit the new senators. The Vice President presided over the election of Senator Hatch to President pro tempore of the United States Senate. The Vice President then called the next order of business, which was to elect the Vice President of the United States of America for the term beginning January 20, 2013. Senator Robert Jefferson Wayne asked that the election of Jordon Scotch be made unanimous, but Senator Booth insisted on a vote by each Member, in alphabetical order, as prescribed by law. Senator Booth's request could not be denied under Senate rules. There was no request for debate.

All one hundred senators were in place, including Senator George Vincent of Ohio. Senator Vincent was the only senator in the Chamber who was uncertain whether he would be sitting as a senator in February. He had chosen the role of spectator / voter for this morning; he voted for Jordon Scotch.

The actual vote was a bit surprising given all of the attention paid to the senators over the past several months and there would be rumors of a conspiracy for decades. The surprise was that virtually every senator from a state that voted either for Senator Vincent or Congressman Roland voted for Jordon Scotch. Voting along these lines produced a fascinating result with Jordon Scotch receiving eighty-four votes and the Vice President receiving only sixteen votes. No one knew with certainty exactly what the message being sent was or to whom the message was being sent.

The Vice President congratulated Jordon Scotch with all of the cordiality he could muster given that one could paint the vote count as a personal repudiation. He entered the Senate Chamber with the intent of being classy and respectful of the body and left having accomplished that mission. In what was a tribute to his parents in raising him to always maintain his poise, the now former Vice President showed neither anger nor his disappointment.

~

In the House of Representatives, the Members of the smaller states did not have any issues determining who voted for who and who their state voted for in totality. This was not the case for the larger states, California in particular, sitting with over fifty representatives. Fourteen states had requested separate rooms for their voting; the remaining states would use the offices of various Members. The Member from Wyoming indicated that if he needed a private meeting, for Wyoming, he would ride his Harley around the Capitol Building a few times. This was all quietly worked out by the individual states as the editorial in the *Washington Post* had gotten everyone's attention. The House of Representatives would try its best not to look like political hacks.

Whether the individual states would conduct themselves in their private meetings like statesmen and stateswomen (or political hacks) would not be visible to their constituents. Word of course would leak out—not always accurate—but word would leak out of the state meetings. One wag did offer that there were leaders of the other political party in his state who he had never met, so he saw the process as an opportunity to "get some autographs." No one knew for certain who it was or if he was serious.

~

Bill O'Brien was in his element. Not only did he have Geekhead and Jennifer Cho, he had former Democratic Senator Richard Dionisio and Senator Blankley. This was Blankley's first appearance on any television panel since the vote of the Electoral College.

"Thank you all for being here this evening. And special thanks to you, Senator Blankley. In my opinion, you have shown enormous class during the past several weeks. What a ride, Senator?"

"Yes, Bill, it has been quite an experience. We gave it our best. Who would have thought that a third-party candidate would win the highest number of electoral votes? The fascinating part to me is that the American Exceptionalism Party did this without any get out the vote effort."

"And where does it leave us, Senator?"

"It leaves Dr. Jordon Scotch as the Vice President of the United States. It leaves me as a Member of the United States Senate. As to the presidency, I do not know. Some of what I hear from the President and on websites is not in concert with what I learned about the Constitution in school. And the riots were truly both unfortunate and inappropriate. This is the United States and we are supposed to be able to pass power without bloodshed and rioting."

Former Senator Dionisio joined the conversation asking, "Why is the President so verbally outside the scope of the Constitution? What he is saying is that he received the largest number of votes and therefore should be President of the United States!"

"Richard, damn it, that is a talking point and you know it. That goes right along with the idiots that denied George Boone was President of the United States because the courts ruled in his favor and of course, ignoring that he actually received the most votes in Florida. You and I both know what the law is and the House of Representatives has the same legal and moral right to opt to re-elect the President, elect Paul Roland or elect George Vincent. That is our system and those are the rules. If you don't like the rules, amend the Constitution of the United States. Part of its brilliance is the ability to amend it." Blankley was not lacking any candor this evening.

"Doctor, what do you think about all of this as an expert on the Constitution, specifically about what the President is saying regarding the fact that he received the most votes?"

"Bill, Senator Blankley has it right on all points. First, if the Founders had been interested in the popular vote, the Constitution would not have had either electors or a procedure with voting by states. One needs to remember that the current rules of the states requiring their electors to vote for a specific candidate are not what was originally intended in the document, yet those rules clearly comport with the delegation of the underlying voting rules to the states. Once it gets to Congress, it was clearly the intent of the Founders that the popular vote not be the key element to the decision. This was predictable and what we would call a *deal point* in 2013. The few voters in several states were not and did not want to join into a nation or a confederation of states where Virginia was going to virtually decide every election. Nothing has changed."

Dionisio retorted: "It is not 1800."

Geekhead forced his way back into the conversation: "You know, Senator, it is not 1800 and the Constitution and its court-determined direction have changed a great deal since 1800. That is the beauty of the document. I think the most important thing is that the Constitution has not changed since the beginning of the election. That is the sign of a democracy. With all due respect, Sir."

Jenn, a bit out of her element needed to become a part of the discussion and as she had been listening to parts of this conversation for months, she was comfortable with her opinion: "North and South Dakota might not be comfortable today having virtually no say in who becomes President."

"Yes, and let me finish the thought about amending the Constitution. Remember, there has been a stealth campaign among the larger states to end-run the Constitution with the National Popular Vote Interstate Compact. This is an effort to backdoor the popular vote into being the electoral vote through forcing the electors to vote for the popular vote winner. This is not being attempted through the Constitutional Amendment system and is probably unconstitutional in my opinion, but it is out there and has been approved by several states."

Bill O'Brien was personally enjoying the discussion, but needed to close for a commercial: "Thank you, my panel, especially you Senator Blankley. It was nice that you had the nerve to come on our show."

~

The President just stared at one of the three televisions in his Oval Office. Sackman and Matta were absolutely silent. Nearly five minutes after the Senate vote, the President asked what was happening. Sackman was succinct: "The every-man-for-himself flag went up in the Senate on November 6. Whether there was some groupthink, which there must have been, the senators are all, each one of them, going to be able to go to their voters and tell them that they thought they were voting as directed by their constituency. We don't know who started that bandwagon, but as I told you, the ultimate result was inevitable and the individual votes were for show.

"The Vice President was so mad at us, it could have been him. He might have told the Democratic senators that he could not care less who they voted for.

"The senators will easily be able to hide behind the electoral vote which favored Vincent with his twenty-nine states. That in itself represented sixty-four senators who logically could follow their voters. So, now we have a vice president who by his own admission was only in Washington D.C. once before, in grade school. This is crazy.

"We are working the House of Representatives, but it is really, really hard. The Republicans control twenty-four states, the Democrats control eighteen states and eight states are tied. Of those eight states, three voted for Roland, three voted for you and two voted for Vincent. You know the drill, but everyone is playing the same game. Bribes, promises, promised bribes, threats; you name it, you got it. We are in there with them, but we are terrified given what happened and what was alleged in Illinois four years ago. Because of Illinois, almost all conversations are taking place through intermediaries. My guess is that this Sarox guy and the new Members are going to be a bitch to move."

The President was a little more controlled this morning than most mornings of the prior couple of weeks. Over the past two months, he was now smoking openly in the Oval Office with his wife in the White House and while no one liked the smoke-filled room look, there was no denying that when troubled and not smoking, the President was impossible on a personal basis. The offset to this was that Mrs. President was making his upstairs life very, very difficult. The guy smelled like someone had dragged him through a room where they were curing pork. His daughters made the situation worse by asking questions and prodding. Of course, they were acting on their mother's instructions.

"Prepare a list in the next two hours of who I should call in which states. I cannot be calling them into the White House yet, but I will make the calls. I want every Republican who is not a Tea Party member and I need to know what we know about them and the same for every Democrat in the swing states. I don't want to be losing anyone on our side.

"Has anyone looked into whether the state legislatures can direct their House Members to act in any particular way on this issue?"

Matta saw this as his turf: "That would be the wrong course of action as too many of these states now have Republican governors and Republican legislatures. While we made some significant gains in the House, we lost ground in the Senate and continue to lose ground in the state legislatures as well. By the way, I am getting nervous that Vincent has already talked to a host of the Congressmen. I talked to a buddy of mine in the Arkansas delegation and he indicated that the senator met with him in September and he had helped host a fundraiser as well. I heard this a couple of other times and it concerns me."

"But this is crazy. I won the popular vote by six zillion votes and if this guy Vincent had not entered the race, I would have won the popular vote by twenty million votes, maybe fifteen million votes and the electoral vote by a landslide. I can't imagine that any Democrat could possibly support this guy. I expect him to be challenged and lose in his next Ohio primary."

Matta, who thought he now knew for sure that he was leaving the administration to write a tell-all book in a few weeks because someone else was President or because he wanted to cash in on the opportunity, felt no job security fear any longer. He was going to get rich and get into good physical condition, in that order. Then he was going to spend some time with his kids and figure out what seemed out of place at home. "Mr. President, get real. We don't have any idea how the election would have turned out without Vincent. For all we know the Republicans could have nominated Bertha Aplin, or Norman Rockwell for that matter, if George Vincent had not started to register his AEP in every state. For all we know, all of those Vincent votes would have gone to Roland. You need to methodically work your way through your lists and see what you can accomplish. No one has been through this drill in over one hundred years. Hell, the last time anyone went through this, it took one vote in the House of Representatives and there were no telephones to contact anyone. Maybe for the people, that was a much better process. This jawboning is just bullshit."

"Mr. Matta," a salutation the President had never used before, "I will remind you who in this room has the title President of the United States. Either you provide a service or you can go back to your office."

Sackman could see Matta's bald head growing red and interceded: "Guys, come on, we need to get through this together. Either we are all going to be out on the street in two weeks or we are going to be working together for another term." *Well not exactly, I will be out of here by April. No way I am going to be here for a second term with fifty-seven Republican senators; life is too short for that drill. I need to find a nice district around Chicago and go back to Congress. Either way, my book is going to give credit for our accomplishments to the right people (or person).* Sackman suspected his thought was not very different from anyone else in the building. He was not clear enough to Matta to know they were marching to the same drummer.

"OK, OK," said the President. Matta just nodded without so much as a word. He would try to avoid at least some of these meetings for a few days.

The meeting went on for a while without any real progress. The threesome still had not arrived at an agreement on talking points and for the first time in four years, and while the President was making telephone calls, the rest of the White House appeared to be staying out of the fray. They were out of the fray not because they chose to be, but because they had a complete absence of meaningful ideas.

~

609

Gershwin Sarox banged the gavel for the first House of Representatives action to elect a President of the United States in 188 years. After the parliamentary niceties, including a prayer from the Chaplain, without speeches or presentations of any kind, he asked for a recess of exactly forty-five minutes for states to organize and vote, waited the forty-five minutes, and asked for the Clerk to call the roll for the decision on the next President of the United States. (The rules had been redistributed long before the meeting.) While there had been speculation at levels that could not be expressed sufficiently in words, no one truly knew what the results of the first vote would be and no one truly knew if there would be a conclusion from the first vote.

Alabama voted first and voted for Paul Roland despite George Vincent's win in Alabama. The internal State of Alabama vote was four for Roland, two for the President and one for Vincent. The message was clear; none of the Republicans and two of the Democrats in Alabama felt no obligation to follow the state as a whole. One Democratic supporter of Vincent voted for Vincent.

Alaska's single voter was a Republican and despite Vincent's win in Alaska, voted for Paul Roland.

Arkansas was another major test for the American Exceptionalism Party and George Vincent. In Arkansas, the state voted overwhelmingly for George Vincent, yet had a three-to-one Republican advantage. The vote: No vote by the State of Arkansas. Two Republicans voted for Roland, one Republican voted for George Vincent and the one Democrat voted for the President. That vote brought a clamber from the Members.

Big Red was broadcasting live and had done extensive homework to go along with her extensive briefing from the young geniuses at OBC. She quickly filled the viewers in on where this vote was going: "Only a few states into the House's vote, we can now guess that the ability of George Vincent to cement a majority is going to be very difficult. Arkansas was the test and he failed that test. Having outpolled his rivals combined by more than 100,000 votes, he only received two votes. Two Republicans voted for Roland and the Democrats, in lockstep, voted for the President. The other important result we can speculate on at this point is that we could be many House votes away from a conclusion. With only two votes per day on normal working days only, if the record of thirty plus votes of 1801 is reached, we could easily be waiting for the proverbial white smoke in April, perhaps April of 2014."

Big Red was the real deal as an anchor. She, her producers and the audience were watching a professional. Robert "Bob" Colony was not forgotten, but was not missed. The men in the audience saw a sensationally attractive woman and the women in the audience saw their *special daughter* becoming an adult. Everyone was happy.

The final first vote was:

	States
The President	9
George Vincent	11
Paul Roland	13
No Vote	17

No Vote was close to the twenty-six votes required to elect a President of the United States.

At that point, the House moved to routine activity, which meant that most of the Members left the Chambers and individual Members made one minute and special order speeches to C-Span. Later in the day, the vote was replicated.

~

Both George Vincent and Paul Roland decided to be quiet after the first vote in the House of Representatives. Everyone knew everyone was working the telephones, so there was nothing to be gained by heading towards a microphone every five minutes.

The President decided to have the Pillsbury Doughboy speak for him at the daily press conference, just as he had for the past two years. When asked how the President felt about the first vote, the Pillsbury Doughboy noted that the President had secured nearly one-half of the Members of the House of Representatives, which he took to be a sign of what Americans wanted when they gave him such a substantial victory in the popular vote. The press secretary went through the votes of the individual Members of the House of Representatives where 206 members out of 435 voted for the President. The Pillsbury Doughboy made a case that if the President received 218 votes from Members of the House of Representatives, he should be President. He did not mention that almost half of his 206 votes were from California, New York and Illinois.

Something tangible had changed in the White House pressroom over the past sixty-five days. The White House press corps was no longer all for the President save one or two. The RBC reporter was first in line: "Mr. Portman, I don't get it. My math says that in theory, the President could get almost one hundred more votes in the House of Representatives and not be very much closer to the twenty-six states needed. Are you suggesting that the President does not believe it should be necessary to win the votes of twenty-six states?"

"Nothing of the sort. I am suggesting that the President believes the citizens of the United States have clearly indicated that he is their primary choice to be President. What more evidence does the country and the House of Representatives need than the popular vote and the 206 initial votes in the House?"

Up popped the Christian Science Monitor with yet another pointed question: "Well, I don't get it either. Didn't seventy-two million voters vote against the President?"

"That is the correct statistic, but we all know that without the AEP candidate, the President would have won in a blowout. Let me finish here, we fully expect the President to be re-elected within a matter of days."

This approach failed as the audience for this presentation should have been Congress, not the media.

~

FRIDAY, JANUARY 11, 2013

From the day's *Washington Post* editorial page by Randy Kraus:

CONGRESS MEETS THIS WEEK TO SELECT PRESIDENT
POLITICAL HACKS - SO FAR

Yesterday, we made but a single request to the House of Representatives: Don't look like a bunch of political hacks.

We are journalists at the *Washington Post*, but sometimes numbers do speak louder than words.

The final first vote, by state, and by Member yesterday was:

	States
The President	9
George Vincent	11
Paul Roland	13
No Vote	17

We see disciplined Democrats by the dozens voting for the President and we mention in passing that George Vincent is a Democrat, but maybe they forgot. Maybe they forgot the voters as well. We understand not at all how the candidate who was last in the Electoral College and the popular vote was the leader after the first vote. The voting only reflects that the Republicans are in the majority in twenty-four states, but says nothing about the election.

Of course the election results were a bit different than the reaction by the House of Representatives:

States Won		Electoral Votes	Popular Votes
The President	12	194	52.5 Million
George Vincent	32	236	46.2 Million
Paul Roland	6	108	30.7 Million

We are not sure what it all means. But, we assume it means that the House of Representatives has far more political types than statesmen, which is a tragedy. We give special negative kudos to the Representatives from states with a single Member in the House of Representatives. It takes a special *Representative* from a state with a single *Representative* to vote for someone other than who the voters of his state selected on the first ballot.

Maybe the adults will appear this Monday.

~

MONDAY, JANUARY 14, 2013

	States
The President	9
George Vincent	11
Paul Roland	13
No Vote	17

No Change.

~

The International Journal had been fairly quiet during the entire election process. It made a lukewarm endorsement of Paul Roland early in the campaign, but had been more of a spectator with respect to the Presidential election than might be expected. As a result, the following Monday morning, January 14, 2013, editorial created a stir from the White House to Wall Street to Main Street.

TIME TO OPEN UP, MR. PRESIDENT

During the election, the RBC broadcasting and newspaper groups did an admirable job of identifying the many areas of non-disclosure with respect to the history and bona fides of the current President of the United States. Both the Republican and American Exceptionalism Party identified these issues and pursued answers without success. We give kudos to the soon to be Vice President Jordon Scotch for his convention speech and its accompanying theatrics.

Where have five years of inquiries gotten the public with respect to the history and bona fides of the President? All such inquiries were dismissed with condescending remarks by the President and his team. Using a term we heard during the campaign, Mr. President, it is time to man-up and make all, not some, of the information available.

We will not speculate on anything that was on the class schedule for the President when he was an undergraduate or what classes he took or what grades he received. We only suggest that this is the time for Congress to give the President the option of providing that information or not expecting the vote of any Member of the United States House of Representatives.

~

Democratic Congresswoman Regina Smith of New York was first to the podium at a few seconds after noon on this cold, snowy Monday morning. There were just under three hundred Members in the Chamber and Ms. Smith had the gravitas to garner their attention. She was a Member who was front and center in committee meetings, always prepared, always polite and very often the worst possible antagonist of a business executive representing a company that had earned recent headlines for the wrong reasons.

She held in her hand *The International Journal*. In every vote to date, she voted with every other New York Democrat for the re-election of the President of the United States. She began: "Mr. Speaker and Members of the United States House of Representatives, I hold in my hand, this morning's *International Journal*. On page A14, *The International Journal* recommended to Members of the House of Representatives that we withhold our votes for the President until, and unless, the President produces his college grades and every other document that those who hold to massive conspiracies have been demanding since it was clear that there was going to be the first black President of the United States."

Ms. Smith, a former social worker in New York City, got to Congress the old-fashioned way. Before running for Congress, she had been a member of the School Board and a state legislator. As she often said, she "had paid her dues and earned her title." Today, she was attired in a brown pantsuit with a flowered top. As always, her hair was cut very short and she was wearing her ever present brown glasses. A graduate of City College of New York, no one could remember so much as a misplaced adverb or a mispronounced word from the often-taciturn congresswoman.

"As a member of the Black Caucus and a representative of a community which is primarily African American, I am certain that there is the anticipation that I will stand here and assault the words, the management and the ownership of *The International Journal*. How could they tell us what to do or assuage the character of the first black President of the United States?

"Regina Smith votes with *The International Journal*. Yes, Regina Smith votes with *The International Journal*. I have been troubled by the lack of disclosure by this President for a long time. I believe that he is a bright, well-educated graduate of Harvard law School. I believe that he has done his best to represent the citizens of the United States since he has come to Washington. I am inclined to favor most of the policies he espouses. But, I think his lack of disclosure injures the reputation of the office which he holds and diminishes his personal reputation. Until and unless he makes the disclosures and more as recommended by *The International Journal*, Regina Smith will be casting her vote for George Vincent, the Democratic senator from Ohio."

The response to her remarks was interesting and time would tell if it was meaningful. She was applauded by both Vincent and Roland voters. There was silence from the supporters of the President. Several members of the Black Caucus turned their backs.

~

"Ok, Dr. Cicerone, why is it that Jenn is wearing an engagement ring and you just sit there with those Popeye forearms and your sleeves rolled up?" Bill O'Brien loved teasing the good academician and the fact that Geekhead always turned crimson when publically teased certainly enhanced O'Brien's personal enjoyment.

With his now customary blue shirt and striped tie, sleeves rolled up and no coat, Geekhead had become a standard bearer of the presidential circus. He was the rules committee for the network.

"Gosh, Mr. O'Brien," sounding more like a twenty-two-year-old than a tenured university professor, "That is the tradition. As you know, you will be in attendance and I will be wearing a gold band when we return from that long honeymoon, you have allowed us beginning on a certain Saturday night as long as we are back here in time for the show that Thursday evening."

"Just don't bring Jenn back pregnant, Dr. Cicerone. We need her here at Fox News." O'Brien chortled and all three of them now turned different shades of red. "So, Doctor, are the comments of Ms. Smith this morning meaningful? They did not result in so much as a single state vote by the end of the day."

"I think Jenn and I will determine when it is the right time for us to have children, Bill. We both want a big family.

"As to Regina Smith, there is no precedent for her remarks this morning as well as everything that is taking place in Washington D.C. this month. Yes, there was an election left to the House of Representatives 180 years ago and yes, Geekheads like me have unearthed every word uttered during that period, but this is very, very different. In this particular case, New York has a majority of twenty or so for the Democrats, so Ms. Smith's vote means little or nothing as to breaking this deadlock. But, Ms. Smith is a leader in the House of Representatives and a leader in the Black Caucus. If either of those groups breaks from the President en masse, then George Vincent will quickly become the President."

"Jenn?"

"I was taken aback by the response from the White House. Attacking a woman like Regina Smith cannot be good long or short-term strategy. Not providing the information generally and now not providing it when this congresswoman is asking sends a lot of messages, none good. Her influence could spill over state lines and voting blocks. Plus, it is a real break on the issue."

O'Brien finished the short segment: "On Sunday evening, Jordon Scotch is going to become the Acting President and the President is going to need to move his family out of the White House. We understand they are moving back to Chicago. That is going to be a meaningful event if it happens. The White House's response that these documents are confidential and personal to the President sounded to me like a comment from General Travis at the Alamo. Of course, General Travis never left the Alamo."

~

TUESDAY, JANUARY 15, 2013

	States
The President	9
George Vincent	11
Paul Roland	13
No Vote	17

No Change.

~

The Pillsbury Doughboy stepped to the microphone for his daily press conference. The first question came from Arthur Ninoah. "Mr. Portman, yesterday morning, Regina Smith demanded that the President make public a series of documents relating to his personal life that he has made unavailable to the public. Will the President do this?"

The Pillsbury Doughboy was prepared for this and responded clearly: "Mr. Ninoah, these documents have absolutely nothing to do with the determination by the House of Representatives of who the American public wants to be President of the United States. Their determination should be about what the American voters told us in November and it was very clear that the President received the largest number of votes and should be President of the United States.

Arthur Ninoah was a bit taken back by the spokesman's response. The White House was not his regular venue; he was covering for someone on a brief ski vacation. He had really expected more than just a declaration that the President was not going to release the documents and that he received the highest number of votes in the election. "Let me follow up, Mr. Portman, are you indicating that the President of the United States is unwilling to provide the same information that most of us need to provide for a first job interview?"

"Now, Arthur, you sound like you are from Fox News. The President does not believe that this information is useful to the discussion and he will not be distracted from the issues."

Ninoah was incensed, but protocol gave him no opportunity to ask another question. The Pillsbury Doughboy looked to Hale Shaw from RBC to bail him out with an unrelated question. Shaw looked at Arthur Ninoah, thought about his career for a second, and knowing that it would make a few headlines, blurted out his question: "Mr. Portman, I don't think it is appropriate for you to diss my good friend Arthur Ninoah. He has served the people of this country for almost forty years and I think his question deserves a more complete answer. You know, Sir, you cannot brand everyone a conspiracist. So, with all due respect, if Regina Smith thinks the President should release this information and she is certainly no flaming conservative or conspiracist, why is the President keeping the information confidential? And let me add to the fire, is there something in that documentation that the President is afraid of?"

The Pillsbury Doughboy was caught by surprise; he laughed and looked at Shaw. "Do you have a serious question or do you want me to remind you that the President graduated with honors from Harvard Law School?"

The water had gotten deeper, but Shaw was now angry too. Sternly, he started: "Hell, that was a serious question. Everyone knows that everyone who graduates from Harvard Law School, graduates with honors. What I want to know is if the President was a minority admit?" Now Shaw was trying to catch the words as they escaped from his mouth. While there had never been a conspiracy not to ask the question, there was certainty that no one would ever ask this specific question in the manner just asked.

The Pillsbury Doughboy, in very uncharacteristic fashion, picked up his briefing book and looked at the White House press corps and responded: "Well, I guess there are no serious issues today." He walked away and through the regular sized door on his right. His direction after he made his right turn was the Oval Office.

~

The President was sitting at his couch waiting for the Pillsbury Dough-boy. He did not ask his spokesman to sit down.

"Now what was that all about?"

"Mr. President, they smell blood. Your term ends in five days and they don't think you are going to be re-elected by the House. With Smith's statement, there really is no defense except to say that you believe they are confidential and unrelated to the key intellectual and political questions. As we talked about last night, Smith obviously thinks that by being tough in New York, she can be elected a senator. She has made her bet."

The President inhaled on his cigarette deeply. "I will find someone myself to run against Smith. If I have to, I'll have my wife rent an apartment in New York and register her there. There is no discussion here. Those documents would ruin my reputation. Grades are not a sign of anything except how much time I devoted to school. As you know, I test as well as anyone on the planet and those test scores always got me through the front door of every school.

"OK, you are no help, that was your last press conference until we are confirmed, I am confirmed, as the president by the House. I've got a large handful of congressional members coming quietly by tonight and maybe we can get past this tomorrow. If not, go to ground. No press conferences. Period."

~

MONDAY, JANUARY 21, 2013

	States
The President	9
George Vincent	11
Paul Roland	13
No Vote	17

No Change.

~

The setting was carefully picked by Jordon Scotch. It was 8:00 p.m. EST on January 21, 2013. His first speech as Acting President of the United States was taking place in the National Archives and directly in front of the Constitution of the United States. He and his wheelchair had already been wheeled into place before he began his speech. In his right hand were several three-by-five cards with a list of issues he wanted to cover. There was neither a podium nor a teleprompter.

The White House was unavailable for Dr. Scotch because the President had, in his heart, always assumed the House of Representatives would get to the *right* decision. He had not so much as packed a toothbrush or moved so much as a favorite pen from the Oval Office. The White House staff would complete moving him out, and Dr. Scotch into, the White House by 10:30 p.m. according to the Pillsbury Doughboy. The White House staff was numbered in the hundreds at the end of the now prior president's term and they were fully involved in moving the President out and the Acting President into the White House.

Acting President Scotch was not dressed in his classic professor outfit. Gone were the sport coat and tan slacks and the ECCO shoes. In their place were a white shirt, button-down and collared, cufflinks, grey pinstriped suit and a red tie. What no one watching would know was that this was his only suit and it had not been worn in well over three years. The good news was that with his exercise program and his attention to his weight, he had not given the possibility that the pants would not fit a moment's thought. The listening and watching audience would also not know that by tomorrow evening, his closet would include eight suits and matching everything. He had provided very specific instructions that he would not be seen in casual clothing at any time Monday through Friday, including any social moments. He was going to dress as he believed a President of the United States should dress.

The green light went on and Dr. Scotch began. "Good evening. For those of you who have been out of the country for the past several weeks, I am Jordon Scotch." A big smile crossed Acting President Scotch's face. "As you undoubtedly know, earlier this month, I was elected by the United States Senate as Vice President of the United States and at midnight last night, I took the oath of office as Vice President. Simultaneously, as all of you already know, I became I the Acting President of the United States.

"As you also know, the House of Representatives has been unable to achieve a majority vote for the now former president, Senator Vincent or

Congressman Roland. Under Article XX of the Constitution of the United States, that means that I will be the Acting President of the United States until the House of Representatives can obtain a majority for one of these candidates or until after the 2016 election, whichever occurs earlier.

"This old Constitution behind me has provided our country rules and procedures for almost 250 years and that is the great marker of this great republic. In the United States of America, we transfer power without the use of a gun; we have peaceful transition of power and have had that since our first President George Washington left office on March 3, 1797.

"It may interest you that I took the oath of office privately because of my respect for the House of Representatives. These individuals are faced with a difficult decision and I believed that having a public ceremony would be inappropriate. That being said, I am proud to be your vice president and part of that job is to serve as the Acting President of the United States. I am proud to be your Acting President.

"I scheduled this presentation two weeks ago when I realized that there was a significant chance the House of Representatives would be unable to timely select a President of the United States. I had hoped that I would be cancelling this presentation. I find it particularly interesting that in theory, in the midst of this meeting, I could get a telephone call indicating that the House of Representatives has reached a decision and my time as Acting President is over. Actually, that is pure theory because the House of Representatives is not meeting at this moment.

"However, since we do not know when the House of Representatives will select a President, the only cell phone that is not on silent or turned off right now is this little American-made Motorola cell phone. It has a telephone number known only to the Speaker of the House. It will always be turned on, twenty-four-seven, during my period of time as Acting President. If it rings during this meeting, we can immediately begin talking about the NCAA tournament prospects for my beloved UCLA Bruin basketball team." Scotch displayed a lovable smile, which endeared him to almost everyone that knew him.

"The business of the United States of America will not stop for a moment. No one needs to worry about my ability to make decisions or those decisions being properly acted upon. I will act timely and appropriately, to the best of my ability. This is the United States of America, an exceptional nation, a nation of exceptionalism.

"But let me talk for a moment about our country and its Constitution. With respect to this wonderful document behind me, I believe that there is unanimity that Congress need take an immediate review of the Constitution of the United States and update the interworking of this process based upon what we have observed over the past sixty days. I will be asking the United States Senate and the House of Representatives to make this a priority, an immediate priority. I don't think we need to radically change the rules and I do not suggest and, in fact, strongly contest the notion that we need to go through a discussion wherein the states with small populations will lose their power in the House of Representatives, the United States Senate or the Electoral College. Those decisions were made two hundred years ago and have served the nation quite well since that time. Those decisions have allowed for the collective decision making of a Congress made up of both urban and non-urban communities.

"I do believe, however, that we do not need to have and should not have specific electors in this highly-educated, electronic society.

"I do not believe that the long-term right answer for the nation is an Acting President. I think the House of Representatives needs a set of rules wherein after some period of time the number of potential presidents is reduced from three to two. That is in the future, but something that Congress needs to consider for 2016.

"I do note that in one of the two previous times when the electors failed to pick a president, the House of Representatives was faced with selecting the President of the United States and essentially agreed to stay in session twenty-four-seven until they picked a President. At some point soon, this might be a very good idea.

"There has been some commentary that if the House of Representatives determines a President of the United States after today, that as the result of Article XII of the Constitution, it would be an invalid decision. I reject that position and believe that the House of Representatives has four years to name a President under Section 3 of Article XX. Let me put that into a couple of sentences without any technical language. If the House of Representatives achieves a majority vote for President based on the rules included in the Constitution for their manner of voting, I will not challenge that decision. There will be no Constitutional crisis on my watch. I hope that is clear to everyone. Jordon Scotch did not run for President of the United States, he ran for Vice President of the United States. I am honored to be the

Vice President of the United States. I am again, pleased to tell you that I am honored to be your Acting President. When and if the House of Representatives selects a President, I will embrace their selection, whether it comes tomorrow or on January 19, 2016.

"Now a few very important things we need to discuss..." the Acting President looked at his three-by-five card for a moment, "...to the rest of the world, the United States of America has not missed a single beat. We will continue to honor treaties under my administration, we will do business, we will not miss a beat. To any predator nations in the world, I leave a single message, which was a guide for this country even before we were a nation: *Don't tread on me!* I do not know how long I will be the Acting President, but I do know that we will respond to all events around the world in a manner which speaks well of the United States of America. And of my stature, Franklin Delano Roosevelt was President of the United States during the worst war in the history of the earth. He also sat in a chair rather than stood at meetings. He was a great president and his disability did not slow him for a moment. This Acting President will do his level best to emulate that aspect of President Roosevelt's presidency.

"The Acting President needs a Cabinet and as a matter of law, earlier today, the terms of every Cabinet officer expired. This is a bit tricky, because many Cabinet members leave Congress to join the Cabinet of the President of the United States and I cannot ask anyone to give up their seats in Congress for what could be just a few days in office. As a result, I have put together a working plan for my White House. I have scheduled telephonic meetings or face-to-face meetings with every member of the Cabinet that was termed out of office today. These will be complete by four o'clock tomorrow afternoon. I believe and hope they will all take my call. All are patriots. Almost all of them will be invited to remain in their positions with the understanding that a president may be selected at any time. I have decided that it is in the country's best interest to select a new individual for several Cabinet appointments.

"At 4:30 p.m. tomorrow, I will hold a brief press conference and confirm for you the individuals who have accepted this opportunity and provide you a list of the additional new individuals I will nominate to be in my Cabinet. In an effort to show respect for every member of the former president's Cabinet, I will not announce who decided not to remain in the Cabinet or who I did not ask to remain in the Cabinet. Please leave all of the existing

Cabinet members alone this evening. I would prefer to provide you with the entire list at one time. One of the things I will tell you in advance is that I will be asking certain senators, congressmen and congresswomen to link up with these individuals as friends and advisors. While I do not want to blur the roles of the executive and congressional activities, I want our team to hit the ground running. I will be asking Mrs. Cloud to return as Secretary of State.

"After tomorrow's press conference, I have asked the Speaker of the House, the leadership of both parties in the House and the leadership of the Senate to join me for an extensive meeting in the Cabinet Room at the White House. Among the things we will discuss is that I will be asking for blanket, or near blanket, approval of my Cabinet. I am hopeful that none of these appointments will be terribly controversial and I will agree that if there are majority votes in the House or the Senate for a Cabinet member to resign, they will either resign on that day or will be fired. That should be fair and keep the country going. I am hopeful that this promise will result in an instantly created Cabinet and an instantly effective government.

"All of the czars and czarinas have been informed that their service was appreciated by the government of the United States and that their service and the service of their entire staffs ended at midnight last night. As I stated during the campaign, I believe that the entire notion of czars is anti-democratic and there will not be another czar, at least not on my watch.

"Let me close with a reminder of why Senator Vincent formed the American Exceptionalism Party and why I was immediately willing to join him in his quest for better government. We did not run as Democrats or Republicans, we ran for office as Americans. I am hopeful that while I am the Acting President, we can accomplish the beginning of rebuilding confidence in the political system and our elected representatives.

"A rebuilding of confidence can only happen with some of the legislation and transparency regarding ethics that the President talked about in his 2008 campaign and we talked about in 2012. And that can only happen if the general public, that is everyone who is listening or has the opportunity to listen, begins to pay attention to his or her country. This country can only move forward towards a higher plain if we trade in our cynicism for proactive interest in our country and its elected leaders. We need to look at every one of our representatives as someone we either trust to act in our best interests or someone we do not trust and replace them with someone who will do right by us. It is an easy formula.

"Thank you and good day! God bless the United States of America!" The Acting President smiled and looked to his side.

Acting President Scotch called to his attendant. "Wheel me up my Scottie, I don't know how long I'll have this job, but let's not lose a minute." Most of the world thought the Acting President believed the microphone was off, but of course, Jordon Scotch knew it was on, and knew with precision the message he was sending.

~

The President was in campaign mode and campaign attire. His campaign attire was the usual open blue, collared shirt with sleeves rolled up, grey slacks and dark loafers. (He and Geekhead dressed as twins.) While he did not have the forearms of Geekhead, he always looked impressive in this attire at a podium. Only when one compared pictures over four years was his loss of weight so evident. Campaign mode was the highly principled, forceful, give-me-a-break style of speaking. Crisp.

The setting was in front of the University of Chicago Law School and the time was precisely 8:00 p.m. Chicago time. The Acting President finished his speech only minutes before and the former president wanted and succeeded in getting the television stations to move from Dr. Scotch directly to him.

"Today, we vacated the White House. Tonight, we are in Chicago, Illinois. Hopefully, tomorrow, we will be returning to Washington D.C.

"As we know, the House of Representatives has been unable to select a President of the United States. As a result," continuing to speak in his clipped style, he paused at this point, "Jordon Scotch became Acting President at midnight last evening.

"As the individual who received the highest number of votes in the election, I should and I expect that within some short period of time"—clipped pause—"we will be returning to the White House. Until that time, we will be spending our time at our home in Chicago.

"This is a great disruption to our family and to the nation. We continue to make this nation great for all, not for some. It is disappointing that Republican politics is trumping good judgment. At some point, the Republicans will have to come face-to-face with the reality that it is not good for the United States of America to have a President of the United States who does not have a single member of his political party in the House of Representatives or the United States Senate, or a candidate who won but a few states. The House of Representatives will have to come face-to-face with the reality that the continuity of our government requires a decision to complete this process and determine that the winner of the popular vote is the President of the United States. The House will need to look at the reality that I received some six million more votes than Senator Vincent and some twenty-two million votes more than Congressman Roland. How hard a decision can it be to listen to the voters?"

As was the President's want, he spoke for another thirty minutes, but added no clarity or additional useful information. He took no questions.

~

The Professor was on the telephone with George Vincent. "Skeeter, this is finally beginning to take place exactly as we game played it. Except of course, Jordon Scotch is even more magnificent than we could have guessed. I thought his speech was damn good and the President's response was pathetic."

"Professor, I think you missed the President a bit. He is playing to a different audience than your intellectual crowd. While I am certain he doesn't want a replay of the riots, the House needs to feel the pressure through e-mails from the crazies who really don't care about the Constitution or the integrity of the House of Representatives. What do you think I should be doing?

"I talked to Jordon last night and he was incredibly cordial. We don't have any palace intrigue here. We did agree that I would be treated like any other senator until the House of Representatives makes its decisions."

"Skeeter, I think you continue to stay low-key, unless the President really goes off the deep end, which is possible. We will know when the time is right to begin calling markers, or whatever. Remember, you talked to and helped a huge number of them. This is the time in the sun for Members of the House of Representatives and we need allow them to be on television and have their say. As a practical matter, we have no control and the rookies running the place seem to have their eye on the ball.

"Let's get Woo fired up and have him ready to have his Twitter people contact their individual congressman. I assume that he can figure out a way to have his Twitterers send e-mails to the right congressman. Let's put him to work building a bit of momentum."

~

From the day's *Washington Post* editorial page by Randy Kraus:

OUR FIRST ADULT
ONE SO FAR

Yesterday, the Vice President of the United States performed like a statesman. What a pleasure it was to have someone speak to Americans as educated adults. What a pleasure it was to have the Vice President speak to the world and explain that the political system of the United States of America was working.

The ongoing comments of the now former President of the United States are far too similar of those of a petulant child. He needs to learn from Vice President Scotch and speak within the framework of the Constitution. We are believers in the President and continue to believe that the House of Representatives should elect him to be the President of the United States. We also believe that whatever decision is made will be the correct one under the law and the President should confirm to the American people that he also believes that is true.

~

TUESDAY, JANUARY 22, 2013

Former Congressman Paul Roland was seated in a small conference room at the Willard Hotel in Washington D.C. Today, it is called the Willard Intercontinental, but everyone continues to refer to it as the Willard. The original hotel at this location was built in 1816, but the foundations of the current building only went back about 110 years. Presidents throughout the past two hundred years have stayed at the Willard starting with Pierce and Lincoln and continued through the centuries. Many presidents stayed at the Willard immediately before their inauguration ceremonies.

Even at 9:00 p.m., Congressman Roland was attired as he always was attired. He was wearing a non-descript expensive grey suit, white shirt and red tie, his standard wear. This might have been a suit that he wore to the office to see patients just a few years before. With his hair in the same traditional middle length it had been over the past forty years, he sat cross-legged in front of about twenty members of the press.

Congressman Roland had decided to hold an informal press conference rather than give a prepared speech. He looked at the assembled group and offered: "Well, here we are. What would you like to ask me?"

There were no shrinking violets in this press corps and the voices all spoke at once. The congressman smiled and said: "You know guys, I am currently unemployed, it's not too late in the evening, so I am in no particular hurry. Let's try to be civilized here and I'll answer a boat full of questions before I head for the unemployment line.

"Congressman, you won 108 electoral votes in the election, the President received 194 and Congressman Vincent received 236 electoral votes.

You were also last in the popular vote, losing to the President by about a zillion votes. Vincent's vice president candidate is the Acting President. Why are you not dropping out of the race? How can all of this be?"

Congressman Roland had far more difficult conversations with patient families. The job of an obstetrician was often far tougher than any conversation could be with the press. Nothing they could ask him would bother him in the slightest and his truthful attitude made this first question pretty easy, a softball for lack of a better term.

"First, let me spin your question more accurately. The *former* president was first in the popular vote and second, by a wide margin, in the Electoral College." He smiled. "Former President, I like the sound of that. I heard him last night standing in front of the Chicago Law School. Same as always, never in doubt, not always right.

"It is no secret that I carry my copy of the Constitution of the United States in my pocket. My copy is signed by Senator Byrd, a man with whom I had virtually nothing in common except an appreciation and respect for the Constitution. Anyone, I repeat anyone, even a former adjunct professor teaching constitutional law at the University of Chicago knows that there is not word one anywhere in the Constitution of the United States that mentions the popular vote. That same anyone knows, or should know, that the reason we have a Constitution that was ratified by the states is because we do not elect our presidents through a popular vote. This was a decision made so as not to have the urban centers of the then thirteen states rule over the rest of the country. Additionally, if you would like me to play academic, there was a concern that Virginia had too high a percentage of the number of eligible voters and if we dig deeper, the founders were not in total agreement as to the appropriate power for the elites and the non-elites, a very significant percentage of who could not read. You can study this at your leisure and a good place to start is with the views of Thomas Jefferson and Andrew Hamilton. None of that has been changed one iota in two hundred plus years. The rules are unchanged and the popular vote is just that, a popular vote.

"As you also know, the rules change once the election moves to the House of Representatives. I don't think anyone, except perhaps the former president, would like to change the Constitution to get to a specific result. Americans want the process to play out as designed in the Constitution.

"As you now know, the House of Representatives, with one vote per state, now needs to elect a president. Or, if we think through this, needs to determine not to determine a president. In its deliberations, my former colleagues will be able to find absolutely no guidance in the Constitution and I have frankly been unable to find anything meaningful written on the subject, even in the late 1700s when the document was written. The House of Representatives is charged with selecting the president from the top three vote getters in the Electoral College. No more and no less. There is no direction as to looking at the number of electoral votes and as I said before, no mention whatsoever of the popular vote. The House of Representatives will, or will not, be able to find twenty-six states to vote for one of the three of us. If they do, that person will become president, if not, until they get to a conclusion, we have an Acting President. And that Acting President could be Acting President until a new Congress makes a decision in 2014 or until the next election in 2016.

"George Vincent selected Jordon Scotch to be his vice presidential running mate because he believed if circumstances resulted in his death or incapacity, he would be a phenomenal President of the United States. Nothing in his mind has changed with respect to the caliber job he believes Dr. Scotch is capable of performing. There is not a single person in the United States that he would choose over Vice President Scotch to be the Acting President. The Senate has confirmed his thinking.

"This is a very long answer and I apologize, but I need more than another minute. I believed the moment I signed up for my first primary that I would be a good president. At least I knew that I would follow my personal philosophy without a beat and the voters could see that philosophy and predict exactly what I would do during my presidency. Nothing has changed. To the contrary of General Sherman, if elected by the House of Representatives, I will serve and I will serve honorably.

"As to the question initially asked of why don't I withdraw, there is nothing to enter or withdraw from. I control none of the Members of the House of Representatives, none of them have or should swear allegiance to Dr. Paul Roland and I am but a bystander awaiting a decision or non-decision.

"Let me answer what should be the second question. Dr. Jordon Scotch is a very impressive man. This man is a story of success, a successful man who succeeded through hard work and brainpower. As I should have mentioned when I questioned the President's storied—emphasize *storied*—success, I should have lauded the transparent nature of Dr. Scotch. So, if Jordon

Scotch were to be Acting President of the United States, to me, he is far preferable to our most recent President."

"Dr. Roland, you aren't holding back what you think, are you?" Everyone laughed, including Paul Roland. "Dr. Roland, we at RBC, and now Congresswoman Regina Smith, have demanded information regarding the history of the former president with respect to his birth certificate, grades and whatever. You have been very non-responsive to this issue even though both you and Acting President Scotch have been more transparent than any candidates on record. Do you have any comment on the former president's continued decision to keep these issues private?"

"Yes, I think it is time I answered this question more explicitly. I do not think it is appropriate for the President of the United States to have anything to hide in his past. Succinct enough?"

"Then why do you think he has not released these documents?"

"Your speculation is as good as mine. The birth certificate was like pulling teeth. As to the class schedules and grades, my guess is pretty straightforward: the reality is less than the advertised genius status. I also suspect that the undergraduate degree was not very intensive with respect to academic intensity. But what do I know? Heck, I think I studied four million hours a day to get into medical school and there were people in my class that seemed to just know everything without studying at all and spent their entire undergraduate careers getting A's and having fun."

"Dr. Roland, what now?"

"I have been a renter in Washington D.C. since being elected to the House of Representatives. I am going home when the lease expires on January 31. Can you give me a call if something important happens? I will be at home, in the office or in the operating room." Paul Roland's press conference ended with a few laughs and handshakes with most of the individual members of the press.

~

FRIDAY, JANUARY 25, 2013

	States
The President	9
George Vincent	11
Paul Roland	13
No Vote	17

No Change.

~

7:00 a.m. Friday morning.

The general looked across the table several stories under the White House and asked Jordon Scotch the difficult question: "What are you going to do with the information, Sir?"

"General, I know you are going to find this difficult to understand after the last four years, but after I have the additional information I need to get comfortable, I will have sufficient knowledge to move forward; you, me and the Secretary of the Navy are going to make a decision. If I knew what that decision was going to be now, I would not have asked you any questions. Is that clear enough for you to understand?"

"Yes, Sir. I will return within three hours with the answers to your questions. I am sorry, but you only want me and the Secretary of the Navy to attend the meeting?"

"Yes," the Acting President responded to the general as he gathered his papers and left the room.

Alone, the Acting President smiled to himself. He and the general just spent thirty minutes on a meeting that should have taken ten minutes if he had been properly prepared and brought recommendations with him. *Who knew that a year after agreeing to run for political office, I would be deciding to conduct a military mission on behalf of the United States and have the responsibility that accompanies such a decision. My model was always Ronald Regan. One bases all decisions on philosophy and power. Philosophy to determine the best pathway, and power...who was that academician from the University of Oklahoma? The one that reminded everyone in his writings that the aphrodisiac is power and that in most societies, the people are far more interested in stability than motivated by democracy.*

~

9:45 a.m.

The Acting President waited in the Situation Room for his general to return with the answers to his questions. In the interim, the general had called twice and begged the Acting President to include every member of the Joint Chiefs along with congressional leadership. Scotch finally allowed the general to bring in his team, without assistants, from the Pentagon and denied his request to bring any member from the congressional leadership. The Acting President reminded the general that he was the Acting President and had the same powers and responsibilities as the prior and future presidents. He was the Commander in Chief.

The generals arrived at 9:45 in full dress uniforms, each with a stern look and a sheath of papers.

After twenty minutes of listening to the general and his team, the Acting President asked, "General, I want you to repeat, in summary form with numbers, your answers in the order which I requested."

The general stood up at his seat and offered the results of the questions in the order asked:

"There is an eighty-five percent chance that we can disable the USS James Pearson between seven and eight miles from the coast of North Korea and a ninety-five percent chance that we can disable it before it reaches the three-mile limit.

"After it is disabled, there is a near one hundred percent chance that we can keep the North Koreans from boarding additional personnel onto the ship. If they attempt to leave the ship with hostages, we believe, but have no certainty, that we can coral their escape.

"There is the possibility that in disabling the James Pearson, there will be casualties on board. We will attempt to destroy its rudder system, but from helicopters it will be a difficult targeting operation. There is very little chance that we will sink the ship and very little chance that the North Koreans would have the ability to target our air resources quickly enough for our people in the air to be in danger.

"We will be able to destroy a minimum of eighty percent of their air force in their bunkers and on the air fields within fifteen minutes of the attack on the Pearson. We have the resources in the area to fire over five hundred missiles into North Korea and destroy nearly eighty percent of their air force regardless of location. We believe that we can also destroy any working missiles in the first five minutes. They should not have time to arm any nuclear warheads. This pathway has been in place for a very long time.

"We know the precise location of the North Korean dictator and could easily place a sea-based unarmed missile in front of the building where he is currently in a meeting. I note we could also take the building out, but that question was not asked.

"I think, Sir, that is it."

The Acting President looked at the impressive array of military commanders and asked for questions. The only question asked was whether he was comfortable that this was the role Congress expected of the Acting President. Jordon Scotch responded that if not, maybe the House of Representatives could elect a President this afternoon.

"Execute the plan immediately. Please arrange for the former Secretary of State and the former Secretary of Defense to come here instantly. This whole organization is so confusing, I assume they are in Washington and believe they are running their agencies even though they have not been officially approved by the Senate. I will have them telephone the Presidents of Russia and China simultaneously with the launching of the missiles, which will be simultaneous with the disabling of the Pearson. This idiot in South Korea will decide very quickly that his men are prisoners rather than jailers. And of course, I want to be talking to the clown when the missile falls in front of his building. You are all dismissed. Keep me carefully informed."

~

12:00 p.m.

The general walked back into the Situation Room. Scotch looked up from his light lunch. "Sir, the Pearson is disabled. There is an air cover protecting the ship and we have had no word from the North Koreans on the ship. Their entire air force and missile systems are apparently destroyed or disabled. If they light up anything in the next few hours, we will react immediately."

"Good, please get the North Korean President on the telephone. Gentlemen, please make your calls," he indicated pointing to the former Secretary of Defense and the Secretary of State. They agreed that the former Secretary of State would also call the Japanese Prime Minister the moment she was done with Russia."

~

12:10 p.m.

"Yes, that is correct. And if you so much as fire a single missile in any direction or launch so much as a bird, more less a missile, I have arranged for eleven nuclear missiles to eliminate you and every major city in North Korea? Any questions?

"And our ship will be returned to control of our officers within fifteen minutes? Yes, thank you. We will transfer your people to a helicopter and leave them with the Chinese by the end of the day tomorrow. And one more thing, don't do anything like this again." The Acting President put the telephone down.

~

12:30 p.m.

Jordon Scotch was at the table with the television camera live and ten senior members of the press waiting to ask questions. He had just explained "How I spent my day" and was responding to the first question: "No, I did not inform the leaders of Congress as to what had happened or what course of action I was going to follow. Every new president or, I guess, new Acting President usually faces a crisis of character within their first year in office. I determined that if time eroded at all, we would have well over one hundred US Navy personnel, men and women, in the custody of the North Koreans. That was not going to happen on my watch and I was not going to let the world think that during this time of enhanced transition that the United States was not going to act with dispatch and decisiveness. I do not know what the former president, Senator Vincent or Congressman Roland would have done; I did what I thought was best. Our understanding is that we are mourning the death of a sailor on Pearson who was killed during the initial North Korean assault. We lost no American lives or assets during the elimination of the North Korean air force. Finally, we have explained to the South Koreans that we will not stand by if they decide to take advantage of the situation and attack a weakened North Korea. Our goal was not to create a war between North Korea and South Korea. Our goals were twofold. First, we will not tolerate attacks on US military assets and second, our intolerance will not be exhibited through words alone."

In answer to the second question, Jordon Scotch responded by indicating that he was expecting the Majority and Minority Leaders of the Senate for a meeting at 4:00 p.m. to explain what had occurred. He indicated that he was performing his role as Acting President during the day.

The third question was the expected question about North Korean response to the action of the United States: "Truly, any answer of mine is going to be purely speculation. My hope is that the North Koreans were testing the Acting President and that I passed the test in their minds. I doubt that they wanted or expected me to pass the test and the cost to them was far more than they could have possibly guessed. I hope they understand that we will not tolerate certain actions and that they, and frankly the world, will understand that while we believe ourselves to be the most peaceful nation in the world, we will react strongly to any issues or events which threaten either our own safety or any treaty commitments.

When asked if he thought his response was disproportionate to the taking of the US ship, Jordon Scotch looked closely at the reporter and answered the question without hesitation: "No, I want the world to understand that diplomacy ends on my watch when the first shot is fired." With that he left the room.

~

4:00 p.m.

Acting President Scotch was waiting in the Oval Office for the Majority and Minority Leaders of the US Senate. He was behind his desk. As Congress had not acted to approve any Cabinet officers, he did not have a Secretary of State or a Secretary of Defense to join him. He thought about asking Senator Vincent to join him, but the politics of that decision were exactly the opposite of his view of an Acting President.

As Senators Mitch MacCone and Chuck Schoore entered the Oval Office, Scotch motioned for each of them to take a seat on the brown sofa. Scotch had done nothing with respect to office decorations or anything else, save for the framed picture of his family on his desk. Scotch had met Senator MacCone during the campaign and had not yet met Senator Schoore.

The meeting began awkwardly with no one in the room knowing exactly what the tradition was, or if there was one, for speaking to an Acting President. Scotch looked up from his wheelchair and offered his hand to Senator Schoore and stated: "Hi, I'm Jordon Scotch. Why don't you call me Jordon, everyone else does?"

"Well, OK, Mr. Acting President certainly does not sound right. Let's get down to business, Jordon. We need to have some kind of working relationship between the Congress and this White House. We don't know how long you are going to be in this office, but we do not want you declaring war on the rest of the world without our input."

"Chuck, let's slow down a bit here. Dr. Scotch responded strongly and positively to an act of war by the North Koreans and I don't think either of us wanted the United States to have an Acting President with seventy hostages in North Korea. Honestly, Chuck, we are here to talk about the future and I for one am glad Jordon Scotch was in this office this week."

"No, Mitch, that is not the point, I..."

"Gentlemen, if you would like me to excuse myself, I can keep busy doing other things, but I have quite a busy schedule today since I have no Cabinet officers or President."

"I'm sorry, Jordon. This is such a strange situation." Offered an uncomfortable Senator Mitch MacCone.

"Let me tell you gentlemen how it is. One, I need a Cabinet to make the country function. Two, I am going to react to international events. If I have a Cabinet, I will involve them; if I have an event that warrants the consent of the Congress, I will involve you, if not, I will not. Further, George and

649

I campaigned against czars and czarinas, so I am not going to backstop the non-existent Cabinet with appointees. As we said during the campaign, we are going to walk the talk. If you want a functional government, you will need to act to allow me a Cabinet."

"No, Dr. Scotch, that is not the way it is going to be. You are going to need to work with us. That is the purpose of the Congress." Senator Schoore now appeared to be very annoyed.

Jordon Scotch yawned. "Gentlemen, I am not a politician, never was, never will be. But to be an economist, you have to be pretty good with a calculator. I count fifty-seven US senators that have an R after their name and a House of Representatives that has a majority for the Democrats. When I look in the mirror, I see a guy who can help this country get righted again and hopefully the Democrats and Republicans will rally around that opportunity. Until then, I am just going to do the best I can. So, Senator Schoore, I am going to look to Senator MacCone here to get my appointees confirmed ASAP and I'll just mope around here with or without your help, I guess. I do caution you to remember that it is the citizens of the United States whom you are denying a fully functioning government if you do not act."

MacCone remained seated, trying to see what his loyal opposition senator would say to an Acting President who had essentially told him *no*, an answer he was not expecting. Schoore thought for a few moments and looked at the Acting Vice President: "Jordon, you are a rookie at this and I guess entitled to a couple of mistakes and..."

"Senator Schoore, this meeting concluded when I finished my last sentence. Your role was to stand up, politely thank me for my time and go back to the US Senate and confirm my Cabinet. There is not one person on that list who should be controversial. Almost everyone is a Democrat and you personally voted for each one of them. I am not a career politician, but rest assured, if the US Senate does not act this week, I will turn up the heat. Last night, I read three books on current politics and I should be pretty knowledgeable by the time I will need to go to a microphone and tell the American people that the Democrats are nothing more than a group of obstructionists. George will love that." Scotch giggled a bit.

"Did you say you read three books last night?" responded MacCone.

"An old habit, yes."

"I don't think I like what you are saying to me, Dr. Scotch," offered Schoore.

"Well, think about it on the way out, Sir. This meeting has gone longer than I planned." With that Jordon Scotch pushed a new button, which had been placed on his wheelchair the day he took his oath of office, and the door opened from his secretary's side. "These gentlemen were just leaving, Betty. Can you validate their parking?"

~

The evening news and talk show conversations were as to be expected. The Democrats were mortified that the President responded with such force to the North Koreans and the Republicans were amazed and generally pleased.

The radio talk show hosts were receiving an earful. Both the left and right side of the radio world was hearing from their listeners that the response by the Acting President was appropriate. Americans were worn down by the political actions of everyone and here, the Acting President charted a course that seemed to work. Only the extreme left, at the voter level, seemed upset.

The United Nations held an emergency meeting of the Security Council. No one, including the British, spoke strongly in favor of the actions by the United States, but few of the major nations in the world spoke at all. Both China and Japan sat wordless and Russia condemned only the proportionality of the action. Each of these nations wanted the small nations of the world to understand that they were just that, small nations. Iran took no position and while a few non-permanent members of the Security Council had harsh words for the United States, there were no motions or actions by the United Nations.

The now former president, George Vincent and Paul Roland read the instant polling and recognized that the American public was in favor of the actions of the Acting President by over two-to-one. Each issued a fairly positive press release.

~

SATURDAY, JANUARY 27, 2013

From the day's *Washington Post* editorial page by Randy Kraus:
JORDON SCOTCH UNLEASHES AMERCIAN POWER
ACTING PRESIDENT?

Who would have thunk it?

Jordon Scotch is a warrior. Jordon Scotch is a decision maker.

He campaigned as an economist and days into his Acting Presidency, he has unleashed the fire power of the United States on North Korea. While we applaud his decision making, we are appalled by his decision. No, we are not appalled by his decision to protect American naval personnel or destroy North Korea's air force. While we are much more inclined to negotiate, North Korea has proved an obdurate opponent on the world stage and we prefer to have our troops home.

We are appalled that Jordon Scotch apparently asked no one in the congressional leadership for an opinion before acting. We are concerned that the Acting President pulled out the *Ready, Fire, Aim* planning book. Yes, he got lucky and we applaud the results. But, and it is a huge but, Jordon Scotch has never held public office and doesn't have any foreign policy experience.

We are scared that the man in charge of the nuclear weapons of the United States does not consult experienced elected leaders before making big decisions.

It is time for the House of Representatives to man up and make a choice.

~

TUESDAY, JANUARY 29, 2013

	States
The President	9
George Vincent	11
Paul Roland	13
No Vote	17

No Change.

~

The Professor sat at one end of the conference table and Senator Vincent sat at the other end. In between them were Molly Tom, Stanley Martin Wade, Milton Woo and Marshall Dankberg. Both The Professor and Molly were missing the first day of the spring semester. The Professor was only teaching one class this semester and had a colleague cover for him. The Professor had written a couple of notes to cover for Molly, but this would need to be her last nonweekend visit to Washington D.C. for a while. Even with the Hawker available for transportation, she needed to be in school for her final semester. While The Professor had not told Molly, he had had a very uncomfortable conversation with the Chancellor that included how much school she was missing and her relationship with Milton Woo. How, exactly, the Chancellor knew about either was not a question that had been answered and The Professor had been a bit taken back about the Milton Woo comment himself. Not that he saw anything wrong with Molly Tom being able to select any man on the planet to fall in love with, he just had apparently not seen it coming—or happening.

The Professor was wearing a coat and tie, which indicated to Senator Vincent that he had other business in town besides this meeting. The meeting started with a rehashing of the events with North Korea. What now, Professor?

"Skeeter, you are a Member of the United States Senate. It is time to take to the floor of the Senate and applaud Scotch's action. You need to indicate that you believe that he acted perfectly regardless of how you may actually feel. I read your press release and thought it tepid. This is your guy."

"Professor, I thought the Vice President or Acting President, whatever, overstepped and I certainly think the senators that are upset are correct. He doesn't have deep experience in world affairs, hell, he could have started a nuclear war!"

"Senator, I don't know if I speak for anyone my age or just me, but if you look at my Tweets and go on some websites where my generation is commenting, we think Dr. Scotch was a warrior and we think that is a good thing. I know there were some protests at Berkeley and Wisconsin, but these were very small and at a handful of Southern universities, the protestors were run off campus.

"Skeeter, he is your guy. Nothing else matters. Don't go crazy, but complement him for his ability to make decisions in an awkward role. As to the House of Representatives, it is still too early to do anything more in the House."

~

WEDNESDAY, JANUARY 30, 2013

	States
The President	9
George Vincent	11
Paul Roland	13
No Vote	17

No Change.

~

"Well, what do they say? When it rains, it pours. What does he expect me to do? I am not going to incinerate an entire nation because of an insult."

The general looked at Jordon Scotch and smiled. "Sir, these types of tests may go on for a couple of weeks. I don't think these guys know the backbone you have in you and I suspect they think you are afraid of Congress. I haven't known you very long, but this looks like a tremendous misjudgment on their part.

"The backbone is there, it is just not perfectly connected. This is easy, I think. This so-called elected President of Iran wants to insult the United States because its Acting President is in a wheelchair?"

"Yes, Sir."

"General, do you mind addressing the press for me. I don't have a press spokesman, which kind of makes it an interesting job to be the White House press corps. I don't have a Cabinet, which makes it kind of interesting to be the Acting President. But, I do have you. Would you mind doing a press briefing and indicate that the Acting President of the United States does not respond to insults, personal or towards our nation. Also indicate that it should be fairly clear at this time that the United States does reply instantly when insults turn to actions. And, Sir, if the Iranian guy comes up again, inform the press that the Acting President would be more than willing to wrestle the man in an arena of his choice if the loser has to make a significant donation to charity and is forced to comport himself as an adult."

The general stood next to his chair and saluted. "Sir, it might be inappropriate, but I want you to know that I would follow you into battle any time, any place. You are a breath of fresh air."

"Thank you, General. Have some fun with this if you want. No reason to be an adult twenty-four-seven."

~

Congressman Grable, the fifty-two-year-old congressman from New York had hardly spoken at the New York meetings for the past month. He went to the meetings, listened to his colleagues moan about the fact that they could not get enough states to vote for the President, cast his vote for the President, and would leave immediately. This afternoon, it was time for change in his mind.

"Let me enter the conversation, folks. In a way, I am with Senator Regina Smith of Illinois. In a way, but in a very different way. We are not ever going to get the President re-elected and we sure as shit are not going to let Paul Roland into the White House. It turns out that the Republicans are far too many in this cockamamie voting system, by state, go figure, to let the President be re-elected.

"Our guy has dissed Regina without so much as a comment on her request for information. Let's get real here. The President is not one of us and couldn't care less about us. He is either a lame duck or he is a former president. Roland is far too conservative than we can accept and this Jordon Scotch, this Jordon Scotch…he may be the lost brother of George Boone, the son. His success should scare us to death. If we have to live with the successes, he could be in the White House, forever. What, eight years if he is the Acting President for four years and re-elected. The people love him and in part, they love him because they hate us. They hate Congress.

"George Vincent is a Democrat, a moderate Democrat, but a Democrat none the less. Let's take our medicine and be realistic here, it is time to compromise before Jordon Scotch becomes too powerful."

The discussion went on for hours and groups of Democrats adjourned to different private conference rooms.

~

The Minority Leader of the United States Senate stood at the microphone. Magnificent in his grey suit, blue tie and black-tie shoes, he looked the part of a senior leader of the government of the United States. Senator Schoore spoke briefly and clearly: "I second the motion to approve every member of the President's Cabinet based upon his word that if we come to a majority vote, as promised by the Acting President and my friend Senator MacCone, we can remove any member of this Cabinet at will. We cannot have an Acting President with no staff. It has been made very clear during the last few days that this Acting President needs adults in the White House to discuss issues. The Cabinet that has been proposed includes Democrats and Republicans and when the House of Representatives chooses a real president, he can bring in his own people."

And fifteen minutes later, the US Senate voted the Acting President his entire Cabinet without five minutes of committee hearings.

~

FRIDAY, FEBRUARY 1, 2013

"No, I was not kidding. I am back on staff and will be assisting in two surgeries today. As I think you know, I maintained my educational and licensing requirements while I was in Washington during both of my periods in Congress, a classic citizen politician, I hope. This is what I love and it is what I do. And today, I will make an exception to my healthy diet rules and sneak downtown for some serious Texas barbeque. I have been away too long. I deserve the BBQ.

"Should the House of Representatives decide that old Dr. Paul Roland is their guy and elect me to the presidency, I will be honored and I suspect the Air Force will provide an airplane to Washington D.C. and a place to sleep for a few nights. That House of Representatives process is something I have chosen not to be a part of and believe that is the appropriate position for all three of us. They are big boys and girls and I will let them figure out what they want to do. Jordon Scotch seems to be doing just fine."

~

Marge Vincent was at home in Cleveland and had been to the doctor every day this week. Her Parkinson's had suddenly gone to a new level and she needed significant changes to her medication. Today, she felt better and called her husband to let him know she was okay and the grandchildren were coming over to see her before dinner. She was happy.

~

At the border between Mexico and the United States, a gun battle had taken place earlier in the morning and at one point, members of two drug cartels were firing automatic weapons at each other across the Rio Grande River.

In the White House, the Acting President was sitting at his desk reading and working. Moments before the general arrived to describe what happened on the border, Scotch looked at one of his aides and indicated, "I just don't know how any president handles this job appropriately and spends hours flying back and forth across the country giving speeches. Didn't the former president average over a speech a day when he wasn't on vacation? I am reading and working twelve to fourteen hours a day and with an hour of exercise, that does not leave too much time to see the family."

As the general entered, Scotch looked directly at him: "Well, General, at least you don't need me in a secure room under the building, what is the problem?"

The General explained that while the shooting over the Rio Grande River had stopped and local SWAT teams thought they had the immediate situation under control, there was no weapon recovery and the local police believed there were significant numbers of automatic weapons that had been used in the firefight on the US side of the border. There was a curfew, but the situation was fluid.

"Yet another test, although I suspect this one would have faced whoever was sitting behind this desk. As I recall, my options are pretty wide. I cannot not respond and leave it to the city and State of Texas, I can call up the National Guard and I believe, although some would disagree, I can call out the Army."

"Yes, Sir. Those are the options, but remember, the Army is not properly trained for this type of event."

"General, this is the same Army that rotates back and forth to Iraq, right?'

A nod.

"Then they are adequately trained for a few days." The White House administrative team was unchanged from January 20 and the Acting President called to his secretary and asked her to get the Majority and Minority Leaders of the Senate on the telephone. "General, here is what you are authorized to do. First, I want you to put troops on the ground today. I want the border within two miles of the shooting incident so quiet that condors

would be comfortable mating in the area. Second, within five days, I want
your people to complete a total review of the situation on the ground and
meet with the National Guard to see how long it would take to get twenty-
four-seven control over the border from Louisiana to San Diego. I want to
understand what will happen when we lose interest in the border and a plan
that will not slowly leak back to where the borders are porous. Let's come
up with a solid operating long-term plan, not a Band-Aid. This might be the
only time that politics will not trump reason. While I will be the target of
the open border people, I find it difficult to believe that the House of Representatives has time to impeach me."

"The senators are on the telephone."

Scotch picked up the telephone. "Gentlemen, in concert with your
recent visit, I wanted you to know what has been happening on the Mexican
border today, what action I have taken, and what I expect to do over the
next seven days. It is also my intent to have another press conference in a
few minutes to explain what we are doing. As you may recall, I have no press
czar, so I will do it myself."

After a few minutes, the Minority Leader began yelling into the telephone: "Good God, you are the Acting President, not the President. This is
a major political decision and we are not going to stand for it."

"Now relax, you know that everything I have explained is in precise
accord with my role as Commander in Chief. Think of this as an opportunity
for you to yell and scream about something that you know we should have
done years ago. We will get this done on my watch without the Democrats
losing a vote or the Republicans being lashed to a yard arm, or whatever
they lash people to."

The Majority Leader would have laughed out loud if the issue were not
so serious. "Sir, we and the American people will support you. My friend on
the other end of this line is just a little excitable and he will see it as a political opportunity. I will remind him that I will not give the first press conference and that my speaking style will make any excessive comments about
the Acting President seem un-American, but say what you choose, Partner."

The Acting President was not particularly happy with anyone on the
telephone and asked if they had any specific ideas or questions. There being
none, the Acting President announced that the call was over and that his
press conference would be later in the afternoon.

~

After the *Washington Post* and *The International Journal*, the first thing many of the Washington insiders look at is the *Daily Presidential Tracking Poll* on Rasmussen Reports. It is free and it gives a daily poll on some five hundred automatic telephone calls. Of interest to those who look daily, there are generally differences on weekdays to weekends with the President's weekend ratings always higher than on weekdays. There were many theories about this, but the best guess among many was that there was an age difference between weekdays and weekends in the polling. No one was sure and Rasmussen was not releasing this information.

The Acting President was at positive levels rarely seen by any president who was doing something. The former president's numbers were always higher if he was not on television or passing legislation. Whenever the President did anything, his negatives always exploded. Suddenly there was Jordon Scotch and he was doing things that apparently most Americans wanted done. He had acted boldly with respect to the North Koreans and now he was responding fully to a problem at the border. Plus, every time he acted, his upward swing in the polls was offset by a softening of the former presidents ratings. While the very negative ratings of the former president were stable, his general disapproval rate increased with this second action by Jordon Scotch.

In Chicago, the President's advisors were without any great ideas. "Mr. President, Jordon Scotch is doing what the people of the United States apparently want him to do. As we know, the *Washington Post* is trying to scare the country to death reporting that the Acting President is acting unilaterally and the Minority Leader is trying to make him look like a part-time dictator, but none of it is sticking to him. The people seem to love him."

"The Army to the border. He is nuts. It is unsustainable and we cannot have the Army internally doing anything in this country. That is un-American."

"Mr. President," Sackman was working eight hours a day on his book without saying a word to the President and in what would be a surprise to him, he was significantly behind Matta who was writing daily about the post-presidency experience already, "I listen to historical tapes over and over again. They remind us that people want stability at the expense of liberty when they are threatened. That is exactly what Scotch is providing."

"But, the long-term effects of this policy will diminish our role in the world."

"Long-term effects, that is the last thing on people's minds. All people knew about health care was that their premiums went up. Same thing."

"I am going to give a press conference and ask the Congress not to provide funding for the army or the National Guard presence on the border. That should lock up the Hispanic vote for generations."

Matta: "Mr. President, that is a high risk maneuver. I think—and you will hate this—if that resolution were to get to the floor of the House of Representatives, it might find itself resulting not in a reduction in the number of National Guard troops, but in the building of a huge wall immediately."

"Not a chance." And the President held his press conference in the afternoon.

~

WEDNESDAY, FEBRUARY 13, 2013

On the Acting President's desk was a bill authorizing the immediate completion of an Israeli type fence on the Mexican border. In the bill was special language listing a panoply of Federal laws that were being specifically suspended or specifically made inapplicable with respect to this bill. As Matta predicted to the President, the House of Representatives reacted to the initial bill, a bill—which had been presented by Members of the House of Representatives from New York and California—to eliminate funding for both the Army and the National Guard at the border by approving additional funding to complete the wall. The Speaker of the House and his cohorts quickly dispatched the former Speaker and her crew and the bill passed the House on a bipartisan basis. In the Senate, it was ratified in moments on a voice vote.

The Acting President opted for a public signing of the bill in the Cabinet Room as the temperature outside was below fifteen degrees. The legislative crowd for the signing included almost every dignitary in the Congress except the Minority Leader who was present day and night on television and radio condemning the bill for its speed and its specific elimination of environmental concerns.

Bill O'Brian had Geekhead across from him the next evening along with a politically conservative lawyer. Their combined view was that the Congress and Acting President had done nothing that would result in more than environmentalists along the border losing summary judgments in Federal Courthouses.

During the same evening O'Brien had the legal and constitutional experts on his show, Big Red opted for the political types. She had Thaddeus Milken and former Congressman Duneaberg. Thaddeus Milken was giddy based on the building of the wall and the clear position of the Acting President that border security was a national priority. Duneaberg was apoplectic about the issues that made Milken giddy. He remarked that, "the United States is no more than that same Gringo bully we have always been." Of course, Thaddeus Milken reacted that the decision to finally build the wall would help both nations. He was certain that if the borders were closed, the drug cartels would move away from the borders and Mexico's border population would have a better chance at a peaceful existence.

~

WEDNESDAY, JUNE 19, 2013

	States
The President	9
George Vincent	12
Paul Roland	13
No Vote	16

Change - Pennsylvania moved from No Vote to Vincent.

~

"Skeeter, as you saw and heard, the dam has finally broken. Now, it is time to execute. Take our list, the one with the mobile telephone numbers and make the twenty telephone calls. Leave your name if they don't answer and keep calling until you talk to each one. Your money and the money of those Max's Place people were the difference in everyone of their races and you have talked to each one of them about this months ago during the election. Actually, you did not talk to them about the outsiders, but we and they now know through their public filings that they were serious players in these elections."

George Vincent: "And we play it just like we talked about. *I intentionally have not contacted you since our conversation before the election. That was our deal, I promised to leave you alone until and unless it was apparent that there was a reason to call. The time is now. The only person who can be elected President of the United States is me and I am ready to serve. As I also said before the election, the only commitment I will make is to be the best President of the United States I can be. So, any questions?*"

"That's perfect, Skeeter, the only thing I can add is that you need to talk to them by name. You have the formal and informal nicknames, use the congressman so and so in the greeting and then quickly move to the nickname. Now, don't talk to me, go to work."

"Got it. Thanks, Partner!"

And George Vincent went to work to become the President of the United States.

~

The former president was speaking to Congresswoman Penelope Atling of Pennsylvania. Her vote tipped the balance in Pennsylvania and her state now had a majority for Vincent.

"Penelope, you are not doing good things for the Democratic Party."

"That may be, Sir, but we need to get some adult leadership in the White House and Senator Vincent is at least a Democrat."

"Vincent is a member of the American Exceptionalism Party, a party which was named after a stray remark I made when I was campaigning in 2008." This was the first time the President acknowledged to anyone that he understood where the name had originated. "He is no more a Democrat than Paul Roland."

"We disagree and down here in the suburbs outside of Philadelphia, that Jordon Scotch is more popular than either of us, Sir. I think my real challenge in the next election is going to come from his supporters, not in a primary, not from the Republicans, but from this new party. And I believe that border security is the key to American culture in the long run. I know you don't want to hear this, but we like our culture in Pennsylvania and we like having jobs for Americans."

"Penelope, I need you."

"Mr. President, this train has left the station. If you run again in 2016, you have my pledge of support."

~

MONDAY, JUNE 24, 2013

	States
The President	9
George Vincent	24
Paul Roland	9
No Vote	8

More Change.

~

"Mr. President, yesterday was a very bad day for you. I think you can get on the telephone to your heart's delight, but you are a former president and will forever be a former president unless you run again in 2016." For maybe the first time in six years, the Pillsbury Doughboy was giving candid, unvarnished advice.

"That just cannot be. I won the popular vote."

"My friend, I know you are not a football guy, but the best analysis I can give you is from football. In college, if you catch a ball with one foot in bounds and one foot out of bounds, it is a catch. In professional football, you must have both feet in bounds for it to be a catch. Maybe in a state election; in a state election, you win if you get the most votes, but the Constitution provides you need the most electoral votes and then in the House, you have these crazy one-vote-per-state votes. It is what it is."

"So, where are my friends?"

"Wrong game, Mr. President. It may yet take two more votes in the House of Representatives, but George Vincent is going to be the president. Once that Smith woman was joined by Grable, your flag was burned just like the French under Napoleon. Your friends became Democratic Senator Vincent's friends and there they will be for four years. None of them want quick trigger Scotch in the White House. Half of them because they think he will blow up the earth and the other half because they are afraid Americans will fall in love with the guy."

"And this is how it ends?"

"Not if you are smart. You have three choices here. You can write books and give speeches for the next forty years and be rich as Crassus. You can run for president again or even Congress; I think it was John Quincy Adams who went from being president to becoming a long-standing Member of the House of Representatives. Or third, you can fight this thing to the end and become a jerk to everyone."

"Nice. What do you suggest?"

"You will hate this. You need to go out and give the speech of your life in support of George Vincent."

~

TUESDAY, JUNE 25, 2013

From the day's *Washington Post* editorial page by Randy Kraus:
IT IS TIME FOR GEORGE VINCENT,
PRESIDENT OF THE UNITED STATES

Yesterday, the dam broke. Only two more states need to give their support to George Vincent and we will have a President of the United States. The nation needs a President and a Vice President and neither the President or Congressman Roland is going to get off the floor in the twelfth round of this fight.

We are perilously close to the beginning of the 2014 Congressional races and the last thing the United States of America needs is for the 2014 election to continue focusing on the 2012 election.

Mr. President, Congressman Roland, it is time for you to throw your support to George Vincent. This is the spirit of America.

~

FRIDAY, JUNE 28, 2013

	States
The President	9
George Vincent	25
Paul Roland	8
No Vote	8

The die is nearly cast.

~

There stood the former President of the United States. He stood in front of the University of Chicago Law School where he had been an adjunct professor. He had decided not to have an arena full of supporters despite the advice of everyone he had talked with. He was in campaign garb with his blue sleeves rolled up in the freezing cold. The former president looked cold and skinny, skinny enough that commentators would be assessing his health for weeks after the formal inauguration of his successor.

He had been speaking for twenty minutes about the evil Republicans and how he should be President of the United States. After twenty minutes of haranguing the Republicans, he gave equal time in his harangue to George Vincent and his American Exceptionalism Party. He then specifically attacked Acting President Jordon Scotch for acting internationally without consulting Congress. He was bewildered that the House of Representatives and the Senate had sat quietly by as he usurped their power.

"But, my feelings on politics and the election must take a back seat to the reality that the United States of America needs a president. While I am disappointed, gravely disappointed in Senator Vincent's decision to run for president as an Independent, I am asking the House of Representatives to elect him as the President of the United States. I will support his presidency while I am campaigning to become President of the United States in 2016.

~

TUESDAY, JULY 2, 2013

At 10:45 a.m., the United States House of Representatives achieved a majority vote of twenty-six states to elect a President of the United States. This vote determined the occupancy of the Oval Office until January 20, 2016. George Vincent took his oath of office at 11:00 a.m. in a private ceremony on the floor of the United States Senate with Jordon Scotch, the Acting President of the United States in attendance. Marge was at the Cleveland Clinic.

A few scholars tried to argue that the Constitution of the United States precluded the House of Representatives from acting after January 20, 2012. These arguments are imbedded in the precise wording of Amendments XII and XX to the Constitution, which were passed in 1804 and 1933. Most constitutional scholars believed the Supreme Court could make short work of any and all challenges, with uncharacteristic speed.

Immediately upon the action by the House of Representatives and the swearing in of the president, Acting President Jordon Scotch moved from the Oval Office in the West Wing to the Executive Office Building. Dr. Scotch and his family had been expecting to move in the Vice President's residence located on the grounds of the United States Naval Observatory. They had lived like hotel guests in the White House living quarters since January 22. Dr. Scotch apparently had already prepared his vice presidential office in the Eisenhower Executive Office Building (EEOB), located next to the West Wing on the White House premises. It was indicated that the telephones would be changed by first thing tomorrow morning and the physical transition of the Acting President to Vice President would be complete by 6:00 a.m. Tuesday morning, July 3, 2013.

The new president's first task was to ponder what had occurred over the past several months and propose amendments to the Constitution of the United States that would make this experience a onetime event in the history of the United States.

President Vincent offered a fairly succinct commentary on this crisis: "We have survived this period of uncertainty because of the will and strength of the people of the United States of America. This should not surprise any nation or peoples of our planet.

"But, we need to ensure that this uncertainty is not repeated. First, the United States of America needs to immediately repair its Constitution to eliminate the uncertain voting in the Electoral College regardless of what Alexander Hamilton might have thought 232 years ago. Second, the United States of America needs to redefine how to select its president if the country determines to continue to have more than two significant political parties or more than two significant candidates for the presidency. Decisions laced with the uncertainty of purely political and parliamentary actions in Congress are not an acceptable finish to any election for the role of President of the United States. I believe that the House of Representatives should have a specific time period to complete their job on the determination of the presidency or on the second Monday of April, the Acting President should become President. It probably makes sense that after a certain period of time, one of the three presidential candidates is eliminated from the voting.

"The United States is blessed to have Jordon Scotch as the Vice President of the United States. I believe it is safe to say, we have certainty of competence if, for whatever reason, I am no longer able to serve as the President."

In completing his remarks, President Vincent indicated that he was asking for a joint session of Congress within the next ten days so that he might address the people of the United States and its elected representatives at the same moment. He indicated that he had been working very hard over the past several months to ensure that his transition would be extremely brief and that he would propose a host of nominations to his Cabinet, Federal agencies and the judiciary within days. He completed his remarks with: "God bless the United States of America!"

~

WEDNESDAY, JULY 3, 2013

President George Vincent sat alone in the Oval Office at 9:15 on Wednesday morning. The Professor was ambling over towards the White House on foot for his 9:00 a.m. meeting with the President.

~

EPILOGUE

June 25, 2013: Immediately after graduation, Molly Tom joined George Vincent's team and moved in with Milton Woo. She told her folks that she was in love with Milton, but not yet sure if marriage was in the cards. This was accepted, but not well received. She became a very young senior assistant to the president on July 3, 2013.

July 7, 2013: Daily missiles began to fall into Israel and the Middle East again became the Middle East.

July 12, 2013: Mr. Sam Dehning, age forty-six, and Ms. Ilana Labowitz, age twenty-two, both naked, were found dead in their suite at the Anatole Hotel in Dallas, Texas. Mr. Dehning had been shot multiple times and Ms. Labowitz had been shot a single time in the head. Police are holding Mrs. Marta Dehning, Mr. Dehning's wife, in custody. Mrs. Dehning, a mother of five children, was found quietly sitting in the hotel room watching Dr. Phil by the hotel maid service. She has allegedly been suffering from Postpartum depression for an extended period of time. In her possession were sexually explicit pictures of Mr. Dehning and Ms. Labowitz. She claims the pictures had been anonymously mailed to her along with the weapon used in the killing.

July 21, 2013: Robert Smith, a Belgium citizen living on the edge of the Amazon Delta, was found tortured to death in his home. There were signs of a struggle. His body had been badly mutilated, apparently after the torture related death. Many weapons were found both in and around Mr. Smith's home. The murder appeared to have taken place in May or June. Brazilian drug enforcement agents are involved in the investigation as Mr. Smith was found to have had tens of millions of dollars in Brazilian and Cayman Island banks. The investigation thus far has produced very little information about Mr. Smith.

November 6, 2013: A very obviously pregnant Mrs. Jennifer Cicerone bid a public farewell to Fox News in anticipation of the birth of her first son. She indicated that her future plans included a very large family and a lifestyle centered around the University of Michigan in Ann Arbor. Jenn Cicerone recently co-authored *The Election of 2012, Disaster on Main Street* with her husband, Dr. Horace Cicerone, the noted constitutional scholar and recent appointee as the Micah Frankel Professor of Political Science at Michigan.

December 29, 2013: Pastor Robert Jackson presided over the marriage of his daughter, Crystal Jackson, to Marc Roland. Doctor and former Congressman Paul Roland was the best man at his son's wedding.

~

AUTHOR'S NOTE

In this fictional account of the 2012 election for the President of the United States, there are legitimate concerns raised about the vitality of the Constitution of the United States if there are more than two meaningful political parties nominating presidential candidates. Without eliminating the requirement that each state has a single vote, the Constitution of the United States needs to be amended to include rules that will assure the timely selection of a President of the United States.

~

Made in the USA
Lexington, KY
02 August 2011